Praise for Laurie McBain

"Good, satisfying fun...McBain's skill at shaping characters and propelling the plot distinguishes her."

—*Publishers Weekly*

"Well-crafted and wonderfully romantic. Readers are rewarded with teeming atmosphere."

—*Romantic Times*

"Ms. McBain's flare for the romantic intermingled with suspense will keep the reader riveted to the story until the last page. Bravo!"

—*Affaire de Coeur*

"Vivid sense of description, colorful characters...I found myself happily lost in the magnificence of the storytelling."

—*Los Angeles Herald Examiner*

"Combines an intricate, fast-paced plot with authentic richness of detail."

—*Publishers Weekly*

What Readers Say about *Tears of Gold*:

"This book transcends the genre. It is a wonderful, lively story—with love, action, adventure, nobility, and a little mystery. Mara is a wonderful, sympathetic character with depth, and Nicholas is the standard to which I hold all my romance heroes. He's Mr. Darcy and Heathcliff rolled up into one delicious and flawed hero."

"Epic romance at its best! One of my all-time favorite romances, *Tears of Gold* has stood the test of time as a classic."

Tears of Gold

Tears of Gold

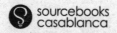
sourcebooks
casablanca

Published by Sourcebooks Casablanca, an imprint of Sourcebooks, Inc.
P.O. Box 4410, Naperville, Illinois 60567-4410
(630) 961-3900
Fax: (630) 961-2168
www.sourcebooks.com

Originally published in 1979 by Avon Books, an imprint of Harper-Collins Publishers.

Library of Congress Cataloging-in-Publication Data

McBain, Laurie.
  Tears of gold / Laurie McBain.
    p. cm.
  I. Title.
PS3563.C3334T43 2011
813'.54—dc22

                        2011023594

           Printed and bound in Canada.
           WC 10 9 8 7 6 5 4 3 2 1

For my mother and father, with love always

The haft of the arrow had been feathered with one of the eagle's own plumes. We often give our enemies the means of our own destruction.

—Aesop

Prelude

1848

"COME AWAY AND LIVE WITH ME, MARA!" JULIAN CRIED, his light blue eyes feverish with longing as he gazed at the beautiful young woman standing proudly before him. Her haughty indifference inflamed him, driving him beyond all caution as he stared into those golden brown, heavy-lidded eyes. Thick, dark lashes shielded her thoughts, but the ghost of a triumphant smile curved the corners of her mouth upward.

The half-smile enticed Julian until he despaired of feeling the soft fullness of her lips beneath his. He gave a deep sigh as he allowed his gaze to linger on her unbound hair, falling like a rich brown mantle of silk to below her hips. Sleek and shiny, it reflected fiery, dark red highlights when touched by the sun streaming through the window. The glistening ivory of her slender neck and the soft swell of her breasts were revealed above the deep flounce of *broderie anglaise* edging her corset. Tightly laced and covered with the crimson silk of her dressing robe, her small waist beckoned a man's hands to encompass it and explore the rounded curves above.

"Mara, my love," Julian spoke hoarsely, forgetting, under the onslaught of her exotic beauty, his intention to remain calm and rational. He reached out suddenly and pulled her against him. The heady scent of lily of the valley invaded his senses as his lips caressed the smooth roundness of her throat.

"My God, Mara, you have to let me love you," Julian whispered raggedly as he nuzzled her ear.

"Julian, do let me loose," Mara sighed in exasperation, her voice cold. "You're being quite ridiculous," she said disparagingly as she laughed, ridiculing his words of love.

Julian's lips found hers, closing over her mouth and muffling the sound of her scornful laughter. He kissed her long and ardently, his hands molding her silk-clad body against his. His fingers found their way beneath the edge of her robe, touching the soft skin of her breast. He pressed the firm swell of smooth flesh. But he could feel no erratic beating of her heart beneath his hand, nothing to match the pounding of his own blood.

Mara stood still. No spark of response glowed in the golden depths of her eyes as she stared coldly over Julian's shoulder. Julian released her reluctantly, his arms dropping to his sides. His blue eyes stared at her in hurt puzzlement as he took in the cool perfection of her features that had remained without a flicker of emotion.

"I don't understand," Julian spoke hesitantly. "Is it that I've taken you by surprise? I can't quite believe that. You know of my love and devotion to you. Is there another man?" he demanded jealously, his voice quivering with anger. Julian grabbed Mara's shoulders and stared down into her tawny, slumberous eyes, feeling frustrated as he failed to understand her quicksilver moods. "I've made arrangements for us to sail to France. My yacht is docked at Southampton and ready to set sail at a moment's notice. We'll spend a month in Paris and then sail the Mediterranean until we tire of it. I can give you anything you desire, Mara."

He gazed eagerly into her face, thinking his words would please her, but she only half smiled and shook her dark mane of hair provocatively over her shoulders. Julian frowned and looked down at his shoes, not wanting to understand the sardonic look on her face.

"Until you tire of me. 'Tis the way of it usually, isn't it, m'lord?" Mara spoke softly as she casually straightened the bodice of her robe. "Well, I think we'll be changing roles this time, for I've tired first of your pathetic attempts at lovemaking."

"Tired of me?" Julian mumbled, a bewildered frown marring his smooth brow.

Mara's golden eyes flickered over him in disinterest. He was a young man, not more than one and twenty, tall and broad shouldered in his superbly cut, blue-striped trousers and matching waistcoat. His frock coat was of a contrasting color and his pale blue silk scarf was casually tied and held with a gold tie pin that reflected his gold hair. His face, now flushed with emotion, was usually tanned and smiling. It was the boyishly handsome face of a sporting gentleman of London.

A cruel light lit Mara's eyes as she said, "Indeed, I'm wondering how 'tis I didn't grow bored with you sooner, what with your constant chatter of horses, hounds, and race-track meetings."

Julian's lips trembled slightly. "You tease me, Mara. Perhaps you are not satisfied with my devotions so far? But this should convince you of my sincerity and help you make up your mind," he said with the confidence of a handsome and rich young man who had always gotten what he wanted out of life.

He withdrew a thin leather case from his coat pocket and held it out to her. When she made no attempt to accept his proffered gift, he snapped it open to reveal a necklace and earrings of blood red rubies.

"They would go well with your coloring," Julian spoke persuasively, "and, Mara, there will be more to come. My mistresses have never had reason to complain about neglect in either trinkets, or in my attentions."

For the first time Mara's eyes warmed with emotion, reminding Julian of the golden flame of autumn leaves. Mistaking the glow for pleasure, he held his gift out to her again, only to have it knocked from his hand. The case hit the floor, the rubies spilling out against the rug like blood stains.

"Mara!"

"Mara!" she mimicked. "How I loathe the sound of my

name on your lips. You arrogant, pompous fool! To think you could *buy* me. How does it feel, Julian, to know that I've been laughing at you all this time?"

Mara stepped closer, knowing her fragrance floated between them as she rubbed the back of her hand against his fiery cheek. "Poor, little rich lord, having to face disappointment for once in his pampered life. You've had too much of a good thing, Julian. *Vous êtes un enfant gâté,*" she ridiculed him, remembering that he had a French mother. "I'm afraid I've had to punish you for it."

Julian backed away from her as though he had been struck. He stared down at her beautiful face, his wide blue eyes dazed. He could not have been more surprised had his pet spaniel turned into a viper before his eyes. "I love you, Mara," he whispered.

"Love?" Mara laughed in genuine amusement. "You don't even know the meaning of love. Lust is all you and your kind know about."

"It was an act? You were leading me on, laughing at me while I kissed you and told you how much I loved you?"

His pained expression and choked voice might have softened Mara had she not at that moment caught sight of the ruby necklace glowing up at her, reminding her of her purpose.

"You were so gullible. It was almost pitiable the way you drooled over the slightest attention I gave you. Did you never wonder why some days I would scarcely glance your way, even though you would try so gallantly to catch my eye? To be sure, you acted the besotted fool better than I've ever seen it played. How you'd tremble when I would accidentally touch your hand or whisper in your ear some amusing piece of gossip. But don't feel too bad. You're among good company. I've lured better and far wiser men than you into believing they could have what they wanted of me," Mara said with a smile of remembrance on her lips. "They all suffered the same fate you did."

"Stop!" Julian moaned and pressed his fingers against his temples. "I can bear no more."

Julian opened his eyes and the tears trickled down his

cheeks, wounded love lingering on his face. He swallowed painfully. "I loved you, Mara. I truly—" he began. Then, uttering a low moan, he turned and stumbled from the room.

Mara stared at the closed door for a moment before she turned. Her foot struck something, and looking down, she saw the ruby necklace.

"Could just as easily be the young gent's blood," a voice commented behind her.

"No one was asking for your opinion, Jamie," Mara retorted.

"Aye, that be for sure, and a shame 'tis ye don't. Ye could be usin' a bit o' sensible advice now and then," Jamie cautioned, "and it'd better be comin' mighty soon."

Mara looked over her shoulder, angry words she knew she'd regret trembling on her lips as she eyed the gray-haired woman.

"And it won't be doin' ye any good to be rantin' and ravin' at me, for I've hardened me heart against it after hearin' it all these many years," Jamie said. Her lined face remained unmoved by the scowl beginning to appear on the younger woman's beautiful features.

"You go too far sometimes, Jamie. Damned, interfering busybody," Mara muttered, resenting the fact that Jamie could still make her feel as guilty as a chastened child. Or was it Jamie making her feel so guilty? Something was pricking at her, something she did not want to face.

Mara picked up the ruby necklace and earrings that still lay at her feet. They were exquisite, Mara had to admit, and, with a sigh of regret, she placed them back in the velvet-lined case.

"Damn!" Mara cried out as the clasp pinched her finger as she closed the lid. She stared bemusedly at the drop of blood on the tip of her finger before putting it in her mouth to soothe the scratch.

"Aye, that's done it. It bodes no good for the likes of us," Jamie said darkly, a grim look on her gaunt face. She came up beside Mara, moving quickly for a woman nearing sixty. Jamie made the sign of the cross, muttering a prayer to anyone who might be listening. Barely reaching Mara's shoulders, Jamie stood silently beside her, her body small and slight, her expression one of long-suffering.

"These are quite beautiful jewels," Mara said thoughtfully, a hint of mischief in her golden brown eyes, "I just might be of a mind to be keepin' them."

Jamie drew herself up to her full four-and-a-half-foot frame, her faded gray eyes snapping with indignation as she rounded on Mara. "Oh no, ye'll not be keepin' these tainted stones. They be stained with blood and I'll not be havin' them anywhere near me, or the O'Flynns. Ye've got enough trouble without something that's been cursed."

"Oh, Jamie, ye do carry on so, I was just teasing you," Mara cajoled. "Only you'd better not let Brendan catch sight of them or he'll be insisting we keep them."

Jamie snorted in disgust. "What Master Brendan don't know can't hurt him. And ye can be wipin' that smile off your face, missie, for I can see the dark clouds gatherin' on the O'Flynns' horizon," she warned before grabbing the case from Mara.

"I'll be seein' that his lordship is gettin' his property back right away," she said smugly as she wrapped her arms across her thin chest, enfolding the offending case beneath them.

"Then ye'd best be takin' the locket too, hadn't ye, Mistress Jameson? And don't be forgettin' the dress, now will ye?" Mara said saucily.

Mara sauntered over to the ornate armoire standing against the wall and, rummaging through it, withdrew a burgundy velvet evening dress. It was superbly cut and without the usual lace frill of the décolletage to detract from its sleek lines. Mara's hand lingered as she smoothed the thick, soft pile. With a sigh of regret and defiance she threw it carelessly across her arm. With a toss of her dark head Mara picked up the golden locket from her dressing table and, swinging it like a pendulum from the slender chain, tossed it to Jamie.

Mara couldn't hide her surprise as Jamie's thin, bony hand reached out and successfully captured it in midair. "Bravo!" she laughed as she conceded defeat and handed the folded dress to the patiently waiting older woman.

"I think I'll be seein' to it personally that these gifts be returned to their proper owner," Jamie told her, her lips firmly set.

Mara shrugged as she picked up her brush and began lazily to stroke the long strands of dark hair. "Do as you wish, the matter no longer interests me," Mara said in a bored tone. "But don't let it detain you too long. After all, we are leaving tomorrow and I'll be needing you to finish packing," Mara reminded her.

"Aye, Jamie'll be back soon enough, so ye've no need to be worryin' on that score," she said over her shoulder as she hurried from the room and the glowering look on Mara's face.

Mara continued to brush indolently the long, silky strands, gazing unseeingly into the mirror as she gave free rein to her troubled thoughts. She felt an unaccustomed guilt when her thoughts lingered on Julian Woodridge's anguished face, but as her own face came back into focus in the mirror, she ruthlessly pushed his image aside.

A terrified cry brought Mara quickly to her feet. Flinging down the brush, she ran into the next room and made her way unerringly across the shadowed bedchamber to the bed in the corner. The little boy lying in it held up his arms, wrapping them around her neck as Mara's warm arms enclosed his shaking body and held him closely against her. He pressed his wet face against the smooth silk covering her breasts, his cries muffled as he tried to explain his bad dream.

"There, there," Mara comforted him. "Nothing is going to eat you, silly-billy."

He sniffed loudly and mumbled against her, "Name's Paddy, not Billy."

"Well, to be sure, you're right. But only silly Billys are believing in giant frogs and mushrooms with ugly faces coming after them. I'm thinking maybe you shouldn't have had that second helping of custard."

"You won't leave me?" he asked tearfully, tightening his hold around Mara's neck.

"No, I'll not be leaving you," Mara reassured him.

"Ever?" he persisted.

Mara smiled indulgently. "Ever."

"Promise?" he demanded.

"I promise. Now lie back and finish your nap."

Mara straightened the rumpled bedclothes and tucked him back in. Sitting on the edge of the bed, one of his small hands clasping hers, she recited nursery rhymes to him until his even breathing told her he had fallen asleep. She tiptoed quietly from the room.

Several hours later Mara comfortably reclined against the silk-covered pillows on her bed and became engrossed in a novel entitled *Jane Eyre* that had been a great success the year before.

"Men," Mara muttered contemptuously as she read. She absently reached out for the teacup sitting on the table beside her bed, and grimaced as she swallowed the tepid tea. She glanced at the clock, wondering where Jamie could be, and was laying her book down when the door opened and Jamie entered. "I was just wonder—" Mara began abruptly, and then noticed Jamie's pale, pinched face.

"What the devil has happened? Are you all right, Jamie?" Mara asked in growing concern as she saw Jamie's quivering lips, and forgetting her book and tea, she left the bed and walked over to Jamie. "Sit down and do tell me what has happened."

Jamie sunk down onto the chair with a deep sigh, her whole body seeming to heave a shuddering breath. "I told ye 'twas bad, didn't I? I warned ye, Mara O'Flynn, that ye was playin' the divil's game. I told ye, time and time again, ye'd rue the day. God have mercy on ye, Mara, if it hasn't come to pass this very day."

Mara paced before her impatiently. "What *has* happened?" she repeated in exasperation, feeling a cold dread spreading through her body as Jamie began to speak in a slow, monotonous voice.

"The young lord went and shot himself. Went crazy with grief they said. They couldn't talk no sense into him, even his friend who was with him at the time."

Mara shivered, hugging her arms about her body as if to protect herself from Jamie's words. "How do you know this? 'Tisn't true, is it, Jamie?"

"Aye, 'tis true enough. Heard the shot o' the pistol meself. 'Twas my doin' too," she added on a sob.

Mara looked down at the grizzled head in disbelief. "*Your* doing? Jamie, you're not making sense."

"'Twas after I delivered the package that he shot himself. Seein' the dress and locket must have driven him beyond all reason. I was down the street a bit when I heard it. Servants was runnin' everywhere, and then coaches started pullin' up, and I just stayed out o' sight, but close enough in a crowd to hear them say the young lord had gone and shot himself dead."

"'Tisn't my fault," Mara whispered worriedly.

Jamie looked up. "Who is goin' to be blamed for this day's deeds—well, I'll not be so righteous as to say. Only, 'tis a good thing we be leavin' London for Paris tomorrow. That much I will say," Jamie said meaningfully, "for there be some who might not be so generous over this matter."

Mara returned her stare steadily, no sign of emotion apparent on her flawless features. "No sense in telling Brendan, is there?" Mara asked calmly, the only indication of nervousness the clasping and unclasping of her hands.

As her lips began to tremble under the strain, Mara turned and walked over to the window. She drew aside the heavy curtain and stared out at the dusky twilight descending over the forested parks and fashionable squares of London. She hid her face from the room as she gazed at the twinkling lights beginning to appear all over the city.

Dear God, what had possessed her to do this? What demons were trying to drive her toward her own destruction? If only she'd left well enough alone. But no, she'd had to toy with the affections of that young lord. Never before had she hated herself for the games she played. Always in the past she had felt justified. But this time it was different. It had ended in tragedy. If only she could go back and change what had happened. But it was too late to say she was sorry. Too late to beg for his forgiveness. He was dead, and it was her fault. That was the ugly truth she must accept and live with for the rest of her life.

A spasm of remorse crossed her face, but no one saw it, nor would they have believed it. For Mara was adept at hiding her feelings.

"No one will be remembering my name, Jamie. Mara O'Flynn's part in this tragedy will soon be forgotten, replaced by some new piece of gossip. When we leave London, we will leave the past behind us. Your word, Jamie, that we never speak of it again," Mara demanded as she turned to face the old woman.

"I'd never be doin' anything to hurt ye, Mara," Jamie sighed. "'Tis forgotten."

✍

"Mara…oh, God, Mara. Please let me love you," the voice pleaded in anguished hopelessness. "She's a temptress, a witch with laughing, golden eyes. Oh, Mara, you can't be saying these things to me.

"Irish bitch!" Julian screamed hoarsely as he writhed with fever in the bed. A strong hand pressed him back against the pillows, holding him firmly against the cool sheets. Sensing the comforting restraint, Julian opened his blue eyes and was lucid for a moment as he recognized the man leaning over him. He reached out his hand and with sudden strength grasped the other man's shoulder in a hard grip.

"She led me on out of malice. She did it on purpose. My God, Nick, the hate I saw in her eyes. If she'd had a knife, she would have stabbed me through the heart. Instead, she used words to wound me." Julian's glazed blue eyes met the man's penetrating stare. "She laughed at me. Ridiculed my love. She said she'd hurt far wiser men than me. I wasn't the only one she'd played the enchantress with, only to deceive in the end. But *why?* Why did she do it? What did I ever do to her, except to give her my heart?"

Julian broke free and hid his burning face in the coolness of his pillow as a tear trickled from the corner of his eye. "She was so beautiful, Nick. There was something so wild and free about her, something I envied. In her moods, she was like an untamed creature. But the danger was worth it. When she'd smile at you, her mouth..." Julian murmured softly, his voice trailing off as his eyes closed.

Nicholas Chantale stood up and drew the blankets closer about his nephew's shoulders. He stared down at the young man, hardly more than a boy, and felt a deep resentment, a barely controlled rage growing within him as he thought of the woman who had so heartlessly driven his nephew into attempting to take his own life. As he looked down at Julian's boyish face, he was reminded of another fair-haired Adonis and a face he'd once known even better than he knew this one.

As Nicholas stood silently, deep in thought, the door opened and the doctor entered, followed by Julian's mother. The countess, Lady Sande, glanced hesitantly at her brother and moved quietly to the side of the bed. At Nicholas's nod she gave a shuddering sigh of relief and gazed down lovingly at her son.

"I do not understand at all," the countess cried. "If only Charles were here. He would know what to do. But at least I have you, Nicholas, and for that I am most thankful. It was fated that you should be in London at this time, for without Charles I am completely helpless."

"Did you send a message to him?" Nicholas asked as he pulled a chair up close to the bed and gently pushed the countess into it.

Turning her tear-swollen eyes away from her son's flushed face, she gazed distractedly up at her brother.

"Charles. Is the earl on his way?" Nicholas patiently reminded her.

"Yes, of course. Charles is coming down from Edinburgh immediately," the countess answered absently as she turned to the doctor. "You will not let anything happen to *mon petit* Julian, doctor? *Il est mon fils, mon enfant unique.* Nicholas," she cried, lapsing into her native French as she pleaded for her son's life.

"That I ever left New Orleans and came to this land I now regret. *Mon Dieu!* I should have listened to Papa and never married an Englishman. My sins have caught up with me for defying the family. I shall lose my Julian and cause the good Charles such pain…My fault, all my fault," she whispered brokenly.

"Denise, please, you're making yourself ill." Nicholas realized he went unheard as she turned to him, a determined glint in her eyes.

"*Mon frère*, Nicholas, you must promise me that you find this person and exact retribution from her. I will not live in peace until you do. And if," she choked over her next words, "if *mon bébé* dies, then you must kill this creature as well. Promise you will seek vengeance for this act of cruelty. Promise!" she cried as she struggled to her feet.

"Madam! You must control yourself," the doctor warned, "or I shall be forced to confine your ladyship to your room. I will not have any emotional outbursts in the sickroom." He noted her rapid breathing and vivid color and sighed. Why couldn't his patient be of an ordinary English family? These French were so volatile. He felt quite drained after every meeting with the countess. Whatever she was saying now was agitating her into a passion, and he didn't care to have a collapsed countess on his hands as well as the wounded son.

The doctor sent an imploring look to the tall French-American. "You really must try to calm the countess down. She will not listen to me. I'm only her doctor, after all. These hysterics are dangerous for both her and my patient," the doctor told him sternly, despite his feelings of unease in issuing such an order to the rugged-looking man towering over him.

"It is enough, Denise. You do no one any good by continuing in this manner. I know you are suffering, but—" Nicholas tried to soothe her.

"*Non!* You do not know what I suffer as I see my only son dying before my very eyes," she interrupted him angrily. "You will promise me, Nicholas—please! I beg this of you, for you are the only one I trust to be ruthless enough to do it. You have no softness in you, Nicholas. You do not forgive."

"Enough, sister. You need have no fear. I will punish this woman. She will regret this day," Nicholas promised in a cold voice devoid of all emotion. "I give you my word that one day she will pay for what she has done to Julian."

The doctor glanced nervously between the brother and sister and felt a shiver of fear at the expressions on their faces.

Nicholas looked down again at his nephew. Would he live? A bullet so near the heart could cause great damage. He might even be left an invalid for the rest of his life…if he survived. Nicholas turned to leave, but was stopped by Denise's hand placed lightly on the hard muscles of his forearm.

"I am sorry, Nicky," she said softly, using her pet name for him. "I know you feel the pain. I remember how deeply you were hurt when François died in your arms."

Nicholas shrugged. "It seems a lifetime ago, Denise. Yet this brings it back as though it were yesterday. Julian is much like our François once was, eh, Denise?" Nicholas said with a sad smile. Then, without another word, he walked from the room, leaving Denise, quietly complacent now that she'd received his promise, sitting beside Julian's bed.

The countess's townhouse was quiet as Nicholas made his way to the earl's study. Pouring himself a brandy, he looked around the book-lined room, taking in the well-upholstered leather chairs, the large mahogany desk, and the rich velvet hangings drawn across the windows. Denise had done well for herself despite their parents' predictions to the contrary. Not that Nicholas would have selected the earl for a brother-in-law. Charles was far too staid and proper.

The good Charles found Nicholas to be lacking these characteristics, and was pointedly absent during Nicholas's brief visit for just that reason. The fact that Julian openly admired his adventurer uncle did little to lessen the strained relationship between Nicholas and Charles.

As Nicholas stood there silently sipping his brandy, he suddenly remembered the parcel that had been delivered and had triggered Julian's tragic reaction. It had fallen beside the desk, still partially wrapped with brown paper. Nicholas tossed off the last of his brandy and picked up the discarded package, placing it on the desk. He pushed aside the concealing paper and looked curiously at the contents. As he opened the leather case sitting on top, he was unable to conceal his surprise at the ruby necklace and earrings. Rage at his nephew's wound prevented him from wondering why an unscrupulous woman would return so expensive a gift.

He removed the bundle of velvet and, shaking it out, held up a dark red dress. The woman who wore it must have the perfect figure. The waist was cut unbelievably small, while the bodice and décolletage curved to conceal and seductively reveal at the same time. By the length of the skirt, Nicholas estimated her to be of average height, standing only as high as his shoulder.

Nicholas folded the dress and placed it back in the wrapping and noticed for the first time a golden locket that must have fallen to the floor when he'd removed the dress. He picked it up and started to add it to the pile when he hesitated and out of curiosity sought the clasp. Beneath the pressure of his thumb it sprang open to reveal two faces. He recognized immediately the face of his nephew. Julian's painted features were a study in blue and gold, but the face opposite was completely unknown to him.

Nicholas's eyes narrowed as he stared at the beautiful, aloof features of the woman half smiling up at him. Despite himself he was intrigued by her face. She was far younger than he'd thought her to be, and far more refined looking than he'd imagined. Her eyes, beneath flyaway brows, seemed to glow goldenly, while the half-smile enticed with soft, seductive promises.

"By God, she is a beauty," Nicholas breathed. "Poor Julian. He never had a chance with someone like this. He was right, there is a certain wildness about her, a damn-your-eyes attitude," Nicholas speculated softly, wondering what thoughts were behind those remarkable eyes. He shook his dark head in exasperation, shaking off the captivating face as he remembered her cruelty. Nicholas stared into the painted face for a moment longer, feeling as though she could hear his thoughts. "When we meet, you'll learn what cruelty really is," he vowed. "And we will meet, Mara O'Flynn. That I promise you."

"Over the Mountains
of the Moon,
Down the Valley of the Shadow,
Ride, boldly ride,"
The Shade replied—
"If you seek for Eldorado."

—Edgar Allan Poe

Chapter 1

MARA O'FLYNN BRACED HER LEGS AGAINST THE ROLL AND PITCH of the ship as it smoothly climbed the waves, only to drop abruptly after clearing the crest into a chasm of blue-black water. The wind cut through her cloak like a dagger of ice, yet Mara reveled in the feel of the brisk, tangy salt spray on her face. She raised her head higher and stared up at the three, far-reaching masts of the ship. Fully rigged, they stretched up into the sky with a profusion of sails filled by the wind.

It had been in the winter of 1850 that they had set sail from the city of New York, leaving behind a storm of snow and howling winds that had blanketed the city in white. But as they had made their way to open sea, they had faced even worse as gale-force winds and snow flurries had raged at the ship, keeping most of the land-loving passengers below decks fighting off attacks of seasickness. Sailors are fond of saying that the sea never remains the same, and they were right, Mara thought in amazement when one morning, after a week of heavy squalls, she had awakened to a calm sea. As she stood on deck now, she could remember the first sail they'd sighted on the horizon, the first sign to her that they were not lost and alone on an endless sea.

"Ship ahoy!" the second mate had cried out from aloft as the strange ship had drawn closer.

"Hello!" had come the reply.

"What ship are ye?"

"The brig *La Mouette*, from Marseilles bound for Boston. Where do you hail from?"

"We're the clipper *Windsong*, from New York bound for California and fifteen days out."

That had been four months ago. Mara now looked across the waves into the distance, staring in disbelief and despair at the bleak shore that was barely discernible, shrouded in floating layers of fog. This was the California coastline. Was this the land they had come to make their fortunes in? Was this the golden dream that had cast its spell upon the world? Mara thought of all the people, like herself, who had been uprooted from their homes and countries to find their fortunes in this land paved in nuggets of gold. Why, on this ship alone were men from places she had never even heard of. Crowded together below deck were fancy European gentlemen in their frock coats and silk hats, speaking French, Italian, or English, disdainfully mixing with flannel-shirted laborers and farmers from Germany and Sweden, Portugal and Greece. The mingling of tongues became indistinguishable and unimportant as they found ways to communicate over the card tables. Their small savings exchanged hands time and time again until they'd all lost something in one game or another.

Mara reluctantly slid her hand from her fur muff and pulled the flapping edge of her cloak closer around her legs. She tightened the ribbons on her green velvet bonnet and touched the matching feathers reassuringly before tucking her icy fingers back into the warmth of the quilt-lined muff. She'd forgotten her gloves, but she'd not go below into the stuffiness of the cabin to retrieve them, not while she could stand here on deck and breathe the sweet, fresh air.

Mara sighed, hoping this was not going to be another one of Brendan's wild flights of fancy. And who was knowing Brendan O'Flynn better than herself? He was her own brother, and the devil take him if he wasn't a charming Irish rogue. His dancing dark eyes and boyish grin charmed people into believing he was everything he wasn't.

Mara returned her gaze to the distant shore. The scene dispelled dreams of easy living. How like Ireland it was! Fog swirled around rugged cliffs. White foamy waves pounded against sharp-edged, vicious rocks, keeping you within your own boundaries, never letting you trespass where you didn't belong. And Mara had a feeling that the O'Flynns didn't belong in this strange land. But how did she convince Brendan of that? Always building castles in the air he was. A fine time he had talking about it too, but seldom did they ever have anything to show for it except debts and their good name held in contempt. Not that Brendan often used his real name when he was up to some scheme of his.

Thinking back, Mara realized that she couldn't help but have become infected with Brendan's enthusiasm as he had planned their journey to America and the faraway land they'd heard was rich in gold. What sane man could resist the image painted of mountains of gold in a land populated by few people? It was yours for the finding, they said. How enticing that was to the poor of Europe, whose ancestors had been born into a life of poverty, and even now their children's children could hope for little better. Not that the O'Flynns were really of the poor, Mara told herself.

The O'Flynns could trace their bloodlines back to the first kings of Ireland, and were part of one of the great families of the land. Of course, it wasn't a legal relationship, for she and Brendan were bastards. But their father, a gentleman of means, had set their actress mother up in a fine house in Dublin. There had always been money for them, and even though they had been excluded from the *haut monde*, Mara and Brendan had been well educated by a succession of tutors, knew how to sit a horse as well as any aristocrat bred to it, and could even comport themselves perfectly over the tea table, should the occasion arise.

But while the children were growing up, their gentleman father had grown tired of his aging mistress. Mara's lovely mouth curled in bitterness as she recalled the abrupt change those circumstances had wrought. Gone was the fine Georgian house that had been their birthplace and held their memories. Gone were the stable of horses and carriages, the army of grooms and hostlers, and the household staff. Jamie, their

mother's longtime maid and confidante, had been the only
servant left to them.

It was not only the loss of material comforts that had
devastated them. They'd lost their happiness as well, for Maud
O'Flynn had made a tragic mistake. After a liaison of close to
fifteen years with her gentleman lover, she had committed the
folly of falling in love with him. She had lost her youth to
those years, but she had never worried about what the future
might hold when her beauty faded. Maud, in her love for
that one man, had forgotten that it was her beauty that had
attracted him in the first place.

Maud O'Flynn seemed also not to have understood that, as
his mistress, she had no rights, that she could be discarded as
easily as a scuffed pair of shoes or an unfashionable hat. She
had believed it could never happen to her. But it had. Mara's
face flamed even now, eleven years later, as she remembered
the humiliation of it all. The packing, the giving up of prized
possessions that suddenly were no longer theirs.

Few such liaisons end in friendship, without scars, and
where love had once blossomed only bitter hatred remained.
Maud was broken by her own dreams, forgotten by a man to
whom she'd given more of herself than he'd asked for—or
had wanted.

Disappointed in her bid to reestablish herself on the stage,
finding it unbearable when the roles she coveted were offered
to younger women, Maud found comfort in a succession of
lovers. Never satisfied, Maud took to traveling, never stopping
long enough to create new memories—or to let the shadows
of the past catch up with her.

And what of Brendan and herself? Mara asked with remembered pain. Did they no longer have a father, now that he had
disclaimed the relationship with their mother? How easy it
had been for him to discard them, for they had no legal hold
on him. They didn't even bear his name. Mara wondered if
he even remembered them.

Maud O'Flynn had died in Paris, her once beautiful face
coarsened by hard living and marred by bitterness. The
voluptuous curves of her body had blurred and faded until

she seemed like a scarecrow. Fever and cough racking her thin form, she finally found her long-searched-for peace in the silence of a cold, February morning. A bleak sun had risen over the rooftops of Paris as twelve-year-old Mara stood before the window, a crack in the glass of one of the dusty panes letting in a small draught of cold air.

Without turning to look into the room behind her, Mara knew what she would see: Brendan weeping against their mother's thin chest that was stilled forever; Jamie huddled in a chair muffling her sobs; the paint chipped and peeling from the walls; and the rough wood furniture in the cheap little room that had become the final resting place of Maud O'Flynn, a once-beautiful Irish actress.

Mara had remained dry eyed as she continued to stare out of the window. Why should she cry now that her mother was finally released from a tormented existence? Maud O'Flynn would no longer be forced to look into the mirror and see her haggard face and ask for the thousandth time, "Why?" But Mara's resolution had nearly failed as she heard Brendan's agonized cries. They had torn her heart from her. Never again did she want to hear a man cry as Brendan had.

As Mara stared at the tragic drama being enacted in that shabby room, at the ugliness which would be her last memory of her mother, she swore that she would never give anyone the opportunity to hurt her as her father and other men had hurt her mother. A vow made by a child, but it was as devoutly made as any priest's.

Brendan had been nineteen that year, and because he knew no other way of earning a living, he followed Maud's footsteps and went on the stage. From then on, the theater had been their life. They traveled to London or Paris, always searching for a better job, and one they hoped would last longer than opening night.

In fact, it had been after their last theatrical engagement, which had been short-lived and had stranded them in Paris without funds, that Brendan had created his latest scheme. Mara had thought he had lost his mind when he had run into their lodgings, a newspaper clutched in his hand, his eyes alight with something she'd not seen in them before. It was a lust not unlike that when he gazed upon a beautiful woman, and yet even that had not been the all-consuming fire that she'd seen in them in that instant.

Gold had been discovered in California. Well, that had meant nothing to her, Mara remembered, for she had never even heard of this place called California. It was on the far side of the United States of America and stretched nearly the length of the coast along the Pacific Ocean, Mara learned from Brendan as he knowledgeably recited the information he'd overheard from others. People were getting rich out there, making fortunes that'd make even a king's ransom look cheap.

And so had begun the fever. Brendan was crazed with the desire to go to this golden land, and the cold facts that they had no money for such a venture did nothing to cool his ardor. But it seemed as though luck had ridden on Brendan O'Flynn's shoulder as he had haunted the gaming houses of Paris and London, making outrageous wagers against the highest of odds and having them pay off in his favor. He'd gambled everything and won. He now had enough money for their fares to America and his dream of gold beyond—but what would they find when they reached their voyage's end? Mara had wondered.

In New York City they had found ships loaded down with gold hunters and supplies leaving daily for the gold mines of California. The rush of the early forty-niners was still going on a year later, but as latecomers, Brendan reasoned, they would learn from the mistakes of the others. There would be no great, rotting hulk of a ship loaded down with gold seekers for the O'Flynns. Brendan had heard the horrifying stories about those overcrowded and poorly provisioned brigs and steamships with their inexperienced crews. Half of the passengers lost their lives even before reaching California. It'd take them only three months instead of the usual seven or more if they sailed on one of the sleek clipper ships, Brendan had declared as he explained away the extra expense such a passage would cost. They usually just carried freight, but they were taking on passengers now, what with the urgent demand to get to California, and they were better equipped and far more seaworthy, Brendan had told Mara confidently. Besides, didn't they want to get to California before all of the gold was found?

Mara was thankful now for Brendan's extravagance, for she was certain they never would have survived the long voyage in a lesser ship. Catching the trade winds that had filled their sails and sent them toward the equator, and the balmy weather as they entered the tropics, had been a welcome change from the thunderstorms and high seas of the North Atlantic. The balmy days had turned into long, hot ones by the time they had reached their first port of call, Rio de Janeiro. Guarding the entrance to the bay and seeming to rise out of the sea was the high peak, Pão de Açúcar. The city itself was nestled between the bay, with its sandy beaches and sparkling blue waters, and the conical-shaped hills that stood small before the gray mountain range in the distance. It was a busy port and the last anchorage for most ships traveling around Cape Horn, especially now that the gold rush was on and ships full of Argonauts landed daily.

The streets of Rio de Janeiro were narrow and twisting as they threaded through the city with its lush parks and public plazas where granite fountains sat attractively in the centers, or as they climbed the hillsides to tile-roofed villas with panoramic views of the bay below. Rio de Janeiro seemed a very civilized city with its museums, cafes, and hotels; its palace of the emperor and empress of Brazil; and numerous cathedrals with their ornate spires rising into the azure sky. There was even a theater, the San Januaria, which had its own stock company of players and circus performers. The shops and businesses of European and American traders intermingled along the avenues and were always open for business. Confectioners and blacksmiths, ship's carpenters and greengrocers had a continuous clientele as ships docked with passengers eager to set foot on land and spend their money.

The people of Rio de Janeiro were just as exotic as their surroundings as they became a blend of the many nationalities that had settled within the shelter of the bay. But the language and customs of the early Portuguese settlers seemed to dominate over the other European colonists, Indians, mestizos, and black slaves that made up the rest of the population of Rio de Janeiro.

The ship's stores had been replenished from the open marketplaces and stalls where gaily dressed black women, often with their infant children strapped to their backs with pieces of cotton cloth, would sell oranges, bananas, lemons and limes, native fruits and vegetables, coffee and tea, or any other goods needed to continue the long voyage. Brightly plumaged parrots and tropical birds, squealing monkeys, and large snakes, coiled in the corners of frail wooden cages, were also temptingly offered for sale.

Mara shivered now in memory of the turbulent sea their ship had encountered as it had fought the cold, gusting winds that had raged as the two great oceans met at the tip of South America—Cape Horn, or so they called it, but Brendan had more aptly named it the Gates of Hell. Poor Brendan, Mara smiled reflectively, he'd turned green with seasickness and fear as their ship had been tossed about like so much driftwood on the tide. Brendan hated the sea. Maybe it made him feel insignificant to gaze as far as the horizon and see only shimmering water, and know that it was something he couldn't exert power over or charm with his good looks or smooth-tongued manner.

It had taken them two weeks to round the Horn, their sails furled as they struggled against the head winds and through the cross seas, the ocean surging into the ship as heavy swells broke over the bow, nosing her under. It was almost beyond human effort just to remain clinging to your berth as the ship seemed to upend itself time and time again until Mara thought it must break in two from the tremendous force of the thrashing waves.

Despite Mara's beliefs to the contrary, the *Windsong* made it around the Horn and into the Pacific Ocean with only minor repairs needing to be made as they sailed northward up the west coast of South America, leaving behind the hailstorms and snow of Cape Horn. They docked briefly for fresh water and provisions in the Chilean port of Valparaiso, a small version of Rio de Janeiro, but without the charm or spectacular scenery, and also their last port of call before reaching their final destination.

It had been a hundred and some odd days now, Mara calculated haphazardly. She'd long ago lost count of the exact number, but soon they must reach San Francisco, for the California coastline couldn't extend much farther, she thought with a feeling of impatience as she stared at the long line of rugged shore stretching northward.

"*Dispénseme, señora.*"

Mara whirled around in surprise. With the creaking of the tall masts and flapping of the sails, she had not heard anyone approach, nor had she expected to see anyone. Few passengers braved the cold wind on deck, preferring to remain securely below in the relative warmth of their cabins. Mara eyed the Spanish gentleman cautiously, her chin raised haughtily to discourage further conversation. There was something about the Spaniard she did not like or trust. She had first observed him in conversation with Brendan, and even then she had felt an instinctive mistrust of the man. Oh, he was charming, Mara had to concede, but maybe that was why she distrusted him. He was too polite, too solicitous of her welfare, too much the gentleman to be true.

Don Luís Cristobal Quintero stared thoughtfully into the defiantly upturned face of the young woman who was backed against the railing. He noted with regret the antagonism in the golden brown eyes. He had been warned to expect this. But he would not have his efforts go in vain, for too much depended upon his success. He had come close to losing everything because of the selfish willfulness of another female, and he had vowed not to allow this one to defeat him. "Should you be on deck in such weather, and unchaperoned, señora?" Don Luís inquired with just the right hint of concern in his voice. Yet Mara sensed the deception in it.

"Strange things have been known to happen at sea. Should you lose your footing," he speculated softly, shaking his head, "why, no one would miss you until it was too late. I doubt that you could survive in this freezing water."

Don Luís shivered delicately at the thought, then smiled apologetically. "But then perhaps you swim, señora? You Europeans seem so accomplished at everything that I am constantly amazed."

Mara turned her face away from the slightly mocking expression on Don Luís's aging, aristocratic features. Despite the reassurance of the sailors clinging to the rigging of the ship as they adjusted the sails high above her head, she shivered, feeling vulnerable as she stood beside the Spaniard.

"That is unimportant, señor, since I have no intention of falling overboard. Now, if you'll be so kind?" Mara made a move to step past Don Luís, but he continued to block her way as he stared down at her.

"Your husband, Señor Brendan O'Flynn, is not as lucky as he would have you believe, señora. Do ask him about it, for I promise you will find his answer most interesting and illuminating. Adiós," Don Luís bid her, mocking his farewell as he bowed exaggeratedly with old-world courtesy. He turned without another word and walked away.

Mara stared at his retreating back in puzzlement, a feeling of unease settling in the pit of her stomach. Could she truly have heard correctly? Had the suave don actually threatened her? It must surely have been her overactive imagination, prejudiced by her dislike of the man. But if indeed Brendan had been lying to her again, then she would be doing more than merely threatening when she had a word with him.

Mara walked unsteadily across the deck to the door leading down to the companionway, a slight smile on her lips as she remembered the Spaniard's addressing her, Señora, he had called her. Another one of Brendan's schemes was to travel as man and wife, and with Paddy along they presented the image of the ideal family. Not only did it protect her from the unwanted advances of unattached males, but it also created an aura of respectability for Brendan. And what could be more perfect, for out-of-work actors were usually looked upon with suspicion. And rightly so, Mara thought, as she remembered all of the unpaid hotel bills they had left behind as they had sneaked off in the middle of the night.

The companionway was shadowy as Mara made her way down it, but she needed no light to pick out Brendan's door. She knocked twice as she heard the sweet, haunting notes on his fiddle. It was the *port na bpúcaí*, which Brendan could play so very sweetly—Irish fairy music that was a part of them all, the superstitions and beliefs that influenced their lives and made them what they were. Mara shrugged off the deeply ingrained fears that were warring within her, and entered Brendan's cabin. She stood tapping her foot impatiently as she waited for the last mournful notes to die into the coldness of the cabin and signal the end of his song.

"Surprised I am to be finding you within, Brendan O'Flynn," Mara began without even greeting him. She threw her sable muff on the foot of his berth and turned to face him. He lounged gracefully against the other end of the berth, a pillow propped behind his shoulders. Brendan looked up lazily from his fiddle, a surprised look on his face at Mara's tone of voice. He carefully placed his fiddle beside him and picked up several yellowed sheets of paper.

"The divil take me if I can remember this cursed play," he complained as he ran his fingers through his hair, leaving the dark, reddish-brown curls standing on end.

"And what are you doing reading a play? I thought we were through working for little pay and even less appreciation? In fact," Mara continued, "I thought we were sitting on a gold mine for sure, the gold just waiting for us to be spending it. And now that I'm on the subject of money, I'll be wanting a look at our savings."

"Will you now?" Brendan murmured softly, masking his surprise as he carelessly dropped the pages to the floor. "And just supposing, little Mara, me love, I'm not in the mood to show them to you?" he drawled.

Mara untied the ribbons of her bonnet and pulled it from her head, smoothing the thick chignon at the base of her neck. The light from the whale-oil lamps shone down on her hair, creating the very misleading illusion of a halo around her head.

"Then I just might be doing without your help," Mara answered back, her eyes darkening with challenge.

"Would ye be doin' that now? Ah, Jaysus, but me own little sister turning against me," Brendan moaned as he increased his Irish lilt to a thick brogue. A sad look crossed his handsome features despite the fact that his eyes fairly danced with mirth. "I'm of a mind not to be tellin' ye a cursed thing, Mara O'Flynn."

Mara watched the smile linger on his lips as he gazed innocently up at her. He was far too handsome for his own good. His profile was reminiscent of Byron's for sure, and his eyes had a devilish tilt at the outward corners that gave him an impish look. It was a face that fascinated the ladies, Mara thought with mingled disgust and admiration at the charming picture he made.

"There's nothing to be worried about, mavournin. Brendan's never let you down, has he?"

"Aye, and the moon be as lovely a green as Ireland. D'ye take me for a fool, Brendan?" Mara asked, her own brogue deepening as her voice began to quiver with anger. "You might be interested in knowing 'twas a Spanish gentleman who called it to my attention."

Brendan, actor though he was, still could not control the stiffening of his body, the momentary flash of anger that flickered in his eyes.

"Aye, I can see you've made his acquaintance, and over the card table too, I've little doubt," Mara taunted. "Well, do I have to be looking for it meself?"

"You'll not be finding a cursed thing, Mara," Brendan confessed. He got to his feet, stretching his lithe body with less energy than usual. He rubbed the back of his neck, then looked up at Mara and shrugged philosophically. "I've gone and lost it, damned if I haven't, Mara."

Mara closed her eyes, giving a deep sigh before opening them to return his look. She stared into his face, so much like her own with the heavy-lidded, thickly lashed, and slightly slanted eyes below sleekly arched eyebrows. Straight, narrow noses and full, sensuous mouths completed the arrogantly aristocratic molding of their faces.

Mara knew before she spoke what her words would be, for

she had recited the same lines over and over again. The setting was the only thing that ever changed. The characters always remained the same, but with each repeated performance her delivery suffered, losing its spontaneity and meaning.

"God help you, Brendan O'Flynn, d'ye care nothing for Padraic or me? You'd be taking the food out of your own son's mouth to lay a bet," Mara threw at him incautiously.

Brendan moved quickly and grabbed Mara by the shoulders, his lean fingers digging deeply into her soft flesh. "I'd kill a man for saying that of Brendan O'Flynn. The day'll never dawn that I can't be putting food on the table for me own son and sister. You be remembering that, *Miss* O'Flynn."

Brendan pushed Mara from him and, with a malicious-looking smile, added, "I seem to be rememberin' a certain uppity colleen who was turning down offers of marriage, even though it'd be helping her family, just because she had not a liking for the gentlemen who'd made the offers. Poor as a church mouse she was, and yet acting as proud as a duchess. The devil take me if I be the selfish one," Brendan berated her. "There am I, a poor widower with a motherless child, fair to starving for want of decent work for a gentleman like meself, and you're turning down the rich gents who could be making our lives a bit easier," he continued cruelly.

Mara flushed angrily. "And would you be having me marry a man old enough to be me grandfather? And the other fine gentleman was twice the widower with a house swarming with children he'd be wanting me to nursemaid. Oh no, Brendan. I'm no martyr, even for you and Paddy O'Flynn. And besides, who was turning down parts because he was thinking them not grand enough for the great actor he is?"

"You're a cold wench, Mara, and you'll end up an old maid if you keep holding out for the gent you think will be matching your uncompromising ideals. Ye be a fool for sure, girlie. Have you forgotten your heritage, Mara? Do you think a fine gent will be wanting to marry a bastard? That's what we are, you and me both, Mara, and don't you be forgetting it. We be the illegitimate offspring of a Dublin actress and a fine gentleman of Ireland who abandoned us when he grew tired of our bonny faces," Brendan said bitterly. "You'll not be faring much better than our dear mother, Mara, if ye be castin' your eyes too high. Fine gentlemen don't marry actresses or bastards, they only take them to bed. You'll not be receiving many offers of marriage, little love."

"And do you think I care? I'll not be taken for the fool that mother was. No one will hurt me like that, and do you know why, Brendan?" Mara asked him softly, her golden eyes glowing. "Because I never give them a chance to. Because I've had their hearts carved to pieces on a platter before me while I smile into their lusting eyes, knowing full well they'll never be dining with me, Mara O'Flynn, and proud of it I am. You say I'm cold, aye, but as least me heart's me own, and in one piece."

Mara looked down at her hands, chafed and red from the cold wind. "So we can be throwing insults at each other until we're blue in the face, but that's not changing the fact that we're out of funds and have no way of paying our way in this San Francisco of yours. Or are we to just be picking these golden nuggets right off the ground, kicking them under foot as we search for the biggest?" Mara asked sarcastically.

Brendan unconsciously stroked a flared eyebrow. It was a nervous habit that meant he was trying to find the right words to convince her of something even he was unsure about. "Why'd you do it, Brendan?" Mara asked tiredly. "We'd made it."

"I took a chance—all or nothing. I had to, Mara. Our money was down too low," Brendan explained, his dark eyes pleading for understanding. "Sometimes I just can't be helping meself. I've got to be feeling them cards in me hands, because I just know I can be winning this time. Sometimes it's almost like a fever in me." Brendan spoke in puzzlement, not understanding this part of himself. "If only I could've won… We needed the money real bad. Our fares cost more than I'd imagined, as does everything else. I swear the world's gone crazy. Why, a man can't even afford to be buried anymore."

"And how about the O'Flynns? Can they afford to go on living?" Mara demanded in a tight voice, her words quivering in the cold silence of the cabin. "Is that why you were learning new lines, Brendan? Are we going back on the stage?"

"Well, in a manner of speaking, yes," Brendan finally admitted. "You know the Spaniard?"

"And what does he have to do with us except for knowing our business," Mara demanded suspiciously. "I've no liking for him, to be sure."

Brendan laughed. "Whether you've a liking for the man or not doesn't matter. He may be our only hope. Besides," Brendan added softly, "he's the one I be owing money to."

"Not him, of *all* people," Mara sighed in exasperation. "So what is it he's wanting?"

"Well now," Brendan replied, rubbing his hands together to warm them, his good spirits returning now that he'd confronted Mara, "it would seem as though he's in a spot of trouble. Come on and sit down while Brendan tells you what he's wanting of us."

Mara reluctantly sat on the edge of the berth and watched Brendan pace before her. His deep voice came easily as he explained.

"Don Luís is a Californian and has a *rancho* somewhere thereabouts—damned if I understood half of the names he referred to—but apparently he needs our help in some business transaction. It has to do with a rather delicate relationship between him and some other gent, and it would seem as though we're the only ones who can help him out," Brendan told her.

Mara gave him a doubtful look. "And since when have the O'Flynns been able to help anyone out of trouble? Into it maybe," Mara remarked as Brendan stopped to pour himself a drink from a half-empty whiskey bottle. "And what's a rancho, pray tell?"

Brendan shrugged. "A big estate, to be sure, only from what I've gathered, on a size that'd make even me swallow me own blarney."

"And is it?"

"Blarney? To hear the Spaniard talk you'd be believing it was," Brendan said, shaking his head in wonderment. "And yet, do you know, Mara, they do everything on a grand scale out here. Some of their ranchos are over a hundred thousand acres! Bigger than County Galway itself, I swear."

Mara stared at him in disbelief. "And what would a person be doing with so much land?"

"Damned if I know," Brendan admitted, "but I'll be saying this. Land is a good thing to be owning. You can always do something with it. And out here there's plenty of land, even for the O'Flynns."

"Well, as to whether Don Luís is telling the truth or not, I have my doubts," Mara commented.

"I'm taking his word for it, and I of all people should recognize a lie when I hear one," Brendan admitted with unusual candor.

"So why is this Spaniard in trouble?" Mara asked curiously.

"Well now, me love, I'm not knowing too much about it, but Don Luís seems to feel that his business deal will fall through unless certain terms of an agreement can be met. It all hinges on one small relationship," Brendan explained with a grin, his mouth widening to create a dimple in his cheek.

"Something tells me that I'm not going to be liking the sound of this," Mara predicted glumly.

"Ah now, mavournin, here I was thinkin' ye be willin' to accept any challenge, that no role was too great for you to tackle." Brendan sighed with regret and disappointment but continued to watch Mara out of the corner of his dark eyes.

Mara stopped playing with the lace of her sleeve and stared up at Brendan suspiciously. "And what kind of a role would ye be havin' me play, Brendan O'Flynn?" Mara asked softly.

Brendan squatted down in front of Mara, his black satin waistcoat hanging open in front to reveal the morocco lining and fine ruffled linen of his shirtfront.

"How would you like to be pretending to be the beloved niece of Don Luís, and be feted at a rancho?" Brendan asked enticingly, his dark brown eyes bright with excitement.

Mara remained silent as she returned his look thoughtfully, a worried frown beginning to form on her brow. She knew she should ignore any scheme of Brendan's, for they always seemed destined to go amiss. "Why am I to be posing as the Californian's niece?" she demanded bluntly. "It doesn't sound right to me. Besides, who'd be taking me, a poor Irish lass, for a Spaniard's niece? I'm not quite that accomplished an actress," Mara scoffed.

Brendan grinned, a secret look entering his eyes. "And who was saying the lass was Spanish? As it so happens, mavournin," Brendan informed her with obvious relish at overcoming her objections, "she is half-English. Her name is Amaya Vaughan, and her father was an English sea captain who settled in California when it was a part of Mexico. He married a local lass, sister to Don Luís, and got himself a parcel of land. Apparently that was the only way you could do it back then. Even became a Mexican citizen and converted to Catholicism to get his land. Unfortunately the lady died a few years later, after giving him only a daughter. The captain, never having a liking for his Spanish in-laws, sent the wee girl off to his own relations in England. When he died a few years after that, well, the girl had no reason for coming back here, now did she? And the good sea captain should have stayed out at sea, for he was a failure as a landowner and ended up selling out just before he died."

Brendan stood up and stretched his long legs, in pale, gray-striped merino, and poured himself another whiskey, taking a hefty swig before continuing his story.

"The only problem was that the young lady had been affianced to a gent while still a child in California, and the Spanish relatives want that agreement legalized. So off goes Don Luís to fetch his niece back to the rancho and her Spanish fiancé. Did I neglect to tell you that the fiancé is the other *ranchero*—that's what these fellows call themselves—who is involved in this business deal with Don Luís? No need to tell you how important this alliance between the niece and this ranchero could be to Don Luís's position."

Mara's interest was caught, as Brendan had intended. "So what happened in England? Did Don Luís find his niece?"

"Yes. In York, to be exact. And a colder, more stiff-laced bunch of prudes you've yet to set your eyes on, or so they appeared to Don Luís." Brendan gave a devilish chuckle. "Can you imagine how the don appeared to them? It must have shook them out of their very proper accents. Sittin' around the tea table, their monocled eyes fair to poppin' as their ladies fainted into their teacups. 'I say, do get the salts, Smythe. I believe her ladyship has fainted. A pity, too, it was a demmed good cup of tea.' I can hear it all now," Brendan laughed, imitating an English lord to perfection.

Mara smiled reluctantly at the scene Brendan had painted so brilliantly. How horror-stricken and affronted they must have been when Don Luís, olive-skinned and very foreign, had walked into their very British parlors and demanded the return of his niece to California. "I can see you've caught the humor of the situation. Miss Vaughan had become quite Anglicized during her residence in England and was barely civil to her maternal uncle. Much less did she entertain the idea of journeying to California with this strange foreigner. Besides, much to Don Luís's consternation, he found her happily contemplating her upcoming nuptials—to an English viscount, no less. Alas, he could not persuade her that she would do better to honor a fifteen-year-old agreement by marrying a Californian ranchero."

Mara shook her dark head, her eyes shading into a rich bronze as she replied discouragingly, "And what would Don Luís gain by masquerading me as his niece? For there's not a ghost of a chance that I'd be marrying this fellow."

"Mara, me love," Brendan laughed easily, "it'd never be coming to that. Don Luís only wants to gain a little time. That's all. Would you be denying him all hope? What harm can it do to be pretending, just for a little while, that you're this Amaya Vaughan? He'll cancel all debts if we agree, and he's even willing to pay us. And, Mara," Brendan added, "think of Paddy and what this will mean for him. It'll keep him from the streets. Ye'd not be havin' an O'Flynn turn beggar, would ye?" Brendan warned in exaggeration, his dark eyes narrowing. "As well as keeping you from the streets, maybe? I've no money, which means you and Paddy have none. And will you be turning Jamie out too? She's too old to be finding herself new employment. And how will we be eating? Especially if Don Luís has me arrested, or killed, for not payin' me debts. This way we've got a chance, Mara. I can get out to where the gold is. Before you know it we'll be rich. I might even be buying this ranchero's land from him. Well," Brendan demanded, "what's it to be?"

Mara flushed angrily. "'Twould seem as though you hold the winning hand, Brendan. But I'll not be playing the game for nothing," Mara warned him as she got to her feet. She picked up her bonnet and muff and turned to face Brendan.

"You'll not be taking me for a fool again. I'll be having your promise that when Don Luís pays us," Mara spoke softly, "I'll be the one keeping our money."

Brendan shrugged good-naturedly. "Sure. 'Tis fine with me. You may be appointing yourself anything you want—as long as you do as Don Luís tells you. He'll be talking to you to acquaint you with your Spanish relatives, so be a good pupil and learn your lessons and we'll be the richer for it. And, Mara, me love," Brendan added warningly, "don't be troublesome. It wouldn't hurt to be polite to Don Luís. Now, now, wipe that thunderous expression from your face, little darlin'. Remember—it's for Paddy," Brendan quickly reminded her.

At Brendan's words a sudden thought struck Mara, and she said abruptly, "Speaking of Paddy, I'll not be leaving him with you, even though you are his father. So where were you planning to be, Brendan, while I'm masquerading as Amaya Vaughan and earning our keep?" she demanded suspiciously.

"Now, now, mavournin," Brendan answered easily, raising his hands placatingly. "You've no need to get your feathers ruffled. Paddy will be going with you as your widowed cousin's son. Don Luís seemed to think I should be along too. Thinkin' we were husband and wife, he thought you might be gettin' lonely for me handsome face and think about leaving before the job was done. I'm thinkin' Don Luís isn't trustin' us," Brendan said with an injured air.

"Then he's smarter than I imagined," Mara answered unsympathetically. "So you're to be me cousin, are you?"

"Naturally. Brendan O'Sullivan, at your service," he replied as he bowed extravagantly. "Your very best friend and trusted companion, protector and chaperone, business advisor—and accomplished dancer as well." Brendan smiled his most charming smile. "I shall be welcomed into the bosom of the family like a long-lost son. However," he paused reflectively, "due to past experience, I thought it best not to be usin' our own name, just in case."

Mara shook her head in exasperation and walked to the door. Before leaving, she turned and added, as a parting shot, "You've always been the better actor, Brendan, me love. Maybe you should be masqueradin' as the niece. Ye've a pretty enough face for it, to be sure." Mara laughed as she slammed the door, catching Brendan's curses in mid-utterance. Her laugh faded quickly as she made her way down the narrow passage to the cabin she shared with Paddy and Jamie. She was troubled, but it'd never do to let Brendan know. He had ways of using your fears to his own advantage. She had to keep her head if she were to hold her own with him.

Paddy was lying on one of the berths, a small replica of Brendan as he stared morosely into space. At Mara's entrance, however, his dark eyes lit up and a wide smile spread across his face.

"You've been ages, Mara. Ye know I've no likin' to be left alone," he complained. He slid his small hand into Mara's as she sat down beside him on the bed. He looked up reproachfully, his dark brown eyes reminding Mara of a fawn's.

"Using your father's charm already, are you?" Mara demanded in mock indignation. "And only six years of age too. I want you to speak English correctly, Padraic," Mara scolded him gently. "I want you to have at least a fair chance in the world, and speaking with an Irish accent isn't going to help you any."

"You talk with one sometimes, Mara, so why shouldn't I?" Paddy asked bluntly. "Sometimes when you get real mad and your cheeks go pink, you sound so funny. I want to sound that way too," he confided. "Besides, Papa talks that way too."

"Well, Master Padraic, you are not your papa, and you should not be trying to sound like him. Your papa and I only speak that way when we're teasing each other, and then only in private. We can speak perfectly good English when we desire to. Sometimes, I admit, when I'm in the heat of anger I do forget myself. Being actors, we can speak many dialects— it's our job—and Irish is just one of them. But you," Mara said, giving Paddy a direct look, "are still young enough to learn English the right way. It's hard enough making a living in the world without having the burden of being an Irishman into the bargain."

Paddy frowned in puzzlement at Mara's words. He struggled to his knees on the berth, steadying himself against Mara's shoulder as the ship lurched and he nearly lost his balance. His small hand found hers again, and spreading her fingers against his, he laughed as he compared his short ones against her long, slender fingers with their oval nails.

"Why's it hard being Irish?"

"Because," Mara sighed, "I've found that few people have the time for an Irishman. Only the Lord, it would seem, remembers that we're his children. And after the famine starving so many families out of Ireland, well, I sometimes wonder if even He has time for us. We've got to make it on our own, Paddy. No one is going to be giving the O'Flynns so much as the time of day," Mara told him sadly. "And I get so tired of the struggle at times. As your papa is fond of saying, 'Jaysus, but it's a fine day for doin' nothin'.' How I do wish that sometimes," Mara whispered.

She playfully pushed the dark, reddish brown curls from Paddy's forehead. "So you be speaking fine, like a fancy London gent, or I'll be having you walk the plank," Mara said. Then, glancing around curiously, she asked, "Where's Jamie?"

Paddy laughed as he was thrown off his perch by another sudden roll of the ship. He sat back against the pillows and answered casually. "Oh, she got sick again. Jamie started to turn green, Mara, and she looked so funny. She said she'd better be doing it over the side, and then she ran out," Paddy explained, then asked hopefully, "Do you think we're going to be liking this place, Mara? I'm awful tired of this ship. There's nothing to do, or anyone to play with. Isn't it ever going to stop somewhere?" he asked with a petulant droop to his mouth as he stared up at Mara expectantly.

"Well, if one is to be believing the captain, then we're supposed to be docking any day now," Mara answered reassuringly. "Of course, he was saying the same thing over a week ago," she added softly to herself.

"What's San Frisco like, Mara? Is it like London or Paris, or Dublin?" Paddy demanded with the knowledge of the well-seasoned traveler.

"Well now, I'm not sure," Mara answered honestly, "but I suppose 'tis as fine a place as London. To be sure, with all of the gold they've found, they must all be living like kings."

Paddy listened thoughtfully, his dark eyes bright with anticipation. "And do they have vanilla meringues and hot chocolate for breakfast if they want to? And they don't have to eat green peas?"

Mara smiled in amusement as she looked down at him. "And why not? Who's to be saying what a rich man may eat or not? Although I think he'd really prefer a plate full of fluffy eggs and chops, with maybe a hot muffin with melted butter and honey to sweeten it…don't you think?"

"Well, maybe," Paddy conceded, "but I like meringues best of all."

"And you'll be getting plenty when we get to San Francisco."

"Can't I have any now?" Paddy asked hopefully. "I'm tired of fish and potatoes."

Mara sighed tiredly. How could she keep an active little boy entertained through the long months of confinement and inactivity? She had run out of stories to tell and games to amuse him, and the bag of sweets she had bought in Rio de Janeiro was almost empty. And Paddy was right, the food on board was awful and monotonous.

Mara reached into the bag now and pulled out the last piece of candy, handing it into Paddy's eagerly outstretched palm. "It's the last one, so make it last."

Taking off her cloak, Mara laid it across the foot of the berth with her muff and bonnet on top and then wrapped a cashmere shawl over her shoulders. The cold dampness of the ocean seemed to permeate everything, making her constantly chilled. Mara slipped her fingers into her waistband pocket and withdrew a dainty gold watch with an enameled back. It hung from her neck on a long, delicate chain.

"Three o'clock in the afternoon," Mara sighed as she tried to make herself comfortable on the hard mattress of her berth.

Frowning at the creases, Mara smoothed down the green velvet of her skirt, then straightened the lace edging the bell sleeves of her bodice jacket. She stared at her nails reflectively, then at her green silk slippers, her eyes wandering from one object to another until she sighed in boredom.

Pulling a large, tapestried bag closer from the edge of the berth, Mara reached inside and withdrew a silver hand mirror. She stared dispassionately at her reflection, trying to see what a stranger might see. She had to concede that her face wasn't one of classic beauty, but it was a beautiful face and she was proud of it. And she knew how to use her beauty, for it drew men irresistibly to her. They could barely conceal the lust on their faces when she allowed them a few, brief moments in her dressing room while she acted out her greatest performance, playing the coquette. Clad in a vividly colored, silk dressing gown that accentuated the smallness of her waist and the firm fullness of her breasts, she would sit before the garishly lighted mirror applying rouge to a soft cheek, or brushing a long strand of dark hair freed from its confining chignon. Standing up and stretching indolently, as though unaware of the hungry eyes upon her, Mara would prowl restlessly before them, her hair cascading in fragrant abandon down her back and swaying with the swing of her hips as her gown parted to reveal a slender length of silk-clad calf.

Mara gazed into the golden reflection of her eyes and felt no remorse for what she did to those men. It was unimportant to her that Brendan hurt women in the same manner as she hurt men. And she did not realize that in seeking revenge, they had both become victims of their own despised memories. All Mara could see were the besotted fools who allowed themselves to be used and who destroyed one another. She didn't differentiate between the sexes—only between the strong and the weak. She had made herself strong, she told herself as a shadow of memory slipped across her mind, darkening her eyes. She felt a momentary sense of approaching panic.

Mara stared into the mirror, seeing two light blue eyes staring reproachfully back at her. She squeezed her eyes tightly shut and shook her head to block out the haunting memory of that young boy. She hadn't meant it to go so far. How could she have known he would shoot himself? Usually the men she became involved with were older and more mature—although just as easily duped—but they didn't kill themselves over her. Strangely, she couldn't even remember the young man's name, or the rest of his face. Just those bewildered blue eyes. Since they had left London the very next day, Brendan had never known about it. That was just as well, for he had warned her often about pushing people too far. If only she could forget...but she couldn't. It was always there at the back of her mind that she had killed a man—no, she had killed a boy—for he'd hardly been older than herself, and she'd been only eighteen at the time. With a muffled curse Mara shoved the offending mirror back into the bag. She had enough to worry about regarding the future without pondering a past she couldn't change.

She couldn't even influence the problem that existed now, Mara thought in growing despair. She wondered how in the world she could go through with this ridiculous plan of Brendan's. What if they were found out? What would happen to them then? She didn't trust Don Luís to support them if her true identity were revealed. In fact, he would be the first to denounce the O'Flynns as impostors, thereby saving himself. But what alternative did they have? Brendan had lost all their money. They were destitute. Well, why *couldn't* she do it? Mara though rebelliously. She was an actress, wasn't she? She had faced difficult roles on the stage. She'd just have to refine her English a bit—and remember to curb her tongue if she were to be convincing as a well-brought-up young Englishwoman.

She would do it, Mara vowed as she glanced across at Paddy. He was playing with his toy soldiers in the ruffled blankets and his mouth was pursed as he sucked his sweet. He had the same tilted, deep brown eyes as his father and the same disorderly curls. Paddy was the only good thing that had happened to the O'Flynns in a long time, certainly the only good thing from Brendan's marriage. Mara had always been curious as to the real reason behind Brendan's marrying Paddy's mother, for Brendan was not the marrying kind. How often had Mara seen heartbroken females hanging about, only to be met by Brendan's callous rejection. But Molly had been different. She had never run after Brendan. Maybe that was what had attracted him to her, that and the instant recognition of a kindred spirit.

When they had first met her all those years ago, she had claimed to be half-gypsy, and had come to London to make her fortune on the stage. She had said she was seventeen, but Mara suspected she was closer to twenty when she joined the troupe of players Brendan belonged to. Voluptuous and fiery, she had stormed onto the stage and made a place for herself despite the jealousies of the older actresses. Mara had been too young then to act with the troupe except in small roles and had spent most of her time backstage running errands, always at someone's beck and call. But that had changed when Molly, without asking leave of anyone, appropriated Mara's services for her personal use. Mara flushed as she remembered how she had idolized the tall, dark beauty, ignoring her capricious whims and vicious temper as she strove to please her.

But Molly was restless, always impatient that life was passing her by. Even Brendan's charm couldn't hold her. When Molly and Brendan had become lovers, it had not shocked Mara. It'd been inevitable, despite the constant arguments and screaming that accompanied the affair. Mara had often wondered which of them was the stronger. They were too much alike for them both to win.

And then Molly had discovered she was going to have a child. Mara still cringed as she remembered the fit of rage it had thrown Molly into. She had cried for days, distraught and moody as she imagined her career was finished. How could she support herself, heavy with child and without a ring on her finger. She'd be thrown out on the streets to starve. She'd get rid of the brat before it came into the world, she had threatened. Whether it was from fear of sinning against God, something Mara suspected Brendan still believed in, or from an attempt to hold onto Molly, or from his own bitterness over being a bastard, Brendan asked Molly to marry him rather than destroy the child.

Jamie had never cared for Molly, and the feeling had been returned in force by Molly. Jamie hadn't trusted her or thought her fit to associate with the O'Flynns. Maybe she had been jealous, too, of Molly's influence over both Brendan and Mara.

But she had been right in cautioning Brendan, for the relationship had worsened with marriage. Molly had hated the child, hated its hungry crying as it reached out greedily for her breast. After catching Molly abusing the child when she was in her fits of temper, Mara had taken Paddy away from his mother.

And then one morning, Molly was gone. She had left in the night, leaving no note, and had taken all their small savings and anything else of value she could get her hands on. Paddy, her son, she had left behind.

Poor Brendan never expected Molly to run out on him. In that one instance when he had lowered his defenses, he had found himself being used and discarded. The experience had served as a warning to Mara, and had strengthened her determination against falling in love.

After Jamie's snort of disgust and muttered "Good riddance, never did trust that thievin' Gypsy," not another word had been said about Molly, and Mara sometimes thought Brendan truly believed himself to be a widower. It was the only way he could accept Molly's desertion. Every so often in some theater they were playing, they would hear her name mentioned by another actor, but they never crossed paths with Molly after that, and in the past few years had not even heard of her again.

Mara looked possessively over at Paddy. She never wanted to hear of Molly O'Flynn again. Paddy was hers, and she wouldn't risk Molly's suddenly coming back into their lives and taking Paddy from her. Mara's golden eyes darkened at the thought. Molly would never get Paddy—why should she? She had abandoned him when he was only a baby, and hadn't she, Mara, raised him like her own child? Wasn't she more of a mother to him than Molly could ever be? Well, she wasn't going to worry about it. Molly was probably dead or had forgotten all about the O'Flynns by now.

But the mere thought of that happening worried her—for with Paddy she was vulnerable. Through Paddy she could be hurt. It was her love for the little fellow, her defenseless, softer self, that was laid bare and exposed for all to see when she gazed at his small dark head. Paddy was the only person Mara could be completely natural with. Even with Brendan she never revealed all of her emotions. It was a battle of wits with him over most things. But with Paddy she could relax and not have to be constantly on guard. She had conveniently forgotten that one day Paddy would grow into a man, and that as a man he might have the power to hurt her. But she wouldn't worry about that; her only concern now was over what Brendan had gotten them involved in and how soon they could extricate themselves from this association. And she had a feeling that it could not be soon enough.

Mara looked up as the door opened and a haggard-looking Jamie entered, a shawl wrapped protectively over her head and a heavy cloak folded around her thin form.

"How are you feeling, Jamie?" Mara asked doubtfully as she noticed the greenish tinge to her skin and the beads of perspiration clinging to Jamie's upper lip.

Jamie gave her a dour look, shivering as she huddled in the corner of the berth. "And how d'ye think I'd be feelin', havin' me insides hung up like sails and blown inside and out," she sniffed. "I've gone from bad to worse on this hare-brained voyage of Brendan's, and if I never be settin' foot on a creakin' hulk like this again, then it'll be too soon."

Mara hid her smile. "I know you're not feeling hearty as a buck, Jamie, but—"

"Hearty as a buck! I'm feelin' more like that gaping-mouthed salmon flapping its tail up on deck," Jamie said with some return of spirit.

"You're silly, Jamie. You're not pink like a fish, you're gray like a big whale!" Paddy cried out as he started making faces like a fish.

"Ye just be watchin' yerself, Master Paddy," Jamie warned him. "Keep making them faces and I'll be givin' ye a dose o' cod-liver oil."

Paddy made an even more grotesque face and subsided into silence on the berth as his toy soldiers caught his attention once again.

"Jamie," Mara spoke quietly. "Brendan's decided that we need more money. In fact, we find ourselves in rather straitened circumstances and need the money rather desperately," Mara tried to explain tactfully.

"Brendan's been gambling again, has he?" Jamie said bluntly, showing no surprise at the news. "Best be settin' our wits to work and figure a way out o' this. Or has Brendan already got a scheme?" Jamie sent Mara a hard look. Her eyes were still as sharp as an eagle's and seldom misread an expression.

"Aye, Jamie," Mara confessed. "Brendan's not wasted any time in getting us paying jobs—acting parts too," Mara added with a half-smile curving her mouth in derision.

"Well, that sounds more like what we was meant to be doin' instead of huntin' for this fool gold mine of Brendan's. What play will we be doin', and what's the pay?" Jamie asked practically.

Mara hesitated, unsure as to how much she should tell Jamie. "It isn't exactly a play, nor will we be acting on a stage in a theater, but we'll be getting room and board, Jamie," Mara admitted as she resolutely continued despite the sour look she was receiving from Jamie. "I'm going to pretend to be the niece of this Spaniard, Don Luís, and Brendan will act the part of my cousin, and—"

"May the Lord forgive me, but I'm not wantin' to be hearin' another word about it. To be sure, I'm not of a mind to be knowin' anything about it, Mara O'Flynn, so don't ye be tellin' me more. The less I know the better I'll be sleepin' nights," Jamie told her emphatically as she shook her gray head in resignation.

"As long as you remember to call me Amaya, and there won't be much else you'll have to say..." Mara paused thoughtfully, a teasing light entering her eyes. "If you'd rather, I can tell them you're a mute, and then you won't have to say anything at all."

"Hrrmph!" Jamie snorted contemptuously. "The day I can't be rememberin' me lines I'll be past breathin'. I may not have acted before an audience in near over a quarter of a century, but I can still be playin' me part. Mute, indeed," she sniffed.

"I have complete faith in you, Jamie," Mara declared innocently, hiding her satisfied grin behind a casually raised hand.

"And don't be thinkin' ye bird-limed me, missie," Jamie snapped. "I knew what ye was up to all along."

"Of course, Jamie," Mara answered.

Later that evening, after Paddy was warmly tucked up and asleep in his berth, Mara left her cabin, Jamie nursing her favorite cup of tea laced with brandy, and met with Brendan and Don Luís in Brendan's cabin. Brendan was staring into his whiskey glass and Don Luís was taking a sip of richly colored red wine when Mara entered. Don Luís rose quickly to his feet and offered her a chair at the table where Brendan still sat, a morose expression on his lean face. Mara eyed him curiously, wondering what had happened to send him into one of his famous black moods.

"Please, señora, will you not partake of some of this excellent wine? I brought it from France." Don Luís poured the dark red liquid into a crystal goblet and solemnly presented it to her. "I am always comforted to have my own possessions around me when I am traveling. Being accustomed to a certain standard of living, I prefer to maintain it no matter how uncivilized the conditions I find myself in."

The incongruity of the crystal next to Brendan's bottle of brown whiskey and plain glass caused Mara to smile. She accepted the wine from the Spaniard, nodding graciously.

"I am reassured, señora, to see your change of spirit," Don Luís commented, misinterpreting the reason for her smile.

"But I must get accustomed to calling you by your new name, Doña Amaya."

"*Doña?*" Mara frowned at his words.

Don Luís's thin lips widened in a grin, but the smile did not reach the black depths of his eyes. He explained, "It is merely a form of address, like miss or madam, and shows respect. You will become used to it. Please, Señor O'Flynn, some wine," Don Luís invited as Brendan was about to pour himself another whiskey.

Brendan shook his head as he filled his glass with the brown liquid. "No, thank you, I can't abide that sweet stuff. It's *uisge beatha*, the water of life, or nothing for any decent Irishman."

Mara shivered as a cool draught of air swept through the cabin and touched her shoulders. She took a deep swallow of wine and felt it lick like fire through her blood. It left her cheeks flushed as the chill left her body.

"It is fortunate that Amaya left California at so young an age. It will not be expected that she would speak Spanish," Don Luís began, his black eyes narrowed to slits as he stared at Mara's flushed face, "and a young girl changes much in the years approaching womanhood. Few will remember exactly what the young Amaya looked like. In fact, I did not recognize Amaya when I saw her in England. And oddly enough, you look more like the Amaya I had expected to see. It will work out fine, and as you are an accomplished actress," he added, his tone sounding insultingly superior to Mara's sensitive ear, "I need have no fears regarding your ability to play the role."

"Then they'll not be expecting me to remember them?" Mara inquired politely, masking her dislike of the man.

"No, it would not be likely that you would know all your relatives after this great length of time. However, you should be aware of the immediate family. I am, of course, your mother's brother, Don Luís Cristobal Quintero," he spoke his name proudly, "and my home is the Casa de Quintero. My wife is Doña Jacinta, and I have a son, Raoul. We will be staying at the Villareale rancho with you. That is the home of Don Andres Villareale; his mother, Doña Ysidora; and a cousin, Doña Feliciana. There are numerous other relatives constantly visiting, but they are unimportant." Don Luís explained all this with patience, despite Brendan's obvious inattention as he poured himself another whiskey.

"Oh—there is also staying at the rancho an American called Jeremiah Davies. He is Don Andres's secretary."

"Is it from the American that you learned your English, Don Luís?" Mara asked, having been surprised by the Spaniard's almost flawless English.

"No, it was from the father of Señor Davies that we learned our English," Don Luís explained. "He was a shipwrecked sailor off one of the fur-trading ships that used to sail our waters, and he decided to stay in California. He was not a sailor by trade, but had been a Yankee schoolteacher in a place called Boston. The father of Don Andres, Don Pedro, had the foresight to hire this Yankee to tutor his children and teach everyone English." Don Luís smiled cynically as he added, "He must have foreseen this invasion by the gringos."

"So the cast of characters have been named, and the players assembled on stage," Brendan spoke suddenly into the uncomfortable silence. "And how long a run are we being booked for, Don Luís?"

Don Luís shrugged complacently. "Of that I am not certain. We will have to let these matters develop as they will. We Californians do not rush through life. We take our time, and consider things carefully. Don Andres and his family will, of course, want to take the time to get acquainted with you. Then there will be the festivities and visits to relatives," Don Luís explained with a satisfied smile curving his thin lips. "All very time-consuming."

"Time-consuming for what purpose?" Mara asked curiously, wondering what in the world she had committed herself to.

Don Luís stared arrogantly down his narrow, high-bridged nose at Mara. "That need not concern you, señora. All that involves you is to successfully act the part of my niece. You will be paid for that, and nothing more. Do I make myself understood?" Don Luís answered haughtily. "You will not meddle in affairs that are none of your business. You will confine yourself solely to acting your part."

Mara shrugged, a devilish glint in her eyes that Brendan recognized and knew meant trouble. She'd like to see the pompous Don Luís cut down a size or two, and with that thought in mind she placed her elbows on the table, propping her chin in her palms as she stared up at Don Luís with a saucy look. Winking at him broadly, she spoke.

"Ye're right, luv. Fer'ow'd the 'ell would the likes o' me, a bit o' fluff, be knowin' about the affairs of gent'men likes yerself? Leastwise their business affairs, if ye knows what oi means," she hinted audaciously. "Why, 'twas bloody 'are-brained o' me to be even askin' such a question. Cooee, what a nerve oi've got, ducks," Mara said in her broadest cockney accent, her voice sounding coarse and vulgar even to her own ears. She picked up her wineglass, silently toasting the don's stunned face. Swallowing a hefty swig, she hid her grimace of distaste behind the back of a hand raised to wipe her lips.

"Mara!" Brendan hurriedly intervened, his dark eyes glinting angrily as he glared at Mara's triumphant and unrepentant face. "Please, Don Luís, you'll have to excuse Mara. She sometimes speaks without thinking of the consequences," Brendan apologized, "but she is always sorry afterward. Aren't you, Mara?"

"To be sure, mavournin," Mara replied, smiling innocently, "I seldom am."

"Mara! How can you—"

"Enough!" Don Luís spoke abruptly, his voice shaking with anger. "I have never been treated with such contempt by anyone, and never by a woman such as this. Were you a true relative of mine, heaven forbid, then you would soon know your place, señora. But this does little good. If I cannot trust you, if you do not do as I wish, then," Don Luís paused, looking at them malevolently, dislike evident on his face, "I shall have no choice but to prosecute Señor O'Flynn for not paying his debts to me. It is hard for a young mother and child alone to make a living in a strange land. I would not envy you, señora," Don Luís said silkily, a contemptuous look in his black eyes as his gaze roamed over Mara's face and body. He turned without another word and walked to the door, his back stiff with outraged pride.

"Don Luís," Mara spoke softly, looking into the dark red depths of her wine. "You need have little fear that I, Amaya Vaughan, will let you down. As your very properly brought-up English niece, I shall do nothing to cause you or your family embarrassment or concern. My conduct shall, of course, be impeccable and above reproach," Mara told him, her voice coolly cultured with just the right hint of hauteur.

Don Luís turned slowly from the door and stared at her in amazement. She sat demurely before the table, her hands folded and her small, chignoned head bent slightly, as though in prayer. The madonna herself could not have looked more serene or pure. Don Luís was incredulous. Mara looked up as she felt his eyes on her. Her tawny eyes were warm and softly luminous as a single teardrop clung to her lashes before dropping to her cheek. Her parted lips trembled slightly as she solemnly returned his stare.

"¡Madre de Dios!" Don Luís exclaimed. "I compliment you, señora, for you are indeed an accomplished actress." He bowed in deference. "You have set my mind at rest, and I have the utmost confidence in your abilities now that I have just witnessed a miracle. Never would I have believed it possible for a person to sound and act so differently," he said, shaking his head in disbelief. "One moment a shrew, and the very next instant an angel."

Brendan laughed, thoroughly enjoying himself. "Mara is full of surprises, Don Luís. I'm sometimes believing she doesn't know who she is, or what she wishes to be, eh, me little darlin'?" Brendan taunted, anger still smoldering behind his dark eyes.

"As long as she is Amaya, that is all that need be important," Don Luís interjected quickly, afraid a row would erupt between these wildly unpredictable O'Flynns. "There is one small thing I must know: The child will not be confused to be calling you Amaya?" Don Luís inquired, a worried frown crossing his high brow. "It would not do to have the little señor give the game away."

"You needn't worry," Mara answered quickly, lest he suggest some alternative arrangement for Paddy. "As an actress, I must be conscious of my public image. I must appear to them perpetually young and beautiful, and having a child of six calling me mama would be quite ruinous to my career," Mara prevaricated as she vainly smoothed the heavy chignon at the base of her neck in an affected manner.

"Of course, it never has been a problem. The boy has always called me Mara, for I am, after all, not his mother. He's from Brendan's first marriage. Oh, you thought he was mine?" Mara laughed, pretending to pout. "But how could you really believe he was mine? Surely I don't look old enough to have a child, Don Luís? Why, I'm hardly more than a child myself."

"My apologies, señora. I naturally assumed the boy was yours. This, of course, will simplify matters. We need have no fear of the child committing some indiscretion. *¡Bueno!* It is all settled then, and soon we shall be in California." Don Luís sighed in evident relief. "With your permission?" he asked as he collected Mara's empty wine goblet, the other glasses, the bottle of wine, and carefully restored them to a leather traveling case, "I bid you *buenas noches*, then," he murmured, and left the cabin with a very contented expression on his face.

The loud clapping of Brendan's hands disturbed the silence and startled Mara from her thoughts. "Well done, Mara, me love. An extraordinary performance, to be sure, and one that nearly threw me behind bars," Brendan said harshly, anger burning brightly in his eyes. "Why d'ye do these things? You dare everyone to call your bluff. I think you enjoy pushin' a person until they're near to their tether's end. One day you'll be pushin' someone too far, and it'll be too much for even your insolent tongue to handle."

Mara remained silent. She had no defense. Brendan was right. Her cursed temper and tongue would be sure to get her into trouble one of these days.

"I'm sorry, Brendan."

"And so you should be. A fine time it is to be playing games, what with our future at stake and Don Luís not havin' much of a sense of humor," Brendan complained, a sour look on his face.

Mara's eyes glinted. "A fine thing indeed, to be blaming me. Who was in his black looks before I even came in? Such a melancholy face I've yet to be seein'. What caused you to be brooding?" Mara demanded.

Brendan hunched his shoulders despondently, then ran a hand carelessly through his hair. "I come halfway around the world to make me fortune, risking death on this damned ocean, only to have the gold out of me reach. I might as well be back in London or Paris for all the good this is going to be doing me," Brendan spoke bitterly.

Mara stared at his dejected expression in puzzlement. "I don't understand? We'll be in California, won't we? There's gold everywhere. You don't have to be going anywhere special to get it."

Brendan snorted in disgust. "A lot you don't know. There's no gold on Don Luís's rancho, or on this other gent's. It's far away in the mountains. The Sierra Nevada he told me. Now, how am I goin' to be getting there if I'm confined to the rancho looking after you? I can't trust you enough to turn my back for an instant," Brendan accused her, shifting the blame easily to Mara.

"That's unfair and untrue," Mara said huskily. "You know I'd never let you or Paddy down. Take it back, Brendan," Mara commanded, a slight quiver of hurt in her voice.

Brendan rubbed his eyes tiredly. "All right, just don't start cryin' on me. I can't abide a woman in tears."

"I never cry, at least not for real," Mara answered shortly as she got to her feet. "We're in this now, so we might as well be giving it our best and hope it's over soon. Then you can get to your damned gold mines."

"Mara," Brendan called out as she opened the door.

Mara turned partly back to look at him, a cold, withdrawn expression on her face.

"It's not a game or a play, Mara. It means everything to us. We can make a place for ourselves out here. It doesn't matter where we come from, or that we don't bear our father's name. We're equals out here. This is our only chance to change our lives, Mara, Believe in me, please."

"I want to, Brendan. God only knows how much I want to," Mara spoke softly as she gave him a half-smile. She left the cabin, the door closing as he slumped into the chair.

The following day Mara stood beside the railing of the ship as they prepared to drop anchor in San Francisco Bay. Paddy was jumping from one foot to another as he peered excitedly over the railing, trying to catch a glimpse of distant land as he dodged Jamie's restraining hand. Mara's shoulders shook with tired laughter as she stared at the bay surrounding them. She heard a step behind her and turned to see Brendan walking jauntily toward them.

"'Tis a fine sight, to be sure, Brendan O'Flynn," Mara said, hiccupping as she tried to control her laughter.

Brendan gave her an odd look and followed her outspread arm to the scene before him. Mara laughed nervously at the ludicrous expression on his handsome features, then turned her own gaze back to the stretch of water between their ship and the shore.

"Jaysus," Brendan whispered as he stared in bewilderment at the abandoned ships cluttering the horizon. Hundreds of masts rose starkly from the rotting hulks of once-proud sailing ships, now deserted and forgotten by crews who had caught the gold fever.

Mara looked beyond the debris-filled harbor and canvas-covered sandhills to the higher hills in the distance. San Francisco. Never had she seen the likes of it before. Frail wooden structures and untrustworthy-looking tents clung precariously to the steep hills that surrounded the city. In fact, Mara thought in amazement, it was the hills that caught your attention, the buildings no more significant than the scraggy, windblown trees dotting the hillsides.

"Is this San Frisco, Mara?" Paddy asked. "It's ugly," he added in disappointment, voicing both Mara's and Brendan's thoughts.

"'Tisn't London, to be sure," Mara replied softly, "Nor is it what you were expecting, is it, Brendan?"

Brendan dragged his gaze from the harbor and silently stared at Mara, his eyes for once lacking their sparkle as he returned her direct look. Mara clenched her fist as she saw his lower lip tremble slightly as he tried to recover. Only once, long ago in Paris, had she seen Brendan so deeply affected. Even Molly's desertion had not moved him as much as this surprising scene.

"Well," Brendan began slowly as he sought for his usual glib retort, only to falter as he looked again at San Francisco, "'tis a young city yet."

Mara glanced away rather than see the defeat on Brendan's face. Vaguely, in the back of her mind, she heard the sound of the ocean as it lapped against the sides of the ship. Overhead the raucous cries of gulls disturbed the quiet as she came to the realization that it was Brendan's dreams that had kept them all going. His looking on the bright side of everything had her believing in the golden dream as well. If Brendan's belief died, then what did they have left?

"The streets may not be paved in gold, more like mud I be thinkin'. But the O'Flynns have never liked things comin' to them easy," Mara said, a laugh trembling on her voice.

Brendan turned to look at her, a hint of mischief beginning to grow in his dark eyes as he caught her mood. He threw back his head and breathed deeply of the salt air, expelling it on a hearty laugh.

"To be sure, ye're an O'Flynn, Mara, and if there be gold out there we'll have it in our pockets," Brendan promised, the old look back in his eyes. He lifted a giggling Paddy onto his shoulders where he would have a better view of the harbor. As the other passengers crowded close to get their first glimpse of San Francisco, small launches began to sail out from the docks to meet the ship and carry the newcomers ashore.

Jamie peered over the railing, shaking her bonneted head as she stared at the crudely built city that straggled in confusion from shoreline to hillside.

"'Tis an uncivilized place, to be sure, that ye've brought us to, Brendan O'Fly—" Jamie began, only to choke on her words. She glanced down into one of the shore boats, staring down wordlessly into the curious eyes of a Chinese boatman. His long braid caught her eye as it swung to and fro in the breeze. Jamie crossed herself and whispered fervently, "May the saints be preservin' us, for we be enterin' a heathen place."

Ah, sad and strange as in dark summer dawns
The earliest pipe of half-awaken'd birds
To dying ears, when unto dying eyes
The casement slowly grows a glimmering square;
So sad, so strange, the days that are no more.

—Tennyson

Chapter 2

MARA O'FLYNN'S FIRST GLIMPSE OF THE RANCHO VILLAREALE came early in the evening a few days later. They had entered a valley of rolling hills, and nestled at the base was the *hacienda*, its adobe walls and red-tiled roof bathed in a golden light from the setting sun.

"The valley is called Valle d'Oro, Valley of Gold," Don Luís spoke beside Mara, "but not, I fear, because of a richness of gold in our hills," he explained contemptuously. "Our forebears so named it because of this very sight."

He followed Mara's gaze to the golden hills and vivid sky above. "They saw the beauty of the land, not its value."

"But you see the value as well, do you not, Don Luís?" Mara asked softly, her golden brown eyes reflecting the last rays of the sun.

"*Sí*," Don Luís admitted, returning her gaze thoughtfully, "and if you are wise, you will see the value in helping me. We can all profit in this valley, Amaya," he reminded her with an emphasis on the name.

Mara smiled cynically. "How fortunate I am to have you, Uncle Luís. I am sure you'll be keeping a fatherly eye upon me."

Don Luís returned her smile just as shallowly "A watchful eye, and I would advise you to keep a guarded tongue, for you speak with temper, and that would not be wise," he warned as he glanced meaningfully at Paddy whose dark head lolled against Mara's breast as he dozed fitfully.

"You needn't fear that my tongue will betray you," Mara told him shortly before returning her gaze to the colorful sky.

The turquoise of it was almost too bright against the crimson of the sun-bathed clouds. The colors clashed as the sunset changed hues. As they made their way into the valley, the sun gradually withdrew, leaving the clouds to float like smoldering coals, their bellies tinged with pink, until they became mere puffs of smoke in a faded blue sky.

"And is this it?" Brendan demanded as he stared out of the coach at the mud walls of the house below. "'Tisn't much, to be sure," he added rudely, unimpressed with the beauty of the valley.

"You think not, Mr. O'Flynn?" Don Luís asked haughtily, eyeing the Irishman with dislike. "The valley, as well as the hacienda, belongs to Don Andres," he reminded Brendan.

Brendan's dark eyes widened. "The whole valley, is it now?"

"Sí, and beyond even the hills in the distance."

"That far? How much land does this Don Andres own?" Brendan asked, unable to conceal his awe.

Don Luís shrugged carelessly. "Who knows for certain? To the south and the rocks shaped like a falcon's wing; to the east as far as the grove of oak; to the north and the lake of clear, sweet water. *Poco más o menos.*" Don Luís smiled at Brendan's uncomprehending frown. "A little more or less."

"But have you no deeds, no papers showing your property lines?" Brendan exclaimed incredulously.

Don Luís turned his head until his aristocratic profile was outlined in the half-light from the coach window. "A man's word is law. His life can be worth no more than that. What need have I, or others, for a scrap of paper telling me what I already know and believe? Who is there to question our rights?"

"You be a trusting soul," Brendan murmured in disbelief. "Seems to me you're asking for a load of trouble and misunderstanding with that attitude, and especially with people being what they are."

Don Luís looked intently at Brendan. "And what are they, Señor O'Flynn?" he asked.

"Why, they're people like you and me, Don Luís," Brendan replied with a touch of malice. "And we know what we are...don't we? You'll be asking me to leave the carriage first, and I, of course, will politely decline by offering you the honor of being first. Neither of us is willing to turn his back on the other, eh, Don Luís?" Brendan mocked.

Don Luís nodded his head in perfect understanding. "I'm pleased that we know one another so well, for now there will be no mistakes or misunderstandings which could result in tragic consequences."

Jamie hunched down closer in her corner of the coach and eyed the Spaniard suspiciously from under the brim of her bonnet. The odd exchange of words was creating an uncomfortable atmosphere.

Don Luís studied the O'Flynns thoughtfully while rubbing his chin as if deciding upon his next words carefully. "Our ranchos are interconnected, in a manner of speaking. It is true that they are few and far between, but many of us are related and there is always someone visiting from another part of the country. We like it this way for we know what the others are about, and know we can count on them for any assistance. One might be led into believing that Don Andres's land stretches as far as the ocean and even as far east as the Sierra Nevada, in that he knows what is happening that far away and even beyond. You understand?"

"No," Brendan muttered abruptly, "I'm a man for simpler words, Don Luís."

Don Luís smiled in derision. "To put it simply, Señor O'Flynn, no matter where a man might run, he would still be, in effect, on Don Andres's land...or on mine perhaps, or on a cousin's or an uncle's. It would make little difference, for there would be no escape."

Brendan laughed. "I stand warned, although you needn't have worried yourself, Don Luís. Mara and I aren't about to be leaving without our pockets full of money for a job well done," Brendan reassured him with a smile, but his eyes had narrowed as he took in the low-lying hills that hugged the mouth of the valley and seemed like a barrier to uninvited visitors. Just as easily the narrow passage, guarded by one or two armed men, could keep a reluctant guest cooling his heels on the rancho. Brendan realized their position with a feeling of growing unease.

Don Luís knocked on the roof of the coach, halting it abruptly. With a slight inclination of his head he left the coach. A moment later he rode past, mounted on the sturdy chestnut he'd ridden for most of the journey.

"Haughty bastard," Brendan murmured beneath his breath as he watched the dust fly up beneath the hooves of Don Luís's mount.

Mara smiled. "I'm surprised he deemed it necessary to pay us a visit at all, unless he thought we might be hatching devious plots in the seclusion and boredom of this coach ride."

"Givin' us a warnin', to be sure," Brendan agreed. "Well, he's met his match in the O'Flynns."

Mara stared at the stiff back of Don Luís as he rode ahead of the coach, and wondered if Brendan might be wrong in underestimating the Spaniard. How different he seemed now as he urged his horse into a gallop, his body moving with the steady stride of the horse as if he'd been born in the saddle. He looked different as well. Gone was the European style of clothing, the long-tailed frock coat and tight-fitting tweed trousers, the tall silk hat and casually tied silk scarf. He wore a short green jacket embroidered in gold, a blue silk vest, and a red satin sash tied about his waist. His trousers were of black cloth that molded his thigh down to the knee, then flared out over his calves, the opened edges decorated with gold braid and revealing white drawers beneath. Deer-skin shoes, richly decorated, and a wide-brimmed *sombrero* with a gilt band completed his costume.

But it was his saddle that caught and held Mara's attention. It was huge in comparison to the smaller and flatter English saddles she was accustomed to. It sat on an apron of leather, stamped and embroidered in bright greens and reds, and had a high wooden horn and long, wooden stirrups. It looked unbelievably heavy.

As the don's colorful figure disappeared, Mara continued

to stare out the window of the coach. She sighed, whether in relief at finally reaching their destination or in apprehension of what lay ahead, she did not know.

She was relieved, at least, to see that Brendan had recovered some of his former high spirits. He had strained at the reins like a mettlesome horse resenting the hard bit in his mouth when they had briefly seen San Francisco. Driving through the streets, Brendan had caught the frantic, feverish atmosphere of the gold-spirited city. To hear the wild laughter and raised voices mingling with the tawdriness of music and song as it drifted to the street from garishly painted wood buildings was a spark igniting the fire in Brendan's blood. His dark eyes had glazed over as he'd stared longingly at the gambling houses they had passed, oblivious to the mud thrown up by the wheels of the coach as it lurched through the debris-clogged avenues of San Francisco that were little more than quagmires. What couldn't be carried or made use of by the transient townspeople was no longer desired or valued, and was dumped in the streets. Iron cookstoves, crates and barrels full of spoiled goods crowded the streets in makeshift bridges across the mud, or ended up in stacks that continued to grow, unchecked.

The streets were crowded with people as well as discarded rubbish. The flannel-shirted figures Mara would find so familiar in future months were just part of the crowd of people that surged and loitered in the streets. Every so often the brightly colored satin jackets of Oriental foreigners would flash before her eyes, then disappear just as abruptly behind the ordinary frock coat of another adventurer hoping to strike it rich in California.

Don Luís, unable to hide his condemnatory expression as he stared at the city around him, hadn't paused to enjoy the sights and sounds, but had urged their party with all possible speed to a steamer docked at Clark's Point that would carry them inland. The steamer had been crowded with overeager, excitable prospectors making their way to the high country of the gold mines. After standing on deck and watching the islands of the bay slide past and catching a last glimpse of the

Pacific through the Golden Gate, the narrow passageway between ocean and bay, Mara had gladly stayed in her cabin, too tired with fatigue and disappointment to do more than peck at her dinner as she found herself, yet again, on another ship. But Brendan had enjoyed the journey, having an opportunity to mix with other hopefuls and some more experienced miners who were still optimistic about making their fortune in gold.

It took them a day to sail from the Straits of Carquinez inland past the sleepy town of Benicia through Suisun Bay, and up the Sacramento River to Sacramento City—the last place to enjoy the comforts of civilization before heading into the gold country and the isolated splendor of the Sierra Nevada.

Sacramento City was a surprisingly well-developed town with two-story wood and brick buildings and tree-lined streets. Their steamer docked among ships, brigs, schooners, and other floating craft that were anchored, some two deep, before the mile-long levee along Front Street. They breakfasted at the City Hotel, with its projecting veranda and balcony, and interior decor of bright colors that clashed with the equally colorful garb of its patrons. Even at this early hour in the morning there was drinking and gambling going on, and out in the street, wagons loaded with supplies continuously rolled past as they loaded and unloaded goods from the ships docked at the levee. Mara had watched in fascination as mule trains, heavily laden with equipment, the picks and shovels, pots and pans, and other paraphernalia balanced precariously on the backs of the shaggy beasts, slowly left town for the northern mines. Dressed in the red woolen shirts, wide-brimmed felt hats, black, knee-length coats, high boots, and baggy trousers that seemed to be the unofficial uniform of the gold seeker, the miners headed up to the mining camps of Marysville and Hangtown. They were seeking virgin land that hadn't been claimed yet, going high up into the steep canyons of the Yuba and Feather rivers that had cut their way down through the High Sierra, carrying with them gold-rich soil.

But Mara and her party headed in the opposite direction. They had been met in Sacramento City by several *vaqueros* from the Rancho Villareale who had been waiting for over a fortnight on the estimated arrival of Don Luís, and after hiring a coach, they had been ferried across the river to continue their journey. They traveled back toward the west across the flat lands of the Great Valley and the coastal range with its rolling hills and valleys covered with wooded slopes and high meadows of golden-yellow flowers. Their progress was slow and arduous, for the road was hardly more than a rock strewn track that they followed into the hills. Don Luís, overhearing one of Brendan's withering denunciations of California civilization as his head hit the ceiling of the coach for the third time, callously had retorted that Californians needed no roads since they preferred to ride horseback and only the old and infirm permitted themselves to travel in carriages. And Brendan's good humor hadn't been restored when they had been forced to spend the night at an abandoned *adobe*, eating a dinner of strange food cooked over an open fire, after which the Californians, including Don Luís, had rolled themselves up in the full, tightly woven wool capes they wore and settled down for a night's sleep. At Jamie's insistence they had slept in the coach, settling themselves uncomfortably for a long night, but resting easier than they would have in the weathered adobe with its dirt floor and unseen crawling inhabitants.

It had been a long night, Mara thought as she yawned. She was jolted out of her recollections as the coach hit a deep hole and the top of Paddy's head bumped her chin.

"Ow!" Paddy cried out as he was rudely awakened. His brown eyes gazed up in reproach at her, but Mara was looking out the window. The coach moved between heavy wooden gates that were standing open, and entered a large courtyard surrounded by high, tile-capped adobe walls.

They had entered what was apparently a stable yard. Mara could see Don Luís's horse being unsaddled while its rider stood patiently awaiting the arrival of the coach. Next to the stables a blacksmith's forge stood before the opened doors of the workshop, but his hammer was still as he watched their arrival. Several women dressed in colorful skirts and embroidered white blouses, their black hair hanging in thick braids down their backs, stood staring silently by the edge of a fountain.

"Welcome to Rancho Villareale, Doña Amaya," Don Luís spoke softly, a gleam in his dark eyes as he indicated his surroundings with triumph.

Mara gathered her skirts together and allowed Don Luís to take her hand as he helped her climb down from the coach. Before she could reach out to help Paddy down, he jumped, landing on his hands and knees in the dust.

"Paddy," Mara sighed in exasperation as she helped him to his feet and dusted off his trousers. She straightened the peaked, flat-crowned hat to a more secure angle on his curls, frowning in mock severity when he laughed up at her and set the cap back farther on his head.

Brendan, having helped Jamie from the coach, now stood staring around him with an absurd expression. He watched a large rooster, less than a foot away, strut arrogantly past him. A mangy-looking dog charged a group of feeding chickens, scattering them in ruffled confusion as they set up a squabbling protest that rivaled the dog's frenzied barking.

"Jaysus," Brendan complained, "but I never thought to be findin' meself in a barnyard and wearin' me best shoes."

Mara hid a reluctant smile behind her gloved hand as he adroitly, with mincing steps, sidestepped the rooster. In an affected manner, Brendan straightened his cuffs, gave a derisive sniff, and eyed his surroundings questioningly.

"Come," Don Luís urged them, a contemptuous look on his face as he watched Brendan's posturings. He did not realize that Brendan was playing the fool, the actor in him unable to resist an audience. "It is time I introduced you to your new family, Amaya."

Mara felt a hand on her elbow and glanced around to see Brendan walking beside her. His dark eyes twinkled irrepressibly down at her as he squeezed her elbow reassuringly.

"Your finest performance, little darlin', is about to begin, and little do they know they're about to witness a show grand enough for a king's pleasure," Brendan predicted, his eyes sparkling at the challenge that lay ahead. "A pity that they're to be an unappreciative public."

"'Tis a pity you're not laying odds on the outcome," Mara commented with a smile.

Brendan's eyebrow lifted in question. "And who's to be sayin' I haven't? I'm an Irishman, aren't I?"

They followed Don Luís through the iron-grilled gate set in the corner of the adobe wall and entered another courtyard. Mara stopped in surprise as she stared at the transformation that had been made in the inner court.

She could feel a change in temperature as she stepped into the coolness of the shadowed courtyard. It was surrounded on four sides by an opened corridor with a low, tile roof supported by rough-hewn posts. In the center of the tiled patio was a double-tiered fountain, its bubbling cascade of water creating a lulling effect as it flowed into the blue-tiled fountain. Gazing around her, Mara felt her senses being assaulted by the bright colors of the flowers and shrubs that filled the courtyard. Planters of fuchsia with their exotic pink and red blossoms and red-leaved creeper with magenta flowers hung from the eaves of the projecting overhang of the gallery. Trellises of deep lavender clematis blended with climbing yellow roses, star-shaped flowers of jasmine, and the carmine and cerise of sweet pea. The bluish purple flowers of a gnarled wisteria drooped from along the roof while below, colorful pottery held hyacinths, pansies, violas, and irises of every possible hue.

It was a fragrant, secluded oasis of color and beauty, protected by the thick adobe walls of the hacienda. As Mara walked along the patio, hurrying to catch up to Don Luís, she noticed the fruit trees. The perfumed orange blossoms engulfed her in fragrance as she hungrily eyed the ripening oranges and pale greens of lemons and limes.

"Don Luís, *mi amigo. ¿Cómo está usted?*" a voice inquired from the shadowed gallery across the courtyard.

"*Estoy muy bien, mi amigo*, Don Andres," Don Luís replied with a wide grin as he waited for the other man to approach him.

Don Andres stopped abruptly as he caught sight of the group standing silently in the shadows of the leafy branches of an overhanging tree.

"*¿Quién es la señorita?*" he asked of the still-smiling Don Luís.

"Es Amaya," Don Luís informed him, smug satisfaction in his voice.

At the name Amaya, and the stunned look on Don Andres's face, Mara came to the conclusion that her intended husband was little pleased to see her on the Rancho Villareale.

Don Andres quickly masked any dismay he might have shown and, smiling a welcome, moved past Don Luís and came to a halt in front of Mara.

Mara returned his stare curiously, drawing strength from his barely concealed uncertainty. A half-smile curved her lips. Tilting her head, she said softly, "Don Andres, it is a pleasure to make your acquaintance."

Don Andres's eyes flickered with a look Mara had come to expect in men's eyes. He said hesitantly, "Amaya?"

Mara's smile widened as she began to master the role of Amaya. "And may I introduce my cousin, Brendan O'Sullivan, and his son, Padraic, and our companion of many years, Jamie." Mara made the introductions easily as she took in Don Andres's appearance.

He was slightly over medium height, slender and dark, very handsome in a romantic way, with sleepy, dark eyes and a drooping mustache. He moved with the easy grace of a dancer in his short, gold-embroidered blue jacket and open-necked shirt. His dark breeches were flared and trimmed in gold braid. He could not be more than thirty, yet there was a gentle authority about him that was evident in his controlled movements.

"Mara, I'm thirsty," Paddy interrupted, his voice sounding muffled as he hid his face in Mara's skirts.

Mara unconsciously rubbed her fingers soothingly along the back of Paddy's neck as she felt his small body lean tiredly against her. "If it wouldn't be too much trouble—" she began uncertainly, yet with a smile calculated to charm and get results.

"Of course not, Doña Amaya. Anything at all I can do for you I will do. You are my honored guests, so please do not hesitate to ask," Don Andres cordially invited, his look taking in all three O'Flynns. "Some refreshment will be brought to your rooms immediately. It is unfortunate that Don Luís did not see fit to send one of my vaqueros ahead to warn us of your arrival. Then we would have had every convenience prepared for you," Don Andres remarked coldly as he stared at an unperturbed-looking Don Luís.

"And ruin the surprise of your fiancée's arrival at Rancho Villareale?" Don Luís replied mockingly. "I have waited for over a year to see the joyous expression on your face when I presented my niece, Amaya, to you."

A thinly veiled hostility between the two men was gradually revealing itself as the two Californians stared into each other's dark eyes. Imperiously Don Andres clapped his hands. "Cesarea! She will show you to your rooms and see to your needs."

"I would like to have my nephew, Padraic, sleeping near to me. And of course Jamie will be seeing to his needs, as well as helping me," Mara explained, then added sadly as she smoothed Paddy's ruffled curls, "Poor Brendan, he's a widower and his darling boy is like a son to me, and even calls me Mara." She laughed huskily. "Amaya was far too much for him to handle. He's quite a dear, and I'm very fond of him. So, if this can be arranged?"

"Of course," Don Andres smiled sympathetically, "I understand, and the young señor will be placed in the room next to yours. Señor O'Sullivan shall be one room farther down the corridor," he reassured her.

"Thank you, Don Andres," Mara replied graciously, her smile sincere this time.

"And thank you, as well, Don Andres," Brendan murmured deferentially, "you are, indeed, too kind to weary travelers."

"When you have rested and settled in, we will meet again, sí. I will have the pleasure of introducing you to my family. But for now you must rest. It has been an extraordinary journey, has it not? I trust that all of your luggage has been brought to the rancho, as we were not expecting you, Doña Amaya. I had sent a couple of vaqueros to Sacramento City to meet Don Luís. He was bringing back several items from Europe for us, so I knew he would need some assistance. I was, however, quite surprised to see exactly what he did bring back with him."

"You were not expecting me to return to California?" Mara asked curiously as she looked at Don Luís, wondering what in the world he was up to.

"We had been led to believe, Doña Amaya, from your relatives' letters in the past, that you would not consider returning. However, you have obviously changed your mind, so..." he let his words drop into the silence. Then, with a flick of his fingers, he ordered the servant to take them to their rooms. He turned to Don Luís who had remained quietly watchful beside him. "You must be fatigued as well, Don Luís. You do not look overly well, and of course you will be anxious to see Doña Jacinta. But first I should like a few words with you."

"My pleasure, Don Andres," Don Luís responded coolly, his voice as smooth as honey and his smile as sweet. Mara and Brendan read the congratulatory look in his eyes as he nodded to them in dismissal. "I will see you later, my dear niece."

"Until this evening, Doña Amaya, Señor O'Sullivan," Don Andres said formally, his initial surprise at their appearance having been replaced by a stiff hauteur.

"Thank you, Don Andres," Brendan answered for them as he urged a puzzled Mara to follow the Indian woman.

Mara's smile encompassed both Spaniards before she turned to follow the servant, Paddy and Jamie trailing along as they hurried to keep up.

"Mara, me love," Brendan said as soon as they were out of earshot, "I'm proud of you. For once you didn't overplay your part. Although you needn't go quite so heavy on the 'poor Brendan' routine," Brendan complained good-naturedly.

"Don't be worrying, my dear. I know how to say my lines," Mara returned confidently. Then, looking up at Brendan with a frown on her forehead, she added, "But what came over Don Andres? One minute I had him charmed with me smile, and the very next he was as stiff as a block of wood."

Brendan smiled cynically. "I'm thinkin' you've had it too easy with your many conquests, little darlin', and the don is a bit deeper than he looks. There's more to him than meets the eye, so don't be getting too puffed up with your success, or you'll be making mistakes," Brendan warned. "I've got a prickling feeling up the back of my neck that's telling me we be treadin' on shaky ground."

Mara gave Brendan a curious look. "It wouldn't seem as though Don Luís and Don Andres are exactly the best of friends either, which should make their business dealings interesting."

"Odd you should be feeling that too," Brendan agreed thoughtfully. "We shall just have to be lookin' out for ourselves. I'm not above keepin' an eye on Don Luís, for he's up to something more than this masquerade, I'm thinkin'."

The Indian woman, with a shy smile, pointed to an opened doorway and indicated that Brendan should enter.

"Apparently this is my room, but damned if I've ever heard of a place this size having just one floor. I'm just hopin' that rooster doesn't wander in on me in the middle of the night, or I'll be puttin' up one hell of a fight," Brendan declared dramatically as he disappeared into his room.

Cesarea pointed to Jamie and Paddy as they passed the next room and then to Mara as she led them to a third room. Then she disappeared across the courtyard in a flurry of skirts.

"Do you think a rooster might really be comin' into my room in the night, Mara?" Paddy asked in awe, a gleam of anticipation in his eyes.

"No, I do not. Your papa was being silly," Mara quickly disabused him of that idea. "Besides, one wouldn't dare, not with Jamie standing guard over the door."

Mara entered her room and stood looking around her in pleased surprise. It was cool and shadowed, and there was little furniture to clutter it. The tile floors were bare, but the bed looked invitingly comfortable with its intricately embroidered counterpane turned back to reveal fine silk-edged, linen pillowcases. Folded across the foot was a gaily colored comforter.

"Don't seem too bad a place," Jamie commented, having followed Mara into her room. She ran her finger along the top of a table, searching for dust. "Cleaner than most of the places we been stayin' in."

Paddy jumped onto the bed with a bounce. "Ummm, it's soft, Mara."

"Well, at least we'll be getting a good night's rest for a change," Mara replied with satisfaction as she took in the cleanliness of the room. Brightly painted pictures of saints hung from the whitewashed walls and the windows were set in deep embrasures, iron bars running vertically across them on the outside. Mara stared at the bars and felt a momentary twinge of panic.

The chink of glass against glass made her turn around to see the Indian servant returning with a tray. She placed it on a long table against the wall before leaving, her long black braid swinging with the movement of her bright skirts.

Mara smiled as Paddy jumped from the bed and ran over to eye the tray from a better angle.

Mara poured Paddy a glass, then another as he quickly emptied the first. Paddy's small hand unerringly found the plate of sweets and with sugar clinging to his chin he made himself comfortable on the bed.

"Now be careful, Master Paddy, or ye'll be spillin' your juice on the lovely spread," Jamie cautioned, gratefully taking a seat and a long swallow of the juice Mara had given her.

Mara sipped her juice and felt some of the dryness leave her throat. "To be sure, I'm thinkin' the O'Flynns haven't done too bad for themselves," Mara commented as she looked around the room.

"And if ye be wantin' it to continue, then ye'd best be guardin' *your* tongue, little darlin'," Brendan said from the opened doorway.

Mara flushed slightly at his reprimand. "I think it's gone quite well so far."

"So far?" Brendan questioned as he moved into the room, his glass of wine half-full. "It hasn't even begun yet. Do you think I could get a glass of whiskey around here?" he demanded and, with a grimace, swallowed the rest of his wine. "At least it'll wash the dust down, and I've got a couple of bottles in my bags."

"Just don't be getting yourself drunk, or we'll be having to watch *your* tongue instead."

Brendan laughed as he rubbed his stubble of whiskers. "I'm an Irishman, mavournin, and Irishmen are never drunk, just a bit blind to the world, that's all," Brendan defended himself.

"That's all?" Mara questioned him with a contemptuous laugh. "More like blind drunk, why, I've seen you sewn up tighter than a—"

"Ye've not!" Brendan interrupted in outraged pride. "I've never been fuddled in me life. But then, ye be so perfect, Mara, me love, that ye've not got any vices, have ye?"

"Enough!" Jamie cut in, an exasperated look on her tired face. "Ye be carryin' on like guttersnipes. A fine example ye be settin' for Master Paddy with your squabblin' all the time. No wonder ye can't be holdin' onto a job longer than it takes to be openin' your mouths."

Brendan stared at the little woman with a jaundiced eye. "One of these fine days I might be gettin' rid of you," Brendan warned, "so you'd best be curbin' your tongue."

Jamie snorted derisively. "Not likely, Master Brendan. Who else but me'd be puttin' up with the likes o' ye and Miss Mara? I ask ye that? To be sure, no one in their right mind would take such abuse from the two of ye, and the pay bein' even more insultin'. If it wasn't fer the promise I made ye mum, God rest her soul, I'd have washed me hands o' the two of ye O'Flynns long ago."

Laughing as he caught the last of her words, Paddy chanted loudly, "Washed me hands o' the O'Flynns! Washed me hands o' the O'Flynns, o' the O'Flynns, washed me hands o' Mara, o' Mara!"

"Paddy!" Mara broke into his made-up song, silencing the childishly high-pitched voice that seemed to reverberate throughout the room.

Scowling, Brendan looked down at his son. "If certain young men aren't knowin' how to behave themselves, then they'll be feelin' the bite o' me hand on the back of their breeches," Brendan threatened.

Paddy stared up at his father, his lower lip jutting out rebelliously. He apologized, but a moment later Mara heard snatches of the same tune beneath Paddy's breath as he sipped his orange juice.

"Well, he's your son, isn't he? What else would you be expecting?" Mara said softly, a smile warming her eyes.

Brendan shrugged. "Seeing how you've more than raised him, I be expecting nothing less," he retorted with a grin. "Of course, there be some people around here, not havin' a likin' for the O'Flynns, who'd be saying 'tis what they deserve," Brendan added with a devilish look of innocence aimed at Jamie.

"Hrrmph. Ye be knowin' as well as me that'd I'd not be happy with anyone but the O'Flynns, so I be deservin' what I get as well," Jamie admitted grudgingly.

Mara had a slight smile on her lips as she turned to refill her glass of juice. As she moved, she became aware of a woman standing in the doorway. At Mara's sudden stillness Brendan turned to find the cause and stared in silence as well.

The woman backed up a step, smiling nervously as Mara and Brendan continued to gaze at her, her smile wavering and fading as she felt their full, concentrated stare.

"Please, you will forgive me for intruding," she spoke softly and slowly, her English heavily accented and barely understandable. "I have waited the long hours of years, wondering if you would return with Don Luís, wondering what you would be like, and you have finally come. You are Amaya Vaughan. You are too beautiful," she added almost to herself as her soft brown eyes took in every detail of Mara's appearance.

Her expression was almost sad as she gazed with longing at the fashionable, striped dress in pale gold colors that accentuated the gold in Mara's eyes, the elegant deep flounce of crisp lace that edged Mara's sleeves, and the fichu that crossed over her breasts and was a perfect frame for her fragile neck.

"I am Feliciana," she introduced herself, and came shyly into the room. As she moved from the shadow of the doorway, the light from the windows fell on her, revealing a small figure dressed totally in black. The perfect oval of her face contrasted startlingly with the rest of her somber appearance. Her eyes were darkly luminous and unreadable behind hastily lowered lashes. Her smooth, wide brow and rounded chin, blending with her soft, slightly curved lips, created a picture of almost untouchable serenity.

"You will not have heard of me, but I am Don Andres's ward, and his third cousin. I live here on the rancho," she said almost defiantly, as if daring them to repudiate her claim. Her mouth trembled slightly as she ran her hands over the black cloth of her gown. In explanation for her dark appearance, she said, "I am in mourning for the death of my father."

"I am very sorry, Doña Feliciana," Mara said inadequately, and for some strange reason she felt guilty as she saw the wounded look on the young girl's face. "This is my cousin, Brendan O'Sullivan, and his son, Paddy."

"And charmed I am to be meeting you, Doña Feliciana," Brendan greeted her, his bold appraisal causing a vivid blush to color her pale cheeks.

She mumbled something unintelligible, then smiled as Paddy said in exact imitation of Brendan, "Charmed I am to be meeting you, Doña Felice-ch—Felice."

"A fine young son, Señor O' Sullivan," she complimented him.

"Please call me Brendan. I am almost one of the family," he said audaciously, continuing despite Jamie's snort, "and we must get to know one another better."

"I must leave," Feliciana spoke hurriedly, looking flustered as she heard voices in the courtyard. "They bring your traveling things, sí? Adiós, Señor O'Sullivan." Her eyes lingered on Mara for a moment before she added on a sigh, "Doña Amaya."

"Well, and what are you making of that?" Brendan declared in amusement as he watched her small figure retreating across the patio, her black skirts rustling provocatively despite her demure walk. "A shy little dove, to be sure," he added, a speculative gleam in his eye.

"And one you should leave in peace," Mara warned softly as she directed the servants where to put her trunks. "You'd best be seeing to yours, Brendan. This one isn't mine."

Brendan scowled. "Do I have to be doin' everything meself? Hey, listen you, wait up! My good man, come back here," he called after the servants as they left. When he got no response, he muttered something and, picking up his own bag, carried it out of the room.

Mara turned to Paddy who was leaning sleepily against the back of the bed. With a nod to Jamie she said, "I think we might have a look at your room, Paddy, and see if your bed is as comfortable as mine."

"I think we could all be usin' a rest after that bone-shakin' ride," Jamie said firmly as she went around the room gathering up Paddy's belongings before guiding him to his own room.

It was later that evening when Mara awoke to find her room silent and dark. She shivered as she felt the coolness of the evening shadows. She curled her toes in surprise as her bare feet touched the smooth coldness of the tiled floor. She yawned, flexing her tired shoulder muscles as she walked to the window and stared through the half-light of dusk at the rolling hills in the distance. Suddenly the twilight silence was shattered by the eerie howling of a coyote. Mara strained her eyes as she saw a doglike shape skulk along the ridge of a hill in the distance.

"Seems a lonely land," Mara murmured as the outline of the hills faded into the darkness and a stillness hung in the night air. She nearly cried out when an abrupt knocking sounded on her door, disturbing the quiet. An Indian servant entered holding a lighted taper and a candelabrum. She shouldered open the door, placed the heavy, silver candelabra on a table, and lit the candles. The flickering flames gradually lit the indistinct shapes within the room and created an illusion of spreading warmth. Another Indian followed her, a towel draped over her arm, bearing a large bowl of water. They hurriedly left, casting shyly inquisitive glances at Mara's silent figure, the jade green silk dressing gown shimmering with threads of gold.

Mara pulled her hair free from its chignon, sighing in relief as she felt the heavy weight of it fall to her hips. She splashed the cool water on her face and hands, working a small, fragrant bar of soap into a lather as she rubbed her face clean of dust and tiredness. She indolently brushed her hair until it crackled with electricity, and tossing it over her shoulder, she sauntered from the room, feeling relaxed without the tight lacings of her corset. She breathed deeply of the night-fragrant garden, its perfumed scents intensifying as darkness enfolded it.

Mara entered Paddy's room, finding him still asleep despite the loud, gurgling snores coming from Jamie, on a small bed next to his.

"Jamie," Mara whispered, but received no response. "Jamie," she said in a louder tone of voice as she leaned closer to her, remembering that Jamie was having trouble hearing. She would not admit to it, of course. "Wake up, Jamie."

Jamie awoke with a start as Mara gave her a gentle shake. "Wh-what time is it?" Jamie demanded as she quickly slid from the bed and straightened her bright orange dressing gown.

Mara smiled. "I don't know. But why do people always ask that when they wake up suddenly, as though they've a guilty conscience or something? Besides, there's nothing you can do about lost time, once it's gone, well…" she said with a shrug.

"Well, I know what I should be doing now, and that's gettin' young Paddy up and dressed, so ye'd best be doin' the same," Jamie told her with a critical look in her gray eyes as she took in Mara's appearance. "It's shameful the way ye be runnin' around half-dressed all o' the time. Ye be askin' for trouble. Why, ye've not even got shoes on. To be sure, ye've got the heathen in your soul, and to think ye was brought up proper-like, to have respect for—"

"All right, Jamie, I'm going," Mara told her as she padded to the door, her bare feet making no sound. "But I won't apologize for liking to feel free," Mara added defiantly as she rubbed the soft silk of her robe, loving the feel of it against her naked skin. "And I am free, Jamie. Free to do as I wish, and no one can say nay to me. 'Tis one of the advantages of bein' born a bastard. There's no one there to give a damn," she said recklessly as she left the room.

Mara knocked on Brendan's door but there was no reply.

After waiting a minute, she opened his door hesitantly, then went inside when she saw him stretched out on his bed, a half-empty bottle of whiskey standing open on the table beside it. How like Paddy he looked in his sleep, Mara thought sadly, his hair in disorderly curls and a slight smile softening his hard mouth. He seemed as innocent as his son.

"Brendan," Mara murmured. "Brendan, wake up now. You'll be wanting to change your clothes."

His shirt was wrinkled and open, revealing the vulnerable column of his throat. Brendan pulled his shoulder away protestingly from Mara's hand and hid his face in his arm as he murmured something.

"What?" Mara asked as she barely caught his sleepily mumbled words.

"Molly, me darlin' Molly," Brendan slurred the name.

Mara's lips tightened at the sound of the name. "No, 'tis Mara, me darlin' Brendan," she said sharply, "and you'd better get up now. You need a shave and a wash. You smell like the inside of a whiskey bottle."

She was leaving the room as he struggled to his elbows and shook his head to clear away the hazy thoughts. "What a hair-raising dream," Brendan groaned as he swung his feet to the floor and held his head in his hands.

"Your hair is standing on end," Mara confirmed. "Even as fine an Irishman as yourself can only be holding so much before finding himself pickled and full of blarney."

Brendan looked up, the light from the candles softening the jaded expression on his face. "Ye've got one fault, Mara, me love, that you ought to be trying to change before someone decides to do it for you. And that's not knowin' when to curb that sharp tongue of yours. In other words, mavournin—shut up."

Mara's lips parted in a half-smile. "To be sure, it gets the right results sometimes in clearing the fog from some people's minds." Turning on her heel she flounced from the room, the half-smile still on her lips as the door closed behind her and she started along the dark passage to her room.

An hour later Mara stared at her reflection in the mirror

as she fastened dangling, jet earrings into her ear lobes and slipped several matching bracelets onto her wrists. In the candlelight her bare shoulders gleamed as luminously as pearls above the pale yellow glacé silk gown. The skirt was gathered in flounces and caught by loops of black velvet ribbon that matched the deep ruffles of delicate black lace that edged the tight-fitting bodice that was cut low and off the shoulder. A caul of black silk net shot with gold was draped over her chignon and caught the light, glowing softly.

Mara touched her favorite scent to the inside of her wrists and the delicate hollow at the base of her throat. Lily of the valley floated around her as it was warmed by her body. Picking up a black satin reticule, she placed a dainty lace handkerchief inside and, drawing the strings, gave her reflection a last, searching look.

She was folding a black lace shawl over her arm when Brendan knocked on the door with his special knock, hitting it once, then again, then twice in rapid succession. He sauntered into the room, pausing to look Mara over critically, a smile curving his mouth as he found nothing to fault in her appearance. He had shaved and washed, and brushed his curls into order. He wore fresh linen and a sky blue silk scarf adorned with a gold pin. In blue trousers and a coat of superfine, with a dark blue velvet collar and a scroll-patterned, gold silk waistcoat, he looked very elegant and highly respectable, quite different from the man of an hour ago.

"Shall we go and face our audience?" Brendan asked in good humor as he glanced around the room curiously. "Where's Paddy? Isn't he dressed yet?"

"Jamie'll be bringing him over," Mara replied patiently. "And if he's looking as fine as his father, then he'll be doing us proud," Mara complimented her brother, smoothing over her harsh words of an hour earlier.

Brendan smiled widely. "D'ye think so, now? I've been thinking, so as not to become too bored with this charade, that I just might be playing me finest dandy. Besides, playing the fool sometimes is the best way of disarming a person. In me role as a Jemmy Jessamy I shall be me lady's fondling, and confidant to all of her secrets. Who knows what I might learn about Don Luís and the others in this household," Brendan said slyly, a gleam of mischievous anticipation in his dark eyes.

"Just don't be overdoing it and scare them off. We really can do without a scandal," Mara reminded him as Jamie entered with a subdued Paddy in hand. Dressed in long trousers, a short, round-edged jacket, and green silk waistcoat, Paddy was a miniature gentleman. His curls had been combed ruthlessly back, although one or two had already managed to escape onto his forehead.

"I'm not sure I'm likin' havin' Master Paddy up so late. 'Tisn't good for him to be eatin' such rich food either. It'll be givin' him nightmares for sure," Jamie complained with a disapproving look at the O'Flynns.

"She's right," Brendan agreed, for once showing more than his usual casual interest in his son. "You know how cranky he gets when he's been up too late."

"Well, it's too late to do anything about it tonight. We'll make other arrangements later on. In fact, you might want to see to all his meals yourself, Jamie," Mara decided as she thought of the richly seasoned food they had eaten on the trail the night before.

"Aye, that I'll be doin', and havin' me own meals in me room, as well," Jamie said firmly. "Thought someone had lit a fire in me insides last night, and 'twas still smoldering most of today as well."

"Good, you are ready," Don Luís spoke from the doorway. His gaze lingered critically over them. "We shall go now."

"I should like some dinner prepared for Jamie and sent to her room. And in future I think she should prepare both Paddy's and her own meals."

Don Luís seemed surprised for a moment and then shrugged agreement. "I suppose the English would find our dishes a little spicy. I'm sure it can be seen to, and it is just as well that the young señor have as little to say as possible," Don Luís decided as he stared at the tired boy. "This is not child's play, and as a gambler, Señor O'Flynn, you will appreciate that the stakes are high. I do not intend to lose. We will now go," he said as he motioned them out of the room with an imperious wave of his hand.

"Our lord and master has given us a command, mavournin," Brendan grumbled in a theatrical whisper. "We'd best not be disappointin' his highness, although I'm thinkin' I might just be doin' some rewritin' of roles in the last pages of this play. Don Luís's is going to become a bit part."

Paddy's small fingers tightened painfully around Mara's as they crossed the open courtyard and neared the lighted windows of the salon. Through the opened doors the sound of laughter and voices raised in conversation drifted into the night air.

Don Luís waited for them to close the distance between them. Then, with the O'Flynns but a step behind him, he made his entrance into the salon as grandly as any stage performer could have. The family Villareale—distant cousins, uncles and aunts, and friends—had gathered. An uneasy silence descended over the previously jubilant group at Don Luís's entrance. As Brendan, Mara, and a reluctant Paddy were ushered in, a flock of fans were raised as the ladies hid their expressions and whispered comments.

With a smile of benevolence that did little to soften his austere features, Don Luís guided Mara to Don Andres, who was standing beside three ladies seated on an upholstered sofa.

"It is my greatest pleasure, Doña Ysidora, to present to you my niece, Amaya Anita María Josefa Vaughan."

"My child, it has been a long wait for your return," said the lady sitting in the center of the three. Though she spoke softly, there was nothing soft about her appearance. She sat with a straight back, almost in defiance of the plush satin cushion, and was dressed in a black silk gown with a discreet edging of black lace around the bodice and cuffs. A heavy, gold cross hanging from a chain around her neck was her only adornment besides the gold rings in her ears and on her fingers. Her dark hair, streaked with silver strands through the temples, was held in a thick pile atop her head with a large, tortoiseshell comb.

Beside her, Doña Feliciana sat quietly, her large brown

eyes full of silent suffering as she looked away from Mara's flamboyant figure and down at her hands demurely clasped in her lap. Her long black braids were draped across her shoulders and fell like ropes of black satin to coil against the seat of the sofa.

"And my wife, Doña Jacinta," Don Luís continued his introductions, "and Doña Feliciana, a cousin of Don Andres."

Doña Jacinta beamed a wide smile of welcome, her round brown eyes shining. Her softly pretty face seemed too small for the large comb holding the heavy twist of black hair on top of her head. She was a startling contrast to the other two women, for her dress was a vivid peacock blue silk and around her neck was a beautiful double string of pearls that matched the pearls clustered at her ears.

"It is my pleasure to meet you ladies," Mara replied, a slight smile curving her lips. "And this is my cousin, Brendan O'Sullivan and his young son, Padraic." Brendan had been standing silently behind Mara, carefully observing each woman in turn.

"Doña Ysidora," Brendan said in a tone of deepest respect as he bowed over her hand, his manners their most polished as he repeated the performance with the other two ladies. "It is, indeed, an honor and a pleasure to gaze upon such unequaled loveliness as I see before me now," Brendan spoke flatteringly, while his lingering gaze caused a delicate blush to spread over Doña Feliciana's smooth skin and Doña Jacinta to smother a pleased giggle behind her fan.

Doña Ysidora's eyes showed a hint of amusement as she accepted the compliment with a slight nod of her regal head. "It would seem as though Doña Amaya takes after your side of the family, Señor O'Sullivan, rather than the Quintero side, for there is a marked resemblance between you," she commented thoughtfully as she allowed her gaze to linger on Brendan's face.

"Sí, there is, isn't there, although I do think she has her mother's chin," Don Luís interjected smoothly. "My sister would have been very proud of her daughter's beauty," he added. Catching sight of a young man standing apart as he conversed with another man, he called out, "Raoul, you have not met your cousin, Doña Amaya. Come here at once!"

The young man flinched visibly at the authoritative tone and, with a careless shrug, sauntered over to where his father stood impatiently waiting.

"*Mi muy estimado padre*," he said sarcastically, raising his wineglass in a toast before draining the contents.

"Raoul," Don Luís spoke sternly, his expression forbidding as he noticed for the first time his son's slightly glazed eyes and precarious balance.

Raoul stared boldly at Mara, his mouth curving in a smile of welcome as he moved closer to her, his eyes darkening to black as they caressed her bare shoulders and throat, lingering on her seductively full lips. "Ah," he breathed regretfully, "a pity we did not grow up together, little cousin," he said, disregarding the fact that they stood almost eye to eye.

He moved suddenly, clipping his arm around Mara's waist. He pulled her against him, covering her mouth with his in a hot kiss flavored with wine.

"Raoul!" Don Luís began angrily, his face turning a mottled red.

Raoul released Mara. "I'm merely welcoming Amaya to California as you requested," he answered innocently.

"You embarrass your mother and me in front of our friends," Don Luís berated him, his hands clenched with suppressed violence.

"Please, Uncle Luís," Mara interrupted, smoothly halting him. "One can forgive a small boy for many offenses. He harms no one but himself, and only makes himself look the fool." Mara laughed, her golden eyes glowing as a look of contrite embarrassment spread across Raoul's handsome face.

"Funny man," Paddy's small voice piped in as he moved closer to Mara, his hand finding hers as he gazed possessively up at her. "Don't kiss her again. She only likes me to kiss her. She only loves me."

"Oh, such a precious one," Doña Jacinta chuckled, relieved to see Raoul turn away before Don Luís could confront him again.

"My son, Paddy, is very fond of Amaya. She is like a mother to him," Brendan said sadly, his expression mirroring tragic remembrances as he continued in a slightly quivering voice, "now that I am a widower. A tragedy, the loss of his dear, sweet mama. Such an angel she was to die so young. And now we are completely dependent on our adorable Amaya, and utterly lost without her. That was why I insisted on accompanying her to this strange land. She is really such a tower of strength to us, and so devoted to little Paddy."

"Very commendable, Doña Amaya," Doña Ysidora commented with a pleased expression on her sculptured features. "It is good that you have a devotion to your family. The young forget too often that once they were cared for by the same old people they now have no time for. They learn new ways and forget what they have been taught." She spoke softly, yet with a hint of condemnation as her eyes lingered on Raoul.

Mara smiled slightly at Doña Ysidora's words. She had wondered if she would let Raoul's conduct go unpunished. Although Don Andres was master, Mara had the feeling that Doña Ysidora still had a lot to do with the running of Rancho Villareale.

"You have not met Jeremiah Davies," Doña Ysidora changed the subject as the man who'd been in conversation with Raoul stepped forward as he caught his name and the look of summons directed his way.

Jeremiah Davies was of medium build with light brown hair and clear blue eyes that stared openly at each face as he was introduced to them. A spattering of freckles spread across his pug nose and rounded cheeks, giving him a boyish quality that went well with the wide grin he frequently flashed in response to the slightest amusing remark.

Mara and Brendan exchanged knowing glances as they watched Don Andres's secretary join in the conversation, ever careful to agree and be attentive to his hosts as he ingratiated himself with all the guests. His boyish, eager-to-please charm might have fooled the others, but being actors themselves, Mara and Brendan recognized all the tricks and nuances of his performance.

"And I'm wondering what young Jerry boy is up to?" Brendan commented curiously as he watched Jeremiah Davies bend attentively to catch Doña Feliciana's softly murmured words. "Are you thinking he might be having hopes in that direction, I wonder."

"That's not for us to worry about," Mara whispered back discouragingly, before turning to greet the others who were now coming forward to be introduced to the long-awaited Amaya Vaughan.

Supper was served on a huge oak table, at least fifteen feet long, that stretched over half the length of the dining room. Benches ran along each side and easily held all of the guests as they gathered around the table to dine. As colorful dishes were placed on the table, Mara looked at Brendan, who with a shrug of inevitability dipped his spoon into the bowl of soup in front of him.

Mara followed his example, expecting it to be as hot as their meal of the previous evening but was pleasantly surprised to find it quite palatable. Paddy, seated between Mara and Brendan, was evidently enjoying it. He hungrily spooned the dumplings that thickened his soup into his small mouth.

Mara eyed the plate of flat *tortillas* and wondered where the usual slices of bread were. She watched curiously as Raoul tore a piece from one and, using it like a fork, scooped *frijoles* onto it and swallowed it all. Paddy seemed to like the idea and promptly copied the Californian, much to Brendan's look of surprised disgust. Large pottery baking dishes covered the table in a profusion of color, the steam still escaping from them.

"Allow me to select something for you, Doña Amaya," Don Andres offered solicitously. He pointed out several odd-looking concoctions as one of the servants filled a plate for her.

"Please, not so much," Mara objected with a worried laugh as an overloaded plate was placed before her.

Suspiciously prodding one of the rolled, cornmeal shapes with her fork, Mara took a bite under the anxious gaze of her hosts and found it delicious, her smile of pleased satisfaction and relief receiving answering grins all along the table.

"It is a *tamale*, and it is filled with meat," Doña Ysidora explained. "For it to be good, it must take two days of cooking. You try also the *enchilada*, and the *puchero*, which has meat and vegetables, onions, and tomatoes. Sí, you will like."

"It is all very good, Doña Ysidora," Mara complimented her.

"*Gracias*. The little one enjoys as well," she said in satisfaction as Paddy finished his beans and took a bite of roast beef.

Brendan gave a shrug, hunger overcoming reluctance, and took a forkful of the thick stew. At his gasp of surprise Mara glanced at him curiously. Her eyes widened as his face turned a bright red and tears streamed from his eyes. He reached out desperately for his wine and eased the fiery burning in his throat.

"May the saints preserve us," Brendan gasped. "'Tis hot enough to be raisin' the dead."

Mara bit her lip in vexation at Brendan's ill-spoken words, but the Californians only laughed loudly, finding his words and beet red face amusing.

"You compliment my mother, Mr. O'Sullivan," Don Andres explained. "We pride ourselves on a spicy dish. The hotter, the better, eh, amigos? My apologies for not mentioning the green *chili* peppers in the stew. And you must watch out for the red ones as well."

Brendan smiled sourly, failing to see the humor in being the butt of the joke.

"Now, Doña Amaya would be different. She has the blood of a Californian mother in her veins," Don Luís taunted, a malicious gleam in his eye. "I wonder if she can withstand the fire of the chili pepper, eh?" he speculated, looking around for support. "Perhaps not, I think."

"Oh, I don't know about that," Brendan said suddenly. "You'd be surprised at some of the hidden talents of Doña Amaya, Don Luís," Brendan challenged. "I'm bettin' she could eat one of them hot peppers of yours, Don Luís, and without flinchin'."

Mara looked at Brendan incredulously and he returned her stare expectantly, as though in little doubt of her answer.

"Of course, it is up to Amaya. If she thinks that she cannot do it…well," Don Luís said patronizingly.

"Please, I will not allow this," Don Andres said laughingly, missing the undercurrent of dislike between the O'Flynns and Don Luís. "Doña Amaya is a guest, and I would not have her thinking ill of us."

"Sí, the child is not used to our food," Doña Ysidora added with a curious look at Don Luís.

"Oh, but I shouldn't like to let Uncle Luís down in front of his friends," Mara replied mockingly as she selected a bright green pepper and, with a shudder, bit into it. She was vaguely aware of being the center of everyone's attention as she felt beads of perspiration gather above her upper lip. Her throat burned with fire and her eyes pricked with tears, yet outwardly she showed little sign of her inner turmoil. A murmur of appreciation went around the table.

"Would you care for one, Uncle Luís?" she asked politely before carefully taking a swallow of wine.

Don Luís raised his wineglass in a silent toast, a look of reluctant admiration on his face.

Brendan's eyes twinkled wickedly at her over Paddy's head, a hint of pride in his glance as he gazed triumphantly at Don Luís.

"I have lived here in California most of my life, having been brought out here by my father when only a child, and I still need to wash down their food with plenty of wine," Jeremiah Davies told Mara with a laugh. "You have proven yourself one of them already, and I am still the outsider even after twenty years of living with them." He complained good-naturedly, but his smile wasn't quite as ready, nor his tone quite so friendly as before.

"Are some of your servants ill, Don Andres?" Don Luís inquired a little too politely as he waited for his empty plate to be removed.

Don Andres's lips tightened and Mara caught a worried look cross Doña Ysidora's usually serene face. "Sí. In a manner of speaking, one might say they are ill," Don Andres answered enigmatically. "They have the gold fever."

"We never know how many servants will be here when we awaken each morning. They do not care anymore that they displease us, or fear the patron's wrath, for they believe they will become rich," Doña Ysidora spoke angrily, a look of disgust on her patrician features.

"Already I've lost a thousand head of cattle because I've not enough vaqueros to guard them," Don Andres spoke wearily.

"It is unbelievable that this could be happening," a gray-haired Californian said harshly, his sun-darkened face weathered by years spent in the saddle. "One never had to worry about thieves in the old days. Our cattle grazed freely wherever they cared to roam. We needed no fences. We had no fears. I remember on our rancho in Santa Barbara, when I was but a child, how excited we were when we saw one of the foreigners' ships come sailing into the harbor. It was late summer once, and all through the year we had raised many fine cattle that were now ready for the slaughter. The *matanza* was a favorite time for us, for there were many festivities that accompanied the hard work. On the hillsides I remember seeing the *ramadas* that shaded the workers as they cured the skins, then stretched the *cueros* in the sun where they were left to dry. We would stack them in the *carretas* with tallow and other goods to be taken to the ships and traded for so many wonderful things. The ships of the foreigners were like treasure chests, their holds full of satins and silks, tea, coffee, and wine and spices that the traders had brought from far across the seas," the old ranchero reminisced sadly.

"We had so few things in that day. We traded for every-thing. Why, some of the furniture in this very room was brought around the Horn by one of those ships. We traded for china and cooking utensils, and even shoes." He laughed, "And then there was so much singing and dancing that it seemed to last for weeks. To me, though, as a young boy, I enjoyed the *rodeo* best. Ah, how the vaqueros could ride back in that day. They were magnificent, dressed in their brightest jackets, with silk handkerchiefs tied across their foreheads; they would do the most dangerous riding tricks imaginable. We would have horse races and bullfights, and ride down to the seaside for a *merienda*, and with baskets full of food we would spend a leisurely afternoon until the ball in the evening, and then we would dance until dawn. And everyone would dance, not just the young, for it was the older and more experienced dancers who could best do the intricate steps of *la jota*. To see them line up in two rows, singing and waving their arms in rhythm to the guitar, then moving right and left, changing partners as they moved their feet in the fancy footwork…But I think my favorite has always been *el jarabe*, and I must admit that I was once quite famous for it. When the *tecolero* would announce that a couple would dance, a large crowd would form a circle around the patio as the *caballero* approached his señorita and escorted her to the center of the patio. After much fancy *mudancias* they would separate, and then the caballero would throw down his sombrero and the beautiful señorita would dance on the brim, much to the pleasure of the clapping onlookers; then, with the captured sombrero on her head, she would return to her seat.

"Sometimes we had *cascarones* filled with pieces of tinsel paper and cologne, and if you were not careful, it was broken over your head, or you might be fortunate enough to break it over the head of a favored señorita, and then she would have to pay the penalty of a *beso*, and it was quite an art to steal a kiss from the señorita under the watchful eye of her *dueña*." Don Ignacio sighed in remembered pleasure, his eyes moist as he recalled the carefree days of his youth.

He shook his grizzled head in disbelief, "I never thought it would change so much. Most of my daughters and sons live in Santa Barbara or Monterey and seldom see a cow. And never did I expect to see so many foreigners! Or that Yerba Buena would become a busy seaport called San Francisco. Have you seen the ships in the harbor?" he asked incredulously, looking around.

Sitting close to Jeremiah Davies, Mara was the only one to hear his smothered snort of derision as he listened to the aged ranchero's reminiscences of the old way of life in California. There was a crafty look in his wide blue eyes as he gazed at the Californians, but it was quickly veiled as his eyes caught her stare, and was replaced with his usual expression of amiable innocence.

"Yes, much has changed, Don Ignacio, and just in the last year or two," Don Andres agreed grimly, a disheartened expression on his face as he gazed on the festive table and his laughing, gossiping guests.

"I was surprised to find the Macias adobe abandoned," Don Luís said curiously. "Where did they go? The place had almost fallen into ruin. Beams and wood were missing; part of the roof had fallen in; it was as though it had been looted."

"You cannot believe it, Don Luís?" Don Andres remarked cynically. "That is one of the many changes that have occurred since your absence. Juan Macias had no vaqueros to ride for him; his servants, the few he had, ran off to the mines, and then, even worse, he had to fight off the squatters. In the end it was too much for him to overcome, and so he moved to Sonora, I hear, and now owns a store. He will do all right there, for his customers will mostly be South Americans or Mexicans, and not too many North Americans there, although they seem to be everywhere else.

"Since you have been gone there has been a continuous horde of *los americanos* swarming into our hills and valleys with a gold lust in their eye. They have no respect for another's land or home. At first I give them a welcome, let them into my home," Don Andres told them, his face mirroring remembered bitterness and anger, "and what do I receive in exchange? A word of thanks? No, only disrespect and contempt."

A hushed silence had fallen over the carefree group as they listened intently in incredulous skepticism and unease to Don Andres's words of bitter truth.

"Did any of you ever believe that one day a Californian would be considered a foreigner in his own land of birth?" Don Andres asked. "You smile, Don José, but I speak the truth. My right, my father's right to own this land, this very hacienda in which we sit now, is being questioned. Why do I have to prove that this is my land? The fact that it was granted to my grandfather by the king of Spain seems not to be of consequence. I have no rights anymore in this new California. I am a greaser."

Mara looked in dismay at the shocked faces around her at Don Andres's derisory word.

"You are surprised? Did you not know that is what they call us? Once the name Villareale was a name spoken with pride, a name looked up to. But to the gringo there is no difference between a Californian, a Chilean, a Sonoran, or a Mexican. A man of dark skin, who speaks with an accent, is an inferior.

"And so how do our runaway servants fare in the mines? Many have returned here to me, beaten men, and I mean that literally. They had been beaten and whipped, degraded and treated like dogs."

"Please, Andres, my son," Doña Ysidora said distressfully, "do not continue. You upset the ladies," she pleaded. She handed a glass of wine to Doña Jacinta who raised it shakily to her trembling lips.

"You will forgive me, my friends, if I have offended any of you," Don Andres apologized, "but I find it hard to swallow my pride and sit quietly by while my land is stolen from me."

"He speaks the truth," Don Ignacio said belligerently. "Have you already forgotten the murder of José de los Reyes Berreyesa and his nephews, Francisco and Ramon de Haro? The rebels shot them on Suisun Bay, and what were they doing but defending their land? And during the war with Mexico, were not Don Mariano Vallejo and his brother, Salvador, unjustly arrested and kept in jail for months while the rebels looted our homes and confiscated our horses and cattle?" Don Ignacio reminded them. "Well, it could happen again."

"I wonder what we can do. Nothing, I think," Don Andres spoke softly, a note of defeat in his quiet voice. "I am only thankful that my father is not alive to see his world destroyed."

"*Silencio*, Andres, you go too far," Doña Ysidora said angrily.

An uncomfortable silence settled over the room for a moment until Doña Ysidora signaled to several men who'd just entered. Grouping together in the corner, they started to play the musical instruments they had carried in with them. The sounds of a violin and guitars filled the silence as the people around the table gradually continued eating, but it seemed to Mara it was with a marked lack of appetite.

Brendan and Mara exchanged glances, their expressions curiously perplexed. They were out of their depth here, for they couldn't fully comprehend all of the undercurrents affecting the Californians. Brendan shrugged, his gesture signifying that it wasn't their problem anyway, and turned his full attention to Doña Jacinta, who could not hide her admiration for the handsome young Irishman.

Most of the guests had finished dining and were sipping their wine when Raoul pulled out a cigar and, lighting it, blew a haze of smoke over the table as he expelled the strong tobacco.

"Raoul. You ask no permission to smoke?" Don Luís reprimanded him, a look of stunned surprise on his haughty face.

"Raoul, do this, Raoul, do that—always some order. Well, I will ask permission of no one if I want to smoke or drink. Madre de Dios, I am a man, *padre*, not a little boy to be continually chastised," he spoke in a raised voice, his face flushed with anger and drink.

"Then act like one, for you bring disgrace on the name Quintero. You still have a few lessons to learn, my boy, and you will show proper respect to your elders or you will leave this table at once," Don Luís promised, a cutting edge to his voice.

Raoul jumped to his feet and, with an angry glance around the room, stalked out, cigar smoke lingering in the air.

Doña Jacinta sighed dispiritedly, biting her lip nervously as she glanced at the empty seat and then at the brooding Don Luís.

"I do not understand what has come over the boy. Never in the past would a son of mine have spoken so disrespectfully to his father. Why have you allowed your son to behave this way, Jacinta?" Don Luís demanded, placing the blame on his dismayed wife.

"The boy is yet young. He will learn patience and his place," Doña Ysidora said soothingly as Doña Jacinta sniffed with threatening tears. "Now we go to the salon, and we laugh and dance, and forget all this nonsense which does not concern us. Sí."

By the time the evening had been called to an end it was after midnight and Paddy had long ago fallen asleep in Mara's arms. With a carefree, whistling Brendan walking beside her, Mara tiredly carried a drowsy Paddy across the courtyard to his room and a disapproving Jamie.

Later, in the darkness of her own room, Mara stood silently contemplating a full, silver moon riding high in the sky above the dim outline of the rolling hills. Mara watched as a few wraithlike wisps of cloud floated across its face. She shivered and pulled the edges of her robe closer together across her bare throat. She felt a prickling fear quiver along her spine. Something was wrong—but what? She felt uneasy about the whole harebrained scheme, but what could she warn Brendan about? He'd only laugh at her for letting childish fears panic her. But she couldn't rid herself of this feeling of doom. Mara leaned her forehead against the coolness of the adobe wall, hoping it would soothe her.

With a smile of self-derision on her lips, Mara turned away from the window and the revealing light of the moon. What did she have to worry about? This was merely another acting job for Brendan and her, and nothing more than that. Already everyone believed her to be Amaya Vaughan. It had been so easy, for they had been so unsuspecting, and after all, she and Brendan were professionals and would not make any mistakes. What could possibly go wrong?

The wheel is come full circle.

—Shakespeare

Chapter 3

THE DAYS OF EARLY SUMMER PASSED SLOWLY IN THE GOLDEN valley of the Rancho Villareale. The pastoral simplicity of the California lifestyle was easy to adapt to as Mara and Brendan played their parts and waited for the falling of the curtain on Don Luís's plans. But it seemed that Don Luís was in no hurry to terminate their contract, and was content to let the somnolent days slide past with no change. But Brendan was not so patient, nor content, as he gazed longingly at the hills to the east, knowing the gold he dreamed of was no farther away, and no closer, than the sun rising above the distant hills each morning.

The leisurely pattern of each day began at sunrise, Mara had discovered upon awakening one morning with a headache; and while relaxing on a stone bench in the patio, she had seen Don Andres striding through the courtyard, his broad-brimmed, flat-crowned sombrero pulled low over his brow. Deerskin leggings protected his calves, and attached to the heels of his shoes were spurs with sharp-pointed rowels that jingled against the tiles with each step.

Mara had followed him silently to the iron-grilled gate and watched unnoticed as Don Andres gave his orders of the day to the workers lined up before him; then, with a vaquero at his side, he mounted the horse saddled for him and rode through the wide gates of the stable yard. Doña Ysidora had also risen before sunrise, and dressed somberly in a plain black gown with a black lace *rebozo* covering her head, she had left the hacienda accompanied by a servant carrying a mat and attended an early Mass in the small chapel on the rancho grounds. On her return she had gathered the household staff together in the courtyard and set them to work sweeping and cleaning the *sala* and dining room, while others began preparing the day's meals, for soon the fragrant aromas began to drift from the kitchen ovens in the outer courtyard.

Each morning Mara was served hot chocolate in her room while she dressed, and then, later in the morning, on the return of Don Andres, the family would gather together for breakfast and an opportunity to discuss the day's events, or, for some, to continue the gossip of the evening before. As there was a never-ending change of faces at the table with the advent of a new arrival, the Californians were kept in touch with the current affairs concerning the entire length of the state. From as far south as San Diego they heard news of the death of a fellow ranchero; of the marriage of a beauty in Santa Barbara; or of government and political activities in Monterey, the old Spanish capital of California.

This morning was to be no exception, Mara thought in resignation as she sipped her coffee and listened inattentively to the conversation around the table. The nagging aftereffects of her headache still lingered as she toyed with her egg and without much appetite took a bite of a tortilla cake of flour and water beaten wafer-thin. Mara pressed her temple with her cool fingers, trying to soothe the dull ache that throbbed beneath the skin. She seemed to be continually bothered by headaches since arriving at the Rancho Villareale, Mara thought in puzzlement, blaming their frequency on her nerves and the tension of the present situation. Mara stopped drumming her fingertips on the table; it was another sign of the unsettling effect these headaches were having on her as she became more irritable and short-tempered from restless nights of disturbed sleep. Don Andres looked up from his plate, a forkful of beefsteak smothered in a rich gravy on its way to his mouth, when Doña Ysidora questioned him about his daily dawn ride across the rancho.

Don Andres shrugged as he thoughtfully chewed his meat. "Another hundred head of cattle are missing, and another family of squatters has settled between here and Casa Quintero," he answered casually.

Doña Ysidora sighed impatiently, a look of exasperation crossing her features at his reply. "And what do you do about it, Andres?" she demanded angrily. "You sit here and calmly eat your breakfast."

"And what would you have me do, *Madre?*" he asked tiredly. "The cattle are gone. Many slaughtered on the spot and half-eaten, their carcasses left for the scavengers to pick clean. And do I take my army of two or three vaqueros and run the squatters off my land? Do I shoot the wife and children, Madre? They will leave under no less a threat. To whom do I take my complaints? The American judges? You think they will listen to me against their countrymen?" He scoffed incredulously.

"You don't seem overly concerned, Don Luís," Brendan commented curiously, continuing despite the cool look he was receiving from the Californian. "I'd be thinking you'd be hotfooting it over there right now to see if the Casa Quintero was still there and hadn't been torn down and stripped bare."

"But it does not—" Doña Jacinta began, only to let her words hang in midair at the gesture for silence from Don Luís.

"As a matter of fact, I was planning to ride over there this very morning. Perhaps, Don Andres, you would keep my niece and Señor O'Fl—Sullivan amused while I am away?" Don Luís asked, correcting his near slip of the tongue without any outward sign of discomfiture.

"Of course, Don Luís," the ranchero answered, a curious look in his eyes. "I do not understand you, Don Luís, but you must do as you wish."

"Perhaps Doña Amaya would care to see more of the rancho, Andres," Doña Feliciana suggested softly. "You ride the horse well, Doña Amaya?" she questioned, a doubtful look in her eyes. "It will be a many-hour journey. Do you think you are good enough?"

Mara smiled slightly, sensing the subtle provocation behind

Doña Feliciana's casual words. "I think I shall manage," Mara answered, the challenge of Doña Feliciana being silently accepted as the two women exchanged glances.

"I must warn you, Doña Amaya, that Feliciana is right," Doña Ysidora added, a concerned expression on her face, "for you will have a hard ride ahead of you. Do you not wish to change your mind? We will all understand."

"No, thank you, Doña Ysidora," Mara replied firmly. "I must become used to this land sometime, and now seems as good a time as any."

An hour later, Mara left her room and made her way along the gallery to the stables. She was dressed in a black cloth riding habit with a long, full skirt and close-fitting jacket that buttoned down the front, revealing, beneath, a plain cambric shirtfront. Mara tipped her black beaver hat with its floating veil over her forehead to shield her eyes from the bright glare of the sun as she stepped from the coolness of the patio into the outer courtyard.

Brendan was already mounted and held a squirming Paddy before him on his saddle, a situation he hardly relished, Mara thought sympathetically as she avoided meeting Brendan's martyred look of suffering. But Paddy was no match for these accomplished Californians, who seemed to have been born in the saddle, and she didn't want an inexperienced Paddy trying to compete with them. Even the smallest of children rode without a sign of fear evident on their cherubic faces as the wind scattered their cries of enjoyment.

Mara gave a start of surprise as she saw Doña Feliciana mounted sidesaddle on the back of a high-spirited black-and-white pinto that danced prancingly under the guiding hand of his rider. She was still dressed in black mourning clothes, but she had changed from the shyly awkward schoolgirl of just an hour ago. Doña Feliciana had come to life as she sat elegantly on the back of her mount, her eyes flashing darkly beneath the rakishly tilted brim of her flat-crowned hat.

Mara grasped the plaited rawhide reins of her horse, her knee hooked around the horn of the saddle and one booted foot fitted in the loop of silk that served as a stirrup, and waited patiently as their group steadily increased in size as more riders joined them and their casual ride turned into a grand excursion, complete with a carreta filled with picnic baskets and blankets.

"It would seem as if the shy little dove has found her wings," Brendan commented, a look of unconcealed admiration in his eyes as he watched Doña Feliciana's small hands skillfully handle her mount with practiced ease.

The colorful cavalcade finally began to make its way from the rancho with a cloud of dust being kicked up, marking its progression from the road and into the gently sloping hills of the valley. The sky overhead was a deep, sapphire blue with a fleecy white veil of clouds floating high above the hills and patterned in wisps by the air currents swirling around them. The horses carried the party through fields of pale yellow and deep orange poppies that blanketed the hillside in a satiny cloak that swayed with the breeze. Groves of massive white oak dotted the slopes, their twisted trunks standing stalwartly as their labyrinthine branches swept the ground in supplication.

Mara's gloved hands tightened on the reins as a long-eared jackrabbit, startled from his hiding place, jumped in front of her horse's hooves and bolted across the sloping hill, his black tail disappearing into the chaparral brush in a flash. They made their way along a dry stream bed, weaving through spiny-branched shrubs and spikes of sage, their laughing voices carrying back into the arroyo as they climbed the rocky slope and galloped across a wide expanse of rolling hill.

Mara glanced back into the valley where the hacienda baked under the noontime sun, its red-tiled roof repelling the heat as the thick adobe walls kept the interior of the house comfortably cool during the hot daylight hours. As Mara's horse disturbed a cluster of greenish-gray chaparral, a gray fox shot out of the dense tangle of underbrush and fled into the safety of the hidden crevices of the arroyo they had just left.

"To be sure, I never thought I'd be finding myself tired of riding." Brendan spoke next to Mara as he maneuvered his mount closer to hers, his face flushed from the sun.

"I seem to remember a certain person groaning about never

having enough time for pleasure, and missing the romps in the park," Mara reminded him with a teasing smile.

"An afternoon's ride with a lovely woman in the park, and this wild ride through the wilderness, I'll have you know," Brendan commented, his voice full of mock grievances, "are two completely different things. I feel as if I should be wearin' buckskin and fringe."

Mara laughed at the thought of Brendan playing the unlikely role of a pioneer. "And don't be forgettin' your coonskin hat."

"Aye, to be sure, 'tis as amusin' as seein' you dressed in a sunbonnet and churnin' butter, mavournin'," Brendan returned with a smirk.

"And thankful I am you're havin' the sense to be seein' that, for that's one role I'd not have a likin' to be taking on. Besides," Mara continued, feigning disappointment, "I've nothing in calico to be wearin'."

Brendan shook his head, a laugh of appreciation trembling in his voice. "You're never at a loss for words, are you, Mara?"

"Oh, look!" Paddy exclaimed as he gazed up at a spread-winged hawk gliding effortlessly above the hills and casting a swiftly moving shadow across the land.

Brendan followed its progress until it disappeared behind the summit of a far-distant hill. Mara caught the longing in his dark eyes as he stared at the empty horizon.

"Why didn't you lose Don Luís when we landed in San Francisco, Brendan?" Mara asked suddenly, curious about Brendan's motives in fulfilling his debt of honor.

"Why didn't I run out on the old buzzard?" Brendan repeated with a thoughtful expression. "Well, you know, I've asked meself that very same question, and you know, I'm not sure."

With a smile of self-derision Brendan continued in speculation. "I could say it was not the honorable thing to do, to run out on a debt, but then we both know I'm not above doing the dishonorable, and turning tail and running. Or I could claim it was because of you and Paddy, seein' how we hadn't a shilling to our names. How could I get a stake going, even get out to the mines without supplies? I couldn't leave you without support in a strange city, especially one like San Francisco. Why, you'd probably have starved," he explained, almost convincing himself it was the truth. But his dark eyes slid away from Mara's as he admitted reluctantly, "But I'm thinking 'twas more the coward in me than anything else. A fear of facing the unknown, you might be sayin'. Maybe even a fear of failing and finding one more hope just as unsubstantial and fleeting as a dream. I can't go on struggling to make barely enough to put food on the table and little more than that. We're not living, Mara, we be merely existing, never gettin' anywhere. Well, that's not the life I'm wanting any longer. I want back that life that was stolen from us, that we're entitled to," Brendan said bitterly, "and if I die doin' it, then 'twas worth the struggle. The only thing I'm worried about now is that at this rate I'll be too old to enjoy it. Has Don Luís said anything to you yet about concluding this charade? I'd like to get paid and be moving on."

"Don Luís isn't one to be saying much, except for us to bide our time and let the Villareales get acquainted with me. The covenant of engagement isn't binding unless we both agree to it now that we're adults. I suppose Don Luís was hoping that Don Andres would go ahead and conclude their business, whatever it is, in anticipation of the coming relationship."

"Well, it all seems just a bit queer to me, and the only thing forthcoming that I want is our money," Brendan declared impatiently.

Mara wiped her brow with the back of her gloved hand and turned to find Doña Feliciana riding beside her.

"You feel the heat, Doña Amaya," she commented casually, showing no visible ill-effects herself from the sun blazing down on them. "We rest shortly unless you wish to stop now?" she offered, a contemptuous look in her eye as she took in Mara's flustered appearance. Mara pushed a clinging tendril of dark hair off her temple and replied with a forced smile that gave away nothing of her true thoughts. "I wouldn't think of it; please let us continue, Doña Feliciana."

"As you wish," she answered shortly, before sending her

horse on ahead, her black skirt billowing out beneath her as she kicked her horse's flank, urging him to greater speed.

"Are you getting the feeling that our little dove doesn't have a liking for Amaya Vaughan?" Mara commented to Brendan as her eyes followed the swiftly moving figure.

"So it would seem, mavournin," Brendan agreed, "although your cousin Raoul isn't feeling near the same," he added with an amused smile curling his lip as the young Californian galloped toward them at a breakneck pace, only to pull up on his reins as he reached them, his horse's hind legs sliding beneath as he came to an abrupt halt. A cloud of dust settled over them as Raoul quickly turned his mount and fell in beside them.

Brendan glared impotently at Raoul, who was oblivious to having caused them any discomfort with his thoughtless exhibition of his equestrian skills. All of his attention was centered on Mara as he rode along beside her, his gaze lingering on her face and long column of neck.

"You ride better than I would have thought for a European, but perhaps it is the Californian blood in your veins that gives you such skills," he complimented her.

"Thank you, Raoul"—Mara politely accepted his compliment despite Brendan's rude guffaw—"but I think Doña Feliciana would disagree with you about my abilities."

"Ah, well, she is just jealous of you, Amaya." Raoul dismissed Doña Feliciana with a careless shrug of his shoulders. "She is spoiled, and it does not help that Andres is her guardian."

"Oh, and why should she be jealous?" Mara asked quietly, showing little curiosity.

"You do not know? Feliciana fancies herself in love with Don Andres. She has always had the grand passion for him and hoped to be his bride one day," Raoul explained unsympathetically. Then, laughing cruelly, he added, "At least she did until mi padre appeared with you on his arm."

"And what of Don Andres?" Brendan asked.

"He will do the honorable thing, the proper thing, and what his madre wishes," Raoul told them with a sneer of contempt. "He still follows the old ways. However, I think he will not mind so much now that he has seen you. I think it will be his pleasure to wed you, Amaya," Raoul added with a suggestive look that slid over Mara's tight-fitting bodice.

So, Mara thought, that is why there is that thinly veiled hostility in Feliciana's manner. She was in love with Don Andres. She fears that Amaya will be the next Villareale bride, and not herself. Mara wondered about Don Andres's feelings toward the lovely young Feliciana, and whether he had given her reason to believe her love might be returned. As far as Mara had seen, he had never given any indication of more than brotherly affection for her. Perhaps it was just a schoolgirl crush and would fade with time.

Mara followed the carelessly scattered group of riders into a hollow formed of low-lying hills where a stream meandered gently through the willow-shaded valley floor. In the distance the slowly moving carreta with its rickety railing and large, solid-wood wheels was making its bumpy way into the valley behind two oxen yoked to the long pole that stretched out in front of the cart.

Don Andres, astride the golden palomino with the ivory mane and long, flowing tail that he often rode, organized the group as they dismounted and found places to rest beneath the drooping branches of the willows. Mara found herself seated beneath a bank of wild irises, the creams, deep reddish purples, and lavender blues creating a perfect backdrop for her beauty as she lounged in the cool shadows of the sweeping willow limbs.

Farther along the bank and closer to the stream, Paddy was peering intently into the clear depths of the water, his small face eager as he searched for frogs and hopped along the slippery banks with several other young children. Mara caught the sound of his laughter and realized that for children there was a universal language that had no barriers as they innocently played together.

Mara gratefully accepted a glass of the cool stream water from Don Andres, who had poured her some from a jug freshly filled from farther upstream.

"The ride was not too much for you, Doña Amaya?" he

inquired solicitously as he stared down in unconscious fascination at the entrancing picture she presented.

"I enjoyed it, Don Andres," Mara reassured him with a
provocative smile curving her lips. "Your rancho is certainly
more than I had imagined, and very lovely."

"Gracias, but it cannot compare with your beauty. I—"
Andres began, only to stop as Feliciana came strolling up
to them.

"Andres," Doña Feliciana interrupted, her lips pouted as
she put her hand possessively on his arm. "Had not you better
see to the fires and your other guests?" she reminded him.

"Doña Feliciana is right, of course, if you will excuse me?"
he apologized regretfully as Doña Feliciana led him away.

"This isn't so bad," Brendan remarked lazily as he dropped
down beside Mara, a glass full of wine held carefully in his
hand. "I could come to enjoy this life of leisure. To be sure, it
fits just fine my ideas of what a gentleman's life should be," he
said on a deep sigh as he stretched out on the fresh green grass.

And Brendan was right, it was a gentleman's life. One
could come to enjoy it very much, Mara mused dreamily. The
afternoon passed languidly. Sides of beef were roasted on iron
spits over live-oak coals, the aromas mingling with the sounds
of fiddles and laughing voices. As the afternoon shadows
lengthened and appetites were appeased, the never-tiring
Californians sought entertainment in a small-scale rodeo.

Demonstrating amazing feats of horsemanship before an
appreciative audience, the rancheros and vaqueros showed off
their prowess. Using the *reatas* hanging from their saddles, they
effortlessly roped any stray steer that wandered near, or played
at a mock bullfight with a rogue bull who angrily charged
his tormentors. Too often he barely missed the shining flank
of one of the horses as the rider's red sash flapped enticingly
before the enraged bull.

Doña Ysidora sat contentedly beneath the shade of a tree
with her ever-present embroidery near at hand and only
glanced up occasionally to see that all went smoothly. She had
ridden her mount as agilely as any young girl of sixteen, never
showing a sign of fatigue as she kept pace with the younger

members of the party. Even the soft, feminine hands of Doña Jacinta had shown strength and skill as she had demonstrated her own proficiency in the saddle, her small, green silk slippers with ribbons tied over the instep peeking out beneath the fine embroidered muslin of her skirt as she spurred her horse relentlessly on.

Raoul sauntered unsteadily over to Mara, pausing before he reached her to take a deep swallow of wine from a highly polished steer horn. Its bottom had a stopper of wood, and it was decorated with bands of silver. Wiping his lips with the back of his hand, Raoul came to stand before Mara.

"You liked my riding, sí? I am the best, I think," the wine emboldened him to say. "I can pick a golden coin from the dust, while riding at a full gallop. Never have I missed."

"You're quite an accomplished fellow," Brendan remarked snidely, unimpressed with the young Californian's revelations. "Now, if only you could be pickin' up gold nuggets from horseback…" he murmured thoughtfully, a devilish twinkle in his eye.

"You do not believe me?" Raoul asked in offended amazement. "I have even, single-handedly, lassoed a grizzly bear. This you can believe. It is the truth. ¿Sí, Jeremiah?" he demanded of the American who had quietly walked up beside him.

"If you say so, Raoul," Jeremiah replied indifferently.

Raoul smiled triumphantly at the O'Flynns, missing the American's patronizing look as he swayed on his feet and took another long drink of the dark red wine, some of it trickling from the corner of his mouth.

"Your madre desires your presence at her side, Raoul," Jeremiah delivered his message, a pitying look in his blue eyes as he watched Raoul straighten his shoulders. "She wishes you to meet someone."

"Bah! She always wants me by her side," Raoul complained. "You tell them of my bravery, eh, Jeremiah, for you have nothing of your own to talk of," Raoul said insultingly and staggered through the milling group of people toward Doña Jacinta and the plump girl standing nervously beside her.

A dull flush spread across Jeremiah Davies's boyish face as

he stared after the weaving figure of the Californian. "The fool," he muttered scornfully.

He returned his attention to the O'Flynns, the determined glint in his narrowed blue eyes fading as he assumed his accustomed expression of humble servility.

"You are enjoying the rodeo and merienda?" he asked politely. "If I might join you, Doña Amaya, Señor O'Sullivan?"

"Certainly. Be our guest," Brendan invited him, an expansive grin on his face. "You must get tired of hearing Spanish all the time," he prodded the American, his eyes innocent as he smiled encouragingly.

"It is part of the job," Jeremiah replied with a slight shrug. "You know, there are now probably more people in California speaking English than Spanish," he commented with a smirk curving his small mouth upward. "Someday Spanish may even become a forgotten language here."

"You seem to find that rather amusing," Brendan said as he heard the American's low chuckle. "Won't you be findin' yourself out of a job then?"

Jeremiah Davies smiled slyly as if at some private joke. "Our fortunes may be bound together, but we shall not suffer the same fates," he remarked enigmatically.

"Ah, you be seein' yourself with a big fortune, now? Have you come into an inheritance, perhaps, or are you hoping to strike it rich with a gold mine?" Brendan asked softly, his interest caught by the momentary gleam of avarice that shone in the deceptively mild blue eyes of the American.

"A gold mine?" he repeated Brendan's query disdainfully. "Why should I search for a gold mine when I have one right under my nose? It just needs the right tools to mine it, that's all."

Brendan's dark eyes glowed with excitement at the American's words. "There's gold on Don Andres's land?" he asked in amazement.

Jeremiah Davies snorted in amused disgust. "You're just like the rest of them. All those people coming to strike it rich, digging the gold out of the earth, spending it overnight. Fools!" he spat contemptuously. "Can't you see that it's the land itself that is worth their toil? Blinded by shiny gold they can't see the value of the dirt they discard. But I have, Mr. O'Sullivan, I've seen it."

The light died out of Brendan's eyes at his denial and strange explanation, and losing interest, Brendan turned his thoughts and gaze elsewhere.

"You'd do better to go back to England, Doña Amaya," Jeremiah Davies suddenly recommended.

At Mara's look of surprise he held up a pudgy hand in supplication and shook his head. "I only meant it as a word of friendly advice, that's all. You're more European than Spanish. You don't fit in here, and besides," he added ambiguously, a slight smile curving his lips, "Don Andres might not be quite the matrimonial prize you were led to believe. In fact, if I were you, I'd be looking around for a rich American husband."

"You seem fond of speaking in riddles, Mr. Davies," Mara replied coldly. "I'm afraid I have neither the time nor the patience to decipher them."

Jeremiah Davies shook his head regretfully. Then, getting to his feet, he gazed for a moment at the laughing Californians spread out in front of him. Their clothing was a kaleidoscope of color—white muslin skirts embroidered in threads of red, green, blue, and purple; rich Chinese shawls and delicate lace scarves; bright silks and velvets embroidered in gold and silver braid. Above their heads was a canopy of brilliant blue sky.

"Look at them. They are little more than children. They laugh and play, and act as though they've not a care in the world. They will not worry about tomorrow until it comes," Jeremiah said derisively. "They live in a fool's paradise. It cannot last forever. Already the change is coming, but they will not accept it. And you wish to cast your fate with *them?*" he asked doubtfully, a smug smile of contempt on his face as he casually walked away.

Mara watched in disgust as he ingratiated himself with a silver-haired Californian, pleasantly exchanging greetings with the old man as he helped him to fill a plate and find a suitable seat.

"The little worm," Brendan commented. "Although I must admit we're losing a good actor by not having him on the stage, not that I'd relish playin' opposite him," Brendan said in mock concern. "Why, he'd probably step all over me lines and steal the scene as well."

"He's more of a viper, so I'd watch my step around him," Mara warned Brendan seriously.

"Don't be worrying, Brendan can be handlin' the likes of him," he reassured her. "Besides, I don't see that we'll be havin' much to do with him, anyway. I don't usually hobnob with servants, my dear," Brendan added with a look of snobbish disdain at the American.

An hour later, as the women began to clear up the remains of the picnic, Mara looked around for Paddy, hoping he hadn't strayed too far off. She walked along the edge of the stream, following its gurgling flow into the cool shadows of the trees hugging the soft banks. Mara glanced around, stopping now and again to listen for the sound of children's voices.

"Paddy! Paddy!" she called out. She kept walking farther from the camp, deeper into a spinney overlooking a clear pool of still water and hidden from view by the bend of the stream.

Mara stopped for a minute, listening to the peaceful silence. As she was about to return to the camp, she heard voices from the far side of an outcropping of large boulders. As she stood there, hesitating, she found herself beginning to listen.

"I do not think I care to be involved in this for much longer," one of the voices stated firmly. "Now that he has returned, he will be suspicious."

"Still scared like a little boy of your padre, Raoul?" jeered a voice Mara recognized as Jeremiah Davies's. "Haven't you enjoyed having a little money of your own for a change, rather than depending on his occasional generosity?"

"Sí, I want money," Raoul declared fervently, but there was a note of doubt in his voice. "But I don't care to get it this way. Stealing cattle from Don Andres is not right, not…honorable."

Mara heard the American laugh. "And is what Don Andres did to your padre honorable and just? It's only right that you should be receiving something from the rich Don Andres. He owes it to you," Jeremiah Davies said smoothly, playing on Raoul's uncertainty and resentment.

"When do I get paid?" Raoul finally spoke in a defiant voice.

"In debt again?" the American asked dryly. Mara could almost see the sly smile curving his small mouth. "You will receive your share of the profits as soon as the cattle are sold in San Francisco. And you needn't worry about being discovered. The brands have been altered, and I hardly think you and I are going to betray each other."

"What do you do with your share, Jeremiah?" Raoul demanded truculently. "I never see you gamble, nor do you spend it on the señoritas. What do you spend it on? You have no pleasures?"

"When I have enough, I'll spend it on what I want, don't worry about that, mi amigo. You'll know soon enough what my real pleasure is," he informed the Californian, laughing at some private joke.

Mara turned, preferring to remain an anonymous eavesdropper. But as she moved her foot, she struck a stone, dislodging it and the loose gravel around it. Mara cringed at the sound the small avalanche of stones made. Quickly, before the now-silent conspirators could detect her presence, Mara hurried back into the concealment of the trees and toward the safety of the camp.

She glanced back once, but saw no one in pursuit. When she emerged from the bank of the stream, she was walking nonchalantly, as if back from a casual stroll.

She breathed a sigh of relief as she saw a tired Paddy leaning against a tree trunk near Brendan, his shoulders sagging wearily as he drowsily watched the cleaning-up activities. His eyes brightened when he caught sight of Mara walking determinedly toward him, the slight smile on his face turning into a broad grin as he held something out to her.

"Look what I found, Mara," he told her proudly as he displayed a wedge-shaped piece of stone. "An arrowhead."

Mara forced herself to look suitably impressed as she handled it. "That's very nice, Paddy. Is that where you were? I was looking for you. We're about to leave now," she told him, not having the heart to scold him as he proudly tucked the arrowhead into his coat pocket.

Mara found no opportunity to speak with Brendan before they began to ride back toward the rancho. It was cool as they galloped through the early evening hours. Twilight lingered in the lengthening days of summer. The wildflowers had closed their petals when the fiery sun disappeared behind the western hills, taking its warm caress with it. They were riding through a field of wildflowers when Mara suddenly felt her saddle slide sideways. She began to lose her balance and fall from the back of her horse. She hit the hard-packed earth with a thud and just managed to roll clear of her horse's flying hooves.

Momentarily stunned, Mara tried to catch her breath. She was struggling to her knees, rubbing a painful elbow when Don Andres, an expression of great concern on his face, dismounted beside her.

"*Dios!* Are you all right? I could not believe my eyes when I saw you begin to fall. What happened? Did your horse stumble?" he asked as he gently helped her to her feet.

"The devil it did," Mara spoke, still shaken as she brushed off her skirt. "It was my saddle. The girth was too loose."

Don Andres stared at her uncomprehendingly. "But that is impossible. I personally checked your mount and it was perfectly secure then."

"Well, it isn't now," Mara said pointedly as Raoul came trotting up, leading Mara's mount, her saddle hanging sideways from the horse's back.

Don Andres shook his head in distress. "I am most sorry, Doña Amaya. I do not understand how this could happen. If you will accept my deepest apologies."

"Accidents do happen, Don Andres," Mara said softly. She did not blame him, but wondered just what had happened. She might have broken her neck.

"Are you all right, Mara?" Brendan called as he rode up beside her, trying to control both his mount and a squirming Paddy, who was staring down tearfully at Mara, his heart in his eyes.

"Lemme go, Papa, lemme go to Mara. She's hurt," he cried frantically.

"I'm all right, Paddy. Now sit still, love, and mind your papa," Mara told him reassuringly.

"There, it is tight once again," Don Andres told her as he resaddled her horse.

"Perhaps Doña Amaya would be happier to ride in the carreta, Andres," Feliciana suggested. She stared down at Mara with a pitying look.

Mara bit back her angry words and allowed Andres to help her onto her mount's back once again. "Shall we continue? It grows late," Mara said, ignoring Feliciana.

"Sí, if you are sure, Doña Amaya," Don Andres agreed. He remounted and urged the group on across the meadow.

"Never seen you take a fall like that before, mavournin," Brendan commented as he kept his mount close to hers.

"That's because I've never had my saddle tampered with before," Mara told him bluntly.

"Tampered with, is it now?" he said softly, a doubtful look in his dark eyes as he looked at her over the top of Paddy's head. "And why should you be thinking that, Mara, me love?"

"I didn't get the chance to tell you earlier, but you had reason to be suspicious of our American friend. I happened to overhear Raoul and him discussing the lucrative aspects of cattle rustling…and need I say whose cattle they've been stealing?"

"The divil, ye say?" Brendan ejaculated in amazement. "You mean to tell me that young Raoul and Jerry boy are up to no good? My, my, there's quite a scheming mind behind that freckled face. And now, me love, just how did you happen to overhear such an interesting conversation?" Brendan asked curiously.

"I was looking for Paddy down along the stream bank and happened to overhear it. They didn't know I was there, at least not until I was trying to leave and stumbled over some loose rocks."

"Rather clumsy of you, m'dear, but do go on," Brendan observed with a thoughtful glance into the group of riders up ahead.

"Well, that's about all there is to it," Mara told him. "I got out of there as fast as I could. I was beginning to believe they hadn't seen me, but they must have. Why else would someone try to hurt me?" Mara demanded.

"I'm thinkin' it's more likely someone's trying to frighten you, mavournin, if indeed it wasn't an accident. These things do happen and you aren't sure that they saw you, are you?" Brendan reasoned. "I wouldn't worry. 'Tis probably just coincidence."

"But what are we going to do, Brendan?" Mara asked.

"Do about what?"

"About Raoul and that little rat Jeremiah," Mara said in exasperation. "Shouldn't we tell Don Andres?"

Brendan sighed. "In the first place, 'tis none of our business. And in the second place, I'm not of a mind to be angering Don Luís when he hasn't paid us yet. I'm not thinkin' he'd be taking kindly to hearing that his son is a thief," Brendan explained patiently. "No, I think we'd best keep this to ourselves, Mara, me love, or at least wait until the time comes when we could use the information against Don Luís, should he decide not to pay us."

Mara nodded. There was no reason to stir up trouble, especially when it could cause further trouble for them. The first star of night was twinkling in the dark blue sky as their party rode through the wide open gates of the rancho. Torches had been lit and flickered eerily from the adobe walls, casting long, distorted shadows across the stable yard. Mara shivered in the cool night air.

Carrying Paddy, Mara moved toward the iron-grilled gate with the others, who were talking and laughing, unaware of anything save their conversation, but as she looked over Paddy's dark head, she saw a shadow move behind the gate. She passed beneath one of the smoking torches, the burning fire highlighting her face and reflecting in the gold of her eyes. She stared into the darkness before her. Mara shivered again, but not from the chill in the air. The shadow moved. Then with a smile of excessive relief, she saw the gate open and Jamie come forward to relieve her of her heavy burden.

"And I hope ye've not brought me a sick little boy," Jamie greeted her with a disapproving look on her small, pointed face.

Leave it to Jamie to banish any imaginings, Mara laughed at herself, feeling foolish. She handed the sleeping Paddy to Jamie, who easily took hold of him. She might be small and wiry, but she was as strong as an ox, she often reminded them, and she proved it now as she walked effortlessly along the corridor, her head and shoulders half-hidden behind Paddy's.

"He probably stuffed himself fair to splittin' and took too much sun as well," she continued as she stomped through the shadows.

Mara glanced around as she followed Jamie's quickly moving figure. She could hear the tinkling of water in the fountain until it was drowned out by the voices of the people crowding into the courtyard.

"Were you standing at the gate watching?" Mara asked, unable to rid herself of that persistent feeling.

Jamie glanced back over her shoulder. "Standing at the gate? No, why should I be doin' that? Been standin' on me feet all day washin' your clothes. Heard all the laughing and knew ye must be back, so I just got to the gate as you came up with Paddy. Why?"

Mara shrugged, a whimsical smile curving her mouth. "Oh, no reason. I was just curious, that's all," she replied vaguely as Brendan came up behind them.

"Curious about what, mavournin?" he demanded, not liking to be left out of anything.

"It was nothing, really," Mara answered carelessly. "I just thought I saw someone lurking at the gate as we dismounted."

"Lurking, was he?" Brendan laughed. "You make it sound mysterious. I'm beginning to wonder about your imagination, m'dear. Panicking at shadows now. It was probably only the stranger," he informed her offhandedly.

"Another relative?" Mara asked as Brendan stopped at the door to his room.

"Damned if I know, but I doubt it. When was a fellow Californian ever called a stranger? I haven't met him. Guess he arrived sometime earlier today. Most likely we'll be meeting him shortly, for unless I'm mistaken, the party's just beginnin', and looks as though it will be continuing until dawn," Brendan predicted as they heard the unmistakable sounds of musicians tuning up. Brendan brushed ineffectually at some of the dust covering his stylish Newmarket riding coat with its one-button fastening. "Would you be believin' this was once a blue coat," he said with a disgusted glance down at the grayish-colored lapels. "Wonder if I can be gettin' some hot water around here."

A half hour later, Mara was smiling in appreciation as she relaxed in the tubful of steaming water that had been prepared for her bath. She rested the back of her head against the curved lip of the tub as she slid down and allowed the hot, fragrant water to slide over her shoulders. Mara sighed deeply as she felt her tired muscles relaxing, and for the first time in many days she was free of the headache that had been plaguing her. She closed her eyes in contentment and wondered if Brendan had fared as well.

A half hour after that, Mara was shifting impatiently from one foot to another. "Do you have to be pulling so tight, Jamie?" she groaned as the little woman's strong hands tightened the back lacings of her corset until the whalebone stays bit painfully into Mara's soft waist.

"Ye want to be gettin' into your dress, don't ye? Thank the good Lord I'm too old to be foolin' with such nonsense as these," Jamie murmured in disgust as she stared at Mara's small, nipped-in waist and swell of breast above the deep flounce of lace and scarlet bows decorating her corset. "Can ye breathe?"

"Hardly at all," Mara sighed as she fidgeted, trying to ease her discomfort.

Jamie gave a smile of satisfaction. "Then 'tis tight enough."

Mara bent over, smoothing the line of her silk stockings with their inset of lace.

"Careful, or ye'll be comin' to grief for sure," Jamie warned as she doubtfully eyed Mara's deep cleavage. "Contraptions like these were made for them folks who haven't got much and need a little help, but on you"—Jamie sighed, raising her eyes heavenward—"'tis like sugarin' candy."

Mara straightened the top of her linen chemise trimmed

with embroidery and then her knee-length drawers with their deep flounce of lace around the hem of the legs. One by one, five ruffled petticoats followed and were buttoned at the waist while Jamie briskly spread out the full skirts. Mara sat quietly while Jamie combed and brushed her long hair into a thick, shining braid that she intricately arranged on top of Mara's head, then adorned with a wreath of artificial red rosebuds. She wove the delicate flowers within the heavy twist of hair that covered Mara's head with the professional skill of her many years as a wardrobe mistress in the theater, a skill she was now putting to effective use as Mara's personal maid.

Mara winced when a firmly placed hairpin scraped her scalp, and she began to grow impatient with Jamie's seemingly tireless ministrations, but then she settled down again as she told herself that Jamie was, in a manner of speaking, preparing her for a performance; and so she stood quietly when Jamie slipped a red silk gown with floral motifs embroidered in silver in the skirt and puffed sleeves over her elegantly coiffed head and, pulling the seams together, began the tedious job of hooking it up the back. The low, curving neckline was edged in Brussels lace and matched the wedge of embroidered silver silk and lace that divided the skirt up the front. Mara adjusted the lace of the décolletage a shade lower, and, finally satisfied with the line of the bodice, she slipped her feet into dainty red satin slippers trimmed with rosettes, and then she swirled for Jamie's inspection.

Jamie smoothed down the hem in back, flicked a pleating of lace into place, and, standing back, nodded her head in satisfaction.

"Ye'll do."

Mara stared into the mirror, a slight frown between her arched brows. She bit her lips, bringing more color to them. "I think I'll add just a touch of rouge. I look so pale," she decided.

"No," Jamie said emphatically. "Ye're not Mara O'Flynn, the actress, but a supposedly well-bred English miss who'd not be wearin' color on her cheeks. Besides," she sniffed self-righteously, "I'll not have ye offendin' these good, Christian folk."

Mara raised an amused eyebrow at Jamie. "And since when have we been caring what others are thinking, Mistress Jameson?"

"Since our livelihood's been dependin' on it, that's how long. And anyway," she added grudgingly, "I kind o' like these Californians. They seem to be honest, God-fearin' people, and they've been treatin' me pretty fairly. To be sure, I can be doin' anything I want to in their kitchens, and always someone willin' to help me."

"Well, 'tis praise indeed, comin' from the almighty Jamie," Mara commented, surprised.

"Lord love us, but was it praise from *Jamie?* Did I hear you right, mavournin?" Brendan spoke from the doorway. Having entered after using his special knock, he now stood before them with an incredulous look of comical disbelief on his face. "To be sure, 'tis a cause for celebratin'," Brendan declared.

Jamie shook her grizzled head in resignation. "To be sure, 'twasn't a cause for celebration the day the two of ye was born into the world. And namin' ye after a saint, indeed," she snorted, giving Brendan a quelling glance.

"Come along, Mara, me love," Brendan said feigning an air of offended pride. "I'll be damned if I'm goin' to stand here and be insulted by little more than an Irish elf."

Mara picked up a shawl of silver gauze woven with silk-embroidered arabesques and a drawstring bag of red silk. She gathered gloves and fan and, snapping the ivory sticks open, winked impertinently at Jamie from behind the sweep of red marabou feathers that she waved before her face.

Brendan took Mara's elbow and escorted her to the party. As they entered and the light fell over them, Mara saw Brendan almost magically assume the role of a rather dandified gentleman as he changed his walk slightly, curved his lips almost poutingly, and angled his head just so. He stood tall and lean in his black, kerseymere trousers, cutaway evening coat, and cream-colored waistcoat of figured silk. His hair had been smoothed back with Macassar oil, the nutmeg fragrance scenting him slightly.

The change in Brendan was barely perceptible, but just enough to alter his character completely.

"Oh, how charming, I do love to dance the night away," he murmured to Doña Jacinta, who greeted them warmly. "But you know, I was so fatigued after the afternoon's jaunt," he confided, pulling a heavily scented handkerchief from his pocket and delicately dabbing at his upper lip, "that I feared I wouldn't have enough strength to attend this lovely soiree."

Doña Jacinta made a moue as she frowned in commiseration, her expression anxious lest her most ardent admirer be absent. "I will see to all of your needs personally," she promised. "A little red wine will do wonders for you. Come, we will sit over here where you may rest, Señor O'Sullivan."

"Oh, please, you must call me Brendan, Doña Jacinta," Brendan urged her as he gave her hand a slight, admonishing pat.

"I see that Doña Jacinta is entertaining Señor O'Sullivan," Don Andres remarked as he came to stand beside Mara.

"Yes, she certainly is keeping him amused," Mara agreed as she caught Brendan's eye as he carefully sipped his wine while feigning attentiveness as he listened to Doña Jacinta's confidences.

Don Andres stopped a servant passing by with a loaded tray of brimming wine goblets and handed Mara one. He made inconsequential conversation with her as his eyes roamed over his assembled guests. Then they returned to rest thoughtfully on her beautiful profile. She was so remote, so coolly detached. Yet there was nothing cold about her, Don Andres thought in puzzlement. There was, despite her aloofness, a smoldering passion in the depths of the golden eyes, a passion she could not disguise. It had yet to be sparked into life, he guessed.

"I am most pleased to see that your fall did not affect you adversely, for you are as beautiful as ever, Doña Amaya," he complimented her, his dark eyes glowing as they gazed down on her pale shoulders.

"Thank you, Andres," Mara said softly, a satisfied smile curving her lips slightly.

Mara watched over the brim of her wineglass as Brendan had a group of women laughing and hiding their blushes behind their fans at his entertaining actions while their menfolk guardedly stood nearby, their faces mirroring mixed emotions as they tried to figure out why this European gentleman seemed to have their women in the palm of his hand. Don Luís had returned from whatever business had kept him absent from the picnic and was now embroiled in yet another argument with Raoul. The young man was looking surly as he casually shrugged a shoulder in answer to some question. Doña Ysidora was overseeing the arrangement of food on a long trestle table. It was loaded down with heavy pottery dishes, stacks of china plates, sparkling glasses, bottles of wine, silverware, and bowls of fruit piled high with apples, oranges, pink-tinged pears, and strawberries.

Mara's slightly bored gaze was caught and held as it would have traveled past a man standing apart from the group of laughing Californians. He was leaning indolently against the wall, his gaze arrogantly aloof as he surveyed the party, evidently looking for someone as his narrowed eyes moved impatiently, it seemed, from face to face. The stranger, Mara thought, wondering curiously, who was he.

She lowered her lashes and covertly watched him. She was partially concealed behind the half-turned shoulders of Don Andres as he talked with Doña Feliciana. The stranger was taller than the Californians standing around him, taller perhaps even than Brendan. He was dressed almost totally in black. He wore tight black trousers that molded his muscular thighs and were a shade above being indecent. A black coat of superfine stretched across a wide expanse of shoulder. His black satin waistcoat was embroidered in a silver floral pattern along the lapel, and in his snowy cravat he wore a black pearl breast pin.

Mara allowed a half-smile to curve her lips as she eyed the brutally handsome stranger. For the slanting planes of his face, the high cheekbones, square jaw, slight indentation in the chin, and the wide, sensuous mouth created a mask of bronze that looked as if it had been molded and beaten by the sun. Thick black hair curled back from a wide forehead above his slightly aquiline nose, and long, beautifully shaped fingers that were now curled around a casually held wineglass gave him a look of breeding. Surely a misleading characteristic, Mara thought uncharitably as she instinctively felt the unleashed power in the man, even across the room. In his own way he was as handsome as Brendan, but not in the same refined and classical manner. There was no tenderness in the chiseled features of his face, nor softness in the sinewy hardness of his lean body. Mara had forgotten to be discreet as she stared openly at the stranger, and now her frank appraisal was being returned by jade green eyes contemplating her intently. Mara waited for the usual expression of appreciation to appear in his eyes but was surprised and slightly piqued when a slow, insolent smile shaped his lips into little more than a derisory grin.

She glanced away, showing no sign of her discomfiture. A boorish provincial, no doubt, Mara speculated with a contemptuous smile, curving her lips as she took a sip of wine, but despite her intentions, her thoughts lingered on the stranger.

"You have not met our new guest, Amaya." Mara heard Don Andres speaking to her. Turning with an abstracted air, she smiled politely up into the stranger's brooding face.

Mara stared in surprise into his penetrating green eyes, wondering at the puzzlement she read in them. They were quickly veiled by thick black lashes. He was just as handsome up close, even more so as the raw power of the man reached out to envelop her. But Mara also saw harshness and cruelty in the face. There was an uncompromising quality in the dark green eyes beneath the heavy black brows, and Mara was suddenly thankful that he was no enemy of hers.

"Doña Amaya Vaughan," Don Andres was continuing, "this is Nicholas Chantale."

Nicholas Chantale stared down into Mara's upturned face, a quizzical expression in his hard green eyes. "A pleasure, Miss Vaughan," he murmured in a deep resonant voice. There was a mocking quality in it that struck a discordant note in her.

"Mr. Chantale," Mara smiled slightly as she assumed her most haughty manner, one that had cowed even the most thick-skinned and ardent of her admirers into silence.

But Nicholas Chantale seemed unaffected by her coolness and the disdainful look she leveled at him. He continued to stare unwaveringly at her.

"Forgive me for staring, Miss Vaughan," Nicholas said in a

voice that was anything but apologetic, "but for a moment—well, I thought I knew you."

Mara tilted her head encouragingly, but her expression left little doubt that he was mistaken. "I'm sure I would have remembered such a meeting, Mr. Chantale. I'm afraid I don't even recognize your name."

Nicholas Chantale nodded regretfully. "Nor I yours, Miss Vaughan. I am puzzled. It's English, and I had assumed you were Californian?" he asked curiously.

"Doña Amaya is only half-Spanish," Doña Feliciana explained with a supercilious look at Mara. "Her father was English."

"But she bears the greatest resemblance to my dear sister," Don Luís interjected as he joined the group.

"I see," Nicholas murmured, a slight frown between his heavy brows. Mara received the distinct impression that he was disappointed about something as he stared at the family group around him that included Mara in it as Amaya Vaughan.

"You are from France, Mr. Chantale?" Mara asked him, wondering about the slight accent that she had heard before. "That is a long way to come to seek your fortune in gold," Mara added, unable to resist taunting him.

"I am from New Orleans, *mademoiselle*," he corrected her smoothly, "and I am a Creole. And indeed," he added with a glint in his eye, "I intend to achieve certain goals while here in California."

"You sound very confident, Mr. Chantale," Mara commented dryly.

"I'm a very determined man, Miss Vaughan, and do not accept defeat easily. Occasionally I am faced with a setback," he answered with a very Gallic shrug, "but ultimately I succeed in my desires."

"How very fortunate for you," Mara said with a polite but dismissing nod of her elegant head as she looked away from the Creole.

Chairs and tables had been pushed back against the walls, clearing a large space in the center of the room for dancing. The musicians had been playing softly in the corner of the sala, but now began a more lively tune as the diners were ready for more active entertainment. Mara stood, silently watching from the sidelines, content just to look on as the two rows of dancers formed and began to move from side to side, stepping intricately as they danced to the music of violins and fiddles. Mara smiled slightly as she saw Brendan's foot tapping in time to the music, and a moment later she saw him with Doña Jacinta on his arm as he led her through the steps on the dance floor. Mara became uncomfortably aware of being watched and, glancing up, saw the green-eyed gaze of the stranger locked on her face. It wasn't the ardent, longing look that she was accustomed to seeing, but a detached and perplexed one. He was certainly a cool one, Mara thought with a vague feeling of resentment as she stared at the arrogant profile now being presented to her.

"You will do me the honor of dancing with me, Doña Amaya?" Don Andres asked politely, his words breaking into her musings. "It would please mi madre greatly, as well as myself," he added persuasively, misreading the frown on Mara's face.

"Of course, Don Andres," Mara agreed as she watched the couples now dancing around the room to a waltz tune. "I see I can at least dance to this and won't embarrass you."

"You could never embarrass me, Amaya," Don Andres replied gallantly before sweeping Mara into his arms and onto the dance floor.

As they waltzed around the room, Mara caught sight of Brendan, who now had Feliciana in his arms, and as they passed by, he winked broadly at Mara before looking down at the dark head that barely reached his chest. No matter what the occasion or situation they might find themselves in, Brendan always managed to amuse himself, Mara thought enviously as she watched his laughing face. He never could stay despondent for long; there was always something to send him into high spirits once again. But long ago she had given up trying to predict his mercurial moods. Mara caught sight of the Creole as she swirled in Don Andres's arms, and smiled thoughtfully, for he presented quite an intriguing puzzle. His reactions struck her as being too studied, too lazily indifferent, for he could not be as unaffected by her beauty as he would have her believe, Mara thought nonplussed. This had never happened to her before, and she could not believe it or accept it, for here was quite a challenge for her.

Mara smiled up into Don Andres's face, flashing a smile that had devastated many an admirer and led him into vain expectations, and she was not disappointed in Don Andres's reaction. It was like a soothing balm to her pride, injured by the sardonic Frenchman.

She was still smiling into Don Andres's eyes when Don Luís stepped forward and, tapping the younger man on the shoulder, cut in, leaving Don Andres no other choice but to relinquish Mara to him. With a slow reluctance he dropped his arms and, bowing stiffly, moved aside for Don Luís.

"It would seem as though you have made a conquest of the self-reliant Don Andres," Don Luís commented sarcastically. "Had I thought you would do so well, I would have contracted you to wed him, for under your spell he might even deed over Rancho Villareale," he laughed.

"Why is it that you've little liking for Don Andres?" Mara asked curiously. "I thought all of you Californians were one big happy family."

Don Luís eyed Mara suspiciously. "What has he been saying?"

"Why, nothing. In fact, Don Andres seldom mentions you."

"So he has said little. Has he spoken of a certain item that belongs to my family?" Don Luís asked casually; yet there was an intent, almost expectant look in his eyes as he waited for Mara's answer.

Mara shook her head. "He has never mentioned anything to me. Why, is it important?"

Don Luís hid his disappointment well. "No, it is of little importance except to me. It is a family heirloom which I would like to have to give to my wife; that is all. It had belonged to my sister and through a misunderstanding had been left in the care of Don Pedro, Andres's father, under the condition that he give it to Amaya. So I must wait a little longer; that is all."

"And how much longer must we be waiting, Don Luís?" Mara asked, "I can't be promising for Brendan that he'll be content to stay any longer. He's getting restless," Mara warned him.

Don Luís stared down his aquiline nose, his lips tightening into a thin, tight line. "And he also will not be getting paid, should he become too restless and decide to leave in the middle of the night," Don Luís replied coolly.

"Maybe you should be worrying about having us gone from here because as Señora Villareale," Mara taunted him, "I could make sure that your business deal never did reach completion."

Don Luís's dark eyes narrowed dangerously. "I think in future I shall have to devote more time to my niece. I do not want you building up false hopes; that would not do at all," he said in a hard voice as he smiled down at her.

"Oh, I think we understand one another, Don Luís," Mara said with an answering smile that did not touch the gold of her eyes.

"I am relieved, then, for I shall see to my part of the bargain, that I promise," Don Luís declared haughtily, "only I cannot succeed without you fulfilling your part. So we are at what they call a stalemate, sí? We work together, and we both profit handsomely. Agreed?"

Mara reluctantly nodded her dark head. "Agreed, Don Luís."

Don Luís smiled in genuine pleasure. "Do not fear, my dear, for all shall work out as I have planned; it is merely a matter of time and patience, and I have enough of that for all of us," Don Luís said confidently.

The rest of the evening passed quickly and gaily, with Brendan fetching his fiddle and joining the musicians for a couple of rousing tunes that harmoniously blended many familiar Irish ditties and strange Spanish melodies into a unique concert, much to the pleasure of the appreciative, music-loving Californians. Brendan, as usual, was the star of the evening and thoroughly enjoyed taking his bows after his impromptu performance and basking in his much exalted position. The merrymaking continued until the pink edges of dawn drew the evening to a close and the revelers slowly made their way to their rooms, many reluctantly, Mara thought as she continued to hear laughter and voices from the sala across the courtyard even as she fell into a deep, untroubled sleep.

❦

Nicholas Chantale stared thoughtfully through the iron grill-work of his window as the first blush of morning lightened the eastern sky, shading it into pink and mauve. He stared, unseeing, as he felt a wave of frustration wash over him. How could he have been so mistaken? He would have sworn that the woman had been the actress, Mara O'Flynn. He had searched the mining camps and finally the ranchos of the coastal range for her, certain at last that his quest was at an end, only to find a woman called Amaya Vaughan instead. What a fool he'd been to think that fate would have played into his hands so easily in that chance encounter.

He laughed derisively as he remembered not having believed his luck when he'd glanced up and seen before his very eyes the face that had haunted him for over two years. Who could have imagined that he would see Mara O'Flynn in the dining room of a hotel in a place called Sacramento City. As a gambling man he wouldn't have accepted the odds, thinking them too high.

Two years. Had it really been so long ago that he'd stood over Julian's bed helplessly watching him suffer, hearing his fever-cracked lips curse the woman who had caused him such anguish? He had gone to her lodgings the following morning, only to find that she had left just hours before for the Continent. He had hired detectives to track her down, even though he hadn't been quite sure of his plans when he did ultimately find her. He'd received a report that she was living in a Paris hotel with a man, also called O'Flynn. Probably a husband who was conveniently absent most of the time, he thought in disgust.

But before he could travel to Paris to confront her, they had disappeared without a trace, running out on their hotel bill in the middle of the night.

Being of the theater, they would have eventually reappeared in either London or Paris, or perhaps even Dublin since they were Irish; but the unexpected had happened and he'd had to set aside his plans for revenge. Gold had been discovered in California, and he, like so many other thousands, had set out to make his fortune. He had roused his longtime friend and traveling companion, Karl Svengaard, from a warm bed and a dalliance with a buxom seamstress. Overcoming the big, raw-boned Swede's initial resentment at having been so rudely interrupted, he had easily persuaded him that it would ultimately prove to have been a timely interruption and well worth his while.

They had made their plans immediately and set sail for New York, arriving in the spring of 'forty-nine. They paid the exorbitant three-hundred-and-fifty-dollar ticket price for their berths on a steamer bound for California via the Isthmus of Panama, well worth the price considering it would take them only little over a month to reach the California shores, rather than the seven-month journey around the Horn. He could remember standing alone on deck as they sailed from New York, no family or loved ones to wave farewell to them from the noisy, pushing throng of people crowding the docks and piers to see off relatives as they began their uncertain voyage and quest for gold.

The overloaded steamship had slowly made its way into the stormy Atlantic and sailed down the east coast to Charleston, past Savannah, and on down the length of sandy beaches and thick, low-lying swamps of cypress and mangrove that choked the shores of Florida. Carried along in the balmy weather of the Gulf Stream, they soon reached Cuba and sailed under the old fortress guarding the entrance to Morro Bay as they docked in the port of Havana. Leaving behind the lush vegetation, slopes of sugarcane, and groves of oranges that belonged to the rich planters who lived in the gleaming white houses on the hillsides, they had sailed deeper into the Caribbean. After stopping briefly in Kingston, Jamaica, they'd had an easy crossing to Chagres, as far as they could go by sea. They would now have to travel up the Chagres River and across Panama to Panama City, where they would be able to catch a Pacific steamer to carry them the rest of their journey. They had traveled the first fifty miles across the isthmus in native dugout canoes poled along the river by Indians as they passed beneath creepers hanging down on them from low boughs of sycamores, and they took shelter from the downpour of frequent storms in primitive huts along the mosquito-infested banks of the river. They had left the river at Cruces and traveled the last twenty-five miles or so by muleback on a rough road cut through gullies and along steep hillsides covered with thick jungle vegetation. It had taken them five days to travel through the tropical forests of Panama, the sudden and drenching rainstorms leaving them struggling knee-deep in red mud, their clothes sticking hotly to their skin as they fought off the armies of gnats and mosquitoes that viciously attacked them.

Upon reaching Panama City they had found over a thousand stranded gold seekers camped in primitive quarters outside the city as they impatiently waited for transport to the gold fields of California. There were few hotels in the ancient and decaying city that had once seen Spanish conquistadors with their stolen Incan gold make plans for conquering the New World. It was now a city of grass-grown plazas, rotting wooden structures, and adobe walls deteriorating under the choking tentacles of jungle creepers and vines. The once heavily fortified fortress for protection against pirates now lay in ruins, and the cathedral was hardly more than a stone shell, ravaged by fire and sword.

Most of the adventurers camped around the city were sick with dysentery, malaria, or cholera caught from the fever-ridden jungles. They gambled and sweated away the endless hours as they waited for the steamer from Peru that would take them the rest of their journey. Adding to the discomfort of mind and body suffered from the squalid living conditions they had been forced to endure, many a dispirited traveler had found his ticket to California had only been good as far as Chagres and had not guaranteed passage to the end of the line. Because of overbooking by the steamship line, tickets were at a premium and being sold at an extortionate price. He and the Swede had been the lucky ones, for they'd had the extra thousand apiece needed to buy their way to San Francisco. The less fortunate, either too sick to travel or too poor to continue any farther, were stranded in Panama and left to uncertain fates.

Nicholas refocused his eyes on the dawn now lightening the California sky to a pale shade of blue. That had been almost a year ago, a year spent in the diggings working his fingers to the bone, standing hip-high in ice-cold mountain streams or raising a pick high over his shoulder under a blazing sun as he searched for those elusive gold nuggets. Existing on beans and bacon, pancakes and pork roasted over an open fire, they had camped high on the western slopes of the Sierra Nevada, where once only herds of elk and black-tailed deer, grizzly bears and rabbits had roamed the forests of virgin pine.

Rising at daybreak, he and the Swede would start panning a stream for gold, standing with the snow-melted waters swirling around their thighs while they rotated a flat-bottomed tin pan until their arms felt like lead and their legs were numb with cold. Working the stream until sunset, they might average around sixteen to twenty dollars, a very small profit when one egg had cost them a dollar, and a pair of boots, forty dollars. They had sweated through the long, hot summer months, showing very little profit for their backbreaking toil, only to be driven indoors for weeks at a time when the rainy season began. They couldn't risk leaving their claims unwatched and had to suffer months of claustrophobic inactivity as they shivered in damp blankets and amused themselves by gambling and drinking. Nothing was constant in the mining camps, for the adventurers were a restless breed who grew impatient if they could not find that promised gold immediately; it was a never-ending search for some unclaimed, gold-rich piece of earth. Rumors were rampant, and a city of tents could be uprooted and disappear overnight, the miners pulling up stakes at the first whisper of a strike in another valley. The streets of the mining camps twisted tortuously along steep ridges or through the bottoms of deep canyons and were dusty in summer, muddy in winter, their rutted surfaces littered with garbage from the miners' casual lifestyle. The most respectable-looking building in the whole town was always the gambling hall, with its long, gilt-framed mirrors and red velvet hangings where exhausted, weather-beaten men could spend their gold dust on whiskey and women.

Nicholas wondered now at the chain of events that had brought him to Sacramento City in time to be misled. He had thought for a while that his good luck had been disguised as bad, but now he was faced with the realization that his mind might have been playing fantastic tricks on him. For how could he ever have thought that the Swede's broken leg could have been anything but the worst luck? They had been working a Long Tom, a fifteen- to twenty-foot-long wooden trough with a perforated iron sheet called the riddle at the lower end, and beneath, the riffle box, a catchall for the dirt and gold that was washed through the trough. Usually it required three to four men to handle the cumbersome device. The two stationed at the head with spades would throw in large quantities of dirt to be washed down with a stream of water to the riddle, which was kept in motion by a man with a hoe. The heavier gold particles would remain in the riffle box while the dirt washed over the sides in a muddy stream of water.

Nicholas mentally kicked himself now for having let the Swede persuade him that they could easily manage the Long Tom by themselves and had little use for two more partners. The Swede had been shoveling the dirt into the long trough while he had stood at its bottom shaking the riddle when the trough had started to slide from its precarious perch on the hillside. The Swede had tried to halt its progress and had succeeded only in falling into it and toppling down the slope with it into the stream bed below, a tangle of waving hands and feet and broken boards. Nicholas smiled reminiscently, for the Swede's clumsy and ill-advised attempt at saving the Long Tom had given him the time needed to jump clear, and he had emerged unscathed except for the stream of abuse and profanity flung at him from beneath the rubble of the Long Tom.

This time he had ignored the Swede's opinion that he could set the bones himself and be healed in no time, and under the threat of being hog-tied had persuaded the big Swede back to Sacramento City. He had seen too many miners die from their wounds after having a leg or an arm amputated by a well-meaning friend and occasional surgeon on the side.

The Swede's leg had been set that morning he had been sitting in the City Hotel and had seen the woman he had thought was Mara O'Flynn. He had been forced to wait another couple of days to make sure the Swede would have no difficulties, and finally had set out to search for the woman he had just briefly glimpsed passing through the dining room. He'd left the Swede contentedly ensconced at the hotel and being consoled by a handsome French faro dealer, her dark eyes attracted to the blond, blue-eyed Swede and his buckskin pouch full of gold dust.

Nicholas hadn't thought he was wasting time, for the Swede would not be going anywhere for at least a month, and this unexpected meeting with Mara O'Flynn had been too good an opportunity to pass up; only now it looked as though it had all been for nothing. Nicholas flexed his shoulder muscles tiredly, and scratching the dark, wiry hair covering his bare chest, he had to admit that he was puzzled, for unless that woman had a twin, she was Mara O'Flynn. Shaking his head, Nicholas walked over to his bed, where he had carelessly discarded his shirt and waistcoat, and now searched through the waistcoat pocket until his hard fingers closed over a smooth metal object.

Nicholas thoughtfully dangled the golden locket from its delicate chain, then opened it to stare at a face he had come to know as well as his own. His green eyes burned into the painted face that seemed to mock his every move. He could almost hear the derisive chuckle coming from that provocative half-smile. And wasn't the stare from the slightly slanted golden eyes becoming more contemptuous with each passing day? Nicholas gave a snort of disgust. By God, he was becoming obsessed with a woman he had never even met, because of that promise made to his sister during Julian's illness. It did not carry quite the same importance it once had. Julian had recovered. But he hadn't left his sick bed completely unscarred. He had learned a valuable lesson, and maybe next time he would be a little more cautious before giving his heart.

A cruel smile curved Nicholas's lips as he thought of the lesson he would still like to teach Mara O'Flynn. The arrogance of the woman irritated him, for she was scornfully indifferent, raising a haughty shoulder in disdain at lesser mortals. He gazed down at the miniature portrait again, a brooding expression on his harshly handsome face as he thought of the woman he had met this evening. She was the portrait in the flesh. But she was not Mara O'Flynn. He was faced with a difficult decision. Did he trust his instincts—which warned him that not all was as it appeared—or did he believe the Californians who claimed her as their relative? Certainly there was no reason why they should lie to him.

Well, it would not hurt for him to stay around here for a while; he could use the rest, and the Swede wouldn't miss him for a week or so. Besides, he had nothing better to do with his time, and he was curious about this Amaya Vaughan who bore such a startling resemblance to Mara O'Flynn.

She fear'd no danger, for she knew no sin.

—John Dryden

Chapter 4

"WELL, I DON'T LIKE IT AT ALL, JAMIE," MARA SAID AS SHE gazed down worriedly at Paddy's flushed face.

"Ye should've been thinkin' of that yesterday, keepin' the little one out under that hot sun, eatin' heaven only knows what, and then ridin' back in that cool night air," Jamie berated her as she straightened the bedclothes over Paddy's small figure in the bed. "Surprised I am ye've not got the sniffles as well, although I can't be sayin' the same for them freckles ye got across your nose. Workin' up a sweat and gettin' cold is the best way to go about makin' yourself ill."

"I don't suppose there's a doctor around here." Mara sighed as she placed her cool hand against Paddy's hot cheek. "Of course, Paddy always seems to be coming down with sore throats; I suppose it's nothing to worry about."

"Seein' how I've raised both Brendan and ye through countless fevers and chest colds, I'm thinkin' I'm capable of seein' Paddy through this as well, so ye needn't be sendin' for one of them know-it-all, uppity doctors, thinkin' they be knowin' more than they do," Jamie said with a snort of disgust for their credentials.

Paddy sniffed loudly, then sneezed, his dark curls bobbing against the pillow. "I don't want to stay in bed, Mara," Paddy complained. "I had ever so much fun yesterday playing down by the creek. Don Andres said I might even ride my own pony like the other boys."

"Oh, he did, did he?" Mara asked in amazement, a doubtful look in her eyes. "Well, I'll be having a thing or two to say about that, and I hope you weren't fibbing about how well you can ride, Paddy?"

"I'm not a baby, Mara," Paddy said stiffly, a resentful look in his dark eyes. "You just want to be spoilin' all of me fun."

"Paddy!" Mara gasped, a hurt look in her eyes. "How can you say such a thing? I think you owe me an apology, Padraic."

"Now don't ye be mindin' what the little one is sayin'; he's just feelin' a bit low." Jamie soothed Mara's rising indignation.

Paddy jutted out his lower lip poutingly as he stared down at the sleeve of his nightshirt and refused to look up at Mara.

"Very well, little man, if that's the way you're feeling, then I'll be leaving," Mara said impatiently, rubbing the ache in her temple. She just was not in the mood to suffer one of Paddy's tantrums. "See that he stays in bed today. I'll be back later in the afternoon."

Without a backward glance, Mara walked to the door, but before she could leave, Paddy called out to her.

"I didn't mean it, Mara, don't be mad at me," he cried, his lips trembling in fear that his beloved Mara would stare at him with that cold look in her eyes that she used when looking at other people.

Mara turned back and walked over to the bed. Paddy had scrambled to his knees in panic, and now knelt in his thin nightshirt, the bedclothes once again rumpled around him. Mara hugged him tightly, kissed each hot cheek before settling him once more beneath the warmth of the covers.

"Ah, Paddy, me love," she murmured softly, "if you weren't such a little rascal, I probably wouldn't love you so much."

Paddy smacked a sloppy kiss on Mara's cheek as he lay back against the pillow, a happy smile of contentment curving his mouth into an impish grin.

Jamie gave a disgruntled snort as she watched them. "Someday someone is goin' to be twistin' ye around their little finger the same way ye do every one of us poor souls, Mara O'Flynn," Jamie warned.

"I think not," Mara replied with an arrogant toss of her

head, her expression remaining unworried as a pleased smile curved her lips.

"Hrrmph!" Jamie shook her head in disgust. "Reckon some people be a bit big for their breeches, and others might have a likin' for takin' them in a size or two," she speculated aloud, a glint in her gray eyes as she added, "I'd be walkin' mighty soft if I were a certain person."

"And a certain person I know is walkin' too near the edge now, unless she learns to curb her runaway tongue," Mara warned, anger darkening her eyes.

"Then let it be on your own head," Jamie mumbled as she began to straighten the bedclothes yet again.

Mara left the room on the promise that she'd return to amuse Paddy shortly, and moving along the gallery, a half-smile curving her lips, Mara made her way to the dining room, where most of the family would have gathered by this time, at least those who could raise sleepy eyelids and brave the bright morning sun. Mara's taffeta skirt and numerous petticoats rustled as she walked across the courtyard as the sunlight streamed down on her smooth, chignoned head.

When Mara entered the dining room she presented a very discreet and ladylike appearance in her cinnamon gown with its high neck and small white collar edged in lace that also matched the lace edging the cuffs of her long sleeves. Her expression was serene as she greeted Brendan, who was sipping a cup of strong black coffee and nodded a good morning to her as he swallowed with a grimace of pain the scalding liquid.

"'Mornin', love," he said as she sat down next to him at the half-empty table. By coincidence Brendan had also dressed in a brown coat with a champagne-colored waistcoat, and with Mara sitting next to him the resemblance between the brother and sister would have been quite obvious to the discerning eye.

"You look a bit peaked," he remarked bluntly, his gaze taking in the slight tinge of purple beneath her eyes.

"Wretched headache again," Mara whispered as she smiled sweetly at Doña Ysidora, politely declining the plate of beef now being offered by her hostess.

"You are much too thin, Amaya," Doña Ysidora told her

sternly as she watched in disapproval as Mara took a sip of coffee. "You must put more flesh on your body; then you will be happier and more content—like Doña Jacinta, perhaps," she added a trifle maliciously, for Doña Jacinta was beginning to show definite signs of plumpness.

Doña Jacinta merely smiled as she helped herself to a second portion of eggs. "Luís has no complaints," she remarked smugly, then allowed her dark eyes to rest on Brendan's handsome features as she added coyly, "and perhaps it is pleasing to others as well?"

Brendan hurriedly swallowed a mouthful of tortilla, washing it down on a gulp of coffee as he replied gallantly, "Madame, you would be in the height of fashion in Europe. In fact," Brendan continued, "you bear a startling resemblance to our own dear Queen Victoria. She is also a small woman, ah, nicely rounded, as well. Charming woman, quite charming," Brendan elaborated further, his tone indicating a personal association.

"And you have met the queen of England?" Doña Jacinta breathed, visibly impressed.

"Well, we have attended several of the same social functions," Brendan explained modestly.

Mara smiled into her coffee cup as she innocently asked, "Was not one of the occasions at the theater?"

Brendan feigned a look of concentration. "Do you know, I believe you are correct, my dear," Brendan replied quite seriously. "'Twas a marvelous performance, I must admit, and especially one actor, he was quite brilliant if I recollect correctly," Brendan mused, his lips twitching slightly as he added, "I'm afraid I really can't quite remember the gentleman's name; handsome devil, though."

Mara had to chuckle, for Brendan was indeed an extraordinary actor. The half-smile still curved her lips and a hint of amusement still lingered in her eyes when Nicholas Chantale and Don Andres entered the dining room. The Frenchman was casually dressed and had apparently accompanied Don Andres on his morning ride, for he wore dust-spattered, knee-length boots over tight buckskin trousers, and a dark green riding coat was opened to reveal a leather vest and casually knotted cravat. His black curls were windblown, and as he laughed at something Don Andres said, he showed even white teeth. Mara drew in her breath sharply, for he had one of the most devastating smiles she'd ever seen. It erased the cynical amusement from his lips as they curved almost boyishly into a wide, unguarded grin, and that was where the charm and danger of it lay. For in its naturalness, its unaffectedness, it was far more sensual and effective than any smile of seduction could have been.

Nicholas sat down across from Mara and Brendan, a plateful of food in front of him. He glanced across at them as he started to dispatch his breakfast with a hearty appetite, staring intently at the two of them before he spoke.

"I don't believe we've met," he said suddenly to Brendan.

"No, we've not had that pleasure, sir," Brendan responded easily. "Brendan O'Sullivan, at your service."

"Irish?" Nicholas inquired, an interested look in the green eyes that seconds before had seemed lazily indifferent.

Brendan nodded slightly, his response more guarded as he answered politely, "Only on my father's side, sir, although I was born in England, and only the name is really Irish. Why, I'm as English as London Bridge," Brendan laughed loudly.

Brendan eyed the stranger more carefully, his manner casual as he asked, "I don't believe I caught your name, sir?"

"Nicholas Chantale," he said, his eyes lingering on Mara's face.

Some instinct warned Brendan not to play the man for a fool. He didn't know why he should feel that way, but he felt an underlying danger from this stranger. Brendan removed his handkerchief from his pocket and languidly dabbed at his delicately flared nostrils as he cast a surreptitious look at Mara, wondering if she realized that the Frenchman was no greenhorn. He would never dance like a puppet on a string, responsive to her every whim. Brendan sighed as he recognized the half-smile curving her lips and the speculative gleam in her tawny eyes as she gazed at Nicholas Chantale. Damn! Well, he'd have a heart-to-heart talk with Mara soon enough and warn her off the Frenchman. He was out of their league, and it would be a damned nuisance to have him fouling things up.

"If I might say so, you bear a marked resemblance to Miss Vaughan," Nicholas remarked curiously.

"It is not unusual. She is Mr. O'Sullivan's cousin," Don Andres explained. "Mr. O'Sullivan accompanied Doña Amaya from England, escorting her on the long journey to California."

"Then you have just arrived here from England? I must have misunderstood, for I was under the impression that you had been raised in California. I should have realized you hadn't been, for you seem so typically English."

"Sí, Doña Amaya and Señor O'Sullivan arrived less than a month ago. Don Luís traveled to England to look for her and to bring her back to California as was her late parents' wish."

"So," Nicholas commented, "you are as much a stranger to these shores as I am."

"Yes, you might say that, Mr. Chantale," Brendan replied stiffly, thinking the Frenchman seemed damned curious about their affairs.

"We were afraid that Amaya would not care to return to California, so we were most surprised, and pleased, when she returned with Don Luís," Doña Ysidora said. "And to find her such a beautiful and charming young woman as well, is most fortunate."

"Then you did not know what Doña Amaya looked like?" Nicholas asked softly.

"Few of us remember her as a child, but she is as we would have wished," Don Andres replied, his eyes warm as they met Mara's.

Doña Feliciana looked on sulkily. "I think Doña Amaya will not wish to stay in California. Nothing is settled yet, and she does not really belong."

"Silencio, Feliciana," Doña Ysidora reprimanded her.

"I only meant that she would not find happiness here," Feliciana explained resentfully as she sent a dark look at Mara. "Besides, she does not seem well. You suffer an illness, Doña Amaya?" she demanded unsympathetically.

Don Andres stared in concern at Mara. "Doña Amaya, this is true? You do not feel well?"

Mara shook her head. "It is nothing, just a small headache which will pass."

"You took too much sun yesterday, Amaya. You must be more careful in future," Doña Ysidora warned her. "And soon, Amaya, we must talk about the future," she added with a meaningful glance at her son.

With a strangled sob Doña Feliciana jumped up from the table and ran from the room. Don Andres sent an imploring look to his mother before he excused himself and followed Feliciana.

"It would seem as though something had upset the young woman," Nicholas remarked. "I trust it was nothing I said?"

Doña Ysidora shook her head with its heavy mass of raven dark hair. "No, señor, the child is troubled by her own problems. She dreams too much of what cannot be. Soon, I think, I must see about sending her to a convent. There she will learn patience and humility. It will be necessary if she takes the vows."

Mara shivered at the determined look on the haughty face of Doña Ysidora. She would hate to think of that autocrat ruling her life. Poor Feliciana! Mara didn't think she would enjoy life as a nun, not after the way she had come to life on the back of her favorite horse. Mara brushed aside the thought that Amaya Vaughan might be the cause of Feliciana's trouble and future destiny.

"And where did you live in England, Miss Vaughan?" Mara heard Nicholas Chantale ask her.

"I was raised in the North Country, Mr. Chantale, and grew up on the wild moors of Yorkshire, near Haworth. I doubt you've ever heard of the village, and indeed, probably have never ventured beyond the comforts of London," Mara replied sweetly, elaborating further as she remembered facts she had heard about Charlotte Brontë, a novelist of renown in England. "Such a bleak place under those gray winter skies, the wind fairly whistling down the chimney and only that wide expanse of moorland stretching away to the horizon to gaze upon. You cannot imagine how lovely these rolling green hills and valleys are to me," Mara sighed, mist clouding her eyes.

Brendan coughed into his hand warningly. Smiling at his hostess, he thanked her profusely for the delicious breakfast. "Although I shall really have to watch my figure if I stay here much longer, my dears, or I'll never be able to button up my waistcoat. You will excuse us. We must go and check on my son, he has a touch of fever."

"I am most grieved to hear of this," Doña Ysidora said, worry crossing her hard face. "If there is anything I may do? I am prepared to care for the sick one."

"You are too, too kind, Doña Ysidora, but our maid is used to caring for him and, to be quite honest, very possessive," Brendan declined politely.

Doña Ysidora nodded in understanding but continued with a determined light in her eye. "If you should need any assistance or special medicine, I shall, of course, be happy to assist. But you will not miss the festivities this afternoon? We are to have a bullfight and other amusements," she told them.

"I wouldn't dream of it," Brendan reassured her. With an all-encompassing smile, he escorted Mara from the room and any further conversation with the inquisitive Frenchman.

"That was a damned, stupid thing to do, mavournin," Brendan confronted Mara as soon as they crossed the sunlit patio. "The Frenchman's no fool. You might be able to overplay your part with the Californians, but I'm thinkin' them green eyes be a damned sight too sharp. Asked a lot of questions too," Brendan remarked in puzzlement. "Too bloody nosey if ye ask me."

Mara glanced up at Brendan in amusement. "Have a little bit of faith in me. I'm no fool either, my dear," Mara laughed softly, her eyes narrowing as she added tauntingly, "I do believe you're frightened of him. I can't believe it!"

"You may laugh, mavournin, but I've run across his kind before," Brendan replied, a frown marring his brow. "I've sat across a green baize table from men like the Frenchman, watching them bet a couple of thousand pounds without a flicker of emotion on their faces. I swear they must have ice water in their veins, for any normal man would have sweated through his jacket. They're arrogant bastards, taking what they want in life and not giving a damn about the consequences. He's an adventurer, mavournin, not one of your scented, well-mannered, play-by-the-rules London gentlemen. You've not met his kind before."

Mara smiled at his words. "You think he would best me in a contest of wills, Brendan, me love, and that my rapier wit would not survive?" she asked him softly.

"I think, Mara, me love, that our Frenchman would carve you to pieces as easily as a slice of beef. You are a mere school-girl compared to his expertise," Brendan predicted.

"And I suppose you would be more successful?" Mara asked.

"Oh, no," Brendan replied frankly, "I know when I've met my betters, my dear. I'm not sayin' he would defeat me; I'm just saying that I'd handle him differently," Brendan mused. "I'd avoid, if at all possible, any direct confrontations with the man. I'd let him think me the fool. 'Tis the best way of getting under his guard. But you'd do well to heed my advice and let him be."

At Mara's preoccupied silence Brendan laughed harshly. "I don't know why I bother, you never have listened to me before. Your problem, Mara, is that you are so arrogant, so blind to your own shortcomings, that you can't admit that someone else might be just as devious, just as determined as you are. I would be interested in seein' your face, mavournin, the day you are faced with having that damned pride of yours smashed beneath someone's feet."

Mara gave Brendan a contemptuous look, her lips curling. "Don't be laying any bets on it, will ye, Brendan? I don't want ye losin' your shirt as well as your courage."

"We'll see, Mara. Someday ye'll be rememberin' my words."

With a careless shrug Mara left him standing in the sunshine and went to see Paddy, soon forgetting Brendan's words of warning as she read to Paddy until he fell into an uneasy sleep.

Mara walked along the corridor a little while later, keeping under the shade of the eaves as she looked out on the glare of the sun. It promised to be another unbearably hot day. Her skirt caught on one of the long, sharp cactus spines, halting her progress. She was bending down to release it when she heard a noise coming from the room opening onto the corridor directly in front of her. Mara released her skirt, glanced past the opened door, and went into the room beyond.

It was apparently Don Andres's study, for bookcases lined one side of the walls and a large desk sat squarely before them. A couple of comfortable-looking chairs had been placed opposite the desk, and against the far wall was an ornately carved pine chest. The room must also serve as an office, for Jeremiah Davies was standing before a map on the wall. His back was to Mara and he was as yet unaware of her presence in the doorway. He alternately studied the map, then a sheet of paper clutched in his hand.

Mara must have made a sound because Jeremiah suddenly turned and stared at her in dismay. It seemed to her that he looked extremely guilty about something.

"Doña Amaya, may I be of some assistance to you?" he inquired politely as he inconspicuously tried to add the sheet of paper to a stack of papers on the desk.

"No. I heard you moving about, that's why I looked in," Mara answered. "I trust I didn't disturb you. You were so intent upon what you were doing. I really must apologize for interrupting."

"Not at all, Doña Amaya," Jeremiah Davies quickly denied, "and no apology is necessary. I was just checking the map to see where Don Andres wants his cattle moved next. I must be able to order the vaqueros to the right section of the property."

The audacity of the man—to be talking so openly of moving cattle, and to her of all people. Mara schooled her features into a look of polite interest. Perhaps he was merely testing her, hoping she would reveal what she knew about him.

Jeremiah moved away from the map and glanced around the room as if checking to make sure he had not left anything out of place. Mara watched him suspiciously, wondering what he really was up to. She was about to leave when Don Andres spoke from the doorway.

"Doña Amaya, this is most opportune, for I would like to speak with you." He smiled down into her face. Then, as he looked beyond her and noticed the American, he frowned slightly. "¿Sí, Jeremiah? I did not know we had business?" he questioned his secretary who was now looking uncomfortable and discomfited under the Californian's stare.

"I left some papers in here. I did not intend to disturb you, Don Andres," Jeremiah apologized nervously, "but I really must have your signature on them."

"Come back later, Jeremiah, we will see to it then," Don Andres told him indifferently as he turned back to Mara. "Please, come in and sit down, Doña Amaya," he invited.

Jeremiah Davies coughed uncomfortably, drawing his employer's attention. "If you please, Don Andres, I really must insist that you sign these documents today. It will take only a moment of your time," he added persuasively.

Don Andres sighed in impatience as he walked over to his desk. "You really can be quite tiresome at times, Jeremiah," he complained as Jeremiah quickly pulled out the large, leather-backed chair and placed the stack of papers neatly in front of the Californian.

"And what exactly are all of these?" he questioned, his pen poised above the first sheet as he hesitated briefly before affixing his signature to it.

Jeremiah smiled as he explained facilely, "Just a few bills and some orders that must be sent out immediately, and a few letters you dictated the other day. Nothing really important. Oh, and the authority to sell that parcel of land."

Don Andres raised his eyebrows inquiringly as he looked up from the paper he was signing. "Then why did you insist upon my signing these at this inconvenient moment?" he demanded of Jeremiah.

The American shifted his weight from foot to foot as a disconcerted expression flickered in his blue eyes. "Don't you remember? I'll be away from the rancho for the next week or two, Don Andres. I must hire a field in San Mateo for when we herd the cattle to San Francisco to sell, and I must do these other errands for you," he explained. He anxiously watched Don Andres quickly sign the remaining documents with hardly a glance at them.

Don Andres laid down his pen with an air of finality. "Enough business for today, Jeremiah. Anything else must wait," he decreed as he smiled up at Mara. "I'm very sorry for keeping you waiting, Doña Amaya."

He waved a dismissing hand at Jeremiah Davies who swiftly gathered together the papers and, with a deferential look at the Californian, hurriedly left the room. Mara walked over to the map the American had been studying over moments before and eyed it curiously.

"Why, this is quite beautiful," Mara remarked in surprise.

"Gracias, I am pleased that you find it so," Don Andres responded warmly to her praise. "It is a *diseño* of the Rancho Villareale and was hand-painted by my grandfather."

Mara stared up at the colorful map that showed the boundaries of the rancho with painted trees, rocks, and other identifiable landmarks.

"And all of this is your land?"

Don Andres nodded his head proudly, "Sí, the land that the hacienda sits on and half of the valley was granted to the Villareales under Spanish rule. However, the bulk of the rancho was granted to us under the Mexican regime in the late eighteen-thirties. It was after the secularization of the missions and all of their properties and holdings in 'thirty-four that much land was given away. We had many more head of cattle, vaqueros, and Indians, as well as a much larger family to support then. So we needed all this land, and it was just sitting empty," Don Andres explained.

"We were most concerned during the war between Mexico and the United States that we would suffer grave retributions. However, under the Treaty of Guadalupe Hidalgo, we were guaranteed legal title to our lands. It said that all property would be respected, and we believed them," he added sadly. "But now, do they remember these promises? No, they begin to demand that we turn over our lands to the United States government, that they be opened to all of the people to come and settle on. Squatters! They steal our land from us and say that *we* are in the wrong. I do not understand the laws of los americanos," he spoke in puzzled anger, a reminiscent look clouding his dark eyes for a moment.

"I can remember so well walking around the property with mi padre as we claimed our land. He would pick up a handful of rich soil, drink water from a stream, or break twigs in a grove of oak as he claimed this land for Villareale. We rebuilt the hacienda, made it much larger to house the family we hoped would live and die on this land for many generations to come. Mi padre even built the chapel, which has seen many baptismals and nuptials, but I think it will not see many more," Don Andres sighed. Then, shaking his head, he laughed self-consciously. "So, as mi madre says, enough of this for it does no good. This is not what I wanted to speak to you about. Just a moment, please."

Mara continued to stare up at the colorful map, wondering what difficulties must surely lie ahead for these kind-hearted Californians.

"Amaya, this is what I wished to show you," Don Andres spoke softly behind her.

Mara turned on the slight quiver of anticipation in his voice. The lid of the carved chest stood open, and Don Andres held a miniature gold chest in his hand. As Mara watched, he took a small gold key and inserted it into the lock. As it clicked, he lifted the lid to disclose a jewel-encrusted gold cross on a bed of purple velvet.

Mara drew in her breath, for she truly had never seen anything so exquisite. It was set with a huge ruby in the center and with groups of smaller rubies and pearls along the edges.

"It is yours, Amaya," Don Andres told Mara, a smile of pleasure curving his mouth as he watched her reaction.

"Mine?" Mara gasped in disbelief.

"Sí, it has belonged to the Quintero family for centuries."

Mara looked up from the jeweled cross in puzzlement. "But why are you giving it to me? Shouldn't Don Luís be the possessor of it?"

Don Andres said something beneath his breath and shook

his head. "The cross belonged to your mother, handed down from her mother and from your grandmother's mother," he explained, his eyes avoiding Mara's as if he expected her next question.

"But why do you have it, and not Don Luís?"

"You must understand that this is difficult for me to say. Don Luís was not given the cross because he could not be trusted to safeguard it until it would become your heritage. Don Luís is a man who likes to gamble and unfortunately does not often win. He has lost many valuables, many treasures that he deeply regrets losing once he is no longer owner of them. He is often in debt. I am sorry, Amaya."

"So that is why Don Luís resents you, because you were given the cross," Mara said thoughtfully. She could better understand Don Luís.

"Sí, for that as well as other reasons. He feels he has many grievances against me, although the cross was given into the keeping of mi padre and I am merely carrying out a promise. Don Luís's resentments go beyond that, but that need not concern you, Doña Amaya. It is now my honor to give you the Quintero cross."

Mara sighed. For once she was sorry she really was not Amaya Vaughan and the rightful heir to this golden cross. It would have solved all of their problems.

"You are not pleased?" Don Andres asked, not understanding the look of regret on Mara's face.

"I can't accept it, Andres," Mara told him bluntly. At his look of incredulous dismay, she prevaricated quickly, "It is too valuable. You must keep it in the chest where it will be safe."

"Ah, I think I understand," he said softly, "that certain people might wish to exert their authority over their relatives and take possession of the cross."

Mara smiled her agreement with him, although she didn't know which relative of hers she really was protecting it from. She could already see the gleam of avarice in Brendan's eyes. And as far as Don Luís was concerned, well, that was another problem altogether.

"You do understand then, that I would not be able to

rest thinking the cross not safely locked up," Mara told him, relieved not to have the responsibility of the priceless heirloom.

"Certainly. I will guard it well, as I have these many years, Amaya, although we have no thieves here on Rancho Villareale," Don Andres reassured her confidently. He replaced the cross in its chest of gold, which was valuable in itself, and locked it. He placed it back in the safety of the large wooden chest against the wall. "Should you wish to wear it some evening, then just ask me and I will be pleased to get it for you."

"Thank you, Andres. Now I must fetch a bonnet if we're to be out in the sun all day," Mara said, adding, "or I shall be quite out of fashion with a freckled face."

Don Andres shook his head. "I do not think that you could ever be that, Amaya." Then he paused uncertainly, as he searched for the right words. "I think soon we must come to a decision, Amaya. You must think about whether or not you wish to stay in California."

He held up his hand as Mara would have spoken. "Please, you need not say anything. I know you must think of this carefully. Whatever you decide upon...well, I will agree to."

Mara stared at this quiet, California ranchero in perplexity. Despite herself, she rather liked him. Never had she met anyone quite so unselfish before. In the world she was accustomed to, a person thought of himself first and sometimes exclusively. But these Californians were a strange race. They opened their hearts and their homes to strangers, unsuspiciously sharing their possessions, their sole purpose to be good hosts. And what were they likely to reap in return? Already they were finding out that not all people were as honest as they were.

How easy it was for Brendan and her to take advantage of the Californians' hospitality. How easy it would be for her to go on pretending to be Amaya Vaughan, marry a rich ranchero who would provide a stable home for Paddy, and spend the rest of her days in this peaceful valley. Mara sighed. What was the use in dreaming, for some instinct warned her that this was not meant to be her destiny.

"What is it that concerns you, Amaya?" Don Andres asked. "You seem saddened."

Mara's lips twisted into an amused smile. "Saddened? No, Don Andres, I was merely indulging in a foolish daydream, that is all."

"Dreams are never foolish, Amaya," Don Andres disagreed with an indulgent smile.

Mara shrugged as she walked slowly to the door. Glancing back at the Californian she said cynically, "Dreams are a luxury, Andres. They don't put food in your belly or shoes on your feet, and they often lead you to false hopes."

"You are quite a cynic and rather world-weary for one so young," Nicholas Chantale remarked in a lazy voice from the doorway.

Mara eyed the Frenchman curiously, a slightly defiant tilt to her chin. "And are you a dreamer, Monsieur Chantale? I would have thought not. You strike me as one who had lost all of the illusions of youth."

Nicholas Chantale straightened his lean body from against the doorjamb and unflinchingly returned Mara's taunting look.

"Ah, now you surprise me, Miss Vaughan. For I would have thought a sheltered, English miss like yourself would have had her every wish granted," he said. "Do you mean to tell me that you are not like the princess in the fairy tale?"

Mara's eyes narrowed in anger kept barely in check, for she was not used to being baited in this insolent manner. "We are not always as we would seem, *m'sieu*," Mara told him coldly. Then, giving Andres a warm smile, she turned back to the tall Frenchman and waited haughtily for him to step aside.

"Are you advising me not to judge you by your appearance, Miss Vaughan?" Nicholas questioned with a sardonic gleam in his green eyes. He obliged her and cleared the doorway.

"I do not expect, or desire, any judgment from you, monsieur," Mara replied in a tone of voice that indicated his opinion was unworthy of consideration and, indeed, of very little consequence as far as she was concerned.

With a patronizingly slight nod of her sleek, chignoned head, Mara left the room, a gleam of satisfaction brightening her eyes as she walked along the gallery and remembered the look of black anger that had flared for an instant in the Frenchman's eyes. And, Mara mused, hadn't there been a shadow of unwilling admiration in those damnably beautiful green eyes?

"You seem mighty pleased with yourself, m'dear," Brendan's drawling voice interrupted Mara's reflections.

"Brendan," Mara said quickly, ignoring his comment as she guided him into his room, "I think we've landed ourselves in a pit of vipers."

"Rattlers," Brendan corrected her as he inattentively straightened the sleeve of his coat where Mara's fingers had wrinkled the material.

"What?" Mara spoke in exasperation as she watched him smooth his scarf. "Do stop fidgeting, Brendan."

Brendan looked up at her with a comical expression of peevishness on his handsome face. "Well, really, did you have to manhandle me so, jerking me into me own room, wrinkling me coat? I'll have you know I've not many in decent shape to be wearing, so do be more careful in future," he told her. Then with a teasing smile he enlightened Mara. "Rattlesnakes would be more likely out here, mavournin. Lying in wait up in the rocks for the unsuspecting, the vicious little devils, although they do give you a warning before they're ready to strike and pump you full of venom." Brendan grinned, enjoying his frightening description and the look of distaste on Mara's face. "Obliging of them, wouldn't you say?"

"Well, 'tis more than most of the people around here are doing," Mara complained.

Brendan eyed her more seriously. "And just what have you been up to while me back was turned?" Brendan demanded suspiciously. "Been tanglin' with the Frenchman again, have you?"

Mara returned his glare coolly as she answered mysteriously. "Among other things, Brendan, me love. However, what I was speaking of was finding Jeremiah Davies sneaking around Don Andres's study, and up to little good. And finding out that our benefactor, Don Luís, neglected to tell us that Doña Amaya would be inheriting a jewel-encrusted cross of solid gold, worth a lifetime's wages," Mara told him softly, relishing the look of incredulity on Brendan's face.

"Damn! A gold cross did you say, mavournin?"

Mara smiled slightly. "It would seem Don Luís is not without his little secrets."

"Well now, suppose you tell Brendan all about this cross of yours," Brendan invited, a thoughtful look in his eyes as he made himself comfortable on the edge of the bed.

"It seems as though Don Luís is a bit of a gambler, and not a very lucky one, for many of the family treasures have slipped through his fingers, so Amaya's father entrusted what heirlooms were left to the Villareales. I was shown this priceless heirloom just a few minutes ago, as well as receiving a rather halfhearted proposal of marriage should I decide upon staying at the Rancho Villareale," Mara told Brendan matter-of-factly.

"Well, things are beginning to pick up around here. Where's the cross? I'd like a look at it," Brendan demanded with a gleam of anticipation in his eye.

"Sorry, love, but Don Andres has it safely locked up," Mara replied innocently, as if it were all beyond her control.

"The divil you say," Brendan grumbled, then glanced suspiciously up at Mara as she remained silent. "I don't suppose you had anything to do with that state of affairs, did you, Mara, me love?" Brendan asked softly, seeing the answer to his question in the slight twitching of her lips. "Ye're a distrustful wench to be thinkin' ill of your own flesh and blood," he ejaculated, a look of anguish transforming his face into a mask of pathos.

"I was merely trying to protect you from yourself, Brendan. Too much temptation is bad for a person," Mara said, remaining unimpressed with his elegant display of dramatics, having seen him use the same expression and gestures while performing on stage. "We might be liars, but so far we've not sunk so low as to start stealing crosses."

Brendan flinched at the bluntness of her words. "Please,

mavournin, must you be putting it quite so crudely? I will admit that we are not above embroidering a bit on the truth, that in the past we might even have been guilty of certain falsehoods," Brendan admitted easily, "but—"

"You lie like a trooper, Brendan, me love," Mara contradicted.

"But," Brendan continued, ignoring her interruption, "*we'd* be fools not to take advantage of the fools who are ripe for the picking, and since playin' a double game comes easy for us, why not make use of our skills?" Brendan stated without a twinge of conscience. "However," he added as an afterthought, "I'm no Jonathan Wild yet, and do not consider myself to be a thief. I do have certain standards, m'dear."

"Well, just keep remembering that, because our fine Californian has his eye on that cross. He must still have some family pride left that he wants it back in his possession, and he'll even lie to get it. He asked me about it, calling it something of little importance."

"To be sure, he must think us the fools," Brendan said sourly. "I don't know what the old fox's game is, but I'm damned tired of playin' it."

"He'll make his move soon, Brendan, and I for one will be glad to leave here," Mara predicted as she echoed his sentiments.

❧

Mara frowned as a loud chorus of cheers echoed around the corral. From her position on the raised platform, built earlier that morning for the afternoon's entertainment, Mara could see the whole area below and the two wild animals insanely fighting in a blood lust. The enraged bellows of the snorting bull and the screams of the giant grizzly bear were almost deafening as they fought each other. The heavy chain that was attached to one leg of each bound them together, not allowing either to get away from his enemy. Mara glanced away from the arena in distaste. The bull, with lowered neck and eyes burning like glowing coals, snorted and pawed the earth before him. The bear sat back on his haunches, his vicious, curved claws flashing through the air. His small eyes glared malevolently at his antagonist. On an ear-shattering bellow he lunged at the bull, trying to leap onto his vulnerable, unprotected neck, but the bull, anticipating the grizzly's move, raised his thick neck and speared the bear through the shoulder with his sharp horns. The grizzly's roar of rage and pain spurred him to lash out in retribution at the unfortunate bull, his deadly claws ripping the bull's lolling tongue in two.

Mara felt sick, not only by the cruel baiting of the animals, but by the expressions of anticipation and enjoyment on the Californians' faces. Doña Feliciana's eyes glowed in excitement, and even Doña Ysidora cheered as heartily as Don Andres as she watched the mauling in the arena. Shaking her head at Brendan, her face pale, Mara signaled that she was leaving and, excusing herself, made her way from the arena, her handkerchief held to her lips.

She closed her eyes for a second, blotting out the bright glare of the sun, and felt her headache lessen somewhat. She stumbled slightly, but before she could fall, a strong hand closed about her elbow. Mara glanced up, a word of thanks on her lips, only to have them trail away as she stared up into the watchful green eyes of the Creole.

"You do not care for blood sports?" he asked casually, his hard fingers still wrapped around her elbow.

"I find very little sport in that," Mara replied as she pulled her arm free from his grasp.

"You surprise me."

Mara stared at him in puzzlement. "Why?"

Nicholas shrugged. "Perhaps I was mistaken, but I sensed a certain strength of mind, a determination and self-reliance," he explained. Then he added with a disarming smile. "And what is it the English say? You have bulldog courage?"

Mara's eyes widened as she sputtered, "B–bulldog courage?"

"I'm sorry. I see I have offended you, mademoiselle. It was not intended. I only meant that you show a certain hardness, a severeness of manner unusual in a woman," Nicholas apologized, his thick lashes hiding the mocking glint in his eyes.

"You find me hard and unfeminine?" Mara asked, hiding her dismay well. "I have never thought of myself in that light, m'sieu. However, to be strong does not always imply that a person is hard."

"Please forget what I have just said. I can see I have angered you," Nicholas smiled.

"Angered me? Not at all," Mara denied even as the anger stained her cheeks.

"Then prove to me that I have not offended you, mademoiselle, and accept my invitation to accompany me on a short ride," Nicholas invited her, his wide, boyish smile charming her as it was meant to do.

Mara hesitated only a moment before she accepted. "Thank you. I should like that, Mr. Chantale," Mara said in the friendliest tone of voice she had yet used with the man.

Yes, she would go riding with him, Mara thought defiantly a few minutes later as she struggled into her riding habit.

"Monsieur Chantale has a few more things to learn about Mara O'Flynn before I'm through with him," Mara muttered beneath her breath as she adjusted her small straw hat.

"What was that ye said?" Jamie demanded as she tried to straighten up the clothes Mara had flung across the floor. "Here's your other hat," Jamie told her, holding up the black beaver hat with the veil. "Why aren't ye wearin' it, it looks better than that one."

"'Tis too hot, Jamie. My head's fair to bursting now with this heat, and I feel like my skin is cracking open. 'Tis so dry. Doesn't it ever rain out here?" she demanded in exasperation as she sat down on the edge of the bed and picked up one of her riding boots.

"Help me on with this, will you, Jamie?" Mara said as she pulled the boot over her toes, sliding her foot down inside.

Jamie had picked up the left boot but dropped it to help Mara in her struggle. Wiggling her foot successfully down inside the boot, Mara started to reach down for her other one when she drew back with a scream. Two exploring claws appeared out of the mouth of her boot as the rest of the body of the scorpion crawled from concealment. Mara jerked her feet up on the bed as she stared in horrified fixation at the tiny pincers waving in the air and the curved, poisonous tail poised dangerously behind.

"Oh, my God," Mara whispered shakily as the many-legged creature moved slowly across the floor. "What the devil is that thing?"

"Whatever 'tis, it isn't goin' to be with us for long," Jamie promised with a threatening glint in her gray eyes. Swiftly she picked up the empty bowl on the table and allowed the scorpion to crawl inside. Then, without wasting any time, she scurried over to the window and tossed the wicked-looking creature out the window between the bars guarding it against larger trespassers.

"That horrid thing nearly scared the life out of me," Mara said breathlessly. "And how did the creature get into my boot?"

Jamie shrugged as she gave the offending boot a vigorous shake. "That I'm not knowin'. Critters creep into places ye wouldn't be dreamin' of lookin', but it won't be happenin' again," she said as she held out the boot for Mara's hesitant inspection.

With a delicate shiver Mara allowed her foot to slide down inside the dark confines of the boot. Then, getting to her feet, she stamped her foot securely in. Picking up her gauntlet-style gloves, she made her way to the door, her nerves frayed as she short-temperedly snapped her whip against her thigh. "'Tis a cursed, inhospitable place."

"Warned ye and Brendan about that when we first sailed into the bay," Jamie grumbled. Then she called after Mara, "And don't be disturbin' Paddy. He's finally asleep."

Mara acknowledged Jamie's injunction with a casual wave of her hand as she made her way to the stables, her mind already dwelling on the ride with the Creole and the fashion in which she would deal with him. Of the outcome she had no doubt, for he would become as infatuated as all of the other fools she had captivated. He was no different from other men.

They rode westward from the rancho toward a line of low, rolling hills spotted with clumps of live oak and flowery buckeye, its blossoms looking like giant white candles amid the emerald leaves. As they climbed higher out of the valley, they passed the neatly laid-out rows of a vineyard. The squat vines were being cultivated for the sweet wine they would ultimately yield.

Mara glanced across at Nicholas Chantale and had to admit reluctantly that he rode magnificently astride a shiny, full-chested roan stallion with a flowing mane and tail. The Creole easily guided his spirited mount past outcroppings of rock and through eroded slides of loose gravel and dirt. His thighs rippled with muscle as he pressed them against the flanks of his horse and the muscular strength of his sun-darkened forearms, revealed by rolled-up sleeves, belied the gentle touch of his hands on the reins. The green eyes beneath the brim of his hat were no less a green than the leaves of the wild blackberry growing across the woodlands and climbing in vines up trunks of oak and pine.

Mara followed Nicholas toward a grove of gnarled oaks and the inviting shade from their wide branches. Several tall fir trees rose above the canopy of branches as if standing sentinel over the small, secluded copse. Spread out far below them in overlapping, straggling rows were orchards of apples, peaches, plums, and apricots. Behind the rancho were the vegetable gardens that supplied the Villareale table.

Nicholas had already dismounted as Mara rode into the cool shadows of the trees. He was waiting to assist her in climbing down. He reached up and Mara felt his hands slide around her waist as he lifted her from the saddle. She placed the palms of her hands lightly against his shoulders and slid into his arms. Their faces were even for a moment as he held her stationary against his chest and allowed his gaze to linger on her face. Mara noticed the fine lines spreading from the corners of his eyes and the thickness of the black lashes that fanned their limpid greenness. She slowly traced the classic outline of his firm lips with her eyes until his mouth curled into an amused sneer. Mara jerked her startled gaze away and struggled to the ground. He released her immediately—as if he could not wait to have her out of his arms, Mara thought with a haughty raising of her chin. She walked away from him feeling, oddly enough, at a disadvantage.

Nicholas watched her intently as she wandered around the glade, his glance missing nothing about her, from the dusty hem of her skirt to the jaunty angle of the straw bonnet.

Mara turned and caught the speculative gleam in his eye and decided to give him something to speculate about. A slow smile curved her lips and she sauntered across to the base of a massive oak tree where one of the twisted limbs curved downward and swept the ground, creating a natural bench of smooth bark. Mara sat down on the mighty branch, smoothing her skirts modestly as she made herself comfortable and leaned back against a profusion of shiny green leaves, only to sit forward again as she felt their prickly edges.

Nicholas smiled as he leaned against the sturdy trunk of the oak. "Magnificent tree, isn't it?" he asked casually.

Mara nodded as she cast a disinterested look at the dome of interlocking branches above her head.

"You don't strike me as the outdoor type, Miss *Vaughan*," Nicholas continued conversationally. "I see you more at home in, say, London or Paris."

Mara smiled thoughtfully. "I seem to present a puzzle to you, Mr. Chantale. Does that bother you?"

"Not really, mademoiselle" Nicholas replied with a glint in his eye. "I enjoy solving problems."

"And you always succeed in finding a solution. How very confident you are," Mara said smoothly. "But I'm afraid I shall have to disappoint you, for I have no secrets," she said directly, her tawny eyes wide and unshadowed.

"Did you never know anyone named Julian?" Nicholas asked suddenly, his body tense as he waited for Mara's reaction. His eyes never left Mara's face.

"Julian?" Mara pondered, a doubtful look on her face. "I think not," she replied innocently, for the name truly meant nothing to her. "I'm sorry, but as I told you, I've led a very quiet life in the country. Is he a friend of yours?"

"It is nothing important," Nicholas lied, hiding his frustration. No expression of guilt or deceit had crossed her face at the mention of Julian's name. "Are you to become the next Villareale bride?"

Mara was caught off guard by that question and stared at him in surprise. "That is something which will be decided by Don Andres and myself. We have reached no decision yet."

"I'm sorry. I had thought you'd come out to California with the express purpose of wedding our handsome ranchero. And unless I am mistaken, he would not find it objectionable."

"Possibly," Mara told him noncommittally, "but as I said, I have not made up my mind yet. Now—I wish to speak of this no more," she said imperiously.

Nicholas inclined his head to her wishes. "Certainly, mademoiselle. What do you wish to speak of?"

"Shall we talk of you, m'sieu?" Mara invited softly. "For instance, did you leave a broken-hearted sweetheart or wife and family behind when you left New Orleans to seek your fortune in California?"

Nicholas grinned widely. "When you want to know about someone, Miss Vaughan, you certainly speak bluntly."

"Why should I not? Subterfuge is only useful when one is being secretive. It's far more expedient to be direct."

"I agree, only some people cannot resist the temptation to mislead others."

Mara smiled, enjoying the exchange. "Ah, but you are guilty of that yourself, m'sieu, for are you not avoiding my questions this very minute?"

For the first time warmth entered Nicholas's eyes, softening their crystalline quality. "I stand rebuked," he laughed as he pushed himself away from the tree trunk and sat down next to Mara on the natural bench. Its gentle sloping caused his thigh to press against the length of hers as he placed his arm along the limb behind their backs. He showed no inclination to give her more space.

"But in answer to your question, I did not abandon a wife and family, nor did I leave a legion of broken-hearted females behind."

"Now that I cannot believe," Mara teased him as she looked up into his hard face, then glanced away uncomfortably under the close scrutiny of his jewel-bright eyes. She could feel the warmth of his breath against her neck. He laughed.

"You flatter me, mademoiselle," Nicholas spoke close to her ear. "But had there been a woman such as you in my arms—then, perhaps, I would never have ventured this far."

Mara kept her gaze locked on the chaparral-covered hill in the distance, ignoring the seductive persuasiveness of his voice. She demanded, "Come now, you don't mean to tell me that a man like yourself had no lady love to regret his leaving New Orleans?"

"There was no one of importance, and I have not seen New Orleans in fifteen years, mademoiselle," Nicholas answered harshly.

At his abrupt answer Mara glanced at his face and was surprised to see a brooding look cross it. It seemed to be an expression of more than bitterness and anger. There was a quality of sadness in it as well, but the look passed quickly and was replaced with one of derision.

"Now you, on the other hand, must surely have left many an unhappy young man who had thought he had your favor?" Nicholas inquired softly. "One as lovely as you must have many admirers."

Mara frowned slightly. "You seem determined to cast me in the role of a coquette. I wonder what she would do if she were here with you in the seclusion of this shady grove," Mara speculated, her golden eyes innocently holding his as she pretended to be puzzled about such a situation.

"If she were indeed with me, she would not have to worry for long about what she would be doing next," Nicholas answered, "for I would leave her in little doubt of what would be expected."

Too late Mara realized that she had set a trap for herself. His meaning hit her and she felt his arm move behind her and caress her shoulder as he firmly but gently turned her to face him on the narrow seat of the tree limb. His other hand moved from her waist up along the row of buttons securing the front of her cambric shirt beneath her riding jacket, lingered against the soft throat before lightly cupping her chin. Nicholas's green eyes were partially veiled behind his lowered lashes, but she could still see the glint in them as he lowered his lips to hers.

Mara prepared herself to feel the pressure of his mouth against hers but was surprised when she felt his lips against her throat and his hard fingers moving to her nape as he

arched her throat backward, exposing the smooth, bare
column to his lips. Mara gave an involuntary shiver as his
mouth moved along her throat, his breath tickling the
fine hairs on her nape before his mouth caressed her ear,
touching it with his tongue before moving leisurely on to
press kisses across her cheeks and eyes, closing them to feel
the thick fringe of lashes. When his mouth finally closed
over hers, it was cool and hard, not hot and moist like so
many of the others' had been. They had been anxious, and
impatient to touch her, but the Creole was taking his time,
seducing her with slow, deliberate passion. Both his arms
now held her wrapped close to his chest, pulling her from
her seat as she leaned against him, her hips pressed to his lap.
Mara felt herself relaxing and was surprised she felt none of
the disgust and revulsion she had always felt before when one
of her admirers tried to make love to her. When she felt his
tongue seek her mouth, she stiffened against it. His lips left
hers, caressing her face instead, teasing her with languorous
kisses. Then, to her dismay, she found herself wanting to
feel the touch of his lips against hers, and for the first time in
her life she sought a man's kisses. Mara opened her eyes, her
lids heavy with passion as her mouth clung to his, but they
flashed wide at the triumphant expression she now saw on
Nicholas's face. Angrily, Mara struggled to free her mouth
from his demanding lips, pulling away from his arms as she
jumped to her feet. Turning her back on him, she walked
over to the edge of the shade, her eyes burning from more
than the glare from the sun-parched earth.

Nicholas watched her curiously as he continued to lounge
against the tree limb. With a frowning sigh, he got to his feet.
At the sound, Mara turned abruptly and stared at him. Her
straw hat was sitting at a precarious angle on her sleek head
as she eyed him warily, and he was surprised to see an oddly
vulnerable look about the mouth he had just caressed.

"You don't kiss very well," he said brutally. The childish
dismay on her face irritated him into hurting her in retaliation
for his momentary feeling of discomfort.

Mara's head jerked back as if she'd been slapped. Drawing a

deep breath, she replied coldly, "And did you expect I would? I am not from the streets of London, Paris, or Liverpool— places you have apparently frequented, rather than the salons of gentlefolk. You offend me, sir," Mara said frigidly.

Nicholas bowed slightly. "My apologies, Miss Vaughan," he said coolly as he rescued her gloves from the ground. "You are correct, it would seem, for I have spent too many years away from polite society. I should have recognized a lady when I met her."

Mara watched him approach her, his long, muscular legs quickly covering the distance between them. He held out her leather gloves, but Mara hesitated an instant before reaching out. Then, grasping them firmly, she snatched them away. But before she could step away she felt his hand against her cheek, then it was quickly and efficiently straightening her hat.

"Your bonnet was crooked," Nicholas explained shortly.

"I think we'd better ride back to the rancho," Mara replied. She avoided his eyes and walked away from him to her mount.

"Will you allow me to assist you, Miss Vaughan?" Nicholas asked softly, but there was an angry glint in his eyes that Mara missed.

"Certainly," Mara assented haughtily, a disdainful expression on her flawless features. "I've no intention of walking back."

"I'll try to control my rakehell lusts, ma'am," Nicholas said mockingly as he placed his hands around Mara's waist and lifted her easily onto the back of her horse. "But can you maintain your decorous behavior, I wonder."

Mara glared down at this insolent Creole, her gloved hands fingering her whip dangerously as anger smoldered behind her tawny eyes. She considered her next action with relish.

"I wouldn't, mademoiselle" Nicholas warned as he stepped out of reach of the whip. "Then you *would* have firsthand knowledge of what goes on in bordellos and bawdy houses."

Mara's hand clenched on the butt of the whip as she turned her horse around, his haunch brushing against Nicholas's chest. "Well, you'll not be getting satisfaction here, Mr. Chantale, for you've come to the wrong woman this time," Mara told

him with a contemptuous smile. She touched her heels to her
horse's flank and trotted from the concealment of the grove.

Mara heard the thundering of his horse's hooves before
she saw him. He rode up beside her as she galloped across
the hillside. She continued to ignore his presence until they
entered the narrow mouth of a ravine and Mara's horse
stumbled on the eaten-away sides of the undermined surface
and slid into Nicholas's mount. Mara fought to steady her
horse, pulling up on the reins as his head nosed the dirt and
he whinnied nervously.

As she brought him under control, Mara turned an angry
face to the Creole who'd managed to gallop clear of her
floundering mount. Losing complete control of her temper
now, she lashed out at him.

"What the divil d'ye think you're about, crowding me so
close," Mara cried out in wrathful indignation.

Mara halted her tirade abruptly at the look of amazed
wonder crossing his features.

"My, my, the little lady certainly has a way with words,"
Nicholas said coldly, a steely glint in his eyes. He stared at her
pale face, cruel satisfaction hardening his mouth.

"You will forgive me," Mara said, recovering. "But I
thought, as you were more accustomed to gutter language, it
was the only way to make myself understood."

"Oh, I think I understand you perfectly, Miss *Vaughan*,"
Nicholas replied with an inscrutable smile.

Mara shrugged away a feeling of disquiet and urged her
horse into a canter. They rode toward the rancho, her
thoughts centering on the score she must settle with the
arrogant Creole. Settle it she would, she promised herself as
she rode through the gates of the rancho.

But those sentiments were harder to act upon than
she'd thought, Mara admitted later that evening as she sat
beside Paddy's bed telling him stories until he dozed off.
The evening had been disconcerting. All her scheming had
gone for naught as she helplessly watched the Creole flatter
Feliciana. He ignored her completely and played the smitten
suitor to the inexperienced Californian. How could she

succeed in making a fool of the Creole when he acted as though she did not exist?

Mara looked down at Paddy's sleeping face. He was still hot, but his breathing seemed easier.

Mara stood up, stretching in tiredness before she tucked the covers around Paddy's shoulders and tiptoed from the room, leaving a sleeping Jamie undisturbed.

Mara paused at the edge of the gallery, leaning against one of the posts as she stared up at the clear black sky where a scattering of stars shimmered in the darkness. She wandered beyond the eaved overhang and silently made her way into the courtyard. The rancho was quieter than usual. A few laughing voices drifted to her from the outer courtyard, but most of the guests had retired for the evening. Mara sat down on the bench that curved around part of the fountain and trailed her fingers in the cool water. She stared across at the darkened windows of the room occupied by the Creole. She wondered if he were within and what he was doing. Was he thinking of her?

Don Luís stared incredulously at the tall Frenchman, unable to hide his dismay. "I—I do not quite understand you, señor," he said on a shaky laugh of disbelief.

Nicholas smiled without humor. "I know it must sound completely insane to you, but are you sure that the woman known as Doña Amaya is really your niece? I suspect that she is an actress masquerading as your long-lost niece. Her real name is Mara O'Flynn."

Don Luís swallowed nervously, his dark eyes sliding away from this strange man who seemed to be able to read his very thoughts. ¡Madre de Dios! What was he to do now?

"I do not know quite what to say to you, except of course that this is absolutely preposterous. To imagine that a strange woman would be pretending to be my niece—well, it is quite impossible, señor, totally inconceivable," Don Luís bluffed as he raised his chin with offended pride.

"Don Luís, please, I mean no offense to you personally. I merely question the circumstances under which you have found your niece," Nicholas tried to explain, realizing he had given great offense. "After all, you have not seen her since she was a small child, is this not so?"

"Sí, but I could not be mistaken in this. She resembles my own dear sister greatly," Don Luís reassured him, "and I did meet her in her own home, with her aunt and uncle present. There really can be no mistake, señor. She is Amaya Vaughan, this I swear on my honor. No one in England knew I would be coming to seek out Amaya, so how could such a deception even be thought of? I think you must be mistaken," Don Luís told him patronizingly, shaking his head in pity.

Nicholas reached into his pocket and pulled out the golden locket, opening it as he handed it across to Don Luís. "Are you still going to tell me that Mara O'Flynn and Amaya Vaughan are not one and the same?"

Don Luís stared down at the picture of Mara O'Flynn, the expression in his eyes masked by his lowered lids. "Dios, there is indeed a certain similarity, señor," Don Luís laughingly admitted, "but I think they cannot be the same person; indeed, how could they be? I do not know who this woman is, or why you should have her picture, but I would swear that they are two different people. Besides, there are things that only Amaya could know, and does know, which would give away an impostor. I am sorry, señor, but you are mistaken."

"So you are convinced she is indeed your niece? I am sorry for having troubled you, Don Luís," Nicholas told him, although he was still puzzled by the likeness and the displays of another personality that this "Amaya" occasionally exhibited.

"You are a personal friend of this woman?"

"No, Miss O'Flynn and I have not had the pleasure. But I have…knowledge of her."

"Then really, señor, how can you be so positive that this woman is the same one when you admit you have never even met her? To base such an accusation on so flimsy an assumption is indeed rather reckless," Don Luís criticized. "I must, however, ask that you do not distress my niece with these unfounded charges, for they will only serve to disturb her and to displease your hosts, the Villareales," Don Luís warned the Frenchman.

Nicholas's green eyes narrowed dangerously. "That sounds almost like a threat, Don Luís," he commented quietly.

Don Luís threw up his hands in alarm as he amiably denied this. "Certainly not! I merely wished to caution you for your own safety and clear conscience, señor. We Californians pride ourselves on our good manners and honor, and when you question me and Doña Amaya, you cast aspersions on the house of Villareale as well."

"I'll bear that in mind." Nicholas nodded as he made his way to the door, his broad-shouldered form blocking it for a moment before he disappeared into the dark courtyard beyond.

Don Luís sank into a chair as the Frenchman disappeared. He looked down at his hands and was surprised to see them shaking—with what? Fear? No, he was not frightened of anything physical this stranger might do; it was just the unexpected suddenness of his dangerous knowledge that had momentarily disconcerted him. Don Luís ran a thin hand through his graying hair as he tried to gather his wits. He did know one thing. That under no condition must the O'Flynns learn of this Frenchman's recognition of them. They were already becoming restless, and at this hint of danger they would surely bolt and disappear into the hills like any cowardly coyote; of this he was certain.

He had succeeded so far in controlling them, but they were very unpredictable, and if they learned certain other facts as well, such as that he was broke and in debt to the equivalent of thousands of English pounds and had no money to pay them, then the situation could become explosive. At least he had no money yet, but as soon as he got possession of the cross and sold it, he would have enough money to pay them off; a pity he even had to do that, but they were the type to cause mischief if double-crossed.

Yes, Don Luís thought in satisfaction, he would soon again own his birthright. He'd been a fool to gamble his land away, but what else could he have done? He needed the money to pay off other debts; besides, he had not thought to lose. Don Andres had pretended not to want to accept the stakes, but he knew differently, for Don Andres had always coveted the Quintero land. Don Luís sighed in remembered pain and despair as he saw again the race that his horse had failed to win. Don Andres had offered to give back the land, but that had been an insult in itself; to be under an obligation to a Villareale, to accept charity from a man younger than himself—why, it was unthinkable.

And that was why he had decided to travel to England to bring back his sister's daughter. Once he had the cross, he could buy back his land and reclaim the honor that had been stolen from him. But he also relished the opportunity the presentation of his niece had given him in causing an upheaval in the Villareale household; for everyone knew that Doña Feliciana had been the expected bride of Don Andres. Most had forgotten the old agreement between Don Pedro and Doña Amaya's father.

Don Luís smiled in satisfaction as he thought of Don Andres's chagrin when Doña Amaya would reject him and return to England. He would not only be humiliated before his friends and family, but he suspected that Don Andres might suffer as well from a heaviness of heart. Mara O'Flynn was a very captivating Amaya, and he had seen the look on Don Andres's face when she entered a room, his eyes following her every gesture, clinging to her face as she spoke. Sí, had Mara O'Flynn indeed been Amaya Vaughan, her future would have been secure.

But the O'Flynns' future was, quite the contrary, anything but secure. It would have simplified matters if he could have told them the truth in the beginning, but he had doubted whether Señor O'Flynn would have felt any sympathy for his loss of his land after having just lost all of his own money. His sentiments would hardly have been charitable; in fact, he had been downright vindictive and insensible of benefits until persuaded otherwise. With the enticement of canceling his debt, as well as being able to earn a considerable sum of money for services rendered, he had induced Señor O'Flynn into acting out the charade. He had deceived the O'Flynns as to his exact circumstances and the true value of the cross, for having been the recipient of the Irishman's charismatic charm, he would not put it above Señor O'Flynn to try to talk his way into owning the cross. The man was a devil with the honeyed phrase. But so far with the exception of the Frenchman's inter- ference, all had gone as planned. Soon he would have the cross, and then, of course, he would have to confront the O'Flynns with the truth and trust that they would be content for a while longer. Of course they would; otherwise they would not get paid. Until then, he must keep their suspicions allayed and hope that the Frenchman heeded his advice.

∽✺∾

Nicholas walked slowly along the corridor, a dissatisfied feeling lingering with him when he thought of his interview with Don Luís. He was still not convinced, despite what the Californian had said, that Amaya Vaughan was not Mara O'Flynn. If only there were some way of proving it beyond all question…But how? Nicholas wondered.

As he passed the fountain he glanced in its direction, its soft splashing bringing back forgotten memories of another fountain in another courtyard years ago. As he stood staring introspectively at the fountain, a shadow moved beside it. He made his way toward the fountain, recognizing the arrogant tilt of the head as his eyes adjusted to the shadowy light.

"Star gazing, mademoiselle?" Nicholas asked.

Mara jerked her head around. "I would have thought you'd accuse me of crystal gazing and conjuring a spell against you," Mara retorted, determined not to be mollified by his friendly tone.

"Now, were we in New Orleans, I might indeed suspect you of such mischief," Nicholas replied, ignoring her sarcasm as he sought to learn more about this perplexing woman.

Mara smiled. "If you deal with others in the same manner as you do with me, then I'm not surprised someone might wish you ill luck."

Nicholas was quietly thoughtful for a moment before he answered in a voice completely devoid of emotion. "At one time, long ago, I did believe I had been cursed. Someone certainly did wish me ill."

"And are you still cursed?" Mara strained her eyes in the darkness trying to read the expression on his face.

"A vivid memory of the past is curse enough sometimes, mademoiselle," Nicholas replied. "Haven't you found that to be true?"

Mara shrugged noncommittally, unwilling to let him know he had touched her. "You sound as though you've no fond memories of New Orleans. Have you no family there?"

"None who would claim me, mademoiselle, but you are wrong, for I do have some very fond memories of my birth-place. There is no other city like it in the world, and I have traveled the world over. Even Paris pales in comparison to the Vieux Carré as you walk down the Esplanade, an avenue lined with grand houses of rose-colored brick, all trimmed in wrought-iron grillwork with balconies overlooking the street. And behind the iron gates you would find the seclusion of a courtyard, much like the one we are sitting in now, where a fountain would flow with cool water. Mellow brick would pave the patio. The sweet scent of magnolia and gardenia, and the beauty of roses would beckon you to stay for a few moments of solitude."

"But you left, m'sieu?" Mara questioned curiously.

"Yes, I left New Orleans, Miss Vaughan," Nicholas answered shortly. "Do you wish to know why?"

Mara shook her head, not caring for his tone of voice. "Please, it really is none of my business."

"You think not? I wonder," Nicholas said obliquely. "However, I should like you to know, Miss Vaughan. I want you to realize what kind of man you are associating with, and to be aware of exactly what I am capable of doing," Nicholas explained in a hard voice. Leaning closer he continued softly, "I was accused of murder, mademoiselle."

At Mara's gasp Nicholas laughed harshly. "That frightens you? It should, mademoiselle, but you're probably wondering why I was not hanged? It was a duel, and although circum-stances alter cases, it is still a rather fine point of law whether or not dueling is a crime. When custom prevails, as in Creole society, where honor is everything and must be defended at all costs, then dueling becomes acceptable. In my case, however, the rules did not apply and I was ostracized by my family and friends," Nicholas said. Then he smiled and added, "Except for one very large, pig-headed Swede."

"I don't think I understand. Why were you different?"

Nicholas shrugged. "It is no longer important. It happened a long time ago."

"In England, duelists used to meet at dawn under the oaks to settle their differences. It sounds a very civilized way of settling an argument."

"There is nothing civilized in killing a man, but you are correct about the dueling. In New Orleans the place is called the Dueling Oaks. Usually, the morning following an argument, when the contestants were sober, they would meet beneath the oaks to fight with either pistol or sword. However, if it was a matter of urgency and the morrow was not soon enough, we could always fight in Père Antoine's garden in the Church of St. Louis. The disagreement was usually over some imagined slight or slur cast upon a name, or most likely over a quadroon one had danced with at the Orleans Ballroom, which was just a few steps from the church. Most convenient, wouldn't you say?" Nicholas asked. "I wonder if you can possibly imagine how many epitaphs in the cemeteries read, '*Pour garder intact le nom de la famille*' or '*Victime de son honneur.*' I think it would surprise you, mademoiselle.'

"What is a quadroon?" Mara asked.

"Usually the child of a white father and a mulatto mother."

"And you fought in many of these duels over a woman?" Mara wanted to know, intrigued despite herself.

"I was a very hot-blooded young man, no different from other callow youths who imagine themselves in love with every alluring woman they see. I made many foolish mistakes, with many tragic consequences," he added softly. "But you wished to hear of New Orleans, Miss Vaughan, not of my past indiscretions.

"Do you not think we Creoles are to be congratulated for creating such a beautiful city as New Orleans from the swamps? New Orleans is in the delta country, a place of flat marshlands where the tall grasses and clouds are blown by the gentle Gulf breezes. Where bayous, the sleeping water, we call them, with their sluggish currents, are full of lotus blooms floating on foot-wide pads, and cypresses with gray moss trailing into the dark water seem to slip deeper into the clinging mud of the swamps. There is a certain serenity, a peace in the delta that can be very misleading. You can be lulled into carelessness as you listen to the shrill cries of the cicadas or the cooing of doves, or pause to watch a raccoon fishing in a stream. With the scent of honeysuckle and verbena filling your senses, you might wander beyond the willows and sweet gum and the safety of a stream bank covered in wild azalea and dandelions. There are many dangers for the unwary in the bayous, for swimming beneath that murky surface might be any number of evils. Should you step into the water, a cottonmouth—a most disagreeable and poisonous snake of the swamplands—might swim past your bare ankle. Or if you were lucky, you might be warned away by the roar of a bull alligator.

"Yes, I do think we should be congratulated on overcoming such an inhospitable land and making New Orleans one of the most important seaports on the Gulf coast. And one of the most interesting, mademoiselle, for we are a blend of many cultures. And, of course, we are slave territory as well. But my heritage goes back to the time of the revolution in France when New Orleans was looked upon favorably by those who would rather become exiles from the court of Louis XVI than lose their heads. Those French aristocrats brought with them a certain standard of living, a way of life they had enjoyed in Paris and Versailles and were unwilling to give up in the new land. With the grandeur and extravagances of our European ancestors we also inherited an exotic flavor from the French who fled the slave uprisings in Santo Domingo. Unfortunately they brought along with their servants their beliefs in voodoo, an insidious sickness which has gained control over many of the slaves, as well as many superstitious Creoles," Nicholas said with a contemptuous laugh.

Mara shivered as a cool breeze touched her shoulders. "And you do not believe?"

"The mind is a very strange thing, Miss Vaughan, suscep-
tible to suggestions, should you let it be. I prefer to think I
am strong-willed enough to resist such temptations. I do not
like to think of another person controlling my life, manipu-
lating my emotions. I think you would not like that either,"
Nicholas guessed.

"You are right, Mr. Chantale, for I am always in control of
my own destiny," Mara told him with assured arrogance. "But
tell me, what did you do for entertainment in New Orleans?"

"Do not sound so doubtful, for we are as cosmopolitan
a city as London or Paris with our theaters and opera, our
nightly *bals de societé*, select soirees, and leisurely afternoons
spent sipping coffee or wine at Vincent's or some other cafe
or coffeehouse along the avenues around the Place d'Armes.
And of course the cuisine of New Orleans is unparalleled. At
large private parties, when all the cousins and distant relatives
would come to visit, we would dine on turkey, soft-shell
crab and oysters, green trout from the bayou, red snapper
from the Gulf, ham cooked in champagne, fresh vegetables
from the stalls of the French market, and Parisian gateaux,
Lafayette cakes, sherbet, and mince pies. All was accompanied
by Madeira, claret, or champagne.

"When the social season was over, we would leave the
city and drive to our plantations in the country, riding along
the Old River Road beneath the oaks draped in Cherokee
roses and gray moss. On one side of the road would be the
low, green banks of the Mississippi, while on the other side
would be the stately, gracefully columned homes and beautiful
gardens of the planters. Odd how one does not appreciate
such things until one can no longer gaze upon them,"
Nicholas spoke more to himself than to her.

"You miss it." Mara was strangely touched by his reminiscences.

"Miss it?" Nicholas asked sharply, and Mara could almost
see him shrug nonchalantly in the dark. "Perhaps, but to
feel nostalgic does not necessarily mean one wishes to return
to that time or place. New Orleans has its ugly side too,
mademoiselle. Just as people do," he said coldly, brushing
aside any compassion she might have offered him.

"Forgive me for thinking anything so naive of you, m'sieu, for you are obviously a very disciplined man and have no place for emotion in your ordered life," Mara told him, stung.

"Oh, but I do have feelings, mademoiselle," Nicholas reassured her. "I have tried to harden my heart against many of them, but I do not go completely unscathed. I was but a boy when I saw my mother die of the yellow fever when the plague took New Orleans. Whole families perished overnight. The streets were littered with the bodies of the dying or dead, many of the corpses half-devoured by packs of dogs, now starving without their masters. I can remember very vividly the roar of the cannons throughout the night and the stench of the tar and pitch fires burning on the street corners to fumigate the disease. Wagons and wheelbarrows full of corpses were rolled down the deserted streets of New Orleans.

"Of course, some people would disagree and say that the real plague was the invasion by the Americans with the signing of the Purchase, which sold the Louisiana Territory to the United States. I wonder what inroads the Americans have made into the Vieux Carré since I have been gone," Nicholas speculated. "We did not associate with them socially. They were considered uncouth and barbarous—the type who would go into the street coatless. Besides," Nicholas said with a laugh trembling in his voice, "they were in trade. They worked for a living, mademoiselle, something much frowned upon by Creoles."

"But you work, don't you?" Mara interrupted. "Aren't you one of the many hoping to strike it rich in the gold mines?"

"If my Creole friends could see me bare-chested, my hands calloused and dirty, standing waist-high in icy water as I panned a stream for gold…well, they would not believe such a thing of the elegant Nicholas de Montaigne-Chantale," Nicholas laughed in genuine amusement, "and would probably call me out for insulting Creole honor."

"So you are no longer a fine Creole gentleman?" Mara asked.

"I thought I had already proven that to you, mademoiselle, but apparently you do not learn quickly," Nicholas reminded her. "I lost the refinement of polished manners and genteel speech as I worked on a flatboat up the Mississippi, learning that it would be muscle and sweat, not my gentlemanly breeding nor drawing-room decorum, which would help me survive. I Americanized not only my name but my thinking as well. In New Orleans today I would probably fit in better with the Americans living uptown along the Faubourg Sainte Marie above Canal Street, or possibly," Nicholas added casually, the darkness effectively hiding his expression but not the contemptuous tone of voice he now intentionally adopted, "in a place called the Irish Channel where all the Irish lived. The men were fit only for working on the docks and their women for burying the dead. They brawled so much there was always a wake being celebrated for some recently bereaved widow. A most quarrelsome race of people, wouldn't you agree, Miss Vaughan?"

Mara remained silent, not trusting her Irish tongue to remain discrete as she smoldered with rage. She'd love to demonstrate to this Creole just how good the Irish really were at brawling.

"Oh—but do forgive me. Your cousin, Mr. O'Sullivan, is part Irish, is he not? I hope I've not offended you," he apologized. Once again Mara caught that faintly mocking quality in his voice.

"Not at all, and I'm sure Brendan would forgive you your lapse of good manners and not challenge you to a duel. Good night, Mr. Chantale," Mara said softly as she stood up, intending to leave with the last word. Before she could step away, Nicholas's hand shot out and found her wrist.

"Since I've no further reputation to lose in your eyes, mademoiselle," Nicholas said silkily, as he pulled Mara closer to him, "I'll not disappoint you. I'll make the most of having a beautiful woman in my arms."

In the darkness Mara couldn't see his face or read his expression, but his arms were warm as they encircled her waist and shoulders, and as she was pressed against his muscular chest, she felt a deliciously languid feeling overwhelm her. His parted lips caressed her mouth and his warm breath mingled with hers. The pressure intensified and he began to kiss her deeply. His mouth moved against hers roughly until she allowed her lips to part invitingly and felt the searching of his tongue in her mouth.

Mara's slim, bare arms curved around his shoulders and she ran her fingers through the thick black hair curling against his shirt collar as she kissed him back, imitating him as she remembered his derisive comment about her kisses earlier that day. She must have succeeded, Mara thought triumphantly as his arms tightened almost painfully around her as he strained her slender body against him before he lifted his searing mouth from hers and buried his face against her throat, breathing deeply of her fragrance before he whispered in her ear, "I was wrong; you do learn quickly, mademoiselle."

In the darkness, Mara's lips curved in a half-smile. She withdrew her arms from around his neck and lightly pressed her fingertips against his chest as he would have sought her lips once again. As he lifted his head, Mara struck quickly, the sound of her hand hitting his cheek echoing loudly across the silent courtyard. "A fairly painless lesson, Mr. Chantale, in remembering not to underestimate the enemy," Mara told him, a nervous quiver in her voice.

"I wasn't aware that we were enemies," Nicholas said coldly as he rubbed his cheek, "but thanks for the warning."

"Let's just say that more time is needed before we become better acquainted," Mara replied lightly. She stepped away, out of reach of his arms.

"I'll remember that and try to oblige you in future. But don't wait too long, mademoiselle, for my time is limited and I might have to look elsewhere for diversion," Nicholas told her in a bored voice. Turning, he walked away, leaving Mara standing alone in the darkness of the courtyard, feeling as though she'd been slapped.

All that we see or seem
Is but a dream within a dream.

—Edgar Allan Poe

Chapter 5

THE STRAINS OF GUITAR AND VIOLIN FILLED THE COURTYARD.
Torches threw flickering shadows across the gathering assembled in small groups around the patio and beneath the shelter of the long gallery. Laughter and voices wafted across the open courtyard and drifted into the cool night air along with the heavy scent from the flower beds.

Don Luís's black eyes were burning with the reflection of the fiery torches, and with covetous yearning for the jeweled cross that now hung, suspended from a gold-linked chain, between Mara's breasts. The tight-fitting bodice of her emerald green gown drew the eye to the cross as well as to the softly rounded curves molded in silk.

It had been Brendan's idea to surprise Don Luís at the party with Mara's sudden wearing of the cross. Don Luís would only be able to gaze longingly at it, unable to get his hands upon something he'd waited a long time to acquire. A cruel smile had curved Brendan's mouth at the thought of Don Luís's prolonged anguish as he would have to sit through the long evening hours making inane conversation with the cross just out of reach. He would know a despair much like that which Brendan had experienced as he found himself confined to the rancho, his eyes straining to the distant mountains of the Sierra Nevada. It had been a diabolical revenge for Brendan.

"I am very pleased to see you wearing the cross, Amaya," Don Andres whispered in Mara's ear. "You bring it to life," he added softly, his eyes lingering on the rounded smoothness of her breasts.

Mara returned his look, staring deeply into his eyes, allowing a flicker of warmth to lighten hers with a golden glow. "Gracias, Andres," she murmured. Then, as she looked beyond him, the gold deepened and her smile became seductive as she stared into the green eyes of Nicholas Chantale. Don Andres drew in his breath at the tantalizing beauty of her face. Even Mara was not aware of the languid look of sensual desire that entered her eyes, curving her lips invitingly, as her gaze dwelled thoughtfully on the Creole.

Andres impatiently drew her attention back to himself as he whispered something in her ear, causing Mara to laugh. The sound drew an amused glance from Doña Ysidora who was sitting nearby, her dark head covered by a lace mantilla draped over her left shoulder. A Chinese shawl, richly embroidered in colorful silks and edged with a deep, knotted fringe, protected her bare arms from the cool breeze. She had shed her figure-shrouding black dress and replaced it with a delicate, yellow silk gown trimmed with lace.

The period of mourning for Doña Feliciana's father must have come to an end, for she, as well, had donned her most colorful dress. Her bare shoulders were revealed above the rounded neck of the close-fitting, pale blue bodice of her blouse. Around her waist was a sash of purple satin, tied on the side. The fringed ends hung to the bottom of her white muslin skirt, which was flounced and decorated with brightly colored ribbons and gold spangles.

Feliciana was not amused as she stared jealously at Mara and Andres. Feliciana's fan snapped shut as she watched Mara place a hand lightly against Andres's sleeve, their heads inclined intimately to catch each other's words.

Suddenly the musicians began to play a livelier tune and Mara and Andres looked up, Andres's mouth opening in surprised disbelief as he saw the scarlet, silk-covered ankles of Feliciana as she lifted the hem of her skirts enticingly and stepped lightly around the patio, her blue satin shoes tapping the tiles in time to the fandango melody.

She danced across the patio, her bare arms raised above her head, tightening the thin lawn material of her blouse across her small, rounded breasts. The ends of her sash swung out in an arc as she twirled around, her skirt billowing around her silken legs. She shook a tambourine, its jingling beat bringing an exotic flavor to the dance.

Feliciana's audience was silent as they watched her dance. Stunned would have been an accurate description, Mara thought in amusement at the disconcerted look on Andres's face and the haughty dismay on Doña Ysidora's proud features. Brendan, on the other hand, was thoroughly enjoying himself, especially as Feliciana seemed to be dancing exclusively for him. She lowered a soft shoulder in his direction and glanced teasingly at him as she whirled. The Creole didn't seem disturbed by Feliciana's impromptu exhibition either, Mara thought as she watched him leaning against a rough-hewn post, his green eyes narrowed in speculation as he watched Feliciana's hips sway.

Feliciana turned a laughing, rebellious face to Don Andres, her steps momentarily faltering as she saw the contemptuous anger in his eyes. She quickly renewed her efforts, increased her tempo, and swirled around faster, her head and shoulders thrown back and her long braids encircling her like twisting black snakes. She was like a small whirlwind as she danced around the courtyard, coming to an abrupt halt near the edge of the patio. Her eyes stared defiantly into Don Andres's, her breasts moving rapidly beneath their light covering. For the first time, the passionate nature of the woman she was flared in her dark eyes.

It was a stunning discovery for Don Andres to see the woman revealed in the young girl he thought she was. Their exchanged looks of wonder were lost in the outburst of applause. Despite the impropriety of such a dance, Feliciana had performed it well and had given the Californians pleasure. Mara was sitting closest to Feliciana, who had sauntered over to the edge of the group to take her bows and was now staring at Mara with a disdainfully superior look. She took a step backward and curtsied deeply.

Mara was the first to see the flames from a torch carelessly laid down lick into the froth of lace at the hem of Feliciana's skirts. The light material was quickly caught in a blaze of shooting flames.

Feliciana's scream of terror paralyzed the startled Californians into immobility for a second, just long enough for the panicked Feliciana to begin to run from the group. She sought to escape the hot flames that were eating away the flammable skirts wrapped around her.

Hardly aware of her actions, Mara left her seat and ran after Feliciana as she tried to stop her from fanning the flames out of control, but Feliciana was beyond hearing. Mara stuck out her leg and tripped the girl, causing her to fall flat against the tiles of the patio. Mara began frantically beating out the flames, rolling the screaming Feliciana over and over, her own hands beginning to feel the heat and pain of the fire. Suddenly water was flung over both of them, the water dousing the fire into a harmlessly smoldering tangle of wet material. Mara glanced up thankfully into the hard green eyes of Nicholas Chantale as he bent over her and helped her to her feet, then shook out what remained of Feliciana's skirts to make sure there were no burning embers.

As Feliciana moaned in shock, the Californians gathered close, all talking in hushed whispers. Andres pushed his way through the crowd and picked up the prostrate form of his ward. Doña Ysidora was issuing orders like a drill sergeant as she sent servants bustling through the hacienda.

Don Andres turned with Feliciana in his arms, his eyes meeting Mara's. He paused for an instant, then said, "We owe you a debt which can never be fully repaid, Amaya. You have saved Feliciana's life. She would have run from the courtyard in her panic if you had not stopped her and then—" he broke off abruptly at the vision of Feliciana engulfed in flames. Gratitude still on his face, he made his way through the gathering with the unconscious Feliciana held closely in his arms.

Mara sagged against the arm she felt slide around her waist, supporting her. She leaned her head against the comforting shoulder, then glanced up into Nicholas's eyes.

"That was a very brave thing you did," he said quietly. For once there was no sarcasm in his voice. "Most people wouldn't have thought so quickly. Don Andres was right, you saved that little fool's life."

Mara shrugged away his praise, feeling uncomfortable playing the heroine and being the recipient of looks of undying gratitude. The Californians thanked her tearfully.

"Are you all right?" Nicholas demanded as he turned her around in his arms and carefully examined her hands, his eyes intently exploring her face and shoulders for burns. She was smudged with smoke and a few stray strands of hair had been singed but there was no serious damage.

"My hands smart a little and my dress is ruined, but I'm all right," Mara said looking down at the stained silk of her gown, wrinkling her nose at the smoky stench.

Nicholas gently guided Mara away from the patio and was leading her across the courtyard when Brendan stepped in front of them.

"I'll take care of Amaya now, Chantale," Brendan said arrogantly as his fingers closed around Mara's upper arm. "Come along, dear. Jamie'll know how to attend to your needs."

Nicholas relinquished his hold on Mara and, with a mocking bow to Brendan, turned and disappeared into the shadows of the corridor.

"Did you have to be so rude, Brendan?" Mara asked sharply, feeling slightly let down that Nicholas had been so easily deterred by Brendan's cavalier manner.

"God, Mara, you could've been killed, or scarred for life," Brendan said roughly, ignoring her question as he wiped a hand across his sweaty brow. "I aged a lifetime when I saw you rush forward. I could scarcely believe me eyes. To be sure, I've sorely misjudged you, mavournin, for I'd no idea you went in for heroics. 'Twas a damned, fool trick," he muttered beneath his breath, unable to admit even to himself that he'd been scared to death when he'd seen Mara attacking those flames with her bare hands. For the first time he realized the depth of his feeling for her.

"And what was I supposed to do? Let Feliciana burn to

death before my very eyes?" Mara retorted, anger sparking her eyes.

"Well no, of course you couldn't," Brendan replied uncomfortably, having the grace to look ashamed, "but couldn't someone else have done it. The Frenchman, for instance? He seems to always be on the spot, taking control of matters like 'twas his right," Brendan complained as he led Mara to her room. "The divil take him anyway. Tried to talk to him about the gold country. Been up there, he has. D'ye know what he tells me?" Brendan demanded in an incredulous voice.

Mara glanced at him wearily. "No, what did Nicholas say?"

Brendan eyed her suspiciously. "Nicholas, is it now? Well, the Frenchman moves fast, indeed he does. But he'll not be getting anywhere with you, will he, mavournin? You're too smart to fall for his fancy talk, aren't you, love," Brendan warned. "So I needn't be worrying about that. But d'ye want to know what he says to me, Brendan O'Flynn, the nerve of the swine. I asked him what the mining camps were like, and how much gold he had found so far. I said once I got there I expected it'd be pretty easy to make me fortune. Well, he gives me that cold, green-eyed stare of his, his lips curled contemptuously—at *me*, mind ye—and says ever so arrogantly that there were hardships suffered by the miners that I couldn't even imagine in me wildest dreams. Spending the rainy season in the High Sierra, tramping through snow drifts, digging and scraping for gold like a pack of wild dogs, was the making or breaking of many a man," Brendan snorted, continuing almost without interruption as Jamie bustled in carrying a bowl of bandages and medicines.

"'It's hell, Mr. O'Sullivan, and very few strike it rich, and then they lose it soon enough over the gaming tables. Do you think you're cut out for it?' he asks me doubtfully, as if takin' me measure and findin' me comin' up short. Damn him to hell, who the divil does he think he is anyway?"

Mara sat slumped on the edge of a chair and stared tiredly into space as she half listened to Brendan's complaints. Jamie rubbed a soothing balm on the tender skin of her hands and wiped a cool cloth across Mara's smoke-smudged face.

"Ye best be gettin' undressed. Master Brendan, I'll be bringin' the curtain down right now on your recitation. Can't ye see that ye've lost your audience?" Jamie demanded as she placed the bowl of dirty water near the door.

Brendan sighed in offended exasperation and shot Jamie a scowling look. "I—" Brendan began, then broke off abruptly as he heard a step outside the door. "What the divil? Damned if I'll take any more interference from that Frenchie. I've had enough of his insolence," Brendan swore angrily as he quickly picked up the bowl Jamie had just set aside. Before either Jamie or Mara could make a move to stop him he had swung open the door and let fly the full contents of the bowl.

A muttered imprecation came from beyond the doorway, followed by a choked, "¡Madre de Dios!"

Mara smothered a hysterical laugh as Don Luís stepped into the light. His dark hair was plastered to his skull and water dripped from the tip of his high-bridged nose as he glared at the stunned occupants of the room.

Jamie's mouth gaped open in surprise as she took a hesitant step backward, then moved quickly around to the other side of the bed. Brendan stood his ground, the empty bowl still held in his hands, pronouncing him guilty as he faced the wet and angry don.

"Damned careless of me, Don Luís. Please accept my most profound apologies," he said with a devilish smile lurking in his eyes, not in the least bit sorry.

Mara bit her lip nervously, her laughter threatening to erupt as she watched a puddle of water form around Don Luís's well-shod feet.

"You will forgive me if I do not linger," Don Luís said frigidly, "but I merely came to claim that which is mine."

He walked over to stand in front of Mara, his shoes making a squelching sound as he moved. A look of distaste and discomfort crossed Don Luís's haughty features at the comical noise.

"The cross, if you please," he said curtly, holding out his hand, palm up, for the treasured heirloom.

"Certainly, Don Luís," Mara acquiesced with a slight smile as she lifted the heavy golden chain off her neck and over her head, then held it out to him.

Don Luís's shoulders sagged slightly as he held the cross grasped tightly in his hands. Drawing a deep sigh, he glanced between the faintly amused-looking O'Flynns. Once more in possession of himself, at least as far as his bedraggled appearance would allow, Don Luís spoke in a soft, menacing voice that very effectively got across his message and wiped the humor from the O'Flynns' eyes.

"You have your laugh, Señor O'Flynn, and play your little games, but remember," he cautioned, "that you have not been paid as yet, and that I am the one you must hold out your hand to."

"Now, now, Don Luís," Brendan protested. "We were just having a spot of fun, nothing more than that. You do have the cross you've been hankering after. What harm was done in givin' you a little surprise?"

"Sí, I have it now. But unfortunately," Don Luís added, looking disconcerted for a moment as he searched carefully for his next words, "I still do not have my land."

Brendan shrugged, his expression unconcerned. He said carelessly, "Well, I don't know exactly what this business deal of yours is about, but all we have to do is to get Mara to ask Don Andres to agree to it. He'll do anything for her, especially after tonight. So the way I see it, our business is concluded, Don Luís, and 'tis time to settle up," Brendan told him as he held out his palm, rubbing his fingertips together suggestively.

Silently Don Luís stared at Brendan, trying to gauge the Irishman's reaction to his next words. "I am afraid, Señor O'Flynn, that until I sell this cross, I am as destitute as you are. You English have a colorful phrase for it," he said with an unsuccessful attempt at an apologetic smile. "To be out at the elbows, sí?"

Brendan's smile faded, his lips tightening into a thin crack as his dark eyes stared in disbelieving anger at the Californian. "'Tis called being duped, gulled, and made an ass of. Damned if ye haven't done a fine job of making me look blunt witted," Brendan said in a tightly controlled voice, the knuckles of one hand showing white as he clenched it angrily.

Don Luís noticed his bunched fist and spread his own hands

out in a placating manner. "I trust that we need not have a display of brute force, Señor O'Flynn, for I am but an old man and your strength is far superior to mine. Nor would it do to alert the other members of the household to our differences. It is also quite unnecessary," he added quickly, lest the Irishman be beyond subtle reasoning, "for you shall be paid in full, this I promise you. You need only wait here until I return with the money, and then you will receive your payment and you may leave the rancho. It is that simple."

"Nothing is ever that simple, Don Luís," Mara said softly as she spoke for the first time. "And just how much longer a visit do you anticipate we will have?" Don Luís shrugged, but his smile came more easily as he turned his attention to the less-intimidating O'Flynn. "One never can be sure exactly, but within the week."

"The divil take ye," Brendan interrupted angrily, "if you think I'm going to sit around here any longer now that I've found out you've no—"

"And how much longer after that must we wait until you get your land?" Mara continued. "I gather that it all depends on Amaya wedding Andres? You needed me, posing as your niece, to get the cross. Now you can sell it to get the money to buy some land that Andres owns," Mara summed it up.

Don Luís's dark eyes shifted away from Mara's direct gaze, settling on a painted saint hanging on the wall. He reluctantly confessed the difficult circumstances he had found himself in.

"I was forced, against my better judgment, into deceiving you on this matter," he began hesitantly.

Brendan's flared eyebrows rose with incredulous disbelief. He snorted loudly, "To be sure, there's nothing new in that."

"I think, under the circumstances, Señor O'Flynn," he continued, "you would have agreed with me that the deception was necessary if I was to enlist your help. The truth of the matter is that I was tricked into gambling my land away on a foolish bet. Unfortunately, I lost," Don Luís told them stiffly. "You would not have been overly anxious to help me out of my difficulties when I had just won all your money, Señor O'Flynn. I could not let you know that I was without funds to pay you."

"Well, well," Brendan murmured sarcastically, "at least we're finally putting the saddle on the right horse. You're damned right I wouldn't have helped you. Can't you pay us with the money you won from me on the ship?" Brendan demanded, his chin thrust out aggressively. "You had quite a pile there."

Don Luís shook his head sadly. "I am afraid that I gambled it away the other day when you and the others left for the merienda and I did not join you. I had gone over to see what I still consider to be my land, and...well, I met up with a few of my old vaqueros and we decided to play a few hands of monte. Some days one's luck is just not with him."

Brendan made a rude noise, his look close to murderous. "My luck sure as hell hasn't been the same since I met up with you."

"But my luck has changed, Señor O'Flynn, since I met you. It is true that I intend to buy back my land with the money from the cross, and that was my intention when I went to England with the hopes of bringing back my niece. I thought I would be able to recover everything. Then, when she would not even consider returning, well, I thought I had lost it all—my land, the cross, everything was gone. Out of my reach."

He glanced between the O'Flynns. "When I first met you on board ship, it had never occurred to me to try and fool the Villareales with an impostor. At least," he said with a slight smile curving his thin lips, "until I won all your money, Señor O'Flynn, and saw your beautiful companion. Then the plan struck me," he laughed softly. "What else could I do but make use of such a providential opportunity?"

"And what happens after you buy back your land?" Mara demanded practically. "How do Brendan and I get out of here?"

"You shall reject Don Andres when he asks for your hand, and say you wish to return to England. The Villareales will never know that a deception has been played on them."

"Well, I don't like it," Brendan grumbled. "There's too many lies and deceptions going on around here to suit me.

Someone's going to get his lines mixed up and then there'll be the divil to pay. I've never been one to overstay my welcome, and I've always preferred walking out on me own two feet rather than bein' thrown out. At least we haven't had any trouble with people being suspicious of us. It's been the easiest role I've ever played."

"You need have no fears of discovery," Don Luís reassured him, even as he remembered the conversation with the Frenchman. After all, the man had only suspicions. What could he do? "Nothing must happen to make Don Andres suspect you. He will readily sell the land to me if he thinks I will soon become a member of the family by marriage."

"To be sure, *we're* not likely to be telling him we're impostors," Brendan said bitterly as he smiled mockingly at Don Luís.

"Good. Just remember that if all goes well, you will receive a large sum of money and be able to leave the rancho by this time a week from now," Don Luís reminded them. "I shall leave in the morning."

With a slight nod he turned to leave the room, the cross tucked in concealment beneath his damp coat. He walked swiftly along the corridor.

"Damn!" Brendan spat as soon as the door closed behind the Californian. "Who would've thought that old slyboots could've taken us in? Have I straw in me hair that he took me for such a yokel?" Brendan demanded half in anger, half in embarrassment at being outmaneuvered by one he thought no match for his own chicanery.

"There's nothing we can be doing about it, Brendan, so you'd better just accept it and enjoy your next week of leisure," Mara advised him.

"Accept it, now? We oughta just pack up and leave. But first, we drop a friendly word of warning in Don Andres's ear. I'd love to see Don Luís's face when he returned to find us gone, a hostile Don Andres unwilling to sell his land, and Raoul behind bars for stealing."

"You know we can't. We still have no money, or have you forgotten that? Besides, I don't want to travel with Paddy until he's over his illness," Mara told him, unwilling to be caught up in yet another of Brendan's schemes.

"Well, if anyone was askin' me, I could've told ye 'twas a mistake to leave Dublin in the first place," Jamie said, having been a silently suffering witness to the scene. "Damned fool idea comin' to this heathen land. Nothin' but trouble is all we'll be findin'," she predicted with an ominous look at the O'Flynns. "I'm gettin' too old for all of these shenanigans of yours. Now get yourself out of here, Master Brendan," she ordered.

Brendan cast a helpless look over his shoulder at Mara as he allowed himself to be dismissed by the diminutive Irishwoman. "Oh, well, what's another week or so going to mean in our lives, mavournin? After waiting this long, I suppose it can't be hurting us to wait a bit longer, now can it?" he sighed.

❦

The next few days seemed to pass in a blaze of heat that beat down unrelentingly on the thick-tiled roof of the hacienda. At night there was some relief as the temperature dropped and a cooling breeze swept through the valley, but Mara felt the week would go on forever. She suffered through Brendan's impatient waiting and her headaches, which seemed to plague both her sleeping and waking hours.

Don Luís had left the rancho the following morning as he had said, and gone as well was the American, Jeremiah Davies. The Creole remained, however, and Mara was receiving her fair share of attention from him; in fact, she felt as if he were courting her, for he seldom left her side, despite the hostility he received from Don Andres, who was still under Mara's spell of enchantment.

As Mara sat within the cool interior of the eaves, she speculated on this change of tactics. She even had to admit that she found it rather enjoyable because for once she was being treated with respect by some man who found her attractive. As Mara O'Flynn, the actress, she had always been prejudged, expected to accept her admirers' attentions without question or protestation, and ultimately to become their mistresses, receiving the lucrative benefits of such a position for the period of time she might be desired by her rich lover. She had been cast in a role that had been predetermined before she'd even been born. There were only two kinds of women in the world: good and bad. And there was no crossing over the rigid lines drawn by this narrow-minded society. Of course, it was easy enough to lose your reputation, but next to impossible ever to retrieve it or create a new one. Anyone who met Mara O'Flynn for the first time, she thought bitterly, would meet her with preconceived ideas of what an actress should be like, and she was never given the opportunity to prove that she might, in fact, be very different. It wasn't her fault that she had to work for a living, that the misfortune of her birth and the selection of a profession had unfairly decided her fate. But they were all wrong, Mara thought defiantly, for despite the fact that she walked the boards of a stage, wore paint, and was considered fair game for any sporting blood of London who wanted a beautiful woman to grace his bed and participate in a discreet liaison, she had never had a lover, but then no one would ever believe that.

Mara smiled softly. For the first time in her life as a woman, a man was looking upon her as something special, not as an object for sale but as someone with feelings and a right to receive consideration. Mara's smile drooped disconsolately as she remembered that after this week she would no longer be Amaya Vaughan, but Mara O'Flynn once again, and that would be the end of respectability. What would the Creole think if he knew who she really was? Could he accept her without doubting her? Or would he assume the worst? Mara wondered curiously. Would the softness she had seen in his eyes, replacing the hardness, change to contempt or, worse, to lustful desire without thought of love? He might still want her, but any thought of marriage would be out of the question, for hadn't he come from an aristocratic French family in New Orleans? When he married, if he ever did, it would be to someone suitable, someone without a tarnished and questionable past.

Mara rubbed her forehead tiredly, a disgusted look curving

her lips in distaste at her self-pitying thoughts. What a fool she was even to be contemplating marriage, especially to one such as he. What had happened to all of her fine ideals, her vows of seeking vengeance and keeping her heart her own? A few weeks of respectability had certainly gone to her head with some high-flown ideas.

Oh, the devil take it and everyone, Mara lashed out in silent defiance. If Brendan struck it rich, then they could do anything they wanted and not have to depend upon someone else ever again.

"Mara! Mara!"

Mara glanced up in alarm when she heard the childish voice and saw Paddy running across the courtyard to where she was sitting.

"What are you doing out of bed, Paddy?" she demanded as he jumped up on the bench beside her, a thick hunk of freshly baked bread spread with jam held in one hand. The jam began to drip over the edge where his small teeth had made inroads into the lightly browned crust. Around his mouth was a dark purple stain.

"Where did you get that?" Mara asked enviously, thinking of the dull tortillas she'd eaten at breakfast.

"Jamie made it for me special, 'cause I've been sick," Paddy informed her importantly, a slight croak still evident in his voice.

"And aren't you supposed to be staying in your room? I don't want you getting sick again," Mara fretted, feeling the heat even in the cool shadows of the corridor.

"I'm tired of staying in my room. Jamie's so cross, and Papa keeps snapping my head off if I even say anything, and you haven't been in to see me either. You're always with *him*," Paddy complained sulkily as he watched the approach of Nicholas Chantale, his large brown eyes reproachful.

Mara followed his glance, her pulse quickening slightly as she met Nicholas's green eyes. "Paddy," she whispered quickly, "remember to call me Amaya."

Paddy smiled, causing Mara to frown, for it was an exact imitation of one of Brendan's devilish grins.

"Maybe I will, and maybe I won't," he said before taking a big bite out of the bread.

Mara glared down at his bent head, itching to give one of his dark curls a yank, her look promising retribution if he misbehaved. As Nicholas paused before them, Mara looked up, her face wiped clear of anger. She smiled. He'd been out riding, and the scent of horses and leather mingled with the sweat trickling down his chest, where a triangle of skin and dark hair was revealed by his opened shirt.

Nicholas stared down at Mara, his mouth curving slightly at the image of cool perfection she created in her pale green gown of shot silk, the softly luminous color reflected in the soft pinks of a single rose pattern running across the material. Nicholas glanced around and, walking over to a rose bush, plucked a single bud from one of its thorny branches. There was a gleam of anticipation in his eyes as he bent over Mara, one booted leg planted beside her on the bench. He leaned behind her and, with gentle fingers, tucked the blossom into the thick coil of hair against her nape.

Nicholas transferred his gaze from the pink bud to Mara's mouth, and said softly, "A Castilian rose whose beauty has been surpassed only by your loveliness."

Mara stared up into the deep green eyes, every nerve in her body conscious of the muscular thigh clad in buckskin that nearly touched her shoulder. Had she dared, she could have reached out and caressed it. Mara touched the rose instead, but something of her thoughts must have shown in her eyes because his hard fingers reached out suddenly, closing over hers. He held her hand softly against his lips. Then, with a provocative look, he pressed her palm to his hard cheek. "I prefer it against my cheek in this manner."

"You're very gallant this morning," Mara remarked when he'd released her hand. It tingled more from the touch of his lips than it had when she'd slapped him.

"If you allowed yourself to know me better," Nicholas responded lazily, his green eyes looking into Mara's warmly, "then you'd discover that I can be, under the right circumstances, very kind and loving."

Before Mara could think of a proper response, Nicholas became aware of Paddy sitting silently beside her. "I don't believe I've met this young man, although he looks familiar." He stared down at Paddy who squirmed under the tall man's penetrating eyes.

"This is my cousin Brendan's son, Padraic. Say hello to Mr. Chantale, Paddy," Mara instructed, but was totally unprepared for his startling response.

"I don't like you," Paddy said in a childishly small voice, his small jaw stuck out pugnaciously.

Nicholas was just as surprised by the unprovoked attack, but after a second's silence he started to laugh, the deep, rich sound filling the courtyard. "I wonder how many people would have given their fortunes to say that to my face as easily as this little fellow did?"

Paddy glanced in worried suspicion between Mara and this threatening stranger who seemed to be able to please her and had even kissed her. In childish fury he threw what was left of his bread and jam against Nicholas's chest, the sticky confection leaving a bluish purple stain against the fine lawn shirt.

"Paddy!" Mara gasped.

But Paddy had sized up his man as well as his target, and without hesitation jumped from the bench and fled across the courtyard as fast as his short legs could carry him.

Nicholas's face was grim, his mouth hardening into a thin line. He looked up from the stain. "I suppose you had nothing to do with this little act of maliciousness?" he asked softly, a humorless smile twisting his lips.

Mara slowly got to her feet. She searched frantically for something to say. But an imp of mischief threatened her composure when she glanced at the widening purple stain. She made the mistake of looking directly into his green eyes, the twinkle of amusement still bright in hers. As Nicholas saw her expression, his hand reached out and curled around her upper arm restrainingly. He effectively blocked her way.

"You find this funny?" he demanded, yet Mara thought she caught a suspicion of a smile around the corners of his mouth.

"Maybe you wouldn't find it quite so amusing if I made you wash the shirt clean for me?"

Mara smiled openly at the thought of her washing his shirts. "Your shirt would be a total loss then. But I'll have my maid do it for you if you wish." Mara shook her head in disgust as she gazed in fascination at the stain. A drop of jam had splattered across the edge of his shirt and landed in the middle of the triangle of bare flesh and tangle of hair. Before she stopped to realize the implications of what she was doing, Mara reached up and scooped the dab of jam from his chest. She licked some of it from the tip of her index finger.

"Not bad. A little salty, perhaps, but not bad," Mara said softly as she looked up at him. Nicholas's eyes glinted down at her. He grasped her hand and very slowly and sensuously licked the rest of the jam from her finger. Mara felt herself leaning closer as her eyes remained locked with his, but she jerked away when she heard the sound of footsteps crossing the patio.

Don Andres stared coldly at Nicholas as he approached them, noticing their closeness. "Is there something amiss?" he asked politely, barely hiding his anger.

"Nothing that can't be washed clean, Don Andres," Nicholas replied evenly.

"I'm afraid Mr. Chantale spilled some jam on his shirt," Mara explained lamely as she tried to regain her composure. The fact that she had lost it in the first place was causing her the most discomfiture.

"I will have my servants clean it, Mr. Chantale," Don Andres offered. "I shouldn't like you to leave here without all your possessions."

Nicholas smiled back at him, his narrowed gaze acknowledging the subtle hint.

"Then you will have it returned to me by the end of the week, when I was planning to leave. Unless of course," Nicholas continued thoughtfully, "there is some hurry and you wish my room sooner than that?"

Don Andres sighed as he admitted defeat. Put so bluntly, he could not in all good manners eject this guest. The Frenchman had very neatly turned the tables on him. With a slight frown, he denied his wishes.

"You are, of course, welcome to stay for as long as you wish, Mr. Chantale," Don Andres said cordially.

"Thank you," Nicholas replied softly, "and you needn't worry. I shall not overstay my welcome. Now…if you'll excuse me?"

Mara watched Nicholas saunter off toward his room. In his tall boots and full-sleeved shirt he reminded her of a swash-buckling pirate. There was something proudly arrogant in the slight swagger of his lean hips, the indolent grace of his stride. Mara could just as easily imagine him striding across the bridge of a privateer on the high seas.

"The Frenchman was not annoying you, Amaya?" Don Andres asked as he noticed the uncertain expression on Mara's face.

"No, not really." Mara paused, then added wryly, "At least, no more than usual."

"I could ask him to leave," Don Andres offered.

"No!" Mara spoke quickly without thinking. "I mean, it really is not necessary, Andres. Please don't," Mara requested, surprised to hear an almost pleading note in her voice.

"As you wish, Amaya. But if he continues to disturb you, I shall not hesitate in seeking his departure," Don Andres said sternly, his dark eyes glowing in anticipation of such an event.

"How is Feliciana?" Mara asked, hoping to change the conversation.

"She is still quite shaken from the incident," Don Andres replied, his voice a blend of anger and softness as he spoke of his young ward.

"You are very fond of her, Andres," Mara said, making it a statement rather than a question.

"Of course, she is one of the family," Don Andres answered. "Come, let us talk of other things. Here are our refreshments," he said as a servant came forward bearing a tray with an earthenware pitcher and glasses. "I thought you might enjoy something cool since you are unaccustomed to our heat."

Mara allowed him to change the subject this time and settled down to an uneventful afternoon although a disquieting one, for she had an uneasy feeling that events were winding down for the final denouement.

❧

Mara rolled over onto her stomach, burying her face in her pillow. It was hot and stuffy and her breathing felt restricted. With an irritable sigh she pulled her pillow from beneath her head and flipped it over onto the cool underside. But it gave her only a moment's relief, soon heating up beneath the warmth of her cheek.

It was no use trying to sleep. She sat up in bed and rubbed her fingertips against her throbbing temples.

Mara threw back the thin sheet that covered her and, dropping her feet to the floor, reached for her robe and wrapped it around her naked body. She padded across the floor on silent feet, fumbling along the top of a bureau for her watch.

Only two o'clock, it was hours yet until dawn. Mara picked up the pitcher of water to pour some into the matching basin beside it, but knew as she lifted it that it would be empty. She pushed back her tangled hair from her face, wishing she could bathe her flushed cheeks in something cool.

The hacienda was so quiet, Mara thought as she stood in the silence of her room, the only sound the faint bubbling of the fountain in the courtyard. A slight smile of satisfaction curved Mara's lips as she made her way from the room and out into the courtyard toward the fountain. The cool night air was as exhilarating as a good wine. Mara sat on the edge of the fountain and let her hand slip down deep into the cold dark water, scooping up a handful to splash against her face. She patted her face dry with a lacy handkerchief and, with a sigh of relief, filled her lungs with the soft, fragrant night air.

With a sigh of regret, Mara began to make her way back to her room, slipping silently through the darkness of the corridor. She yawned widely, her eyes closed shut for a second. She continued walking until she suddenly struck something hard and immovable and was knocked sideways.

"What the devil?"

Hard hands saved her from falling as they reached out and grabbed her. They brushed against the softness of her breast as they grasped her around the waist. "Are you all right?'

"I'm fine," Mara answered huskily, not needing to hear the voice or see the face to know that it was Nicholas. She had known instinctively.

Mara could see the dim outline of his face in the darkness of the passage and knew he was straining to see her face. "Amaya," he said softly, and Mara felt an instant's regret that she couldn't hear her own name on his lips.

"Are you certain I didn't hurt you?" Nicholas asked again. Mara would have sworn there was genuine concern in his voice. "I must have knocked the breath from you. I've never heard you quite so silent before. Come, let me get you something to drink. Why, your hands are like ice," he exclaimed as he guided her along the corridor, away from her room, to his door. "If you won't be offended by coming into my room, I do have some cognac. That should warm you up." His room was dark, and Mara stood silently by the door, refusing to give in to the nervousness she felt flicker along her spine. As Nicholas lit the candles, the room was thrown into a warm yellow glow that intensified the shadowy furnishings and corners of the room. Mara heard the rattle of glasses. A tumbler of golden liquid held in his hand, Nicholas turned and stood still, seeing her revealed for the first time. Almost leisurely, his green-eyed gaze roamed over her startling dishabille as Mara's jade robe shimmered in the flickering light, the rich silken fabric clinging to the softly rounded contours of her body.

Mara drew in her breath slightly as she watched his eyes slide down her shoulders to the opened lapels of her robe where the white curve of her breast was revealed. Burning with embarrassment, Mara pulled the gaping edges of her robe together and tied the sash tighter around her slim waist, nervously realizing he was very much aware that she was naked beneath the robe.

Nicholas moved slowly closer, stopping barely a foot in front of her as he held out the glass. Mara reached out and accepted it, feeling it might indeed calm her nerves. Mara glanced up into his face as she sipped the fiery brandy, her eyes locking with his. She looked away, swallowing the last of her brandy quickly. What was wrong with her? Hadn't she wanted him to look at her this way? Hadn't she flirted with him, led him on? She had never been emotionally affected in the past when men stared at her in this way. Now that she did have his full attention, she was afraid. He was different from the others, and she had to admit that she was different as well. He had managed to entice and excite her in the same way she had always bewitched men.

"Little did I imagine when I stepped outside for a brief moment to enjoy my cheroot, that I would find you wandering alone in the dark half-naked," Nicholas said softly, his eyes lingering on the unbound glory of her hair.

He reached out and took Mara's empty glass from her unresisting fingers and placed the two glasses side by side on the table. Mara glanced down at her bare feet, staring at her toes as if seeing them for the first time. She felt at a disadvantage with Nicholas. It was something she had never felt before. She was definitely out of her league with this man, and she had a feeling she should have heeded Brendan's warning.

"You puzzle me, Amaya," he spoke close to her ear, his breath warm against her cheek. "I would have expected a proper English miss to be securely wrapped in a high-necked nightdress, her chaste body enveloped in yards of fine linen." His hand moved up her arm inside the loose-fitting sleeve. "But here you are in a silk wrapper that displays your charms most tantalizingly."

"Have you ever been in a young Englishwoman's bedchamber when she was preparing for bed, m'sieu?" Mara managed to ask with a sardonic smile curving her lips. At his shake of his dark head Mara shrugged. "Then how do you know what a woman like me would wear to bed?"

"A woman like you?" he repeated, his eyes questioning her. "And what kind of woman are you? Or are you still just a little girl playing at being a woman?"

At his words Mara's cheeks flushed angrily. But before she

could give vent to a stinging retort, he continued unrelentingly. "Your heart is racing. With what? Excitement? Fear? Do I have the power to disturb you, my dear," he demanded as his hand moved from her arm to her shoulder. It slid beneath her robe, cupping her bare breast, his thumb rubbing against the soft nipple until it hardened under his probing. His other hand slipped down her slender back and along her spine until coming to rest on the curve of her buttocks.

Mara looked up into his narrowed gaze, her golden eyes widening in surprise as his hand pressed her hips against his muscular thighs, molding her pliant flesh against his hardness. Mara was breathing rapidly. She'd be damned if she'd show him how innocent she really was, how lacking in actual experience. She moved her arms slowly up to his shoulders and then around the strong column of his neck, her fingers locking together at the back of his head as she tilted her face upward. Her lips parted slightly as she steadily returned his gaze.

Nicholas allowed Mara to pull his head gently toward her upraised face until their lips touched, their breaths mingling. Mara felt Nicholas's tongue lick against her mouth, and she returned the caress, enjoying the sensation of its velvety softness touching hers. Under Nicholas's practiced hands Mara was experiencing waves of sensuous desire, spreading through her as he pressed and molded her against his hard body. His lips moved down her throat, leaving a trail of fire. His hard hands gently untied her sash and parted her robe without her being aware of it, revealing the beauty of her body to him.

Mara trembled slightly as she felt her robe pushed from her shoulders and dropped to the floor at her feet, the cool air of the night rushing over her bared flesh.

Nicholas breathed deeply of her scent, his face pressed against her breasts as his hands wandered persuasively around her small waist and across her taut stomach. His knee spread her thighs and he pressed himself intimately against her, making her aware of his rising passion and need.

Mara impatiently pulled his head back up to her mouth as she sought his lips, wanting to touch him and caress him as he was her. She rose on her toes, straining herself to him, rubbing her breasts against his chest.

"Despite my better judgment I've always thought you were an unbelievably beautiful woman," Nicholas whispered as he swung Mara up into his arms and carried her to the bed. He gently laid her down. Mara's dark mane of hair cascaded across her shoulders, shielding her breasts from his all-encompassing gaze. Drowsy with desire, Mara scarcely heard his words.

With casual ease he stripped naked before her widening eyes, standing boldly in front of her, unashamed of his nakedness. Her golden eyes roved in hypnotized fascination over him. They moved unchecked from the wide shoulders and chest that tapered down in a rippling of muscle and hair to lean hips and proud masculinity, then followed the long length of firmly muscled thigh to his feet planted slightly apart on the tiled floor.

Walking with the easy grace of a stalking cat, he came to the edge of the bed and stared down for countless seconds at Mara before the bed sagged beneath his weight. His hands lifted the heavy mass of luxuriant hair aside as he pressed his lips to the pink crest of her breast, now revealed to him. He slid against her on the bed, his hard body touching hers, pressing along the length of her as he rolled her beneath him. Mara stared up into his green eyes, staring deeply into their glowing depths as she felt a languorous feeling spreading through her, leaving her weak and pliable under the gentle pressure of his hands as they stroked her slender thighs, and he rubbed himself against her hips as she arched closer to him.

Mara sighed in satisfaction as his mouth closed over hers again, his kisses deepening with his growing passion. He was deliberate as he kissed and caressed her willing and ardent body. At last, smoothly, Mara parted her thighs and allowed him to become a part of her flesh. At Mara's sudden cry of pained surprise he stopped. He was about to withdraw from her, but Mara wrapped herself around him tighter, urging him to continue, until his steady rhythmic movements brought her to a startling climax that consumed her in a blaze so great that she thought she would faint. She cried out. She wasn't even aware

of his own release as she lost herself in lovemaking. Even after
he had parted from her, he continued to fondle her gently, his
fingers smoothing back the tangle of hair. He caressed her face
with light kisses, licking the salty tears from her flushed cheeks.

Mara returned his kisses passionately, her fingers trailing
through his thick, dark hair, her breasts pressed against
him. She buried her hot face against his neck. "I love you,
Nicholas," she whispered shyly, her tongue tickling his ear.

With a deep sigh Nicholas moved away from her, reaching
out for his cheroots on the table beside the bed. Lighting one,
he sat back against the headboard, pulling the pillows more
comfortably behind his shoulders. Mara looked up at him
curiously as he stared silently into the shadowy darkness of the
room. The flickering light from the candles danced across his
face, but rather than softening it, the candlelight threw into
prominence the high cheekbones and strong line of jaw. His
features suddenly looked cruel.

"Nicholas," Mara questioned softly as she ran her fingers
lightly along his rib cage and through the thick, wiry hair
covering his chest. Nicholas drew deeply on his cheroot.
Then, curving his arm around Mara, drew her up against the
pillows until her head rested on his chest just beneath his chin.
Mara relaxed against him, her thigh riding intimately across his
lap. She rubbed her cheek against his hard chest and heard the
slow beating of his heart beneath her ear.

"I think I said once before that you puzzled me, but now…
well…I must confess to having been completely fooled. I
think I owe you an apology," Nicholas finished abruptly.

Mara snuggled closer, her eyes still softly golden. "An
apology?" she asked lazily.

"Yes. I'm sorry about tonight."

Mara pushed herself away from him, her breasts just teasing
the surface of his chest as she brushed a long strand of hair
from her cheek. "You're sorry you made love to me?" she
asked in confusion, her lips looking softly vulnerable as she
nervously moistened them with her tongue.

Nicholas smiled down at her and, unable to resist the
temptation of her parted lips, lowered his mouth to hers,

kissing her deeply as he felt the fires of passion stirring again in his loins.

"No, I'm not sorry about making love to you. I enjoyed that very much," Nicholas told her as his fingers traced a delicate pattern along her inner thigh. "I'm just sorry that you were a virgin. Everything about you, from the arrogant angle of your head, to the way you move your hips, to that derisive half-smile, tantalizes a man until he either makes love to you or goes insane. You have very practiced ways. That led me to believe you were more experienced in the ways of love than you really were."

"I'm experienced now," Mara reminded him as she lay back against him, nibbling along his chest before biting his shoulder.

Nicholas stretched out his arm and stubbed out his cheroot. Then, turning back to Mara, he gathered her close against him. She could hear the soft rumble of laughter deep in his chest as he said, "You've only just learned the rudimentary techniques in pleasing a man, *ma petite*."

Mara stared deeply into his eyes, hers full of promised pleasure. "And will you teach me these ways, Nicholas?" she inquired huskily as she rubbed her lips against his throat.

Nicholas ran a hand through his hair, an expression of mock indecision on his handsome face. "I'm not sure if I'd be doing you a favor or not. Or indeed, if the man you'll eventually wed would appreciate my initiating you into the finer arts. You'd certainly be one hell of a wife. But unfortunately, not for me."

Mara bit her lip, feeling a sharp pain at his casual acceptance of her with another man. She caressed his powerful shoulders and with a soft smile curving her mouth moved so she lay on top of him, surprising him by the sudden boldness of her ploy. She languidly stretched out full length along the top of his body. She could feel the growing hardness of him under her thighs and, staring up into his green eyes with a quizzical look in hers, she whispered, "Are you sure you're not the right man for me?"

"If I were still the gentleman I'd been raised to be,"

Nicholas sighed, "then I would probably ask you to marry me, but I really am not the right man for you, ma petite. My way of life is no life for you. You'd be far happier here on the rancho with the good Andres. He'll give you the love you deserve. Your love, Amaya, will be returned in full by him. That is something I can't give you," Nicholas offered honestly.

Mara swallowed painfully. "You feel nothing for me?" she whispered huskily.

Nicholas lifted her down-bent head up to his face. "I'm attracted to you more than to any woman I've met in a long time, my dear. You're a beautiful woman, a damned bewitching one, and one I want to make love to," Nicholas told her, staring deeply into her wide, tawny eyes, "but I can promise you no more than that. Can you accept that?"

Mara bit her lip and nodded. "I won't demand any—"

Nicholas's mouth cut off the last of her words as he smothered her lips with his mouth, his tongue searching hers as he explored the softness of her mouth, his hands cupping her buttocks and pressing her to him as her awakening body responded in frank eagerness.

Mara pulled her mouth away from his lips and stared down at his hard face, his lips softened with lovemaking and curving in a slight smile of satisfaction as he lay beneath her curious gaze, his thick lashes masking his thoughts.

"What did you mean that I puzzled you?" Mara asked, suddenly remembering his earlier comment. "It seemed to me that even when you met me for the first time you were surprised. Perhaps you've dreamed of me all of your life," she said provocatively, "and were astounded to meet the woman of your dreams in the flesh."

Nicholas smiled as his hands lingered against her soft breast. Then, with a reluctant sigh, he slid from the bed and walked over to his vest, which had been thrown across a chair. Mara watched him in puzzlement as he drew something from one of the pockets. She allowed her gaze to roam freely over him in admiration as he came back to the bed.

"I don't know if I dreamed of you or not, although I wouldn't be surprised if that face hadn't haunted my dreams as well," he said oddly, "for it certainly has been in my thoughts. That face could be yours."

He held out the delicate gold locket, flicking it open as he placed it in Mara's palm. Mara stared down at her portrait. She could feel the muscles of her face tightening. Her own half-smile and golden eyes gazed enigmatically up at her, beside the blue eyes she remembered so vividly.

Nicholas stared at Mara intently, but detected no sign of emotion or discomfiture. "You can see why I seemed startled when I first saw you, for you could be her double."

"Who is she?" Mara managed to ask, her voice so low that Nicholas had to lean close to catch her words.

"No insult intended, my dear, but she's an actress, Mara O'Flynn," he answered shortly.

At the contemptuous note in his voice Mara glanced up, noting the cruel expression in the dark green eyes as he stared down at the picture in the locket.

"You hate her, don't you." It was a statement, not a question.

"I vowed I would find her one day and seek revenge for something she did," Nicholas explained as his eyes moved to the picture of Julian.

"Who is the boy?" Mara forced herself to seem calm.

"My nephew," Nicholas said abruptly as he took the locket from Mara's opened hand.

Mara stared down at her bare thighs as she knelt on the bed, her thick hair hiding her expression. "Why do you want to hurt her? What did she do to you?"

Nicholas was still staring down at the faces in the locket as he replied casually, "It doesn't matter. Since you are not Mara O'Flynn you have nothing to fear."

Mara felt her lips tremble as she fought to control the urge to run from his room. Dear God...if he ever found out who she really was? Mara risked a glance at him through a strand of hair and swallowed nervously at the intense look on his face. She clenched her fists beneath the covers as she realized the enormity of the situation she found herself in. She had fallen in love with that unfortunate boy's *uncle*. Julian. Yes, Julian.

She knew now she hadn't truly forgotten his name. She rubbed her aching temple, wondering what she was going to do. She knew she couldn't stay in his bed a moment longer and still keep up the charade.

Mara jumped in surprise when she felt Nicholas's arm slide around her, cupping her breasts as he nibbled along her shoulder and neck, his demanding lips impatiently pushing aside the heavy curtain of silken hair.

"Enough talk of the past," Nicholas breathed against her ear, nipping the soft lobe, "I'm more interested in you and me, not some other woman who has nothing to do with us."

Mara nearly choked at the casually dismissing words that made a fool out of him as he made love to that very woman right now. Mara shuddered as she thought of the black rage that would throw him into, and vowed that she would be miles away before anything could happen to enlighten him concerning her true identity.

She resisted as he pulled her back against his bare chest, his hands caressing the curve of her hip as he pressed his face into the mass of fragrant hair. "Please, Nicholas, don't," Mara objected as she tried to release herself.

At her words Nicholas lifted his warm mouth from her shoulder and turned her around in his arms, cradling her as she lay against his chest and he stared down into her pale face. Her golden eyes looked up at him luminously, and he could have sworn he saw a flicker of fear in them before she lowered her lashes.

"No?" he demanded softly as he lowered his mouth to her parted lips and kissed her deeply, savoring their soft sweetness as he rubbed his lips against hers. But Mara could stand no more and struggled to free her lips from his as his sensual mouth ravished hers, creating a tide of rising passion that she seemed to have little control over as she felt herself wanting to respond wantonly to him.

As she opened her eyes, she felt sanity begin to return to her as she saw a pale dawn beginning to break over the dark horizon, soon to glow goldenly through the bars of the window. Her mouth free at last as he lowered his head to nip softly with his teeth along the soft curve of her breasts, Mara said huskily, "It's dawn, Nicholas. I must go; please let me leave you now. I mustn't be seen leaving your room. Please, Nicholas," Mara repeated helplessly, gasping in surprise as he fondled her boldly and intimately, molding her against him to make her aware of his desire.

"And what if I say no?" he asked softly, hugging her naked body to him. "I think I'll keep you prisoner here in my room for the whole day, making love to you over and over again."

"You wouldn't embarrass me so, Nicholas." Mara could hear the desperation in her voice as her eyes locked with his.

Nicholas smiled regretfully. "No, I suppose I'm still that much of a gentleman." Nicholas sighed as he released Mara and lay back against the pillows, an amused expression softening his features as he watched her untangle herself from the bedclothes and struggle to her feet.

As Mara found her robe on the floor, she felt his green eyes burning into her slender back. As she turned, wrapping the robe around her naked body, she caught his gaze sliding over her, possessive pleasure in his eyes.

Mara hooked her thumbs into the silk sash tied securely around her narrow waist. She couldn't find anything to say as she stood unhappily tongue-tied before him. He lay stretched out on the bed, his feet casually crossed, his muscular arms folded behind his head as he silently watched her, noting her uncomfortably flushed face and nervous shifting from foot to foot.

She dragged her eyes away from the sardonic look on his handsome face. "I'm leaving."

But before she could reach the door, Nicholas had risen from the bed and caught her from behind. She could feel him against her through the fine silk of her robe. His arms slid around her waist, pulling her hard against his chest and thighs. He pressed soft kisses along her neck and jaw, his hands finding their way beneath the thin covering of silk. He caressed her tender breasts. With gentle determination Nicholas raised her chin, arching her throat against his shoulder as his lips closed over her mouth.

"Just to make sure you remember me, ma petite," he

whispered. Finally, he let her go, his hand lingering against her buttock as he opened the door for her, glancing out first to see that they were alone. Turning her into his arms, he kissed her with slow deliberation before letting her leave the room.

Mara stood for a moment in the gloomy darkness of the corridor, her lips still tingling with his kiss as the door closed softly behind her. Then she ran silently across the courtyard to her room as if the hounds of hell were on her heels.

She fell across her bed and buried her head in her arms. What cruel twist of fate had brought Nicholas Chantale into her life?

"Damn, damn, bloody damn," Mara swore beneath her breath as she tried to erase the night's events from her mind. But it was useless. The Creole was as much a part of her as she was of herself.

Mara's bitter laugh was muffled by the bedspread. She realized that Nicholas had had his revenge on her without even being aware of it. "And 'twas far crueler and more vindictive than you could ever have planned otherwise," Mara whispered, "for I've fallen in love with you, just as Julian did with me. And you wouldn't be any kinder to me than I was to him."

Mara closed her eyes, blocking out Nicholas's face, wishing it were just a dream she was waking up from but it wasn't, for her skin still tingled from the touch of his hands.

"Why is nothing ever as it seems?" Mara murmured into her pillow, her eyes finally closing in exhaustion as she dozed fitfully.

All farewells should be sudden.

—Byron

Chapter 6

MARA OPENED HER EYES TO THE SUN STREAMING BRIGHTLY through her window. She could hear the singing of birds. She rolled over, momentarily forgetting the previous evening until she felt the soreness of her breasts and noticed the faint bruises covering her body.

She was about to get to her feet when there was a knock on the door. She scrambled quickly beneath the covers, her shoulders disappearing behind the sheet. Mara expected to see one of the servants with her usual cup of morning chocolate. Feliciana entered instead.

Mara eyed her suspiciously as Feliciana awkwardly handed her the cup from her still-bandaged hands, her dark eyes avoiding Mara's unblinking stare. She stepped back from the bed. "This is unusual, isn't it?" Mara asked coldly, taking out her mood on the young Californian for whom she felt little affection anyway.

"I must tell you…confess…what I have done," Doña Feliciana said hesitantly, an embarrassed flush staining her cheeks.

"You've come to the wrong place for confession, haven't you? The church is next door," Mara reminded her unsympathetically. "Listen, thank you for the chocolate, but I've got a blinding headache and I'm just not up to any gossip. So if you don't mind?"

Feliciana clasped her hands together nervously, grimacing in pain as she forgot her burns. She was still undressed and wearing a robe over her long, white nightdress, her hair hanging loose about her shoulders. "It is my doing that you have suffered discomfort since coming to the rancho," she admitted, shame on her face as she looked quickly away from Mara's golden eyes, now narrowed in interest.

"What do you mean?" she asked quietly.

"You fall from your horse, sí? I loosen the strap. You never say, but I am the one who planted the scorpion in your boot." She paused diffidently, then asked, "You have suffered from the headache, sí? You have not slept well? It is because I placed the crushed laurel leaves beneath your pillow and rubbed the essence into the silk where you would place your cheek. You have breathed deeply of it. I am sorry. I ask—no, I beg your forgiveness. It was wrong of me, but I hated you so. You seemed to have everything. You would have taken Andres from me. I could not bear it." Feliciana's dark eyes pleaded for absolution. "You saved my life. You did not have to, but you did. I have been so horrible to you, and yet you risked yourself for me."

Mara laughed shortly in disbelief as she began to realize the depths to the seemingly demure Feliciana. She and Brendan had underestimated everyone around here, their own arrogance and intricate strategies allowing them to ignore and overlook the more simple and open hostilities. At least she was relieved to learn that it hadn't been the mischief of Jeremiah Davies and Raoul, for that would have indicated a more serious threat to her because of her knowledge of their unlawful activities; instead, it was just malicious mischief by a jealous girl.

"You must forgive me, instead," Mara said, "for I seem to be the one who wronged you, Feliciana. I thought you a weak nonentity, hardly worth a second thought."

"I do not understand," Feliciana said as she came closer to the bed, the cynical, amused smile on Mara's face confusing her. "You forgive me, please?"

"Certainly," Mara said, suddenly tired of playing with other people's feelings. "As long as I don't suffer any more unexplainable accidents. And you will see that my headaches disappear, won't you? Of course, as I'm not planning on a protracted visit, that won't be any problem," Mara added softly.

Feliciana nodded her head eagerly. "Sí, and you do not hate me? I will accept you as Andres's wife and even leave the rancho should you desire," Feliciana assured her in a trembling voice, properly humbled for her misdeeds.

"Please," Mara sighed, holding up a slender hand. "You are forgiven, although I'm thinking 'tis me who should really be asking *your* forgiveness. So please, no more of this." Mara wished Feliciana would leave now that she'd cleared her conscience.

"I do not always understand what you say, Amaya," Feliciana said in puzzlement, "but as long as I am forgiven, then I will feel free to enter the convent and make my pledge to God."

Mara eyed the young Californian thoughtfully. "I'd advise you to wait awhile before committing yourself to a life of wearing black for the rest of your days. Who knows what could happen soon to change your mind?" Mara asked. She thought of the certain future for Feliciana, at the hacienda as the wife of Andres and the mother of a brood of small Villareales.

Mara was to remember her fateful words on the morrow.

All the rest of the day passed quietly enough, although Brendan was openly curious as he watched Nicholas and Mara at lunch, aware that something was going on between them. He was not sure he liked it whatever it was.

"Damned impertinence of the man," Brendan complained as he accompanied Mara on a ride later that day. He stared over his shoulder at the Creole who was riding a discreet distance behind them, then stared hard at Mara's averted face. "What's going on between the two of you? It's not decent the way he's been looking at you all day."

Mara raised her slim eyebrows in disbelief. "*You're* complaining about someone not being decent? Surely my ears are deceiving me," Mara retorted, masking her embarrassment with sarcasm.

Brendan snorted derisively. "Even a fool couldn't miss it."

Mara smiled slightly. "And you're certainly no fool, are you, Brendan? Perhaps, however, a bit fanciful. And what do you mean, 'couldn't miss it'?"

"He's making love to you with his eyes. The way they rove over you, as if he has some intimate knowledge of you. It's damned insolent of him."

"Don't be absurd, Brendan," Mara scoffed, her face flushing a bright pink.

"Ridiculous, am I?" Brendan demanded angrily. "Just don't go and get involved with that Frenchman. It can only mean trouble, mark my words. Besides, he's not rich. It wouldn't be worth your time, my love," Brendan added warningly.

"Listen, I wanted to talk to you about something," Mara began hesitantly. "Can't we leave the rancho now? Do we have to wait for Don Luís to return? How do we know he will? He could be lying to us again, couldn't he? You do want to get to the gold mines, don't you?"

Brendan stared at Mara incredulously. "What the divil's got into you anyway? And just how are we to leave—on foot? And what explanation are we to give our host? And where will we put up for the night? Are we to pay our bill with our good looks? I think not, my love. You've been the one cautioning me to be patient, and now all of a sudden you're having qualms about the whole thing?" Brendan eyed Mara suspiciously. "Has it something to do with the Frenchie? Has he found out something?"

Mara bit her lip indecisively. Should she tell him? He could become so unreasonable, and the last thing she wanted was a confrontation between Nicholas and him.

"You might as well tell me. You've never been good at lying to me." Brendan sighed.

"Very well, Brendan, you might as well learn the truth," Mara gave in. "The Creole recognized me from London. He suspected I was a certain actress, called Mara O'Flynn. He remembered seeing me on the stage."

"The divil he does!" Brendan exclaimed incredulously.

"At least he did suspect the truth. Now I think I've convinced him that I am not Mara O'Flynn, but I've only allayed his suspicions temporarily. And it certainly wouldn't do to have him find out the truth."

"Well," Brendan speculated, "if worse comes to worse I suppose we could always take him into our confidence, even offer to pay him to keep his silence. He's blackguard enough to accept."

"No!" Mara cried out in dismay. "You mustn't tell him the truth. You see he has little respect for the O'Flynns and would relish the chance to expose us, even see us prosecuted."

Brendan frowned thoughtfully. "Damned if I remember him. We've never met him, have we? Why should he hate us? To be sure I'm a friendly fellow, and no one's bearing a grudge against Brendan O'Flynn." He pondered the disturbing thought, then shot an accusing look at Mara's flushed face. "Or is it Mara O'Flynn, not 'the O'Flynns,' that he's no liking for, mavournin? He just wouldn't happen to be one of your discarded swains? No," Brendan answered his own question as he laughed harshly, "I can't see the Creole letting a woman get the best of him, so it's got to be…let me see…a friend of a friend, out to even the score?" Brendan took a lucky guess, not realizing how close he came to the truth.

"I can truthfully swear that I've never met him until now, and I really don't know why he bears a grudge against me," Mara lied, unwilling to have Brendan know the whole truth. "But you can see why I'm uneasy and do not care to be around should he discover I really am Mara O'Flynn."

"Well, I wouldn't worry unduly about it, because Don Luís should be here anytime now. Then we'll be gone from here. And while we are still here, what can he do? Don Andres would hardly take kindly to slurs cast upon his adored Amaya. Why, he'd probably have the Creole thrown off the rancho!" Brendan declared, a gleam of anticipation in his eyes. Mara nodded in agreement, looking away from Brendan. How could she possibly tell him that she had fallen in love with Nicholas? He would laugh in her face, be stingingly contemptuous of her weakness, amused that the proud and disdainful Mara had finally succumbed. Brendan could be merciless in ridicule if he wanted to be. She wouldn't have her love for Nicholas subjected to that.

"I just hope you're right and we do have the time," Mara finally murmured as she urged her horse back toward the hacienda.

"Now, now, you're not to be worrying. The O'Flynn luck is riding with us, I can feel it," Brendan promised with a laugh as he rode along beside her.

In fact, for the rest of the evening Brendan stayed close to Mara's side, giving Nicholas no chance to move up closer for conversation. The one time he tried, Brendan acted the consummate bore, monopolizing the conversation and rudely interrupting. Finally Nicholas had turned away with a slight shrug, and for the remainder of the evening Mara was presented with a view of his wide-shouldered back, while her fingers itched to run through the dark curls that just touched his collar.

Mara didn't know if she had expected a knock on her door after midnight or not, and so she wasn't sure if she was disappointed or relieved when it never came. She ignored the fact that she had sat for over an hour brushing her long hair until it crackled and shone in the candlelight, or that she had touched more of her favorite scent between her breasts and on the inside of her wrists where the pulse beat erratically. Finally she gave up waiting and snuffed out all the candles but the one flickering beside her bed. As Mara climbed into bed she noticed for the first time something tucked just beneath the edge of the cover of her pillow. Curiously, she pulled back the spread and stared down at a single rose.

How? How had he planted this in her bed? As she slid beneath the covers, she heard a rustling, and feeling down lower, her hand encountered a piece of paper. Her lips curved in a smile as she read the carelessly scrawled message:

I thought your watchdog might be guarding your bed as well, so this lonely but very fortunate rose shall have to take my place. Bon nuit, ma petite, and dream of me.
    N.

The arrogance of the man, Mara thought with a grin as she

held the fragrant rosebud to her nose and breathed deeply of it. She blew out the flame and settled down under the covers. She kissed the soft petals of the rose, and pressing it between her breasts, she curled up and fell to sleep, dreaming of Nicholas.

The following morning, Mara was dressing when she heard loud voices from the courtyard. Her curiosity urged her to the door of her room. It might be Don Luís returning.

Brendan had come from his room as well and was already standing on the edge of the patio, an interested onlooker to what was happening in the center of the courtyard.

At Mara's approach he glanced up from the apple he was neatly peeling with his penknife and shrugged a shoulder in the direction of the voices as he asked curiously, "And what do you make of that, mavournin?"

Mara's eyes followed his gesture and opened wide as she stared at the small group gathered in the center near the fountain. The most startling person was Jeremiah Davies, for once the center of attention as all eyes focused on his startling change.

He was dressed in a beautifully cut frock coat with velvet collar and cuffs, and as he pulled out a heavy gold watch from his pocket, Mara could see the expensive satin lining and the fine, striped silk of his waistcoat. An ornate breast pin was stuck in the folds of his cravat. Several rings now adorned his stubby fingers. He was tapping an ebony cane with an agate head against the unmarred leather of his shiny new shoes. His sandy head was now covered beneath a tall silk hat, but as Doña Ysidora joined the group to stand regally beside her son, Jeremiah doffed the hat and bowed.

"Well, well," Brendan murmured thoughtfully, "it looks as though Jerry boy has come into an inheritance. I wonder where he discovered this newfound wealth. To be sure, I'd no idea cattle stealin' was so lucrative."

"It would seem as though a lot of people are curious about his finances," Mara said as she saw the looks of incredulity and confusion mirrored on the Californians' faces. By now Raoul had sauntered up to the group, as well as Feliciana, Doña Jacinta, and other guests.

"I can't say that I think much of his taste," Brendan

remarked as he eyed the two garish females standing behind Jeremiah. They were dressed in gaudy gowns of striped silk adorned with a profusion of ruffles and bows, their faces painted heavily with rouge and powder that didn't cover their lines of age and dissipation. Each one's hair had been dyed a different but equally brassy shade of red.

"Jerry boy has quite an entourage with him," Brendan remarked as he noticed for the first time the three hulking figures standing warily around Jeremiah Davies and his two female companions. "Lovely trio of ruffians I'd not enjoy the pleasure of meeting," Brendan commented dryly. He quickly took their measure, noting their broken noses and the pugnacious expressions on their battered faces. They stood menacingly behind the American, their heavily booted feet planted firmly apart, their large-knuckled hands curled into casual fists.

"They remind me uneasily of the type who come to collect debts," Brendan added with a look of acute distaste. "Most disagreeable individuals," he murmured. Then, glancing down the corridor, his eyes narrowing, he added sarcastically, "And speaking of disagreeable people…"

Mara had been so intent on the group gathered in the courtyard that she hadn't been aware of Nicholas approaching along the corridor behind her. She jumped nervously as she felt a hand lightly caress her arm, her nerves tightening even more as she stared up into Nicholas's green eyes.

Brendan eyed the Creole disdainfully. Then, with a malicious look, he nodded toward the three cutthroats. "Friends of yours?"

Nicholas grinned thoughtfully. "No, although I do recognize the one with only half an ear. His name's Patrick O'Casey, Irish, wouldn't you say?" Nicholas asked softly.

Brendan stabbed the knife into a thick slice of apple, then bit it off before he could utter the profanities that burned on the tip of his tongue as he glared impotently at Nicholas.

"¡Madre de Dios! I cannot believe this," Mara heard Don Andres say, his tanned face paling as he stared at his secretary.

"You'd better believe it, Don Andres," Jeremiah replied easily, his blue eyes glittering. "Now I came here in friendliness. I mean, if we are to be neighbors, I don't think there should be any hostilities between us. After all, here is the bank note for the sale of the land," Jeremiah said, a triumphant smile curving his small mouth. "Everything is legal. You have the money, and I have the deed to the land and a receipt."

"But this is impossible!" Don Andres said in disbelief. "I never signed such a document. All you had authority to sell was the land in the southeast quarter, not this. What have you done?"

"Ah, but you did sign the proper documents, and it is all quite legal, I assure you. In fact," Jeremiah said, his tone patronizing as he smiled sadly at the Californian, I even have a witness to the transaction." He looked over to Mara. "Amaya Vaughan is my witness."

Mara's mouth parted in surprise as Don Andres and every other person stared at her. She began to shake her head in disbelief, returning Andres's stare in puzzlement.

"Don't you remember, Miss Vaughan? You were in the study the other day when Don Andres signed several papers for me," Jeremiah reminded her, "and he told me to sell the land to get money to pay his taxes."

"I-I do remember being there," Mara admitted reluctantly, "but I didn't see what you signed."

"There, you see!" Jeremiah cried. "She would have to swear in court that you signed it over to me of your own free will, that I exerted no force against you."

Jeremiah Davies looked around at the stunned faces and with an expansive smile declared, "I am therefore, the undisputed owner of over half of the next valley and of the hacienda that sits there, the Casa Quintero. Now I shall have to think of a more American name for it," he said with a derisive look at Raoul Quintero, who was standing as if turned to stone by the words just uttered by Jeremiah Davies.

Doña Jacinta gave a small moan of despair and fainted, her plump body falling almost soundlessly to the ground. Doña Ysidora called out for her servants, while several men carried the prostrate form of Doña Jacinta to a long bench. They rested her prone body along its length. Raoul remained where he was, oblivious to all but the gloating face of his traitorous friend as the implications of his own perfidy began to sink in.

Mara felt Brendan's look even before she turned to stare into his dismayed eyes, their expressions simultaneously mirroring the direction of their thoughts.

"Jaysus," Brendan whispered, his face paling slightly as his mind quickly traveled over the outcome of all this. Don Luís would soon return and find his land sold out from under him.

Mara began to feel some of Brendan's panic, especially as she became aware of Nicholas standing close beside her. Mara glanced up at him, but he was unaware of Brendan and Mara's agitation.

"And so you see, Don Andres," Jeremiah was saying in a hatefully self-satisfied voice, his chest puffed out bravely with the support of his hirelings, "there is nothing you can do. Indeed, it would be most unwise of you to challenge me on this. In fact, you should really be grateful to me."

"Grateful to you?" Andres asked incredulously, his usually gentle face hardened in anger. "You are insane! How did you imagine you could get away with this act of thievery?"

Jeremiah sneered openly, his obsequious manner gone completely now that he believed himself to be a landowner. "You're the one who's the fool. Anything can happen in California today. Come out of your golden valley and look around you. The state is wide open, with thousands coming to stake a claim on what is rightfully theirs. Your days are numbered, Spaniard. You can take me to court and try to prove I cheated you, but we'd be tied up in a legal battle for years. It would become very expensive as you hired your lawyers and I hired mine. How would you pay their expensive legal fees? You could only pay them by giving them some of your land, and little by little it would be eaten away. The outcome would be the same, only you'd be losing more land than you are now," Jeremiah reasoned smoothly. "Besides, I don't think you need the government questioning your right to this land. They will hardly look favorably on your claim to land you won in a bet, especially when the land is now owned by a true American. They might even begin to wonder about the validity of the Rancho Villareale. I think you'll have enough worries in the future, trying to pay your taxes on all this land, and even more worry in trying to keep it," Jeremiah warned.

"Dios, but I am stunned," Don Andres mumbled. Then looking directly into Jeremiah's blue eyes, he questioned, "How could you do this to me? What did I ever do to harm you, Jeremiah, that you would hate us so much?" he said, shaking his dark head. A sudden thought struck him and he demanded with narrowed eyes, "Where did you get the money? How could you afford to buy land? You are not a rich man. And these clothes, these women?" he asked, gesturing disdainfully at Jeremiah's female friends. "How?"

Jeremiah smiled, his eyes sliding over to Raoul. "We all have our secrets."

Raoul apparently could stand no more. His own guilty conscience forced him out of control and he cried out.

"Dog! You tricked me! Used me to steal my own land! You will never live at the Casa Quintero," Raoul cried, glancing around him for support. As his eyes clashed with Don Andres's, he forgot his own part in the cattle rustling and confessed, "He steals your cattle, Don Andres. That is how he becomes rich. He is a thief. He should be hanged!"

"Prove it," Jeremiah snarled. "Who will take the word of a drunken mama's boy who can't even stand up straight?" he jeered.

Raoul gave a bellow of pure rage and charged the amazed American like one of the bulls in the corral. He fumbled for his knife as he staggered forward, but before Raoul could come within arm's reach of his victim, the bunched fist of one of the American's brawlers had connected with Raoul's smooth face, sending the stunned Californian forcibly backward with such power that Raoul's head hit one of the posts of the corridor with a sickening impact. It sounded like a pistol shot. Raoul crumpled to the ground, senseless, dark red blood beginning to seep from the back of his head and trickle from his nose.

"¡Madre de Dios!" Don Andres exclaimed as he rushed over to the fallen Raoul and knelt beside him. He placed a tentative hand over Raoul's chest as he gazed worriedly into the still face. Don Andres slowly struggled to his feet, his knees wobbling slightly as he turned to face the others. "He is dead."

His startling words hung in the strained silence of the courtyard as many shocked glances were sent to the still-unconscious Doña Jacinta. She had been spared the agony of witnessing her only son's death. Don Andres was the first to shake off the numbness. He took a threatening step toward the American but found his path blocked by Doña Ysidora who flung herself in front of him.

"Andres, my son," she cried, "nothing can be done now. Let it be. What good will you be if you are maimed or killed by these brutes?"

"Listen to your madre, Don Andres," Jeremiah warned nervously as he glanced around the ring of angry faces surrounding him and his bodyguards. "It was self-defense. He was going to knife me. You all saw it," Jeremiah blustered.

Don Andres continued to glare at the American. The other Californians grumbled threateningly, willing to back him up in whatever move he made as they crowded closer around him, the ladies moving back to safety within the corridor.

The three huge men hired for protection by Jeremiah Davies prepared to earn their wages as they closed ranks around him, their faces showing a mixture of ugliness and anticipation.

Suddenly the loud report of a pistol rang through the court-yard, echoing like the ringing of a chapel bell calling people to mass. Mara and Brendan jumped in alarm at the sound, for it had nearly deafened them by its closeness. Turning in surprise and fear, they stared at the smoking pistol held negligently in Nicholas's hand.

"You'll forgive me for interfering in what is not my business," Nicholas apologized, "but there has already been one death and I don't think you wish the ladies to become involved in this."

One of the hired thugs made a reach for the gun strapped to his hip. Before his thick fingers could even close over the butt of the pistol, Nicholas fired again. This time his well-aimed shot stung the man's fingers. It left a bloody trail to mark its passage.

"I think it's time you three and the little man said your farewells and left," Nicholas advised in a cold voice. "And the *ladies* too," he added, a cruel smile curving his lips as they loudly protested their outrage.

"¡Sí!" Don Andres agreed as he saw the wisdom of Nicholas's words. "You will leave my land at once!" Don Andres ordered, promising himself that he and his friends would seek retribution in their own good time.

"A pleasure, Don Andres," Jeremiah agreed, casting a malevolent look at the tall Creole and the wrathful faces of the Californians. He turned with his disreputable party and left the courtyard.

Brendan coughed, attracting Mara's attention. He signaled her to follow him. As Mara started to follow, Nicholas turned his attention to her, his green eyes stopping her as effectively as if he'd caught her arm.

"I'd like to talk to you, somewhere private," Nicholas suggested softly.

Mara swallowed nervously. "I must check on my nephew. He was probably frightened by the gunshot," Mara stalled. "Later?"

"Very well. Later," Nicholas acquiesced, his eyes softening as they rested on her flushed cheeks.

But Mara didn't see the gentle tenderness in his gaze. She only remembered the murderous look in those green eyes as they had stared piercingly at the man he'd shot. He had dealt swiftly and ruthlessly with the troublemaker, showing no pity. If that was the way he reacted when he wasn't even personally involved, how would he react should he find out who she really was? Mara trembled on a wave of desperation and fear.

Brendan had entered Paddy's room and was pacing restlessly as Mara entered. Mara ignored him as she went to Paddy who was standing wide-eyed in the center of the room, his red and white painted toy soldiers spread out in various formations across the tiles. The make-believe battle was now forgotten as Paddy demanded, "What happened? Did somebody get killed?"

"There was an accident, that's all, Paddy," Mara said sharply. "A gun went off by mistake."

"But I heard two shots, Mara," Paddy persevered.

"Saints be praised," Jamie breathed thankfully. "I thought for sure one of ye had finally pushed someone too far. What with all of the raised voices, I'm surprised not to find ye both in the middle of it."

Brendan gave her a quelling glance as he stopped his pacing and ran a nervous hand through his thick hair. He frowned, chewing his lower lip thoughtfully as he put both hands deep into his pants pockets and stared down at his shoes.

"What are we going to do?" Mara demanded, her eyes clinging to Brendan's worriedly.

"What the divil d'ye think? We're getting out of here before there's any more bloodletting," Brendan said with a determined look in his eye. "I'm not of a mind for it to be any of mine."

"You mean someone would want to shoot you, Papa?" Paddy exclaimed in awe, only to fall silent under the threatening look from Brendan.

"The divil with getting paid, mavournin. I think 'tis time we made an exit, without taking any curtain calls. Can you imagine what will happen when Don Luís arrives back to buy his land? I don't want to be anywhere near here when Don Luís discovers his son murdered by the man who now owns the very land he's been scheming to regain. And who do you think the good Don Luís will blame? None other than our host, who was duped into signing over the deed. I doubt whether anything Don Andres could say will convince Don Luís that it wasn't done out of anything but malice. Don Luís doesn't strike me as one to suffer alone. He'll try to bring us all down with him, and one of the best ways of hurting Don Andres is to reveal to him that he's been made a fool of with a phony Amaya. I'm also thinkin' the climate will be a bit hot around here for foreigners. I don't think Jerry boy will be enjoying his richness for long either, for despite those half-witted muscleheads he's hired, there's a lot of open country around here where a man could easily have a fatal accident."

Mara nodded numbly. "Start packing, Jamie," Mara directed. "Well?" she demanded, uncertainty sharpening her voice, as Jamie continued to stand there staring, arms akimbo.

"And I suppose ye'll be wantin' me to carry all our luggage on me back?" Jamie asked. "For although I've heard fine reasons for leavin' here—and 'tis about time—I've yet to be hearin' how."

Mara turned expectantly to Brendan, but he shrugged his shoulders in answer to her silent query. "Don't be looking at me. I can't be coming up with answers to everything."

Mara sighed in exasperation. "Now's a fine time to be running out of ideas," she complained, tapping her small foot nervously on the tile floor.

Brendan pulled out a cigar and was lighting it, the match flaring briefly, when he suddenly gave a cry of pleasure. "Damn! I've got it!"

Mara eyed him with suspicious curiosity as he blew a large puff of smoke into the room and a wide grin spread across his face. "You will collect, mavournin, on a debt from Don Andres."

"He owes me nothing," Mara replied.

"You collect on Feliciana. Or have you forgotten how you so courageously saved that young woman from a fiery death? Anything you want, mavournin, he'll give you."

"But what will I tell him?"

"Anything you like except the truth, love. I prefer not to push our luck too far," Brendan advised.

Mara nodded absently as she turned to the window overlooking the courtyard and stared out. What would she say to Don Andres? The courtyard was deserted. Even the place where Raoul had met his tragic end had been scrubbed clean, erasing at least the physical memory of his dreadful death. Mara was still gazing at the spot when she recognized a dapper figure striding through the courtyard.

She drew in her breath audibly, the ragged sound drawing Brendan's attention. "'Tis too late."

Brendan looked over Mara's shoulder at the man just disappearing into the hacienda. "Was ever an entrance quite so ill-timed?" Brendan breathed. "Don Luís of all people."

"Brendan, what are we going to do now?" Mara wailed, admitting for the first time in her life that she was frightened, as she remembered a pair of penetrating green eyes.

"The hell with our baggage, let's just get the divil out of here," he said with no pretense of showing a bold face. "Not that I think there's anything they can really be doin' to us. However, it's bound to become a bit uncomfortable around here when the truth is known."

"Now ye're talkin'," Jamie said as she began to bustle around the room, quickly picking up the scattered belongings. "We can always send for our possessions when things die down a bit."

"Don't pack more than what you can carry on horseback," Brendan ordered as he made for the door. "I'll see about some horses. Meet me in the stable yard in fifteen minutes. And try not to look too panic struck and obvious about it, will you, Mara? I'd prefer not to be hanged as a horse thief."

Mara managed a tight smile. "Oh, no, I shall be as calm as if I were going out for an afternoon stroll."

The sound of Paddy imitating a cannon drew Mara's attention to him as he knelt on the floor and intently moved each soldier into a different position. "We don't have time for you to be playing games, Paddy," Mara reprimanded him, taking out her fear in impatient anger at Paddy.

Paddy pouted as he angrily swept all his wooden soldiers into a disorderly pile.

"Now don't be actin' naughty, Master Paddy," Jamie intervened smoothly as she handed him the small chest the soldiers were stored in. "Ye put them away carefully now, while I pack your clothes."

"Hurry. We haven't time to neatly fold everything," Mara reminded Jamie. She turned in the doorway and watched as Jamie folded with slow precision a small jacket and shirt of Paddy's.

"Ye just get yourself busy and don't be mindin' about us. And don't take time tryin' to pack things yourself. Ye'll just be slowin' us up," Jamie retorted without even glancing at Mara.

Mara hurried along the corridor to her room, thinking that Brendan didn't even know half of the danger they found themselves in. She thought of Nicholas's promise of vengeance. She had reached her door when she became aware of voices raised in anger coming from the study just a few doors down the corridor. Hesitating just briefly, Mara tiptoed along the passage, coming to a halt just before the opened door of Don Andres's study. She could hear the voices within, but she couldn't understand the conversation for they spoke in Spanish. The tone, at any rate, left little to the imagination. When she recognized her own name, and not the one she was currently known by, Mara knew it was all over.

She quickly fled to her room and began to throw together the more necessary items of clothing, stuffing them in bundles into the large tapestried bag she had previously carried for odds and ends. She placed her jewelry boxes inside, along with her beauty aids and brushes and combs. Mara began unhooking her dress, wishing Jamie would show up to help her as she struggled with the fastenings, her arms twisted behind her uncomfortably for what seemed hours. Finally, with a feeling of triumph, she undid the last hook and pulled the endless yards of gown over her head.

She was pulling out her riding habit when a knock sounded on the door. Mara held her breath, her heart beating errati-cally, until the first knock was followed by Brendan's special tap. Mara sighed in relief as she opened the door, her tremu-lous smile fading when she saw who stood there.

"Nicholas," Mara soundlessly mouthed his name.

Mara backed up as Nicholas stepped into the room, closing the door behind him with finality. Mara's eyes were locked on his hard, bronzed features. His eyes glowed like the emeralds Mara had once seen in an ancient mask of gold. Those eyes had held no warmth either. Mara could feel the hatred and suppressed rage that burned in them now without even having to hear his voice. It flicked her like a whip.

"Mara O'Flynn," he said softly. "So we meet. No more secrets or masquerades between us. I have your..." Nicholas paused questioningly, "*cousin*, is it, to thank for allowing me such easy access to your room. I heard him use his special knock the other evening."

Mara licked her dry lips nervously, backing up another step as she widened the distance between them. Nicholas followed her deeper into the room.

Nicholas took in her scantily attired body, not missing the rapid and uneven movement of the swell of the breast above the lacy edge of her corset or the trembling of her parted lips. His gaze slowly traveled across her small waist and rounded hips to the pale slender thighs revealed by the opening on the inner part of her drawers. Her silk-clad calves and delicate ankles showed enticingly beneath the lacy hem edging the bottom of her drawers, while on her narrow feet she wore red broché silk slippers with slender straps tied around her ankles.

He came a step closer and held out something. "Why don't you get dressed, ma petite?" he said softly, a cruel smile curving his sensuous lips.

Mara stared in amazement at the thick red velvet material thrown across his arm, and as she watched in fascination, he unfolded it. She gasped as she recognized the red velvet dress Jamie had returned to Julian that fateful day so long ago.

"I thought you might remember it. It did belong to you, didn't it, Mara O'Flynn?" Nicholas lingered over her name as if he relished the sound of it. "A pity it's never been worn. Put it on," he ordered and threw it across to her.

Mara reached out instinctively as it was flung against her, her eyes widening in horror as she felt the soft fabric touching her skin. She stared into Nicholas's green eyes, glowing with vengeful anticipation.

"I've always wondered how you would look in it," he was saying in a reminiscent tone, but as Mara remained still it sharpened harshly. "I said put it on," he warned, "if just to humor me. Just think of all of the trouble I went to, carrying it around all these years. But something told me not to throw it away, that I'd one day have the satisfaction of seeing you in it."

Mara backed farther away from him, dropping the gown. She stared at him in trembling defiance.

"How did you find out?" Mara asked faintly. "Did Don Luís tell you?"

Nicholas smiled humorlessly. "You shouldn't have run away so quickly from eavesdropping at Don Andres's study door. I saw you, but before I could call out to you, you had disappeared in a rustle of skirts into your room. I followed, only to stop in surprise as I heard the conversation in the study. It was a most revealing discussion," he explained coldly. "Didn't you know I spoke Spanish? How remiss of me not to have told you. Of course, there are a lot to things about me you have no knowledge of, but I did warn you, ma petite, what kind of man I am. A pity you did not heed my advice.

"I don't know why I should be at all surprised to find you involved in a conspiracy, knowing your past indiscretions as I do, but I am amazed at the coil you've managed to entangle yourself in. Life with you must be a constant struggle. No wonder Don Luís looks so ill, besides finding his land swindled and his son dead. He must have aged a century trying to keep an eye on you and your cousin," he speculated. Shaking his head in disgust, he continued thoughtfully, "I can see now why Don Luís denied that you were Mara O'Flynn. He was in on the charade all along, and certainly didn't want to be exposed before he could buy back his land. Mon Dieu, I must have shaken him when I mentioned your real name."

"You spoke to Don Luís about me," Mara demanded, adding almost beneath her breath, "and he never warned us?"

"Certainly my good fortune that he had no more faith in you than I do. Just imagine," Nicholas taunted, "if you'd known, you could have been gone from here by now and never had the displeasure of having to face me with the truth."

"You can't do anything to me," Mara told him bravely, wishing desperately that Jamie or Brendan would come.

"Can't I?" Nicholas said, his eyes narrowing dangerously. "You and I have a score to settle, and you are the one owing up."

"I'm sorry about your nephew. How was I to know he'd go and kill himself over me?" Mara said defiantly. Looking beyond Nicholas's shoulders to the door, she missed the surprised expression in his eyes.

"Yes, you killed him, Mara O'Flynn," Nicholas lied, preferring her to continue to believe she had been the cause of a boy's death and suffer the responsibility of it on her conscience—if she had one, which he doubted. "How does it feel to be a murderess?"

Mara gasped. "I didn't kill him! It wasn't my fault, Nicholas!"

"Maybe you didn't hold the pistol to his heart," Nicholas said harshly, "but you might as well have pulled the trigger."

Nicholas glanced down at the dress lying at Mara's feet. "I think I deserve to see Mara O'Flynn in all her glory, don't you? Put it on."

"No," Mara replied huskily.

"Very well," Nicholas said grimly. Without warning he moved so quickly that he had grasped Mara's arms before she had a chance to cry out. She felt his hard hands jerking her around, and picking up the dress, he forced it over her head. Pulling it carelessly over her shoulders, he gathered it together at the waist and she could feel his fingers against the soft skin of her back. He began to hook it up. Her hair had come loose during the struggle and now hung across her shoulder in a thick wave.

"How you must have laughed when I showed you the locket and your picture." Mara felt his warm breath against her neck. "I knew I should have trusted my instincts when I first saw you and knew you were Mara O'Flynn."

"Where did you see me?" Mara whispered.

"One of those fateful meetings. I happened to see you in a Sacramento City hotel. It must have been when you had just arrived in California."

Mara bit her trembling lip as she felt his fingers viciously tightening the dress around her. She jumped as she felt the cold metal of the locket against her skin as it dangled between her breasts.

He turned her around, holding her at arm's length as he stared down with a look of satisfaction.

The bodice was cut low and off the shoulder with the décolletage more daring than any Mara had ever worn before.

The soft line of velvet barely covered the smooth swell of her breasts, pushed up by the stiff molding of her corset. Her skin seemed to glow with a pearly translucence in contrast to the rich burgundy of the velvet material. The gown hugged tightly to her waist, the velvet skirt falling in heavy folds to the floor.

"A perfect fit I'd say," Nicholas remarked cynically, his fingers still biting into her upper arms beneath the small puffs of velvet that served as sleeves.

Mara's eyes seemed to smolder with molten gold as she stared up into Nicholas's hard face, her exquisite features still not revealing any of the fear that quivered within her.

"How can such a beautiful face hide so cold and calculating a mind?" Nicholas asked. "You would think some of your ugliness would show, but it doesn't. Does it, Mara O'Flynn? You're the consummate actress, always performing before the poor wretches fool enough to believe what those soft, lying lips are saying, or to fall under the spell of those bewitching golden eyes."

Nicholas pulled her closer against his chest, his fingers tightening painfully on Mara's arms until she cried out softly. "And were you acting again when I held you in my arms and made love to you, Mara O'Flynn? Did you feign that sweet response to my kisses and caresses? Or, for once," Nicholas paused meaningfully, his green eyes fathomless, "were you the cat's paw?"

Mara dragged her eyes away from the pitiless cruelty she saw in Nicholas's face, her mind seeking desperately to hold onto reality. She must never let Nicholas know how his words wounded her. If he knew how deeply she loved him, he would be merciless in revenge, her love leaving her defenseless against him.

"Look at me, Mara O'Flynn," Nicholas said harshly, his hard fingers closing around the point of her chin and forcing her face up to his. "Do you think the disdainfully haughty Mara O'Flynn, brilliant actress and beautiful deceiver, finally fell into a trap of her own making? Perhaps you really do love me?" Nicholas speculated silkily. "I pity you if you do, Mara O'Flynn."

"Do not pity me, for 'twas an act and I do not love you," Mara whispered brokenly, her face reminding Nicholas of carved marble, so cold and emotionless was it.

"No," Nicholas said, a sneer curving his lips. "You wouldn't know how. You like to bait a man, tease him and play with him until he would gladly die for one smile from those cruelly insensitive lips or just one glance from those insolent golden eyes. But this time you played the game recklessly. You were too confident of your own charms, too arrogant to even imagine that a man might not be attracted to you. That you might be just another pretty face, someone to spend a few amusing hours with. It was your own trap, Mara."

Mara felt her skin burning as if it were on fire as his hateful words struck her in her most vulnerable place, and a venom-tipped arrow could not have pierced her heart more deeply or fatally. But Mara dared not show this inner turmoil to Nicholas, and so her face remained unmoved even as Nicholas's penetrating gaze searched it for some sign of emotion, a flicker of hatred or a shadow of tears in her eyes, but there was nothing except the cold mask.

"How does it feel to know that I've made a fool out of you, Mara O'Flynn?" Nicholas asked curiously. "You've always held yourself aloof from the men you've tormented, until now. I still find it hard to believe that you were an innocent. Does it hurt to know that the man you finally gave yourself to would turn out to despise your very name? Ironic, isn't it, that you should lose your virginity to me, Nicholas Chantale, a man who had cursed your name, gazed on your face with nothing but loathing, and felt only revenge in his heart. I've stolen something from you that can be given only once. I'm only sorry I wasn't sure at the time you really were Mara O'Flynn, or I wouldn't have been nearly so gentle," Nicholas said coldly.

Neither of them had seen the door open, or a figure enter stealthily and creep up behind the broad shoulders of the Creole. Too late Mara cried out as she saw the heavy butt of the pistol come down forcefully on the back of Nicholas's head. There was a stunned look of surprise on his face before he fell into Mara's arms, pulling her down with him as he hit the floor.

"Dirty swine," Brendan spat as he stared down at the unconscious body of Nicholas Chantale. "You may have deserved some of his hatred, but no one treats an O'Flynn like dirt beneath his feet," Brendan spoke in a hard voice, his eyes softening slightly as he saw the stricken look on Mara's face. "I think you've been through enough, mavournin. Come on, 'tis time we were leaving."

Mara stared down at Nicholas's pale face and touched the back of his head with trembling fingers. As she withdrew them, she felt the sticky wetness and then saw the bright red blood.

"Oh, God, Brendan, you've killed him," she breathed as she looked up in horror.

Brendan frowned. "To be sure, I just tapped him," he denied the accusation, but a worried look had entered his dark eyes. He bent down on one knee and felt Nicholas's wide chest for a heartbeat. "He's alive, but he'll have one hell of a headache when he wakes up," Brendan said, sighing in relief, "and I'd rather not be around when he does."

Mara lightly touched Nicholas's face with her fingers, tracing the line of his lips and feeling the softness of his lashes as she memorized his every feature.

"Come on, Mara," Brendan urged her, his eyes narrowing as he noticed for the first time the red velvet dress she wore. "What the divil d'ye have on?"

Brendan helped her to her feet as she tried to pull the skirt of the dress from beneath Nicholas's heavy body. "I'll change as fast as I can, Brendan," she told him raggedly.

Brendan swore beneath his breath as Mara struggled to unhook herself, his hands pushing hers aside as he quickly unfastened her, freeing her. "I don't know what's going on around here," he complained as he stepped back, "but I'm thinkin' everyone's gone crazy in the confusion." Brendan looked around thoughtfully, then took the sash from Mara's robe and with quick efficiency tied Nicholas's hands behind his back. "Don Luís practically knocked me down as he ran into the stable yard. He was staggering and holding his chest, dramatizing the situation for sure, and I don't even think he knew who I was. I was going to ask him to pay us. It wasn't any fault of ours that his scheme fell through," Brendan defended himself at Mara's look of disbelief. "But I didn't. In fact, I was just as glad he didn't see me, for he had a murderous look in his eye as he called for a groom. Ready?" Brendan demanded as Mara pulled on her riding jacket.

"I'll be right with you," she told him breathlessly. She sat down to pull on her boots. "You go and get Paddy and Jamie. I'll meet you in just a minute."

Brendan frowned. "Well, hurry up with it before the whole damned rancho knows we're impostors. And don't worry about him," he said, casting the prone form of Nicholas a contemptuous look, "he won't be bothering anyone for a while."

After Brendan departed, Mara quickly finished dressing. Closing the tapestried bag, she looked around the room, her eyes lingering on Nicholas, who still lay quietly on the floor. "Oh, Nicholas," Mara whispered, her eyes mirroring her pain now that there was no one to witness it, "if you only knew how well you succeeded in your revenge, how deeply you have hurt me. I love you. But you will never know that."

Without a backward glance Mara opened the door, closing it softly behind her as she started along the passage. She didn't see Brendan, or Paddy and Jamie, and assumed they had already left for the outer courtyard. Mara walked across the stable yard, looking cool and unflustered in her severely tailored riding habit, the tapestried bag carried easily at her side. But as she entered the stable, her step faltered slightly. She saw a sullen Brendan standing with an uncomfortable-looking Jamie and curious Paddy, while Don Andres and several of his vaqueros stood nearby.

"Don Andres," Mara said with no sign of discomfiture at his inopportune appearance.

"You are leaving, Ama—" Don Andres began, only to correct himself with a forced smile of apology that didn't reach his eyes. "Forgive me, it is not Amaya, is it? I believe your real name is Mara?"

"Yes, Mara O'Flynn," Mara admitted, lifting her head proudly as she tried to gather together the pride that had been stripped from her by Nicholas only minutes before.

"It is best that you and your party leave the rancho before my family and friends discover this deception," he surprised Mara, his voice cold. "I suppose I cannot really place the blame on you. It was Don Luís's plan, and he was the only one who could have benefited from it. Unless of course," he added bitterly, "you would have accepted my proposal. But I think that was not in the plan, sí? I am afraid that you will not be receiving any payment for your performance. You see, Don Luís has collapsed. That is why I was called to the stables, and how I discovered your rather sudden plans for departure. It is over now, and Don Luís has paid a higher price for his folly than he could ever have imagined. I accept part of the responsibility for this tragedy as well. I am not only dishonored by what has happened to Don Luís's land, but ashamed of my feelings for you. Dios, what a fool I have been."

Mara bit her lip at the pained embarrassment revealed in his voice. "You had little chance against the combined efforts of Don Luís and myself. You expected no trickery. Do not blame yourself too harshly. And what you felt for me, well, 'twas just a brief fascination. I'm an actress by profession. It's my job to fool people. You found me beautiful and alluring, as you were meant to. After a while you would have grown tired of the glamour and discovered that it is Feliciana you truly love. I saw the way you looked at her the night of the fire. You care for her, genuinely care, and she loves you. Don't shun that, Andres. Forget me and the unhappiness I've brought to your house," Mara told him honestly. "I've lost my chance at happiness. Take care you do not lose yours, Andres."

Don Andres stared deeply into Mara's eyes, seeing a vulnerable softness he had never seen in them before, and a breathtaking beauty that was perfectly natural. And one that Mara was completely unaware of herself, Don Andres realized.

His wounded pride and anger, mixed with his grief, warred with the attraction he still felt for this strange woman.

"Even if I had not already decided to allow you to leave the rancho, I do owe you a debt, as your brother has reminded me. So you are free to leave. Horses and several vaqueros will ride with you to guide you from the valley and safely to wherever it is you go. I will see that your baggage is sent."

Mara heard Brendan's audible sigh of relief, and with a nod of farewell, she followed Brendan to her mount. Jamie was helped onto the back of a sturdy but docile-looking pony, while Paddy was placed with Brendan on his mount.

Don Andres himself helped Mara to mount her horse. For a moment he stood silently staring up at her, his thoughts unreadable. Then, with a slight bow, he stepped back and gave her horse a gentle tap on the rump.

As they rode from the stable yard, through the wide gates of the rancho, Mara glanced back and saw Don Andres standing alone. Then he raised his arm slowly in farewell and Mara thought she caught his words floating to her through the dust.

"*!Vaya con Dios!*"

May God go with you, he had wished them even after all the misery they had caused him. The devil would be a more likely partner, Mara thought, as they followed the vaqueros across the dusty hills and left the Valle d'Oro behind them. It was no longer a peaceful valley, no longer untouched by time.

After a hard day's riding, the Californians never seeming to tire, they reached Sonoma, where they took rooms at the Blue Wing Inn. It was a thick-walled adobe structure, two-storied, with a gallery on the second floor with rooms opening off it and a railing with wisteria clinging to it running along its length. The hostelry overlooked the main plaza, which was lined with other tile-roofed adobe buildings.

Mara was unpacking her tapestried bag when Brendan entered the room, and she could have sworn that he seemed uncomfortable as he paced restlessly around the room.

"I was wondering how we're going to pay for our rooms," Mara said as she folded a shawl and placed it on the bed.

"For once I had enough to pay for our stay. You needn't worry about that," Brendan reassured her. "I won a few hands of poker against Raoul, so we'll have enough for a few days." Brendan paused, then coughed, clearing his throat nervously. "At least there will be enough to see you and Paddy and Jamie to San Francisco."

Mara stopped her unpacking, feeling a shiver of apprehension shoot through her. "And what does that mean?" she asked outright.

"It means that I'm going up into the Sierra Nevada, where I should have gone in the first place. I'll manage someway to get enough money to buy equipment. Hell," Brendan spoke with excitement, "all I need is a tin pan to wash some gold nuggets from a stream bed. Then I'll have enough profit from that to buy some real equipment."

"And what are we supposed to do while you're up in the mountains somewhere?" Mara demanded in a cold voice that couldn't hide the anxiety she was feeling.

"You'll be fine in San Francisco," Brendan said easily, adding persuasively, "the mining camps are no place for the three of you. Life is damned rough up there, and you wouldn't want to subject Paddy to such an unsavory place. He'd never survive the winter up there. Why, they have snow drifts twenty feet high."

"And you expect to find gold beneath all that snow?" Mara asked. "Why don't you wait until the spring?"

"It'll be too late by then. I've got several months until winter comes on, and I intend to strike it rich before the first snowflake falls," Brendan promised. "Listen, mavournin, 'tis the only way. I can't take you and Paddy with me. I'm sorry I haven't more money to give you than this," he said, actually flushing in embarrassment as he handed a small pouch over to Mara. "It's all I have. I've already made arrangements for you to stay here until our baggage arrives and I've paid your way to San Francisco as well."

Mara stared down dumbly at the not very heavy pouch of leather. She couldn't believe it. Brendan was abandoning them. Mara looked up into Brendan's anxious eyes. She knew he'd already made up his mind. He would leave regardless of whatever protestations she made. "When?"

"Tomorrow at dawn," he told her, his voice trembling with excitement, "You wait for me in San Francisco, and as soon as I strike it rich, I'll join you there. Find some lodgings and I'll find you when I get there."

"How?" Mara asked quietly.

"Mara, me little love," Brendan spoke with a twinkle in his dark brown eyes, "you've never been one to go without notice. Should you not have made yourself famous in San Francisco by the time I arrive, then I'll just pay a visit to every boardinghouse in town. Eventually I'll find you."

"Try to stay out of trouble, will ye, Brendan?" Mara said softly.

Brendan had walked to the door, but he turned as she spoke, and coming back he gave her a quick, awkward hug. Then, an irrepressible dimple in his cheek, he winked at Mara and walked jauntily out the door, leaving her standing in the early twilight filtering in from the window of the silent room.

Mara sat down on the edge of the bed, her shoulders sagging tiredly under her dispirited thoughts. Everything had gone wrong. It'd been a venture doomed to failure from its very conception. And had they never gone to the rancho, she might never have met Nicholas.

Nicholas. Why should she love him? She who had been so contemptuous of others who she had assumed were weak, had fallen irrevocably in love with a man who cared nothing for her. Well, Mara thought, she had let herself live, and now she was hurting. Nicholas had been successful in administering retributive justice. And now she couldn't escape her memories. She wondered if he was all right. What was he doing now?

❧

Nicholas rode eastward from the Rancho Villareale as he made his way back to Sacramento City. His thoughts lingered on the past and his expression was grim.

He had awakened from unconsciousness to find himself trussed up like a holiday turkey, a throbbing lump on the back of his skull, his pockets picked clean and the O'Flynns having taken to their heels. He'd managed to free his swollen wrists and, rubbing them to get the circulation back, had stumbled to the door. He found the hacienda in a state of uproar. Servants ran to and fro while the guests milled around the courtyard in small, whispering groups. Some of the women were weeping, and every so often one of the mourners' voices could be heard above the others raised in anger and grief. Then a hushed silence would envelop them once again. Nicholas walked along the corridor to his room unnoticed as the Californians remained absorbed in each other and their grief.

It hadn't taken him long to pack his belongings, then seek out his host, Don Andres. He had found him in his study with Doña Ysidora, who was dressed in black, her haughty features no less austere than her gown. Her hands expressed her thoughts eloquently as she talked.

"And what happens now?" she demanded. "Don Luís is seriously ill. How will he be able to support her? Her grief overcomes her, my son. I am so worried. We shall, of course, despite Don Luís's dishonorable behavior, offer them a home with us."

Don Andres shook his head tiredly. "That will not be necessary."

Doña Ysidora stared at her son incredulously. Her tone sharp, she asked, "What do you mean? Where else will Jacinta and Luís stay? Their rancho is stolen by this," she paused, her thin lips tightening with suppressed rage, "this Judas. I still cannot believe that one who had lived beneath our roof for so many years would betray us. And to find out that Luís, as well, had deceived us. It was so unnecessary, Andres. He could still have lived on his rancho. You would have sold it back to him. Something could have been worked out.

"And it saddens me that she was not Amaya. I liked her, whoever she was. She was strong, Andres. She would have given you many fine sons. But this cannot be. It seems that one never truly knows another person. Even one you know for a lifetime," she said with a shrug of inevitability, "you do not know who he is, what goes on inside him." She shook her head.

"Don Luís and Doña Jacinta will need no help, Madre,"

Don Andres told her with a sad smile. "You forget the cross. It had been Don Luís's intention of buying back his land with it They will most likely return to Monterey. It is Jacinta's home. She has many relatives there and they can buy a house in town, for Don Luís will probably never leave his bed again."

"Excuse me, Don Andres," Nicholas spoke from the doorway. "I think it is best that I go. This isn't the time to have strangers under your roof. Thank you kindly for your hospitality."

Don Andres nodded courteously. "It is my pleasure, Señor Chantale, although you are welcome to stay as long as you wish," he added, always the gracious host under any circumstances. "These will be sad days for us, however, with no festivities."

"Thank you," Nicholas answered, "but I've a friend to meet in Sacramento City, as well as some unfinished business I must see to."

As he rode along the trail, across gently sloping hills beneath a blazing sun that steadily moved toward the western horizon, he thought about that unfinished business and how he'd been duped by the O'Flynns—masters of the art of deception, it would seem. As he rubbed his hand across the tender knot on the back of his head, he smiled in expectation of bruising the flawless profile of one Brendan O'Flynn. And what of Mara O'Flynn? he thought, his lips savoring the name as he saw her beautiful face. She had managed to play him for a fool, bruising his ego in the process, and the image of the O'Flynns' laughing faces as they once again managed to extricate themselves from a difficult situation without any acceptance of responsibility rankled him.

Well, Nicholas thought with a gleam of anticipation in his narrowed green eyes, he didn't doubt that he would run across the O'Flynns once again, and when he did, they would pay in full measure.

The melancholy days are come, the saddest of the year,
Of wailing winds, and naked woods, and meadows brown and sere.

—William Cullen Bryant

Chapter 7

MARA STEPPED BRISKLY ALONG THE PLANKED SIDEWALK, HER footsteps muffled by the thick coating of mud clinging to the soles of her half-boots. A northwest wind was blowing in ice-cold gusts against her, molding her mantle to her shivering body. The wool seemed to absorb all the cold dampness in the air. Mara tucked her gloved hands inside her muff trying to warm them. She could taste the salt spray on her lips as she licked them to ease the tender, chafed skin. The wind had driven the usual morning fog, which was like a fine Scotch mist hanging low and dense over the city, into the distance and the high hills that surrounded the San Francisco Bay.

It had been over a year since they had set sail from New York City. Soon it would be spring again in San Francisco, the city of canvas tents and wooden hovels she and Brendan had first seen when the *Windsong* had docked in the bay. In just under a year the city had doubled, and the canvas-lined streets were beginning to be edged out by two-storied, wood and brick buildings of more stable construction.

The streets were still crowded with people—Mexicans, Europeans, and Kanakas from Hawaii; Malays, Chileans, and Yankees from the East Coast of America. They intermingled in a mass with one common goal—to strike it rich. Gold fever was the one thing that never changed in this city. Saloons and stores, hotels and houses of prostitution were built practically overnight, creating within one day a whole new street to raise hell on. The city was a hive of activity and noise as workers hammered and sawed. Chinese workmen with long bamboo poles across their shoulders balanced mortar and bricks swinging by ropes on each end, and carts and drays pulled by sturdy horses carried goods through the widening city limits, straggling to the tops of the surrounding hills. Vendors called out along the muddy avenues and open areas fronting the docks. New arrivals landed daily on the countless ships sailing through the Golden Gate, the sailors and adventurers alike hungry for a change of diet and the excitement to be found in this boomtown by the bay. The vendors also found eager customers among the tired miners, rich in pocket, who streamed in from the mines as frantic for ways to spend their gold dust as they had been to find it.

Mara came to the end of the sidewalk and stared down at the ocean of slimy mud that stretched between her and the other side of the street. Various crates and boxes, and anything else that wouldn't sink, made a temporary bridge across the quagmire. But deep pools of muddy water from the downpour the night before had already submerged some of the makeshift supports, leaving gaping holes in the roughly made crossway.

Mara glanced back at Portsmouth Square and the post office, where hundreds of people were milling about as they impatiently waited their turn to find out if any long-awaited letters had arrived. Twice a month, when the Pacific Mail steamers sailed into the bay, the crowd would grow to over five hundred. Mara didn't know why she had gone down there. She knew there would be no letter from Brendan. But she supposed she hadn't given up hope.

Since parting so abruptly at the end of the summer, Mara had not seen Brendan. He had spent the autumn and winter months somewhere up in the Sierra Nevada searching for his gold mine. He'd been gone such a long time that every so often she wondered whether he were still alive. Mara thought of the inhospitable winter months she and Paddy and Jamie had spent in San Francisco with the rain and fog, and icy winds that never seemed to die down. At least they had a roof over their heads. But how had Brendan fared up in the high country? Poor

Brendan. Mara remembered some of the horrendous stories she'd heard about life in the isolated mining camps. Drinking and gambling were the standard forms of amusement when the inclement weather kept the miners holed up in the village of tents and huts. That would be the worst life for Brendan. He would enjoy both to the fullest and probably manage to get himself involved in a fight or two. When in his cups, Brendan was not apt to guard his tongue. Nor was he above dealing from the bottom of the deck. In the mining camps, where there were no representatives of the law to carry out justice, the miners had found their own ways of dealing with cheats.

Her gloomy thoughts were interrupted as she warily eyed two drunken miners stumbling across the muddy street, heading toward where she was standing. One had a pair of suspenders holding up his baggy pants, as well as a thick leather belt around his waist with the butt of a six-shooter stuck underneath. There wasn't much of his face visible beneath the wide brim of his sloppy hat and the thick beard. Both men were wearing the high boots and red flannel shirts favored by miners. The other had, besides a holster and gun, a large bowie knife suspended from his wide belt. They seemed oblivious to the light drizzle as they slipped and slid their way across the mud. Their carefree voices were raised in a merry song, albeit off tune, that they seemed determined to serenade the town with, in rambling, disjointed verses.

> A bully ship and a bully crew
> Doodah, doodah,
> A bully mate and a captain too,
> Doodah, doodah day.
>
> Then blow ye winds hi-ho
> For Californ-y-o.
> There's plenty of gold so I've been told
> On the banks of the Sacramento.
>
> Oh around Cape Horn we're bound to go,
> Doodah, doodah,

Around Cape Horn through the sleet and snow,
Doodah, doodah day.

I wish to God I'd never been born,
Doodah, doodah,
To go a-sailin', round Cape Horn,
Doodah, doodah day.

As they caught sight of Mara watching them with her contemptuous golden eyes, they quickly broke into another song:

Hangtown gals are plump and rosy,
Hair in ringlets, mighty cozy,
Painted cheeks and jossy bonnets—
Touch 'em and they'll sting like hornets!

With wide, satisfied grins they came closer to stand gazing up at her. Their bloodshot eyes traveled over her neat figure wrapped securely in the tobacco-brown cloak trimmed with wide strips of pale gold ribbon around the hem and arm slits. As Mara glanced away in disinterest, her profile became etched against the soft brown velvet brim of her bonnet.

"'Tis the fairest creature in all Fran Sancisco!" one of them cried as he bowed low, nearly falling to his knees in the mud. "'Twould sheem ash though I," he paused, frowning for a moment, then smiled triumphantly, "George Abraham West, could be of some asshistance to the lovely lady."

"I think not, thank you," Mara replied coolly.

The spokesman's friend gave a hoot of laughter at her snub, elbowing his friend in the ribs as he mimicked Mara's haughty refusal. "'I think not, thank you.' Well, I'll be damned if she ain't a lady, that one," he chuckled, "and mark my words, mate, she knew the man fer her when she set them bonny eyes on him."

With that sure statement, he stepped in front of his open-mouthed companion and introduced himself as he pulled his grimy hat from a headful of matted hair of unknown color.

"Freddie Watson, ma'am, born within spittin' distance of Bow bells, but more recently of Sydney, Australia," he explained with a knowing wink, "due to a slight misunderstanding with the law."

Quite a misunderstanding, Mara thought as she noticed his battered features and the crafty look in his eyes. He moved even closer and Mara could smell the whiskey fumes that seemed to permeate his clothing as well as his insides.

"How about you and me, luv, finding us someplace nice an' warm," he suggested, the look in his eyes turning lascivious as he added, "I ain't seen a piece as fancy as you since bein' transported from London. Got plenty o' gold in me pockets, luv, so ask yer price."

Mara turned away from the two drunken lotharios with an expression of repugnance crossing her features.

"Knew her man, did she!" the cockney's friend guffawed loudly. "Knew him for the wenching rascal that he is, I'd say."

But his friend wasn't listening as he stared in drunken anger at the slender caped figure starting to move away. "Too bloody good for the likes o' Freddie Watson, are ye? I've seen plenty o' yer type in London, so damned high and mighty, crossing to the other side o' the street when they sees me comin'," he spat, an ugly glint in his eye. He put one booted leg up on the edge of the sidewalk and made a grab at the hem of Mara's cloak, only to find himself falling wildly backward, a booted heel in the middle of his chest.

He struggled to rise in the slippery mud, a bellow hovering in his throat until he noticed the quietness of his friend. Following that fellow's fixed gaze, he stared up in bemused cowardliness at the rest of the six-foot-five body attached to that boot.

"Speaking of crossing to the other side of the street, gentlemen..." the stranger suggested in surprisingly quite tones, but then a man the size of a mountain seldom needed to raise his voice.

Mara watched in silent satisfaction as the two wretches picked themselves up and widened the distance between themselves and the giant. Mara turned to her rescuer. Looking up at the big man, a half-smile curving her lips, she said, "Now they certainly knew their man."

The big man smiled in appreciation, his broad face split with a widening grin of unholy amusement. "A man my size can usually bluff a smaller man."

"Well, thank you very much," Mara said with a warm smile.

"My pleasure, ma'am. Now if I may be of assistance to you," he said hesitantly, "I believe you wanted to cross the street?"

Before Mara knew what he was about, the big man scooped her up effortlessly and was striding purposefully across the muddy thoroughfare. Mara gazed incredulously into his face, not sure whether she should be outraged or thankful. But as Mara's eyes met his clear blue ones, she relaxed, instinctively knowing she had nothing to fear from this man. He was dressed well enough in a pair of light gray trousers that looked newly bought and a dark blue frock coat worn over a some-what gaudy, tartan-check vest. His thick blond hair was shiny, if a bit shaggy, and he sported a magnificent blond mustache of stunning proportions. Mara's eyes traveled on down his ruddy-complexioned face, taking in the strong line of jaw and the thick neck that proudly supported his leonine head.

He set Mara down carefully on the wooden boards of the sidewalk after staring hard at anyone unfortunate enough to be standing nearby. He reminded Mara of an overgrown watchdog.

"I think I'll be all right now," she reassured him. "I've been in San Francisco long enough now to know how to protect myself, especially with my little friend here," she added with a dangerous gleam in her eye. She pulled open her purse to reveal the small, pearl-handled derringer tucked within.

The big blond's blue eyes narrowed in thoughtful surprise. "Yes, ma'am, I can see that he would speak loudly and in your favor. But it's always good to know you've a friend around," he continued easily, "Though I reckon you know how to use our little friend there."

"Indeed I do," Mara replied lightly as she pulled shut her purse and began to move through the crowd. She felt a hand cup her elbow as the big man escorted her along the congested sidewalk, his bulk automatically clearing the way ahead. "I really can take care of myself," Mara told him as she craned her neck upward to see his face.

"Well, I've nothing better to do, ma'am. Thought I'd just see you to wherever you were headed," he explained with a wide grin. Mara couldn't help but respond warmly.

"Thank you," she said softly, smiling slightly as he glared at someone unwise enough to step in front of them. He was certainly a strange mixture of brawn and gentleness, Mara thought in amusement as they turned up Clay and moved away from the busy plaza and the big gambling saloons and hotels that lined it. Mara finally stopped before the plain doors of the boardinghouse in which they had been rooming. "This is where I shall leave you. Thank you again, and good-bye."

The big man glanced around curiously at the unassuming, two-storied wood and brick building. It was definitely a respectable house.

"I was pleased to be of service to you, ma'am. If you ever need me, the name's Karl Svengaard, but my friends call me the Swede."

"I'll remember that," Mara said, her golden eyes full of laughter as she smiled up at him. Then, with a slight nod, she turned to enter the boardinghouse.

The Swede quickly held the door open for her and called in after her, "I'm staying at the Parker House on Kearny."

Mara glanced back at him patiently. "Good-bye, Swede."

The Swede stood staring at the closed door a minute before turning and walking back down toward the plaza. Now there was a fine-looking woman, he thought. She was different from the brazen and coarse females who usually walked the streets and haunted the gaming halls, and yet she wasn't one of the strait-laced, sunbonneted women who'd come out across the plains to pioneer in the new land. No, the Swede speculated, she was definitely different. Maybe not respectable, but certainly a lady, and unfortunately not for him. She was more Nicholas's type, he thought with a grin as he imagined the Creole's green eyes meeting hers. Well, Nicholas would have to find her for himself. The Swede chuckled as he entered the saloon on his left, the loud music and laughing voices beckoning him inside and out of the cold wind.

Mara shivered as the door closed behind her. The hall was only slightly warmer than outside with draughts whistling in from the many cracks and ill-fitting boards.

As she stood there fumbling to remove her gloves and bonnet, she became aware of the proprietress of the boardinghouse standing quietly at the back of the hall. As she caught Mara's gaze, she smiled, softening the harassed look on her thin face as she closed the door to the kitchen behind her and came forward.

"Good afternoon, Miss O'Flynn," she greeted her. "Here, let me help you with that."

"Thank you, Mrs. Markham," Mara sighed as the woman helped her remove her heavy cloak.

"Please, I wish you'd call me Jenny," Mrs. Markham asked. "I feel like I know you better than anyone else in this fool town. After all, you have been here longer than any of my other boarders."

"Thank you, and my name is Mara. You're welcome to call me by it if you wish," she invited the other woman who couldn't be more than four or five years older than she was. Mara had often thought if Mrs. Markham would smile more, she would be quite an attractive woman. Of course, she didn't have much to amuse her, working from dawn until midnight trying to run a boardinghouse and raise her three young children. Mara shook her head. Jenny Markham hardly looked old enough to be the mother of that trio of roughneck, gamin-faced boys ranging in age from three to seven. With her fine-boned face under that incredible mop of tousled red hair, she seemed so young and innocent, as if she shouldn't have a care in the world.

Now Jenny Markham's eye avoided Mara's in embarrassment, her face flushing uncomfortably as she held Mara's cloak in her work-roughened hands. "Well, I'd be mighty honored, Miss O'Flynn, but for some reason it just don't seem right to be calling a person by their Christian name when they're a paying guest," she explained, shrugging her shoulders as she smiled shyly. "But I hope you'll call me Jenny still."

"Of course," Mara said with a cynical smile curving her lips as she accepted her cloak from Jenny, who seemed to be flustered as she saw the expression in Mara's tawny eyes. "If you'll excuse me, I want to take these sweets to Paddy."

"Oh, Jamie stepped out for a short spell, Miss O'Flynn," Jenny Markham called after her. "She took Paddy and a couple of my boys along. She said something about buying some new boots for the boy."

"That's right, I forgot they were going," Mara remembered.

"Ah, Miss O'Flynn," Jenny spoke suddenly. "I was just fixing myself a cup of coffee. If you'd care to join me…well, I'd sure like that."

Mara stared down at her in puzzlement. As she thought of the tempting coffee, she nodded her dark head in assent and followed her hostess into the room that served as a dining hall for her boarders. A long table that could probably have seated at least thirty or forty people stretched almost the length of the room, while a long bench ran the distance on each side. In the middle of the table were stacks of plates, cups and saucers, and cheap silverware.

A tray with an earthenware coffeepot and two matching cups and saucers and an unmatching sugar bowl had been placed on the end of the table near them. A plate with several small slices of cake had been added as well, and it was to this that Jenny Markham gestured in embarrassment.

"It's the last of the set. Most all of it except for a couple of plates and cups got broken on the trip out here, along with most everything else. I thought maybe you wouldn't mind having coffee in here, and maybe we could talk while I'm setting the table," she said hopefully.

Mara nodded and sat down with a curious look on her face. It seemed as though Jenny had been expecting her.

"I was hoping I'd see you when you came back in," Jenny answered Mara's silent query, "and we'd get this chance to talk. My smallest one is sleeping and most of the other boarders are out right now, so I've got a few moments for myself."

"Talk about what?" Mara asked as she waited for Jenny to pour the dark, freshly brewed coffee.

Jenny looked down into her cup thoughtfully, obviously ill at ease. "Just now when I said I'd rather call you Miss O'Flynn," she began, looking up frankly into Mara's golden brown eyes, "it wasn't because you're an actress, or that you work down at the Eldorado."

Mara's eyes began to warm a little as she listened to Jenny Markham's awkward explanation.

"I admit that when you first came here seeking rooms," Jenny said nervously, "I didn't think the kindest thoughts about you."

"I had gathered as much," Mara commented dryly as she took a sip of coffee.

Jenny's dark blue eyes traveled over Mara's elegant figure, not missing the pearl buttons closing the front of Mara's bodice jacket of dark brown velvet, or the edging of fine lace around the collar and cuffs. She made a wry face as she looked down at her own plain wool dress and practical apron. "I guess I was partly jealous. You're so pretty, and dress so fine, that I never gave myself a chance to like you. I thought you'd have a lot of men friends calling, and be real uppity. But no one ever comes to call on you, and I seldom see you with a man at least until today," Jenny corrected herself as she remembered the curly blond head that had been stuck inside the door with Miss O'Flynn.

"The gentle giant," Mara laughed as she remembered her rescuer. "He came to my assistance and rather handily routed two amorous drunks from my path. He says he's called the Swede."

Jenny smiled in understanding. "Even with my brood of redheads tagging along, I get proposals of marriage on nearly every street corner. I suppose if you're looking for a husband, it's the best place to be, but for us who'd rather be left alone, the shortage of females is a hazard. Besides, they just want someone to wash their shirts and fix them a decent meal. Do you know some of them actually send their dirty linen all the way to China to get washed?" Jenny demanded incredulously.

Mara shook her head in disgust, thinking it must be true if they were as helpless as Brendan. She could not imagine her brother fixing himself a meal, much less washing out his own clothes.

"I misjudged you, Miss O'Flynn," Jenny confessed, "and I wish you'd forgive me. I can tell you're a good person by the way you treat the boy. You love him a lot, and I reckon a person has to make a living the best way they can. So I hope you and I can be friends?"

"I'd like that, Jenny," Mara responded, "but don't expect too much of me, or paint me something I'm not. I'm not always a nice person, and I've made a lot of mistakes," Mara told her abruptly.

"All of us have things we'd like to forget," Jenny spoke softly, a look of remembered pain in her eyes.

"My brother Brendan's favorite saying is, 'I've got the divil ridin' on me shoulder, so don't be blamin' me.' And besides that," Mara laughed, "we're Irish."

"I'm afraid I don't have that excuse, although you would've thought as much the way I raised hell with John, my husband, when he told me about coming out here to California," Jenny confided with a rueful laugh. "I couldn't believe it when he told me he'd gone and sold the farm. We had a real nice one back in Ohio, and his folks lived nearby. We were doing pretty good, or so I thought. But I guess John just got kind of restless, wanted more out of life than he could ever get on the farm. It was just a small one and we'd never have gotten rich on it. But we were happy and making a decent living off it."

"You're a widow aren't you?" Mara asked gently.

Jenny nodded, sending numerous unruly curls cascading over her brow. "Yes, been one now for little over a year I guess. Funny how you lose track of time when you've got nothing to look forward to. You just live each day as it comes," she reflected sadly. Then, taking a sip of coffee, she continued on a lighter note, "I guess, you being from Ireland, you came around the Horn? A lot of people say that's one of the worst ways of doing it, but don't ever let someone talk you into coming across country. That's the way John and me did it. We joined up with a wagon train heading west from Council Bluffs on the Missouri River. We had a wagon and a team of oxen and what supplies we thought we'd need for the journey." Jenny laughed with a grimace of remembrance. "We had all our possessions packed in the wagon as well, including furniture. I even had my grandmother's fine cherry chest-of-drawers, but it went for firewood about two months out. In fact, most of the furniture ended up in the fire 'cause the wagon needed to be lightened. We left Iowa in May and started out across the plains knowing we'd have to make at least sixteen miles a day if we were to make it across the mountains before the snows came. Nobody wanted to get trapped up there like the Donner party did in 'forty-six. We were up at daybreak getting breakfast, burning buffalo chips when we couldn't find enough kindling, packing, and hitching up the wagons to move on a little bit more each day. There was always a river to be crossed or a water hole to be reached before we could stop and get some of the dust out of our eyes. Of course, there was always the threat of Indians attacking us, but I think it was the sudden storms and the sickness that scared me the most. I thought for sure the heavens were going to fall in one day when it rained so hard and the thunder was deafening, but it wasn't until the next day when we had to cross the rain-swollen river that I realized how awful it'd really been when one of the wagons got swept downstream by the current. I guess we were lucky that we even got as far as that; a lot of people died when the cholera hit the train and took twenty people in one night, and it seemed as though there was always a grave to be dug for someone who'd caught something or hurt himself in some accident. Since we didn't have a doctor along, there wasn't much that we could do."

She shook her head. "I remember how happy we were to cross the Rockies, little realizing we still had deserts to cross and another mountain range to climb before we even got to California. That's when we started losing more of the wagons and the animals began to lag behind, finally dropping dead beside the trail, just too tired to go on. But we had to keep going on. We couldn't turn back. There was no place to go. I didn't think we'd ever get through that desert. I stared out on miles and miles of sand stretching away into the distance, and seeing the skeletons of wagon trains that hadn't made it—the bleached bones of their animals, all the graves—well, it still haunts me. But finally we got across, and John and me and the three little ones actually made it to California."

Jenny placed her empty coffee cup on the table. Noticing Mara's empty cup, she refilled it and offered her a piece of cake.

"What happened to your husband?"

"Don't seem right somehow for a man to come through all that alive and then get killed here in San Francisco by a runaway freight wagon as he stepped outside for a breath of fresh air. Such a senseless sort of thing to happen."

"I'm sorry, Jenny," Mara said and reached out to touch Jenny's hand. It was the first gesture of comfort Mara had ever made to a stranger.

"Well, it's over now, and I've got to make do with what I have."

"Did you never think of going back home?"

Jenny shook her head. "I suppose I thought about it, but what's back there for me now? My folks have been dead for years, and John's folks are too old and poor to support me and the kids. I guess here's as good a place as any to raise a family."

Jenny stood up as she heard the front door open and the sound of voices. Mara gathered up her cloak and bonnet as she recognized Jamie's shrill brogue.

"I'd better go see what Paddy's up to. Thank you for the coffee. I enjoyed our talk."

"I'm real glad we had it, Mara," Jenny said, deciding suddenly to forego convention. "Have you heard from your brother yet?"

"No, and I'm not likely to either," Mara responded. "Brendan will show up in his own good time."

As Mara walked to the door, two redheaded little boys rushed in, nearly knocking her over. "Sorry, ma'am," the tallest of the two said as he dodged past her and ran up to Jenny. "Gordie and me got new boots too, Mama! Same kind as Paddy!"

Paddy was only a step behind his friend, but Mara was quicker and managed to grab hold of him as he careened into her. "There is such a thing as walking like a gentleman into a room, Padraic," Mara spoke in exasperation.

"I'm sorry, Mara," Paddy apologized quickly, then grinned up at her with Brendan's dimple showing in the softness of his cheek as he added proudly, "Did you see my new boots!"

Mara looked down, putting on a show of carefully inspecting their color and shape. "Very nice, Paddy," Mara approved. She had to admit they were more practical than shoes in these muddy streets. He seemed so grown up in them. Indeed, he had grown a lot in the past year, besides turning seven years old.

Jamie entered and now stood behind the three boys as they lined up proudly before Jenny, showing off their brand new, knee-high boots. Both Jenny and Mara wondered how Jamie had managed to pay for all three pairs.

Jenny looked between Mara and Jamie, then back at her two boys, a look of regret on her face as she shook her head. "I don't see how we can pay for these. I'm sorry, boys, but you'll have to give them back," she told them.

"Now, now," Jamie interrupted the cries of protest from Paul and Gordie. "There's no need for that. I got them all on sale from a man who'd bought a whole wagon load of them, only to find most of them too small for his customers. He was sellin' them real cheap, ma'am," Jamie explained, "and to be sure, all the boys needed new boots. Thought 'twas too good a chance to be passin' up. Ye can be payin' Miss Mara back sometime later. There's no hurry."

Jenny stared down at her boys' pleading faces and nodded in agreement. "Very well, but I'll want an exact billing for it, Jamie, and thank you," she added with a grateful smile as the three boys started jumping around the room, Gordie and Paul copying the Irish jig Paddy was dancing.

"Got them real cheap indeed," Mara whispered to Jamie as they left the room. "If those are the ones I saw in the window of the general store around the corner, they cost more like forty dollars a pair."

"Closer to twenty-five," Jamie admitted, "but they were marked down, bein' so small, and her boys needed them real bad."

"I suppose so," Mara agreed, not seeing the surprised look on Jamie's face as she failed to make an issue out of the expense. The little woman followed Mara upstairs, shaking her grizzled head in disbelief.

"I'll just have to smile more seductively at my customers tonight and look a bit longer into their leering, bloodshot eyes if I'm to make up the difference in tips. You'd be surprised how much they pay for you to just sit and have a drink with them."

"Wish ye weren't workin' in that place," Jamie said, not for the first time. "And I'm not likin' that gambler ye be workin' for either."

"Jamie," Mara said, trying to make her understand, "you know I can't earn enough in the theater to live on, much less support you and Paddy. I can earn more in one night by just sitting at Jacques's tables, drawing the customers to him, than I could half a year on the stage. He pays me well enough, Jamie. I'm not complaining."

"Well, I still don't like it. 'Tisn't decent workin' in a place like that, all of them men ogling ye and pawin' ye," she said even as she shook out Mara's gown for the evening and set aside the accessories to be worn with it.

"And do you think I like it any better?" Mara asked as she looked out on the rain that was falling more heavily now. Soon the whole street would be under a river of muddy water. "It won't be for too much longer. Brendan'll be coming soon. He'll come, Jamie, just you wait and see."

❧

"Come along, monsieur, place your bet, perhaps *ce soir* is your lucky night, and this your lucky numbaire," Mara said, feigning a light French accent. The gentlemen seemed to find the Frenchwoman the most attractive and alluring, showing their preference in the size of their tips. Mara spun the roulette wheel around, her golden eyes watching in cynical amusement as the miners' eyes watched hopefully for their lucky number to come up. The small ball sped past each number until finally rolling to a stop in one of the numbered compartments. "Sorry, monsieur. I guess tonight wasn't your lucky night, after all."

It seldom was, Mara thought as she collected each miner's money and gold and gave the wheel another spin. She glanced around the large room crowded with green baize tables and every sort of individual imaginable, his race or dress unimportant as long as he had gold in his pockets. At one end of the room was a long bar lined with cut-glass decanters. A small band of musicians played on the edge of a stage nearby, and a troupe of dancers was performing a lively number, much to the pleasure of the front row of spectators. Mirrors and suggestive paintings hung on the wall-papered walls, while rich, crimson curtains draped the long window. Above the gamblers' heads hung ornate glass chandeliers, their light filtering down through the smoke that floated up from the countless cigars and cigarettes. The thick, heavy air was filled with whiskey fumes, sweat from unwashed bodies, stale perfume, and the Chinese punk that smoldered for the convenience of smokers.

This saloon was no different from all of the others that lined Portsmouth Square. Whether it was the Eldorado, Bella Union, Parker House, or Verandah, they all offered the same attractions—all for the price of gold mined in the Sierra Nevada.

Mara was rudely startled from her thoughts as she felt someone kiss her bare shoulder. She turned around sharply, ready to deliver a scathing set-down, and found herself staring into the dark eyes of Jacques D'Arcy.

He smiled slightly as he noted the antagonism in Mara's eyes. "Mara," he softly scolded her, "you never smile for poor Jacques. Yet you smile so enticingly for these fools."

"That is what I'm getting paid for, remember?" Mara said coldly, pulling her arm free of his possessively caressing hand.

"I could pay you, ma petite, for certain favors," Jacques said very softly, his dark eyes glowing. They seemed to burn into Mara's skin as they slowly traveled across the smooth swell of breast revealed by the décolletage of the red velvet dress she had worn for the first time tonight.

Mara silently cursed herself for being so stupid. She knew it had been a mistake to wear the dress. In fact, it had caused her nothing but trouble since she had first set eyes on it back in London. She had been speechless with surprised dismay when Jamie had unfolded it from her trunk. It must have still been in her room when Don Andres's servants packed her things. Naturally they had assumed it was hers. Jamie's gasp had been slightly louder, for she hadn't seen the dress since returning it to its owner on that fateful day long ago. When she'd learned who Nicholas really was, she'd just sat down on the edge of the bed, shaking her head, saying nothing.

Mara supposed she had worn the dress because she had wanted something different to wear, something besides the same few dresses she had worn over and over again. And partly out of defiance. She had wanted to prove to herself that she could forget Nicholas, that the memories associated with the dress meant nothing to her any longer. But she had been wrong. Even the feel of the soft velvet against her skin made her think of Nicholas's hands as they had caressed her in love—and of their hurting strength when he'd grabbed her while in a black rage upon discovering her true identity.

"No thank you, Jacques," Mara replied sweetly, "I'm not that desperate yet, and I'm not your petite."

Jacques's smile curved into a cruel sneer, "Someday you will want me, Mara, and then you will have to beg for my favors. But until then, ma petite," he said purposefully, "you either do your job, or I fire you."

"I do my job well, Jacques," Mara replied tartly. "And besides, you wouldn't want me working for another gambler, would you? Taking away your business? Because you know I would."

Jacques stared into her defiantly upraised face and the contempt she didn't bother to hide. She smiled that enticing half-smile of hers. "No one would want a woman with a scarred face to sit at their table and deal faro or drink with the customers…eh, ma petite?" Jacques spoke softly, running the tip of his finger across Mara's smooth alabaster cheek. "And the lover who once, I think, must have called you his petite would no longer care to look upon you. Just remember that you work for me, and no one else," Jacques warned. Then, shaking his head, he added, "I don't know why you waste your time here at the tables when you could be asking five hundred dollars a customer upstairs. You are a foolish woman, ma petite, to be so selective about who shares your bed."

"I'm not a courtesan, Jacques," Mara told him coldly as she glared up into his sallow face. For the first time, she felt a deep fear of this Frenchman. She had managed so far to repulse his attentions, for he knew her value as an employee. But as time had passed and his pockets filled, he became bolder. Mara knew that soon she would not be able to laugh away his advances.

"Come, I want you at the faro table. There are some big players anxious to have you deal for them," Jacques told her as he signaled for another woman to take over the roulette wheel.

Mara followed Jacques across the room, conscious of the eyes following her figure in the revealing red velvet dress. But even she wasn't aware of the full impact of her startling beauty on the love-starved miners, many homesick for wives and sweethearts, others longing for the companionship of a beautiful woman. Yet there was something about Mara that stopped them from reaching out and grabbing greedily at the soft velvet skirts that rustled past their legs, or touching the pale, scented skin of her bare shoulders as she threaded her way through them. There was a ladylike quality about her, an air of breeding that made a man keep his distance.

Mara sat down at the green baize table, accepting the long-stemmed glass of champagne placed at her elbow as she smiled at the gentlemen sitting across from her. She placed a complete suit of spades in a thirteen card layout on the table and waited for the players to place their bets on the card of their choice. Then, the faro box in front of her, she played the banker and prepared to withdraw from the box in pairs the cards that decided whether a man won or lost. If he placed his gold by the eight of spades in the layout and the eight of hearts were turned over first, then he lost. If the eight didn't show up in either card turned, his bet remained. But if it were the second card turned, he won his bet and the dealer had to pay.

Mara had acted as faro banker for more than two hours and was beginning to grow tired. The smoke and noise pressed in on her. Several of her customers had grown as tired of losing and were withdrawing their bets and moving on to other games of chance. Mara paused for a moment to take a sip of champagne while their places were quickly filled, and didn't even bother to glance up into their expectant faces. After a while they all looked the same.

"If monsieur would care to place his bet," Mara spoke in her mock French accent as she filled the faro box with cards, "this could be his lucky night, perhaps monsieur will even win a fortune, one nevaire knows in a game of chance."

Mara glanced up, a smile softly curving her lips as she stared into the gaze of the player who'd just filled the vacant seat in front of her. The smile stiffened painfully as her eyes locked with the mocking green eyes she knew so well.

"Well, well, I didn't realize you were French as well as Irish, English, and Spanish," Nicholas Chantale said. "You do have a colorful past, Mara. Or are you going by another name? Perhaps Angelique, or Desiree?" Nicholas laughed in pleased amusement at the shock she could not hide. "You seem startled to see me. You didn't suppose that vicious blow to the back of my head had killed me, did you?" Nicholas asked in a voice that only she could hear as the music and laughing voices swirled loudly around them.

"Come on, now. I've placed me bet. Let's deal," a man on Nicholas's right called out impatiently.

"Yes, mademoiselle, please do not waste my time," Nicholas agreed with a hateful curl of his sensuous lips, "for you must please me if you want a generous tip for your gracious hostessing."

Mara ground her teeth as she dealt the cards and watched in increasing annoyance as Nicholas won turn after turn.

"The mademoiselle is a fortune-teller as well," Nicholas laughed as he collected his winnings after an hour's successful play. "She predicted that tonight would be my lucky night."

Nicholas reached out and grasped Mara's wrist with hard fingers as he added in a soft voice that only Mara could hear,

"And I insist that the mademoiselle share a glass of champagne and a light supper with me."

"I think not," Mara said in a tight voice as she tried to pull her wrist free. As she glanced around helplessly, she became aware of Jacques standing nearby and watching her table with curious eyes.

"There seems to be some trouble here?" he asked smoothly as he came up behind Mara's chair. "I can assure the monsieur that I run honest tables, and my dealers are above suspicion. If you think you have been cheated, then I will certainly deal harshly with this woman."

Mara glanced up in surprise at Jacques's suddenly subservient manner. He was practically falling on his hands and knees before Nicholas, Mara thought in dismayed anger.

"That won't be necessary. As you can see, I have no complaints," Nicholas said as he gestured to his pile of winnings, "but I should like the lady to join me at my table for a drink. It would be well worth her while, as well as yours, monsieur," Nicholas said silkily. "I believe you take a percentage of the mademoiselle's tips?"

Jacques smiled slightly, his eyes showing a momentary flash of anger at Nicholas's contemptuously spoken words. But he only nodded. "The mademoiselle is free to join you, monsieur." Mara glared up at Jacques, disbelief showing in her eyes as he snapped his fingers and a blond woman appeared to take Mara's place at the table.

"Go with him, Mara," Jacques ordered her. "Michelle will take over for you here."

Mara had little choice, unless she wished to make a scene. With Nicholas's fingers still wrapped around her wrist, she got up from the table and followed him to a table in the corner of the room. She adopted her haughtiest demeanor and ungraciously declined a glass of champagne.

"I thought a table against the wall the safest," Nicholas began, catching Mara's attention with the fury in his voice, "just in case that *cousin* of yours happens to be lurking under the floorboards."

"He was only trying to protect me from your attack," Mara defended Brendan. "And he happens to be my brother."

"I should have guessed at the closer relationship, considering his lack of character," Nicholas jeered. "It certainly lends credence to the saying, 'as thick as thieves.'"

Mara frowned. "And just what is that supposed to mean? Brendan and I are not thieves."

Nicholas raised his heavy eyebrows questioningly. "Aren't you, Mara O'Flynn? It doesn't surprise me to learn that you are a liar as well as a thief. You O'Flynns are incredible, completely without conscience, to hit a man from behind, and then steal him blind while he's unconscious."

Mara licked her lips, her mouth uncomfortably dry as she suddenly remembered the money Brendan had given her in Sonoma. Mara's face showed her confusion and dismay as she looked up into Nicholas's pitiless eyes. "I—I didn't know about the money, Nicholas. I swear I didn't. You must believe me. I did not know Brendan had taken it. I'd never take your money. You know I wouldn't."

Nicholas lightly clapped his hands, his even teeth showing as he grinned mockingly. "Your protestation of innocence is brilliant, my dear, with just the right touch of suffering in those beautiful golden eyes. Did I not know you better, I would surely believe you knew nothing of the theft. A nice try, but I remain unconvinced."

"You bastard," Mara said softly, trying desperately to hide her love and the hurt she felt at his sneering words. "Who the divil d'ye think you are, that you can harass me this way," she said to him in a quivering voice. She fumbled inside her purse, her shaking fingers closing over the pile of coins she'd received in tips for the evening. With an eloquent gesture she pushed them across the table to Nicholas. "This should more than repay you for your money."

"Tch, tch," Nicholas said with a satisfied smile, contemptuously ignoring her proffered restitution, "your Irish temper is showing, ma petite. But it's most enlightening, so do continue. I look forward to meeting the true Mara O'Flynn at last."

Mara sighed in exasperation. "Nicholas, leave me alone. Haven't you had revenge enough against me?"

Nicholas stared at Mara's delicate features. Though she was

thinner than the last time he'd seen her, she was more beautiful than ever. She glared at him in defiance, her full, lower lip trembling slightly. "Perhaps what I want from you is more than just your virgin's blood," he speculated softly, his green eyes as cold and hard as emeralds.

Mara moved her hand, feeling the smooth, crystal stem beneath her fingers as she picked up the goblet of champagne and threw the whole contents of it into Nicholas's arrogant face. She stared in bemusement as the pale liquid fell in drops onto his white shirtfront, staining the clean linen. Mara got shakily to her feet as he pulled out a handkerchief and began to wipe the champagne from his face, his eyes never leaving her stunned face.

"You never disappoint me, Mara," Nicholas said.

But Mara waited to hear no more. Turning, she began to frantically make her way through the room, finding her path blocked by gamblers milling around the room, some almost too drunk to stand as they staggered aimlessly from table to bar and back again. She finally managed to push her way through the noisy throng, but as she neared the back entrance, she jumped in alarm as hard fingers closed over her arm. Turning to face her captor, Mara stared, almost in relief, into the dark eyes of Jacques D'Arcy.

"Mon Dieu!" he exclaimed as he pulled her into the quiet darkness of the hallway. "I could scarcely believe my eyes when I saw you throw that champagne into Chantale's face. I would bet my life that no one has ever done that to him before—and lived to talk about it," Jacques said, his face still registering disbelief at the odd scene he'd just witnessed.

"You know Nicholas?" Mara asked dully.

"Nicholas, is it?" Jacques demanded, his gaze sharpening as he stared down at her pale, distraught face. "Well, well, I should like to hear more about this relationship with a man you obviously dislike and seem to fear. But in answer to your question," Jacques continued with a reminiscent look in his dark eyes, "oui. Anyone who'd ever lived in New Orleans would have heard of Nicholas de Montaigne-Chantale. When I saw him in Paris a few years ago, he had dropped part of the name. He belongs to one of the richest and most aristocratic families in all of Louisiana. Or at least he used to, until he was run out of town. The de Montaigne-Chantale plantation, Beaumarais, was famous throughout the state."

"Nicholas told me he had to leave New Orleans, fifteen years ago, I think," Mara said. "Because of a duel."

Jacques smiled. "Oh, but it was not just any duel, *ma chérie.* You see," Jacques explained as he lowered his voice confidingly, "he killed his brother, François, who happened to be not only the heir to the de Montaigne-Chantale fortune, but the fiancé of the beautiful Amaryllis Sandonet. It had been rumored that it was Nicholas she really loved. It was said that they had been lovers before the lovely Amaryllis's papa affianced her to the heir to Beaumarais. Some say that Amaryllis wanted both Beaumarais *and* Nicholas, and that they continued to be lovers—discreetly, of course. But you know how these secrets have a way of becoming known," Jacques said with a wink, "and then one day before the marriage could take place, there was a duel between the two brothers. What the disagreement was about one can only speculate, although Nicholas Chantale claimed there was no argument, that they were only practicing. But what better way to rid oneself of a bitter rival? In an instant," Jacques spoke softly, snapping his fingers sharply, "Nicholas de Montaigne-Chantale gained both the plantation and the woman. Unfortunately, though, François had been his papa's favorite. He could not even bear to gaze upon the son who had killed his heir. So he banished him from Beaumarais, never to set foot there again, refusing to recognize Nicholas when they met in town. After a while, no door in all of New Orleans opened in welcome for the infamous Nicholas Chantale. A sad tale, *non?*"

Mara listened in disbelief, shaking her head. "He killed his own brother? I can't believe it," Mara whispered.

Jacques's fingers grasped her chin as he raised her face. "You are in love with him, aren't you?"

"No!" Mara denied fervently.

"Bah! You lie," Jacques spat. With a strange light in his

dark eyes he asked, "But what does Chantale feel for you, ma chérie? It would be most interesting to find out."

"He means nothing to me," Mara cried, grabbing Jacques's arm as she forced him to listen, "and I mean even less to him. In fact, he hates me. So I wouldn't be talking to him about me if I were you."

Jacques smiled unpleasantly as he moved closer to Mara. He pressed her back to the wall, holding her against it with the weight of his body. "I think in the future you will be much nicer to your admirer, Jacques, non? You are a very beautiful and intelligent woman who knows who her friends are."

"What do you mean?" Mara asked, turning her face away from the closeness of his lips.

"It is most simple, ma chérie. I do not think you would wish for Monsieur Chantale to know where you live, eh?" Jacques asked softly, his eyes glittering as he lowered his lips to her mouth, his fingers holding her chin in a hard grip.

His mouth was greedy as it devoured hers. Mara could feel the painful press of his teeth into the softness of her lips. His kiss deepened in intensity as he strained her closer against his body, leaving her in little doubt of his passion. Mara managed to free her lips from his suffocating mouth as she gasped for breath, only to feel Jacques's hard, brushing kisses along her throat. His hands fumbled to push the red velvet from her shoulders, leaving the soft, tender skin bared to his searching mouth.

When she felt his tongue slide along the crest of her breast, she could stand no more. Raising her knee, she quickly and accurately kneed him in the groin. As Jacques let out a surprised gasp of pain, doubling over, Mara escaped from him. She moved out of reach down the hall.

"You can find someone else to work for you. I quit," Mara flung at him as she searched for her cloak, hanging with an assortment of outer garments on a rack near the door. "Go on and tell Nicholas Chantale anything you wish. I don't care what you do as long as I'm not having to suffer your foul hands pawing and fondling me all the time. *Bon soir*, Monsieur D'Arcy," Mara called defiantly as she stepped out into the night and the fresh, cold air. She slammed the door behind her with finality.

The next morning Mara had a twinge of doubt about her hasty actions. But as she remembered the feel of Jacques's lips, she gave an involuntary shudder of disgust. Now she was faced with the disagreeable problem of finding employment, for unless she had misjudged her man, Jacques was not one to forgive and forget. He would see that no other gambler hired her...as well as possibly making good his threat. She touched her smooth cheek with a shiver.

Well, she wouldn't worry about it now, Mara decided as she made her way downstairs. She had enough saved to live comfortably for at least a month, and she'd prefer not to cross paths with Nicholas again—especially as he had yet another grievance to add to the long list he carried against her. Mara wrapped her shawl closer around her shoulders as she sought more warmth from the finely woven, white wool garment she wore over her simply cut yet elegant blue and white gown of shot silk.

Mara heard voices coming from the room Jenny had designated as the salon. It was a plain room with six or seven straight-back chairs, a sofa of questionable origin, and a scarred-top table. Jenny had done her best to create a homey atmosphere, and Mara had to admit that it wasn't all that bad, especially with a cheery fire crackling in the fireplace.

Jenny was sitting near the fire, her lap cluttered with odds and ends of clothing. She glanced up, smiling behind the end of the needle and thread protruding from her mouth. Taking the needle from between her lips, Jenny shrugged good-naturedly. "If it's not washing and cooking, then it's mending. Especially," she said with a laugh as she eyed her youngest crawling under the sofa in search of a toy, "if they're on their hands and knees all day long."

Mara eyed Paddy who, with Jenny's two oldest boys, was playing with his toy soldiers. She sidestepped through strategically placed troops as she made her way to Jenny's side. "I suppose boys just have to get dirty or tear something if they're going to have fun," Mara remarked casually as she sat down across from a chuckling Jenny.

"Hey! I take exception to that remark," a deep voice spoke from behind the sofa, startling Mara. She turned around to see the Swede's blond head rising above its cushioned back. "I dare you to find a tear in my coat, and damned if—pardon me, ma'am—darned if I'm going to get these new breeches dirty," the Swede said as he stood up to his full height and came around from behind the sofa, the retrieved soldier's red hat just barely peeking out of his large hand.

"Now don't let this fellow wander off again," he warned Peter who eagerly reached out for the brightly painted toy soldier.

"Come on, Petey," Gordie called out, "you're holding up the war!"

The Swede was smiling broadly as he stepped gingerly over a whole regiment of dragoons. Easily lifting a chair, he placed it near Mara's and sat down. "Don't need to tell me which three are Mrs. Markham's. That red hair's a sure giveaway, and I don't need to ask who the dark one belongs to, 'cause he gave me hell when I nearly stepped on one of his troops," the Swede laughed. "'The divil take ye!' he told me, and damned if I've ever heard it spoken any finer than that," the Swede said. Then, glancing uncomfortably between Mara and Jenny, he added, "I'm sorry, ladies. I guess I'd better mind *my* tongue as well."

"That's quite all right, Mr. Svengaard," Jenny told him. "I'm used to that kind of talk by now. It's hard to close your eyes and ears forever to a town full of fun-loving miners."

"And Paddy's probably just copying what he's heard me say, so I can hardly fault you, Swede," Mara told him with a slight smile.

The Swede grinned engagingly, his eyes locked on Mara's face as he took in the creamy complexion and golden eyes that were partially hidden behind a thick fringe of dark lashes. He sighed as he took in her beauty, his eyes noticing the smallest detail about her appearance, from the delicate gold earrings to her small, blue satin shoes.

Jenny gave an inaudible sigh as she discreetly watched the big man openly admire Mara. She bit her lip when she carelessly jabbed her fingertip with the needle. It served her right for daydreaming about things that never would be, or could be, she thought in self-disgust. What man would even glance her way when someone as beautiful as Mara O'Flynn was sitting in the same room? Besides, what man would desire a bride with three small sons? It might be true that women of good reputation were scarce in California, and that just about any woman could find a husband, but that didn't mean she would accept a proposal from just any man. She could make a living for herself and her sons until she found the right man, and until that day she didn't mind living on her own. Even so, her dark blue eyes noticed the wide breadth of shoulder and the gentle expression in the Swede's blue eyes. "The gentle giant," Mara O'Flynn had named him. She was right. There was a gentleness in him which was surprising in so large a man. She had been amazed at his patient attention to her boys and Paddy as they'd run noisily around the room, creating havoc in their exuberant play.

"Are you staying here in San Francisco permanently, Swede?" Mara inquired conversationally, wondering if perhaps he owned a store or a business of some kind in the city.

"I'm living here for now. Maybe forever—who knows? But I'm just recently down from the Sierra," the Swede told her, then added casually, "me and my partner struck a rich vein of gold and thought we'd celebrate."

A spark of interest lit Mara's eyes. She leaned closer toward the big man, and the Swede felt an instant's disappointment that she would be so obvious. He expected to hear her ask him how rich he was, but was surprised when he heard her say, "Did you ever meet a man named Brendan O'Flynn? He was going up into the mountains to mine for gold late last summer. I thought you might have run into him, or have heard something about him."

The Swede shook his head regretfully. "I'm sorry, I don't believe I know him. O'Flynn? Your husband, is he?" he asked, unable to mask the disappointment in his voice.

"No, he's my brother, Paddy's father," Mara explained.

"Oh, I see," the Swede beamed, relieved. "Of course, just because I don't remember his name doesn't mean I might not have met him, or even bunked with him, or played a hand of poker with him. You see so many men up there coming and going, you lose track of them after a while and don't even bother to catch a name. I can see you're worried about him, Miss O'Flynn, but you really shouldn't be. The camps aren't half as bad as they've been painted by those who haven't been there."

Mara eyed the big Swede thoughtfully as she wondered if a man like him ever found anything difficult. With his sturdy constitution she doubted if he even felt the cold discomfort surrounding him. Brendan, on the other hand, would feel each raindrop, each meal burned over an open fire, each blister on his hands from raising a pick, as insults meant for him personally. "Brendan is less hardy than you," Mara tried to explain her fears without insulting the big Swede, "more delicate and—"

"More refined, ma'am," the Swede said with a chuckle. "Not a big, lumbering ox like myself."

Mara had to smile at the accuracy of his description. "I wouldn't have put it quite that way. However, Brendan is less familiar with physical labor than most, having been raised a gentleman and earning his living as an actor. I seriously doubt whether Brendan's ever held a pick or shovel in his life."

The Swede laughed as he remembered other dandies he'd seen sweating away their refinements as they hunted for gold. "I've seen too many men change their silk vests for red flannel and their patent leather pumps for heavy boots while looking for gold, to believe your brother won't as well. He may learn the hard way, but he'll learn," the Swede assured her.

Mara frowned slightly as she remembered the echo of another man's voice telling her how he'd gotten rid of his gentlemanly ways. And she had personal, firsthand knowledge that he'd succeeded, Mara thought unhappily. "I suppose you are right."

"Oh, I am. In fact, a friend of mine was once quite a dandy, but you'd never believe it to see him now. Of course, Nicholas would probably be even more handsome to the ladies in New Orleans now than he even was years ago when every skirt in town was after him," the Swede said with a reminiscent smile. He stopped as he saw the stunned look crossing Mara's face.

"What's wrong, Miss O'Flynn?" he asked in concern, hoping he hadn't offended her. He was always so damned clumsy.

Mara hesitated before she asked softly, "Your friend wouldn't happen to be Nicholas Chantale, would he?"

The Swede nodded slightly, puzzled by her sigh of tired disappointment. "Do you know him?" he asked, then shook his head mockingly. "I should have realized Nicholas would know a woman as beautiful as you. I never have been able to get the jump on him yet. I don't blame him for not having mentioned you, 'cause I didn't say anything about you to him either," the Swede admitted sheepishly.

"Then you don't know anything about me?" Mara asked carefully, her tawny eyes watching his face.

The Swede continued to stare at her openly. "And what more should I know about you except that you're one of the most beautiful women I've ever met?" he said earnestly, having forgotten for the moment the presence of Jenny, across from him. He stared deeply into Mara's eyes, a look of longing in his soft blue eyes.

As Mara recognized the look, she suddenly realized the extent of her power over him. Using her beauty as an intoxicant, she might even be able to destroy the friendship between the Swede and Nicholas, planting doubts and lies in the Swede's mind about Nicholas. But the feeling faded. Mara knew that she couldn't do it. Instead, she would probably lose the Swede's friendship, for Nicholas would not leave him in the dark about her for long, once he knew the Swede was seeing her.

"I'm afraid Nicholas thinks me anything but beautiful," Mara told him bluntly, deciding to geld that stallion before he could become too troublesome. By telling the Swede the truth about her relationship with his friend, Nicholas could not completely prejudice the Swede against her.

"I can't believe he'd think that," the Swede protested in disbelief. "Nicholas isn't blind, and he's always had a deep appreciation for a beautiful woman. And no offense intended, ma'am, but I can't quite believe you repulsed his advance either, for Nicholas can be a very determined man."

Mara smiled reluctantly. "I've found that out, much to my discomfort, Swede. Nicholas is also an unforgiving man, and when he takes a dislike to a person and feels there's a debt to be paid...well, he's quite relentless in collecting what's due him, isn't he?" Mara asked in a tight voice.

The Swede sat quietly watching her, aware that she was losing her composure as she talked about Nicholas. He glanced uncomfortably at Jenny but was relieved to see her busily sewing, her red head bent as she worked. He glanced back at Mara, leaning forward on his knees. "You don't need to tell me anything if you'd rather not, but I really can't see Nicholas wishing you ill, or doing you any harm. He's a reasonable man, and an honorable one, despite any rumors you might have heard to the contrary," he defended his friend.

Mara laughed abruptly as she looked around the room, avoiding the Swede's honest gaze as she admitted, "I suppose he has reason to hate me. You see...I caused the death, no suicide, of his nephew Julian in London a few years ago. He swore he'd make me pay. And he has."

Mara finally looked into the Swede's eyes, surprised to see a puzzled frown in them. "I'm confused, Miss O'Flynn. Are you sure you couldn't have misunderstood Nicholas? The only nephew Nicholas has named Julian, and living in London, is alive."

Mara's lips parted slightly in surprise. "Alive? Julian's still living? He didn't die from the gunshot wound?" Mara repeated in a whisper more to herself than to the Swede. "And all these years I had his death on my conscience." Mara's eyes suddenly seemed to glow with a bronzed light as she angrily remembered what Nicholas had allowed her to believe. "He let me go on thinking I killed Julian," she spoke more loudly as she glanced up into the Swede's worried face. "How could he hate me so much he'd have me believe Julian dead?"

"Nicholas told you that?" the Swede asked in disbelief. "That doesn't sound like him. Are you sure we're talking about the same Nicholas Chantale?"

"Mocking green eyes, cruelly sneering mouth, and a sarcastic tongue in a ruggedly handsome face," was Mara's brief description.

The Swede nodded his big blond head in agreement, a smile of appreciation curving his wide mouth upward. "That's the Creole, sure enough. But I'll be damned if I've ever heard of him acting quite so vindictive before."

Mara looked over at Jenny who had given up pretending to mend the socks still held in her hands. She openly listened now to the conversation. "You might as well hear the worst of it too. I'd rather it came from me than an unfriendly party."

"I can leave," Jenny offered in embarrassment as she started to rise.

"No, please," Mara said, waving her back into her seat. "I believe I told you once before that I'd made mistakes. Well, this is one that has come back to haunt me. You see—I was the cause of a young man taking his own life. Or at least," Mara corrected herself, "I thought he'd taken it. Of course, the undisputable fact is that he tried, and I was the reason why. I played a very cruel game with his love, spurning him, ridiculing him, but you must believe me," Mara told them, her eyes unconsciously pleading with them, "I never meant him to try and take his life. I was wrong, I know that now, and I deeply regret how I treated him. I can't excuse my actions. They were vicious and calculated. Nicholas has every right to hate me. But I have been punished for my sins, and Nicholas unknowingly has had his revenge, so must I go on paying for a mistake?" Mara demanded defiantly as she stared at the two silent people. "If you want to tell Nicholas where I am, then go ahead. He'd probably find me soon enough anyway. And if you'd rather not continue to visit me, then I'd not blame you. After all, Nicholas is your friend."

The Swede rubbed his chin in perplexity. "Thank you for telling me all this. You needn't have, but I admire you for your honesty."

Mara laughed in genuine amusement. "No one has ever paid me that compliment before. I'm afraid I'm not very good at confession. I'm quite out of practice."

"Well, I don't think any of us likes to admit we've been wrong. I know I don't," the Swede laughed, easing the tense atmosphere with his deep chuckle. "You didn't by any chance happen to run into Nicholas last night as well, did you?"

Mara nodded. "Yes, as a matter of fact I did. Why?"

"I just wondered. He was in such a foul mood that I was curious. Nicholas isn't one to speak aloud his private thoughts. That's why I've never heard of you before. And although I knew about Nicholas's nephew, I never knew the exact details concerning the incident. I didn't know you then, I only know the woman you are now, so I won't judge you on the past. What is between you and Nicholas is none of my affair," the Swede told Mara, but he made up his mind to hear Nicholas's version as well.

"Since I'm clearing my conscience, I probably should tell you of Nicholas's latest grievance against me, which involves a deception played on him and the loss of his money. I knew nothing about his money—not that he believes a word I say—but he has reason to be angry once again, so I don't think he shall ever forgive me. Too much has happened to destroy whatever faith in me he might once have had."

Mara glanced over at Jenny and shrugged. "I told you I wasn't very nice. Do you still want to be friends?"

Jenny pushed a bright red curl from her forehead as she smiled gently, realizing for the first time that behind the facade of hauteur she protectively wrapped around herself, the beautiful Irishwoman was really very vulnerable. "That's what friends are for, aren't they? To stand behind you when you need them, give support, and," she added bluntly, "to accept each other's faults. 'Cause Lord knows we all have enough of them."

"Thank you," Mara said simply, humbled by a type of loyalty she'd never experienced before.

"Well, I'd best be on my way," the Swede said regretfully as he stood up. "I'd like to call again, if I might?" he asked tentatively, his wide smile broadening at Mara's pleased nod.

And so during the next week the Swede continued to visit as if that revealing conversation had never taken place. Whether or not he had spoken with Nicholas, Mara wasn't sure, for his attitude of obvious adoration continued. He asked her to dine with him one evening and Mara accepted. She knew it was a first step into a different relationship, but perhaps she wanted to see if it could develop into something more than friendship.

She dressed with care in a pale green brocaded silk with layers of Brussels lace falling from the décolletage and framing her shoulders elegantly. A wreath of artificial spring flowers sat like a crown on top of her head. The Swede turned out to be a perfect host, entertaining her throughout their dinner with amusing stories of incredible, if perhaps exaggerated, adventures he'd had and seeing to her every need with gentlemanly courtesy.

As they stood in the hallway of the silent boardinghouse, the shadowy light from one of the oil lamps flickering on their faces, Mara thanked the Swede for an evening she had truly enjoyed sharing with him.

"I haven't told Nicholas I'm seeing you, Mara," the Swede told her honestly. "It's not that I'm afraid of what I might learn about you, or that I haven't believed you," he said with a frown, "but Nicholas is my best friend, and he might say some things about you that I won't like. He can be insultingly cutting—vicious in fact—when he's at his worst. I don't want to have that between us just yet."

"I understand," Mara said, touched by the difficult position the Swede found himself in. "I'm sorry it's been so difficult for you, Swede. I wish there were some way I could help, but I'd only manage to make things worse," Mara sighed. Then, holding out her hand, she said softly, "Good night, Swede."

The Swede's big hand engulfed hers as he took it gently into his. Staring down longingly into her face, he breathed her name. He pulled her unresistingly into his arms. His mouth came down on hers.

The kiss started out with tender passion, but as the Swede felt her response, his arms tightened, enfolding her slender form against his muscular body. His lips moved hungrily over hers and he breathed the intoxicating sweetness of her fragrant skin.

Mara allowed herself to be pressed closer to him as she tried to respond to his kiss, but it was useless. She felt none of that excitement that seemed to set her blood on fire when she was near Nicholas.

The Swede's lips parted from hers with lingering sweetness, and as he stared down into her face, his worst fears were confirmed. The truth was revealed in her clear eyes, their golden depths unshadowed by passion. He shook his leonine head sadly. "It's no good, is it?"

Mara stared up into his wide blue eyes and knew she could not lie to him, or pretend a love she did not feel. "I'm sorry, Swede," she said gently.

The Swede smiled crookedly. "I was just fooling myself. I knew the first day I saw you that you weren't for me, but a fellow can't help dreaming," he said gruffly. Then, as he stared down at the sad longing in her eyes, he said oddly, "Are you in love with someone, Mara?"

Mara stepped away from the Swede as she tried to compose her features and erase whatever it was he had read in her eyes. "Well now, with a town full of rich miners and fast-talkin' adventurers I just might be, to be sure, there's enough of them to choose from." Mara laughed with a mocking glint in her eyes.

"I'm sorry, Mara," the Swede said softly.

"Sorry? Now whatever for?" she asked curiously, feigning ignorance.

"It's Nicholas, isn't it?"

Mara stared at him in humiliated silence, her face mirroring confusion and anguish. "Is it so obvious?" she asked in self-derision, her voice shaking.

"No, my dear," the Swede reassured her, "but I'm more sensitive, being half in love with you myself. It's our secret."

"Thank you," Mara said with dignity. She turned and started for the stairs, but at the foot she turned and asked diffidently, "I hope you will still be my friend?"

The Swede nodded, forcing himself to grin naturally. "You won't be getting rid of me so easily."

"I'm glad to hear that," she smiled.

And sure enough, the very next morning when Mara came

downstairs, she found him enjoying a cup of coffee while he laughed with Jenny over Peter's antics.

"Good morning," Mara greeted him casually, her cool beauty showing no sign of the sleepless night she had spent. "'Tis a good sign to see the sun shining for a change," Mara predicted. She waved Jenny back as she poured herself a cup of coffee and prepared to enjoy the half hour of talk that had become almost a daily ritual since the Swede started calling.

Mara was laughing at one of the Swede's endless supply of anecdotes when a loud voice sounded in the hallway and Mara heard her name being called.

"If you'll excuse me, please," Mara said. She quickly left the room, recognizing the voice imperiously summoning her as Jacques D'Arcy's. She had allowed herself to forget him as the week passed, but apparently she had been lulled into a feeling of false security by his silence. Her step faltered slightly as she entered the hall and saw the man standing beside Jacques.

He was called the Count. Nobody knew his real name. Despite his elegant style of dress, he had a mean look about him that repelled close contact. He wasn't a large man like the Swede, but there was a toughness about his firmly muscled body and a cunning wariness in his eyes that warned a smart person not to cross him. Nothing had ever been proven against the Count, but Mara knew the unsavory rumors about him were true, for too often, someone who had displeased Jacques had suddenly been found murdered, or had suffered a strange accident that left them incapacitated for months.

"What do you want?" Mara demanded bravely.

"I think you know what I want, ma petite," Jacques answered her, an unpleasant gleam in his eye. "You and I have some unfinished business to settle, and I would advise you to come quietly," he said meaningfully as he gestured toward the room Mara had just come from and where the laughing voices of small children could be heard. "I know you would not wish for your little boy to get hurt by mistake. Accidents are often fatal, ma petite. So you will come with Jacques and the Count, eh?"

Mara backed up a step as the Count moved forward, a cruel smile curving his thin lips. His eyes were without expression or emotion, reminding Mara of the opaque eyes of a reptile. She watched in fascination as one of the Count's heavily ringed hands slid beneath the fine woolen cloth of his coat and reappeared a second later with a very thin-bladed, evil-looking knife. The hilt of carved ivory was held caressingly in the palm of his hand.

Mara felt a faintness wash over her as the Count continued to close the distance between them, the sickeningly sweet cologne he wore engulfing her.

"The Count likes pretty women," Jacques taunted softly, "and he has always been especially fond of you, Mara. It will hurt him when the cool steel touches that warm, soft cheek."

Jacques shook his head regretfully. There was a look of sadistic anticipation in his eyes as he said, "I'm afraid you must learn a lesson, ma petite, for no woman rejects me and goes unpunished. Perhaps later, when other men turn away from your once beautiful face in distaste, you will welcome my kisses. Only, then I will make you beg for my lovemaking, and then even I might not be able to face your ugliness, for the Count is very thorough. So come now, ma petite. I might even reconsider should you be very generous with your favors to the Count and me. We will see," Jacques said as his eyes traveled slowly over Mara, his thoughts mirrored in his smile. "So, do not be difficult, ma petite," Jacques said. He and the Count closed in around her.

"She may not prove difficult, but I sure as hell will," came a calm voice directly behind Mara's shoulder.

Never had she heard a sweeter sound, Mara thought as she recognized the deceptively soft voice of the Swede. She could almost feel the strength of his large body as he moved silently past her.

Jacques and the Count seemed momentarily discomfited at the unexpected entrance of so huge an adversary. He deftly placed himself between Mara and her would-be abductors before either Jacques or the Count could make a move to stop him. Their victim was now safely out of harm's way with nothing less than a mountain standing sentinel before her.

"Come now, my big friend," Jacques spoke in a friendly tone of voice even as he took a judicious step backward, leaving the Count standing alone to face the giant. "This is none of your concern. Just a small matter to settle between me and the lady, hardly worth coming to grief over, eh?"

The Swede smiled grimly. "One, I'm no friend of yours. Two, the lady and you have just concluded your business. And three, I expect to see the back of you and your friend by the time I count to four."

"You speak pretty brave for a man alone. The Count here, he doesn't like your tone of voice, not at all," Jacques warned, his tight smile stretching grotesquely as he nodded toward the Count

Jacques was feeling brave because he knew the Count's skill at quickly disabling a man, a proficiency for which he'd become notorious. But Jacques had misjudged the Swede, never imagining a man of such great size could move so agilely or think with such quick cunning.

The Swede anticipated the Count's murderous attack. Even as the Count's arm raised, the knife blade flashing, wickedly, the Swede had reached out and grabbed the smaller man's wrist in his viselike grip, turning it so suddenly, and at so unnatural an angle that Mara heard the sharp snap of bones breaking, followed by the cry of excruciating pain. The Count's weapon was jammed between two loose-fitting boards in the wall and then snapped clean in two by the Swede.

Jacques wasn't a man for wasting time. As he witnessed his surprising change in fortunes, he decided to make his escape. But he had delayed too long, for the Swede was close behind. As Jacques cleared the front door, he found himself flying through the air with the help of a huge hand clamped to the seat of his pants. He flew headlong into the foul-smelling mud of the street below.

"And just remember," the Swede spoke down to the sprawling figure now covered in mud, "if anything ever happens to this lady, if you even come near her, I'll spread-eagle you in the sun, carve your beating heart out with my bowie knife, and feed it to the coyotes while the vultures pick clean your rotting eyes."

"Jaysus," a voice commented softly, "I trust we are on the same side?"

The Swede turned at the sound of the amused voice and stared curiously at the thin, tanned face of the lean man standing just clear of the doorway. He narrowed his eyes in puzzlement, feeling a second's recognition of the stranger.

Mara had followed the Swede to the door, giving wide berth to the unconscious form of the Count as she passed him stretched out on the floor. Now she stepped out onto the porch, staring in curiosity at Jacques as he struggled to rise from the ignominious position in which he found himself as bystanders stood around, laughing at his predicament. Mara became aware of the Swede's puzzled gaze and turned to see what he found so interesting.

"Brendan!" Mara cried out in amazement as she flung herself into his outstretched arms, wrapping her arms around his neck as she ecstatically hugged him and spread kisses across his face. "Brendan! Oh, Brendan! You're alive!" Mara whispered, still not believing he was actually there.

"Well, to be sure, I had a hard enough time tracing you. As soon as I saw the ruckus, however, I knew I'd found you, mavournin," Brendan laughed as he swung Mara off her feet and swirled her around.

"Papa!" Paddy screamed as he ducked past Jenny's arm. They all crowded into the doorway, Gordie and Paul gawking first at the prostrate form of the Count, then in admiration at the Swede who still stood with hands on hips, feet planted firmly apart. He surveyed the chaos with wry amusement.

Brendan released Mara to capture Paddy as he threw himself against Brendan's hips, nearly knocking him off balance with his embrace. "To be sure, but you've grown at least a foot since I last set me eyes on you," he laughed as he stared into Paddy's upturned face.

Jacques managed to escape unnoticed as the reunion caught everyone's attention, but as Jenny invited them inside to continue their merrymaking, the Swede remembered the fallen Count and shook his head with regret as he declined the invitation.

"I think I'd better remove our unwelcome guest here," the Swede said as he nodded his big head at the Count, who was beginning to show signs of life as he moaned his way back into consciousness. "I don't think you want him at the party."

Mara broke away from Brendan's arm and hurried over to the Swede. "I don't know how to thank you, Swede, but I'm in your debt," she told him. On sudden impulse, Mara stood on tiptoe and placed a soft kiss against his hard cheek, her golden eyes warm with friendship as she stared up into his surprised blue eyes.

Brendan and Jenny seemed just as surprised by Mara's uncharacteristic gesture of affection as the big man himself appeared to be. But as the groans from the Count grew progressively louder, the Swede put aside any other thoughts he might have voiced and quickly hoisted the elegant figure over his shoulder as carelessly as he would have a sack of potatoes. With a casual nod he made his way from the boardinghouse.

"Whew!" Brendan declared in amazement. "Now there's a mountain masquerading as a man, and relieved I am to be finding you on such good terms with him, mavournin. Who *is* he?"

"He's called the Swede, but as to his continued allegiance," Mara added with a speculative look, "that's questionable. You see, he happens to be a friend of one Nicholas Chantale. You do remember *him*, m'dear?"

"The divil take him, now," Brendan said with a grimace. "I knew there had to be a worm in the apple."

"Oh, Brendan, it's so good to hear your mocking voice again," Mara laughed, pushing aside all other thoughts as she gazed at him. She became aware of the unnatural thinness of his face, and the slight slumping of his shoulders. He looked tired, as if he'd been ill and hadn't quite shaken the effects of his illness from him. And even though his face seemed healthily tanned, there was a slight yellowish tinge to the skin. Mara could see the beads of perspiration breaking out on his forehead as Brendan made himself comfortable on the sofa.

"You haven't been well, Brendan?" Mara asked worriedly.

"'Tis nothing now, my love," Brendan reassured her. "I caught a chill, that's all. In fact, most everyone does up there, and considering what a hellhole it is, why, surprised I am even to be alive."

"Master Brendan!" Jamie cried from the doorway as she rushed into the room, her gray eyes suspiciously moist as she stared at Brendan's lounging figure. "Holdin' court as usual, dominatin' the conversation, cussin' away as always—ah, but 'tis good to be seein' ye, that it is," Jamie greeted him with a watery chuckle. Then, with narrowed eyes she continued, "And I can see ye've not been eatin' properly, nor takin' care of yourself the way ye should. Ye're lookin' like death himself."

"You never do stop mother-henning me, eh, Jamie?" Brendan laughed, pleased by her show of concern even though he didn't care to have her clucking about him.

"Ye need a good meal in ye, boy. How about a cup of coffee? There's fresh bread as well, and—"

"It's all right, Jamie," Mara interrupted, "Jenny's gone to fix something, although by the smell of him, I'd say Brendan's already stopped off somewhere for a whiskey and a bath," Mara guessed with a knowing look.

"Mavournin, you wouldn't have cared to see me the way I was looking on me arrival here in San Francisco. I looked and smelled worse than a grizzly," Brendan said in horror, "and you can't begrudge a man for wanting to wash the dust out of his mouth."

"I'll go help Mrs. Markham," Jamie said as she bustled from the room, but not before she'd given Brendan an all-encompassing stare that missed nothing of his appearance.

"Same old busybody," Brendan commented with a laugh as he stretched out his long legs, drawing Mara's attention to his expertly tailored pants and fashionable shoes.

"To look at you now one would imagine you'd just been out for a stroll through St. James's Park," Mara remarked, adding curiously, "and certainly not just back from the mines. How long have you been in San Francisco, for I don't imagine those were the clothes you arrived in?"

Brendan laughed. "Indeed not, mavournin. I was elegantly clad in red flannel and baggy breeches—held up by suspenders, no less—and sporting the shaggiest, most disreputable beard this side of the Rockies," Brendan declared dramatically. "Ah, my love, you'd not have recognized me handsome face nor, indeed, have cared to claim the relationship."

"Then where did you find the clothes?" Mara demanded.

"If a man has enough gold in his pockets, then anything is possible," Brendan said smiling, his dark eyes twinkling with excitement as he waited for Mara's reaction. "I snap me fingers and my smallest wish is granted. Like having a tailor working all night sewing me my new suit. Or, for instance, having a lobster salad and fillet of beef smothered in mushroom sauce, a magnum of champagne, and a beautiful woman sent up to me room."

"Brendan," Mara said softly, "you struck it rich?"

"To be sure, I did," Brendan replied offhandedly, yet his eyes were shining with suppressed happiness.

Mara just sat silently staring at him for a minute, not quite believing what she heard. How could it be true? They were actually rich. Brendan had succeeded in finding his fortune. It was incredible! It was a soft, hazy dream she must surely awaken from into the cold, clear light of day.

"No, 'tis true, mavournin," Brendan broke into her thoughts, having accurately read her mind. "I wouldn't lie to you about this. We're rich. Jaysus, but we're rich!"

"Oh, Brendan, Brendan, you did it!" Mara cried with happiness and pride as she watched Brendan throw back his head and laugh for the pure enjoyment of it, his face flushed with success. They exchanged glances, not having to speak their thoughts as each felt the past years slide away. Under the heady onslaught of their newfound wealth, the past could finally be forgotten.

No matter how fair the sun shines,
Still it must set.

—Ferdinand Raimund

Chapter 8

MARÍA VELAZQUEZ STARED AROUND HER PINK-TINTED BOUDOIR in vain appreciation of the elegant adornments serving as a backdrop for her exotic beauty. Gilt-framed mirrors on every wall reflected sparkling glass chandeliers suspended above the thick carpet. White lace fluttered against the glass of the windows, which were draped in heavy, red damask. Satin-upholstered rosewood chairs and an overstuffed, deep-buttoned chaise longue were strategically positioned around the room. But it was the large four-poster with canopy draped in red velvet that dominated all else and drew the eye, as indeed it was meant to do. With its matching spread of dark red velvet and a fur rug folded at the foot, it seemed a haven of warmth and security to a man just down from the loneliness of the Sierra or weary from a long sea voyage. The lovely room and the woman were available should he have the right amount of gold in his pockets.

And María Velazquez always made sure they could pay before she shared her favors with them. Time was money in this city full of prospective customers. María stared out the window at the rain falling in windblown sheets against the clapboard sides of the buildings. Making a moue of distaste, she turned away from the window, wrapping her diaphanous peignoir of pink silk gauze around her pale body. Shivering delicately she pulled the fur rug from the bed and wrapped it around her body, rubbing her hands sensuously over the dark glossy sable.

With a bored sigh she walked over to one of the side tables loaded down with fine imported liqueurs and brandy, champagne, claret, and port, and poured herself a full goblet of champagne. San Francisco had been a slight disappointment to her on her arrival here from Europe less than a month ago. But she had quickly seen beneath the crude glitter and discovered the real gold mine of opportunities for a beautiful woman. Anything could happen here and everything was possible, especially for an ambitious woman. And María Velazquez was most ambitious.

With a provocative swing of her hips, a contrived movement that had now become second nature to her, María moved to the large wardrobe with its marquetry-paneled doors standing slightly ajar. Pushing the doors wider, María stared in disagreeable silence at the colorful assortment of gowns presented for her inspection. Her calculative gaze traveled over the silks, satins, and velvets, until finally coming to rest on a deeply flounced black velvet figured gown of purple silk. She pulled it free from the confining space of the wardrobe and spread it out on the bed. Her amethyst necklace and earrings would go well with it, and her dark purple velvet cape lined in mink would keep her elegantly warm. She was taking a great deal of trouble with her appearances tonight, but then she was dining with someone very special and she had every intention of captivating her host. Jacques D'Arcy was definitely a man going somewhere in the world. He also possessed a certain sophistication, a savoir-faire, that was glaringly absent in most of the population here. They might be able to don fancy clothes and pay for expensive entertainment, but gentlemen they were not. Nor would they ever be. They were still farmers, store clerks, schoolteachers, and bookkeepers—some even deserters from ships and army regiments. Most were still the same dull louts they had always been, with plenty of money and drink bringing out the worst in them.

María had achieved some of her goals as the mistress of princes and counts, generals and bankers, all men of importance and wealth in European society. And like her idol, Lola

Montez, she had even exerted some political influence over her lovers. She enjoyed a life of luxury, surrounded by servants who would jump to her slightest whim. But the sacrifice of her beautiful body to elderly, debauched voluptuaries—in hope of their generosity—had become too great.

As María Velazquez rang for her maid, she swore to herself that things would be different in San Francisco. Once she made her fortune, she would never have to submit to the insults of those who thought themselves better than she, or bow submissively before them as she fearfully awaited their pleasure, or displeasure, and whatever handout they deigned to give her.

Well, she would show them all and someday laugh in their faces when she returned to Europe a wealthy woman. María tapped her foot impatiently. Where was that damned maid? Must she constantly have to suffer fools around her? She rang the bell again, vigorously shaking it until the door opened and an appropriately cowed servant with a harassed expression entered.

María picked up her hair brush from her dressing table and viciously threw it at the diffident young girl who served as her maid, the brush hitting her in the shoulder before she could sidestep it. The pale girl flinched in pain and nervously caught her lower lip between her teeth as she faced her volatile mistress.

"And where have you been?" María demanded. "You're here to see to my needs, not to entertain some rutting Don Juan down on the docks," she bullied. The thin girl was hardly more than a child with her underdeveloped body and pale blond hair that hung in lank wisps around her pinched face.

"B–but—" the girl began tearfully, her lips trembling.

"I don't want any more of your lies, Ellen. It's disgusting the way you go around mooning over anything in breeches. At least you ought to get them to pay for it," María said crudely. "Now prepare my bath and set out my things for this evening."

With a sullen look Ellen obeyed her orders, her mind forgetting her hurts as she handled the delicately beautiful garments that would soon adorn her mistress's voluptuous body. They were far too elegant for the likes of her, Ellen thought resentfully. Her thin fingers fondled the soft cambric of María's chemisette. She cast a sly, malevolent look at her benefactress from pale blue eyes dulled by years of drudgery and subservience.

"And this time don't forget to perfume the water, you little fool," María continued her harangue. "And it'd better be hot or I'll sell you to one of the houses on the docks. The sailors can teach you your place," she threatened without even bothering to glance up from her jewelry. She wasn't aware of her browbeaten servant's look of terror as the young girl pressed her hand against her mouth in silent suffering.

María finally glanced up to see Ellen still standing there, indecisively. "Well? Are you some bloody statue or something? Get a move on, girl. If you ruin this evening for me, I'll beat you black and blue," she warned as the girl ran from the room. With a smile of satisfaction she turned back to her jewelry and her thoughts of this evening.

❧

"Mavournin," Brendan called impatiently up the stairs, "are you dressed yet? To be sure, 'twould be nice to dine before dawn."

Upstairs, Mara was ignoring his sarcastic plea as she delicately touched scent behind her ears and to the hollow between her breasts. She thought of the startling change in fortune Brendan's arrival had brought. Strange how a large chunk of metal could make you rich overnight. For that was what Brendan had stumbled across—one large gold nugget worth forty-five thousand dollars.

Brendan was on top of the world. Never had Mara seen him look happier—or quite so ill. The search for his elusive gold had robbed him of his health. He had always been on the delicate side, and the cold, wet weather, combined with excessive drinking and poor diet, had left its destructive mark on his thin body. But Brendan contemptuously brushed aside any suggestion that he should rest until he regained his health. He was enjoying his newfound riches with a spending spree that must have run into the thousands of dollars already.

Not that Mara could complain too much, for she benefited

from his unrestrained spending. He had bought her a whole new wardrobe of dresses and cloaks, hats and shoes, jewelry and any trinket that caught her eye. No one could possibly accuse Brendan of being parsimonious, for he thoroughly enjoyed spending his money in a devil-may-care manner that was his style. Mara was uneasy as Brendan spent his money so freely. They should save some of it. They had been close to ruin too many times for her to enjoy seeing money tossed around so casually. But Brendan only shrugged and reassured her that he could easily find more gold.

She had stood firm against him in only one thing, and that was over moving out of Jenny's boardinghouse. He had taken rooms at the St. Francis, one of the best hotels in San Francisco, but Mara thought that environment would be unhealthy for Paddy, besides which, he had friends to keep him amused at Jenny's. And Mara preferred to stay discreetly out of sight as much as possible, remembering her last meeting with Nicholas.

Brendan had given in to her demands easily, not admitting that he preferred to have the care of Paddy out of his hands. Too, it was preferable not having a sister hanging on to his coattails when he entertained his lady friends or lost money in the gaming halls. He remained in constant touch with the family, though. He insisted upon Mara's dining with him several times a week, still finding her his best confidante and most amusing dinner partner.

Tonight was one of those evenings. They had also persuaded a reluctant Jenny to join them for dinner at Delmonico's. She had volubly protested, proclaiming herself no more than a farmer's widow, hardly fit company for the O'Flynns at so fine a restaurant. But Jenny had never come up against so irresistible a force as the O'Flynns when determined to have their own way. So she found herself dressing for this evening as if there'd never been any doubt about it.

Mara turned from the mirror and looked Jenny over critically, a smile of satisfaction growing in her eyes as she stared at the startling transformation the new gown and different hairstyle had made. Jenny was beautiful. And perhaps that was what frightened her, Mara perceived, as she noticed Jenny's shy glances at her reflection, her blue eyes widening in disbelief each time she caught sight of herself. Always hardworking and practical, she had seldom had the opportunity to indulge herself, money to spend on herself, or reason for glamorous clothes. This was her first glimpse of what luxury could do for her, and she had found to her dismay that she liked it.

"You can see now, can't you," Mara began, "that the blue silk wouldn't have done for me at all? It matches the color of your eyes exactly," Mara continued persuasively. The gown had, in fact, been made for Jenny, but Jenny must never know that. It was perfect for her, with its three flounces edged with delicate blond lace that matched the inset across the bodice. Jenny's bright red hair had been swept back, curled into ringlets over each ear, and decorated with delicate white flowers. Around the column of her neck was tied a blue velvet ribbon and small cameo, which drew the eye to the soft swell of breast above her lacy bodice.

Mara gestured to the blue silk cloak that matched the dress. "You might as well wear the whole outfit. It doesn't match anything I have," Mara added, casting a dubious look at the plain gray cloak Jenny carried over her arm.

"Well," Jenny said softly, then smiled widely. "I've gone this far. Why ruin the dress with this old thing?"

"Shall we go?" Mara said with a last look in the mirror. "Brendan will leave without us if we don't." Mara picked up her cloak and purse and followed Jenny from the room. The ladies were greeted by Brendan's whistle as they descended the stairs.

"To be sure, Brendan O'Flynn has never had two more beautiful women than these on each arm," he declared in appreciation as he escorted them to the carriage hired especially for tonight.

Brendan knew he was the envy of half the men in the restaurant as he sat between his two partners, playing the charming host, not letting on that neither was his paramour. Having two beautiful women sitting at his table certainly didn't hurt his image, and he had to admit that Jenny Markham was doing him proud. He had, in fact, been pleasantly surprised by her altered appearance and for a second had even speculated on a dalliance. He'd quickly changed his mind about that as he remembered her three sons. The only way into Jenny's bed would be through marriage.

Brendan ordered a second bottle of champagne as their dinner was served, despite the wine that would accompany each course. He played the entertaining and expansive host to more than just Mara and Jenny as he gradually gained the audience he craved. Other diners became quickly aware of the handsome man and his two beautiful companions.

Nicholas Chantale and the Swede were two of the diners very much aware of the other party in the restaurant, each for a different reason, and with differing reactions.

They had finished their dinner and were sipping brandy. Nicholas waited patiently for his dinner companion, an attractive blond faro-dealer at the Bella Union who had gone to freshen up.

"I've been meaning to ask you about her," the Swede broke into Nicholas's contemplation of the O'Flynn party, noticing the Creole's narrowed gaze when resting on the dark-haired woman in the white lace evening gown. Her shoulders gleamed softly above the daringly low neckline, the lace fluttering at her breasts caught and held with a large jeweled brooch that matched the earrings dangling from her ears and the delicate gold-and-enamel necklace set with pearls, rubies, and turquoise around her neck.

Nicholas pulled his gaze away from Mara. Turning to the Swede, he asked softly, "Which woman did you want to know about?"

"About Mara O'Flynn," the Swede told him bluntly.

"And what do you know about her? I wasn't even aware you knew her?" Nicholas said quietly.

"I met her here in San Francisco. I understand that you met her a number of years ago, in London."

Nicholas smiled unpleasantly. "And just what lies has our fair beauty been telling you, I wonder."

"I think she's told me the truth, Nicholas," the Swede

replied, undaunted by the cruel look on his friend's handsome face. "She told me about Julian. She admitted that she'd wronged him. She's very sorry about it, Nicholas."

Nicholas laughed humorlessly. "Sure she is, now that her past indiscretions are being disclosed. But she hasn't changed. Look at her now, enjoying herself, feeling nothing for anyone or anything—except the gratification of her desires."

"You're wrong about her, Nicholas," the Swede said flatly.

Nicholas turned his narrowed green eyes on the Swede's broad face. "Don't tell me you've fallen for her? I can't believe you'd be such a fool. She's no good, Swede. Can't you see that? She and that conniving brother of hers were masquerading as two completely different people on a rancho near Sonoma just last year. They ran out on the place when things got out of control, but not before they knocked me out and robbed me of my money."

The Swede frowned thoughtfully as he mulled this over.

Nicholas smiled grimly. "I can see she neglected to confess that to you. I wonder what else she didn't tell you."

"She told me something of that incident. But she doesn't have to explain herself to me, Nicholas. I'm certainly not here to judge her. Mara O'Flynn made a mistake," the Swede said compassionately. "My God, she couldn't have been but a young girl when she met Julian. Younger than you when you made many mistakes you'd like to forget about, Nicholas. Can't you forgive her? I think you've misjudged her."

"Quite the contrary, Swede. In fact, in the past three years she's had time to refine her talents, and I wonder how many other fools she's duped. Considering what I've had to put up with from her, I think I've been exceptionally reasonable."

"I think your problem is," the Swede remarked casually as he watched Nicholas's gaze return to Mara's laughing face, "that you do like her. No, don't try to deny it. You can't. You find her damned attractive. I can see it when you look at her. It's just a shame that you had already made up your mind about her before you met her, for I think the two of you together would be something to see." Then he added with a laugh, "Like dynamite and matches."

Nicholas smiled derisively. "I thought you had more sense than to fall for such an obvious type of woman. But then, I should have remembered that Mara O'Flynn is not to be underestimated. She's quite the little actress. Just don't make too big a fool of yourself, Swede. She's not worth it," Nicholas warned.

"You're the one fooling yourself, Nicholas," the Swede advised in turn, "and you just might discover the truth once it's too late."

"I'm not your nursemaid, Swede," Nicholas said as he paid his bill. He saw his lady companion returning to the table and prepared to leave. "Are you coming?"

"I'll be along shortly," the Swede excused himself.

Nicholas shrugged and started to walk away with the blonde snuggling herself against his shoulder. But after only a few steps, Nicholas turned and said, "You're wrong, Swede. You know I've always had a preference for blondes." And with that final retort he strolled off, the blonde gazing up at him in adoration, her mercenary hopes confirmed as she heard his remarks.

The Swede shook his head, a smile lingering in his eyes as he hoped Nicholas would find his hands full with his blond friend after that remark. Usually Nicholas was perceptive and his judgment could be trusted, but where Mara O'Flynn was concerned Nicholas couldn't think straight. Poor Mara, the Swede thought with a tender look in her direction. Maybe she was right about Nicholas and he would never forgive her. That damned Creole pride of his was still as touchy as ever. There had to be more between the two of them than either one had said and he wondered curiously what had happened out there on that rancho.

Mara O'Flynn was laughing at one of Brendan's funny caricatures of life in the mining camps when she glanced up and saw Nicholas leaving the restaurant with the blonde. Mara watched in jealous fascination as Nicholas drew the woman's cape over her shoulders, his fingers lingering against the soft swell of breast.

Yes, do help her with her cape. We wouldn't want the

poor dear to catch her death of cold in that skimpy gown, Mara thought. She saw Nicholas's dark head bending down to the woman's overly rouged face as she whispered some endearment in his ear, her hand fondling a curl on the back of his neck. Mara dragged her smoldering gaze away from them and stared down at her plate of food. Only moments before it had looked so appetizing.

"You're not laughing, mavournin," Brendan complained. "Have I lost me touch as a storyteller? Jenny here is the best audience I've played to in years."

Mara glanced up, forcing a smile to her stiff lips. "Forgive me, Brendan. I wasn't listening."

Brendan sent a suffering look heavenward. "You seldom do these days, Mara, me love."

"And if I was listening to you all the time, I'd be stone deaf for sure," Mara retorted with a laugh, making an effort to be better company.

"I'm glad I came," Jenny said. She wasted no time cutting into the tenderloin of beef and washing it down with a sip of champagne. "But the way you two carry on," she chuckled, her red curls bobbing and catching the light.

"Here, try some of this wine. 'Tis really what's supposed to be proper with beef," Brendan suggested, pouring some into Jenny's glass. But Jenny shook her head.

"Oh, no, not me. I've never had champagne before so I'm not going to fill myself up with something else when I can have this instead."

Brendan laughed as he took Jenny's glass and emptied it into his. "Can't stand to see liquor go to waste."

"Now tell me again about that polecat who strayed into your tent that rainy night," Jenny begged, thoroughly enjoying Brendan's exaggerated descriptions.

With a broad smile Brendan obliged her, his eyes dancing with mirth. "And who am I to be denying me public?"

They were still laughing over his story when a tall shadow fell across the table and they glanced up to see the Swede standing before them. "Might I join you for a drink?"

"Certainly," Brendan invited cordially, "'tis the best way of making friends. And as I said once before, I'd not care to have you for an enemy."

The Swede sat down and graciously accepted a glass of champagne from Brendan. He smiled at Mara, hiding the longing in his blue eyes as he turned to Jenny. "I don't believe we've met, ma'am," he said politely. "I'm Karl Svengaard, called the Swede."

Jenny laughed as he introduced himself, her laughter confusing him. "A fine memory you've got, Swede," she teased him, feeling emboldened by her fine clothes, and perhaps the champagne bubbling inside her, "unless you purposely would like to forget about causing a brawl in my boardinghouse?"

The Swede's mouth dropped open as he narrowed his eyes. Comprehension flooded through him as he recognized Jenny Markham. She didn't look like Mara O'Flynn's landlady now. "I should have guessed. That red hair is like no one else's," he laughed, but there was another look, not so humorous, as he continued to gaze at Jenny's amazing transformation.

Why had he never seen her beauty before? It wasn't the same kind of exotic beauty as Mara O'Flynn's, but there was a delicate fineness in the bone structure of her heart-shaped face, and her lips were full and soft below a slightly retroussé nose. But what really gave beauty to her face was the warmth shining from her dark blue eyes and the hint of mischief trembling at the corners of her lips. She was definitely a changed woman, the Swede thought. "I guess the joke's on me. Sorry, ma'am, for not recognizing you."

"Sorry!" Jenny exclaimed. "I'm not. Going to all this trouble to get dressed up would have been for nothing if I looked the same."

"More champagne!" Brendan ordered from a passing waiter.

Mara glanced at him worriedly. His hollow cheeks were flushed, yet she couldn't tell if it was from too much wine or with fever. His dark eyes were glazed. He emptied his glass, yet his plate was still loaded with food.

Mara sighed, knowing from years of experience that

nothing she could say would make any difference to Brendan. She took a sip of champagne and glanced idly around the crowded restaurant. Her golden eyes moved over the wide assortment of people without much interest until they made contact with a pair of eyes staring piercingly at her.

"Brendan," Mara mumbled beneath her breath as she blindly reached out and grasped his arm, her fingers tightening around it in a surprisingly hard grip.

❧

María Velazquez silently watched the party of four gathered around the crystal- and china-cluttered table. She recognized only two of the diners. They had changed a great deal in the years since she had last seen them.

The O'Flynns. It had to be. She'd thought she had forgotten that name, as well as the brother and sister she had known in London so many years ago. María Velazquez's dark eyes lingered nostalgically on Brendan's handsome face. He was still devilishly attractive, but he was far thinner than he used to be. The years seemed to have made a more cynical and experienced man of him. María's eyes moved to the dark-haired woman beside Brendan, and she shook her head in disbelief. The fledgling chick had grown into a swan. But she shouldn't be surprised. The O'Flynns had inherited their good looks from Maud O'Flynn, who in her day had been a famous beauty of the stage. Remembering the portraits she'd seen of the famed actress, María had to admit that Mara O'Flynn had surpassed her mother's beauty. Her features were more refined, with just a touch of the exotic in the tilt of her eyes.

María Velazquez wondered if either of them would think she had changed much over the years. Would they remember her?

Brendan looked down at Mara's fingers clenching his arm and then up into her face. Following her rapt stare, he looked to the object of her fascination.

Rubbing his bleary eyes, Brendan focused them more clearly on the woman sitting across the room. "Jaysus," he breathed, "'tis Molly."

Mara shook her head. "No, it can't be her. It just can't. Brendan, it isn't her. Tell me 'tisn't," she pleaded, a premonition of danger snaking through her. But Brendan apparently felt none of her fear as he continued to stare at Molly O'Flynn, his dark eyes examining every detail of her appearance. For a breathless instant Mara had a feeling of dread that Brendan might still be in love with her. She needn't have feared that, for when Brendan finally spoke, he was anything but complimentary.

"Who would've thought Molly would run to fat?" Brendan said contemptuously as he allowed his gaze to settle on the full breasts straining to escape from her low-cut bodice. "To be sure, the years haven't been overly kind to her. Damn, but she looks older than me."

Jenny caught Brendan's sneering words and looked curiously between the two O'Flynns, noting their discomfiture. They stared at the strange woman at the other table, but it was Jenny who noticed Molly O'Flynn's companion first. "Isn't that the man you threw out of the boardinghouse?" she demanded of the Swede.

The Swede glanced across at the two people who seemed to be causing a slight stir at his table and shrugged. "Looks like the same fellow, although I see he's keeping his distance tonight," the Swede remarked, his eyes glowing in remembered satisfaction. "The woman, I think, is María Velazquez. Made a name for herself in Europe doing some kind of gypsy dance, although she's more famous for her abilities as a courtesan than as a dancer," the Swede commented casually. Then, remembering the company, the big man flushed uncomfortably. "I beg your pardon, Mrs. Markham, Mara, I forgot myself for a moment."

"María Velazquez?" Brendan repeated thoughtfully, a slight shadow of doubt entering his eyes. "Gypsy, hmmm?"

"I suppose she could have changed her name," Mara said.

The Swede looked between the brother and sister thoughtfully. "You seem to know her."

Brendan became aware that both the Swede and Jenny were staring at him curiously, suspecting something was amiss.

"I thought she was someone we knew long ago, but the name isn't the same."

"As you well know, that doesn't prove anything," Mara said softly.

"To be sure, it doesn't," Brendan answered. Then, throwing his arm around Jenny's shoulders, he cajoled, "Now come along, drink up, let's all forget the past and enjoy this evening. The divil take me if I'm going to walk out of here sober," Brendan warned mockingly as he refilled the Swede's glass and Jenny's. "I'd be interested in finding out how much a man your size can hold. Half of the whiskey in County Cork, I'd swear."

The Swede smiled. Despite his reservations, he had to admit that Brendan O'Flynn was a charmer, full of blarney perhaps, but nonetheless entertaining. "Only County Cork? I'd have reckoned on all of Ireland."

Brendan laughed in appreciation. "Now that's what I like, a man with confidence, as well as one who can lie straight-faced."

Mara listened to the joking, knowing Brendan was overdoing it as he sought to gather his wits about him. Neither of them believed that woman was not Molly. Mara cast a surreptitious look at the woman who sat talking with Jacques D'Arcy, their dark heads close together, and wondered worriedly what they were saying. Jacques D'Arcy, who bore a grudge against her, was the last person she wanted trading confidences with Molly.

"You seem rather interested in the O'Flynns," Jacques remarked casually, his eyes resting on María Velazquez's face. Surprise, disbelief, dismay, and finally speculation had moved over her features. She was thoughtfully chewing her thumbnail as she turned to him.

"So…they really are Brendan and Mara O'Flynn," she said. Her husky voice trembled with underlying excitement. "What do you know about them, except that Brendan O'Flynn seems to be made of money? I can see that for myself," she demanded as she saw Brendan order another bottle of champagne.

Jacques shrugged, an ugly look crossing his face. "He certainly spends it like there was no tomorrow. I suppose it doesn't matter to him though. Heard tell he found a chunk of gold worth a hundred thousand dollars or more and is now living like a king at the St. Francis. He gambles away thousands of dollars nightly, not seeming to care whether he wins or loses—losing more than winning most of the time, I might say."

"So Brendan's rich," Molly spoke softly, her eyes shining like black onyx.

"Brendan?" Jacques asked curiously. "You know the gentleman?"

Molly eyed the Frenchman with an enigmatic look. "María Velazquez, do you like the name?"

"Nothing wrong with it," Jacques said impatiently. "Even sounds exotic."

"Exactly. That's why I made it up a couple of years ago," Molly told him, laughing. "Did you know that Lola Montez, a personal friend of mine, was actually born in Ireland and her real name is Eliza Gilbert? And don't you think that María Velazquez has more mystery to it than Molly O'Flynn?" she asked coyly.

Jacques almost choked on his cheroot. "Who did you say?"

"Molly O'Flynn," she reiterated clearly, "Mrs. Brendan O'Flynn—at least until I ran out on him."

"Mon Dieu," Jacques said beneath his breath.

"Tell me," Molly asked, suddenly remembering. "Is there a small boy with them by any chance?"

Jacques grinned, fitting the pieces of the puzzle together as he added María's relationship to the O'Flynns. "The boy Mara O'Flynn is mothering is your son, isn't he?"

Molly laughed harshly. "So Mara is still playing the role of the little mama? Well, if the brat's around six or seven, then he's most likely mine."

"Motherhood apparently didn't agree with you, ma chérie," Jacques remarked with a smirk.

"I had other ideas at the time," Molly replied vaguely, then added with a determined glint, "but I just might have different feelings about that now. Brendan always did have a weakness for me."

"What are you plotting, ma chérie?" Jacques asked suspiciously.

Molly smiled unpleasantly. "Could be that rumor will soon have it that Brendan and his little sister abandoned me, stole my son from me, and left me destitute. I *am* still his wife, and I think public opinion would be on my side and demand I share in their wealth," Molly speculated. "But I will only resort to that if Brendan shows any reluctance to take me back. I do not fear that happening, however, for I am more beautiful today than I was years ago when he loved me."

Jacques eyed her professionally, silently agreeing that she was a beautiful woman. She lacked the refinement of Mara O'Flynn, and already her looks were beginning to suffer. The skin around her eyes was puffy from late nights and heavy drinking, while the heavy dusting of powder and rouge did not hide the faint lines of age. The steady thickening of her voluptuous body would probably continue until she eventually became grotesque, Jacques speculated as he watched her spooning a rich dessert into her mouth.

But for now, she needn't worry. There was an earthy quality in her beauty, a certain bawdy suggestiveness about her that told a man he would get his money's worth with her.

"I wonder if they recognized me," Molly asked thoughtfully. "I stared right into those damned gold eyes of Mara O'Flynn's, but not a flicker of emotion or recognition crossed her face. Either she didn't know me, or she's turned into a damned fine actress," Molly fumed, wondering just what her next move should be.

"Mara O'Flynn is the cool one, ma chérie," Jacques informed her as he eyed their table. Then, as he uncomfortably recognized the big blond man sitting with them, he suggested, "I think we should give careful thought to this rather interesting development and wait until tomorrow to act upon it. By then we should have come up with a workable plan."

"*We?*" Molly questioned caustically as she cast a doubtful look at the Frenchman. "I had no idea *you'd* been married to Brendan as well."

But Jacques ignored her sarcasm, his fingers rubbing along her thigh beneath the table as he replied suavely, "*Mais oui, ma chérie.* You will need someone you can trust, who can make sure the O'Flynns don't cheat you once again. I am a very influential man in San Francisco. I could possibly be of service, should the O'Flynns become difficult about sharing their good fortune," Jacques told her with a smile. It hinted that he almost wished they would.

Molly ran her hand along his arm as she smiled softly up into his face. "I can see the value in having you as a partner, my love."

"I thought you might," he said, his dark eyes lingering on the O'Flynns as they prepared to leave the restaurant. He couldn't resist nodding his head in casual acknowledgment as he caught Mara O'Flynn's eyes on him. She acted as though she had not seen him, looking away from his table without a sign of recognition on her beautiful face.

❧

"My God, Brendan," Mara was saying the following morning when she joined Brendan for a late breakfast in his rooms at the St. Francis. "I can't believe it. Molly. After all these years."

Brendan sipped his coffee, his face haggard and pale as he stared morosely at his plate of food before pushing it away disinterestedly. "To be sure, I never thought to be seein' her face again."

"And with Jacques, of all people," Mara frowned.

"That fellow who was being rather forcibly ejected from Jenny's by our mountain of a friend the day I arrived," Brendan noted.

"Yes, and he's a treacherous cutthroat who isn't likely to forgive and forget."

"And how is it, mavournin, that you should have an acquaintance with such a lack of character?" Brendan demanded.

"I had to earn a living while you were looking for gold, didn't I? He's a gambler, and I was one of his faro dealers. We had a difference of opinion and I quit just shortly before you arrived."

"A difference of opinion, was it? The same old story I

suppose. You played games with him and he turned nasty when repulsed?" Brendan speculated.

Mara sighed in exasperation. "Please give me credit for having more sense than to tease someone like him. I never encouraged him, Brendan, never. I find him quite despicable. That's why I quit working for him."

"Well, it's still the same thing. He's no friend of ours, and come to think of it, I'd like to keep it that way."

"Brendan," Mara said, deciding to voice an idea she'd thought about for some time now, "I've been wondering if we ought not to invest some of the money in a business or something like that. You know, we could even open a boardinghouse. Or maybe build our own hotel? What do you think, Brendan?" Mara asked hesitantly as she saw the incredulous look on Brendan's handsome face.

"My dear, your sense of humor is extraordinary. Of course, I am giving you the benefit of the doubt and assuming it was a joke. Can you imagine Brendan O'Flynn *in trade?* Why, the mere thought is preposterous. I suppose you'll want me to open up a butcher's shop, tie an apron around me waist, and hawk slabs of beef? Or perhaps open a laundry? Or even better, become a haberdasher." Brendan looked at Mara, shaking his head in disbelief. "My dear, I really must get you back to London. These Americans with their peculiar class mixtures are really going to your head. Oh, dear me, I can even see the newspaper story now: 'Mara O'Flynn, one-time famous actress who gave up the stage in favor of opening her own little hat shop, married a redheaded greengrocer and is raising a family of little carrot-tops of her own.' Doesn't sound too excitin', mavournin. To be sure, it sounds damned dull," Brendan told her with a pitying look.

Mara stared down at her fingernails, Brendan's cutting remarks touching her on the raw as she fell into a mortified silence.

"Mavournin, knowin' you the way I do," Brendan continued, realizing he'd hurt her feelings, "you'd be bored within a fortnight without fine restaurants and fancy dress balls and the elegance of—" Brendan was interrupted by a firm knock on the door of his suite.

Mara glanced at Brendan. "Were you expecting someone?"

"Not that I know of. Can't remember issuing an invitation, but then, my women friends haven't always waited for one when wanting to further the acquaintance," Brendan said half-seriously as he reluctantly got up.

Mara was glancing idly through one of the newspapers stacked on the end of the table when she heard voices and looked up to see Brendan sauntering back to the table followed by a female visitor.

Up close Molly O'Flynn had indeed changed a great deal since the last time Mara had seen her. Mara shook her head, wondering in amazement how she could ever have idolized this coarse creature. Molly was dressed in a bright red taffeta gown trimmed with black bows and bunches of artificial flowers, the décolletage unsuitably low for a daytime dress and partially concealed by a fur stole draped across her shoulders. She had one hand tucked into a fur muff that matched the stole. In her other hand she was carrying a delicate fringed parasol of red taffeta that she spun like a pinwheel behind her shoulders.

"Look who's come to pay us a visit, mavournin," Brendan said coldly. "The long-lost, and almost forgotten Molly."

"Never at a loss for words, are you, Brendan, my love?" Molly said acerbically. Then, remembering the reason for her visit, she smiled sweetly. She approached the table where Mara sat watching her. "My, my...how you have grown, Mara. I always predicted you would be a beauty someday," she said grudgingly, her smile tight. Molly recognized a natural grace and elegance in Mara that she herself had not achieved.

"Why have you come, Molly?" Brendan asked bluntly, pointedly not inviting her to join them at breakfast. He sat back down and picked up one of the newspapers, his look impatient. "Well?"

Molly, laboring under the misconception that she still held Brendan's love, looked down at him out of the corner of her eye, her lips curving provocatively. "Brendan, my love, is that all you've got to say to me after all these years? I've missed you dreadfully. You must believe me," she cried as she fell to her knees before Brendan, her hands grasping and clutching at his. She stared beseechingly into his austere face.

Mara stared in disbelief. If she hadn't been so shocked by Molly's reappearance, she would have laughed, for Molly always had been a terrible actress and still was as she overplayed her part once again, her gestures exaggerated and almost comical.

"I was so young and foolish. I really didn't know my own mind until I had left London, leaving my beloved husband alone, to raise our sweet child without a mother's love. Oh, Brendan, I've been such a fool," Molly spoke in a quivering voice, a hint of tears glistening in her eyes. She pulled a dainty handkerchief from her bodice and dabbed at her dry eyes. "I came back, looking for you, but you had left London, and I didn't know where to look. I barely had enough money to live on, much less to search for you across Europe."

Molly bent her head in an attitude of repentance, twisting her handkerchief nervously in her hands as she waited for his reaction. As the silence lengthened, she felt the need to add more to her part. She gave a deep sob. "Oh, Brendan, when I saw your handsome face, I knew what I had been missing all these years. I knew that our love had not died, that it never could die. Brendan, I have been so alone, so in agony without you, my love. It is fate that we should find each other once again," Molly cried, risking a glance from beneath the brim of her silk bonnet.

The lacy handkerchief ripped between her hands as she saw the look of sardonic amusement on Brendan's hardened features. Throwing back her head haughtily, she faced the O'Flynns. Never before had they been able to put her out of countenance, but now, as she saw the contempt they didn't bother to conceal, she felt herself squirming. Her presence was being suffered politely, like a maid's intrusion into a room where her betters were having a private discussion.

"Try again, Molly m'dear," Brendan told her unsympathetically. He casually lit a cigar, rudely blowing the smoke between them.

Mara gave a silent sigh of relief. For a moment she had worried that Brendan might fall for that pack of lies and take Molly back, but Brendan had rid himself of her ghost.

Molly glared at Brendan's aloof countenance with a pang of regret. Not only was Brendan still handsome, he was now filthy rich.

"I am still your wife, Brendan. You haven't forgotten that, have you?" Molly demanded belligerently as she struggled to her feet. "Other people will not forget so easily when it gets around town that you stole my child from me, running off and leaving me destitute and in grave health."

Mara gasped at the effrontery of the woman, drawing Molly's attention to her. Molly's eyes narrowed dangerously as she stared at Mara's exquisite face and felt the hatred of envy through her.

"I shall demand the return of my son. He should be with his mother," she threatened. "You wouldn't like that, would you, Mara? You think of him as yours, don't you? Well, you'd better get used to the idea of being without him."

Brendan got to his feet. Mara was surprised to see his hands shaking with anger as he faced his one-time love, a murderous look in his dark eyes.

"Don't threaten us, Molly," Brendan warned quietly. "You walked out on me and Paddy, and from that day forward you ceased to exist for me. So you might as well go on pretendin' to be María Velazquez, because you're nobody to me," Brendan told her coldly. "And I'm not thinkin' anyone in his right mind, after setting eyes on you, would believe that make-believe of yours, or allow an adulteress anywhere near a small boy. What you are is plain to see, and you're no fit mother. Give up, Molly," Brendan finished.

"Brendan, please, I beg of you. Take me back, forgive me," Molly cried in one last, desperate attempt to persuade him, her fingers closing over his arms like claws.

Brendan shook off her clinging hands and stepped away from her, shaking his head in disgusted pity. "Don't degrade yourself any more than you already have, Molly. I never could stomach beggars."

"Damn you to hell, Brendan O'Flynn!" Molly screamed, dropping her unlikely pose of humility. "Still the arrogant bastard pretending to be the fine gentleman? You're from the same gutter as me, boyo, and don't you be forgettin' it, will ye now? I'll be here to remind you, and before long people won't be bowing and scraping as they rush to open doors for you—they'll be shutting them in the face of Brendan O'Flynn, my fine lover."

Molly swaggered to the door, turning as she reached it, her hand poised above the door knob. "I'd think over that reconciliation, Brendan, me love. It just might cost you less now than 'twill later. 'Tis up to you, remember that."

"There always was just one role you could play to perfection, Molly, m'dear," Brendan said. "And that was the one of the foul-mouthed whore who comes to grief in the last act."

An ugly sneer curled her lips as Molly turned with a swish of her skirts and opened the door without another look at Brendan. The sound of the slammed door almost deafened Mara and Brendan as they silently stared at each other.

Mara rubbed her cold hands together as she shivered in reaction, thinking how lucky they were she'd run out on them when she had. She'd turned vicious, Mara thought in revulsion as she remembered the brightly painted mouth that had uttered such horrible lies and accusations, her heavy, cloying perfume still lingering in the room even after she'd left.

Mara got up and opened a window, breathing deeply of the cool air. As she turned back to the room, she became aware of Brendan slumped tiredly in his chair, his head resting heavily in his hand as he propped his elbow on the table.

"Are you all right, Brendan?" He looked so pale, almost feverish.

Brendan sighed. "I think seein' Molly again after so many years has affected me more than I thought," he explained with a half-smile that faded quickly. "Actually I feel like hell. I think I'll lie down for a while, Mara. Maybe I'm just getting older and can't take these late nights anymore," he joked. As he reached the door, he paused. Glancing back at Mara with his old, devilish smile, he said curiously, "You know...I feel good about one thing."

"What's that?"

"I really told Molly off, didn't I? I feel like I've exorcised that bitch for good and all after all these years. I said all the things I wanted to say seven years ago, only I didn't have the chance then. Jaysus, but I feel good about that."

"To be sure, I was proud of you, Brendan," Mara said softly, her eyes warm with understanding. For Mara had learned how a face could haunt you.

Brendan shook his head in confusion. "You know, mavournin, a year ago you'd probably have come back at me with some sarcastic remark. You've changed in some way, Mara, and I don't know quite what to make of it. But Molly was right about one thing. You have grown into a very beautiful young woman," he said. He eyed her quizzically. "Maybe *that's* the difference, mavournin, you've become a woman, haven't ye now?"

Mara nodded her head regretfully. "A woman, with a woman's fears and heartaches. I'm all too human, Brendan, and I ache with the realization of it sometimes."

Brendan nodded in understanding, his eyes bleak for a moment before he smiled softly and entered his room, closing the door behind him.

Mara stared at the closed door in silence for a moment, making up her mind to call in a doctor for Brendan whether or not he approved. So far Jamie's homemade remedies weren't helping him. Mara gathered together her things and left Brendan's rooms, her mind on Molly and the trouble she might cause them. Mara walked down the stairs and through the lobby of the hotel, not noticing the interested glances she drew from the men hanging about as she walked straight through without looking around. As she neared the doors, an arm reached out and held them open for her to pass through.

Mara glanced up, a polite thank-you framed on her lips when she recognized the man. Nicholas Chantale. She made no protest as his fingers closed over her elbow. He guided her along the street until, passing a quiet alley, he pulled her into its gloomy depths. The odor of rotting garbage filled the air with a breathtaking stench.

"Lovely," Mara murmured.

"You'll accept my apologies, mademoiselle, but I desired privacy," Nicholas explained suavely, as though merely apologizing for spilling punch on her skirt at a cotillion, instead of dragging her into a stinking, rat-infested alley.

Mara shivered, for among the piles of refuse she could hear the shrill squealings and scratchings of the long-tailed, gray rats who prowled the city in thousands.

Mara glared up into Nicholas's green eyes, repressing a cry as one of the beasts scampered out of an overturned barrel and into the hidden crevices of a crate. It would only give Nicholas satisfaction to see her fear, Mara thought in defiance. She controlled the urge to fight her way free of him and the alley.

"Not squeamish, my sweet?" he asked softly, his breath warm against her face.

"Of what? You, or the rats?" Mara retorted without hesitation.

Nicholas smiled despite himself. "Ah, Mara, you certainly never bore me. Irritate, provoke, insult, and enrage, yes, but never do you bore me."

"What do you want, Nicholas?" Mara demanded, her chin raised aggressively as she faced him, refusing to be intimidated by him any longer.

"So you've finally grown tired of subtleties, and are for plain speaking. Very well," Nicholas said sharply, "I want you to leave the Swede alone."

Mara stared at Nicholas incredulously. "You're warning me off your friend? Does he know you've appointed yourself his watchdog?" Mara asked contemptuously, hoping her wounded feelings didn't show. "I don't think he'd appreciate your meddling. He is a grown man, and most capable of taking care of his own affairs. Nobody likes a busybody, m'sieu," she ridiculed him, deciding he could just go on thinking what he wanted about her and the Swede, for she wasn't about to tell him that they were merely friends. Let him worry and make a fool of himself, Mara thought angrily.

Nicholas's mouth tightened. "I'm just giving you a friendly word of advice, Miss O'Flynn. Don't play any of your cruel games with the Swede. Remember, I know who you are, and should anything happen, you can't slip away to Paris the following morning. I'll be watching you, and waiting for the least misstep."

Mara smiled up into his face, her eyes glinting with anger. "My, my, we do love to threaten people, don't we? How do you ever find time for yourself, or for polishing your halo?" Mara demanded. "Well, you're worse than me, Nicholas, because you're a hypocrite and a liar."

"Careful you don't go any further than name-calling, Mara," Nicholas warned her as he noticed her clenched fists and remembered the feel of her hand against his cheek.

"I wouldn't touch you for all the gold in California. You lied to me. You let me go on believing that I'd been responsible for your nephew's death. That was despicable," Mara whispered as she stared up at him. "How you must hate me, Nicholas."

Nicholas was silent for a moment, then said coldly, "It didn't hurt you to feel a little remorse for once in your life. Just maybe you might learn to respect the emotions of other people. Not that I expect any miracles where you're concerned, my sweet," he added.

Mara couldn't think of anything to say, and without a word she turned on her heel and walked away from him, her shoulders sagging slightly. She would never be able to change his opinion of her. Never. Nothing she could ever do would ease his bitterness. She never even had a chance. She hurried down the busy street, her cloaked figure disappearing into the crowd.

The next few days passed quickly, with no word from Molly. But Mara was not lulled into believing that Molly was out of their lives. She was just waiting for the right time to strike. They would have to be prepared for her scandal-mongering, for that was the only way she could hurt them.

Brendan seemed unconcerned by the incident and continued his partying and late nights. In fact, Mara thought, he might even be trying to show Molly just exactly what she had lost out on, as he entertained lavishly. Mara finally began to wonder how long it would last at the rate Brendan was spending it but she wasn't worried, for as Brendan had told her often enough, there was more gold out there just waiting to be picked up by some enterprising fellow.

Tell me not, in mournful numbers,
Life is but an empty dream
For the soul is dead that slumbers,
And things are not what they seem.
Life is real! Life is earnest!
And the grave is not its goal;
Dust thou art, to dust returnest,
Was not spoken of the soul.

—Longfellow

Chapter 9

"WAKE UP, MARA! WAKE UP!" A VOICE WHISPERED URGENTLY. Mara burrowed deeper into her pillow, pulling the blankets up over her head as she closed out both the annoying voice and the chill of the room.

"Go away," Mara mumbled sleepily, but the persistent arm kept shaking her. Finally Mara sat up in bed to face her tormentor. "What the devil?" Mara demanded.

"Mara, there's someone downstairs wanting a word with you," Jenny told her, her voice still urgent. "I think it's important. You'd better see her."

"Her?" Mara asked groggily as she climbed out of bed. By now Jenny had lit the oil lamp, and a dim light was spreading throughout the room. Mara found her robe and slipped it over her nightgown, something she had finally given in to wearing in the cold, damp climate of San Francisco. She followed Jenny's woolen-robed figure down the stairs.

In the hallway below a single figure huddled, and although Mara couldn't see much of her bundled-up form except for a bunch of blond curls, she knew she didn't recognize the woman who stood waiting for her.

Hearing footsteps, the caller glanced up in relief and came toward the foot of the stairs, her wind-chaffed hands twisting nervously. "You Mara O'Flynn?" she asked eagerly.

Mara eyed her curiously, wondering what in the world she

could want with her at this hour of the night. "Yes. Who are you? What do you want?"

"He sent me," she said breathlessly.

"Who?" Mara asked, looking at Jenny in bewilderment.

"Yer brother's Brendan O'Flynn, ain't he?" the woman demanded. "Well, he's sick, and real bad too, I reckon. He didn't seem himself tonight when we was out on the town. Won a heap of money too, but he just didn't seem to care. Then, when we was back at his hotel, he just faints dead away. That he did, I swear. I don't usually get myself involved in other people's business, but Brendan...well, he's a real gent'man. Treats a body like a lady, even if he is payin' fer it. So I figured I'd tell you like he asked me to. He says, 'Get Mara. I must see her, and the divil take ye if ye don't.'"

Mara had grown pale. She believed her and now she turned to Jenny with a determined look. "I must go. Will you take care of Paddy? I'll need Jamie with me."

"Of course. And if there's anything I can do, you must let me know," Jenny reassured her.

"Well, I guess I'll be on my way," the strange woman said.

"Thank you. If you'll wait a minute, I want to give you something for coming out of your way to tell me," Mara said, indebted to the woman for not ignoring Brendan's plea.

"Nah, ain't necessary," she replied with a sniff. "Did it fer a friend. Besides, he'd already paid me. Like I said, a real gent'man he is. Hope he gets better right soon. 'Night."

Mara quickly roused Jamie and dressed. Together they made their way to Brendan. Lights still shone out of the gaming saloons into the night and were reflected into the dark pools of water filling the potholes in the streets. They made their way to Brendan's hotel without incident, for by this time in the early morning most of the revelers were either being entertained or had drunk too much to notice two unescorted females.

They passed without comment through the lobby of the hotel where a few latecomers were straggling in. The desk clerk dozed behind the register, his pince-nez precariously balanced on the tip of his nose.

"For once Brendan showed some common sense in pickin'

this hotel," Jamie whispered as they walked along the quiet corridor to Brendan's room.

"Brendan's always had the best of taste, Jamie," Mara said automatically, "and now he can finally afford it."

Mara tapped lightly on the door of Brendan's room. After waiting a second, she and Jamie entered the silent room. Several pink-tinted lamp shades cast a rosy glow over the room with its elegant furniture and rich carpeting. Above the mantelpiece a clock was ticking away, the only sound in the room until a faint moan drifted to them from the other side of the sofa, the high, carved back having hidden Brendan from their view.

Mara rushed around to the other side and stared down in shock at Brendan's sweat-drenched body. His breathing was coming raspily, then he suddenly started to shiver, curling up his body as he tried unsuccessfully to find warmth.

"Brendan," Mara whispered as she pushed the hair from his brow. She was surprised by the cold dampness of his skin.

"We gotta get him into bed with plenty of hot bricks and blankets. And get something hot inside of him too," Jamie said as she eyed Brendan worriedly. "Never would stay out of the rain, fool boy, always wantin' to go out and play. Guess he never changed none."

It was hard to lift Brendan's weight into the bedroom, but they managed between them to get him settled in bed. Mara pulled up a chair and sat down next to the bed, watching as Brendan alternately shivered and sweated. A painful cough would rack his body every so often, leaving him weak and pale against the pillows as he gasped for breath.

His delirium continued through the next day, Jamie or Mara keeping watch while the other rested. Mara began to lose count of the hours. With the thick velvet drapes pulled across the windows, night could be day. The activity down on the street seldom let up, and the only time she could accurately guess was the period preceding dawn when most people were abed.

Jenny came the following afternoon with a change of clothes for Mara and other items she thought they might need. The Swede had come with her and sat uncomfortably on the edge of the sofa, not knowing how to help, or even what to say. His eyes showed his concern as he stared at Mara's haggard face and reddened eyes.

"If there's anything I can do, Mara," he offered as he was about to leave, "well, don't hesitate to ask. I'd like to help if I can."

Mara smiled tiredly. "Thank you, Swede, but I think we're doing all that can be done. I appreciate the offer," Mara told him.

"How's Paddy doing?" she asked Jenny, wondering what he'd been up to while she was away.

"Oh, he's been real good, Mara, no trouble at all, just playing with Paul and Gordie," Jenny reassured her. "Yesterday, Swede took them all down to the docks to watch the ships."

"Thank you. That was certainly kind of you," Mara said, relieved. "Have you heard anything about us around town?" Mara asked casually.

"Like what?"

Mara smiled. "If you don't know, then I don't have to worry," she responded enigmatically.

As they were about to leave, the Swede paused at the door and said carefully, "I have heard a few rumors, Mara, but if you think it's Nicholas spreading them, then you're wrong."

Mara sighed. "So it's started," she said softly. Shaking her head, she looked at the Swede. "I know it's not Nicholas. He may despise me, and at times can be hateful, but he doesn't sneak around behind someone's back. That's not his style."

"Good," the Swede answered, relieved that she hadn't lost complete faith in Nicholas, that her love hadn't turned into hate quite yet. With a nod of understanding he left with Jenny.

Mara was dozing fitfully when she woke abruptly to hear the clock in the sitting room chiming the hour. She counted five. Soon it would be light, and Brendan would have passed another night. But as Mara listened intently, she became aware of a difference in Brendan's breathing. It sounded laborious, as though he were having a great deal of difficulty catching his breath. Mara stared down at his handsome face, so pale and thin. Around his lips was a faint tracing of blue. Mara lightly touched his face, jerking back her hand at its coldness. His eyes seemed to have sunk in his head, and his soft curls hung limply over his forehead. Suddenly he opened his eyes and stared up at his sister. He looked lucid for the first time in days.

"Mara," he whispered hoarsely.

Quickly Mara filled a glass of water and, carefully holding his head, let him sip a little of it. He smiled thankfully and lay back against the pillows.

"No whiskey?" he joked, reminding Mara faintly of the old Brendan.

"Not until you can hold your fill, me love," Mara told him. "I wouldn't be so cruel as to give an Irishman a mere swallow."

"I'm so tired, Mara," Brendan said. "I seem to ache all over. Did anyone beat the daylights out of me while I wasn't looking?" He choked back a cough that rumbled up from his chest and left a reddish brown phlegm staining the cloth on his pillow.

Mara wrung out a fresh cloth in the bowl of water on the bedside table and pressed its cool dampness against his hot forehead.

Brendan stared into the distance. "Never knew I could spend money so fast and enjoy it so much. I've been thinking, mavournin, that I'll go back up to the Sierra and find myself another chunk of gold. I know where to look, you know," he confided, then continued dreamily, "and then I think we'll return to Ireland. I rather fancy going back to Dublin and buying back our old house. Of course, we might be wantin' something grander than that. Wouldn't it be something if the old man's ancestral estate were for sale, and we, the illegitimate offspring, bought it? 'Twould only be fitting after all we've been through because of him, Mara," Brendan sighed.

"Ah, it'll be grand, Mara, me little darlin', you wait and see. Brendan did it for you, like he promised. We struck it rich, livin' the life of a king, for sure. I can see meself in London now, with a townhouse in Grosvenor Square and a small place in Bath—quite the place to be during the Season, you know—and we'll have a fine stable full of horses that'll be the envy of half of London. We'll be quite respectable, riding out every morning along Rotten Row, and damned if we won't catch an earl or even a duke for you, Mara. Ah, mavournin, 'twill be grand to be living fancy again, never having to worry about payin' the bills; and people sayin', 'there goes Brendan O'Flynn, a fine gentleman, to be sure,'" he said softly. He closed his eyes with a deep, contented sigh.

Mara tucked the blankets around his shoulders, brushing from his forehead the soft curls that reminded her so much of Paddy's. She placed a light kiss against his brow before settling down in the chair beside his bed. She picked up the book she'd been reading and tried to find her place once again, but her heart wasn't in it. Soon she fell asleep, the book still open in her lap.

Mara awoke suddenly, the pounding of her heart the only sound in the room. It was dawn. She could see the glare of light through the parting of the drapes and hear the stirrings of sound from the street below, but there was an unnatural stillness in the room. With a feeling of dread Mara looked down into Brendan's quiet face and knew he had died.

The slight smile of contentment still curved his lips even in death. Mara continued to stand silently staring down at him, her face frozen. Swallowing hard, she whispered her brother's name for the last time.

She was still standing there when Jamie bustled in half an hour later. The old woman stopped abruptly as she took in the strange look on Mara's face. With a deep sob Jamie ran forward, her gray eyes moving quickly between brother and sister, both so unnaturally still.

Jamie's wail cut through the numbness of Mara's mind. She refocused her eyes and gazed lovingly down at Brendan's features for the last time. She gently covered his face with the sheet and, without a backward glance at the shrouded figure, walked from the room and closed the door. But still she could hear Jamie's sobbing, and with a muttered curse she pressed her hands over her ears, determined to shut out the sound that brought back memories of her mother's death in Paris.

It wasn't the way of the Irish to hide their grief. During the night-long wake that preceded the burial of Brendan O'Flynn, his friends paid their respects. Many of these were Irish and they stayed the night long, sitting vigil over the body.

But some of the faces crowding the room Mara had never seen before, and she suspected they were fellow Irishmen who had never met Brendan O'Flynn. They were homesick for the old country and its customs, and hoped to find solace with a glass of whiskey and the gentle, melodic brogue of the mourners murmuring softly around the coffin.

That Mara received her share of curious glances and speculation she didn't doubt, for she sat in stony silence throughout the long hours of the wake, never smiling, crying, or speaking except for a word of thanks and a slight nod now and then as she received condolences. Brendan had been a popular fellow, and he'd have been proud of the send-off his friends gave him. From the dissipated looks of many of the mourners, Mara judged that they would shortly follow in his footsteps. They staggered drunkenly into the night still humming snatches of song from the evening's festivities. A wake was meant to be enjoyed by all but the dead.

The following morning, as a light drizzle fell under leaden skies, the mourners gathered around the open grave on Russian Hill, and Brendan Michael O'Flynn was laid to his final rest in the land that had promised him riches beyond his wildest dreams.

Dressed in black bombazine trimmed with crepe, a bonnet with a heavy veil obscuring her face, Mara looked like a statue. The only movement she made was in the slight lifting of the edges of her cape as the wind caught it. A subdued Paddy stood beside Mara, his small hand tucked inside hers. He solemnly watched the proceedings, a slight frown on his forehead as he listened to the priest's droning voice, not understanding the Latin the man was speaking. Jamie stood on the other side of Paddy, her small body hunched over as she cried continuously into a soggy handkerchief. For the first time, Jamie looked really old. Jenny and her boys stood nearby. For once, they seemed to have been impressed into silence, but it might have been the intimidating presence of the Swede standing just behind them that formed their admirable behavior.

But it was as Mara stared across the grave that she felt a black rage rise almost uncontrollably inside of her. On the other side, suitably dressed in black, stood Molly O'Flynn, the grieving widow, there for all the world to see. Behind the concealing folds of her veil Mara's eyes glowed with fury, the first stirrings of emotion she'd felt since she'd stood over Brendan's deathbed. Mara unconsciously tightened her fingers around Paddy's small hand and watched in disgust as Molly sobbed loudly. Jacques D'Arcy patted her arm every so often, perhaps warningly, as Molly's wails threatened to drown out the priest. As the eulogy ended, Mara bent on shaky legs and, picking up a handful of the soft, damp earth, let it trickle onto the coffin, staring down in fascination at the dark hole. She felt a strong hand beneath her elbow as she swayed, and then was led away from the graveside by the Swede. Mara drew strength from his comforting presence. Without looking back at Molly on the far side of the grave, Mara allowed the Swede and Jenny to escort the little party back to the boardinghouse.

At the foot of the stairs Mara turned to Jenny and the Swede and held out her hands. "You've been so kind to us. I want you to know I'll never forget it—never. I really don't know how I'd have gotten through it all without you. I think I'd prefer to be alone for a little while now, if you don't mind," Mara said, her face as white as ivory with the black veil framing it.

"Can I stay down here with Paul and Gordie?" Paddy asked hopefully as he eyed Mara's black-clad figure and grim expression with an apprehensive shudder of confusion. "I'll be real quiet."

"It'd do the little fellow good to forget for a while, Mara," the Swede suggested. "I'll be here to keep an eye on them." He watched with concern as she sagged against the banister. "Go on up, Mara. You could use some sleep. Everything will be all right down here."

He signaled to Jamie but her nose was buried in her hand-kerchief. She seemed incapable of even finding her own way upstairs, much less helping Mara.

But Jenny quickly and efficiently took charge. She hustled the Swede and the boys into the parlor with strict instructions not to make a sound, and then guided Mara and Jamie upstairs.

"See to Jamie, I'll be fine," Mara told Jenny as she headed for the quiet of her room.

Mara lay back against the pillows on her bed and gazed up at the ceiling. What was she going to do? Always, in the past, Brendan had been there. Or at least she had known he *would* be there in case she should need him. Now he was gone. It seemed impossible that he would never come striding through the door, a devilish grin on his face and some disastrous scheme lighting up his eyes. Brendan had always seemed indestructible. She'd never even imagined a life without him.

She felt such emptiness that it ached inside her. Mara wearily rubbed her eyes wishing she could put it all out of her mind. But she could not do that, for soon she would have to decide what to do. Mara smiled wryly. Brendan had, in his final and greatest scheme ever, left them wealthy. For once money would be no problem. She would just have to worry how to spend it, Mara thought drowsily as her head rolled on the pillow. She fell into a deep, dreamless sleep, the first she'd had in days.

Jenny backed out of Mara's bedroom on tiptoe, closing the door silently behind her. She made her way back downstairs with the tray. The sleep Mara had found would be far more beneficial than food.

"Isn't she well?" the Swede asked immediately on Jenny's reappearance with the tray. "Should I send for a doctor?"

Jenny shook her red curls in exasperation. "No, that's all I need is someone else to bump into on the stairs. She's getting the best thing she can right now, and that's sleep. Best cure I know for troubles of the spirit and the flesh."

"I suppose you're right, although she seemed a mite strange to me," the Swede commented. "Aren't women supposed to cry? I swear I never once saw a tear in her eye. I thought she and her brother were mighty close."

Jenny sat down, pouring the tea out for them rather than waste it. Busying herself with stirring in a spoonful of sugar, she shrugged tolerantly. "People have different ways of grieving. Some fall to pieces, ranting and raving, until they're not much better off than the dead. Other folks don't show much emotion, which don't mean they aren't grieving inside. It hurts them real bad, and it's worse for them since they can't release the grief. I figure Mara O'Flynn is like that. Not that she can't get in a rage about some things. Why, that look she gave the widow was enough to put her in the grave next to her husband. Something strange there. Funny her showing up now. Wasn't she the woman we saw at Delmonico's? They acted like she was a stranger or something. I don't remember what they called her, but it sure wasn't 'Molly O'Flynn.' And did you see, she didn't even glance at her son once," Jenny said, astonished.

"I gather this Molly O'Flynn ran off and left them, her son only a couple of months old at the time," Jenny declared shaking her head in disgust. "Can you imagine that?"

"From what I know of the woman, it's most likely true," the Swede said, not feeling quite the same degree of outrage as Jenny did.

"Well, I think she's horrible, and I just hope she doesn't intend to cause trouble," Jenny said worriedly as she handed the Swede the plate with several pieces of apple strudel on it that he'd been eyeing for the past minute and a half. "I don't see what she can do," the Swede said in unconcern as he bit into the freshly baked pastry. "Besides, I'm here to protect her, should the occasion arise."

"Well, I just hope it doesn't. Now, shssh," she warned her sons as their voices were steadily rising, hiding a smile at the momentary look of surprise that had crossed the Swede's face as he'd thought she'd meant him.

Mara slept undisturbed through the afternoon and night and awakened the following morning feeling more of a mind to make decisions. She felt a momentary twinge of guilt over the neglected Paddy, until she heard laughing voices and sighed in relief, for that was definitely Paddy's giggle.

Mara was halfway down the stairs when Jenny came from the dining room and, glancing up, stopped in surprise. Mara continued down, pulling on her gloves as she reached the last step.

"I have to see to Brendan's business affairs—see what needs to be taken care of," Mara explained.

"Are you sure you feel up to it? I know the Swede was going to pay a call today to see if he could assist you," Jenny offered helpfully.

"I can handle it. And I'd just as soon get it over with."

Her business was, in fact, concluded far more quickly than she could possibly have imagined. But then, there was very little to see to, and very little money to worry about. Brendan had only a couple of thousand dollars left of the huge fortune he'd discovered. And there were some personal possessions, which she collected.

What had happened to it all? Mara made her way back to the boardinghouse, stunned. She began to remember the clothes, dinners, parties, and the nights spent gambling. Well, she shouldn't really be angry. It'd been Brendan's money, and he'd had a right to spend it as he pleased. She was glad that he'd lived his last days like a king, and had not died a pauper's death. No, she didn't begrudge him those last weeks.

Mara paused for a moment on the edge of the sidewalk, waiting for a loaded wagon to be pulled slowly past before she could cross to the other side. Suddenly her attention was caught by a familiar figure striding along the street on the far side. Nicholas, Mara whispered, her eyes clinging to his broad back as he stopped and bought a paper, one of many for sale on each street corner and only a few months old, having been brought in one of the mail steamers. Mara watched as his figure moved along the walk. He didn't even glance her way. As Mara felt the people crowding her closer to the edge of the sidewalk, she stepped back to avoid being knocked into the muddy street. They pushed rudely against her. Mara disdainfully glanced around her, then brought down the heel of her boot on the instep of the man standing next to her, smiling apologetically at his groan of surprised pain. He'd not take another liberty too soon, Mara thought in satisfaction as he limped away.

The street was clear of traffic now and the people started to pick their way carefully across. Mara started forward but was halted by an arm sliding around her back, the hand biting painfully into her waist. Mara turned a look of outrage on the person. It was Jacques D'Arcy.

He leered down, undaunted by her anger. His grip tightened and he said warningly, "You wouldn't deal so harshly with Jacques, would you, ma chérie? I am not so careless as your unfortunate admirer of a moment ago, so do not anger me. Accompany me without making a scene, and I promise you will not be hurt," Jacques told her with a broad smile. His eyes glinted in malicious anticipation. "A certain person only wishes to have a word with you—that is all. You have my word as a gentleman," he promised with a grin.

"How many dead men believed that?" Mara asked as she tried to hide her fear and revulsion.

"Ah, ma chérie, you are so cruel to poor Jacques, who only desires to be kind to you. Now come, we have talked too long. The Count grows impatient." He drew her attention to the elegant figure of the Count, who stood watching them a few feet away. He eyed Mara coldly.

"And, ma chérie, a small word of advice, don't let the Count's broken hand lull you into thinking he cannot do his job. He is just as efficient with his left hand, and already he is most displeased with you—and with your big friend."

Mara had little choice. The crowd of people had scattered, and should she try to call out to a passerby, Jacques would find some way of circumventing her. Even now she could feel the painful pressure of his hand beneath her rib cage and knew he'd not hesitate to use the knife she now saw gleaming in his other hand.

Jacques nodded to the Count who closed in on the other side of her. They moved swiftly along the sidewalk. They had walked only a short distance when they turned off the main street and into an alley, Jacques quickly leading her to a door in the side of one of the buildings, a key from his pocket soundlessly opening the door. Mara faltered as she stepped inside, her eyes adjusting slowly to the dimness of the narrow hallway. The Count pushed her and she stumbled against the wall, reaching out to save herself from falling. Mara cursed beneath her breath as she straightened, rubbing her arm where it had come into painful contact with the wall.

"Let me guide you, ma chérie," Jacques offered gallantly as he put his arm around her waist and guided Mara to the stairs, holding her closer than was necessary as they climbed. His hot breath brushed against her cheek as he smiled down into her face. "We are here, ma chérie," he said with a low laugh, and grandly swung open the door.

Mara blinked, staring around her at the opulent gaudiness of the room. She was not really surprised to find Molly O'Flynn reclining on a chaise longue, clad only in a pale pink negligee. Molly indolently brushed a long strand of black hair. She glanced up, a welcoming smile parting her lips.

"My dear, how lovely of you to accept my invitation," she said mockingly. Then, curling her legs under her, she patted the cushion invitingly. "Do sit down, Mara, for we must become reacquainted after so many years apart. My maid is bringing tea. You must be chilled. Do share a cup with me, I insist."

Mara eyed Molly suspiciously, ignoring her request as she stayed where she was. "What do you want, Molly?"

Molly's eyes narrowed, her smile now curving into a sneer of dislike as she laughed rudely in Mara's face. "You never were one for sweet talk, eh, Mara? Once, at a snap of my fingers, you'd have come running, begging to be of some help. I used to think you were such a sweet child. What has happened to you, my dear?"

"I've grown up, Molly. I've seen the world," Mara answered boldly, "and I've learned to tell the difference between rhinestones and diamonds."

Molly's lips tightened, her eyes flashing as she caught Jacques's appreciative snicker. "You and Brendan always did have a certain caustic wit. A pity you don't know how to use common sense as well. That's why I left Brendan—he was a loser."

"Yes, you were indeed wise, Molly. Brendan would

surely have become bored with you after too much longer," Mara said casually as she made a point of looking around the room, the distasteful look on her face hiding her purpose. She searched for a route of escape. "He never could abide a woman with little intelligence and no style."

Molly swept her feet to the floor, her movement affording both the Count and Jacques an unrestricted view of her shapely thighs. Mara blushed as she realized Molly wore nothing beneath the negligee.

"Very well, Mara. Shall we forget any idea of becoming friends? You're still one of the high and mighty O'Flynns, and better than me, aren't you?" Molly spat as she moved to within a foot of Mara's face. "Well, I'm an O'Flynn too. Or have you conveniently forgotten that? As the widow of Brendan O'Flynn I demand the right to his fortune."

Mara didn't bother to control her laugh.

"Damn you! You think it's funny, do you? Nothing ever seems to pierce that damned arrogant O'Flynn pride. Always ridiculing your foe. Let's see how hard you laugh when I reclaim my son, Mara O'Flynn," she threw at Mara, a spiteful smile curving her mouth.

Mara stopped laughing. Shaking her head, she said, "I'm only laughing because, as usual, Molly, you've mistimed your entrance. You see," she told her earnestly, "Brendan spent it all. I've just come from the bank. There is no fortune for you to claim."

Molly's mouth dropped open. "Liar!" she exclaimed, the disbelief in her eyes replaced now by ruthless determination as she said in a softer tone, "You must really think me a fool if you expect me to believe that."

"It's the truth," Mara told her simply.

"He *was* spending a great deal of money, María," Jacques said, the name he first met Molly under coming easier than her real one.

"Shut up! When I want your opinion I'll ask for it," she yelled as she turned on him wrathfully.

"You'd do well to listen to him, Molly," Mara advised her, not intimidated by the other woman's temper.

"You'd like that, wouldn't you," Molly snarled, her face becoming mottled with anger. "To have me believing there was no money so you could have it all. He couldn't have spent it all. They said he was worth hundreds of thousands of dollars."

"There was never that much, and now there's hardly more than a thousand dollars left," Mara tried to tell her, only to have Molly reach out and grab her shoulders, her fingernails digging into Mara's soft skin as she shook her.

"Damn it! Where is the money? If you don't tell me where it is, I swear I'll have the Count carve the information out of you," Molly swore as she stared down into Mara's pale face before pushing her against Jacques who was standing just behind Mara.

Mara jerked away from the contact and, her golden eyes full of hatred, fumbled with the drawstrings of her purse as she searched for the small bag belonging to Brendan that she'd just claimed from the bank.

Pulling it from her purse, she held it up to a curiously watching Molly and, with a bitter smile, opened it and threw gold dust into Molly's face. It clung to her eyelashes and glittered on her cheeks.

"You can have this cursed gold," Mara cried. "Take it and weep, Molly. Cry tears of gold, for that's all you shall reap in return. This dream of riches leads only to despair and death. That's all Brendan found…a cold grave on a lonely, wind-swept hill in a strange country."

Molly stood stupefied, her face and hair covered with the fine gold dust. She blinked, her eyes watering. A tear fell and mixed with the gold as it ran down her cheek.

Mara became aware of the full implications of what she'd done as she felt Jacques move behind her, his hand closing over her shoulder painfully, holding her immobile as Molly stared with burning eyes into Mara's face. She took a step forward, her hand raised to strike when a door tucked away in the side of the room opened and a thin girl dressed as a maid entered carrying a heavy tea tray loaded down with a silver teapot and cups and saucers.

"Where do you want this, Miss Velazquez?" Ellen asked timidly as she nervously looked around, shuddering when she recognized the two men.

"I don't want it anywhere you stupid fool!" Molly screamed.

"B-but you told me," Ellen began shakily, only to fall silent as she stared incredulously at Molly's gold-splattered face. Molly's arm swung out and viciously knocked the heavily laden tray from the girl's straining arms. Ellen gave a cry of pain as the boiling water splashed across her arms and chest. The china cups and saucers, silver teapot, and plate of sweets all crashed to the floor. Ellen started to cry, her sobs rising loudly as she rushed from the room. Mara found herself free and, without hesitating, darted off to the side and followed the maid. Slamming the door shut behind her, she quickly locked it.

Mara glanced around her curiously. The room she'd run into was a parlor, and apparently seldom used for it was stuffy and dust thickly covered what little furniture there was. She went quickly to the window which overlooked the back of the house, as well as another building close behind, one that was lower and onto which she could possibly jump.

Mara was hesitant to try it, but there was no other alternative. She was about to raise the window when she heard a whimpering sound coming from behind one of the large overstuffed chairs in the corner. With a sigh she hurried over to it, peering down into the concealing darkness to see the maid whose timely interruption had allowed her to escape.

"Are you all right?" Mara asked, anxious to flee. The girl had stopped crying and sniffed loudly as she hesitantly got to her feet, not standing much higher than the back of the chair. She nodded.

Mara looked at the pathetic creature. Her life must surely be hell if her livelihood depended on the whims of Molly. Mara dug into her purse and pulled our several silver dollars. Grabbing the girl's bony hand, she placed them in her palm. She hurried back over to the window while the girl stood staring down into her hand, looking at the small fortune she suddenly possessed.

Mara was about to climb over the sill when a tremulous voice halted her. "There's a back staircase, ma'am," Ellen told her as she came out from behind the protection of the chair. She pointed to another door partially concealed by a heavy curtain.

Mara hurried across to it, pushing aside the curtain and opening the door that led to the stairs. "Thank you," Mara said quietly, yet with a depth of feeling the word had never held for her before. Then she disappeared behind the door.

❧

"It won't open," Jacques said as he tried the door Mara had disappeared behind from Molly's bedchamber. "I'll have to break it in."

"Wait, I have a key for it somewhere." Molly stopped him as she rushed over to her dresser and began to sort through the cluttered surface where her perfume bottles, brushes, beauty aids, and small bunches of artificial flowers, ribbons, and feathers, all covered with a thin coating of powder, were crowded together. "It'd cost me a fortune to get that door repaired."

Jacques watched her impatiently as she continued to dig without success in the disorder of her dresser. "Mon Dieu! She'll be in Paris by the time you find that key, ma chérie," Jacques swore.

"Oh, break it down, then. I'll be able to buy a thousand doors when I get my hands on that damned fortune of Brendan's," Molly told him as she gave up her fruitless search for the key.

Swearing beneath his breath, Jacques stepped back from the door he'd just charged, rubbing his painful shoulder as he glared at the offending obstacle. Taking a deep breath, he took a step and kicked hard against the door, the lock giving with a splintering of wood as he and the Count rushed in, only to find an empty parlor.

"She must have gone out of the window," the Count said in disappointment at losing his quarry when he noticed the window as a cold draft swept through the room.

"Never mind," Molly spoke from the doorway, a look of

cunning replacing the frustrated expression on her face as she continued in a soft voice, "we'll settle the score with Mara O'Flynn later, and at the same time, get my fortune from her."

⤷⤶

Mara reached the relative safety of the boardinghouse without incident, her breath coming raggedly as she stepped inside and closed the door firmly shut behind her. She was still standing before the door when Jenny entered the hall, her smile of welcome changing to a look of alarmed concern as she became aware of her friend's agitation.

"What has happened? Are you all right?" Jenny demanded as she grasped Mara's arms, pulling her away from the door and into the parlor. She pushed her down into a chair.

"What on earth has happened?" Jenny asked once again when Mara had caught her breath.

Mara made an effort to gather her thoughts together. "I'm afraid Brendan didn't leave me as well off as I imagined. In fact, it will take all there is left just to leave for Europe," Mara told her with a worried frown. She checked her watch. "I must go to one of the shipping lines and book passage on a ship leaving immediately for England."

"You're leaving San Francisco! But why, Mara? You can find a way to live here, can't you? Will it really be any better in London or Paris? You can make a new life for yourself and Paddy out here, Mara. Why don't you give it a chance?"

Mara replied dully, "It's no good here for me. It's funny—that's just what Brendan used to tell me, that we could make a new life for ourselves out here. That the past didn't matter anymore."

Mara shook her head, a bittersweet smile curving her lips. "He was wrong, for it seems as if the past caught up with us out here. Molly wants Brendan's fortune, and she wouldn't believe me when I tried to tell her that there isn't any. She won't leave me alone until she gets everything, or at least what she mistakenly believes there is. I've got to get away from here, Jenny. She scares me, as well as that Jacques D'Arcy and the Count. They'll use Paddy to try and get what they want, and I don't want him hurt," Mara told Jenny desperately. "I can't stand this city anymore. It's brought nothing but misery to the O'Flynns. I will be sorry to leave you, though. I guess you're the first real friend I've ever had.

"Brendan and I traveled so much, and—well, in our profession you just don't make many friends," Mara said with a shrug as she got to her feet and glanced around the plain little room. "Maybe someday we'll come back and see how you're doing. I believe I'll actually miss this place," Mara said wryly. "I've got to find Jamie now and start her packing. I don't believe she'll be sorry to leave. She never did like it in California."

Jenny watched Mara walk from the room, a sad look in her eyes as she realized she'd probably never see Mara O'Flynn again. There would be nothing in San Francisco for the beautiful Irishwoman to return to, nothing except sad memories.

∽

Nicholas Chantale picked up his winnings from the faro table and made his way out onto the street, breathing deeply of the crisp air after the stuffy gambling saloon. He strode effortlessly along the congested sidewalk, groups parting as he shouldered his way through, his wide chest and strong jaw only hinting at the strength that lay beneath.

Nicholas stopped at the corner, pausing long enough to buy San Francisco and New Orleans newspapers. Without sparing a glance for his surroundings, he moved along and quickly found his way to the restaurant on Dupont Street where he was meeting the Swede for lunch. While he waited, he began to thumb through the newspapers. He'd almost finished his wine when he started to read the New Orleans paper.

His wineglass had been refilled but was still close to the brim when the Swede pulled out a chair and sat down at the table, casting a curious glance at Nicholas who was still staring thoughtfully at his newspaper.

"Something interesting in there?" the Swede asked as he ordered a whiskey. Then, noticing that the paper was from New Orleans, he said, "A New Orleans paper? Don't tell me the Mississippi's flooded its banks again?"

"I bought it out of curiosity," Nicholas said quietly. "I'm returning to New Orleans as soon as possible."

The Swede stared, astounded. "You're going home? I thought you swore you'd never set foot in New Orleans again? What's happened to change your mind?"

"I received a letter from my father, forwarded from London by Denise. My family hasn't the slightest idea where to find me," Nicholas told him dryly. "You can travel a long way in fifteen years."

The Swede shook his curly blond head, a look of amazement crossing his broad features. "Your father wrote to you?"

Nicholas smiled crookedly. "Seems hard to believe, doesn't it?"

"After the way he practically ran you out of New Orleans, yes, it does. But I guess time heals all wounds," the Swede said, not really comprehending such hatred, especially a man's hatred for his own son. But then, these were Creoles, and never had he met such a thin-skinned bunch of folks. They imagined slights right and left of them. Even Nicholas could stop a person cold with one of his looks.

"Time didn't heal this one, Swede," Nicholas told him, drawing an envelope from his pocket. "Only the truth permitted him to write to me. His pride and honor wouldn't allow him to continue to accuse me falsely. So he swallowed both and wrote to me," Nicholas finished. He handed the letter to his friend.

The Swede banged his glass of whiskey onto the table. "You mean he finally believes you?"

"Yes," Nicholas answered shortly, a troubled expression settling on his brow.

The Swede opened the letter and began to read, the formal wording bringing back vivid memories of that aristocratic old gentleman.

> September 11, 1850
>
> My dearest son, Nicholas,
>
> I have gravely wronged you, my son. I have recently discovered the truth of François's tragic death. To write this letter brings me both pain and joy, for in facing the true evil,

I realize that I've been a foolish old man whose grief drove him to turn against his beloved son and send him from his heart. I can only ask that you forgive me. Will you return home and take your rightful place as heir to Beaumarais? I will be changing my will in your favor, and should anything happen to me before you return, I shall have written it all down in my diary. There you will find the truth. I beg your forgiveness and long to see your face.

    Your loving and penitent father,
    François Philippe de Montaigne-Chantale

"Well," the Swede commented, handing the letter back to Nicholas, "if I hadn't seen it with my own eyes I wouldn't have believed it possible. I wonder what he found out to change his mind."

"I don't know, but you can understand why I would wish to know who really killed François and let me be accused of it. That's why I'm going back to New Orleans," Nicholas told him, his lips thinned into a grim line as he stared at the letter.

"You want me along?" the Swede asked bluntly.

Nicholas eyed him curiously for a second before saying softly, "It's up to you, Swede. Maybe you have a special reason for not wanting to leave San Francisco? You thinking of looking for more gold?" he asked carefully.

The Swede shook his blond head. "No. Actually, I was figuring on maybe buying myself some kind of business, maybe a restaurant or a small hotel," the Swede confided with a broad smile. "Turning respectable, you might say."

Nicholas nodded, a cynical smile playing over his face as he asked casually, "Thinking of settling down in San Francisco, are you?"

"Been thinking about it for some time actually," the Swede answered just as carefully. He watched Nicholas, knowing not to accept that smile at face value. "San Francisco seems my type of town, what with all the whiskey and women around. Now that I've got some capital behind me, I'd like to be in on the building of this town. I think it could be quite a place one of these days, if the right people have a hand in its growth."

"You sure it's not just one woman who has you wanting to stay here?" Nicholas asked him suddenly. "A certain acid-tongued Irishwoman whose golden eyes probably reflect the gold in your pockets instead of love?"

The Swede's big fists bunched. "You know, Nicholas, if you weren't such a good friend you'd be picking yourself off of the floor right now and nursing a sore jaw. But knowing you as well as I do," he added with a humorless smile, "I can forgive you for your short-sighted, cruel, and just plain stupid attitude toward Mara O'Flynn."

Nicholas laughed without amusement. "My, my. She really does have you bewitched. When's the wedding?"

The Swede glared across the table at his exasperating friend. "You're the one bewitched, and it's blinding you to the truth. My God, Nicholas, what does she have to do to prove to you that she's a decent woman? Or don't you want that? Because then you wouldn't have an excuse to hate her, and you might even find that you actually liked her. Isn't *that* the truth, Nicholas?"

"You're becoming quite a philosopher, Swede. Better be careful or they'll start calling you the Preacher instead."

"You may think you've lost your old attitudes, Nicholas, but you're just as arrogant and narrow-minded as you were as a young dandy in New Orleans. You're destined to learn the hard way, Nicholas, and then it's likely to be too late."

The Swede stopped long enough to give his order to the hovering waiter. Then, looking his friend straight in the eye, he stated clearly, "Just to set your mind at rest, I have no plans to marry Mara O'Flynn."

"Well," Nicholas interrupted, "now you're showing some sense."

"If she'd have me, I'd wed her tomorrow. But she's never led me to believe that she cared for me in that way. I'm just a friend to her, someone she can depend upon, something she's had too few of I'd say. You know her brother died? That she's been left alone to care for his son?"

"Yes, I heard," Nicholas replied. "But I wouldn't worry too much about Mara O'Flynn. Her brother must have left her a fortune, although for some people it's never enough. And so now she's after your money and your pity."

"You're entitled to your opinion, but don't make the same mistake your father made, Nicholas, and turn your back on someone before they are given the chance to explain themselves."

"I'll remember your words, Swede," Nicholas said lightly. "So you'll not be coming with me?"

"No, I don't think so. Besides, what could I do? I never was welcomed with open arms at Beaumarais, and when they catch sight of your casual ways, I will never be invited inside. Reckon I'll just keep an eye on things around here. Maybe you'd even care to invest some of your money in a business with me?" he speculated, a hopeful look in his blue eyes as he offered the partnership to the Creole.

Nicholas smiled. "I'd like that, but only as a silent partner, I can't quite see myself as a storekeeper."

"Good as done!" the Swede laughed, holding out his hand. "Let's drink to our new partnership. When you return, I'll own half of the town," the Swede boasted. Then he eyed Nicholas suspiciously. "You are planning to return, aren't you?"

"I'll be back, Swede, if just to make sure you're not swindling me out of my fair share," Nicholas told him as he raised his glass in a toast to his longtime friend.

"When are you planning on sailing?" the Swede asked.

"Day after tomorrow. There's a ship leaving for New York via New Orleans, I'll sail on her. That'll give me time to take care of our business and enjoy one last night in San Francisco," Nicholas said. "Let's make it a night we're not likely to forget."

Life's uncertain voyage.

—Shakespeare

Chapter 10

MARA WALKED SLOWLY ALONG THE HALLWAY OF THE PARKER House as she searched for the number of the Swede's room. She had debated upon the propriety of calling on him in his hotel, but since time was short, she had decided to seek him out in order to bid him farewell and thank him for his kindness. She couldn't just leave San Francisco without saying good-bye to him.

Mara stopped before his door, pausing briefly before knocking. She hadn't long to wait. The door was opened quickly by the Swede, a broad smile lighting his kindly face as he recognized his visitor.

"Mara!" he said as he opened the door wider. "Come in, please. This is certainly an honor."

Mara stepped inside hesitantly. "I could come back at a later time if I've inconvenienced you?" she asked as she eyed his unbuttoned vest, his ruffled shirtfront showing beneath.

The Swede's broad face flushed in embarrassment. "Please, don't go. I was just dressing," he explained, "I'm sorry the place is in such disorder."

"I know you're probably going out to dine, so I won't keep you. I just wanted to say good-bye," Mara told him.

"Good-bye?" the Swede repeated.

"I've decided to leave San Francisco. In fact, there is a ship leaving this evening that I've booked passage on. This time next year we should be settled in London. It's where I belong, Swede, not out here," Mara explained.

The Swede managed a shaky smile. "I'll miss you, Mara. Are you sure you want to leave? I'm going to make my home here in San Francisco, and...well, I thought we could at least be friends."

Mara smiled sadly. "I would have liked that, Swede, but things don't always turn out the way you'd wish them to."

"You're not leaving San Francisco because you're frightened of someone, are you?" the Swede demanded belligerently. "That French gambler hasn't been bothering you again, has he? If he has, I'll twist his fingers so he never shuffles another deck of cards as long as he lives." Mara knew it was no idle threat.

"No," Mara lied, for what good would it do to get the Swede involved in this. It really didn't matter now. "I want to leave, and this way there won't be any trouble, either with Jacques or Molly. It really is for the best," Mara told him gently. "Now I really must go."

The Swede nodded, a look of disappointment that he could not hide darkening his blue eyes. "I hope you find what you're looking for, Mara, and you know I wish you happiness."

"I know, Swede, and thank you for remaining my friend in spite of certain things you know about me," Mara told him, smiling warmly as she stood on tiptoe and kissed his cheek.

The Swede's muscular arms slid around her as she would have stepped away from him, and lowering his head, he touched her mouth with a kiss. It was sweet and sad, for they both knew that nothing would come of it.

But to Nicholas, standing with blackened brow in the opened doorway, there was nothing innocent about it. It looked like a kiss of passion.

"Excuse me, but I did knock," he said in a cold voice as the Swede released Mara. "I had no idea you'd already started your evening's entertainment, Swede," Nicholas said as his green eyes ran insolently over Mara's flushed face. "You should have a most enjoyable evening, Swede, for I can swear from personal knowledge that she'll be worth every penny you pay her."

At Mara's gasp of disbelief and the Swede's look of

outraged confusion, Nicholas smiled and said, "Didn't she tell you we'd been lovers? A pity. You really should remember to try and tell the truth, my sweet. I guess I won't be seeing you at Delmonico's later," he said to the Swede. With a pitying glance, he left the room, closing the door firmly behind him.

Mara bit her trembling lip, her eyes full of pain and longing as she stared at the closed door. The Swede took her arm and turned her around to face him, staring down kindly at her mortified face.

"I'm so sorry, Mara. I didn't know it had been that serious between you and Nicholas. I knew there was more to your relationship than either of you told me, but I had no idea..." he let his voice trail off lamely.

"As far as Nicholas was concerned, there never was very much to it," Mara said bitterly, her voice muffled by the Swede's chest as he comforted her. "I'm a fool to still be in love with him, but I can't seem to help myself, Swede," Mara confided hopelessly. "I love him so much I ache with longing, and I know I'm just tormenting myself because he'll never return my love. He loathes me."

The Swede shook his head. "I don't understand Nicholas. He's never acted quite this way before. It's that damned Creole pride," the Swede said savagely. "I think he doesn't hate you as much as he'd like you to believe, Mara, and that's why he's so angry. Maybe he's even jealous of us. You confuse him, and he doesn't like that. Maybe if you two had more time together, to really get to know each other, you might be able to start fresh. But you don't have any more time," the Swede sighed, "for you're headed to London and he's going back to New Orleans."

Mara stared at the Swede. It stunned her to know that Nicholas was leaving San Francisco as well. She'd accepted the fact that she'd never see Nicholas again once she'd left San Francisco, but somehow it comforted her to know that she could at least imagine him here in the city, picturing him in familiar places, among people she knew.

"He was my first lover, Swede, and he knows that. He knows I'm not what he tried to make you believe just now.

Well, he'll never know of my love now, and maybe one day I'll be able to forget him," Mara said. She looked at the Swede and managed a slight smile. "Good-bye, Swede."

Mara hurried back to the boardinghouse, hoping Jamie would have Paddy dressed and ready to leave for the ship without much delay. She pulled off her bonnet and gloves as she entered the hall and called out into the cold silence.

"Jenny? I'm back. I hope we have time for a cup of tea before we have to leave. I'm sorry it took longer than I thought, and—" Mara broke off as she walked into the dining room and found the dinner dishes still crowding the table.

"Miss O'Flynn?" a hesitant voice spoke behind Mara's back.

Mara spun around, her heart pounding at the suddenness of the sound. "You gave me a fright, Gordie! Where is everyone? It's so quiet in here."

Gordie's lower lip quivered and a huge tear fell as he sniffed. "Upstairs. A man hurt my mama. Took Paddy too. He was real mean. He made everyone cry, and kicked Jamie real hard. I been hiding on the stairs waiting. Mama told me to watch for you, Miss O'Flynn," Gordie confided importantly.

Mara's eyes widened in horror as she listened. With a groan of despair she ran past Gordie and up the stairs to Jenny's room. She could hear crying and voices coming from within.

Mara pushed open the door and stood staring in disbelief at the small group of people huddled together protectively, her eyes quickly taking in the dishevelment of both Jamie and Jenny, who was rocking a hiccupping Peter on her lap, tears still streaking his chubby face.

"Oh, my God," Mara spoke beneath her breath as she gazed in stricken fascination at Jenny's swollen right eye and bruised lip, then at Jamie who was holding her arm at an awkward angle, her eyelids partially closed in pain.

"Mara!" Jenny cried out as she became aware of Mara's cloaked figure standing in the doorway. "Thank God you've come back!"

Mara walked slowly into the room, Gordie shooting past her as he entered the room and rushed to Jenny. Paul was standing on the other side of the chair, like a soldier at attention.

Mara glanced between the two women with a feeling of dread, knowing already what she would hear.

"They came in here and asked for Paddy," Jenny said huskily. "I recognized them from the time before, only this time the Swede wasn't here to stop them."

Jamie began to wail, cradling her arm to her chest as she rocked back and forth. "Took Paddy, they did. They took Master Paddy, and him kickin' and screamin' bloody murder all the while, till suddenly he was quiet. What did they do to him, what did they do to him?" she cried. "'Tis that she-divil's fault. Never did trust her. May her soul be damned to hell for what she's done!" Jamie cursed as she began to sob.

"We tried to stop them, Mara," Jenny added with a frustrated look that caused her to wince in pain. "I'm sorry, if only there'd been someone here, but I've lost so many guests. With spring here, they're all back at the mines, and the ones still here never stay in at night. We just couldn't stop those two men. What do they want?"

Mara couldn't believe this was happening. Molly had sent Jacques and the Count to kidnap her own son, holding him for ransom. They had beaten two defenseless women who had never harmed anyone. "There's going to be the devil to pay for this," Mara said in a hard voice, her eyes glowing with a murderous rage. "Are you all right?" she asked abruptly.

"A little shaken up, but I'll be all right," Jenny reassured her. Then, with a worried look at the older woman, she added, "But I think they broke Jamie's arm, Mara."

Mara nodded and walked over to where Jamie was sitting, staring at the floor as she continued to mumble Paddy's name. Mara knelt down before her, looking into her reddened eyes. "I'll find him, Jamie. I swear this on Brendan's grave. I'll bring Paddy back safely to you."

Jamie sniffed and glanced up, staring deeply into Mara's hardened eyes as a look of relief began to settle on her haggard face. "You will get Master Paddy back? You'll get him away from her?" she asked, then nodded as if reassured by what she saw in Mara's face.

"I'll be back soon. I'm going to get a doctor first. His office is close-by," Mara said as she started to go. "You'll be safe now. They have what they want."

"B-but, Mara," Jenny called after her disappearing figure, "shouldn't we call the authorities? Get the Swede, he'll help us. Mara! Come back!" she cried, but Mara was gone.

Finding the doctor in his office, Mara sent him to Jenny's boardinghouse and now stood across from Molly's house. Finally satisfied that all was quiet, she ran across the street and into the blackness of the alley beside the house. Slipping around to the back of the house Mara stumbled over discarded boards and rotting garbage as she searched for the entrance to the back staircase.

She held her breath as she opened the door and peered up into the darkness of the stairwell, the stale air rushing over her as she stepped inside. Barely making a sound, Mara slowly climbed higher into the house, catching her breath in panic when a rat ran across her foot. She forced herself to keep going higher, taking each step one at a time until she stood before the door that opened into the room she had escaped from only the day before.

Taking a deep breath, Mara opened it carefully and slid inside. She frowned, realizing they might not be here. Walking faster now, she crossed the room, pausing at the door to Molly's boudoir as she listened for voices. She could hear nothing. It was too quiet. Pulling out her derringer, Mara pushed open the door, noticing for the first time the splintered wood around the door knob as she looked inside. Molly's bedchamber was dark and chilly.

Mara's hand fell to her side as she looked around help-lessly. The house was deserted. They hadn't brought Paddy back here. She'd been so certain she could rescue him. It had never entered her head that they might take him somewhere else.

"Nobody's here," the voice seemed to shout from the darkness behind her, causing Mara to scream in fright as she whirled around to face the sound.

"Who are you? Where is Paddy? What have you done with him?" Mara demanded.

"Dunno who you're talking about, but I saw you crossing the street from my window and recognized you," the voice continued. Then a match was struck, and Mara blinked as one of the oil lamps was lit and the owner of the voice was revealed.

Ellen stood silently staring at Mara across the room. Then, a smile curving her mouth, she said, "I did hear them talking about taking the little boy to a warehouse down on the docks."

Mara's shoulders sagged wearily as she was overcome with feelings both of relief and apprehension. Now she had an idea of where he was being held, but she also knew she couldn't possibly rescue him without assistance.

"Did you hear the name of the warehouse?" Mara asked hopefully, thinking of the rows and rows of plain wooden buildings lining the waterfront.

But Ellen shook her head. "You was nice to me, that's why I'm telling you what they said. Anyway, I hate her—*Miss* Velazquez," Ellen said bitterly. Then she added, a pleased expression lighting her lackluster eyes, "Did hear one of them say something about putting him in a keg of nails if he started causing trouble."

With a quick thanks to the pitiful creature Mara hurried from the house and out into the fresh air, taking deep breaths as she ran toward Portsmouth Square. She had to find the Swede. He would help her; he would save Paddy. As Mara reached the plaza and heard the raucous, discordant music blaring out from the gaming halls as the beckoning lights streamed out onto the square, she remembered Nicholas's last biting words when he'd misinterpreted her farewell to the Swede earlier that evening.

Nicholas had said he guessed he wouldn't be seeing the Swede at Delmonico's later. That was where she'd find him, Mara thought in elation as she walked on past the Parker House and left the plaza, hurrying down Merchant Street to Montgomery and Delmonico's restaurant.

The restaurant was as crowded with diners as the last time she'd dined there. She glanced around nervously but could see no sign of the Swede, or of Nicholas. With a frustrated sigh she turned around and was about to leave when she saw a waiter placing a bottle of champagne in a silver cooler of packed ice and walked over to him with desperate determination.

"Have you seen a large man with blond hair? He's called the Swede and I need to find him. It's of the utmost importance," Mara told him.

The waiter carefully wiped his hands on a linen towel and eyed her with a supercilious look as he disdainfully informed her that he had no knowledge of the gentleman in question. Mara ground her teeth as he haughtily turned his back on her and continued with his careful preparations.

"Then have you, perchance, knowledge of a certain gentleman called Nicholas Chantale? I am dining with him this evening, and he does not care to be kept waiting, m'sieu," Mara lied in a last, desperate attempt.

The waiter turned back to her with a knowing smile that Mara longed to wipe from his face. "Why didn't the mademoiselle say as much in the first place? Monsieur Chantale is dining upstairs in one of our private dining rooms. You should have used the other entrance, *madame*," he advised her insolently. He snapped his fingers and a young waiter came running. "Show this *lady* to Monsieur Chantale's table," he said with a discreet gesture to a door at the back of the hall.

Mara followed the waiter up the stairs and into the dimly lit hallway of the second-floor suites. Here, a man and his dinner partner could dine in luxurious privacy and then enjoy a few hours of dalliance on cushioned sofas.

Mara stood nervously behind the waiter as he knocked discreetly on the door, her fears for Paddy overcoming her reluctance to face Nicholas again. He might hate her, but he could at least tell her the whereabouts of the Swede.

Mara heard Nicholas's deep voice bidding them enter. She did so, the door closing firmly behind her as she stood facing an incredulous Nicholas Chantale.

Dressed in her heavy cloak, with her bonnet still covering her head, Mara felt horribly overdressed. She stared at the embarrassing dishabille of the blonde reclining languorously on the velvet cushions, a glass brimming with champagne held in one hand as she looked up dreamily. The softness left her eyes as she became aware of Mara.

"Who the hell is she?" she demanded angrily as she struggled to pull up her bodice. "Lord, but you should've warned me you had a jealous wife who might come barging in."

The sound of Nicholas's rich laughter filled the room as he moved away from the sofa to where Mara was standing. He stood silently in front of her for a moment, watching her. He had discarded his coat and vest, and his finely ruffled, linen shirt was partially open, revealing the dark hair covering his muscular chest.

"I should really be surprised to see you here, but knowing you, I'm not," Nicholas remarked softly. "What do you want? Not looking for the Swede, are you? I am surprised you'd let him get away from you. You're losing your touch."

"I don't care what you think, Nicholas. I've got to find the Swede, he's the only one who can help me," Mara cried, her hands clenching in front of her. "Jacques and the Count have kidnapped Paddy. They're holding him in a warehouse down at the docks. I've got to get him back, Nicholas. Molly won't believe that Brendan spent all his money. There's nothing to give her. I don't know what she'll do when she finds out," Mara told him, the story spilling out in tangled confusion. "Where's the Swede? Damn it, Nicholas, tell me!" Mara begged as she raised her fists in a fury of frustration.

Nicholas grabbed her arms and held her away from him as he stared into her panic-stricken face, trying to read the truth. She'd lied to him so many times in the past that he didn't know what to believe.

"Nicholas," Mara whimpered. "*Please*. Help me. I'll do anything you ask, but please, please help me."

Nicholas looked deeply into her eyes for a moment longer before nodding thoughtfully. "All right. I believe you, Mara. Come on, let's find the Swede," he said abruptly. Gathering up his coat and vest, he started from the room.

"Hey! What about me? A fine gentleman you are to leave a lady in the middle of dinner! I've got half a mind to—" she began, only to fall silent as Nicholas threw a bag of coins into her lap.

"For wasting your valuable time, mademoiselle," Nicholas apologized gallantly. He pulled Mara after him, out of the room and down the hallway to another room. Without bothering to knock he stepped inside, leaving Mara in the hall.

Mara opened her mouth to complain, then stopped abruptly as she remembered the state of undress Nicholas's dinner partner had been in. She heard voices beyond the door, and a second later fell back as the door opened and Nicholas and the Swede stepped into the hallway.

"Are you all right, Mara?" the Swede demanded as he took her arm and guided her down the back stairs and out into the noisy street below. "Paddy was kidnapped, is that right?"

Mara nodded in the darkness. She was helped inside the carriage Nicholas had signaled to. As she settled down between Nicholas and the Swede on the carriage seat, the Swede asked, "What happened, Mara?"

"Yes, would you care to tell me exactly what I'm becoming involved in?" Nicholas asked quietly. "You weren't too explicit when you interrupted my dinner."

"The person causing all the trouble is Molly. She was Brendan's wife, only she abandoned us years ago. Paddy is her son. We never thought we'd see her again, and we didn't until a couple of weeks ago here in San Francisco. She demanded money from Brendan, said she'd cause trouble, spread false rumors about us if we didn't give her the money she wanted," Mara explained quickly. As they passed a gaily lit building, the light shone through the carriage window and revealed her pale, haunted face. "Then Brendan died, and no sooner had he been laid to rest than she demanded his fortune, but, Swede, Brendan spent it all. There isn't any fortune to give her."

"You mean you're penniless?" the Swede asked in growing amazement.

"Not quite, but close to it. I spent most of it for our passage on the ship. I was desperate. You see, I knew they wouldn't believe me about there being no money. Yesterday, Molly sent Jacques and the Count to bring me to her, and that's when she demanded the fortune. I tried to tell her there was none, but she wouldn't believe me. I managed to escape from them, but I had no idea they would take Paddy," Mara said in a trembling voice. "I knew they would continue to cause trouble. That's why I decided to leave San Francisco immediately. It was while I was saying good-bye to you tonight that they went to the boardinghouse and took Paddy. They broke Jamie's arm and beat Jenny," Mara told them, her voice throbbing with anger.

"My God!" the Swede expostulated, his fist bunching with suppressed violence, "they hit the old woman? And Jenny?"

"They're animals, and Molly's the worst, to do this to her own son," Mara cried in despair. "I've just got to find him."

"How do you know where to look?" Nicholas asked as he glanced outside the window. They were nearing the wharves.

"I went to Molly's house, thinking they would have Paddy there. I knew a back way in."

Nicholas looked over at her in surprise, his eyes narrowing as he stared at her profile. "You went to rescue him by yourself? And just what did you hope to prove by that fool stunt?"

"I'm not completely helpless, Nicholas. I have a weapon, and I know how to use it," Mara told him coldly. "Paddy's like my own son. I'll do anything to get him back."

"I believe you would, Mara," Nicholas spoke softly, beginning to sense for the first time some of the determination and strength in this enigmatic woman.

"I wish you'd told me about your trouble, Mara," the Swede said unhappily. "I would've helped you. You didn't need to run away."

"I didn't want to get you involved in this. You might have gotten hurt. And anyway," Mara said with a tired sigh, "I thought we'd be gone from here before anything more could happen."

"Do you know what warehouse we're looking for?" Nicholas interrupted as he halted the coach.

"The only thing I know is that they talked about nails, nothing more than that," Mara told him with a frown.

"Well, it'll have to do," Nicholas commented. "You'd

better wait here with the coach. In fact, he'd better take you back to the boardinghouse. You can wait for us there," Nicholas ordered.

"No," Mara said, jumping from the safety of the carriage into the muddy street before either Nicholas or the Swede could make a move to check her flight. "I will not wait. I'm going with you," she proclaimed, "and you can't stop me. I have to be there, Nicholas."

"You might as well let her come," the Swede advised. "I'd rather she were with us than sneaking around in the dark behind us."

Nicholas shrugged as he paid off the coachman, promising him a large tip if he'd wait. With the Swede and Mara on each side of him, he began walking down the street.

It was quiet along the row of warehouses, although farther along were the rowdy grog shops and bawdy houses that attracted the scum of the waterfront with the cheap whiskey and cheaper women to be found inside the gloomy and squalid shacks that huddled together against the cold winds off the bay. They moved slowly along the front of the warehouses trying to read the lettering painted on the outside. They passed by fine hardware and woolen goods, printing materials and paper, ship's stores and glass, all the large buildings darkened at this time of night. The next one they passed, however, had a glimmer of light showing from a small window at the back. And painted in huge letters across the front was the advertisement for building materials.

"They're probably in the small office at the back of the building. I think the best thing to do is for you to go around to the back. There's most likely a door from the office leading out into the alley. I'll enter through the door next to the main part of the warehouse," Nicholas spoke quietly. "That way, we'll have them between us. Do you remember that Indian yell you used to cut loose with when we'd pass other boats on the Mississippi?" Nicholas asked suddenly.

"Sure do," the Swede answered with a broad grin as he understood Nicholas's idea.

"Give me a few minutes to get inside, Swede, then come

through the door when you're ready," Nicholas said. Then, without another word, he slipped into the darkness.

Mara jumped nervously as a hand was clapped to her shoulder. Then she heard the Swede's deep voice speak softly in her ear.

"We'll get him back for you, Mara. I swear we will," he reassured her, and then strode off to position himself outside the door.

Mara pulled her little derringer from her purse and followed them along the side of the building until she was just below the window where the square of light was shining through. There was no sign of Nicholas, and the Swede had disappeared around the far side of the building.

Nicholas had paused before the outside door and halfheartedly tried the door handle, controlling his start of surprise when it turned beneath his palm and the door opened. Apparently the kidnappers thought themselves so secure that they never imagined someone tracking them down, nor suspected a surprise attack. They hadn't even bothered to lock the door.

Nicholas stepped inside. Although it was dark, he could just barely make out the bulky, rounded shapes of large barrels and stacked crates. He cursed as he tripped over the handle of a shovel that had fallen across the passageway from the line of shovels, picks, and saws leaning against the wall. He sidestepped several wheelbarrows in the center of the floor. At the back of the cavernous warehouse Nicholas could see a thin strip of light showing from beneath the door.

Nicholas stood silently waiting just outside of the door, knowing that any minute now a bloodcurdling scream would shatter the silence of the night, and then the Swede himself would follow his bellow of rage into the small room as all hell broke loose.

Nicholas heard a cough and then a rough laugh followed by a woman's voice behind the door. Suddenly he hoped that they had the right warehouse, and the people inside the office weren't just working late on accounts. For they'd never be the same after hearing the Swede's war cry. But then, it must be nearing eleven o'clock, and no merchant would be working so late, Nicholas reasoned, and certainly not with a woman or a child, Nicholas added grimly as he distinctly heard a small child's squeal of fear.

Suddenly a savage, inhuman cry ripped through the stillness of the warehouse, causing even Nicholas's flesh to creep as he swung open the door at the precise instant that the outside door split into pieces under the force of the Swede's broad shoulder.

The occupants of the room had been temporarily immobilized with terror by the sound and the suddenness of the attack. Nicholas and the giant Swede charged into the room from either side.

Molly fainted dead with fright, her body slumping in the corner of the room as the Count and Jacques turned to face their attackers.

As Jacques recognized the almost satanic face of Nicholas Chantale, he almost gave up. But because he knew he'd receive no mercy from this foe, he pulled his pistol from his coat pocket and took hasty aim at the figure flying at him. But Nicholas was faster and dived at Jacques's legs, knocking him off balance. They fell to the floor in a tangled heap, Jacques hitting out at anything he came in contact with, his feet kicking viciously at Nicholas as they rolled across the floor.

The Swede had, in one clean punch, knocked several of the Count's front teeth down his throat, breaking the man's jaw with the same powerful blow. He now stood spread-eagled over the Count's bloodied body, his arms akimbo, watching with enjoyment as Nicholas fought Jacques. It seemed as if Jacques D'Arcy was getting the worst of it as the Swede saw Nicholas's fist connect with the Frenchman's nose. Suddenly the Swede caught the flash of steel, but before he could call out a warning to Nicholas, Jacques had struck, the knife blade piercing through the flesh of Nicholas's shoulder.

Jacques was on his feet in an instant, Nicholas having lost his hold on him, but before he could reach the door, Nicholas called out for him to stop. Jacques turned with an evil grin crossing his bloodied face as he raised his arm, ready to throw the deadly dagger through the air. But this time Nicholas hadn't been caught off guard. The ear-shattering report of his pistol filled the room with noise and smoke as the bullet struck Jacques, sending him backward against the wall. He fell to the floor dead, the look of surprised pain still on his face.

"You hurt bad, Nick?" the Swede called as Nicholas struggled to his feet.

Nicholas grimaced as he looked down at his blood-soaked shirt and coat. "I'll be all right. Where's the boy?"

The Swede and Nicholas glanced around the room, their eyes traveling quickly and without interest over the prostrate form of Molly as they searched for the little boy. Suddenly Nicholas stepped forward as a bundle of blankets piled in the corner moved slightly. Flinging aside the suffocating cover, he stared down in disbelieving anger at the little boy tied up beneath. His dark curls were tangled above fear-widened eyes as he blinked up at the tall, savage-looking man looming above him, blood smearing his hands.

He cringed in horror as his round eyes caught the rustling movement of Molly just behind the tall man standing over him. Nicholas's attention was drawn to the sound as Molly, having regained consciousness and discovering she'd lost, was trying to slip unnoticed from the room. As the Swede made a move to stop her, Nicholas shook his head, signaling him to let her go.

"She lost, and she knows it," Nicholas said as he turned back to the little boy. "I don't think we need worry about her any longer."

"If she tries to cause any more trouble, I'll make her wish she'd never set foot in California," the Swede promised, an angry glint still darkening his soft blue eyes.

When Mara had heard the Swede's terrifying scream, she had stood aghast, paralyzed with fear, until she heard the sound of a scuffle, and then the roar of a pistol. She had finally come to her senses and started toward the breached entrance to the office, when a figure suddenly emerged from it and Mara came face-to-face with Molly.

The two women stared at each other in silence for a

second, before Molly gestured contemptuously at the small gun Mara held pointed at her.

"You won't shoot me," Molly spat. "But if I were holding the gun, I would kill you without a qualm: You think you've won, but you haven't. You may have gotten help this time, but those two can't always be around to protect you," she warned with a sneer. "Just remember that I intend to get that fortune, and that I'll be here waiting. I can get fifty more friends who'd like a share of it. You haven't won, Mara O'Flynn...but I will, eventually," she promised as she gave Mara a vicious push against the wall and rushed past her down the alley, disappearing into the street.

Mara breathed a shuddering sigh and hurried to the debris-scattered doorway of the office. "Paddy!" she cried as she stood looking around her in dismay.

Paddy's silence crumbled as he heard Mara's voice, and with a cry he started to struggle from his bonds.

Nicholas stepped aside as Mara rushed into the room, her eyes seeing only Paddy's little body huddled in the corner. The Swede squatted down and quickly cut the ropes binding Paddy's wrists and ankles. Then Mara had him in her arms. She held him pressed tightly against her breast.

"She said she was my mama. She isn't, she isn't, I hate her!" Paddy cried, his sobbing muffled against Mara as he wrapped his arms around her neck. "She's ugly and awful and I hate her!"

"There, there—it's all right now. Mara's here, isn't she? Have I ever let anything happen to you? Now come on, Paddy, we're leaving here and you'll never have to see her again, I promise you," Mara told him as she struggled to her feet, Paddy's weight dragging her down.

"Here, let me take the little fellow," the Swede said as he scooped Paddy up in his arms and grinned down at him.

Mara turned around and stopped in surprise as she saw, for the first time, the blood on Nicholas's shirtfront. "Oh, Nicholas," she breathed softly as she hurried to him. He swayed slightly.

Putting her arm around his waist, she steadied him, ignoring the quizzical look in his green eyes as she helped him to the door. They left behind a crumpled Count and the late Jacques D'Arcy.

Nicholas now leaning heavily against her, Mara followed the Swede's bold stride out into the night. She could feel Nicholas's breath warm against her forehead. "Are you all right? Do you want to rest?"

Nicholas glanced down at her face, her eyes wide with concern as she stared up at him. "Do you care?" he asked cynically.

"Yes, I do," Mara answered simply as they stepped out into the street. She nearly collided with the Swede's heavy bulk. He stood stock still, staring at the skyline.

"My God! The city's on fire!"

Mara and Nicholas followed his gaze in disbelief as flames shot upward above the rooftops of San Francisco, the crackling heat engulfing everything. Nicholas's arm tightened instinctively around Mara's shoulders as they stood watching the heavy smoke billowing up above the city, the whole sky lit by the fire.

"It looks like it started over toward Portsmouth Square, but it's spreading fast," Nicholas said worriedly.

"Jamie!" Mara cried out as her eyes stared in dazed horror at the flames shooting up into the sky. "And Jenny and the boys, they're right in the middle of it. We've got to get to them!"

People were crowding out onto the street to watch the fire, and in the distance they could hear the clanging of fire engines.

The Swede stared down the street where they had left their carriage. It was gone. A man was climbing up onto the seat of a wagon across the street and the Swede hailed him. "Give us a lift uptown?"

At the man's nod they hurried across, the Swede tossing Paddy up first, then lifting Mara in before jumping up himself. Holding a hand down for Nicholas, he helped him climb aboard. Seated in the back of the wagon, they rode toward the heart of the fire, not bothering to question why their driver should be riding right into it. At least they didn't wonder until they passed several wagons loaded down with goods of every description, and realized that looters were already at work, scavenging at the scene of the disaster.

As they neared the fire, the heat intensified, becoming almost unbearable. Their eyes began to burn and they coughed as they breathed in the thick layer of smoke that hung over the city. They quickly fled their transport as they neared the fire, not caring to be shot as looters. As falling timbers crashed to the street with a shower of sparks and spooked the already frightened horses, they moved to safety on the side of the road. A minute later a team of screaming horses, pulling what remained of a wagon, fled past, their eyes rolling in fear as they raced through the streets.

Buildings were collapsing all around them. In the distance they began to hear loud explosions as the desperate men fighting the fire dynamited. It was a vain attempt to stop the fire's march as it was fanned by a northeaster blowing it into the most densely populated part of the city. They passed the burned-out ruins of restaurants and hotels where all that was left were melted piles of twisted silverware and molten glass among the smoldering embers.

Hundreds of people were crowding into the street, some crying for help, others moaning in pain from injuries suffered in trying to save their belongings from the destruction of the fire. The sky above them was smothered in a dense black cloud of smoke that rolled across the flame-lit city and blended with the dull orange glow that looked like a false sunrise. The air was thick with choking, sulfuric fumes from the blasting that was going on in a last-ditch effort to halt the fire. The water supply had long ago run out and now the firefighters could only stand helplessly aside while building after building fell prey to the voracious flames.

The fire raced along Kearny from the plaza, already ablaze, and down Montgomery toward the wharves along the bay. Incredibly enough, some of the buildings in the plaza still stood, among them the El Dorado, its gaming tables and roulette wheels still safe. But where the Union Hotel had once stood, now only smoldering bricks remained, and the Parker House was lighting up the sky with its flames.

They wearily made their way up the hill, pushing their way through the throngs of panicked people fleeing the roaring heat. The wind increased as they climbed the hill toward Jenny's boardinghouse, praying they would find it still standing. With a cry of happiness Mara saw the plain, little building outlined against the backdrop of distant flames.

The Swede rushed ahead, pushing through the door with Paddy clinging around his neck. Mara and Nicholas, following close behind, entered the hallway in time to see the Swede vaulting up the stairs two at a time as he called out, his voice bellowing through the silent house.

Jenny appeared at the top of the stairs with a bundled-up Peter in her arms, his little red head covered by a cap. Gordie and Paul crowded close, their arms full of their most prized possessions. Jamie had come out behind them, her arm in a professionally wrapped sling as she peered over the railing, her wizened face seeming to split open with a thousand wrinkles as she caught sight of Paddy.

"Come on, we've got to get out of here," the Swede urged them as he helped to guide the heavily laden group down the stairs. "We should get to a safer place higher on the hill."

Jenny smiled stiffly around her bruises as she stared up at the Swede and Paddy. The Swede herded them from the boardinghouse, Jenny glancing back sadly at her home as she slowly made her way up the hill.

Below them the city of San Francisco continued to burn through the early morning hours. A blood red sun rose slowly over the city and revealed the devastating destruction. The fire was finally beginning to die out, and people were starting to return to their homes, hopeful that they would still be standing.

"We missed our ship," Mara said suddenly as she stared out over the bay and saw the tall masts of the sailing ships standing starkly against the hazy sky. "It sailed last night. I forgot all about it."

"You needn't leave now, Mara," the Swede spoke beside her. "The danger is gone and you've got Paddy back."

Mara shook her head, still not believing it was over. She remembered Molly's threats. "For how long? I can't always run to you, Swede, when I need help. Molly's down there, just waiting. Now more than ever, she'll need the money to get herself started again," Mara told him as she chewed on her lower lip. "I'd always be worrying about Paddy, wondering where he was, if he were safe. No," Mara said softly, "I've got to leave."

The Swede put his arm around her shoulders comfortingly as they stood there and stared silently at the ruins of the city. Nicholas's eyes narrowed thoughtfully as he noticed the warm smile Mara gave the Swede before she turned away and walked over to see how Jamie and Paddy were doing. Both had succumbed to sleep and were snuggled close together under a blanket.

"I've got a proposition to put to you, Mara O'Flynn," Nicholas said as Mara knelt down next to him and checked his bandaged shoulder. "I'm leaving for New Orleans today, and I want you to come with me."

"What?" Mara gasped, her golden eyes staring at him in amazement.

"You heard me," Nicholas said calmly. "You want to leave San Francisco, and I can pay for your passage, as well as the boy's and your maid's."

Mara eyed Nicholas suspiciously, wondering if their uneasy truce was over. "Why the sudden interest in my affairs?"

"With the right woman," Nicholas said with a look at Jenny, who was now standing beside the big Swede, Gordie holding onto one of his huge hands, "the Swede could find happiness here in San Francisco. I just want to give him that chance."

"And you think I might interfere with the course of true love?" Mara asked wearily.

"Let's just say that your beauty holds a certain fascination which might blind him to another, less-alluring woman," Nicholas said softly. "You also, my dear, are a dangerous woman to know," Nicholas said, alluding to the many misadventures that seemed to happen to people around her. "I don't think the Swede needs that worry as well."

Mara smiled tightly. "Still acting the guardian angel for him? You needn't worry, there's nothing between the Swede and me. I have tried to tell you that, so you needn't burden yourself with me," Mara told him proudly. "And what makes you think *you* could survive being anywhere near me, if I'm as dangerous to be around as you say?"

Nicholas smiled. "I lead a charmed life. You might even bring me good luck, instead of bad. Well?" he asked, his green eyes narrowing on her profile as Mara stared down at the glistening bay. "Do we have a bargain? You did say that you'd do anything I asked if I would help you find your nephew." Nicholas reminded her unfairly, but he was determined to have her sail with him when he left for New Orleans.

Mara nodded as she turned back to look at him, her tawny eyes staring deeply into his with a feeling of premonition as to her future destiny as she placed herself in Nicholas Chantale's ruthless hands. "I'll go with you," she said simply.

As they were rowed away from the pier later that day, Mara glanced back at the city shrouded in a mixture of smoke and fog. She really would miss Jenny and the Swede. She wondered if perhaps Nicholas was right and someday the Swede and Jenny might make a life together. Jenny still had her boardinghouse, and she would certainly have a horde of borders, including the Swede—until some of the hotels were rebuilt. He'd lost most of his possessions with the destruction of the Parker House. There were moments when she wished things had worked out differently and she would be staying in San Francisco too, but it wasn't meant to be. Never had been, Mara thought sadly.

As she stared at the line of waves curling against the shore, and at the hills in the distance, she suddenly heard Brendan's laugh ringing across the water, his dark eyes flashing with the light of adventure, his handsome face mirroring his dreams of riches. This new land was to have changed the destiny of the O'Flynns.

"Good-bye, Brendan, my love," Mara whispered, her lips barely moving as the sound of his voice faded from her mind. The shoreline grew fainter and was swallowed up by swirling fog, as they left the golden shores of California.

Like glimpses of forgotten dreams.

—Tennyson

Chapter 11

"WHAT THE DEVIL IS THIS?" MARA MURMURED AS SHE curiously picked up a shirt that had been tossed onto the berth in her cabin.

"It happens to belong to me," Nicholas spoke lazily from the doorway as he entered the cabin, closing the door softly, yet firmly behind him as if he intended to stay.

Mara turned and stared at him incredulously. "Haven't you mistaken your cabin?" she asked politely, one sleek eyebrow arched in question. She watched in growing alarm as he removed his coat.

"No," he replied casually as he began to undo his shirt.

"No?" Mara repeated skeptically. "That is all you have to say? But this is my cabin," Mara informed him coldly.

Nicholas smiled thoughtfully. "Actually, it is *our* cabin."

"The devil it is," Mara expostulated, her cheeks flushing hotly with both anger and embarrassment.

Nicholas laughed. "How elegantly you express yourself, my dear, but I'm afraid I shall have to disabuse you of that idea. You see, since I had no prior knowledge that you would be traveling with me when I booked passage on this ship, I took only one cabin. Space being rather limited, I was most fortunate in finding even one extra on such short notice. That cabin is now occupied by your nephew and maid," Nicholas explained to Mara as she watched uncertainly as he removed his shirt, grimacing slightly as he flexed his stiffening shoulder, the bandage over his wound a bright patch of white against his bronzed skin. He scratched his chest reflectively. Mara could have sworn she caught a mischievous glint in his green eyes as he continued blandly, "And since we have shared a bed before, I thought you wouldn't mind sharing this cabin with me."

Mara opened her mouth, but no sound came forth. She glared at him in stunned silence.

"I see I have shocked you. I'll have to think up some more surprises, for it's rather entertaining to have rendered you speechless," he teased her, his smile of enjoyment confusing Mara even further as she gazed at him with growing suspicion, wondering what his game was.

"Besides, this will be quite convenient for you," he continued smoothly. "You're going to need someone to play the part of lady's maid, what with your own maid suffering a broken arm, and all those exasperating hooks up the back of your gowns."

"And you see yourself filling that role?" Mara asked in a carefully controlled voice.

Nicholas feigned surprise. "And who else? In fact, I'm quite looking forward to it."

Mara smiled stiffly. "I beg to differ, m'sieu," she told him haughtily, "for I shall be perfectly capable of seeing to my own needs, thank you. A pity to have to disappoint you, but perhaps you will be able to find a more accommodating female elsewhere on the ship."

Nicholas shrugged complacently. "I'm quite satisfied with you, Mara, but we'll see." He calmly poured water into the washbasin and splashed his face with it, his broad back turned to her. She continued to watch him, her confusion showing on her face as she wondered uneasily about this change in his attitude.

"I thought you merely desired my absence in San Francisco," Mara challenged him, determined to get to the truth of the matter. "But now I see you really desired a bedmate. You could have been more honest about forcing me to accompany you."

Nicholas laughed. "You certainly put things bluntly, my dear."

"It's the truth, then?" Mara asked, not fooling herself that he could feel anything more than lust for her.

"The truth is that I wanted you out of San Francisco. In fact, I wonder if the distance of two oceans is indeed far enough. But," he paused, a light entering his green eyes as they slid over her face, lingering on her lips, "I thought, as long as we are confined in such close quarters, why shouldn't we make the most of this voyage?"

"Oh, I see. It is to be the mere gratification of mutual lusts?" Mara asked angrily, her eyes blazing. "Your self-conceit is astonishing, m'sieu. I had no idea I had given you reason to assume I cared to share your bed."

Nicholas frowned thoughtfully. "My pardon, mademoiselle, but it seemed the only natural thing to do. After all, we are a man and a woman who are attracted to one another."

Mara drew in her breath, covering her discomfiture with a scornful laugh. "Indeed, I have been mistaken. I had thought you disliked and distrusted me." Mara said mockingly. "Could it be that you have changed your mind about me?"

Nicholas smiled. "Perhaps, now that I know you better, I have a more complete understanding of Mara O'Flynn than I had some years ago. I find I can overlook certain... character flaws."

"*I*, on the other hand—now that I know Nicholas Chantale better—find that I cannot overlook his arrogance, his dictatorial manner, or his insolent effrontery."

"Since you know me so well, Mara," Nicholas said, not in the least concerned by her outburst, "you know that I shall ultimately win."

Mara stared at him coldly, her heart fluttering. "And what will you win, Nicholas?"

Nicholas shook his dark head, his green eyes narrowed in speculation as he gazed at her slender figure, stiffened with outraged pride. "I'm not really sure. Perhaps I'll become acquainted with the real Mara O'Flynn. I think I have yet to meet the complete woman."

"Nor shall you," Mara told him stonily.

"I wonder," Nicholas responded softly, a determined glint in his eye as he gazed at Mara, not missing the nervous wariness in the way she faced him. "You have reason to be concerned, my dear, for you are most accurate in reading my character. I am a very persevering man, especially when presented the challenge of a beautiful woman. I admit that you fascinate me, and have done so since I first saw your face in that damned locket. You've haunted my thoughts for far too long. I should warn you," he added grimly as he threw down the towel he'd dried his face with and came to stand directly in front of her, "that I never yield an inch. I'm a very tenacious and stubborn fellow."

Mara stood her ground despite his closeness, and stared up into his green eyes, losing herself for an instant in their luminous depths. She sought desperately to fight the almost overwhelming attraction he held for her.

"Do you think you can resist me, Mara?" he asked softly as he lowered his lips to the side of her neck, breathing in the heady fragrance. He rubbed his rough cheek against her soft skin. He felt her warm breath tickling his ear as she sighed. Pulling back, he stared down at her and shook his head. "Even dressed in black mourning you still look more beautiful than other women in their finest gowns could ever dream of. In fact," he added almost resentfully, "you are even more beautiful for there is no color, no frills to distract from the stunning, almost pure beauty of your face."

A slight flush spread across Mara's face. She'd never before been subjected to a Nicholas bent upon seduction, and she was determined at all costs not to reveal any weakness. She raised her chin haughtily, allowing a slight smile to curve the corners of her lips as she gave him a disdainfully provocative look. To Nicholas staring down at her, she was the miniature portrait coming to life before his eyes.

"So you are no different from any other man," Mara said as she purposely allowed her gaze to travel over him pityingly, "and have become a victim of your own lustful nature, letting that rule your head. A pity. I thought you were made of stronger stuff, or at least," she added tauntingly, "so *you've* told me."

Nicholas's hard fingers closed over Mara's chin as he forced her face up to his and looked deeply into her eyes. "You are mistaken, madam, if you think I am not different. I am no callow youth carried away by the breathlessness of your beauty, nor some bourgeois lout who has never seen such perfumed and silken loveliness before," he told her with a grim smile, his thumb moving along the line of her jaw. "I cannot be fooled by you, and although I might desire your body, I have no illusions about you, Mara."

Mara pulled free of him as she stepped away and said, "Nor I of you, Nicholas."

"It should prove an interesting contest of wills," Nicholas remarked, and Mara could have sworn he was actually enjoying himself and even looking forward to their next confrontation.

Mara unconsciously shook her head as she said firmly, "Since we shall be parting company in New Orleans, I prefer to keep our relationship as casual as possible by not falling prey to your baiting."

"I won't need to bait you, my sweet, for do you really imagine that you and I can share a narrow berth without becoming intimate? You are either very trusting, or dangerously naive, for nothing has, nor ever will be, casual between us," Nicholas told her; yet he didn't seem angry or even disappointed by her refusal as he pulled on his clean shirt and proceeded to fasten it carelessly. "You do have spirit, though, and that I do admire," he said suddenly; then, picking up his coat, he left Mara in the silence of the cabin.

Her stern resolve for noninvolvement was much easier said than done, Mara was to think later as she prepared for bed and realized that the close confines of the cabin did not allow for privacy—in fact, very little at all, she swore as she bumped her knee against the berth while struggling into her nightgown.

The first night, Nicholas was still on deck when she prepared for bed, and by the time he returned she had already claimed her half of the berth and had even managed to erect a barrier down the middle in the shape of a rolled-up blanket. Mara pretended to sleep when she heard him enter the cabin, ignoring his snort of contempt when he saw her makeshift wall. But it held, with only the contact of cold feet during the inhospitable night. Mara awoke the next morning feeling refreshed and quite rested, but as she rolled over, she found Nicholas's half of the berth empty.

She was still standing in her petticoat when Nicholas entered the cabin a short while later, his skin roughened from the cold air up on deck and his black curls windblown as he shrugged out of his heavy overcoat. He didn't look as if he'd had too comfortable a night's rest, and as he saw Mara standing in her lacy underclothing, her skin glowing like soft silk, his mood blackened even more. Mara's satisfied feeling of superior smugness faded, however, as, she pulled her dress over her head and attempted to hook it up, straining tiredly to get her arms behind her, and after a struggle of five minutes, with only a few fastened hooks to show for her efforts, she gave up. Mara stared silently at Nicholas's broad back, for he'd turned his back on her as he read a book with increasing absorption, ignoring her and her futile attempts to dress herself.

Mara tapped her satin-shod foot indecisively for a moment before sighing in defeat as she walked over to him. "I find that I *am* in need of your services after all, if you'll be so kind?" Mara informed him as she turned her back and waited for him to assist her.

Nicholas turned and stared at the slender back stiffly presented for his inspection, and a devilish glint entered his eyes as his gaze traveled up to the back of her neck and the fine, silky hairs on her nape just below the smooth, chignoned head held so arrogantly aloof.

"Of course. My pleasure. But," Nicholas said as he stood up and, pulling the two gaping edges of material together, continued, "my services are no longer being offered for free. I shall expect payment."

Mara looked up at him over her shoulder. "What do you mean? I don't have very much money; you know that."

"But you do have two very soft lips, and I think a kiss would be sufficient payment for my time and trouble," Nicholas told her softly as he stared down into her tawny eyes, which were still locked with his.

Mara turned around, breaking that suffocating contact with him, as he continued to close the back of her gown, his fingers touching her skin every so often—perhaps unnecessarily, she thought resentfully as she felt his hand linger against the curve of her shoulder as he completed the last of the hooks.

Mara set her face firmly and turned around once again to face him, even though he still stood close behind her.

"Well, do I receive payment?" he demanded.

Mara knew she needed no urging to kiss him, yet she wouldn't let him see that it would be an exquisite agony for her, so she cocked her head sideways as if in contemplation, her lips pursed thoughtfully. "Hmmmm, I suppose."

A look of amusement showed briefly in Nicholas's green eyes as he smiled. "How gracious of you, my dear, to bestow such a great honor on me," Nicholas said lightly before suddenly pulling her into his arms and kissing her long and hard. Mara's parted lips clung to his breathlessly as he lifted his mouth, his warm breath fanning her face as he stared down into her golden eyes, partially masked by her passion-heavy lids.

"I look forward to this evening when we dine with the captain and you have to change for dinner," Nicholas said with a speculative gleam in his eye.

That day, Mara waited on Jamie for the first time in her life. Jamie seemed far more put out about that state of affairs than she was about the relationship developing between Nicholas and Mara. On first hearing of the cabin arrangements, she had seemed momentarily surprised, then suspicious, and finally almost pleased.

"I really can't understand your attitude, Jamie," Mara questioned her in perplexity. "I thought you didn't like Nicholas Chantale. Doesn't it bother you that I'm sharing a cabin with him?"

"Nope," Jamie answered, with a shake of her head. "Don't really know the man, so can't say whether or not I like him. And what goes on in that cabin between the two of ye, well, 'tis no business of mine. Besides, I figure 'tis about time ye got yourself a man, and a good one at that. He's a fine man, to be sure, and he's proven he can be trusted. He saved Paddy, didn't he? Aye, seems to me ye was destined to come to this, what with him bein' mixed up in that London affair, knowin' all about ye, comin' to look for ye, and then meetin' so strange like in California—twice too. Just seems as though ye paths were fated to cross.

"Anyway, it's no good bein' a woman alone, especially a beautiful one like you, just askin' for trouble. I like the feelin' of havin' a man around now that, well..." Jamie trailed off huskily, both of them knowing what she had been going to say. Brendan was no longer with them. They needed a man.

Mara glared at the self-assured Jamie. "Perhaps, Mistress Jameson, since ye've such a likin' for the man, you should be sharing his bunk instead of me," she recommended. Jamie's wizened face turned beet red with embarrassment.

"Well, I never!" Jamie sputtered. "I can see that someone's goin' to have to teach ye to curb that wicked tongue of yours," Jamie warned. "Ye've got the worst of your mama in ye, God rest her soul. She could cut loose with a phrase or two that'd have ye reelin' with the shock of it."

"But I don't intend to follow in her footsteps, Jamie," Mara told her, feeling a momentary flicker of fear at the memory of Maud.

"Ye won't," Jamie said with assurance. "Ye be stronger than Maudie ever was."

Mara stared at the little woman and wondered if it were true. At one time she might arrogantly have thought so, but where Nicholas was concerned, she was pitifully weak. If he only knew how vulnerable she really was. Then there would be no contest of wills.

"Mara!" Paddy said again as he tried to attract her attention. "Will you play soldiers with me?" he asked hesitantly, jealous of all this talk about the big man who was taking up all of Mara's time.

Mara smiled as she sat down on the edge of the bunk. "Which am I, the French or the British?"

"The French, of course," Paddy replied happily now that he had captured Mara's full attention. Soon her men would be his as well, for the English always won in battle, and his side always flew the English flag. Their first week out at sea stretched into a second and then into a third as they sailed southward toward the tip of South America and the passage around Cape Horn that Mara dreaded even worse than the first time, for now she knew what she could expect with stormy sea and weather, but she was less certain what to expect from Nicholas, even though he left her to sleep undisturbed beside him night after night. The only contact between them was the kiss she bestowed upon him each time he helped her to dress, although of late the last kiss of the day when she was unhooked from her gown before climbing into the bunk had evolved into something more than a kiss as Nicholas held her without the barrier of her many petticoats between them, his mouth caressing hers with such tantalizing sensuousness that she felt herself drifting against him, with only an awareness of Nicholas filling her senses as she allowed him to mold her closer to his muscled chest, her soft breasts pressing against his flesh as his lips devoured hers.

As their first month at sea came to a close, Mara realized that it was truly no ephemeral attraction she felt for Nicholas Chantale. She had fallen irrevocably in love with the dark Creole. It was a love deeper than mere physical lust and appreciation of his handsome features. As the weeks of confinement lengthened, so did the time spent together, and gradually Mara came to know the man Nicholas was. That was what finally captured her heart, along with his determined effort to befriend Paddy.

Nicholas had surprised her by his sincere attempts to include Paddy in their activities. At first his moves toward friendship had been met with total rejection, as Paddy eyed this rival for the attentions of his beloved Mara with a deep wariness. But a lonely little boy of seven was no match for a charming, experienced man almost thirty years his senior, and soon Nicholas had Paddy hanging on his every word as he told him tall tales about fierce alligators in the deep water of the swamps, of fishing along the banks of the Mississippi River for catfish, and of poling into the backwater of the bayous as they hunted crawfish. Nicholas even managed once to almost change history as his Napoleon came close to beating Paddy's Duke of Wellington at the Battle of Waterloo played out in deadly seriousness on a mock battle-field on Paddy's bunk.

By showing just a little bit of attention and interest in Paddy, Nicholas had made an easy conquest of Paddy's hero-starved imagination. Brendan had only felt like playing the father when the mood suited him. He had loved Paddy, but he'd been too absorbed in himself to take much time with him. And as Nicholas gave of himself to Paddy, Mara fell more hopelessly in love with him. Here was a man who would accept Paddy as his own, making a home for both of them. Mara suddenly felt envious of the easy affection that now existed between Nicholas and Paddy. She wished it could be as simple between them.

One stormy afternoon Mara was trying to decide whether to lay down the ace or the queen, Nicholas having already won the last couple of hands, when she stopped and sat as if turned to stone. Nicholas looked up, staring at the strange look on her face.

As Mara continued to hear the faint notes drifting to her from the corridor outside their cabin, she got slowly to her feet. "But he's dead," Mara whispered brokenly, her compo-sure falling from her as Nicholas watched in fascination. The haughty demeanor disappeared as her shoulders slumped tiredly. "Brendan," Nicholas heard Mara mumble as she stood dazed, her eyes focused on something beyond him and the cabin. "He always hated the sea. He used to laugh and say it was strange that he should be named after St. Brendan the Navigator. He used to play his fiddle when it became too much for him," Mara remembered aloud. When the notes from the fiddle became louder so that even Nicholas heard them, Mara put her hands over her ears. Finally she ran from the cabin.

Mara followed the music down the passageway. Opening the door to the cabin, she stared in disbelief at the fiddler. Not Brendan. But the fiddler had the same dark reddish brown curls and laughing eyes. Paddy! He was playing Brendan's fiddle. Mara had forgotten all about Brendan's sole legacy to his son—his prized fiddle.

Paddy glanced up as he felt the eyes on him, his dimple deepening as he saw Mara standing in the doorway.

"I surprised you, didn't I?" Paddy laughed.

"I didn't know you knew how to play, Paddy," Mara said huskily.

"Papa taught me. Well, he let me play his fiddle sometimes and I just remembered from watching him," Paddy explained proudly, unaware of the fright he had given Mara, or of the memories conjured in her mind as he played with the same natural gift that Brendan had had.

Mara felt a hand slide along her shoulders and glanced around to see Nicholas standing behind her in the doorway, his eyes soft with compassion as he pulled her gently against his chest.

"Brendan played the fiddle so beautifully," Mara whispered.

"I know. I remember hearing him play once," Nicholas answered simply, knowing there were no words of comfort he could offer.

Mara spent the rest of the dismal day in a brooding silence that matched the weather. Thunderclouds piled high across the horizon, promising rougher seas ahead. She was almost relieved to be able to lose herself in sleep after she crawled under the cold, damp blankets later that evening.

It felt like she'd only just closed her eyes when the ship seemed to drop into an endless pit, and Mara woke up reaching out for support. Coming in contact with Nicholas's warm chest she fell against him in rising terror.

"Nicholas!" Mara cried.

Nicholas's comforting arms closed around Mara as she pressed against him, but she couldn't get close enough to him, the bolster blocking any movement she made to feel the warmth of his body. "Hold me close, Nicholas."

Swearing beneath his breath, Nicholas yanked the rolled-up blanket from between them and tossed it across the cabin. He pulled Mara against him, warming her shivering body with his. Mara could hear his heart beating under her ear as she rested her head against his chest.

"It feels as if we're going to sink," she whispered as the ship rode precariously to the crest of a huge wave.

Nicholas's hand rubbed her shoulder and back with a soothing motion that began to relax the taut muscles as he said softly, "You don't really think I'm going to allow this ship to sink now that I've finally gotten that damned bolster out of our bed?"

Mara snuggled against him, pressing her cold nose into the warmth of his throat. "Your nose is like ice," Nicholas complained as he rubbed his cheek against hers. And then, in the darkness, their lips met and clung, and parted only to return.

Nicholas's hands began to slowly search the concealing folds of her nightgown, finding the soft swell of breast, the nipple beneath rising hard with excitement as his other hand slid the material over her thighs until her hips were bare against his. His hard, muscular thighs moved against hers. Cold was no longer the cause of Mara's shivering, her flesh now burning where it came into contact with his as his hands explored with leisurely thoroughness the alluring curves of her body.

As the violence of the tempest raged outside with turbulent seas and shrieking winds, Mara gave herself up to the wildfire sweetness of Nicholas's lovemaking. She lay beneath his warm body as he once again filled her with an exquisite pulsating hardness as he became a part of her, knowing her with such intimate knowledge that he could control her pleasure with his movements inside of her until she thought she would burst with the pure joy and rapture of it. To be one with him again was worth the despair she would ultimately feel on the morrow, Mara thought feverishly as she returned his kisses with such unrestrained and natural eagerness that it surprised Nicholas as well as inflamed his desire to know every soft, fragrant inch of her beautiful body.

But for now he was content with the softness of her parted lips as his tongue moved against hers with velvety sinuousness. He gave Mara no opportunity for words as she began to speak, keeping her lips beneath his and her thoughts solely concerned with responding to his next arousing caress, the fury of the storm forgotten and fading into insignificance under the onslaught of emotion generated by Nicholas's fierce, all-devouring passion.

✦

Mara slept, waking only when the feel of the ship changed as it gently rocked on a tranquil sea, the violence of the squall having abated sometime before dawn. Mara yawned and stretched, her elbow coming in contact with a firmly muscled chest and reminding her of the night past. Mara stared at Nicholas's face, the hardness of his expression softened in repose. Unobserved, she allowed the truth of her feelings for him to be revealed on her face. Mara's golden eyes captured for memory every endearing feature of his face, from the dark lock of hair that had fallen across his brow, to the beautifully chiseled lips that had kissed hers so hungrily only hours before. She laid her cheek against his chest, the thick covering of black hair tickling her nose as she gazed at the rest of his naked body, her hand straying across the taut, flat belly while her eyes followed the line of his thigh, the powerful muscles hardened from years of vigorous physical activity that went beyond mere horseback riding. Mara cursed that he should be so devilishly handsome, and that she was so desperately in love with him.

Two hard arms wrapped themselves around her, and then she was on her back, staring up into Nicholas's bright green eyes that reflected a warm lustfulness as they roamed across her face and down to her rounded breasts.

"Nicholas, please, I must talk with you," Mara said softly as she avoided his searching lips, pressing her hands against his chest as she fought the rush of feelings his touch evoked inside of her.

Nicholas rose, a slight frown marring his brow as he stared down at her withdrawn expression. "Your timing is ill-conceived, for you arouse me with your touch and the feel of your warm body pressed intimately against mine, and then you wish to talk?" he exclaimed softly, not quite believing her words of refusal as he lowered his mouth to hers and began to kiss her with seductive slowness.

"Nicholas," Mara gasped, pulling her mouth free, her heart pounding erratically. "We need to have an understanding."

Nicholas sighed and rolled over to his side of the berth and Mara felt like crying out in protest as the contact of his warm body left hers, but she held her tongue, for she had carefully thought out what she must say and she was determined to set things straight between them before any more time passed and she lost her advantage.

"What's troubling you, Mara?" Nicholas asked. "Are you still fighting the truth, that you and I are attracted to one another and that you have responded naturally to me? There's nothing to be ashamed of," he told her gently, his hand rubbing her thigh.

"I'm not ashamed," Mara told him truthfully—for how could she be ashamed of her love for him?

"Then what is bothering you?" he asked curiously. Then, as a sudden thought struck him, he turned to face her, peering into her face. "Oh, I see. You wish to talk of certain financial matters pertaining to our relationship?" Nicholas spoke softly, yet there seemed to be a hard note in his voice as he sat up against the pillows. "It's hardly in good taste to have broached the subject so soon, and in bed. However..." he paused reflectively.

Mara drew in her breath raggedly and, jerking away from him, sat up. Facing him, she balanced on her knees. "Damn ye, Nicholas Chantale," Mara spat. "You don't understand me and you never will. I take nothing from you, no money, no gifts, nothing. You were right, and I am attracted to you. There is no payment due. You insult me by offering it. I'll not play the whore for you, Nicholas. I never shall. Not for you or any man. I give my body to you because I want to, not because I expect anything in return. I will not be your mistress, you will not be supporting me, Nicholas, and when we tire of each other...I go my way, and you yours. You do not love me, and I," Mara swallowed painfully, "I do not love you. So do we agree? Once in New Orleans you will have your family to return to and I shall make plans to return to England. I shall be free of any entanglements with you, free to go my own way," Mara told him bluntly, her chin raised proudly.

Nicholas was quiet for what seemed an endless time. "You are certainly cold about the whole affair," he finally commented.

"I'm merely being practical," Mara defended herself, then managed a slight laugh as she added wryly, "for it might prove embarrassing to have me acting the clinging vine and making outrageous demands when you return to New Orleans. How much easier to just bid me adieu."

Nicholas frowned in the darkness. He had the impression that he was, in some subtle way, being maneuvered by her. Yet, could he really find fault with her reasoning? He never had cared for the breaking off of relationships, finding the angry accusations and tearful pleadings distasteful. But Mara O'Flynn was a woman of surprises. He didn't, however, like having his life arranged for him, and this arrogant Irishwoman was definitely trying to guide their relationship along the lines she desired.

"You're right, of course," Nicholas agreed easily, masking his irritation, "for it will be a relief for once to have no jealousies and sad partings when the time comes. But I insist upon paying your fare from New Orleans. After all, it is due to me that you find yourself in this predicament. I won't take no for an answer," he added as Mara started to speak.

Mara shrugged, giving in to him on this at least. Indeed, it was his fault that she found herself in this position. He was the one who'd had the vendetta against her. She hadn't asked to fall in love with him. In fact, her life had been perfect until he'd stormed into it, she lied to herself. It was the least he could do for her, she decided as she graciously accepted his offer, making Nicholas feel as though he'd been granted an honor of some kind.

The next couple of months passed all too swiftly for Mara as she found their more intimate relationship more satisfying than she had ever dreamed of. She grew even more alluring as she matured with love. Nicholas was a demanding lover who could be fiercely passionate, bringing her to the heights of sexual awareness, and possessively tender, catering to her every need. Mara came to envy the woman who would one day be given his heart. But for now, Mara savored each day she spent with Nicholas, her golden eyes glowing with love. She refused to think of the day they would dock in New Orleans.

By the time that day came, they had entered a new year, major repairs on the ship having kept them anchored in Rio de Janeiro for almost two months. Mara hadn't resented the continued delays, for they had prolonged the sweet agony of having Nicholas as her lover, a part of her life she would always remember and cherish, but one that would come to an end. Mara stood on deck now, watching as their ship docked along the crowded miles of levee. The docks bustled with activity as ocean-going ships, keelboats, and flatboats from upriver docked to unload one cargo and load another. The double stacks of the steamboats, their triple decks decorated with fancy, carved scrollwork and painted a gleaming white, stood tall above the buildings of the city. Their paddle wheels rested quietly in the still water. Bales of cotton were piled high along the levee, while heavy drays, low carts pulled by mules, were piled high with goods before setting off at a reckless pace through the city. Pedestrians and fellow dockworkers, curses trembling in the air, jumped for safety out of their way.

Their ship docked at the landing on Canal Street and while the crew and dockworkers fell headlong into the business of unloading the ship, Nicholas hired a carriage and made arrangements to have their luggage picked up later.

Jamie and Paddy were settled in the open barouche. Although the air was cold with the nip of winter in it, there was a brave sun shining down from a bright sky of vivid blue. Wrapped in their warm coats, they would find the drive through the city in the open carriage far more enjoyable than sitting in the stuffiness of a closed one.

Nicholas handed Mara inside. Then, turning to the black driver awaiting instructions, he asked casually as he lit his cheroot, "Which hotel do you recommend?"

"Well, reckon that depends on how much a gent's willing

to pay, sir," he answered seriously as he rubbed his chin and eyed Nicholas with professional scrutiny, thoughtfully taking his measure and not missing the casual elegance of the man nor the natural arrogance that almost always denoted a wealthy, aristocratic background. He also didn't miss the beautiful woman sitting inside the coach, and there was nothing cheap about her, he thought as he recognized not only the quality in the small amber velvet cap she wore and the matching velvet jacket with its gilt buttons, but also the way she held her head, showing a definite air of breeding. Yes sir, here was a lady of quality, he decided with approval.

"The price is unimportant as long as I get quality," Nicholas told the man carelessly.

"Well, *in that case*," the coachman grinned as he thought of the large tip he would most likely be receiving, "either the St. Charles or the St. Louis in French Town. Both are mighty fine hotels, yes, sir, although the St. Charles is fancier and uptown. See the white dome in the distance? That's her. Can see for miles across the city and river from up there—or so they say. Got fourteen columns running across the front. The St. Louis only got six," he informed them, the fact obviously impressing him.

"I assume when you speak of *French Town*," Nicholas asked softly, "that you are referring to the Vieux Carré?"

The coachman's eyes opened wide with surprise. "Yes, monsieur, that's what some folk call it," he explained. There was a new note of respect in his voice, for the man must be a Creole—he had to be, the way he'd pronounced his French. And they were the true gentry of New Orleans, not like these rough Americans who ordered a fellow around without any idea of proper manners and didn't tip much either.

"The St. Louis then, and tell the man over here to send our luggage there," Nicholas instructed as he climbed up into the barouche beside Mara, his hard thigh touching hers on the leather seat. "Would you care for the rug across your lap?" he inquired politely, but Mara shook her head and placed it across Paddy's and Jamie's knees. Paddy had sneezed twice. He couldn't find his own handkerchief and Mara handed him hers. As he loudly blew his nose she watched him with a worried look, afraid that he was coming down with another of those foul colds that would no doubt last for weeks.

As they drove along the crowded thoroughfare, Nicholas looked around him curiously. "It would seem as though a few things have changed since I've been away," he commented. On one side of the avenue he recognized the narrow streets and pale yellow, green, and peach stuccoed houses of the Vieux Carré. On the far side of Canal Street toward the Faubourg Sainte Marie, however, were large ornate mansions set within lush grounds, their gardens full of tropical plants and colorfully blossoming shrubs.

"This place has certainly grown since I last saw it," Nicholas remarked, loudly enough for the coachman to overhear. Not wishing to appear lax in his job, nor being above enjoying a bit of conversation, the driver replied, "Yes, sir, there's a lot of money in the Garden District. Real big homes in there. Want to drive through?" he questioned, carefully hiding his eagerness to increase his fare.

"Why not?" Nicholas acquiesced. He glanced at Mara who nodded in agreement as she looked around.

They drove along the wide, tree-lined streets where grand mansions with imitation towers, rococo gingerbread trim, and stained-glass windows were partially concealed behind grounds as large as a city block, full of live-oak, magnolia, and palm trees. The carefully laid out gardens were full of roses, camellias, and jasmine.

Where once there had only been swampy ground, now stood a small town of theaters, hotels, churches, and private residences.

"This is Lafayette Square," the coachman told them, "and that's the city hall facing the square."

"You don't even recognize it, do you?" Mara spoke suddenly as she watched the surprise and disappointment reflected on Nicholas's face. They continued into the Vieux Carré in silence. Mara caught the sounds of the names, Bourbon, Chartres, Dumaine, and Royal, as they traveled up and down the streets bordered by quaint houses with ornate iron grillwork decorating their balconies.

Mara heard Nicholas's gasp as they emerged on a beautiful square where an old cathedral with three spires rose with stately dignity into the blue sky. In the middle of the flower gardens and walks stood an equestrian statue. The square was flanked by twin brick buildings with lacy ironwork.

"What a lovely square," Mara remarked with pleasure as they traveled past. She was reminded of some of the small parks dotting London.

"The Place d'Armes. I don't know why I should be surprised that it too has changed a great deal since I last strolled through," Nicholas said, a sadly reminiscent look on his hard face.

"'Fraid not, sir," the coachman corrected Nicholas respectfully. "It's called Jackson Square, now. Statue of the old general himself right there."

"Seems I was indeed wise in hiring a guide," Nicholas added wryly. "I never thought to be a stranger in the city of my birth. There used to be a double avenue of sycamores along there. At least they didn't tear down the St. Louis Cathedral, or the Calbildo and Presbytère," Nicholas commented as he gestured to the buildings adjacent the cathedral.

"It was the Baroness who did all of this. Just finished it too," the coachman informed them. "The Baroness de Pontalba, that was her name. And my, my, but she was something to watch, yes, sir," the coachman chuckled. "Riding her horse through town every day to oversee the rebuilding of the square, that red hair of hers catching fire in the sunlight."

"And why did she rebuild the square?" Nicholas inquired curiously.

"Well," the coachman paused a moment as he carefully considered the gentleman's question, "reckon 'cause the place was near to ruins. Most folks had moved and all the businesses had gone on up to Canal St. where they could do some real selling for a change. Yes, sir, the place was deserted, excepting maybe for a few rats. Then the Baroness comes along and changes all that, and now, as you can see, the square is a real fine place once again."

"And where is the Baroness?" Mara asked as she looked around, hoping she might see this extraordinary woman.

"Gone back to France, ma'am. The St. Louis Hotel, sir?" the coachman asked after they had left the square.

Nicholas nodded, his eyes partially concealed by his thick lashes, his thoughts unreadable as he stared at this city in which he was now a stranger.

The St. Louis Hotel was, as the coachman had said, one of the finest in the city. Nicholas stayed with them only long enough to sign the register, not noticing the discreet lifting of the clerk's eyebrows as he read the guest's name, his smile obsequious as he assured Monsieur de Montaigne-Chantale that the rooms he had reserved were the very best in the hotel. The lady would be most comfortable.

Nicholas grasped Mara's elbow as she would have followed the bellboy to their rooms. "I have to see some people, I'll be back later, Mara."

"You needn't hurry on my account," Mara told him carelessly.

"Later," Nicholas repeated as he turned and walked through the lobby of the hotel, disappearing into the street. Mara watched forlornly, wondering if he would indeed return.

Nicholas stood on the street a moment, then hired a carriage and returned to the heart of the Vieux Carré, not noticing his surroundings this time. His thoughts centered on his next meeting.

The driver stopped before the house Nicholas had indicated, accepting his fare with a curious look. "Want me to wait, sir? Don't look as though there be a soul around. No, sir, there sure don't."

Nicholas looked up at the quiet front of the house, the drapes drawn across the windows. Shaking his head, he signaled to the driver to go on. Nicholas stared at the pale peach stucco of the house and the ornate, wrought-iron grill-work that ran along the gallery and balcony above the street. He walked up wide steps to the entrance and, knocking on the white paneled door, received no answer. He had suspected he would not. He walked along the gallery to the side of the house and, without hesitating, opened the wrought-iron gate that led through an arched stone passage beneath the lower part of the house.

Nicholas stood in the center of the courtyard as he glanced around at the silent fountain and patio paved in brick, weeds now growing up between the moldings. Had it been summer, the double doors would have been standing open to catch the cooling breeze along the two levels of gallery that ran around three sides of the courtyard. The low building in back that housed the slaves was quiet. Several oleanders were still in bright bloom while a large tree with waxy green leaves would flower with creamy magnolia blossoms in the spring. Nicholas looked around sadly at the faded splendor of the once beautiful courtyard. Walking across to the double doors of the dining room, he tried the latch, knowing it would give if turned a certain way. The large mahogany dining table where his family had once dined en masse was now covered with a dust sheet, while the sideboards were thickly coated in a layer of dust.

Nicholas stepped from the dining room into the long entrance hall where faint light filtered in from the fan-shaped window above the door. On his right were three great square rooms. He entered the double parlor and gazed at the rosewood sofa with its pale green brocade cushions, the fireplace and marble mantel, the occasional tables and delicate chairs. The crystal chandeliers and gilt-framed mirrors reflected the neglected atmosphere. Across the hall was the long ballroom where the late-night soirees and masquerade balls had been held. Very formal affairs they had been, with an orchestra hired for the occasion.

But it was painfully obvious to Nicholas that there had been no balls in this house in a long time. No laughing, flirting couples had danced past here, he thought as he swiped at a cobweb dangling from a mirror frame.

He made his way back into the hallway and stared up at the curved staircase with its handrailing of smooth, dark mahogany, hearing the voices of his past.

"Betcha can't ride all the way down to the floor without

falling off," François challenged him, his ten-year-old's voice full of contemptible goading.

"My pony and new fishing pole says I can," Nicholas heard his own eight-year-old's voice challenging his brother, and he smiled slightly as he remembered that hair-raising ride down the slick banister that he'd negotiated successfully. He remembered looking up daringly at François, waiting for him to descend in a like manner. But François had landed off balance at the foot of the stairs, breaking his arm.

And then there had been the Sunday mornings when they were invariably late dressing for church and had been hurried down the stairs by a scolding maid.

"If yer mama could hear you now, Master Nicholas, why, whut would she say? And whut you got stuffed in that pocket, Master François? Mercy!" Nicholas could still hear her shriek of horror. "And whut were you goin' to do with that frog? Lordie, but all hell would've broke loose in the congregation o'er that."

Following mass, they would have had a big breakfast, shared with many friends invited to spend the day with the family. Then they would have attended a matinee, usually a light opera, and afterward have returned to the house for dinner. Later the carpets in the parlor would have been rolled back, the furniture pushed against the walls, while an aunt played the piano and the young couples danced. Punch and light refreshments would have been served to the thirsty, and finally, the day would have come to a close around midnight.

With a last look up the empty staircase Nicholas left the deserted townhouse and walked back through the streets of the Vieux Carré. At least they had not changed drastically over the last fifteen years. Maybe it was all a little shabbier, but it still retained that special charm he remembered. As he strode along the narrow streets, he became lost in thought. He tried to find the answer to the puzzling question of why the de Montaigne-Chantale house had been closed up, and apparently had been for a long time.

Mara looked around the hotel suite Nicholas had taken for her and wondered if it was *her* room, or *their* room? Perhaps this was his way of bidding her farewell? For unless she was mistaken, he was at this very moment being welcomed home with open arms by his family, and that meant the end of their liaison. She hadn't wanted to question him about his sudden decision to return to New Orleans, for he seemed very reluctant to discuss the details. He had just told her that he'd had a letter from his father asking him to return. She had left it at that, but her curiosity had been aroused. She hadn't cared to admit that she'd heard the gossip about his past and the questionable circumstances involving his departure from New Orleans which went far deeper than the duel he had once mentioned to her.

No, Mara suddenly decided, she doubted very seriously whether Nicholas entertained the idea of returning to the St. Louis Hotel and sharing a room with her. It was about time she made some plans of her own, for she was free to do as she wished. That had been the arrangement between them. A pity Nicholas hadn't thought to leave her enough money to pay for their fares to Europe before he'd disappeared.

Mara glanced around the hotel room, hoping he'd at least paid for it, and a pretty penny he'd pay, too, Mara thought as she admired the European style of decor with its mahogany and gilt Neo-Rococo furniture, the chairs elaborately carved and upholstered with scarlet silk cushions. Gilt-framed floor-to-ceiling mirrors and heavy crystal chandeliers added light and sparkle to the room and reflected the bright colors of the Turkish carpet.

"Where's Uncle Nicholas?" Paddy demanded as he returned from his inspection of the street below. "He promised me we'd go fishin'."

"Paddy, me little love," Mara said with a softening smile, "you really shouldn't call Nicholas 'Uncle,' and he didn't promise you he'd take you fishing, now did he?" Mara asked skeptically, trying to prepare him for disappointment. "Besides, I think we'll be leaving New Orleans before you'll get a chance to do any fishing."

Paddy stamped his foot angrily. "He promised! He told me we'd go fishin', and he told me I could call him uncle if I wanted to," Paddy told Mara defiantly, his hands on his hips as he jutted his chin out stubbornly, his dark brown eyes flashing with spirit. Suddenly he reminded Mara so much of Brendan that it was painful to look at him.

"I just don't want you to be disappointed, Paddy," Mara said shortly. "Nicholas has his own family and friends here, and he'll be spending most of his time with them. We're not his family, Paddy, nor very important to him, love."

Paddy's lower lip trembled slightly as he blinked back his tears. "Why can't *we* be his family? He likes you, and he likes me, and I know he wouldn't go off and leave me without saying good-bye," Paddy reasoned simply as his small shoulders sagged. "Nobody ever stays with us, Mara. Don't we have anybody?" he asked pathetically. "Papa's gone, and the Swede, and Gordie and Paul. Nobody really cares about us, do they?"

At this startling question Mara looked away from his forlorn figure. She then glanced back and saw him standing there in his blue sailor suit looking like a little man who carried the weight of the world on his shoulders.

Mara hurried over to him and hugged him to her as Paddy wrapped his arms tightly around her waist, holding onto her as if his life depended upon the warm contact between them.

"You've always got me, Paddy," Mara told him huskily, "and I'll never leave you. You believe that, don't ye?"

"I love you, Mara," he whispered, pressing his face against her.

Mara bent down and kissed the top of his head, wondering if she could live up to his faith in her. She felt a momentary fright as she realized the responsibility of accepting someone's love. It was such a fragile feeling and could be damaged so easily by a careless word or action.

Mara glanced up to see Jamie standing in the doorway watching them with suspiciously bright eyes, her sharp features softened as she saw the love between Mara and Paddy. As she became aware of Mara's eyes on her, Jamie sniffed loudly and began to bustle about the room, breaking the melancholy atmosphere.

Paddy was napping on the sofa an hour later when Mara could stand the confinement of the hotel room no longer and said, "I can't stand being cooped up in here. I'm going out for a breath of fresh air."

"'Bout time. Your pacin' is gettin' on my nerves," Jamie told her, "Ye go on now. I'll watch Master Paddy."

Mara looked over at Paddy's sleeping form. "I think he's coming down with another cold. He sneezed several times during tea," Mara told Jamie as she put on her bonnet and picked up a parasol of amber and green mosaic-patterned silk with a deep fringe along the edge. "I won't be longer than an hour."

Mara walked along the corridor from her room. Hearing voices across the rotunda, she paused at the railing of the gallery that overlooked the lofty space of the gallery on the far side, which was crowded with people. A marble counter stretched around one-half of the circular area that was paved with a marble floor, while countless barkeepers were kept busy behind the bar with its colorful array of decanters full of alcoholic refreshments. The other side of the barroom was given over to solid fare; a lunch table was crowded with tureens of soup, plates loaded down with sandwiches, hors d'oeuvres and other enticements. But it was another table that caught and held Mara's eyes as she stared in perplexed curiosity at the half-dozen or more young black women neatly clad in plain dresses who were sitting on the table surrounded by laughing and conversing groups of men.

The black girls seemed interested in the proceedings as they the groups of men with wary glances. Then a man stood up on a chair and, gaining the attention of the lunchers, began to auction off the young girls. It was a slave sale, Mara thought in horrified amazement as she watched the proceedings. Then, with a sickening feeling, she moved on. She had begun to draw speculative glances from several men standing nearby.

Out on the street Mara opened her parasol to shield her face and made her way along the banquette, past interesting shops along Royal Street and then down street after nameless street. She enjoyed the exercise after being confined on the ship.

Mara continued her tour until she ended up in a large square where long colonnades of tawny stucco lined the market-place and stalls of fresh fruit and vegetables, meat and fish, shrimp and crabs, freshly caught from the Gulf and bayous, were being sold. Mara turned up a narrow street, leaving behind the market square and the crowd of women with baskets over their arms as they argued down the price of a pound of string beans or with doubtful eye scrutinized the color of a tenderloin of beef.

Mara's steps carried her away from the busy marketplace, her eyes wandering across the colorful facades of the houses with their profusion of greenery and flowers peeking over the edge of grilled balconies. Gradually though, she became aware of a change in the neighborhood as she skirted the garbage-clogged gutters and avoided eye contact with the disreputable men she began to pass on the banquette.

As she passed a run-down-looking building, a sailor came flying out to tumble headlong into the street, his hat following close behind. Something unintelligible in French followed as well, but Mara didn't need to understand the strange patois to know what it meant.

She hurried on uneasily. Suddenly a hand grabbed her shoulder and spun her around.

"*Où allez-vous, ma petite mademoiselle?*" a swarthy-skinned man demanded with an engaging grin, his eyes roaming over her with an undisguised leer.

Mara shrunk back from his whiskey-foul breath as she tried to free her shoulder from his hard grip. "Please release me, monsieur," Mara requested tightly.

"*Ah, vous êtes une americaine,*" he declared, undaunted by her cold rebuff. "*Combien?*" he asked with crude bluntness as his eyes roved suggestively across her breasts.

"More than you could ever pay, *mon ami,*" a cold voice said behind Mara. "Besides—she's spoken for."

The amorous Frenchman glanced up with an ugly glint in his eye, but as he took note of the hard green eyes and cruel sneer on the speaker's lips, he decided that the beautiful mademoiselle was better off in other hands than his.

"*Mille pardons!*" he said with an ingratiatingly apologetic smile as he removed his hand from Mara's shoulder and backed carefully away. "*Au revoir, mes amis.*"

Mara sighed in relief as she turned to look at Nicholas, her smile fading slightly as she met his angry gaze. "Merci, m'sieu," she said lightly, trying to ease the tension, but only fanning his anger.

"What the devil are you doing down here?" Nicholas demanded as he wrapped his hand around her elbow and guided her along the street.

"I was just out for a walk," Mara explained defensively.

"On Gallatin Street? You could hardly have selected a worse place for a stroll, my dear," he said with a sarcastic bite, "unless you'd chosen the Swamp above Canal Street where you'd probably have been raped by a keel-boat crew."

Mara drew in her breath, angry at herself and at him. She knew she shouldn't have walked through town unescorted.

"Do I shock you? Good! It might keep you out of trouble for once," Nicholas said grimly, his rage still simmering. "Do I have to keep my eye on you every minute to assure myself that you are not up to some mischief?"

Mara glanced up at him as she responded to his attack. "I am no responsibility of yours, Nicholas Chantale. In fact, I had wondered if we would be seeing any more of you at all, now that we've reached New Orleans," Mara commented pointedly as she pulled against his restraining grip.

Nicholas stared down thoughtfully at Mara, her eyes seeming to glow even more goldenly as they reflected the amber velvet of her bodice jacket. "We will discuss your position later," he said abruptly.

"*My* position?" Mara questioned, her own anger beginning to rise as she was pulled along beside him. "I hadn't realized I'd been hired on, especially as I'm not hearing a jinglin' in me pockets."

"You know, I've always thought the Irish far too glib for their own well-being," Nicholas remarked smoothly as he signaled a carriage.

"Rue des Ramparts," he instructed the coachman as he

assisted Mara into the carriage and sat back, his stony expression silencing her.

"Where are we going?" she asked at last.

"I need some explanations," Nicholas told her uncommunicatively.

"I'm surprised to see you. I thought you'd still be celebrating your return to New Orleans with your family," Mara remarked. "You did go to see them, didn't you?" Mara asked boldly.

"Apparently they are not in New Orleans at this time," Nicholas explained, adding softly, "which is strange, for now is the season they would be living in town so they could attend the parties and theater. They must still be at Beaumarais."

Mara caught the softening of his voice as he mentioned the family plantation. "What is Beaumarais like?"

Nicholas smiled. "She has no equal. There is a strange grace and beauty in the six columns running across her facade. Sweetbriar climbs up to the covered gallery above and with each sunrise her walls of rose stucco glow delicately. One's first glimpse of Beaumarais is from a long stately drive, lined with live oak draped in gray moss."

Mara stared at Nicholas's face, the hardness of his features softened. The love for his birthplace was visible, and Mara could see now why people might have suspected him of killing his brother in order to inherit the family estate. "And so now you've been invited to return home," Mara said softly. "You must be very happy. Did your father find out who really killed your brother?"

Nicholas turned and looked at Mara sharply. "What do you know about it? And where did you hear about François?" he demanded, then nodded immediately as he realized the answer. "The Swede."

Mara shook her head. "No. It was Jacques D'Arcy who told me about it. He'd lived in New Orleans for a time and recognized you at the El Dorado."

"I see," Nicholas said with a frown. "The rumors still follow me. What did he tell you?"

Mara shrugged, uncomfortable under his steady gaze, "I'm sure you've heard it all before."

"Yes, I have, but I want to hear what *you* have heard about my disreputable past," Nicholas said, his eyes narrowing with determination.

"Very well, if you insist," Mara said shortly. "Jacques D'Arcy told me that the man you killed in that duel was your brother, and that you killed him because you wanted Beaumarais as well as his…"

"Do continue, my sweet," he urged softly. "As well as…?"

"As well as his fiancée, if you must know," Mara told him defiantly. "He said you and she had been lovers, but that your father and hers had made a match between your brother and her."

Nicholas lit a cheroot with apparent unconcern.

Mara glared. "Well, doesn't it bother you to have people tell lies about you?" she demanded.

Nicholas cast her an amused glance. "Why should it when it's the truth. At least," he clarified as she gasped, "the truth that most people know. But I'm curious, Mara, why did you say, 'lies'?"

Mara stared at him for a moment. Then, clearing her throat, she began, "Well, for one thing I don't believe you'd kill your brother. And anyway, Jacques D'Arcy said you claimed you hadn't shot him. I believe you," she ended lamely, shrugging as she turned from him.

Nicholas shook his head in disbelief. "Now why should you believe that? What I wouldn't have given fifteen years ago to have heard those three words spoken by just one member of my family. But no. They all believed the worst of me. And now, finally, someone believes me, and yet I don't know why she should. Your blind faith in me, Mara, is quite touching. But I would have thought that with your unfortunate experiences with me, you would be the first to believe me capable of such a monstrous act."

"I think you capable of many things, Nicholas," Mara told him bluntly, "but not the cold-blooded murder of your brother."

Nicholas stared deeply into her golden eyes. She didn't turn away from him. Her belief in his innocence was clearly revealed. Nicholas was the first to look away, feeling oddly moved by her faith in him. Suddenly, he felt obligated to tell her the whole of it, almost as if testing her loyalty in the face of the sordid details.

"I was a hotheaded, arrogant young man, Mara, and I met many a man in duels over imagined slights and—now that I look back on it—for unworthy and ridiculous reasons. I was a different man from the one I am now, so you mustn't judge the two together. Also," he added with a challenging glint, "you have not seen Beaumarais…or Amaryllis."

"And was she so very beautiful?" Mara asked, feeling a wave of jealousy wash over her.

"At one time I would gladly have given my life for her," Nicholas told her simply, without a sign of embarrassment.

"If you say you were innocent, then I believe you," Mara repeated, her resolve unshaken in the face of his self-criticism.

"I wish it had been so simple, but I'm afraid I was my own worst enemy. My reputation, which I had created over the years, was what really convicted me. I was the infamous black sheep of the family. Most families have one, and I was ours. François was the fair one, much like Julian. That is why I reacted so strongly when Julian was hurt, and I suppose I was taking out some of my self-hatred on you.

"How many times, in my mind and even in my dreams, have I gone over that fateful day? I know in my heart that I could never have killed François. Yet, in moments of weakness the doubts creep in," Nicholas said softly, his eyes focused within, rather than on the scenes passing by outside.

"Maybe I really did shoot him. Did my bullet actually strike him down? I aimed to the left of him, as he aimed to the left of me. It was a game, a foolish trick we had played as boys. But this time, they said, envy overcame my brotherly affection and I shot him. It was a perfect setting for murder, for I could always claim it was an accident—and who could have proven otherwise in a court of law? But I couldn't fight public opinion, or the condemnation from my own family, and that is what finally drove me away.

"I always have wondered what François must have thought

when he felt the bullet strike him," Nicholas said in a low voice, pain shadowing his eyes. "Did he believe I had shot him? I was with him when he died, and the last time he opened his eyes and stared up at me I felt as if he were trying to tell me something. He was facing me when we dueled, and he would have seen behind me," Nicholas spoke thoughtfully, then shook his head in frustration. "François may well have seen his murderer. If only he could have spoken to me. The look of affection and love in his eyes when he died was all I've had to believe in all these years. He didn't die cursing me."

"And what of Amaryllis?" Mara asked softly. "She didn't leave with you?"

Nicholas sent her a sardonic look. "Amaryllis, an outcast to society? I think not. Besides, what could I have offered her? I had very little money, and even less prospect of earning any in the future. I couldn't ask a woman to share that uncertain future with me—not that Amaryllis would have chosen to. Amaryllis has always known what she's wanted, and a life of straitened circumstances had no place in it. We grew up together, but it wasn't until she attended her first ball that I became aware of her as a beautiful woman. Her family's plantation, Sandrose, and Beaumarais border each other, and so the families were constantly thrown together on outings and picnics. I'm sure it was hoped that a match between members of the families might be made. I suppose I was considered an acceptable suitor by Amaryllis's father until her brother died in a riding accident and Sandrose became Amaryllis's inheritance. After that it was François who became the preferred de Montaigne-Chantale to court Amaryllis. What could have been more perfect than to have the two heirs wed and join the two great estates into one holding? Far more desirous a union than one with the rakehell younger brother."

"And you agreed to this? Didn't you tell them that you and Amaryllis loved each other?" Mara asked, feeling pity for the intolerable position the young Nicholas must have found himself in.

"Of course I rebelled against it, and I'm sure my father expected as much from me. But what could I do when he told me that my beloved Amaryllis had readily agreed to the engagement with François? I preferred to think at the time, bemused still by her loveliness, that she had been forced against her will into agreeing to marry my brother. But Amaryllis had not been so blinded by love that she would pass up the chance of being mistress of Beaumarais, as well as benefiting from our family's wealth. The Sandonet family seemed always to be short of money. I suspect also that François was no less immune to Amaryllis than I, and was fast falling in love with her. As Amaryllis and I had always been very discreet, I think he did not realize the depth of our affection," Nicholas told her, then with a speculative look added, "and I wonder if that was not Amaryllis's intention, even then—to have me as a lover and my brother as her legal mate. I thought I was protecting her reputation, but actually I was making it possible for her to turn from one brother to the other with her halo intact. Maybe she would have wed me—I don't know—but when she inherited Sandrose it became imperative for her to marry money just to keep her plantation from falling into ruin and the hands of creditors. The only thing Amaryllis had miscalculated upon was that once she became my brother's betrothed I would not touch her again, for I was not quite as debauched as people thought and still had some decency."

"You said you received a letter from your father asking you to return. Why now, after all of these years?" Mara asked curiously.

"Because my father apparently found out who really shot François," Nicholas said softly.

"Who?" Mara asked breathlessly.

Nicholas smiled, shaking his head regretfully. "That, my father did not tell me. Perhaps he feared I would not forgive him and would not return to Beaumarais, so he held back that piece of information as enticement, knowing I would not rest until I knew the truth." The look in his eyes chilled Mara's blood, and she shivered despite the warmth of the sunlight shining down on them in the carriage.

Mara glanced around her at the row of small, one-storied houses, then looked at Nicholas in surprise. He halted the carriage at the corner, near a flower seller. He jumped out and stood in conversation with the black woman whose cart was loaded down with fragrant blooms. Mara saw the woman gesture toward a group of houses farther along the street. Nicholas pressed money into her hand and accepted a bouquet, climbed back into the carriage, and directed the coachman.

Nicholas glanced over at Mara and, with a slight smile, tucked a single yellow rose inside her bodice just above her breast. The sweet fragrance floated up to her.

The carriage stopped before one of the small houses. Paying off the coachman, Nicholas and Mara stood staring at the pale stuccoed house, its pink shutters gleaming discreetly through the lush garden that enclosed the front.

Nicholas strode up to the house without hesitation, knocking firmly on the pale pink door. He glanced around with interest. The door was opened by a uniformed black butler who politely inclined his head but stood blocking the doorway. He waited for Nicholas to speak.

"Tell Mademoiselle Ferrare that Nicholas de Montaigne-Chantale is calling," he announced as proudly as he must have spoken the name fifteen years before.

The butler's downcast eyes flashed up for a moment in surprised recognition. Stepping aside, he led them into a parlor and went to inform his mistress.

"You needn't have brought me along if this is some private matter, Nicholas," Mara said stiffly, feeling out of place. She sat on the edge of a satin-upholstered chair. "I can find my way back to the hotel."

"You're here now," Nicholas commented, "so you might as well relax."

Mara sighed in exasperation and sat back. She glanced idly around the parlor, finding herself surprised by the almost faultless elegance. The room could have rivaled any parlor in a Paris townhouse. A marble mantel held a gilded, ormolu clock and a pair of rose- and gold-colored Sevres vases, while several porcelain biscuit figures and two beautiful silver candelabra graced a Louis XV commode of tulipwood. A tall bookcase held many volumes of elegantly bound books, one of which still lay open on the cream-colored satin seat of the settee. A delicately painted music box, its lid open, played a tinkling melody.

"Nicholas?"

Mara turned toward the doorway at the sound of the incredulous voice, the husky attractiveness of it drawing her eyes to the woman who now threw herself into Nicholas Chantale's outstretched arms, laughing and hugging him, pressing warm kisses across his face as he lifted her slender form off the floor.

"Françoise," Nicholas laughed, "still as impulsive as ever. I expected to be greeted by an aloof sophisticate," Nicholas teased her as he returned her kiss.

"It is over fifteen years dropping from my age at the sight of your handsome face that does this to me. When I was just a child I was so much in love with you," she complained with a deep laugh. "Ooh la, what a curse that was for me."

Mara had gotten to her feet and now stood in forgotten silence watching the happy reunion between the two Creoles. Mara had to admit that this lady was one of the most beautiful women she had ever seen. She moved with the natural and easy grace of a gazelle, the long, slender column of her neck supporting a smooth, dark head that was now tipped backward as she stared up at Nicholas. Her heart-shaped face had the soft color of a sun-kissed peach, while her almond-shaped eyes were a pale blue green with delicately arched brows above a straight, narrow nose. The nostrils flared slightly as her perfectly proportioned lips curved into a smile. Dressed in a simple, pale green afternoon dress of sprigged muslin with a square neckline and bishop sleeves that enhanced rather than detracted from her breathtaking beauty, she exuded charm and poise as she scolded Nicholas with a mocking look.

"After such a long time, Nicholas," she said, disbelief still showing on her face, "you show up here so suddenly, as if you'd been gone less than a week instead of sixteen years. Mon Dieu, but you are the one for surprises."

"*You* are the one to give surprises," Nicholas retorted with amusement as he held her away from him and looked her over, "by growing up on me and turning into a ravishing beauty without benefit of my guidance."

Françoise threw back her head and laughed. "My dear Nicholas, it is fortunate for me that you were not here to guide me, for I can see that you are still the same arrogantly handsome Nicholas who snaps his fingers at convention and would have led me down the road to ruin. But now I think you are even more dangerous, for you were just a boy then. Now you are a devilishly attractive man with a mysterious past. The ladies will be fainting and—" Françoise suddenly became aware that she and Nicholas were not alone. Stepping away from him, she stared at Mara through narrowed eyes, missing nothing about Mara's appearance. "And who is this, Nicholas?" Françoise asked softly.

Nicholas walked over to Mara and, placing his hand lightly on her shoulder, said with possessive pride, "Mara O'Flynn."

Françoise arched one of her fine eyebrows quizzically, amusement showing as Nicholas neglected to volunteer any more information about Mara. With a mocking smile she said politely, "It's a pleasure to meet you, Miss O'Flynn."

Mara inclined her head slightly as she replied coolly, "Mademoiselle." Nicholas laughed softly. "Mara, this is *ma petite cousine*, Françoise Ferrare, and she is dying to know more about us—especially about you."

Mara felt some of the antagonism fade. There was nothing between them, nor had there ever been. She realized as well, upon closer inspection of Françoise Ferrare, that she was quite a few years older than she'd first thought. She guessed her to be about thirty.

"I think I shall be able to contain my close-to-bursting curiosity until I have at least offered you some tea," Françoise said as she rang for the butler and gestured for them to be seated, pausing as Nicholas produced the bouquet he'd bought for her. Françoise held the fragrant blooms to her face. "Ah, Nicholas, you remember how I love flowers," she murmured softly.

The butler appeared with a maid and the tea service already prepared and stood watchfully beside the table as the maid placed the delicate china cups and saucers in position for her mistress.

Françoise shook her head at the butler. "He is always a step ahead of me and can read my mind better than me I think," she laughed. Then, spreading her hands, she added, "And see, he adds the bottle of brandy for the gentleman. There is no one quite like my Peter," she said affectionately, and Mara could see the pleasure on the old man's face. "See that these flowers are arranged in water, Colette," Françoise told the maid after she had finished setting the tea table.

"Lemon, or cream, mademoiselle?" Françoise asked as she poured the tea, then shook her head with an apologetic look. "Ah, but please forgive me, I forget that you English always take the cream, non?"

"Actually I'm Irish, but cream will be fine," Mara explained as she accepted her cup of tea.

"And she happens to be very proud of that heritage, and pity the poor fool who makes light of it in her presence," Nicholas added with an almost affectionate look in his eyes as they met Mara's.

Françoise noted the intimate exchange of glances as she watched Nicholas and the Irishwoman and wondered just how good a friend this Mara O'Flynn was to him. "And how did you know where to find me, Nicholas?" she demanded curiously.

Nicholas shrugged. "I thought if you were not living permanently in Paris, then you would most likely be living along here somewhere, so I asked of you from the woman selling flowers on the corner."

Françoise sighed in exasperation. "That old woman knows everything that goes on around here. I cannot go out without her—" Françoise was saying when she was interrupted by a small child who came running unannounced into the room, her dark braids flying out behind her as she jumped across the carpet and came to a breathless stop before Françoise.

"Mama! Mama!" she cried as she backed up a step. "*Regardez-moi!*" she commanded as she executed a perfect pirouette.

Nicholas's clapping hands disturbed the silence and for the first time the little girl became aware of her audience and blushed a bright pink that rivaled the pink satin of her dancing skirt.

"*Très bien, ma petite danseuse*," Nicholas complimented the little girl. She couldn't have been more than five years old.

"Chérie, how many times have I told you it isn't ladylike to charge into a room like a wild Indian?" Françoise scolded gently as she smoothed back a stray curl from the miniature ballet dancer's forehead. "Now say hello properly to your cousin Nicholas and Miss O'Flynn," Françoise instructed her.

"*Bonjour, monsieur, mademoiselle*," she said softly, her dark blue eyes hidden beneath lowered lids as she hunched her narrow shoulders.

Françoise smiled, her blue green eyes glowing with pride as she looked into Nicholas's face and said, "My daughter, Gabriella, who is just back from her dancing lessons and must demonstrate her newest step for her mama. Now, *ma chatte*, run along and change," Françoise told her.

"Au revoir," she said politely as she curtsied, then ran from the room in a flurry of pink petticoats. "She is a charming little girl," Nicholas said as he watched her disappear. "She reminds me of you at that age, Françoise."

Françoise smiled. "And you were always teasing me, and Gabriella has two brothers who see to it that she is reduced to tears whenever they are around," Françoise said disapprovingly.

"I would like to meet them," Nicholas told her, gesturing away the plate of cakes she offered him.

"It is a shame. I would have liked that," Françoise began with a regretful look, "but they are studying in France and will not return until the spring. But perhaps you will still be here then?"

At Nicholas's slight frown Françoise continued, afraid that he would think her too inquisitive. "Jean-Pierre, my eldest, is very musical and has already composed several pieces of music. But Henri, he is the wild one, much like his papa. He shows much brilliance with words, also like his papa," she laughed. Then, catching the politely quizzical look in Nicholas's eye, she answered his unasked question. "They are de St. Jaubert's."

"Armand de St. Jaubert is their father?" Nicholas asked, a smile of pleased recognition at the name.

"Oui, and I have been Armand's *placée* for almost fifteen years now," Françoise spoke quietly and with great dignity.

The truth dawned slowly on Mara. Françoise's was saying that she was this Armand's mistress. Mara cleared her throat uncomfortably, drawing Françoise's attention to her. "This is really a private conversation and I know you would prefer to be alone with Nicholas," Mara began as she started to rise. "After all, it has been many years and you must have much to discuss. I'll step into the garden."

"Please, it is not necessary," Françoise argued, then added with the same cynical look Mara had often seen on Nicholas's handsome face, "unless of course you find this conversation embarrassing and would prefer not to sit in my presence?"

Mara opened her mouth to hotly deny such an accusation, knowing full well that she herself was in no position to make judgments on Françoise Ferrare, but before she could speak Nicholas spoke for her.

"I'm sure Mara thought nothing of the sort, Françoise," Nicholas explained in her defense.

"I merely desired to give you a chance to be alone," Mara said as she began to retreat behind a wall of cold reserve.

Françoise smiled, realizing she had misjudged the Irishwoman. "Please, forgive me, but you are not a Creole and do not understand the system we have here in New Orleans. It is a time-honored one, and one which works quite well for us. I live quite openly as the mistress of Armand de St. Jaubert. He supports me and our children, and will continue to, throughout our lives. He will always provide for his sons and daughter, even though they are a second family for him. You see, he has children by his legal wife. It is really most civilized," Françoise said with a slight laugh. "But I do not expect the Americans or British to understand."

Mara bit her lip. "Oh, but I do understand." Seeing the doubtful look on Françoise's beautiful face, Mara made a quick decision and defiantly uttered the truth she and Brendan had always kept to themselves. Now she wished to shock, especially Nicholas, and so she said bluntly, "I am the product of such a union myself. The difference is that when my father grew bored with my mother, he abandoned us, leaving my aged mother, my brother, and myself to fend for ourselves. So you see, I find your system has certain advantages. Of course, it all depends upon the manner of man one chooses, doesn't it? My mother chose a rich, titled Irishman, but I think she would have done better by a farmer or perhaps a fisherman. I have found it far wiser not to depend upon anyone—just myself," Mara finished as she stared challengingly into Nicholas's eyes. If she had expected to see disgust written across his face, she was disappointed. Instead, she encountered a gentle expression that confused her.

Françoise shook her head and smiled sadly. "But, mademoiselle, that is not always possible. One cannot explain the ways of love. Why should one be attracted to a certain person? But me, I have been fortunate, for I have found the man I love."

"My mother thought the same," Mara said, unable to hide the furious resentment she still felt after all those years.

Françoise smiled pityingly as she gazed at the defiant young Irishwoman whose wounds hadn't healed. Suddenly, she felt so much wiser than this child. Mara seemed so young to her now, with her attempt to appear indifferent to that which she didn't understand. "One always takes a chance when one gives with the heart, mademoiselle. It is not always a wise move, nor one that ends happily. But it is a chance one must take sometimes if one is to know love."

"And are you happy, Françoise?" Nicholas inquired.

"And why shouldn't I be? I have lived in great happiness with Armand, and I have two fine sons being educated in Paris and a small daughter who will grow into a beautiful woman one day," Françoise spoke proudly. "I may only be the placée, but Armand loves me, and that is more than can be said by his wife. It was a *mariage de convenance*, and so there has never been any love between them. In fact, they dislike the very sight of one another. She is always traveling to Europe on one of the ships he owns, and so is seldom here to make demands upon him. She would do so just to annoy him," Françoise said with a shrug. "More tea, Mademoiselle O'Flynn? It's still hot. But what I want to know, *mon cousin*, is just what you are doing here in New Orleans?" she demanded with an arch look as she poured Mara a fresh cup. "Oh, your papa, of course," she sighed.

Nicholas frowned at her tone. "You know of the letter?"

"*La lettre?* Non, I know nothing of this," Françoise said thoughtfully, "although I suppose they could have written to you about his death through your sister."

Françoise glanced up to see a shocked expression spreading across Nicholas's face and she gasped in dismay, her hand pressed against her mouth. "Oh, Nicholas, I am so sorry, but your papa, *il est mort.*"

"When did he die?" Nicholas asked quietly.

"Ah, let me see, it is so hard to remember exactly," Françoise said reflectively as her slender fingers tapped the table. "Why...it was over a year ago. It was in the autumn and I remember thinking that it was a time for dying, so somber and bleak a season it was."

"How did he die? Did he suffer any?" Nicholas asked gently, finding it hard to believe that his father was dead. He remembered the vigorous lust for living that had made Philippe de Montaigne-Chantale one of the most admired Creoles in Louisiana.

Françoise avoided Nicholas's steady gaze as she answered his query with a strange hesitancy. "It was a tragedy, one of those senseless accidents. He fell from the levee and into the river. He drowned, Nicholas. It was too late. When they found him, he'd been carried downstream from Beaumarais. A fisherman caught sight of his body along the river bank."

"My God," Nicholas breathed.

Mara watched him in silence, aching to reach out and comfort him. She had seen Nicholas livid with rage, laughing in boyish amusement, sarcastic and cruel, and sensual with desire, but never before had she seen that vulnerable and hurt expression.

"I don't understand," Nicholas said with a disbelieving frown. "He was a strong swimmer. Many times I've seen him climb from the river after a long, tiring swim. He was a powerful man and knew every inch of that levee. He wouldn't fall in."

Françoise shook her head sadly. "Nicholas, he was not the same man you remember. He had changed greatly in the years that you were gone. I think he still grieved deeply for the loss of his sons. It preyed upon his mind. It destroyed him, Nicholas. He was a broken old man the last time I saw him, just before his death. In fact, I remember thinking that this could not possibly be the once-great master of Beaumarais. He seemed troubled, but he kept whatever it was to himself. He was only in town that one day I think. The next thing I heard was that he was dead."

Nicholas ran a hand through his dark curls as he tried to assimilate this new picture of his father, his old memories fighting the painful truth. "He wrote to me. He had forgiven me, Françoise, and said he knew what had really happened when my brother was killed," Nicholas spoke in a hard voice as he looked up at his cousin, his eyes a shiny green. "He said he knew the truth at last. The letter must have been written just before he died. He knew who murdered François and he was going to tell me. I wonder…" Nicholas mused softly, leaving the rest of his words unspoken. The implication was horrifyingly clear to both Françoise and Mara.

"Oh, Nicholas, non!" Françoise cried. "His death was an accident. It must have been. You cannot believe that someone would…Oh, non. This I cannot believe," she whispered, shaking her head in complete rejection of such an idea.

"It remains indisputable, Françoise," Nicholas continued, "that my brother is dead. And now my father. Both under questionable circumstances, but this time I was not here to take the blame."

Mara felt a shiver of dread spread through her as she recognized his tone of voice, knowing he was in a black rage.

"I should have realized something was wrong when I went to our old townhouse only to find it practically boarded up. But I suppose the family is still in mourning for him."

Françoise busied herself with fixing a fresh cup of tea before saying delicately, "I'm afraid that the townhouse has been closed for longer than that. In fact, it has been unused by the family for many years."

"And why is that, Françoise?" Nicholas asked, not allowing her to sidestep his questioning.

Françoise sighed. "It has not been so good a time for many Creole families, Nicholas. Your father, he was a proud man, and he would never have had it known that he was no longer the wealthy man he had once been," she told him bluntly.

Nicholas stared at Françoise's pitying expression in growing dismay. "What are you trying to tell me? That the de Montaigne-Chantales are beggars?"

"Non! Never that, Nicholas. Please, you misunderstand me," Françoise explained desperately, not wishing to offend him, but knowing he would not like to hear what she had to say. "Not long after you left New Orleans there were several bad years for the sugar cane. Prices dropped drastically when the government reduced the tariff on imported sugar, and so there was not so much money anymore. As a result, many of the banks had to close their doors. Many large planters lost their plantations and their whole fortunes."

"Beaumarais?" Nicholas asked quietly.

"It is still there, and still belongs to your family," Françoise reassured him, "but things were never the same after that. The lost fortunes could not be completely recovered. Times change and now it is the Americans who have all the money in New Orleans."

"I've already seen some of the more obvious changes around town," Nicholas remarked as he remembered the new buildings uptown.

"Yes, there have been changes, Nicholas, not only in the way we live, but in the way we think as well. I'm afraid we have become very old-fashioned in our beliefs, and now it is the Americans who are so outrageous in their behavior. It is hard for the old ones to accept the changes they see in their New Orleans. You remember René Cabrole, who owned Carrefour near the Bayou Teche?" Françoise demanded.

"Yes, I visited there often as a boy. It was one of the

most magnificent plantation houses I've ever seen. Why?" Nicholas asked.

"Because René Cabrole lost it all when the prices fell. He could not bear to lose Carrefour so he took his own life and now his family is living very quietly in an unassuming little house on Frenchman Street. All the beautiful furniture and silver, family portraits, and prized possessions are crowded together in a few rooms. And that has happened to many families, Nicholas," Françoise ended, her smile bitter.

"And what of mine, Françoise?" Nicholas wanted to know.

"What have you heard over the years?" Françoise avoided a direct answer.

Nicholas's green eyes turned to gaze directly at her, their intensity making Françoise wish she had not asked. "I have heard news about them occasionally from Denise when I visited with her in London. I know that I have two half-sisters. One is named Nicole, and would be about sixteen now. And the other one, who was not even born when I left," Nicholas said with a smile, "would be eight or nine."

"Damaris, she is eight, and quite a handful for your step-mama," Françoise informed him, then added carefully, "but you do not mention the youngest, your half-brother, Jean-Louis?"

Nicholas could not have looked more surprised. "A brother?"

Françoise nodded her sleek head in amusement at his incredulous expression. "Mais oui, only he will need a long time before he becomes master of Beaumarais, for he is only two years old."

"It's incredible," Nicholas murmured.

"It was a surprise for everyone, especially after such a long time, for your stepmama was not meant to have many children and nearly died giving birth to the little Jean-Louis. But your papa, oh, he was so proud, so happy to have another son. He seemed like his old self. And then suddenly, he was like a man haunted by the past again, almost overnight he aged a lifetime."

"I see," Nicholas sighed. "Thank you for telling me, Françoise."

"What will you do, Nicholas?" she asked with concern.

"I shall go to Beaumarais," he said quietly. There was a determined note in his voice that Mara knew well.

Françoise reached over and, placing her hand lightly on his arm, said, "There may be no welcome for you there, Nicholas. Even if it is true that your papa found out the truth about François's death, he would still not have told Celeste. She would have still been too ill from having borne him his son, and he would not have spoken with his two daughters about such a thing. Nicholas, no one may know the truth. They might still believe you guilty. I am sure that is the way it still is. I have heard nothing exonerating you of guilt, and such news would travel fast, *mon cher*," Françoise told him sadly.

Nicholas looked down at Françoise's beautiful face, her concern touching him. "As long as I know that my father forgave me and knew the truth, then I can face whatever awaits me at Beaumarais. And I've really no other choice, Françoise. I must find out the truth," he told her as he bent down and lightly touched his lips to her forehead. "Don't worry, ma petite, for I'm very thick-skinned and have lived with dishonor for many years. I shall be all right."

Mara bit her lip at his display of tenderness. He had seldom shown this side to her. She realized once again that here was where they must part company, for she would not be wanted at Beaumarais. Mara turned her tawny eyes away from their figures silhouetted closely together in the doorway and suddenly knew herself to be an intruder.

"Nicholas!" Françoise exclaimed, suddenly remembering something. "Alain. Alain will be able to help you in your search."

Nicholas frowned. "Your brother? How could he help me?"

Françoise shook his arm in excitement. "He is overseer at Beaumarais now. He will know everything that is going on around the plantation. You can trust him, Nicholas," Françoise spoke with an entreating note. "You know he has always been a friend to you."

"Perhaps I shall speak with him," Nicholas said ruminatively, "for it would be good to have at least one friend I can count on. I shall probably be met with hostility."

"Not by my papa, Nicholas," Françoise corrected him with a knowing smile. "You have always been a favorite of his."

"Etienne is at Beaumarais?" Nicholas asked with pleased surprise.

Françoise threw up her hands in defeat and said mockingly, "He always says he will leave, and he goes to Paris, London, Vienna, or even St. Petersburg, which was where his travels took him last time. And yet always he returns to Beaumarais and is happy living nowhere else."

"I'm glad he's there. I look forward to seeing him again, for it has been far too long since our last meeting. I saw him in Venice many years ago and he had changed little."

"Papa never seems to age, but then perhaps it is because he is never aware of time passing. To him one day is the same as the next, and all he is interested in are his paintings and music—and collecting treasures from all over the world," Françoise said with an indulgent smile.

"He used to enjoy riding with me upriver along the boundaries of Beaumarais. Perhaps we will find the opportunity to do that again."

Mara was the first to notice Françoise's discomfiture and waited for her next disclosure. Nicholas became aware of Françoise's hesitancy as well and, folding his arms across his wide chest, stared down at her patiently.

"You might as well tell me."

"Much of that land is no longer Beaumarais property. Some of it had been sold off during the years, but it was just last year, after your father's death, that…" Françoise paused nervously under the narrowing of Nicholas's eyes. Then, taking a breath, she continued quickly, "…the whole northeast quarter was sold."

Mara could see the muscles in Nicholas's jaw tighten. He said quietly, "The land bordering Sandrose."

"Yes. Amaryllis still lives there," Françoise told him as she watched him closely.

Mara was watching Nicholas's expression as well, wondering if he still felt anything for Amaryllis.

"I thought she had married a man from Natchez? Denise told me she left New Orleans shortly after I did," Nicholas remarked without any sign of emotion.

"Even Amaryllis's beauty couldn't overcome the scandal of that time, and so she fled north to Natchez where she quickly found herself some poor, rich fool and inveigled him into marriage," Françoise spoke contemptuously.

Nicholas eyed her thoughtfully. "You never cared for her, did you?" he asked softly.

"Non," Françoise admitted, "and I still do not. She always acted like I was the dirt beneath her slim, satin shoes. And I never forgot when she pushed me—on purpose, Nicholas—into the bayou."

Nicholas smiled, remembering the incident. Françoise could only have been about ten years old and Amaryllis around thirteen. "I believe she claimed you slipped."

"Slipped!" Françoise cried indignantly. "Slipped with the palm of her hand in my back. That is the truth! But she was always a liar."

"Enough, Françoise," Nicholas said abruptly, halting in mid-stride Françoise's diatribe against her old enemy. "Why is Amaryllis back at Sandrose?"

Françoise sniffed. "She bled her poor husband dry, spending his money on a big house up on the bluff in Natchez, acting like a queen when she visited New Orleans. But most of all she used his fortune to keep Sandrose alive and thriving. Her husband didn't fare so well, however, for he drank himself into his grave just to escape her and her incessant demands. He was in debt when he escaped her greedy clutches," Françoise said with a malicious look.

"So she is a widow," Nicholas commented with a curious look in his green eyes.

"With two nearly grown children," Françoise added. "She would like to forget about their existence while she tries to ensnare a rich American banker into becoming her second husband. It is rumored that it was her new suitor's bank which loaned her the money to buy Beaumarais land, and," Françoise added portentously, "they say she is after more than the land belonging to the de Montaigne-Chantales. She wants Beaumarais itself."

Françoise looked away from Nicholas's emerald green eyes,

squirming uncomfortably under his gaze. Françoise's eyes rested speculatively on the beautiful Irishwoman who sat apart from them, and she wondered just what the relationship was between her and Nicholas. Could it survive the test of Amaryllis?

"We must be leaving, Françoise," Nicholas said, breaking into her thoughts, his own eyes resting momentarily on Mara before he turned back to his cousin. "By the way, who inherited Beaumarais?" Nicholas asked curiously.

"No will was ever found, so Celeste did, as guardian for Jean-Louis, since you were not here and François was dead," she told him. Then she added with a pleading note, "Nicholas, please, you are not angry with me? Say you will come and visit again?"

Nicholas smiled. "You mock me, for you know I can never stay away from you for long." Nicholas kissed her cheek. "Au revoir, ma petite cousine."

"Nicholas," Françoise said seriously, "you will be careful?"

"I am always that," Nicholas replied carelessly as he guided Mara to the door.

"It was a pleasure meeting you, Mademoiselle Ferrare," Mara said politely as she held out her hand.

Françoise seemed momentarily surprised, then clasped it firmly. She shook her head. "Françoise, please—and I think it was not so much a pleasure this time, but I hope you will come and visit me again. Oh, Nicholas, do give Papa my love and tell him to come and visit me. His granddaughter asks constantly for her *grand-père*."

"I will, Françoise," Nicholas promised as they started along the path to the street.

"Peter tells me he took the liberty of ordering my carriage for you," Françoise called after them with a laugh. "He noticed that you dismissed yours. So please, allow my coachman to take you wherever you are going," she offered with a wave. She quickly disappeared back inside her house before Nicholas could argue.

There was an awkward silence in the carriage as they rode back to the hotel. Mara glanced over at Nicholas's brooding face knowing he was suffering both grief and anger at the news about his father's death. The silence became unbearable for Mara, yet she knew there was nothing she could say. She sought another, safer subject.

"Your cousin is a very beautiful woman," Mara said suddenly. Despite Nicholas's continued silence, she went on. "She seems very happy. If you are going to Beaumarais, you should have invited her to accompany you. She would like to visit. You'd think her father would—" Mara stopped abruptly as she became aware of Nicholas's amused glance.

"You really don't know, do you?" he asked with a strange expression on his face.

"Know what?" Mara demanded defensively, not caring for his amused look.

"Françoise is a *femme de couleur*, an octoroon," Nicholas said quietly. "She and Alain are the children of my uncle Etienne and a quadroon. Olivia, Françoise's mother, was unbelievably beautiful. I have only a boy's memory of her. Once, when my parents were in Europe, she arrived with Etienne to stay on the plantation while they were gone. Even then I recognized the unusual beauty of the woman. I can understand why my uncle never married and is still devoted to her memory."

"What happened to her?"

"She died a long time ago. After that Etienne would often bring Alain and Françoise to the plantation when he came to visit, and that is why I know Françoise so well. But now that she is a grown woman it is different. She would not be comfortable at Beaumarais."

Mara shook her head, still unable to believe his startling disclosure about Françoise. "I had no idea. I never guessed. Why, she looks like…" Mara's impulsively spoken words trailed off.

"She looks like you or me," Nicholas finished her thoughts aloud. "If she chose to live in France, she could very easily pass for white, but she chooses instead to live here in New Orleans with her lover, and here she is considered less than equal, even though she is a free woman. But she will remain. This is where she was born, and where she will raise her children, and where she will die. She has too much Creole blood in her ever to be content anywhere else."

Mara looked out on the street passing by and knew that Nicholas had come home too. She wondered if he could ever be happy anywhere else either.

The carriage stopped before their hotel and Nicholas escorted her through the crowded lobby and up to the corridor leading to their room.

"You will no doubt be leaving for Beaumarais almost immediately," Mara began, "and as I wish to sail for Europe as soon as possible, I would like to make the necessary arrangements for our passage without any further delay."

At her casual words and cool tone Nicholas halted beside the railing of the gallery, his hand closing around Mara's elbow and bringing her to a sudden stop beside him.

Mara gazed up at him in amazement which quickly turned to confusion as she noticed the cruel look entering his green eyes. "What is wrong? I would have thought you'd be rather relieved to have our liaison come to an end so smoothly," Mara taunted him, hiding her unhappiness behind caustically spoken words.

Nicholas's lips curved into a humorless smile. "You seem in a hell of a hurry all of a sudden to rid yourself of my presence. Don't you care for the idea of being seen with me, now that I find myself still the outcast?" Nicholas sneered.

Mara stared in growing frustration, realizing that he was in no mood to be reconciled. "You know that is not true," Mara denied. "You, of all people, should know that I don't care about appearances. I just want to return to Europe. It is what we agreed upon, Nicholas."

"And just how do you expect to buy passage, my dear?" Nicholas inquired in a voice that sounded far too soft for Mara's comfort.

"You'll forgive me for reminding you so bluntly, m'sieu, but as your memory seems to need prodding, you did offer to pay for my passage to Europe," Mara told him tartly. "Or is it your intention to renege on the agreement?"

Nicholas's eyes narrowed dangerously as he replied smoothly, "And if I did?"

"I only accepted your charitable offer in the first place to humor you. I didn't fancy sailing halfway around the world with someone staring daggers at me, and so it relieves my mind considerably not to have anything further to do with you. I shall sell some of my jewelry to buy passage," Mara declared.

"That, my dear, would possibly get you a bunk in steerage, hardly a private cabin," Nicholas said. "But you may set your mind at rest for I have no intention of reneging on our agreement. I only question when you will be leaving. It doesn't suit my purposes for you to leave at this time."

"The devil it doesn't," Mara said shortly, anger simmering as she glared up at him. "You seem to be laboring under a misconception that you've got some say in me life, when ye haven't, M'sieu Chantale," Mara said with growing indignation as she tried to ridicule him with a mocking Irish accent. "Ye seem to have very little faith in me natural abilities."

Nicholas smiled grimly. "Oh, I've never underestimated you, Mara, *me love*," Nicholas mimicked her.

With a sigh of defeat Mara dropped her pretense. "Just what is it you are playing at, Nicholas? All of a sudden you seem to be acting as if you own me, like one of those unfortunates over there being sold to the highest bidder." Then with a derisory look around her, she added, "Of course, that might not be such a bad idea. With a personal reference from you, why, who knows? I might even be able to make me fortune."

Mara winced as Nicholas's fingers tightened painfully around her elbow.

"So you wish to be bought and paid for, like one of those young women across there? Did you know that in many slave sales the bidders demand a full inspection of the goods. You would stand before a room full of men, stripped of your clothes and dignity, while they stared at your beautiful body, your rounded breasts and slender thighs. You would have to suffer their gloating inspection and ribald remarks as they walked around you, their hands itching to touch that soft curve of buttock as they raped you with their eyes."

Mara flushed with mortification, refusing to look at him even when his fingers closed over the point of her chin and lifted her face to his.

"Well, my dear, my gold is as good as the next man's," he bit out, his insulting words flicking her like a whip. "Come," he said as he became aware of the stares they were beginning to draw.

Mara went along with him to their room.

"To be sure, I thought ye'd fallen into the river, or worse," Jamie greeted Mara. "And ye was right. Looks like Master Paddy's comin' down with a churchyard cough for sure. Goin' to rub some more salve on his chest right now," she said. Without waiting for an answer, she bustled back inside, firmly closing the door to Paddy's room behind her, but not before nodding to Nicholas.

Nicholas watched Mara curiously, wondering what was going through that beautiful head. He could see her slipping away from him now, just as everything else had done. In less than an hour he had heard of the death of his father and the threatened sale of Beaumarais. And now Mara O'Flynn was demanding her freedom.

His emerald gaze traveled across the distance of the room and locked on Mara's averted profile, lingering on the soft, full curve of her lips as he remembered the taste of them beneath his; yet even then, with her clasped against his heart, she still kept herself apart. She always seemed to be holding something back from him and he never felt as if he possessed her completely. She was an enigma, as indeed she always had been. Maybe because of that, she excited him as no other woman ever had. He had never felt this almost unreasonable need for possession, this ache in his loins whenever he was close to that damned Irishwoman, but could he really blame himself, for she was, after all, an actress, and it was that very fine art in acting of creating an illusion that Mara O'Flynn seemed to excel in. In her very complex nature she presented a challenge to him, and he was determined to solve the puzzle of her, he swore beneath his breath as he made his first move against the wall of reserve she had erected between them.

"How much is Paddy's life worth to you, Mara O'Flynn?" Nicholas began his attack on that which was dearest to her heart. "Is it worth coming with me to Beaumarais? You don't hate my touch so much that you couldn't endure it awhile longer for someone else's sake. Paddy and Jamie are both fatigued from the months at sea and could use a rest on dry land for a change. You wouldn't, for your own selfish reasons, deny them an opportunity to recuperate?" Nicholas argued both persuasively and unfairly, knowing full well that Mara would never risk her nephew's health. "Think of spending those long hours in a damp cabin as you cross the stormy Atlantic to Europe, Paddy suffering a chest cold and the old woman's rheumatism acting up," Nicholas added. "I really would have to advise against such a journey at this time."

Nicholas paused for a moment to allow his words to sink in, his eyes never leaving her face as he watched for some sign of weakening. The expression on her flawless features never changed.

She would never endanger Paddy's health, and he knew that. But what he didn't know was that she wasn't as self-sacrificing as she would have him believe. Her heart had jumped with excitement and joy when he first suggested her accompanying him to his home. And if she agreed to go to Beaumarais, was it really enough to be with him just a little longer, or did she perhaps hope for a more permanent relationship?

"Maybe the real reason you wish to leave New Orleans is that you have come to enjoy my lovemaking so much that you desire to run away before you become my slave," Nicholas taunted softly, his expression deliberately contemptuous as he goaded her into acting rashly, knowing that once she gave rein to her temper she would speak without stopping to think.

"Become a slave to you, Nicholas?" Mara scoffed, humiliation and anger coloring her cheeks. "Never."

"Then come with me to Beaumarais," Nicholas said. "It's one way of proving me wrong, isn't it? And you always enjoy doing that, don't you, Mara?"

Mara's lips trembled slightly as her tawny eyes, carefully wiped clear of all emotion, met Nicholas's stare. She nodded. Whatever her motives were, she had made her choice.

Chapter 12

"'TIS LIKE A FLOATING HOTEL," MARA REMARKED IN AMAZE-ment from the top deck of the big, ungainly-looking steamboat as it made its way upriver, the thick, black smoke pouring out from its twin stacks. Huge stern paddles stirred up a torrent of frothy, white water in its wake. Mara looked across the wide, muddy river with its flat banks and thought it must be a mile from shore to shore.

She stared down into the swift current, past the lower decks where she could see the hands and heads of curious passengers sticking out as they strolled along the wide decks and enjoyed the view. It wasn't really like a ship at all Mara thought, wondering at the large, elegant stateroom Nicholas had taken for them with its thick carpeting, heavy chandeliers, ornately framed oil paintings, and mahogany furniture. There were several enormous salons, all expensively endowed with velvet hangings and satin-cushioned sofas and chairs. In the numerous dining rooms the service was as excellent as the food. There was also a main saloon where the men could gamble and drink while the big paddle-wheeler made its way upriver toward Baton Rouge, Memphis, and St. Louis, stop-ping as well at numerous small-town levees and plantations to let passengers on and off.

Back in her stateroom Mara pulled off her bonnet and rid herself of her shoes. She padded around the room in her stockinged feet. Soon her skirt and bodice jacket, petticoats, corset, and drawers had followed suit to lay forgotten across the bed as Mara soaked in the hot, perfumed water of a large tub that had been filled by a small troupe of maids. Closing her eyes, she hummed a soft melody. A satisfied smile curved the corners of her mouth.

"Glad you came?" Nicholas asked from the doorway where he had been standing quietly as he watched her bathe. His coat was thrown carelessly across his arm and his vest was hanging open to reveal his ruffled shirt-front. He came slowly toward the tub.

Mara eyed him suspiciously over the broad brim of the tub. "To be sure, I'd not have missed floatin' upriver in a ship as fine as a king's palace," Mara retorted uncomfortably as Nicholas continued to stare moodily down at her.

Nicholas wanted to reach out and touch the rich, dark hair piled high on top of her head. The steam had curled delicate tendrils of hair around her forehead and temples. The long, slender column of her neck and curve of shoulder glistened above the water while just beneath the surface he could see the soft outline of rounded breasts.

"You may wish you had stayed in New Orleans instead," he said oddly as he glanced away.

"If I recollect properly, you didn't give me much say in the matter," Mara responded, wondering what she had done to displease him that he would suddenly wish she were not here.

"I know I didn't," Nicholas answered shortly. Then, reaching down into the tub, he grasped her arm and pulled her to her feet facing him, the water lapping gently around her thighs as she stood shivering in the middle of the tub. "A man is seldom reasonable when he wants a woman's company, and that is what you're here for, my dear."

Nicholas's arms closed around Mara's wet, dripping body and pulled her against his chest. "So comfort me now," he ordered as his mouth closed over her slightly parted lips and he began to kiss her passionately, his hands moving along the curve of her back, then up to cup her warmly damp breasts. His jade green eyes burned into her flesh as they roved over her pink-tinted body. With deliberate slowness he moved his palm across a hardening nipple, then to her shoulder, brushing the back of his hand caressingly against her jaw before he pulled loose the mass of dark hair and let it fall to freedom down her back. He ran his fingers through its satiny length, stroking the long strands of hair indolently, as if he enjoyed the feel of its softness in his hands. Suddenly his languid manner disappeared as he cupped the back of Mara's head and kissed her fiercely, his lips moving against hers, forcing them open. She gave herself up to the languorous sensations spreading through her body.

"You'd better finish bathing," Nicholas spoke abruptly as he freed his mouth and pushed Mara from him, his shirtfront clinging damply to his chest from contact with her wet body.

Mara stared at his retreating figure in hurt confusion. She sank back beneath the warm waters of her bath, the long ends of her hair floating around her shoulders as she soaped her body, the pleasure of her bath having vanished.

Mara awoke close to dawn to feel the bed beside her empty. Looking into the gloomy darkness of the room, she saw the solitary figure of Nicholas standing silhouetted against the open door of their cabin, his shoulders slumped against the doorjamb as he stared out on the moonlit banks of the Mississippi. Mara saw the tip of his cheroot glow red in the darkness. What was going through his mind, as he stood alone and prepared to face Beaumarais? Mara watched him in silence, keeping him company without his being aware of it. When finally he returned to their bed, she waited patiently until he had fallen asleep. Then, moving slightly, she cradled his head against her breast as he rolled over restlessly, turning to her naturally while he slept.

"But I don't want hot milk and oatmeal!" Paddy complained nasally, his lower lip jutting out precariously as he looked across the breakfast table at Mara. "I want sausage balls, waffles, pork chops, and hot chocolate," Paddy stated firmly.

"Now, Master Paddy, ye know ye've got the sniffles and ye shouldn't be stuffin' yourself," Jamie said just as firmly as she eyed the menu, a pair of hastily donned spectacles on the tip of her nose. "How about some nice stewed chicken and buttered toast?"

"No, don't want chicken," Paddy mumbled grumpily as he sniffed loudly.

"Paddy," Mara interjected with a reproving note in her voice that told him to not make a scene, "be a good lad and do as Jamie asks."

"Won't eat anything then," Paddy decided with a mutinous look around the table.

"Let the boy have what he wants," Nicholas commented easily. "You should be relieved that he is hungry, for he can't be too sick if he's willing to put away all that food."

"Thanks, Uncle Nicholas," Paddy beamed as he cast both Mara and Jamie a smug look.

"Now apologize to your aunt and Jamie," Nicholas commanded lazily, but his green eyes warned Paddy he'd be wise to obey.

"Sorry," Paddy said contritely, then brightened visibly as the waiter arrived to take their order.

Mara shook her head in amused exasperation. "Very well, order what you want, Paddy," Mara gave in as she looked down at the menu and tried to decide what to order. After the long months on board ship, it was a treat to be able to choose from such a wide variety. She could have ham, beefsteak with onions, beefsteak with tomatoes, beefsteak à la Creole, mutton chops, or calf's liver; fried fish, fried potatoes, fried onions, mush, codfish balls, hominy fritters, or plantains; grits, stewed potatoes, potatoes fricasseed, hash, or jambalaya; waffles, muffins, flannel cakes, buckwheat cakes, corn bread, dry toast, buttered toast, or graham rolls. For liquid refreshment there was green tea, black, or oolong; coffee, Java or mocha; milk, hot chocolate, or claret.

Mara signed, knowing for a certainty that she didn't wish for fish or potatoes, having had her fill of those two dishes on the voyage.

"Will you trust me to order?" Nicholas suggested. With quick efficiency he selected for all of them except Paddy, who had already placed his order.

Sipping the last of her coffee a little later, Mara glanced casually around the crowded dining room and suddenly became aware of a stout woman dressed in pale mauve and pearls staring boldly through her lorgnette at Nicholas.

"You seem to have caught the eye of a certain diner," Mara commented softly, drawing Nicholas's attention to his apparently bemused admirer.

Nicholas turned and stared curiously at the woman. She seemed to become flustered by his direct look. She definitely was not one of his admirers, for as she saw his full face clearly, the dull red of her blush turned mottled with suppressed outrage. Mara could see the woman's bosom heave with indignation as she pushed back her chair and hauled herself to her feet. Although she wasn't very tall, she gave the impression of being so by the way she regally marched across the room, the tortured flesh of her tightly corseted body quivering beneath the material of her gown as she made her exit, her stiff back retreating eloquently through the door.

"She obviously remembered me," Nicholas said with a sardonic look.

"Who was she?" Mara demanded, thinking that Brendan could have described her beautifully in a few choice words.

Nicholas shrugged. "I don't remember her name, but the look of disapproval seems vaguely familiar. Shall we go?" he asked smoothly, apparently unconcerned by the woman's scornful actions as he seemed to put the incident from his mind.

But Mara couldn't seem to, for if this stranger who had barely known Nicholas still ostracized him after all of these years, then how would his own family react when they saw him? Mara had time to wonder and worry about the reunion as the next few hours passed in lazy idleness as the riverboat made its way up the Mississippi.

"When will we arrive at Beaumarais?" Mara finally asked rather cautiously after lunch. Nicholas had maintained a preoccupied silence for most of the afternoon.

"In about an hour, although it took a little material persuasion to get the good captain to dock at Beaumarais," Nicholas explained with ill-concealed contempt. "It seems the steamboats are accustomed to stopping upstream at the Sandrose landing now, instead of at Beaumarais."

Within the hour the riverboat had berthed at the river landing of Beaumarais, the paddle-wheeler's whistle having heralded their arrival. Their luggage was quickly unloaded onto the small pier, and as they stood in a silent group surrounded by the piled-up trunks, the riverboat moved sluggishly out into the main current of the river and continued its journey north.

Nicholas looked around at the familiar landing, which once had groaned under bales of cotton and bundles of sugar cane, stacked and waiting to be loaded.

Jamie was perched on one of the large trunks, her feet barely touching the wooden boards as she kept a watchful eye on Paddy.

"Now don't ye go and fall in, Master Paddy," she warned him as he slipped in the slick mud, nearly losing his balance before stepping back higher along the bank. "I don't want to have to go and fish ye out like an old boot."

"The house sits back from the river a fair distance, and as we are not expected..." Nicholas left the rest of his sentence unfinished as he looked around the deserted wharf.

"We have a short walk ahead of us?" Mara queried.

Nicholas grinned. "I hope you wore your walking boots. Or if you think you're not up to it, you can always wait here for me to return with a carriage," he offered with gracious hospitality, but his eyes held a challenging glint.

Mara returned his look with a slight smile. "And miss the grand reunion? I think I can manage, thank you," she said coolly, then glanced around at Jamie. "What about it? Do you want to wait here for a carriage or walk up to the house with us?"

"I want to come too!" Paddy cried as he came running back, his shoes caked with mud and his cheek and upper lip streaked with dirt where he had wiped his nose.

"Don't fancy sittin' here all day," Jamie said with an impatient look as she got to her feet. Grabbing hold of Paddy's hand, she began walking.

They moved up the narrow road that wound through the thick belt of trees that stretched away from the river. Mara pulled her cape closer around her as she felt the coolness in the air. She glanced up as the honking cries of geese overhead drifted to her. They congregated in the marshes and swamps where they would spend the winter months after their long flight from the northernmost reaches of the country. Mara stayed toward the center of the road, avoiding the thick underbrush extending into the shadowy depths of the willows and poplars.

Nicholas pointed to a tall tree standing above all of the rest and around the far side of the curve of the road they were following. "The sycamore stands just before the grounds of the house. It's not too much farther now."

They rounded the curve and came to a sudden halt as they found themselves face to face with a solitary figure seated bareback on a beautiful horse, apparently waiting for them.

Nicholas's green eyes narrowed speculatively as he sized up the small girl sitting astride the big red bay, his shiny coat no less a flaming auburn than the girl's two, long braids. She sat with the indolent ease that only a confident rider could manage, her bare legs dangling from beneath the muddied hem of her skirts, one hand in the pocket of a blue velvet jacket as she watched them approach from her vantage point on the big horse's back.

"We don't take kindly to strangers trespassing on Beaumarais land," she spoke suddenly, her childish voice cutting through the quiet afternoon shadows.

"And what makes you think that I'm a stranger to Beaumarais, little one?" Nicholas retorted easily.

The girl nudged her horse slightly with her bare heels as she came forward for a closer look at this impudent stranger. He stood in the middle of the road with his long legs planted firmly apart, looking as if he owned the territory.

"I don't know you," she said arrogantly as she tossed one of her braids over her shoulder disdainfully. But her remarkable gray green eyes had narrowed suspiciously as she gazed, at Nicholas's face. "And since we aren't expecting guests, you might as well turn around right now and leave."

"And what has happened to the famed Beaumarais hospitality?" Nicholas demanded.

The young girl straightened her narrow shoulders proudly as she lifted her chin and stared down at Nicholas. "And what would you know of Beaumarais hospitality? I doubt whether it has ever been extended to you before," she commented.

"Is that your horse?" Paddy couldn't resist asking as he watched the animal in awe.

The girl's wide eyes turned on the little boy who couldn't hide his envy. She smiled indulgently. "He's mine. His name's Sorcier, and nobody but me rides him. He's the fastest in the parish—maybe even in the whole of Louisiana," she declared.

"He seems like a lot of horse for such little hands," Nicholas commented, unimpressed.

"You think I'm just a braggart, do you?" she said with a challenging glint in her eye. "Well, I'll show you, m'sieu, just who is full of hot air and who isn't."

With a superior look at Nicholas she turned her horse around and galloped back up the road, veering off as she headed toward a high gate in a fence that surrounded the grounds.

Mara glanced at Nicholas as he stood watching the little figure, her auburn braids flying out behind her as she urged the big bay over the high railing. His hooves easily cleared the gate. Nicholas's green eyes were narrowed in what Mara knew from past experience was simmering anger, and she hoped for the sake of the small equestrian that she turned out to be no close relation. She would be in constant trouble if she fell under Nicholas's discipline.

The flying hooves appeared once again over the gate, not clearing it by such a margin this time. The girl returned to the group of strangers, expecting praise.

"You might as well enjoy him now, for you will not be riding on his back for much longer," Nicholas promised coldly. "An irresponsible little fool like you should only be allowed on the back of a pony."

The little fool in question stared down at this stranger, her mouth hanging open in disbelief. No one had ever dared to speak to her in such a tone before. Two bright spots of color appeared on her pale cheeks as wrathful indignation began to rise. "Get off my property right now. You don't have any right to be here, whoever you are," she spat.

"And just who are *you?*" Nicholas inquired with deceptive softness.

"I am Damaris de Montaigne-Chantale. Who are you?" she asked insolently.

Nicholas smiled. "I'm Nicholas de Montaigne-Chantale." The young girl's hands clenched on the reins and her horse neighed nervously as he felt the tension in his mistress's muscles.

Mara watched as different emotions flickered across the elfin face. She was too young to be able to hide what she was feeling, and so the surprise, disbelief, dismay, and finally the wary curiosity were vividly displayed for all to see as she stared down with huge gray green eyes at this half-brother she had never met but had heard about in whispered stories.

"Well, *ma petite demi-soeur,*" Nicholas said almost gently as he realized her confusion, "am I to be welcomed back to Beaumarais?"

A fleeting smile curved Damaris's lips, then was gone. "Maybe by some," she said enigmatically, and suddenly seemed very adult.

"And by you?"

Damaris shrugged. "I haven't decided yet. Who's she, your wife? Is the boy your son?" she demanded inquisitively as she stared down at Mara and Paddy from her perch high atop the big bay's back.

"You ask a lot of personal questions," Nicholas said disapprovingly.

"If you don't, you won't get any answers," Damaris returned with childish logic.

"You still may not get any answers, Damaris," Nicholas warned.

"You want me to ride back up to the house and send a carriage?" Damaris asked, deftly changing the subject.

"No. If I remember correctly, it isn't too much farther. Do you mind continuing?" he asked Mara, who'd been watching and listening to the exchange between brother and sister with growing amusement. "No, not at all," she told him truthfully. "In fact, I'm rather enjoying myself," she added with a look that left him in little doubt about what she was enjoying.

"Where are you from?" Damaris asked Mara. "You sound different even from the Americans in New Orleans." She rode along beside them as they resumed walking up the road.

"I'm from Ireland," Mara told her.

"Is that where you've been all these years?" she questioned Nicholas.

"I've been all over the world," Nicholas answered.

"We just came from California," Paddy informed her importantly, "and Uncle Nicholas is rich. Richer than you I bet," he added for good measure as he jealously sidled closer to Nicholas, trying to match him stride for stride.

Damaris's eyes flashed angrily as she glared down at Paddy's sailor-capped head. "We've got a lot of money and a big house. Do you? Why did you call him uncle? You're not my cousin, are you?" she demanded. "Is he?"

"No, but he has my permission to call me uncle."

Damaris thoughtfully considered his answer for a moment, not understanding the relationship between these strangers. She gazed at Mara in open admiration and without any sign of embarrassment for staring so rudely. Then her eyes slid over to Nicholas, and she subjected him to the same critical appraisal until finally seeming to come to a conclusion.

"She's too pretty to be your wife," Damaris uttered simply. "Is she your mistress?"

Jamie drew in her breath abruptly and choked, drawing Paddy's attention from Damaris's startling comment. Mara felt a warm blush spreading across her face. The casually spoken words of a child had the power to hurt her. Nicholas's lips had thinned ominously.

"Apologize to the lady, Damaris," Nicholas ordered in a cold voice. For the first time in her life Damaris was fearful of someone.

As she looked over at the flushed face of the beautiful woman, she mumbled contritely, "I'm sorry, mademoiselle. I truly meant no harm."

Mara managed a smile as she looked up at the little girl who had only spoken the truth. "I know you didn't, it's just that people sometimes don't care to hear the truth about themselves. Some things are best left unsaid, Damaris," Mara advised her. Damaris nodded. "I suppose so, but I don't always understand why, mademoiselle," she said with a frown before urging her horse on ahead. Galloping to the tree-lined entrance of Beaumarais, she pulled up on the big bay's head and sat silently waiting for them.

Nicholas's stride seemed to quicken as they neared the drive leading up to the house. Paddy and Jamie, their short legs working double-time, hurried to keep up with the fast-moving figure. Mara lengthened her own stride as she began to feel some of Nicholas's excitement.

Nicholas came to an abrupt halt at the foot of the long, stately drive. Outstretched oak boughs formed a natural, living arch above the roadway leading up to the house. It was as Nicholas had described it, only there was a strange sadness in its rose-stuccoed walls that could not be described, only felt. Gleaming white shutters framed the long French windows, which were set back in the deep shadows of the wide galleries running across the front and around the sides of the two-story structure. Six massive white pillars marched across the front and supported the high cornice that rose in proud magnificence above the treetops.

"Beaumarais," Nicholas murmured softly as he stood staring at his birthplace.

"You've been away a long time," Damaris's childish voice interrupted the silence that had fallen over the small group. "I wasn't even born when you left," she said in awed tones.

Nicholas didn't seem to hear her. He continued to stare at Beaumarais. "Shall we go," he said at last as he started up the long walk.

Through the moss-draped trees Mara could catch glimpses of the plantation grounds, of colorful gardens thick with flowers and patches of green lawn spreading down toward the river. In fact, they were far closer to the muddy waters of the river than she had realized, for the road they had traveled to the house had curved gradually through the trees and back again to the river.

Suddenly Mara heard Paddy giggling as his dark eyes filled up with the wonder of his surroundings. "They're like old men with long gray beards, Mara!" he laughingly exclaimed as he ran over to the base of one of the gnarled oaks and grabbed a handful of the spidery moss that covered it.

When they were halfway up the drive, Damaris, having dismounted, gave Sorcier a slight nudge and sent him on ahead. She ran beside him to the entrance. Then her hurrying figure disappeared up the wide, low steps set between two tall columns.

The white paneled door opened and several people came out to wait for them. The arrival of guests at Beaumarais seemed to be a rare occasion, for a group of black workers had gathered around the bottom of the steps, their chores apparently forgotten as they whispered among themselves and up to the group of house servants in the gallery behind.

Mara saw Damaris standing slightly apart from two women who stood squarely in the center of the wide steps. They silently watched the arrival of the unexpected guests. One of the women was just a young girl, not more than sixteen, with black hair and magnolia skin. There was a petulant droop to the sulky mouth that hinted at what her true character might be. A pale blue satin slipper was tapping impatiently beneath the hem of her flounced skirt, while the ends of a matching pale blue ribbon tied around her small waist flickered slightly in the breeze.

The older of the two women was dressed in mourning, but the rich auburn of her hair mocked the somberness of her gown and thoughts, and marked her as the mother of Damaris. She was pale and thin, but at one time she must have been a great beauty. Her face still bore faint traces of it, but ill-health and grief had done their best to erase any sign of happiness from her expressive gray eyes. Her thin hands moved constantly and a fretful look had settled on her brow. She stared down at Nicholas with disbelief and anger, recognition coming with a flash of apparent pain.

"Nicholas," she spoke her stepson's name in a raspy whisper as her gray eyes seemed to swallow up his figure. Then she gave a feeble cry from deep within, as if she'd seen an apparition.

"Mama!" the dark-haired girl suddenly screamed.

Nicholas vaulted up the steps in time to catch his step-mother as she slumped forward in a faint, her slender neck arching back across his arm as he swung her up against his chest. Clearing a way through the servants crowding close, he walked boldly through the opened door of Beaumarais.

"Who are these people? What is happening? Oh, mon Dieu, she is dead! I cannot bear this," Nicole cried out, her black curls bouncing around her face as she glanced around wildly.

"Oh, Nicole, she is not," Damaris said, even as her eyes worriedly followed Nicholas's figure. "She's just fainted. But *you'd* better not because *I'm* not going to catch you," she added warningly, well used to Nicole's dramatics.

Nicole turned on her young sister, indignant anger mirrored on her flowerlike face. "You horrible little beast. You know nothing about these matters, or anything else," she berated Damaris. Reaching out quickly, she slapped her sister's face. "All you know about is that old horse of yours. Mama ought to sell him."

Damaris's lips trembled slightly and the imprint of Nicole's punishing hand showed red against her pale cheek, but she stood her ground, proudly facing up to Nicole's wrath as she defended Sorcier. "He isn't old, and nobody's ever going to sell him."

"What shall I do if Mama becomes indisposed? She must not fall ill again," Nicole fretted. "We were just beginning to discuss designs for my wedding gown. Oh, it is impossible," she cried, stamping her foot in angry frustration.

Mara gazed between the two sisters amazed that they could be related.

"If we might go inside," Mara began tentatively yet firmly, with polite rebuke for having been kept standing on the front steps. "We are rather fatigued after our walk from the river, and I believe I did hear somewhere about a certain Beaumarais hospitality? It wasn't just a rumor, was it?" Mara smilingly asked the dark-eyed young girl who was staring at her as if seeing her for the first time.

"Since your mama is not feeling up to it, you shall have to act as our hostess," Mara said, her eyes telling the upset Nicole that she understood perfectly what that young woman must be suffering at this moment. "It will be good practice for when you have a home of your own. I did hear you mention your upcoming marriage?" Mara continued on a practical note, her voice soothing the frayed nerves of the girl as she found herself being charmed out of her bad mood by this strange woman. "I do know something about the latest fashions. And, my dear, I have just come from New Orleans. There I saw some of the most divine gowns. Do let us discuss them over a cup of tea. I can see already what colors would suit you," Mara spoke dreamily, then pretended to run a thoughtful eye over Nicole's figure. "Ummm, yes, of course, cerise will most definitely be your color."

Nicole brightened under Mara's expert handling as she basked in the attention. "Oh, mademoiselle, I should be so delighted to talk with you of such things," she beamed, her good spirits rapidly returning. "And of course Beaumarais welcomes you with open arms. I shall see about rooms for you and your party." She paused uncertainly. "You are staying here? *Bien*," she continued as Mara nodded. "Now, I shall order some tea immediately. Then we must talk, please, mademoiselle," she said with a smile she knew was her prettiest.

Mara caught Damaris's eye, the girl's smirk letting her know that at least she had not been deceived, even if Nicole had. "I'll have a wagon sent for your trunks, mademoiselle, but first I must go and see how Mama is."

"Finest bit of actin' ye've done in many a year," Jamie muttered as she walked beside Mara through the door of Beaumarais.

Mara stepped inside the mosaic-tiled entrance hall and, pausing briefly, admired the painted landscape that papered the walls and the crystal chandelier that gleamed high overhead. A grand staircase of rich mahogany climbed to the second floor while a pier table with a vase of deep red roses was reflected in the ornate, gold-leaf mirror hanging above it.

"Please, mademoiselle, in here," Nicole invited Mara as she led the way into a spacious parlor carpeted with a pale gold Aubusson carpet, gold-brocaded curtains draping the row of long French windows opening out onto the gallery. It was only as Mara stepped onto the carpet that she noticed the worn spots, and the frayed hems of the drapes. Nicole gestured to the pale blue sofa before sitting down gracefully in one of the matching satin-upholstered chairs.

But Mara's eye had been captured by the portrait that hung above the molded mantel. Mara walked over to stand just below it as she stared up in fascination. The man with the hawkish face bore the same sensuous lips and boldly staring green eyes as Nicholas. Only the expression was softer than the one his son wore. This was Philippe de Montaigne-Chantale, the proud master of Beaumarais who'd banished his son from his sight.

Nicole sat silently watching Mara, biting her lip nervously before she asked hesitantly, "Is it true? Is that man really Nicholas? Is he my half-brother?"

Mara turned and eyed the young girl. "There can be no denying the resemblance, and your mama's reaction should be proof enough."

The butler entered carrying the silver tea service while two maids followed behind carrying trays, one loaded down with enticing confections and the other with a silver chocolate pot, the hot chocolate giving off a rich aroma. The tray was placed near Nicole.

Paddy's eyes brightened as he caught sight of the trays, his dark brown eyes feasting on the dainty cakes. Without waiting to be invited closer, he stationed himself at Nicole's elbow as she prepared the tea.

"Paddy," Mara said softly, signaling him to seat himself beside her on the sofa.

"It is all right, mademoiselle," Nicole said with a charming smile, "for I have a sweet tooth too, and I understand the little one's impatience. I always have chocolate in the afternoons," she confided as she poured out a cup. "You wish to have the chocolate, Paddee," Nicole teased him, her pronunciation of his name causing him to make a comical face. He eagerly accepted the cup, then placed it with a regretful sigh on the table as he waited in patient silence beside Nicole. She raised her eyebrows questioningly. "Tea for Jamie, please, ma'am," he said politely, surprising Mara by his thoughtfulness. Jamie had positioned herself near the corner of the room where she could sit unobserved, her gray eyes missing nothing of what went on even as she worked the embroidery in her lap. Her role as maid, companion, and governess left her in a vague social position and so she preferred to keep quietly in the background.

She was deeply touched as she watched Paddy balancing a delicate china cup and saucer brimming with tea in one hand and a plate full of carefully selected sweets in the other. His eyes glued to the sloshing contents of the teacup, he slowly placed each foot in front of the other as he made his way to Jamie's side, then returned for his own treat.

"Why did he come back? What does he want?" Nicole spoke suddenly, worried apprehension etched across her rounded forehead as she handed Mara her tea. "The scandal of it all! Oooh, he shall ruin everything. My fiancé is a most important person, mademoiselle. Jean-Claude is heir to Belle Saulaie near St. Francisville, and his family also has townhouses in both New Orleans and Natchez. I am very fortunate in becoming a member of their family," she informed Mara importantly, a smile of satisfaction curving the corners of her mouth slightly upward. "I am to be wed in the spring. It will be the wedding of the year, and such a grand occasion. It will take place in the St. Louis Cathedral, and there will be a detail of Swiss Guards who will precede me up the aisle. Since Papa has died, Uncle Etienne will escort me. Oh dear," Nicole added worriedly, looking at Mara with huge dark eyes full of anguished horror, "do you suppose *he* will wish to attend? It will be most uncomfortable if no one will speak with him, and then he will be forced into defending his honor should someone insult him. It is not fair, mademoiselle. He is a horrible man to do this to me," Nicole cried, forgetting that Mara had arrived with that horrible man.

"I'm sure he doesn't mean to cause you any inconvenience, Nicole," Mara tried to reassure her.

"It is just as well that we will not be coming here after the wedding but will be starting our married life at Belle Saulaie instead. In fact," Nicole added, her eyes narrowed in speculation, "none of my new family need ever meet him. We will be going to Belle Saulaie in a couple of weeks and will stay there with Jean-Claude's family until we wed. So I needn't worry. Nicholas will have had to leave by then," she concluded with a triumphant smile. With a sigh of relief she changed the subject before Mara could inquire why Nicholas should have to leave by then.

"What kind of gowns are they wearing in Europe now, mademoiselle? My dearest friend, Leonore, is just back from Paris, and she says they are all wearing demi-trains now. My best colors are a deep rose and a pale yellow, and when I am wed, I will be able to wear bright colors and much more daring gowns. I grow so tired of this white all the time. Did you know that Brussels lace…"

Mara tilted her head as if attentively listening to Nicole's views on fashion, but she let her thoughts drift away as she wondered what was going on upstairs between Nicholas and his stepmother.

❧

"Why did you come back?" Celeste demanded weakly as she reclined against the pillows of her canopied bed, her slender hands fluttering nervously over the satin quilt tucked up around her. "My God, but you look like Philippe. It is like seeing a ghost," she continued without waiting for his answer. "When Damaris called for me to come see who had arrived, why, I never imagined it could be you, of all people. And now, of all times. And then when I recognized you, I thought to myself, no, it cannot be, and yet the eyes and mouth, so much the same," she spoke haltingly. She shuddered delicately as she rambled on in a faint voice. "I knew Philippe was dead, but there was that moment of horrible doubt as I stared at you. Why?" she demanded beseechingly, pressing her hands to her cheeks. "Why come back now? How can you dare to show that wicked face of yours in New Orleans? After all the misery you have caused for this family, I cannot believe that even you would be so cruel to return."

"Celeste," Nicholas spoke his stepmother's name quietly as he said gently, "I was asked to return by my father."

Celeste's gray eyes widened in disbelief. "What? *C'est impossible.* He never spoke your name in this house after you left. He forbade mention of your existence. You were dead to him, the same as François. You lie. Now that he is dead and cannot send you away you think you can return and become master here? Well, you have no rights here at Beaumarais. You no longer belong here," she said hoarsely, the vein in her temple pounding with excess emotion.

Nicholas reached into his pocket and carefully withdrew the treasured letter he had received in San Francisco. "This does not lie, Celeste. I would not have returned otherwise. I swore never to return the day I was driven from my home," Nicholas told her coldly. "This is the *only* reason why I have now broken my vow."

Celeste stared at the letter as if it might reach out and strike her, but finally she put out a shaky hand and accepted it. Nicholas watched in silence as she pulled the frail sheet of stationery from the envelope and began to read. The letter began to shake uncontrollably as she neared the end, and she held the back of her hand against her trembling lips.

"Mon Dieu, what does this mean?"

"It means, Celeste, that my father knew of my innocence. He knew the truth of François's death. He had forgiven me and wanted my forgiveness of him," Nicholas said without hesitation, eyeing her intently as he watched her reaction.

The letter dropped from Celeste's stiff fingers. She had instantly recognized the handwriting as Philippe's, and the straightforward look in Nicholas's green eyes that were too familiar convinced her that he was not lying.

"B–but he never spoke of it. Never did he say a word of this to me. Why?"

"You have been ill?"

Celeste nodded absently, then looked up at Nicholas with just a touch of bitterness in her expression as the corners of her mouth turned down with discontentment. "Do you know what it has been like for me all these years to be the second wife of Philippe de Montaigne-Chantale? I think I have always been pitied by my friends, for everyone knew how much Philippe loved your mama, the very beautiful Danielle. He was heartbroken when she died. I think he never had a whole heart to give to me. I could never compete against her memory," Celeste said sadly, "and when I could not give him the sons he needed, well, he was disappointed in me. This I know."

"You can't be blamed for that, Celeste," Nicholas dismissed her claims.

"You wait and see how you feel when you have no son to inherit what is yours one day, then you will feel different," Celeste accused him bitterly. "It is the same with all men. But when I found I was with child after so many barren years, oh, the joy of it all! I knew that this would be the son that Philippe had wished for since…well, for so long. He was so happy when Jean-Louis was born. It was feared that I might lose him, but God was watching over us."

Celeste pressed her aching temples, shaking her head as if still unable to believe what had happened. "One day he returned from his daily ride filled with such rage and hurt. I could not reach him. He would not speak with me and he locked himself away in his study the whole night. He was a changed man the next day and even little Jean-Louis could not bring a smile to his lips. He went to New Orleans the next day, and then…" Celeste whispered tearfully, "he had not even been back for two days before he died."

"And you have no idea what he had found out to cause him such anguish?" Nicholas probed gently.

But Celeste could only shake her auburn head sadly. "Non, I knew nothing, not even that he had forgiven you, Nicholas, but I am glad for his sake that he did before he died. It had grieved him for so many years," Celeste said generously even as certain doubts began to darken her eyes to a cloudy gray color. "Nicholas," she said looking him directly in the eye, forcing her voice not to quiver, but failing as she said quickly, "it changes nothing. He may have forgiven you, but there was no will that named you heir as he said he would do. I am owner of Beaumarais, this you cannot change," Celeste warned him as if ready to pit her feeble strength against his.

"There are many things we need to discuss, Celeste," Nicholas began, only to be interrupted as Celeste sunk back against the pillows and raised a weak hand in protest.

"Not now, Nicholas," she pleaded. "I must rest. I grow fatigued so easily since my illness. This news has upset me greatly. We will talk more, Nicholas, this I promise you. But later, please. Not now," Celeste said as she closed her eyes wearily, the gesture dismissing him as effectively as words.

Nicholas stood up, but before he left he asked one last question. "The diary? Do you know where it is?"

Celeste opened her eyes as she stared up at her stepson in confusion. "The diary? Non, now that I think about it, I haven't seen it. He used to write so many things down in that book. It was always in his desk. You will have to ask Etienne, or Alain, for they handle the business affairs of Beaumarais now, and they have access to the desk. They might have seen it."

Nicholas nodded thoughtfully, then turned and quietly left the room as her head lolled sideways on the pillow. He was standing at the head of the stairs when he was startled by a well-remembered voice calling out his name.

"Nicholas! They told me, but I could not believe such a miraculous thing."

"Uncle Etienne," Nicholas said softly as he stared down at the silver-haired man who stood waiting at the foot of the stairs, his beaming expression one of open welcome. "You haven't changed," he laughed as he quickly made his way down the grand staircase.

And, indeed, with the exception of his silvering hair, Etienne Ferrare looked exactly as Nicholas remembered him from their brief encounter in Venice almost ten years ago. He was a slender man of slightly less than medium height who had an air of elegance about him that was as natural to him as breathing.

"You flatter me by kindly overlooking this silver mane of mine," he said as he stretched out and hugged the broad-shouldered form now towering over him, "something I can no longer pretend to do when I look into the mirror. To see you walking down the stairs in the hall of Beaumarais once again, that brings back the happiness of my youth."

"It is good to see you, Etienne," Nicholas said as he gazed down warmly at his mother's brother.

Staring up at Nicholas with the blue eyes that reminded Nicholas of his mother, Etienne said, "It is no less a pleasure for me to see you standing beneath the portraits of your ancestors. I never thought I would see this day."

Nicholas glanced around. "I thought never to step foot inside Beaumarais either, but I have." The words sounded almost like a vow never to leave again.

"Has Celeste seen you yet?" Etienne asked with a worried frown. "This will upset her greatly I fear."

"It already has," Nicholas told him regretfully, "for at first sight of me she fainted into my arms. I'm afraid I remind her much of my father."

Etienne nodded in understanding. "Yes, I suppose your sudden arrival would come as a shock. In fact," he added with an apologetic smile, "I must admit to being extremely curious myself about your return. Incredible timing," he murmured beneath his breath.

"It would seem as though my father confided in no one about his letter asking me to return home."

Etienne could not hide his surprise. "Philippe sent for you? B-but that seems most extraordinary. Forgive me, Nicholas, but in all of these years he has never once spoken your name to me. Why should he send for you?" he asked.

"Because he wanted my forgiveness, Etienne. He finally discovered the truth about François's death," Nicholas told him simply.

Etienne remained thoughtful for a moment. His slender fingers caressed the head of his cane as he tapped it lightly against the tiles. "And what was the truth, if you do not mind an old man's curiosity?" Etienne inquired softly.

"That I am innocent of all guilt, or at least of fatally wounding François. For having taken part in such a fool's game...of *that* I am guilty. But not of killing my brother. My father knew this in the end. He knew who had really killed François."

Etienne's cane had stopped its tapping. He now stared up at his nephew, a very intent expression hardening the gentle blue eyes.

"But he did not confide this information to me. He left a diary, and in this he said that he had written down the whole story," Nicholas said, then added with lazy indifference, "but unfortunately it seems to have disappeared. You haven't by any chance seen it?"

Etienne shook his head. "A diary? Non, this I have never seen," he said in a disturbed voice before a sadly mocking smile touched his lips just briefly. "You will forgive me, please, Nicholas."

"Forgive you? For what?"

"For believing ill of you. Oh, I did not believe that you had cold-bloodedly murdered François, but I did believe that it was the bullet from your pistol that had struck him down. I thought it was an accident. And you were so young. It is hard for the young to admit they have done wrong. But if this is indeed true..." he murmured. Nicholas could hear the doubt in his voice.

"I know it is hard to believe, because if *I* am innocent, then someone else is guilty. And that person let me take the blame. Who would do this, and why?"

Etienne stared into his nephew's hardened face, seeing a ruthless implacability in the green eyes. He had matured into a hard man, unforgiving of many things. Etienne knew instinctively that Nicholas could be a deadly adversary. "I do not know the answers, Nicholas," he told him.

"I don't either, at least," Nicholas added quietly, "not yet."

"Come, I hear voices from the parlor and the tempting sound of china," Etienne suggested as he began to move toward the double doors that stood slightly ajar, "and I am never one to turn down an aperitif. It is so much more pleasant to converse over a leisurely drink, don't you think?" he asked with an encouraging smile as he held wide the parlor doors and waited expectantly for Nicholas to follow.

"Oh, Uncle Etienne," Nicole cried out when she saw him enter the room, "the mademoiselle here has been telling me all about the latest styles, and I must have—" her voice halted abruptly as she noticed who was with her uncle. Her dark brown eyes mirrored her uncertainty and resentment at his unexpected arrival. She raised her shoulder haughtily and glanced away from his intimidating and almost overpowering presence.

Nicholas seemed unimpressed by her snub as he continued into the room and accepted a brandy from Etienne, who had with a natural familiarity poured two glasses, then selected a chair and made himself comfortable, completely at ease in the parlor of Beaumarais. He sat down next to Mara on the satin-upholstered sofa, his eyes meeting hers briefly before he said, "You might as well get used to my face, Nicole, as I intend to be around for a while."

Nicole flounced around and stared at this half-brother stranger who had returned uninvited and was now trying to ruin her wedding. "Why have you returned here? No one wants you at Beaumarais. You have no right to be here," she accused him angrily. "You shall ruin everything, just like you did before."

"Enough, Nicole," Etienne reprimanded her. "You know nothing about his reasons for returning. And he is your brother," he reminded her gently.

Nicole jumped to her feet, a pout forming on her lips as she threatened both Nicholas and Etienne. "I shall go to Mama. She will not allow this intruder to stay a moment longer."

"You will not disturb her with your petty grievances," Nicholas said in such a coldly authoritative tone of voice that Nicole was stopped effectively in her tracks as she would have left the room.

She turned around with an incredulous look on her face. "Y-you are ordering me in my own house not to speak with my mama?" she stuttered, disbelief darkening her brown eyes to black. "H-how dare you!"

"I dare," Nicholas retorted quietly. "Your mama is resting, and if you cannot keep your selfish needs to yourself, then you will go to your room. Or you may sit back down and finish your tea."

Damaris had returned to the house and had just entered the parlor in time to hear Nicholas's threat. She recognized the signs of one of Nicole's magnificent tantrums, but she knew that for once Nicole would not succeed in getting her way.

"I'd take his advice if I were you, Nicole," Damaris said, curling up on the rug before the hearth and suddenly feeling sorry for Nicole.

Nicole turned her tragic eyes on her little sister, who was now unconcernedly trading pinches with Paddy, who'd squatted down next to her. Nicole's big brown eyes lingered on Mara, but on receiving no encouragement from her—and, in fact, feeling as though the golden eyes were seeing right through her and into her mind—she stamped her satin-shod foot in frustration.

"Oh, you are all horrible," she cried and ran from the room.

Nicholas glanced mockingly over at Mara. "You could teach her a few things about acting, my dear."

Mara smiled slightly, not knowing whether he meant that as a compliment or, more likely, as an insult, but either way she had to agree.

"Mon Dieu," Etienne suddenly spoke, his voice full of contrition, "but in all of the commotion I seem to have neglected my manners. My pardon, mademoiselle, but I am Etienne Ferrare, Nicholas's uncle," he introduced himself, bowing politely over her hand with a suave sophistication that seemed second nature to him. He glanced over at Nicholas almost accusingly. "Now you must introduce me to this ravishing creature."

"Mara O'Flynn," Nicholas said with a smile of enjoyment,

as if taking personal satisfaction in watching the effect she had on people meeting her for the first time.

"Ah," Etienne sighed, as if that explained everything. "Irish. They say Ireland has some of the most beautiful women in the world," he flattered her gallantly.

A slight smile curved Mara's lips as she responded in kind. "You've been to Ireland, then? And here I was thinkin' that only the Irish were kissin' the Blarney stone," Mara said with a friendly laugh.

Nicholas's laugh drowned out Mara's as he explained to an appreciative Etienne. "Now *that* is the true Mara O'Flynn. Don't let her beauty fool you into believing she hasn't a sharp tongue in her head, for I carry around enough scars to bear witness to it," Nicholas complained good-naturedly.

Etienne held up his brandy glass in a toast. "It is truly a pleasure to meet you, Mademoiselle O'Flynn, for now I shall be able to enjoy your conversation as well as your beauty," Etienne complimented her sincerely.

"Is Ireland very far away, Mademoiselle O'Flynn?" Damaris inquired excitedly as she stared up into Mara's amused eyes. "I've never been out of Louisiana. I've been downriver a couple of times when we stayed in New Orleans, but never much farther." She sighed. "I want to sail all the way around the world, but," she added with a bright light in her eyes, "only after I've raised my horses."

"I've sailed around the world. Well, almost," Paddy told her, his small shoulders raised and squared proudly.

Damaris's gray-green eyes widened. She was visibly impressed and eyed this strange boy with a keener interest than before. Here was someone who could satisfy her insatiable desire to hear about the world.

Mara sipped her tea as she divided her attention between the two conversations going on around her. Half listening to Etienne's amusing accounts of travels, she wondered what had happened between Nicholas and his stepmother.

Mara heard footsteps approaching rapidly across the tile floor of the entrance hall, and glancing toward the wide doorway, she saw a man clad in riding boots and breeches pausing uncertainly, as if unsure of his position among this gathering. As his hazel eyes met Mara's curious gaze, he shifted uncomfortably, embarrassed by the state of his sweat-stained shirt and muddy boots. He looked only a few years older than Nicholas and was slighter of build, but with a wiry strength well evident in the muscles bunched up beneath the rolled-up sleeves of his shirt.

"Alain," Etienne called out with pleased surprise as he saw his son standing in the doorway.

Nicholas got to his feet and walked across the room to where Alain stood. The overseer's tanned face showed a variety of emotions, not the least of which was relief when he recognized who Nicholas was. "Nicholas. I heard you were here, but I could not believe it until I saw for myself," Alain spoke softly, his hazel eyes crinkling with pleasure as he shook Nicholas's hand. "It is good to have you back, Nicholas," he welcomed him simply.

"Thank you, Alain," Nicholas replied, "it has been a long time. Françoise said that you would probably welcome me, which makes it easier for me because there is much I shall wish to know about Beaumarais."

"I will tell you whatever I can," Alain responded. Then, glancing around apologetically, he added, "But I would prefer to change before I completely offend the lady."

"I'm sure Mara doesn't mind," Nicholas told him with a smile of remembrance for all of the bedraggled gold miners they had seen in California. He then introduced Mara to him, Alain bowing elegantly and with gentlemanly courtesy despite his field-hand appearance.

"Actually, I would rather discuss these things in the morning after I've had a chance to ride over Beaumarais. If you'll meet me afterward, I'll have more of an idea of what changes have been made since I last saw the property," Nicholas suggested easily, his eyes narrowing at the brief look of consternation that had flickered across Alain's face. "I have a few things I wish to do now before it gets dark."

"Of course," Alain said as if he understood completely, "and I'll be free anytime you wish tomorrow. Just send word down to me," he said. With a slight bow to Mara and a glance at his father, he added, "I'll be off then. Good evening."

"Alain works so hard," Etienne told Nicholas with a sad shake of his head as he watched his son's figure disappear. "I wish he would learn to enjoy life's small amusements as I do. But he assures me that he is enjoying walking knee-deep in mud, or helping a newborn foal into the world. Another brandy, Nicholas? And what is this about ma petite Françoise? You have seen her? When? You must tell me all about it, eh?"

"If you'll excuse me," Mara began as Nicholas accepted another brandy from Etienne, "I should like to see my room and rest for a while. I am rather tired, and I think Paddy should come along as well," she added, despite the annoyed look he shot at her.

"Of course," Nicholas said as he noticed for the first time the faint shadows beneath Mara's eyes. "I'll have a—"

"No, please, allow an old man the pleasure of a beautiful woman's company for just a brief while. It is not often anymore that I have such an opportunity," Etienne interrupted as he got quickly to his feet. "Besides it grows late and you did say you wished to do something before dark. I will leave you to it. If, of course, Mademoiselle O'Flynn has no objections?"

"I would be honored, Monsieur Ferrare," she accepted his offer, and gathering up her cloak and bonnet Mara allowed him to escort her from the room. Jamie saw to it that Paddy wasn't far behind.

"Etienne, please—I will answer to nothing else," he appealed to her with a charming smile. Mara suspected he used it often when he wanted his way.

Mara smiled slightly. "Only if you will call me Mara, Etienne," she told him, her smile widening to match his.

Etienne patted her arm in an almost fatherly manner. "My dear, we shall get on admirably, just admirably," he chuckled. "If I may be so bold as to say so, I can see now why that nephew of mine is so fond of you. You are remarkable, my dear. Now come, child, let me show you to your rooms," he said as he led her across the hall, not giving Mara the chance to respond to his incredible observation about Nicholas.

"And what do you think of Beaumarais, Mara?" he inquired expectantly as he climbed beside her up the stairs. "Is it not the most beautiful house you have ever seen?" he answered before she could reply.

"It is indeed beautiful," Mara told him, "but I had expected as much, for Nicholas was very expressive about it."

"And you were not disappointed, were you." He smiled wistfully, glancing up proudly at the ancestral paintings guarding the stairs and watching their progress with expressionless eyes. "Even before my sister, Danielle, married into the family, I loved this house. There is something special about it, is there not? Yes, it is as though the house lives." He spoke softly, a dreamy look in his eyes as they lingered on the high, molded ceiling, then back down into the hall below to almost caress the entrance to what he must consider sacred ground.

"This is your room, Mara," Etienne stopped before an open door, bowing slightly as he took her hand and lightly touched his lips to it. "I hope you will be comfortable during your stay at Beaumarais."

"I'm sure I shall, Etienne. Thank you," Mara nodded. "I will see you this evening?"

"Of course, my dear mademoiselle. Although I do not sleep under the roof of Beaumarais, I do often dine here," he told her with a look of anticipation in his blue eyes.

Mara showed her surprise. "I'm sorry. I thought you lived here?"

"I do, but not here in the great house. I live in the garçonnière, it is a detached wing of the house where we old bachelors live. I have my servants and all the comforts of a home. Alain lives there as well, and we are quite comfortable. Yes, indeed, most comfortable. Now I shall bid you adieu until this evening. Your nephew's room is next door to yours," he added.

Mara stood silently watching him saunter off, thinking he was certainly a harmless and very charming gentleman. A smile still played around her lips as she entered her room, feeling that Nicholas's homecoming had gone rather well so far.

Paddy rushed past her and into the room, looking around curiously as he raced to the French windows. Pushing them open, he skipped out onto the gallery.

"Now mind how you lean over that railing," Jamie warned him as she approached from the room next door. "Master Paddy and me have a fine room next to ye," she informed Mara as she marched in.

Jamie sniffed, unable to find any fault with the arrangements so far. "And ye better be gettin' yourself back inside, Master Paddy," she called out to him. "Ye're lettin' in all the cold air, and I don't want ye comin' down sick now. 'Twould seem as though Mr. Chantale be a real fine gentleman after all," Jamie commented with a nod of satisfaction as she glanced around the room, with its high-post mahogany bed draped in pale green and gold silk hangings. Matching upholstered armchairs and an Empire mahogany sofa were grouped around the Turkish carpet that filled up the middle of the room. A marble-topped washstand and large wardrobe stood conveniently close and faced the fireplace on the far wall, where a small fire that had just been lit was struggling to warm the chilly bedchamber.

"Did you ever doubt that he was anything less?" Mara asked with a sardonic expression in her eyes as she glanced around the room, not quite able to disguise her own surprise at the rich surroundings she found herself in.

"No, not really, but I'm suspectin' ye might have at one time," Jamie retorted, undaunted. "Ye'd best let me help ye out of your gown and loosen that corset. I swear ye're lookin' paler than a ghost."

Mara sighed. "I am rather tired. If I could just lie down for a bit, I'd feel better, and don't pull my corset so tight this evening, will you, Jamie? My back's been aching all day long," Mara complained as she stood still while Jamie helped her undress.

"Haven't tied it any tighter than usual. Reckon ye just might be eatin' a might more than 'tis ladylike."

Mara shrugged, unwilling to pursue the argument. She stretched and breathed deeply as she felt the restrictive corset fall away from her waist. A few minutes later, in just her chemisette and drawers, she settled down on the thick, soft mattress with a grateful sigh.

Mara lay back against the lacy pillows and stared around her pensively. A slight shadow passed over her face as she allowed a worrying doubt to surface, then willed it away as she gazed out through the square panes in the French windows at the tops of the trees beyond. How could her life have taken such a strange turn, she wondered as she now fondly remembered the relatively smooth existence of her life in London with Brendan. How odd it was that now when she looked back on those days they didn't seem so bad anymore. Mara was jolted from her musings as she heard Paddy's sneeze, and, focusing her eyes, she saw him standing beside the bed.

"Well, take off your shoes and come on up with me," she invited him as she patted the empty space beside her, but Paddy needed no encouragement as he quickly removed his shoes; then, glancing quickly, almost apprehensively over his shoulder, he jumped onto the bed and snuggled down next to her.

"Won't he mind?" Paddy whispered.

"Who?" Mara asked lazily.

"Uncle Nicholas," Paddy informed her. "He usually sleeps with you, doesn't he?" Paddy declared with childish bluntness. Mara could feel a hot blush spreading over her skin.

"Well, he won't now that we are at Beaumarais," Mara told him a trifle shortly.

"Why?"

"He just won't, and I don't want to hear you discussing this matter anymore, or with anyone else. Do you understand, Paddy?" Mara asked him, feeling more uncomfortable than angry.

"I won't say anything, Mara," Paddy promised as he sighed and happily rested his dark head against Mara's shoulder, his eyelids beginning to droop sleepily as he mumbled, "but do you think Uncle Nicholas will be mad that I'm here instead of him?"

Mara smiled as she hugged Paddy's warm body closer. "No,

silly-billy, and what Nicholas doesn't know can't hurt him," she murmured softly as her own eyes began to grow heavy and she felt herself drifting off to sleep.

༸

Nicholas hesitated for a moment outside the family cemetery. He pushed open the wrought-iron gate and made his way toward the graves. His mother had died of yellow fever when he was only twelve years old. Two brothers had been stillborn. Nicholas stared down at the smooth marble marking François's resting place, and then shifted his eyes to the newest headstone. The once-empty plot next to his mother's was now filled. Philippe de Montaigne-Chantale had joined his wife. What knowledge did you take with you into the grave? he wondered. He caressed the hard stone as if trying to read a sign that might be written there.

He continued looking at his father's grave and then his brother's again, and he wondered who had put them there. Why? Whom had you been suspicious of, he asked silently of his father. What truth had you discovered that caused your death?

He looked up at the great house and knew the answer. Beaumarais. He thought of all the years he'd spent traveling the world, seeking escape from his memories, doubt eating away at him until he had, in his weakest moments, believed himself to be a murderer. But his father's letter had laid those doubts to rest, and now he had faith in himself again.

Who had done it? Celeste? She'd always been jealous of Danielle's children, especially of her sons. Perhaps she'd thought the child she was carrying at that time was going to be another son for Philippe, and had sought to secure an inheritance for him. But she hadn't had a son, not then, nor the next time, when Damaris was born. And finally when she did give birth to a son, Philippe died. But Celeste didn't know much about firearms and always swore they frightened her.

Amaryllis, on the other hand, despite her gentle upbringing, was as good a shot as he was. What would have been her motive? As the fiancée of François, she was already destined to become mistress of Beaumarais one day, and with the lands of Sandrose combined with Beaumarais, she would have been one of the wealthiest women in the state. Recalling the passionate lovemaking they had once shared, he wondered if she had truly loved him so much that she would have murdered his brother in order to have her heart's desire as well as everything else. But even Amaryllis could not be so evil, or so he tried to convince himself.

If she were not the one, then who? Etienne? Nicholas shook his dark head, dismissing the thought with contempt. Etienne was not interested in owning a vast plantation, for he had sold his own family's land after he'd inherited it in favor of having the money and freedom to travel. In fact, he was seldom at Beaumarais longer than it took to rest and repack his trunks. Etienne was a gentleman who valued his code of conduct above all else. True, he also enjoyed the finer things in life. As long as he was surrounded by beauty, he had no complaints. Nicholas looked again at the great house, the last rays of the sun gilding it into breathtaking beauty, a beauty that Etienne was almost obsessive about. But *Etienne?* No, he couldn't believe that. No wiser than before, he walked slowly back to the house, wondering if he could really trust anyone. What did he really know about any of them after over fifteen years? A slightly ironic smile twisted his lips as he realized in amusement that the only one he could trust was Mara O'Flynn. How she would laugh if she could hear his thoughts.

He was still brooding when he entered Mara's room a few minutes later and found Mara and Paddy together asleep on the bed. Nicholas stopped in surprise, then walked softly over to the bed and gazed down at them in sardonic amusement. Mara O'Flynn was such a strange mixture of woman—and hardly even that for she couldn't be long out of her teens. He still found it hard to believe sometimes, when he held her close against his heart, that this woman was the Mara O'Flynn he had once sworn vengeance against and set out to destroy. He looked down at her, his eyes lingering on the full lips softened in sleep and slightly curved with pleasant thoughts.

Mara stirred in her sleep, reaching out to enfold Paddy

protectively in her arms, and Nicholas felt a strange envy as he watched the naturalness of the gesture and wondered with longing what it would be like to be loved by Mara O'Flynn. For an instant he speculated on how it would be if she responded to him out of love and not just in response to his passion. She never whispered words of love into his ear, nor was there ever a softening of the golden eyes when they stared up into his. Nicholas suddenly felt a desire to know that love, but a second later he contemptuously discarded the idea. Too much unpleasantness had passed between them to allow the delicate nurturing of a real love. Besides, was that something he really wanted?

Nicholas moved closer to the bed and stood silently staring down at Mara as she slept, her breasts moving slightly, all of the old antagonisms wiped clear of her face, and he felt himself reaching out a tentative hand; then he withdrew it as if he'd been burned. He felt the familiar resentment for Mara O'Flynn flare briefly and wondered how he had let this beautiful Irishwoman come to mean so much to him. There she lay like some innocent babe, completely oblivious to the raw emotions that were tearing him up inside, for he couldn't, nor would he, admit that someone, especially Mara O'Flynn, was important to him. After he'd been driven away from all the people he'd loved, seen them turn their backs on him, he had never allowed himself to feel deeply for anyone. Yet ever since first setting eyes on Mara O'Flynn, he had found himself drawn deeper and deeper into the intrigues surrounding her. Of course, he couldn't really blame anyone but himself for the position he now found himself in, for he forced her to accompany him to New Orleans, and finally to Beaumarais despite her wishes to the contrary. With a sneer of self-disgust he stepped away from the bed and the tantalizing picture Mara made.

Mara knew nothing of these sentiments as she sat across from Nicholas at the dinner table later that evening and eyed him thoughtfully over her tomato and rice soup. Every so often their eyes met and Mara was disturbed to see the familiar expression of contempt hardening into a jewel-like quality. Mara sighed and glanced away, her gaze lost among the

colorful china and crystal that crowded the surface of the table
and reflected the glow from the pair of silver candelabra set at
each end of the long, oval table. The sideboards were covered
with large silver platters full of chicken and lobster salad, baked
ham and oysters on the half shell, tenderloin of beef and duck,
and assorted vegetable dishes in sauces and gravies. A pastry
centerpiece in the shape of a pyramid constructed of nougats
and surrounded by squares of marzipan occupied the center
of the table.

"Oh, mademoiselle! Your gown, *c'est exquisite*," Nicole
breathed in awe as her dark eyes clung to the delicate black
Spanish lace that edged the soft mauve silk of Mara's dress.
"Never have I seen such a beautiful shade of purple before. It
is from France, *n'est-ce pas?* Oh, mademoiselle, it would go so
well with my coloring, *non?* Oh, Mama, I must have a gown
of that exact color," Nicole pleaded as she sent an imploring
look to Celeste, who had recovered enough to join the family
for dinner.

She was still quite pale, the black of her gown accentuating
it even more, but she seemed in control of her emotions.

"I cannot bear your whining this evening, Nicole. We will
discuss this matter later. Not that you haven't enough clothes
as it is," she said firmly, ignoring her eldest daughter's pout
and silencing her with a coldly disapproving stare.

"You will forgive my daughter's somewhat ill-mannered
behavior, Mademoiselle O'Flynn, but she becomes carried
away in the excitement of her wedding," Celeste explained
somewhat apologetically, then purposefully looked over to
Nicholas who was sipping his wine in ruminative silence. "It
is a good match for Nicole," she added. Her thin hands were
clasped nervously together in front of her, yet there was a look
of determination on her face that Mara had not seen before.

"It has always been considered an honor to marry a de
Montaigne-Chantale," Nicholas commented matter-of-factly,
his look focusing on his stepmother's strained features at the
note of defiance in her voice.

Celeste smiled cheerlessly. "Times change, Nicholas, and
even though the de Montaigne-Chantale name is an honored

one, it is only that. No longer does the name also imply great wealth," she told him with sad dignity. "If Nicole were not the beauty that she is, then," Celeste shrugged as if it were obvious, "I would find it hard to marry her off. As it is I am grateful for any offer. Damaris," she added with a doubtful look at Damaris's auburn head and elfin features as she made a face at Paddy, "will be most difficult to wed. She is different, with not the classical beauty of Nicole. And she is not wealthy, so what will attract a man to her?"

"Well, I don't wish to wed any old man anyway," Damaris said arrogantly, a look of purpose in her greenish eyes. "I'm not going to have time. I'm going to travel all over the world."

"I believe you shall, my little tiger-cat," Etienne said fondly. Catching Celeste's eye, he shook his silvered head. "You are right, she is different. But can you not see that she is special, that your wild little Damaris will one day have an unusual beauty? That, combined with her spirit, will have the men running after her. You will not have to go begging to get offers for her hand, Celeste."

"It is the long years in between now and this special beauty you speak of that I worry about," Celeste told him with a note of uncertainty in her voice.

Nicholas frowned at her words, nor had he cared for the note he'd heard in her voice when she'd spoken of Nicole's upcoming wedding. "I know things are not as they once were, but I did not know that the de Montaigne-Chantale pride was gone as well," he accused. "You sell Beaumarais land to our neighbors, and does the family now grovel at their feet as well?"

"Oh, Nicholas," Celeste said tearfully, shaking her head in despair. "You have too much of Philippe in you to ever understand. You have not lived here to see the changes and know that if we are to survive then we must change as well. It is very easy to sit in judgment on us, on me, yes, but you do not know what I have been through, especially now that Philippe is gone. Do you know that all along the river they are already speculating on how long it will take before Beaumarais is reclaimed by the swamp it was stolen from? How can I fight that?" Celeste shook her head. "I cannot manage any longer. We are so in debt, with barely enough money to buy food for the table. You look surprised, but it is the truth. It was vital to sell the land, and to Amaryllis. Who else would want it? She made *me* the offer for it, I did not go begging. But I would have begged rather than see my children grow hungry." Spots of bright color stained her cheeks.

"How much did you get?" Nicholas asked quietly, and when Celeste told him he swore. "Damn her, she stole it from you, Celeste."

"Beggars cannot be choosers, can they, Nicholas?" Celeste quoted with bitterness. "And so when she comes tomorrow to buy all of Beaumarais, I shall sell it to her. It is my right," Celeste added defiantly. "No, let me continue," she pleaded as Nicholas would have interrupted, his eyes blazing.

"You have returned at your father's request. So be it. But if you have returned to receive something from the estate, then I am sorry, for there is nothing here for you. You cannot expect us to support you, or give you money, for there is none. What money I receive from Amaryllis for the sale of Beaumarais I shall use to take Jean-Louis and Damaris with me to Charleston. It is my home, it is where *I* belong, not here at Beaumarais, a place where I have seldom known any happiness. Oh, I accepted living here in Louisiana when Philippe was alive. It was different then, but now," she paused, her eyes brightening suddenly with a fierce determination, "I want to go home. So," she said with the tired look returning to her gray eyes, "I am sorry, but do not ask anything of me, Nicholas. I can give you nothing."

"But he doesn't need anything," Damaris piped in as she quickly swallowed a mouthful of mashed potatoes. "He's rich! Paddy says Nicholas has thousands and thousands of dollars, and whenever Paddy asks, Nicholas will give him as many five-dollar gold pieces as he wants," Damaris informed the startled party. Paddy turned a bright red as he felt Nicholas's eyes on his down-bent head.

"This is true?" Celeste asked faintly, her eyes widening with astonishment.

"For the most part it is," Nicholas admitted.

"*C'est incroyable*. I cannot believe such a thing. How?" she demanded, incredulous doubt still evident on her face.

"I've been in California. You have heard that gold was discovered out there. Well, Karl Svengaard—you remember him, don't you?—" Nicholas asked with remembered amusement of his family's disapproval of the Swede, "—and I were fortunate to find some of it."

"Mon Dieu, *le grand blond?* The American who stood so tall? You and he found gold? Much of it?" Celeste asked, her frail voice trembling.

"Enough to make my life comfortable for quite a while. So you see, there is no need to worry that I have returned home to demand money from you."

Etienne propped his chin in his hands, his elbows on the table in defiance of the rigid code of manners he believed in, as he allowed his amazement to show on his face. "You struck it rich?" he demanded with all of the excitement a child would have shown. "That is simply amazing. I am astounded. I have heard many tales from California, but never have I actually met anyone who found gold."

"My papa found one piece of gold and we were rich," Paddy told the silent group proudly.

"This is true?" Etienne asked doubtfully.

"Yes, Brendan found a piece of gold worth close to fifty thousand dollars," Mara backed up Paddy's story.

"Mon Dieu," Etienne mumbled as he took a deep sip of wine. "I just did not believe it was possible that those stories could be true." He glanced over at Nicholas. "And you, Nicholas, you found such a chunk of gold?"

Nicholas shook his head regretfully. "Only the very lucky ever find chunks of gold worth that much, and even those men had probably spent months, maybe years up in the High Sierra looking for such a find. It didn't come as easily as it sounds. The Swede and I worked several streams for months at a time before we had even half that amount saved up, and we were luckier than others," Nicholas told them.

Celeste stared. Nicholas was still arrogantly handsome, and

charming when he chose to be, but beyond that he was not the same. There was a hardness to the man that had not been there before, and yet there was also a dependability about him as well as a gentle strength that he had not possessed when he'd been the rakish, young dilettante son of Philippe de Montaigne-Chantale. He had become far better a man in the years spent away from Beaumarais than he would ever have been had he never left. Pampered and privileged, he would have grown into manhood never having to find the strength of will that'd helped him to survive beyond the secure surroundings of his Creole upbringing.

Nicholas's reticence could not stem the flow of questions from his family, and so the rest of the meal was devoured along with stories of California that Nicole, and especially Damaris, listened to avidly, their eyes alight with excitement as they heard of a strange world beyond the wide Mississippi, a world completely different from Europe and the rest of America, or any other place they had ever read about in their schoolbooks.

Mara sipped her wine, her own memories of California still too painful for her to comfortably participate in reminiscences. She was almost relieved to notice Paddy's nodding head as he slumped down in his chair.

"If you'll excuse me, I think I should see my nephew to bed," she interrupted and got to her feet.

"Mon Dieu, I had no idea how late it grows," Celeste fretted. "You must think our manners quite deplorable, mademoiselle. Nicole, Damaris, it is time you retired as well."

"Oh, Mama, please," Damaris protested even as she struggled to keep her eyes open, "it is so interesting. Let us stay up a little while longer, non? Please..."

"There will be other times, little one," Nicholas told her as he pushed back his chair, his attitude unrelenting despite the entreaty in her wide eyes. "Do as your mama says."

Mara moved close to Nicholas as she guided Paddy from the room. As she passed by him, she felt his hand on her arm. He said softly, "Celeste and I have matters to discuss. You will find all you need to be comfortable in your room. If not, then do not hesitate to ring for a maid," he told her.

It sounded like a dismissal and so she responded coolly, "I shall be quite comfortable, thank you." With a curt nod she made her way from the room.

After tucking Paddy into bed, his eyes closing almost as soon as his head touched the pillow, Mara was standing on the gallery, staring into the dark depths of the tangled mass of oak branches above the drive to Beaumarais. Mara wrapped her arms around the smooth silk of her robe and shivered. There was a strange sense of decay about the house. Mara breathed deeply as she tried to shake off the melancholy mood that had seemed to grip her since setting foot inside the hallowed halls of Beaumarais. She laughed softly, for it was probably just the rich, moist soil of the swamp with its thick undergrowth that gave her this feeling of death. She glanced down to see pale light streaming out from what must be the drawing room or study. Apparently Nicholas was still cloistered with Celeste.

Mara sighed, feeling oddly dispirited as she returned to her bedchamber, her body shaking with cold. She quickly flung off her wrapper and climbed beneath the warm quilt. It was to be the first night in a long time that she slept without Nicholas's warm body beside her, and she wondered if it would be the first of many to come.

Doubts are more cruel than the worst of truths.

—Molière

Chapter 13

MARA TURNED OVER LAZILY, STIFLING A YAWN AS SHE snuggled deeper under the quilted silk covers. The rattling of china sounded just beyond the door, and then there was a hesitant knock and the appearance of a young maid with a tray.

"'Mornin', mademoiselle. I'm Belle, and if there's anything you need, just call me," she spoke quietly, smiling shyly as she put the tray on the table beside the bed and quickly found Mara's bed jacket, helping her into it as Mara struggled to prop herself up against the pillows. She looked slightly startled as she noticed Mara's bare shoulders.

Mara smiled wryly with the realization that, by noon, the whole household would be aware that Master Nicholas's lady friend slept without a nightdress.

"Thank you, Belle," Mara said as the young girl placed the tray across her lap and stood back to await any further instructions. "Do you know if my nephew and maid are up yet?" Mara inquired as she took a tentative sip of the steaming coffee.

"Master Paddy is out playing with the young Miss Damaris, and that maid of yours, well," Belle continued in a grievous tone of voice as she shook her kerchiefed head, "she was in here giving me orders last evening when I was turning down your bed. Telling me how *she* liked your things folded and put away. I reckon she thinks I was raised in the fields or something," she said with an injured sniff.

Mara smiled, her eyes mirroring amusement as she tried to picture the diminutive Irishwoman issuing orders to this tall, slender girl. "You'll have to forgive Jamie her bossiness, but she has cared for my family for so long that she is very proprietary about my things," Mara soothed.

Belle put her hands on her narrow hips and shrugged, a smile lurking in her dark eyes. "She reminds me a lot of ol' Mama Marie out in the kitchens, never letting a body touch nothing without her eagle eye watching every move. Lord, but it's worth your skin to even go in there. Now, when you're ready to bathe just pull the bell and I'll be comin' up with some hot water, mademoiselle." She was about to leave when Mara choked, turning pale as she tried to keep down the little food she had eaten so far. Belle quickly reached for the washbasin and held it beneath Mara's head.

"Oh, no," Mara moaned as she leaned back against the support of the pillows and waited for the nauseous feeling to pass. She smiled thankfully as she felt the cool compress Belle held against her brow. "I'll be all right now. It just came on me so sudden," Mara said in puzzlement.

Belle nodded wisely. "It's a real shame, but that's the way it is with some womenfolk when they start to grow big with child."

Mara felt another wave of nausea rise inside her. Her worst fears, ones she had not even dared to contemplate, couldn't be ignored any longer.

She was carrying Nicholas's child. She had suspected as much last month but had kept hoping that nothing was wrong. No longer could she ignore the tenderness of her breasts or the growing heaviness between her hips. Mara continued to stare numbly at Belle until the young girl began to move uncomfortably under the golden-eyed stare.

"I want your word that you will not mention this to anyone in this house. Do you understand, Belle, that no one must know about my condition," Mara told her. "Promise."

Belle's brow cleared. "I can keep a secret, mademoiselle, even if others I know can't," she assured Mara. "You can trust Belle."

After Belle had left the room, taking the now-unappetizing

tray of food with her, Mara sighed in relief and lay back against the pillows, her arms folded across her breasts.

Nicholas's child. He had gotten her with child, and suddenly Mara felt a deep resentment flare inside her. Why should she have to be the one to suffer for the pleasures they had shared? Why was she now to be branded, as if being punished for wrongdoing? By next month—her third month of pregnancy, she calculated—she would begin to "grow big with child" as Belle had so descriptively put it, and then everyone would know.

What would Nicholas do, Mara wondered. How would he react to the news that she was carrying his child? No, Mara decided with firm resolution, Nicholas must never know. She wouldn't let him find out. It would be the final humiliation. He might even pity her, and that she could never bear, not from Nicholas. And what if out of some perverted sense of decency and honor he offered her marriage? Could she accept him under such circumstances, Mara shook her head sadly, knowing that Nicholas would never do anything so quixotic.

Oh, Brendan, me love, what am I going to do? Mara thought desperately, wishing she could turn to him for advice and see that devilish smile light up his face as he set about making plans. If only she weren't stranded on this plantation.

A short while later Mara descended the stairs, looking as if she had nothing more to worry about than the weather. She paused briefly before the mirror in the entrance hall and stared at her figure, fearing that her condition might be evident, but her waist was still narrowly enclosed inside the pale green foulard silk of her morning dress. A lacy fichu crossed over her breasts and effectively covered the tightness she was beginning to feel as the material of her gown stretched across the increasing fullness. Mara straightened the lace edging her bell sleeves and, smoothing a deep wave of dark hair back from her forehead, turned toward the parlor.

"Mademoiselle O'Flynn," Celeste greeted her. "I thought I heard someone come down the stairs. Won't you please join me? I was having a cup of tea while I try to get Jean-Louis to take a nap," she explained as she rocked the blanketed bundle held closely in her arms. Mara could just barely see the top of a dark head.

"Thank you, madame," Mara accepted, thinking a cup of tea would taste good since she hadn't had much breakfast. She was also rather curious about the almost startling change of appearance in Nicholas's stepmother. It seemed as if overnight she had undergone a transformation from the nervous and harassed woman Mara had first met into the relaxed and quite friendly hostess who was now waiting for her.

"Please, you will call me Celeste," she invited as she indicated a chair near the tea table. "I know tea is usually an English drink, but when I was expecting mon petit Jean-Louis, tea and toast were all I could eat in the mornings," she said as she beamed down at the small head snuggled against her breast. "Please, mademoiselle, you will pour."

Mara filled two cups with the fragrant brew and sat listening to Celeste speaking proudly of her only son. Mara eyed her curiously, wondering if the sight of her son always caused her to chatter nonsensically to strangers. Yet, perhaps there was something else. She seemed almost to be waiting for something to happen. There was a sudden stillness when she thought she heard something from the drive in front of the house, and then a faint excitement, or anxiety which Mara could see in her eyes, led her to believe that Celeste was awaiting the arrival of someone important.

"I am afraid Nicholas left early this morning to look over the property, but he will no doubt return soon," Celeste said suddenly, as if Mara were waiting for an explanation.

"I see," Mara answered, feeling oddly relieved. She couldn't face Nicholas yet and be relaxed. "I suppose he would be very interested in seeing the plantation again after so great a time."

"Oh, yes, he is most interested. But it is good that he looks now, for soon we will be having more rain and it will be difficult to get around. The river will most likely flood its banks again, and with Beaumarais so close to the river, we always suffer a little flooding."

Mara looked at her in concern. "Is that very often?"

Celeste sighed, nodding regretfully. "Every year, it would

seem, although some years it is worse than others. A few years ago it was especially bad and the river flooded the ground floor with so much water and mud that everything was ruined. I thought Beaumarais would never be the same. There was so much damage, and I loathed the snakes that found their way in as well," Celeste told Mara with a delicate shiver. "Mon Dieu, but the sight of them swimming through my parlor was enough to nearly cause me to lose Jean-Louis. We were afraid that we would have to have extensive repairs made to the foundation, for the river current cut right into it, but it was filled back in and rebuilt in places, and *voilà*, it is as good as new. Beaumarais will probably be here longer than the old sycamore in the swamp," she said with a small chuckle.

"You don't fear the flooding?" Mara asked doubtfully.

"Yes, I fear it, but it is something you grow used to after a while," Celeste said practically. "When I first arrived from Charleston and came out here to Beaumarais, I was frightened to death of the swamp and that mighty river so close. I would have nightmares about it all swallowing me up. I think one must be born here to ever feel at home. The rest of us will always be intruders."

Mara shivered, for she had experienced the same feeling about Beaumarais.

"Belle told me that my nephew, Paddy, had come down earlier?" Mara sought to change the subject.

"Ah, yes, he went off with Damaris. Not that I think they will be gone long when she discovers—" she paused as she listened attentively to certain unmistakable sounds of anger issuing from the front of the house. "Yes, Damaris is most displeased," she predicted correctly as the little redhead flew into the room, an expression of outraged anger on her small face.

"Mama! He is on Sorcier, Mama! He took my horse. He's riding Sorcier! How dare he do this," she cried almost incoherently as she stamped her foot in frustrated rage.

Paddy had followed her more quietly into the room and now stood silently watching his new-found friend, his dark eyes round as he listened to her tirade against Nicholas.

"I gave him permission to ride Sorcier, and as you well

know, Damaris, he is not your horse. Your papa bought him for himself, and it is only because no one else cares to ride him that you have come to believe him yours. You know your papa would never have allowed you anywhere near him if he were still alive."

"But I am the only one who can ride him," Damaris protested volubly. "He likes no one *but* me."

"Exactly," Celeste responded. "He is an evil horse. He is uncontrollable and dangerous. You know I have been of a mind to sell him for many months now. In fact, if Nicholas wants him, which I doubt, then I will sell that devil horse to him."

"No! No, you mustn't. I won't let you," Damaris cried as tears began to fall unchecked from her eyes. "I hope he throws Nicholas! He has no right, no right at all to take my horse. Oh, I wish he had never returned!" she cried as she ran from the room and out of the house. A second later they heard the front door slam loudly.

"My pardon, mademoiselle, her behavior is inexcusable," Celeste said angrily, her mouth tight with displeasure. "She is completely without sense sometimes, and I seem to have very little control over her. She has always been a stubborn little troublemaker. If only she were more like my Nicole, who would never dream of carrying on so over a horse and spends most of her time worrying over what color hair ribbon to wear each day."

Mara smiled slightly, thinking that if it came to a choice, she personally rather liked the little firebrand the best.

"Paddy," Mara said quickly, stopping him as he would have followed Damaris from the room. "I think you'd best let her alone. Why don't you get your soldiers and set them up somewhere?" she suggested. With a disappointed look Paddy nodded. Excusing himself, he left the room, an intent expression already forming on his face as he planned his military maneuvers.

"Nicholas told me that you are the little one's only family now that his papa has died," Celeste spoke gently as she looked down at her own son's dark head. "It is good that you care for him, mademoiselle," Celeste told her with a look of approval. "Nicholas also tells me that you were left stranded in San Francisco and that he offered to escort you as far as New Orleans. It is a pity you did not arrive in the spring. Then your nephew would have had a far quicker recovery under our warm sunshine. But I think it wise you did not continue immediately on your long voyage back to London." Celeste paused as she stared at Mara's face. "Perhaps you might wish to stay in...non, I will not interfere. Forgive me, mademoiselle," she apologized. "It is none of my business."

Mara frowned slightly, thinking Nicholas must have neglected to inform Celeste that she was an actress. Celeste would hardly have been chatting so amiably over the tea table with her had she known. Mara was grateful for Nicholas's thoughtfulness in protecting her reputation. On the other hand, Nicholas would not have jeopardized his position at Beaumarais by introducing her as an actress. They would have automatically assumed her to be Nicholas's mistress. Presented to them as a young woman trying to care for her orphaned nephew, she had been given respect and hospitality. How strange a world it is, Mara thought ironically. Once she would indeed have deserved that respect, and yet, now Nicholas was her lover, and—

"Mademoiselle," Celeste spoke suddenly, "was that a carriage? I thought I heard one arrive."

"Would you like me to look?" Mara offered as she stood up and walked over to the long French windows facing the drive.

Mara watched as the carriage Celeste had heard came to a halt in front of the wide steps leading up to Beaumarais. It was an elegant barouche with the collapsible top down and a liveried coachman sitting smartly on the driver's seat, his gloved hands easily controlling the team of spirited bays hitched to the harness.

A young footman hopped down and quickly opened the carriage door for the solitary woman sitting inside. Wearing a fine, merino wool bodice jacket and matching skirt of palest blue with a fur stole draped over her shoulders, the woman stepped down from the carriage. Mara could just barely make out her features behind the wisp of veil that concealed the side of her face and decorated the dark blue velvet bonnet that didn't completely cover the paleness of her blond head.

With a small, fringed parasol tipped casually over her shoulder, she disappeared up the steps toward the house, Mara losing sight of her as she walked beneath the covered gallery.

"It's a woman," Mara told Celeste as she turned away from the window and reseated herself by the tea table.

"Ah," Celeste murmured as if Mara's words only confirmed what she had been expecting.

"Madame St. Laurens," the butler intoned in a deep voice from the parlor doors.

"Celeste, how well you are looking this morning," Madame St. Laurens greeted her as she made her way into the room on a wave of heavily scented perfume, her gauzy veil floating out behind her and revealing the delicate beauty of her face. And an undeniable beauty she is, Mara thought with a strangely growing feeling of dislike. She didn't like the patronizing note in the slightly amused voice, nor the offhand way the woman threw down her gloves and stole on the sofa as if she were mistress of Beaumarais.

Narrow blue eyes, no less pale than her gown, were now turned on Mara with curious inquisitiveness as the woman helped herself to a cup of tea. Celeste caught the look, smiling with strange satisfaction as she noticed the hostility in the newcomer's light eyes as she assessed Mara O'Flynn, the Irishwoman's stunning beauty disconcerting her.

"Amaryllis, Madame St. Laurens, this is our guest, Mademoiselle Mara O'Flynn."

"Mademoiselle," Amaryllis said coolly, nodding her blond head regally, then insultingly turned her attention to Celeste.

So this was Amaryllis, who had once held Nicholas's heart in the palm of her hand—and perhaps still did.

"And what may I do for you, Amaryllis?" Celeste inquired politely, yet distantly as her gray eyes slid away from the coldly amused look in Amaryllis's pale eyes.

"You ask *me* that?" Amaryllis asked, some of her amusement fading as she sensed a subtle change in the older woman's attitude. Glancing over at Mara pointedly, she said, "Shouldn't we discuss this in private?"

But Celeste only shook her head. "Soon we will have no secrets here. What do you wish, Amaryllis?"

"I am not amused," Amaryllis told her brusquely. "Do you hope, perhaps, to drive the price up more by pretending unconcern about my visit? Well, I do not play the game, Celeste," she said in a hard voice. "You either accept my offer for Beaumarais now, or sooner or later the creditors will be here on your doorstep and then Beaumarais will have to be auctioned off. Then you will be sorry, for it will not fetch much. Who but me would want it anyway?" Amaryllis took a sip of tea.

"Bien, I think we understand one another," she said in a businesslike voice as she pulled a large envelope from her muff. "Here are the papers already drawn up. Sign them, now," Amaryllis told her as she placed them on the tea table with barely concealed impatience.

༄

Nicholas let Sorcier have his head as the big bay stallion's hooves sent the thick mud of the road flying in all directions. Clearing the topmost rail of the fence Nicholas sent Sorcier across the sloping field until, climbing to the top of a small rise, he halted the big horse's headlong flight. He stared out over the wide river gleaming in the sunshine below. He glanced along the levee, knowing that somewhere along that length of red bank his father had fallen into the swift current of the river below and drowned. Nicholas's green eyes stared hard at the now-empty levee. If only he could see what had actually happened. With a sigh of frustration Nicholas nudged Sorcier with his heels and sent him along the riverside as he slowly made his way upstream until finally coming to what used to be Beaumarais land. He pulled up just short of the new fence that now divided the two properties. On the far side lay fields that would, during the long, hot summer months, yield white cotton along the straight rows stretching away into the distance. Field hands would work from sunup to sundown with long sacks thrown over their shoulders, dragging the ground behind as they threaded their way through the rows of cotton, picking the tufts and filling their bags.

Nicholas glanced back at Beaumarais land, and the fields that had been left unplanted, tall weeds growing unchecked across the land. Nicholas's hands tightened unconsciously on the reins as he remembered the past glory of Beaumarais, when they had sent the biggest crop of cotton downriver to New Orleans. Turning Sorcier around, he cut across the fields and headed back toward Beaumarais, stopping briefly at the rows of slave quarters now standing empty and silent, doors gaping open, some off their hinges. Chickens roosted in the rafters.

Only the slave quarters nearest the great house were still occupied by the house and yard servants. The abandoned slave quarters, as well as the barren land, told the story about Beaumarais. There would be no more big crops this year or next for Beaumarais. Most of the slaves had been sold, something Celeste had neglected to mention to him.

Nicholas rode along the narrow dirt road running beside the great house and noticed for the first time the run-down appearance of Beaumarais. He could see the water line staining the walls where the flood waters had risen higher than ever one year, the rich earth still looking sunken around the foundation. The low kitchen wing hadn't been repainted or repaired in years, while overgrown shrubs choked the formal walks leading through the gardens where roses, gardenias, and crepe myrtle would have once flourished. Too many idle hands, Nicholas thought as he eyed several young men sitting near a large banana tree.

Nicholas dismounted in front of the stables and saw to the unsaddling and rubbing down of Sorcier himself. He was making his way along the gallery when he noticed for the first time the carriage sitting in front of the house. The sharp, staccato sound from the heels of his riding boots marking his progress, he entered the entrance hall of Beaumarais. He ran a careless hand through his black hair as he walked without hesitation into the parlor. Sweat glistened on the wiry, dark hairs of his chest where the fine lawn of his shirt was opened, and his thighs rippled with muscle under the tight covering of his leather breeches.

"I'm afraid Celeste is no longer in a position to sell Beaumarais, Amaryllis," Nicholas spoke suddenly from the doorway, a sardonic look entering his eyes. "For you see, I am now the owner, and I'm not interested in selling."

Amaryllis spun quickly around, surprised by the abrupt interruption.

"Nicholas?" she whispered, her light blue eyes widening in disbelief as he obliged her by moving closer. Mara's fingers clenched painfully as she watched the look of surprise on Amaryllis's face change into something else. Her eyes traveled over every inch of Nicholas's tanned face and casually attired body. Mara thought Nicholas had never seemed more attractive nor more out of reach as he stood there with the easy grace of a man who knew where he belonged.

"Satisfied?" he asked softly, his own eyes lingering with almost insulting familiarity on Amaryllis.

"You came back." Her voice sounded strangled, her cool sophistication crumbling away from her as she continued to stare at him. Amaryllis sank down on the edge of the sofa.

"Y-you own Beaumarais? How? I don't understand? When?" she demanded, finding her tongue on a wave of growing anger.

"Last night," Nicholas informed her as he walked over to stand behind Celeste, who was nervously watching the confrontation between these two arrogant, determined people. Her thin hands fluttered over the tea set in agitation. "I thought it best to keep Beaumarais in the family."

"Last night?" Amaryllis repeated shakily, turning frosty blue eyes on Celeste. "My God, you knew I'd be coming today to make you an offer, and yet behind my back you sold the place?"

"It was not really behind your back, Amaryllis," Nicholas said, and it seemed to Mara that his voice softened over her name. "After all, I think I've more right to Beaumarais than you. And," he added with a cynical look at Celeste's lowered head, "I doubled your offer—which was surprisingly low, my dear."

His words were deceptively soft and silky and Amaryllis

flushed guiltily. "The way the plantation has gone downhill," Amaryllis defended herself, "Celeste was lucky to receive an offer at all. Well," Amaryllis drew a shaky breath, "I seem to have received quite a few surprises this morning, as well as a rather large disappointment. If you will forgive my rudeness, Nicholas," she said as she tried to regain some of her composure, "what are you doing back here?"

"Philippe asked him to return," Celeste found the courage to answer Amaryllis. "He wrote him a letter and told him that he knew Nicholas had not killed François."

Amaryllis's razor-sharp gaze met Nicholas's as she absorbed this. "So, this is true, Nicholas? Your father believed your story of so many years before? It is most curious after such a long time. What did he know?" she asked bluntly.

Nicholas smiled as he shook his head and denied her any satisfaction. "That is a family matter, Amaryllis, but soon the truth will be known to all," he baited her, watching her reaction with a speculative gaze.

"I see. Forgive me for intruding," Amaryllis responded, not in the least bit sorry. "I still cannot believe that you are here talking to me," she said, intentionally linking their names together.

"He is also a very wealthy man, Amaryllis," Celeste delighted in telling that piece of information to her fair-haired neighbor. "He's been out in California where they've had the gold rush. Nicholas struck it rich." Celeste repeated the phrase she'd heard used the evening before and which sounded to her very remarkable.

"Well, well," Amaryllis murmured as she got slowly to her feet and walked over to Nicholas, stopping less than a foot away from him as she gazed up into his eyes. "I suppose I can forget some of my unhappiness in losing Beaumarais since it is *you* that I lost it to. You are here at Beaumarais where you have always belonged. It has been a long time. May I welcome you home, Nicholas?" she whispered softly, her eyes losing their brittle quality as she placed a slender, well-cared-for hand on Nicholas's arm. Standing on tiptoe, she pressed her lips against his mouth in a lingering kiss.

Mara's fingers wrapped around the arm of her chair, her nails scoring the soft underwood as she stared in pain at the blond head held so close to Nicholas's dark one.

Amaryllis stepped back, her hand slow to leave his arm as she returned his look from lowered lids, her pale eyes glowing through the dark fringe of lash covering them.

Nicholas was the first to glance away, and Amaryllis seemed startled by the ease with which he broke the contact between them.

"Have you met Mara O'Flynn?" he asked casually as he left her side and made his way purposefully to Mara's.

Amaryllis frowned slightly. "Yes, I have, Celeste introduced us," she answered, her tone of voice leaving no small doubt that she thought Mara of little importance. But as her eyes caught the movement of Nicholas's tanned hand covering Mara's shoulder, then moving to caress her cheek, her estimation of the Irishwoman began to undergo a change.

"I thought she was Celeste's guest," Amaryllis said abruptly as it began to dawn on her that Mara was Nicholas's friend.

"Did you? Mara and I have known each other for several years, and we are quite close friends," he said softly, looking down at Mara's dark head almost tenderly, the look confirming Amaryllis's suspicions.

Mara's golden eyes met Amaryllis's cold stare, and she knew she had an enemy in the pale-eyed Frenchwoman. Many years had passed since Amaryllis and Nicholas had been lovers, but the feeling had not faded with time. Mara knew instinctively that Amaryllis hadn't given up trying to win either Beaumarais or Nicholas.

Amaryllis found her composure with difficulty this time. After a second she managed to smile. "You must come to my small party tomorrow night at Sandrose. I shall enjoy reintroducing you to society, Nicholas. Celeste, Mademoiselle O'Flynn," she added politely, with feigned hospitality, "you will attend as well?"

Celeste glanced up from cuddling Jean-Louis, a doubtful look on her face. "I will see. I am still not up to much entertaining, as well as still being in mourning for Philippe."

"Yes, of course. But you must have Nicole come with Etienne. I invited him last week and he said he'd come, so," she concluded as she adjusted her fur across her shoulders, then picked up her parasol and muff, "I shall expect to see you tomorrow evening, if not sooner." Her provocative glance at Nicholas was a blatant invitation. For now, she seemed content to have him escort her to her carriage. "Au revoir," she said with a satisfied smile as she tucked her hand in the crook of Nicholas's arm.

Mara followed their progress from the room, her face showing her feelings as her eyes mirrored her unease. So Nicholas had bought Beaumarais. He had made his decision. Mara glanced around the stately room resentfully, knowing that his ties to Beaumarais were stronger than any he could ever feel for her. He would never leave here, she thought despondently. He had come home, and here he would stay. And here was Amaryllis, who was just as beautiful as Mara had feared.

Mara stood up. "If you'll excuse me, Celeste, I would like to rest for a while," Mara said as she caught Celeste's curious gaze.

"But of course, mademoiselle," she answered, unaware of Mara's turmoil as she looked back down at her son and sighed with relief. Her confrontation with Amaryllis was over, and indeed, it had gone much easier than she had anticipated. But then, Nicholas had been here, and the Nicholas who had returned to Beaumarais was no longer the hotheaded young man he had once been, but a cold-blooded and ruthless man of the world. Yes, Celeste thought with deep contentment, he was quite capable of handling Amaryllis.

Mara entered her room thankful for the quiet she found there, but she couldn't relax and found herself pacing aimlessly back and forth. She thought of Paddy and decided to see what he was up to. But Paddy's room was empty, his soldiers left scattered and forgotten across the floor. Mara returned to her room and, selecting a knee-length mantle, stepped out onto the deserted gallery and silently made her way down the outside staircase to the brick path below. It winded through what must once have been a beautiful garden but now was overgrown with weeds and shrubbery that choked the path. Mara lifted her skirts aside as she swept along the neglected walkway. A sudden gust of wind caught at Mara's skirts and blew them around her ankles. She glanced upward at the blue sky and saw in the distance clouds that were growing steadily higher and darker by the minute as they boiled into thunderclouds that would bring rain to Beaumarais by afternoon.

Mara continued walking until she broke from the lushness of the garden and came out before a low structure. Architecturally, it matched the great house, but was only single-storied. Mara stood there curiously staring at it and was spotted by Etienne as he stepped from the entrance.

"Mademoiselle O'Flynn!" he exclaimed, his eyes lighting with apparent delight.

"I'm sorry if I'm intruding. I just realized this must be your own private wing," Mara apologized, making a move to leave.

"Oh, please, it is so nice to have a lovely woman calling on me," Etienne cajoled, his hand sliding around Mara's elbow persuasively as he guided her toward the door. "Please, let me show you some of my treasures. You will have a cup of tea or glass of sherry with me, non?" he invited with a hopeful look in his eyes.

Mara hadn't the heart to refuse, but she declined his offer of tea as she accompanied him into his bachelor quarters. "I've just had tea, thank you."

Etienne eyed her closely. "The way you say that, I think perhaps it was not most enjoyable, eh?"

Mara smiled, for despite his air of polite inquiry he was very curious. "You are very perceptive, m'sieu."

Etienne fondly patted her hand as he apologized. "I'm sorry, my dear, but it is not that I am so perceptive, but that you are so expressive. One word, one look or gesture from you is worth a thousand words from another," he told her with delight. "You have the same gift that many people of the theater possess," he complimented her with an innocent look in his blue eyes, but Mara wondered if she should allow herself to be hoodwinked by this charming, yet wily old gentleman.

"There was a visitor," Mara admitted. "A Madame St. Laurens."

"Ah, Amaryllis," he breathed softly, then cast Mara a mischievous look. "I think that must indeed have been an interesting tea party. Amaryllis would not have been pleased to see you, mademoiselle, not at all."

Mara arched an eyebrow quizzically.

"Because, ma chérie, she has always hated anyone who was more beautiful than she, and," he added with a wicked wink, "especially younger. Did she happen to see Nicholas?"

Mara's smile faded slightly. "Yes, they had quite a reunion, only I do not think it was quite as pleasant as it might have been under different circumstances."

"Ah, yes," Etienne replied with a slightly malicious wink. "She would have discovered, much to her dismay, that Beaumarais had already been sold. Such a pity for her, eh?" he chuckled. "I am only sorry I overslept and was not there in time to see Amaryllis's face when she discovered both that *and* Nicholas."

"You are pleased?" Mara asked.

"That Nicholas bought Beaumarais? But of course, my dear, for it means that I shall not be evicted. I most certainly would have been had Amaryllis become mistress here," he said with a look of relief, then frowned as if an unpleasant thought had suddenly occurred to him. "Of course, I suppose that possibility still remains for our Amaryllis is a most attractive, unattached widow. She is also very determined," he murmured in worried speculation, then shook his mane of silver hair as if refusing to contemplate such a disastrous event. "If Nicholas were any lesser a man, well, I should start packing my bags immediately."

Mara smiled slightly in response to his grin and glanced around Etienne's parlor. It was a beautiful room, brilliant with color from the many pieces of fine furniture, paintings, and *objets d'art* that Etienne had collected from his years of travel. A lacquer and ebony secretaire, a marquetry commode of satinwood and tulipwood, the finish warm and rich, a baroque table supported by four bronzed statues serving as legs, and an ormolu-mounted console table all fought for the eye's attention while heavy, crimson drapes curtained the windows and blended with the jewel-like reds and blues of a Persian carpet. But it was a delicate armchair, its carved frame hand-painted to match the floral motif of its silk cushions that caught and held Mara's eye.

"I was told when I bought that poor little chair that it once belonged to Marie-Antoinette," Etienne offered when he saw Mara's interest.

"It's exquisite, Etienne," Mara said with admiration and awe.

"*Merci*, I only wish you could see the rest of my collection in Paris. I have a small house there where I have the greater part of my small treasures," Etienne told her proudly, pleased by Mara's appreciation.

"You mean you have more?" Mara asked incredulously as she glanced around at the cabinets loaded with beautifully carved ivory figures, richly detailed Oriental vases and prints, and countless boxes, tankards, bowls, and candlesticks of gleaming silver.

"My dear, I have so much that it would really take most of the great house of Beaumarais to do justice to it all," Etienne laughed. "But let me show you my latest acquisition," he whispered excitedly as he hurried over to a table and picked up an elaborately engraved silver cup. He held it gently in the palms of his hands, for it had no handles. "I have just recently returned from St. Petersburg, and it was there that I found this," Etienne beamed, "a loving cup, mademoiselle."

Mara lightly ran her fingertip over the flat lip of the cup and wondered idly if it had indeed brought good fortune to the people who had drunk from it. Mara smiled. Etienne was like a small boy, surrounded by his favorite toys and eager to show them off to his friends.

"Someday I shall show you my fan collection too," Etienne promised as he carefully replaced the loving cup, "for I've just added one to it that I was assured belonged to Catherine the Great herself," he confided. "Are you sure I cannot offer you a cup of tea?"

"No, thank you. Actually I was looking for my nephew,

Paddy. He was supposed to be playing indoors, but he seems to have disappeared." Mara told him. "I really should find him, especially as it looks as if it is going to rain."

"Perhaps I may be of some assistance. Shall we look in the stables?" Etienne suggested as he picked up his gloves and cane. Settling his black, silk top hat on his silver head, he escorted her outside. "When I was a child, the stables always held a certain fascination for me," Etienne commented with a puzzled frown, "although for the life of me I can't understand why. They're such dirty, smelly places."

Paddy was indeed to be found in the stables. Mara heard his giggle and squeal of delight, and following the sound, she discovered his small figure hunched over something in the corner of one of the empty stalls. Alain was leaning against the rough wood of the partition, a slight smile curving his lips as he watched Paddy in amusement. At the rustling sound of Mara's skirts Alain turned, shaking his dark head.

"One would think the boy had never seen a bitch and her pups before," Alain spoke in amazement.

"I don't suppose he has," Mara realized. "We have always lived in the city, and having traveled so much, well, Paddy has never had pets."

Alain nodded in understanding. "Don't touch her," he warned Paddy as they heard a snarling growl from the stall, "or she'll bite your fingers off."

Paddy jumped back as if indeed he had been bitten, his dark eyes wide with concern. "I only wanted to touch one of the little babies," Paddy said wistfully.

"She's very protective over her brood, and she doesn't know you don't mean them any harm," Alain explained.

"Mind what the gentleman says, Paddy," Mara told him as he backed against her skirts and eyed the bitch warily.

"Perhaps the boy would care to see a more agreeable stablemate," Alain suggested as he led the way down the row of stalls to one occupied by a gentle-looking mare and her newborn foal. Alain lifted Paddy up to the top railing, where he allowed him to perch, safely out of reach of any harmful hooves.

"Mara was telling me that Beaumarais had a visitor this morning," Etienne told his son with a smile of wry amusement.

"Madame St. Laurens from Sandrose," Alain spoke softly. His hazel eyes returned Etienne's amusement as they shared a private joke between them. "I would have given a year's wage to have seen that."

"You may think we are a bit harsh on Amaryllis," Etienne tried to explain, "but in the past our dealings with the young madame have not always been mutually agreeable."

"Yes, the mistress of Sandrose often forgets who she is speaking with and continues to crack the whip above our heads as if we were her slaves," Alain elaborated further, a note of resentment entering his voice. He was a free man and valued that position highly.

Paddy sneezed and Mara glanced up at him worriedly. "Come on, Paddy, I think we'd better go in."

"Oh, Mara, let me stay just a little while longer," Paddy pleaded. "It was only the straw that tickled my nose. Please, Mara?" he asked, his anxious brown eyes never leaving her face.

"It will be all right, mademoiselle," Alain assured her, "for I shall keep a close eye on the boy."

Mara hesitated a moment, but gave up when she caught Paddy's eye and hadn't the heart to say no. "Very well, but I want you back in the house in half an hour."

"You do not mind, mademoiselle," Etienne said apologetically, "but I wish to have a few words with Alain?"

"No, of course not, I can find my way back to the house," Mara reassured Etienne as she turned to leave, but not before giving Paddy a warning look reminding him of her words.

The wind had increased. A storm approached and was blowing in gusts as Mara made her way across the stable yard toward the great house. She hurried up the steps to the gallery, her head lowered as she held her hair in place. She didn't see Nicholas as he stepped out from one of the wide columns, his hands reaching out and grabbing hold of her as she made her way down the shadowy corridor.

Mara jumped as she felt the strong hands gripping her

shoulders. She looked up into his face and wondered what he was thinking behind that bronzed mask.

"So, you bought Beaumarais," Mara said lamely. Even to her own ears it had the sound of an accusation.

"Yes, I am the owner of Beaumarais now," Nicholas answered quietly.

Their eyes met and they stared in silence at each other for what seemed hours.

"Congratulations, Nicholas," she said softly, managing a slightly twisted smile as she added, "when would you like me to leave?"

Nicholas's heavy eyebrows raised in surprise. "I thought we had discussed this question once before."

Mara gave a sigh of exasperation, realizing that Nicholas was going to be difficult. "That was in New Orleans, before you became master of Beaumarais. Things are different now," she told him calmly, not showing any of the trepidation she was feeling over how different things really were.

"Are they?" Nicholas asked doubtfully as his hand softly caressed her cheek, the look in his eyes daring her to refute his claim. Mara suspected Nicholas knew his touch was causing her heart to race within her chest.

Mara drew herself up proudly, jerking away her flushed cheek from his persuasive touch. "I would have thought your interests lie in a different direction now?"

Nicholas smiled lazily. "And which direction would that be, my dear?"

"Amaryllis," Mara told him shortly.

"Ah, Amaryllis," he said with a speculative gleam in his green eyes. "She is quite a beauty, isn't she?"

Mara's hands clenched at her sides. "Indeed she is, if you care for that type," Mara answered frigidly, "but I will not be used to make her jealous."

Nicholas's eyes blazed with sudden anger. "And you think that is what I'm doing by keeping you here with me, making Amaryllis jealous? You underestimate my skills if you think I need to resort to such a stratagem in order to get a woman."

"I underestimated you once, Nicholas, but never again,"

Mara retorted. Swallowing what little pride she had left, she gazed up into his hard eyes, her hands pressed against his chest almost beseechingly. "Please, Nicholas, let me go now. 'Tis the best thing for everyone concerned."

Silently Nicholas stared down into the golden eyes which for once were gazing at him clearly and earnestly. He felt a moment's uncertainty, but only for a second, for the old suspicions returned as he caught a triumphant gleam in the tawny eyes. Mara had noted his hesitation. "Of course," Nicholas spoke mockingly, his jade eyes running over Mara's figure almost contemptuously, "even a gentleman of my talents needs some time to complete his seduction, and so until then, my dear," he said, his voice intentionally dispassionate, "you'll have to continue in the role of devoted paramour."

Mara raised her hand to strike that mocking look off his devil's face, feeling so much rage that she went faint with it. Nicholas's hand closed around her wrist like a vise, and he held her hand just inches from his face.

"You might as well give in gracefully, Mara, and accept your fate," Nicholas suggested arrogantly, watching her intently.

Mara glanced away, well aware that it was almost impossible anymore to hide her thoughts from him. When Mara looked up again, she was the picture of resigned acceptance.

"Very well, Nicholas," she replied carefully, "you win. You are master here, aren't you?"

Nicholas smiled with genuine amusement. "Coming from you, that sounds more like an insult."

"I only treat you as you treat me."

Nicholas turned her chin up so he could see her eyes. "I wonder if we shall ever fully understand one another, my dear. Or even perhaps become friends one day?"

"Friendship is based on trust, and we don't trust each other," Mara said sadly. "We never will."

"I suppose you're right." Deep regret crossed his face for just a second.

"May I go now?" Mara demanded.

"To your room?"

"And where else would I be goin'?" Mara replied with a

challenging look. As she felt herself freed from his grip, she walked quickly past him, disappearing into the house without a backward glance.

⁓

Mara smoothed down the soft velvet of the red gown that held so many memories for her. Tonight Amaryllis would be the center of attention, especially when she presented her special guest, the notorious Nicholas de Montaigne-Chantale. Amaryllis would be sure to play the hostess well, and all eyes would no doubt be focused in curious speculation on the one-time lovers. But when Nicholas's eyes would fall on the red dress he would remember other times. Times that only Mara could share with him.

Mara glanced at the time, the porcelain figure clock on the mantel ticking the minutes away all too quickly, hastening the departure for Sandrose. Mara had seen little of Nicholas most of the day. It had rained steadily and he had holed up in the study with Alain, going over the accounts.

Mara breathed in deeply as Jamie fastened the back of the gown, the red material pulling tight across her breasts and pushing their fullness precariously close to the edge of her bodice.

"Don't know why ye be wearin' this gown tonight when ye've got so many other pretty ones to choose from," Jamie complained as she closed the last hook and eye. "Well, guess ye might as well wear it now since ye won't be able to get into it much longer," she added with a sniff.

Mara turned around and stared at the little woman. "And just what is that supposed to mean?" she asked softly, hiding her discomfiture behind a haughty look.

But Jamie was not cowed. Folding her thin arms across her chest, she said in a voice of carefully nurtured indignation, "D'ye think I've not got eyes in me head? I'm seein' a might clearer than ye be these days, missie," she snorted.

Mara sighed and then laughed. "To be sure, 'tis a fool I am to be thinkin' I could be keepin' such a secret from you, Mistress Hawkeye," Mara said, but there was no sting in her words. She smiled pathetically down at the old woman, the friend who had always been there when she needed her. "'Twould seem as though your fine Creole gentleman has dealt me more than threats this time, Jamie. Soon everyone will know I am carrying his child." Mara muttered beneath her breath as her hands moved shakily over the velvet covering her hips.

Jamie could sense Mara's uncertainty and fear. She frowned and, patting Mara's slender hand, said, "Now don't ye be frettin' none. Master Nicholas will do right by ye. He'll not abandon ye, missie. He's a good man, that he is."

Mara jerked her hand away and turned angrily on the little woman, her eyes blazing as she saw the pity on Jamie's wizened face. "Don't be feelin' sorry for me. That I will not have," she whispered brokenly. "My God, if you pity me, what will Nicholas think? I would rather die before I'd have him look at me with pity," she swore. Mara reached out and grasped Jamie's shoulders. "Swear on Maud O'Flynn's grave that you will never breathe a word of this to Nicholas. Promise me, Jamie, Promise!"

Jamie swallowed nervously. "It'll be as ye wish, Mara. Ye know I'd do nothin' to hurt ye," she told her quietly, her gray eyes watching Mara's trembling lips in astonishment. Mara turned away and walked over to the French windows, staring into the darkness. But before she'd hidden her face, Jamie had seen the bewilderment and hurt there.

As Jamie stared at Mara's rigid back, she thought suddenly of the vulnerable little girl in Paris who'd stood at that dirty window and stared out on an unfriendly city the morning her mother died. The same golden eyes had been turned on her for understanding then, but she hadn't been able to give the numbed child the answers or comfort she had so desperately needed, and it seemed to Jamie that after that morning Mara O'Flynn had never been the same. She became so different from the sweet child she had once been, with her laughing eyes and infectious giggle, a bright velvet bow tying back a mass of unruly dark curls. She could charm the life out of you even then, Jamie remembered with a reluctant smile as she saw a six-year-old Mara sitting on her father's knee, gazing up at him adoringly as he read to her. How many times had she seen that small figure dressed in lace dancing around the salon as she performed for her father before being given a box of her favorite chocolates.

But that had been so long ago, when they had been living happily in Dublin. Years later, when she had left Paris with Brendan and Mara, they had also left that little girl behind. It was the ghost of that child Jamie was seeing now. It was all so long ago, Jamie thought sadly, then cursed the name of Mara's father as she thought of what he had done to Maud's little darlings. Brendan was dead now, his life never having been really happy, and now Mara was faced with raising not only her own babe, but Paddy as well. All alone. She glanced down in disgust at her gnarled hands and knew she wouldn't be here much longer to help Mara. Why couldn't things be different for Mara? she prayed. They just had to be different, she made up her mind against all reason, they would be.

Mara turned away from the window. "I'll make sure we're gone from here before anyone can guess about the child. It'll be our secret. Then, when I can't hide it anymore, it won't matter."

Jamie frowned suspiciously. "And what d'ye mean we will be gone from here? Just where are we goin' I'd like to be knowin'?"

"Does it really matter?" Mara asked tiredly. "London, I suppose. And if I'm still with child then, I'll buy myself a cheap ring and pretend I'm a poor, Irish widow. Who's to be knowing any different? I might even call meself Mara Chantale. It has a nice sound to it, to be sure," she said mockingly.

"And just what are ye meanin' when ye say, 'if the child's still with ye,' I'll be wantin' to know?" Jamie demanded with a glint in her eye.

Mara's golden brown eyes looked away uncomfortably. "Women have been known to lose their babies early, haven't they? Maybe I can't be havin' children?" Mara was defiant.

Jamie placed her hands on her hips and stated matter-of-factly, "There's an old sayin', missie. 'Hips good and wide, the lass was born to be a bride; full breasts for a man's joy, she'll be birthin' a boy.' Seems to me ye've met both requirements just fine."

Mara gave her an exasperated look. "And it seems to me you've been listening to too many old wives' tales."

Jamie smiled smugly. "We'll see, missie. We'll see who knows what they be talkin' about." She started folding up stray articles of clothing.

Mara was about to deal a stinging retort when Nicholas strolled into the room, just as if he had the right.

"Do come in, m'sieu," Mara spoke bitingly, taking out her frustration on him. Jamie quickly excused herself.

Nicholas arched an eyebrow. "My, my, we seem to still be in a bit of a temper," he commented lazily, his green eyes narrowing as he carefully watched her reflection in the mirror.

Keeping her back to him, Mara steadily returned his gaze in the mirror. He was dressed in the black he seemed to favor, the rose embroidery along the border of his black silk vest the only touch of color except for the white shirtfront and cravat.

Mara became aware of a flat case he was holding negligently in his hand. As he caught her questioning look, he came forward to stand just behind her. Mara could feel his warm breath against her temple, then the soft touch of his lips. She jumped as she felt cold metal against her throat and breast.

Mara caught the glitter of jewels in the mirror and stared in amazement at the gold filigree, ruby, and diamond necklace now draped around her neck. Five settings of the exquisite stones glowed against the paleness of her skin. The necklace held the most beautiful ruby pendant Mara had ever seen. Before she could find words, Nicholas had enclosed her wrists in matching bracelets and was putting the drop earrings into her ears.

"The family jewels, ma petite," he murmured with a wicked look. "They once belonged to my mother, and in answer to your next question, no, Celeste will not mind. She has never worn these. She has her own jewels. These were kept by my father, with the intention that one of his sons would give them to his wife. But since I have no wife, and there happens to be a very beautiful woman here dressed in red velvet, why…what could be more perfect?"

Mara turned around, her fingertips lightly touching the cold stones pressing into her flushed skin. "I don't understand. Why should you wish to have *me* wear them?" she asked faintly. Then, noticing how well the ruby necklace went with her gown, she glanced up at him in confusion. "And how did you know I would be wearing red? I almost wore my turquoise gown."

Nicholas smiled indulgently. "I think I know you better than you know yourself, my dear. I suspected you might pull out that red velvet creation which seems to haunt our lives. When you feel threatened, you always lash out at something, or someone. That red dress seems to represent rebellion for you."

Mara glared up at him, knowing he was right. "So?"

Nicholas laughed. "So, I'm at least thankful it happens to be a beautiful gown and not a pair of breeches you slip into when you feel the need to get rid of some of your frustrations," he said silkily, his fingers tracing a delicate pattern across the curve of breast above her gown. "It's extraordinary, but you seem to grow more beautiful each day. Surely I should grow tired of seeing you in this gown, but oddly enough, I don't." His eyelids grew heavy and his mouth suddenly lowered. His lips took hers in a kiss that seemed almost punishing. Mara's mouth clung to his as she wrapped her slender arms around his neck and savored the contact. It seemed so long since they had last kissed so deeply and completely, but suddenly the remembrance of what a kiss like this usually led to, and what the end result of Nicholas's lovemaking was leading to for her, caused Mara to free herself and jerk out of his arms.

Nicholas's irritated glance followed her velvet-clad figure across the room, noticing her nervousness as she sorted through her gloves and studiously avoided looking at him.

"I'm not sure I shall accompany you this evening. I'm not feeling well," she spoke suddenly.

"I see I haven't completely persuaded you from your fit of temper. We must soon discuss this tiresome tendency of yours. Shall I meet you downstairs in, say, ten minutes?" Nicholas ordered softly. When she nodded, he gave her a puzzled look and left the room.

❧

The rains had let up as their carriage made its way from Beaumarais to Sandrose along the seldom used road between the two great plantations. Celeste had declined to attend but had allowed Nicole to accompany them. Wearing her best party dress of white silk tulle embroidered with tiny flowers and tied with a red ribbon belt, her red satin dancing slippers tapping constantly on the floor of the carriage, she kept up a continual chatter, uncaring that no one bothered to answer her. Etienne, acting as chaperone, sat back in his corner of the carriage in patient silence, making a comment only when politeness decreed. Nicholas, on the other hand, didn't feel so inclined, and maintained his silence until the carriage turned up the drive to Sandrose, the team of horses slowing their pace as they neared the house.

To Mara, seeing it for the first time, Sandrose looked as if it had risen out of the swamps like a giant crab. It appeared to squat grotesquely on its many brick pilings, the flickering torches along the drive casting giant shadows over the narrow, two-storied structure. Light poured forth from the many French windows across the galleried front of the house, while faint strains of music and voices could be heard floating down from the high veranda encircling it.

Liveried servants lined the steep flight of steps to the double-doored entrance. As Nicholas escorted her inside, Mara glanced up at him, curious of his reaction to seeing Amaryllis. But his face was expressionless except for that sardonic smile.

Mara's cape was spirited away and she found herself standing beside Nicholas beneath the warm glow of the hundreds of candles burning brightly in the wall sconces and crystal chandeliers overhead. A grand staircase, the banister decorated with trailing roses, stretched up to the second floor and was crowded with giggling, gossiping young girls rushing up and down from the privacy of dressing rooms provided for their preening.

"Nicholas!" Amaryllis's cool voice greeted them as she swept toward them in an elegant gown of turquoise, the bright color of her hair no less a shining gold than the brocaded silk threads in her dress. A spray of diamonds sparkled in her soft curls, while matching necklace and earrings adorned her pale, white throat and ears. Suddenly Mara was thankful for her borrowed rubies.

"I was beginning to wonder if you had lost your way, or perhaps your nerve," she pouted as she slid her arm into Nicholas's. "*Bon soir.* Etienne. Nicole, how charmingly sweet you are looking, my child," she greeted them, her praise effectively stripping Nicole of her confidence. She saw herself now as a mere schoolgirl beside Amaryllis's sophisticated elegance.

"Everyone is absolutely dying to see who my special guest is, for no one knows you have returned, mon cher. It really will be priceless. Oh, you must meet Edward," she said suddenly as she caught sight of a man standing hesitantly in the doorway, watching them intently. At her imperious gesture he came forward. "This is Edward Ashford, a very good friend of the family," she introduced him. As Amaryllis hesitated slightly over the introduction, Mara noticed the surprised look on Edward Ashford's face.

He was shorter and stockier than Nicholas, and older. The receding hairline was beginning to show traces of gray. In another five years he would be quite bejowled, but there was an irrepressible twinkle in his brown eyes as he greeted them with a broad smile and extended his hand in welcome to Nicholas. But Mara thought the twinkle dimmed slightly as he registered the name.

"Nicholas de Montaigne-Chantale?" he repeated. "Of Beaumarais?" he asked almost dumbly, and Mara felt an instant's pity for this man, now faced with the realization that he could never compete against Nicholas for Amaryllis. Mara could see it was a very bitter pill.

"Yes," Nicholas replied with a smile of pure enjoyment, his green eyes showing a devilish gleam. "Didn't Amaryllis tell you that I returned just in time to ruin her plans to purchase my home? I'm afraid I've inconvenienced her greatly."

"No, Amaryllis neglected to tell me," Edward Ashford answered slowly. "But then, I've just arrived today from

New Orleans, and what with all her party plans, I suppose she forgot." He said this with a shrug, but there was reproof in his face as he glanced at Amaryllis. "Of course, I've never quite understood her desire to buy your plantation when she has a fine one of her own. The land, yes. But the house? No, that I can't understand," Edward said with an indulgent smile at Amaryllis. "But then, I'm a hardheaded businessman who never lets sentimentality rule my mind."

"Ashford?" Nicholas pondered for a second. "The banker?"

Edward Ashford beamed proudly. "One and the same. Opened one in St. Louis last year, and making plans for one in Natchez next year. I'll have a whole string of banks along the Mississippi one day." Mara now realized why he might indeed be a successful businessman, for his genial and mild-mannered outward appearance actually masked a deceptive strength and quick mind, the gentle brown eyes missing nothing.

"You shall have to begin to court Nicholas, Edward," Etienne said with a sly smile of amusement at the banker's sharpening interest. He explained, "Nicholas has returned from California a very wealthy man. But I don't suppose your banks would have room for all his gold, eh?"

"You've recently come from California, Monsieur de Montaigne-Chantale?" Edward inquired with keen curiosity, his opinion of this particular Creole undergoing a quick revision. Here was a man who actually had money in his pocket. "I would be interested in discussing your adventure, m'sieu— especially if you tell it truthfully and without making it sound too exciting," Edward pleaded with a suffering smile, "for I have been trying for over two years now to talk my young brother out of sailing for California."

"I'm afraid a man must find that out for himself, Monsieur Ashford," Nicholas told him dryly, "for the lust for gold and adventure burns too strong to be extinguished by words."

"Well, you must speak with him anyway," Ashford continued. "And please, call me Edward," he invited with an ingratiating grin. "I do hope we might find the time to discuss your financial situation. I know of several investments you might be interested in, and of course," he added as if the thought had just come to him, "if you are newly arrived here in Louisiana, you'll want to open an account. I think you and I could come to a mutually satisfying agreement."

"Please, Monsieur Ashford," Nicholas replied with a dismissive look. "I wouldn't dream of insulting my hostess, or the ladies, by engaging in business while being so graciously entertained. I think Nicole grows impatient standing here while she sees her friends dancing in the other room. Shall we join the others?" he inquired softly, his manner stopping any further mention of business.

"Oh, Edward, you've not met Mademoiselle O'Flynn," Amaryllis quickly eased the tension, but her pale blue eyes seemed to reflect the hardness of the diamonds around her throat when she noticed for the first time the rubies glowing against Mara's breast.

"No, I've not had that pleasure, mademoiselle," Edward returned gallantly as he bent over her hand. "And I doubt whether there has ever been a lovelier beauty than yours to grace the parishes of Louisiana," he complimented as he assessed her in a single sweep, no doubt setting her worth as his pudgy hand lingered against hers for just a second too long.

Amaryllis frowned with displeasure at his fulsome flattery. She caught sight of an attractive man making his way toward the group, and with a smile of triumph that widened into one of excessive welcome, she reached out and captured his arm, turning his attention to Mara O'Flynn.

"You've not met Edward's brother. Carson Ashford," Amaryllis declared as she maneuvered him closer to the red velvet figure, "this is Mara O'Flynn, and she's been to California. You must get her to tell you all about it. Now, if you'll excuse us, I must introduce Nicholas to the rest of my guests. Come along, mon cher," Amaryllis neatly separated the group, leaving Mara to handle the ardent glow in Carson Ashford's brown eyes.

After only a moment's conversation with him Mara had concluded with unerring accuracy that the man was a pretentious boor who was long overdue for a crushing set-down.

Mara raised an eyebrow superciliously as he touched her arm with familiarity and handed her a glass of champagne. His eyes roved over her bare shoulders with speculation.

"And here I was envying ol' Edward," he said with a leer, "but ma'am, you make Amaryllis pale by comparison. Is it true that you've actually been out to California? Heard tell there aren't many women out there, excepting for some sunbonnets. Meaning no offense, mademoiselle," Carson said with an odious little smile, "but you sure don't look like any pioneer woman I've ever seen! I don't believe I saw who accompanied you here this evening, ma'am?" he inquired. His eyes never left her face, letting her know that he had every intention of becoming her escort for the evening.

"With that man over there," Mara said lazily, nodding her sleek head in the direction of Nicholas.

Carson glanced around carelessly, but as his eyes came into contact with the green eyes staring so intently at him from across the room, the bluster and swagger seemed to escape him like hot air from a deflated balloon.

While he stood there looking stricken, Mara made her escape and wandered off into a crowd milling aimlessly around the room. Nicole was holding court and gossiping with a group of her contemporaries on a sofa in the corner of the parlor while, across the room, Mara caught sight of Etienne's silver head bent attentively over a bejeweled woman who seemed to be holding a one-sided conversation.

Although Sandrose was not near so beautiful and gracious an establishment as Beaumarais, it had been better maintained. The rugs were obviously new, their colors still bright. The wallpaper was not faded. There was a feeling of gloss over everything in the room. Undeniably it was an elegant room, but not one that exuded warmth. Vases of exotic blooms filled the mantel and tables and blended with the heavy scent of many perfumes. Across the wide hallway Mara could see couples dancing in the ballroom where the orchestra played a gentle waltz. Mara steered clear of the small groups of laughing, chatting young matrons, the disapproving dowagers seated in chairs along the sides of the room as they kept watch over their granddaughters or over stray males who emerged from the smoke-filled study where the gentlemen had gathered to drink and joke. Mara contented herself with sampling some of the hors d'oeuvres being passed around by the waiters and sipping her champagne as she watched with the objective interest of an outsider the various dramas being enacted around the room. Mara had just finished a small, hot patty filled with oysters when she felt someone beside her and looked up to see Nicholas smiling sardonically down at her.

"You seem to find something amusing, my dear," he commented softly.

"I should really be grateful to you for bringing me this evening. I've always wondered how the other half lived," Mara remarked mockingly, a look of amusement in her eyes as she added, "and just think how this experience will help my acting the next time I play a society lady."

"You, my sweet, could be giving some of these women lessons in deportment and the fine airs a genteel lady should adopt at all times," Nicholas laughed.

As Nicholas stood beside her Mara became aware of curious stares being sent both openly and discreetly their way, some admiring, most hostile. "Could it be me dress, d'ye think?" Mara asked as she pretended concern.

Nicholas stared at her blankly for a moment before understanding dawned. He followed her amused glance to a middle-aged woman whose thin body vibrated with indignation as she stared with imperious disdain at Nicholas's tall figure.

"I'm afraid, my dear, that not all people are of a forgiving nature. Quite a few of the disapproving are here this evening," Nicholas told her quietly as he allowed his eyes to roam freely over the rudely staring woman's person. She turned a bright red with mortification. "Some of these people never forgive or forget," Nicholas commented impersonally as he glanced around the room.

"But they will have to when they hear that your father sent for you," Mara reassured him. She hoped he wasn't being hurt.

Nicholas covered her hand briefly before he said with a derisory look around the room, "It wouldn't matter even if I paraded the real murderer around the room. They would still prefer to believe the worst of me. It makes for far more interesting gossip. I have been cast in the role of villain, and that is where they will keep me. They are all probably dying to know just who the devil you are, my dear, and just what the relationship is between us. Come," Nicholas said abruptly as if suddenly making up his mind. Taking her champagne glass and placing it on a tray passing nearby, he pulled her with him from the room. "Shall we give them something new to discuss?" he asked as he swung her into his arms. Their closely moving figures joined the other dancers. "Let them talk about your beautiful silken ankles for a change, and the shocking manner in which I hold you pressed so close to my body," Nicholas laughed in Mara's ear as he swirled her around the ballroom, Mara's red velvet skirts billowing and revealing a tantalizing length of silken leg.

Around midnight supper was served on a huge oak table covered in a rose damask tablecloth. An ornate epergne, holding assorted sweets and flowers, sat squarely in the center. One end of the buffet held stacks of plates and silver, while the rest of the table was filled with silver bowls of salads, tureens of soups, large platters of whole turkeys, roasts, and hams, brimming dishes of vegetables and accompanying sauces, and rich cheeses. Should the diners still have the appetite, pies, cakes with thick icings, creamy custards, and mounds of ice cream were within arm's reach. Champagne and wine flowed freely.

After the guests had eaten their fill, the orchestra struck up a livelier tune and the dancing continued until the early dawn hours.

Mara stepped out on the gallery after a while and breathed deeply of the cold, wet air. It was so stuffy and crowded inside. She needed just a few minutes respite from the constant chatter, as well as a break from the persistent attentions of Carson Ashford. He couldn't seem to keep his hands to himself. Mara had not seen Nicholas since being separated from him shortly after they'd dined. She wondered how much longer he intended to stay, hoping he hadn't planned on participating in the traditional gumbo and black coffee she heard was always served at dawn.

Mara sighed, thinking she'd better return, for it was quite cold and damp and she didn't have her wrap. Mara remembered seeing Etienne in the parlor and she was thinking about seeking him out when she heard voices from the partially opened door behind her.

"Why, it's absolutely scandalous, my dear. Can you imagine it? After all these years he's come back!" an incredulous voice demanded. "He is a handsome devil, isn't he, Marie?"

"Some might think he is. But that's not surprising, is it?" Marie snickered. "Who *but* a devil would shoot his own brother?"

"I'm surprised he had the nerve to come back. But then he always did do the most daring and outrageous things, my dear," Marie spoke again. "But he will find it pretty rough going this time. Some people have not forgotten, or forgiven him. The Fouches won't acknowledge him, nor will the Bruniers. In fact, they left early. They all remember him well, let me tell you."

How right Nicholas had been. No matter what he did, they would never let him forget. It was so unfair, she thought angrily, wishing she could slap some sense into those gossiping women.

"Of course Amaryllis says that he was invited back by his papa, old Philippe, but who can say. He's dead. Besides, everyone knew he wasn't the same toward the end. Did you hear that Nicholas bought Beaumarais from Celeste? It's incredible."

"And what do you think Amaryllis said to that?"

Mara cocked her head to hear the answer, her interest caught despite herself.

"Well, I'm not really sure. If it had been anyone but Nicholas, then I'd say she'd have felt murderous, but..."

"Exactly," the other woman continued, and Mara could just see the exchanged looks passing between them. "We all know how she once felt about him. They were lovers, you know. Yes, I'm sure of it. And now that he's back, and they are both unmarried…And they say he's a millionaire. Struck it rich in the gold fields out in California. And, my dear, do you know, they say he even has calluses on his hands. He actually worked out there, like some common…*laborer*," she added, her voice full of horror.

"Well, I don't know what could stand in their way now."

"Perhaps that dark-haired beauty in red velvet he arrived with, and who happens to be his guest at Beaumarais," Marie's voice spoke coyly. "Amaryllis was looking quite put out. He danced so many waltzes with her and he sat with her at supper. I heard she is wearing his own mother's jewels."

Mara automatically touched the rubies around her throat, her face burning.

"I was expecting to hear an announcement of Amaryllis's engagement to Edward Ashford this evening. I mean, my dear, he is paying for everything, even the clothes on Amaryllis's back. I would think he is expecting a return on his investment," Marie said archly.

"If I were him I wouldn't be holding my breath. I just saw Amaryllis and that devil step outside, and after the way they've been looking at each other all evening, well…"

Mara moved away from the door, wishing she hadn't eavesdropped. She walked swiftly along the dark gallery. Seeing something move ahead of her she stopped and stepped deeper into the shadows. She was shivering with cold as she stood there, but she couldn't move as she watched the black shadow break apart and turn into two people. The two figures moved together toward the revealing glow from one of the French windows, the light catching the turquoise of the woman's gown. The tall figure of the man remained dark. He was dressed totally in black. Mara saw his face for just a second as he glanced her way, the candlelight shining on those hawklike features she'd come to love so dearly.

When Mara entered the ballroom moments later, couples were circling the floor in slow, sweeping steps. She remained unnoticed for an instant before being spotted by the eager Carson Ashford. He rudely left the side of the young girl he'd been engaged in conversation with and hurried over to Mara's side, stopping only briefly to snatch a goblet of champagne from a tray. With a great show of ceremony he presented her with the champagne, acting as though it were his heart.

"I'm hoping to bribe a smile out of you, mademoiselle," he said softly as his eyes lingered on her soft lips. He swallowed his surprise as he saw the mouth widen in a half-smile that tantalized him as the golden eyes looked deeply into his.

"And how could I resist one so kind as you, m'sieu?" Mara replied with a provocative look.

"I should like to be more than just kind, mademoiselle," Carson said thickly, his eyes feasting on the enticing curve of breast above the red velvet.

"Please, if we are to be friends, you must call me Mara," she invited with a seductive smile now curving her lips.

"Mara," he repeated, his eyes glowing with the privilege. Under the heady excitement he dared to reach out and touch her cheek in a light caress. "Would you dance with me, Mara?"

Mara nodded slightly. Setting down her untouched goblet, she moved into his embrace and they joined the dancers.

Nicholas watched as the two figures moved past him, his green eyes never leaving the red-velvet figure as she waltzed around the room, her slender ankles showing every so often. Nicholas had seen the intimate gesture made by that besotted fool and felt a strange anger rise in him. As he watched her smile up at the flushed face of Carson Ashford, he saw the old Mara, the seductress out to ensnare some poor, unsuspecting, lovesick man's heart. Carson Ashford, no matter how accomplished a rake he thought himself, didn't stand a chance if Mara set out to capture his affections. Just a look from those sultry, golden eyes could make a man burn, his lusts eating away at him until he would gladly give his life to feel the soft, fullness of her lips beneath his. Wearing that damned red dress like a matador waving a red cape at an enraged bull, she dared a man to take what he wanted.

Nicholas's eyes traveled on to the golden head of Amaryllis. She was still a very beautiful woman. He had wondered about her all these years, sometimes even imagining them together.

But now that he was here, and there was a very real possibility of that happening, he found that Amaryllis left him cold. What he had found attractive and maddening as a hot-blooded young man, no longer had the ability to arouse him.

Mara O'Flynn's delicate scent remained strong in his memory despite the cloying fragrance Amaryllis wore. When he kissed Amaryllis, he felt none of that wildfire sweetness he did when caressing Mara. Could he possibly be in *love* with Mara? In sudden amazement, he felt jealous rage whip through him. Carson Ashford was pressing his hot lips against Mara's ear. Nicholas's smile widened, but it was not a nice smile. What a weapon he'd be putting into Mara's hands if she knew he had fallen for her, just like all the other fools.

Nicholas shook his dark head. She must not know. He would be a fool if he let himself fall prey to Mara. For how could he ever know what she truly felt? Would she be merely seeking revenge against him if he revealed his feelings to her? No matter what she might say, he would always have doubt.

With a purposeful stride he made his way through the dancing couples to where Mara and her ardent admirer were waltzing, and with a cavalier tap on the shorter man's shoulder, he cut in, taking Mara away from her gaping-mouthed partner before he could raise an argument.

"You seem to have found yet another lapdog to amuse you, my sweet," Nicholas said softly as his arms tightened around her waist. He brought her closer than was considered proper even for the waltz.

Mara stared up at his strong chin and profile. "No less amusin' than the little cat you've been stroking all evening," Mara retorted shortly, still smarting from what she had witnessed.

Nicholas glanced down. "Jealous? I think I shall have to beware of *your* claws rather than Amaryllis's."

Mara looked away, refusing to be baited. "Don't be absurd. I should have to care about you to feel jealousy, and since I've no great passion for your kisses, nor patience to stand in line for them, the whole idea is ridiculous," she said.

Mara nearly lost her step as Nicholas suddenly swung her around, his hand tightening painfully around her fingers as his other hand bit into her waist. Mara glared up at him impotently, wondering why he should react so strangely. Then, glancing around, she saw Amaryllis dancing closely in Edward Ashford's arms and knew Nicholas must be feeling the pangs of jealousy as he saw his beloved laughing up into the rich American's face.

It was nearly dawn when, despite Amaryllis's pleas that they stay for an early breakfast, they headed back to Beaumarais. Mara stared tiredly for a few minutes out of the carriage window and into the chilly darkness of the early morning hours.

Beaumarais was in silent darkness as well when they pulled up before the entrance, having let Etienne out near his quarters. As their carriage came to a halt, the front door was thrown wide and a welcoming stream of light spread across the wide steps as the butler stood patiently awaiting them.

"Go on to bed, Daniel," Nicholas ordered the grizzle-haired old man who managed, despite the lateness of the hour, to stand rigidly erect. "Send everyone else to bed as well. We won't need them."

Daniel nodded, and Mara thought he seemed to give a sigh of relief. But like Jamie, his pride wouldn't allow him to admit even to himself that he might be tired. Only Nicole's ebullience was showing no signs of faltering as she hurried up the staircase, still humming one of the waltz tunes from the evening.

"Oh, mademoiselle," Nicole cried out, making no effort to lower her voice. "I have no one to unhook me. Could you possibly be so kind and assist me?" she asked with her small hand raised beseechingly.

Mara sighed. Turning back toward Nicole, she left Nicholas.

"Oh, mademoiselle, it was magnificent, *n'est-ce pas?*" Nicole breathed excitedly as she spun around the room she shared with the sleeping Damaris, whose auburn head was barely visible beneath the silk comforter. "I shall give wonderful parties like that when I am mistress of my own home. We do not have so many here anymore. But once, Beaumarais was famous for its balls and grand picnics on the lawns."

Mara quickly and efficiently unhooked the chattering Nicole from her gown. With a warning to go to sleep before her beauty faded, she left Nicole frantically struggling into her nightdress as she shot worried glances into the mirror.

It wasn't until Mara had nearly reached her own room that she realized that without Belle she would have the devil of a time unhooking herself. She wasn't about to disturb Jamie. Mara was reaching out to open her door when a tanned hand closed over the doorknob ahead of hers and Nicholas pushed open her door, stepping aside politely for her to precede him into the room.

Mara eyed him suspiciously for a moment as she stood in the middle of the doorway.

"It grows late," Nicholas spoke quietly.

"I'm well aware of that, m'sieu, so I shall bid you good night," Mara returned just as softly as she swept past him and into her room.

"And do you intend to sleep in that damned dress?" Nicholas inquired. Closing the door behind him, he followed Mara into the room. Mara turned around in surprise at his tone. He seemed to be looking for a chance to argue. "I'm tired, Nicholas, and I have no intention of engaging in a senseless quarrel with you. You may either assist me, or not, but I'm going to bed."

"Indeed, my dear," Nicholas said very softly, "that is exactly what I had in mind."

Mara felt his hands unhook her gown and then move to the clasp of the ruby necklace. Mara removed the earrings and bracelets and, turning around, handed them to him. "Thank you, Nicholas. It was an honor to wear them this evening," she surprised him by saying graciously.

Nicholas nodded slightly, and then, without even bothering to say good night, he walked from the room. Mara bit her trembling lips, then quickly disrobed, spending several minutes brushing her long hair free of tangles, until it spread out over her shoulders in smooth waves. She stared at her reflection in the mirror for a moment before getting up and padding in her bare feet over to the long French windows. Pulling aside the heavy drapery, Mara stared out into the blackness of the night. She heard a distant sound of thunder, then a flash of lightning cut through the sky overhead. Mara shivered. Letting the curtain fall back in place, she untied the sash around her waist and tossed her silk robe across a nearby chair before climbing into bed. The cold sheets caused her to shiver again.

"Shall I warm you up, my sweet?" Nicholas spoke quietly from the darkness of the room. Then he was there in the bed beside her, his warm body pressing against hers and warming her as he had promised.

"Nicholas," Mara murmured in surprise as she felt his hot breath against her face, then his caressing hands moving with familiar boldness over her breasts and hips. "Ni—" Mara began, only to have his name smothered as his mouth took hers in a long arousing kiss.

"So you feel no passion for my kisses?" he whispered as he lifted his mouth from her parted lips. His hands roved over her and entwined in her long hair, twisting the silken strands through his fingers as he held her face captive and rained kiss after kiss across it, closing her eyes with the touch of his lips as Mara became drugged with sensuous pleasure.

❧

The fire in the hearth was little more than smoldering ashes as Mara stared into the dusky silence of the room. The only sound she heard was the deep breathing of Nicholas beside her, his head heavy against her breasts as he slept peacefully. Mara rubbed her cheek against the softness of his hair, and moving slightly, she felt his warm body pressed closely along the length of hers.

"Oh, I do love you, Nicholas," Mara whispered, her lips moving in a caress against his hair before her thoughts grew drowsy and she drifted into an uneasy sleep.

❧

Nicholas pushed back his chair and stretched. The last drawer of his father's desk, and still no sign of a diary or a will. He stood up and, walking over to the windows, stared out morosely on the wet lawn. The storm had struck them early this morning, and for most of the day it had been raining steadily, but now there was a break in the clouds to the south and it looked as if the storm was over.

"Uncle Nicholas?" Paddy said hesitantly from the doorway.

Nicholas smiled as he turned and met Paddy's huge brown eyes. "Yes?"

"I was wondering if I could set up my soldiers in here. I can't play in my room 'cause they're all in there dusting and cleaning and giggling," Paddy added in disgust. "They kept knocking over my troops, then setting them up in the wrong position. Besides, you've got a fire in here. It's nice and warm," he added with a wistful look at the crackling flames.

"Go ahead," Nicholas consented. "I'm through for now, but don't touch my desk," he warned as Paddy hurried into the room with his treasured box of soldiers beneath his arm.

"I promise," Paddy said excitedly as he fell to his knees and began to unload his armies.

Nicholas watched for a moment in amusement, remembering how much enjoyment he had once had playing with toy soldiers. Then as he recognized the arrogant tilt of Paddy's small dark head as he stationed his generals along the front line of his troops, he remembered another dark head of the night before and knew he'd never trade his pleasures of the present for those of childhood.

Nicholas moved into the hall, intent upon finding himself a brandy, when he heard laughter. Recognizing the amused voice, he followed the sound into the parlor. He paused as he saw Mara sitting beside Etienne on the sofa, a cup of tea raised to the lips he'd devoured with his the night before. There was no visible sign of his possession of her, and suddenly he felt irritated by her coolness and apparent inviolability. One would think she were as innocent as a nun, Nicholas thought resentfully as he watched her sitting, so demurely, in a plain silver gray merino dress.

"I was just telling Mara about Lady Annabelle who drank too much and fell into the Grand Canal in Venice. No one missed her, you see, and so the gondola continued on without her. Luckily, before she could drown, another gondola came along and rescued her. Only it was filled with vegetables and farm animals being brought in for sale. It was quite a sight, my dear," Etienne chuckled with remembered delight, "for she was such an obnoxious harridan anyway, and after that no one could quite look her in the face without seeing those pens of squealing pigs all around her."

Nicholas poured himself a brandy and sat perched along the arm of the sofa, his thigh riding next to Mara's shoulder, his arm lying along the back of the sofa and just touching her neck. "Doesn't Mara remind you, Etienne, of one of those Italian beauties painted centuries ago?" Nicholas said conversationally. Mara was sensitive to the biting quality in his voice. "Someone who is part Madonna, and part—" Nicholas paused, listening intently for a moment before getting to his feet. The sound of horses' hooves and barking dogs grew closer. Nicholas opened the French windows and stepped outside as a young boy ran up to him. The fellow pointed out to the drive where a group of riders sat impatiently calming their mounts. Mara glanced at Etienne questioningly, but he shrugged his shoulders and, with a wry grimace, got to his feet to see what the commotion was about. He led Mara out onto the gallery. They stood slightly behind Nicholas, staring at the group of riders and hounds.

One of the riders broke free from the others when she spotted Nicholas and rode up closer to the gallery. "Care to join us?" Amaryllis invited.

"What are you hunting?" Nicholas asked softly, his eyes registering distaste as he eyed the heavy-set riders who seemed to be in charge of the baying hounds. Several of her guests from the night before were in this party, including Carson Ashford, who was valiantly trying to catch Mara's eye.

"Runaways," Amaryllis pronounced in cold contempt. "A whole family of them took off late last night. They can't have gotten far, and these hounds have already gotten their scent. I'll have them in less than an hour," she predicted. A hard light grew in her pale eyes as she snapped a wicked-looking whip against her gloved palm.

"I think not," Nicholas replied as he indolently leaned against one of the columns.

"You haven't changed, Nicholas," Amaryllis spoke disparagingly, shaking her head. "You never did like tracking down runaways. Of course, I do prefer hunting fox. It's a much more exciting chase, for at least the fox has some chance of escape and gives us a good race. But these fools just stumble through the swamp leaving a trail a mile wide behind them, and if the gators don't get them, I always do. It's no contest at all.

"And, of course, they never do it again. They can't get very far hobbling along on one foot. I don't know why they bother, or what they expect to find in New Orleans or upriver somewhere. They've got my brand on them, anyone can see that they aren't free. Of course that doesn't seem to stop some of the Northerners turning a blind eye to it," Amaryllis complained. With a regretful look at Nicholas, her eyes narrowing as she saw Mara, Amaryllis lifted a casual hand in farewell and whipped her horse into a gallop down the drive.

Appalled, Mara hugged herself, shivering as she thought of those slaves being hunted down like animals. Amaryllis, Mara suspected, rather enjoyed the whole thing.

"Come, let us forget this unpleasantness," Etienne advised kindly as he guided Mara back inside, Nicholas following without a backward glance.

❧

"Surrender, or face destruction," Paddy ordered as his troops surrounded the enemy army. Kneeling in the large leather chair in front of Nicholas's desk, Paddy surveyed his regiment's position on the battlefield, deciding that desperate measures must be taken if his side was to be victorious.

Climbing down from the chair he scooped up several toy soldiers and transferred them across the room to the window-sill where he perched them rather precariously near the edge. As the battle progressed and further troops were rerouted to the top of the make-believe escarpment, one of his soldiers lost his footing and became a casualty of the war. Paddy sighed in exasperation as his soldier hit the floor. Getting to his feet, he stomped over and retrieved the wounded soldier. With the toe of the soldier's boot broken off he couldn't stand properly, so Paddy wedged him in the crack along the sill. But as he pressed the soldier's heel deeper into the crack, it widened and began to slide back to reveal a space beneath the flat surface of the windowsill.

Paddy gasped in surprise, his mouth forming a soundless circle as he stared at the secret compartment. "You'll get a medal for this, lieutenant," he declared as he put down the toy soldier and began to push back the wooden panel.

Paddy peered down into the hollow sill, but it was dark and he couldn't see much. Sticking his small hand down inside he felt around the bottom, his eyes lighting up as his fingers came into contact with something.

"Secret orders!" Paddy whispered in triumph as he withdrew the small leather-bound book and several documents tied with ribbon. They looked very important. He replaced them in the secret compartment without even glancing at the contents. Then, reaching down, he grabbed the wounded soldier and placed him on top of them to stand guard. No one would know of this secret hiding place, he vowed. He jumped back into the center of his armies and resumed the battle with renewed vigor.

"You still playing with those toy soldiers?" Damaris demanded as she sauntered into the room, her frilled drawers just peeking out below the hem of her plaid skirt.

"It's raining," Paddy replied unperturbed.

"The sun's come out," Damaris informed him airily.

"So?"

Damaris eyed him calculatingly, a secret smile curving her lips. "So maybe you might be interested in doing something besides this…child's play?" she hinted. There was an if-you-dare note in her voice.

Paddy glanced up. "You wouldn't know about playing with soldiers. You're just a girl. Girls play with dolls," Paddy told her patronizingly as he bent his dark head back to his soldiers, missing the brief flaring of anger in Damaris's eyes. "Besides, I have a secret that even you don't know about, I bet," Paddy taunted. "And I'm only going to tell Uncle Nicholas about it."

"Then I guess you're not interested in going for a ride on Sorcier?" she said indifferently. She started to leave, one of her half-boots carelessly knocking over one of Paddy's soldiers.

Paddy's head shot up. "You're going to take Sorcier out?" he demanded in disbelief even as admiration glowed in his eyes. "But Uncle Nicholas said you weren't supposed to ride him, ever again."

"Oh, pooh to what *he* has to say," Damaris dismissed Nicholas with a shake of her auburn braids. "Sorcier is my horse and I can take him out whenever I wish, *and*," she paused enticingly, "I can ask anyone I want to ride with me on him. Of course, that certain person would have to be pretty brave and not be frightened of horses."

"I'm not afraid!" Paddy exclaimed as he jumped up and hurried through his soldiers, knocking them over as he ran after Damaris's retreating figure. "Will you really give me a ride?"

Damaris turned, eyeing him doubtfully. "I might."

"Oh, please, Damaris, please," Paddy begged as he followed on her heels from the house.

Mara watched their progress across the yard from the gallery outside her room. The rain-drenched air felt good. Mara wrapped her cashmere shawl closer around her shoulders and frowned slightly when she noticed Paddy hadn't put on his greatcoat and Damaris had on only a short velvet jacket over her skirt and blouse. She was about to call out, then decided against it, for they were probably going directly to the stables to see the puppies or the new foal.

Mara walked back inside, and closing the doors behind her, she made her way to the fireplace where a good-sized fire was burning. Holding out her chilled hands, she rubbed them together before the flames, and lifting her skirts, she let the warmth penetrate to her legs.

She sank down into a chair near the fire and wondered,

again, what she was going to do. She couldn't just stay around until her condition became obvious. After last night she was more concerned than ever, for Nicholas was still not tired of making love to her. Mara pressed her fingertips against her temples. She couldn't understand Nicholas at all. Why was he continuing to keep her here? It was painfully obvious that he could have Amaryllis if he wanted her, so why keep Mara around? Mara stared into the flames, deciding on a last attempt to persuade Nicholas to allow her to leave. If he would not, then she would escape Beaumarais without his permission.

"I knocked twice, but you're brooding so deeply that you didn't even hear me," Nicholas spoke beside Mara, the sound of his voice startling her. She jumped to her feet.

He was dressed for riding, his boots shiny and black and reflecting the jumping flames of the fire. "You have a very guilty expression on your face, my dear," he spoke quietly. "Have you reason to feel so? What devious plans have you been devising in here by yourself?" he asked, a warning note in his voice.

Mara swallowed nervously. There was something so intimidating about him sometimes that it was impossible to meet his eye. That made her seem even guiltier.

"I want to leave Beaumarais, Nicholas," Mara said quickly, her golden eyes widening with an almost pleading look.

"I thought we'd already gone over this argument?"

Mara glared up. "Why?" she demanded. "Why keep me here any longer when I'm sure the widow would be more than happy to warm your bed. Or is it that you are still unsure of her and wish to make her jealous? You flaunt me before her with the de Montaigne-Chantale jewels around my neck while you play your sadistic games. I think it's despicable."

Nicholas laughed. "Now that is something, coming from you, Mara O'Flynn. But I don't know why you should be so impatient, my dear, for if, as you say, my kisses mean so little to you, why should you mind staying as a guest in a lovely home, having nothing better to do than to worry about which gown to wear to dinner?" Nicholas asked. "And yet here you are sounding like a jealous woman being mistreated by the man she loves," he ended silkily, his eyes glowing.

"I just don't like being used, that's all," Mara denied the truth of his words. "The theater is my life and I'm anxious to return to it. Besides," Mara added, her tawny eyes looking seductively up into his as she caressed his hard cheek with the back of her hand, "how am I ever goin' to be findin' meself a rich husband stuck way back here in the swamps?"

Mara was startled to feel his jaw clench beneath her hand. His fingers wrapped viselike around her wrist as he lowered his face closer to hers. She could feel his breath against her lips. "Someday, Mara O'Flynn," he bit out in a barely audible whisper that made Mara think more of a growl, "you're going to push me too far. And then, my dear, you're going to wish you'd never opened that insolent mouth of yours."

"So what else is new? You've never spared my feelings before. Or maybe *you* fear pushing *me* too far, and then you'll be hearing a few painful truths about yourself," Mara taunted.

But before she could utter another word, his mouth had closed over hers, shutting off her tirade more effectively than any angry words he might have spoken. It wasn't a gentle kiss, for there was a brutality in it that hurt her far more than his words could have. It was a hot and searing kiss, an insulting kiss without any real warmth.

Just as suddenly she was free of his embrace. They stared angrily at each other for countless seconds, then Nicholas had dropped his arms and, turning on his heel, walked from the room.

Mara stared blindly after his disappearing figure, her hands clenched painfully at her sides as she began to shake.

She was still standing in the middle of the room a few minutes later when she heard voices raised in anger coming from the front lawn. Stepping out on the gallery, Mara leaned over the railing to see Nicholas in conversation with several young stableboys. They were stepping nervously from foot to foot and looking around at each other as if stepping the blame for something.

Nicholas seemed to tower over them in his black boots

and narrow riding breeches, his hands placed firmly on his hips as he listened. Something must have caught his attention then, because he turned his head as if listening to a distant sound. Turning around, he stood waiting. Mara craned her neck to look along the drive but she could see little. Suddenly a flash of color caught her eye, and as she stared in amazement, the big bay, with two children clinging to his back, jumped the railings of the fence edging the drive, then shot onto the spacious lawn and trotted toward the front of the house. Mara could scarcely believe her eyes as she looked down at Paddy's dark, windblown curls and his thin arms wrapped around Damaris's small waist. His legs were sticking out like matchsticks as he bumped up and down on the rump of the frisky stallion. But before Damaris reached the path, she caught sight of Nicholas standing before the house, his face grim with angry silence as he stared at the two small figures perched atop Sorcier's broad back.

Mara's breath caught in her throat as she recognized that look of cold rage on Nicholas's hardened features, and knew that no thought of leniency would enter his mind as he punished them for disobeying his orders. Damaris and Paddy had earned his full wrath and would now pay for their defiance. With the thought of getting to Paddy first, Mara hurried along the gallery to the outside stairs, hoping she could get there in time.

Damaris stared down at Nicholas unrepentantly, not showing a flicker of the fear that was causing her heart to race alarmingly in her small breast, and whether it was this fear that was transmitted to the big horse, or the excitement of having too many people come too close to him, he reacted violently. Rearing backward, his forelegs pawing the air viciously, he unseated the startled Paddy. Nicholas reached out and scooped Paddy before he hit the ground, Paddy's frightened yelp echoing to Mara as she turned the corner of the house and saw him falling from the back of the big bay. All she could think of were the heavy hooves coming down with deadly accuracy on both Nicholas and Paddy.

Mara stopped short as she saw Nicholas swing Paddy out of reach of the horse's rage.

"I thought I told you, Damaris, not to ride Sorcier," Nicholas said, his voice vibrating with fury. "Paddy could have been killed or maimed for life because of your recklessness."

Damaris stared down at Nicholas in growing fear, knowing deep down inside that she shouldn't have taken Paddy up with her on Sorcier's back. But she wouldn't admit that she couldn't control the big stallion. "You aren't my father! Sorcier's mine, and I can ride him whenever I wish," Damaris defended herself even as she fought with all her strength to keep control over the bay.

Nicholas saw the determined effort she was making to keep her seat on the spirited horse, but he knew it was only a matter of seconds before her grip weakened and the reins became slack. Then Sorcier would be off. Nicholas could sense it in the way his eyes rolled.

Nicholas reached out to grab hold of the reins. Damaris, seeing his intentions, jerked back on them, causing Sorcier to snort angrily and rear up once again. Nicholas swore beneath his breath as he sidestepped the flying hooves. Moving quickly, he pulled Damaris from Sorcier's back, swinging her to the ground before she knew what had happened. As Sorcier felt the disturbing weight leave his back, he began to settle down. Now he was content to stand easy while one of the more-experienced grooms patted his sweating neck and talked soothingly to the big bay before leading him away.

Nicholas still had hold of Damaris, and as he felt her squirming in his arms, he let her feet just touch the ground before he pulled her along beside him to the steps of Beaumarais. He drew her across his knee and spanked her with the hard palm of his hand, continuing despite her shrieks of rage as tears welled in her eyes and, overflowing, fell down her burning cheeks.

Nicholas released her, stepping back just in time to avoid the toe of her boot as she kicked out at him. Then, with a mortified look around her, she ran crying into the house.

Paddy stood frozen to the spot as he saw Nicholas walking

toward him, his intention clear in the green eyes. Before
Nicholas could reach him, Paddy had taken to his heels and
raced up the steps and into the relative safety of the house.
Even Mara's reassuring arms were no haven for him against
the cold anger of Nicholas.

"Nicholas!" Mara said as Nicholas started to follow Paddy.
"Don't you dare touch him. He's not your child. I will have
a word with him," Mara told him as she hurried to catch up
with his long strides.

Nicholas glanced down at her briefly but didn't slow his
pace. "Words aren't enough this time, Mara. Paddy needs
to learn that he can't do whatever pleases him regardless of
the consequences. He needs to learn the lesson now, or he
never will. I only wish I'd been around when you were his
age and could have given you a similar lesson," he added
shortly, as if he sorely missed having had that opportunity.
"It would have saved a lot of unhappiness all around. Now
stay out of this, Mara," he warned her grimly, "or I may yet
have that pleasure."

Mara stopped in her tracks, staring after him in disbelief.
By the time she moved after him, he'd already reached the
top of the stairs.

Mara stood at the bottom of the stairs indecisively, trying
to think what she should do. Jamie stomped down wearing a
look of puzzlement on her face.

"What the divil's goin' on around here?" she demanded.
"And just what the divil's he doin' to Master Paddy?"

"Paddy was riding Sorcier with Damaris and Nicholas
caught them," Mara explained, wondering why it was so quiet
up there.

"Well," Jamie sighed regretfully, "reckon he needs to be
taught a lesson."

"Jamie! He's whipping Paddy," Mara cried.

"'Twill be doin' the lad good to know a man's keepin' an
eye on him," Jamie said. Then, as she heard a cry of pain, she
sniffed and walked toward the kitchen wing. "Think I'll be
gettin' meself a cup of tea."

It is too silent, Mara thought. She moved up a couple of

steps, then hurriedly climbed the rest as she made her way to Paddy's room. Before she reached it, she heard voices from a partially opened door and, pausing, found herself listening to the words.

"No one can always do as they want to, Damaris," Nicholas told her gently.

"I always have," Mara heard a muffled reply. "No one has ever cared what I did around here."

"I care," Nicholas said, "and that is why I didn't want you riding Sorcier. I'd hate to see that little neck of yours broken," he added with shocking bluntness.

"Why should I listen to you? Why should you care about me? Nobody else ever has."

"That's not true, Damaris."

"It is so. Papa never had any time for us. We were just *les petites filles*. Never did he talk to me, never did he smile at me as if he would want me to kiss him good night. And then Nicole, she has always been Mama's favorite, at least she was until *le petit* Jean-Louis was born. But she does not care because she has a fiancé now and will be living in her own home. Mama only has eyes for Jean-Louis. So did Papa when he was alive. Never did he gaze at me that way. Sorcier has always been mine. He is my *only* friend, Nicholas, he is *all* I have. Why are you being so cruel to me?" Damaris demanded tearfully. "You must hate me so much to do this to me. Why are you taking him from me? Why?"

"Oh, Damaris, little one," Nicholas spoke softly, with a gentleness that Mara had never heard before. She knew he was touched by his little half-sister's pathetic confession. "I'm sorry I wasn't here to know and love you, for I think you would have been my favorite."

Mara risked glancing into the room as she tiptoed past and was surprised to see Damaris, auburn head resting against Nicholas's broad chest as she cried. Mara opened Paddy's door to see him standing before his bed with a solemn expression on his tear-stained face. He glanced up nervously as he heard the door, then when he saw it was Mara, he ran to her and wrapped his arms around her waist.

"I hate him," Paddy cried, his voice muffled in Mara's skirts.

Mara smoothed Paddy's ruffled curls soothingly. "I'm sorry you had to be punished, but you know what you did was very dangerous. How do you think I would have felt if something horrible had happened to you? You know that Nicholas is master here, Paddy, and when he lays down a rule it must be followed. You did disobey him."

Paddy sniffed. "I only did it because Damaris dared me to. I was frightened," he confessed as he hid his flushed face against Mara.

"And you won't be riding that horse again?"

"No! Never!" Paddy answered without hesitation, and Mara wondered which had frightened him more, the thought of the horse or Nicholas's anger and swiftly painful retribution.

Mara bent down and kissed Paddy's forehead. "I suspect Jamie'll be up soon with some milk and a piece of that pecan pie you like so much, so why don't you just play up here for a while," she suggested.

Paddy nodded his head. "All right, I think it's going to rain again anyway," he said as he found his favorite book of illustrated fairy tales and sat on the edge of his bed. "I'm not goin' to tell Nicholas my secret now either," he said to himself as he opened his book.

Evil is easy and has infinite forms.

—Pascal

Chapter 14

THE FOLLOWING DAYS PASSED IN A FLURRY OF ACTIVITY AS
Celeste made her final preparations for leaving Beaumarais.
Plans had already been made in advance for Nicole and her
family to spend the rest of the month with her future in-laws
on their plantation upriver, and then to travel to New Orleans
with them to enjoy the rounds of balls and soirees accompanying the Mardi Gras season. Word had been received that
her fiancé, who'd been traveling in France, was due back any
day. Nicole was in a state of euphoria that kept her on her best
behavior through the busy days. Packing and sorting clothes
and possessions had the household in complete disorder.

Except for certain personal items of sentimentality and
favorite pieces of furniture, Celeste chose to leave the furnishings of Beaumarais to Nicholas. She was a very wealthy
woman now, thanks to Nicholas's more than generous terms
for Beaumarais. When she arrived in Charleston, she would be
able to start fresh and purchase all new furnishings. She wanted
few reminders of the past when she left Louisiana, and even
though Nicholas assured her that it wasn't necessary to leave
in such haste, it was Celeste's wish to finish everything now so
that she would not have to return to Beaumarais. And so, in
compliance to her wishes, Nicholas made sure that everything
ran smoothly for her, seeing to her every need.

During the intervening days Amaryllis found reason to
consult Nicholas on all manner of business. Often her elegant

figure could be seen wandering in and around the house, her blond head bent close to Nicholas's shoulder as she attentively listened to his opinion about something. Paddy on the other hand studiously avoided any contact with his one-time hero, his dark brown eyes full of reproach whenever they happened to linger on Nicholas's tall figure.

It was the night before Celeste was due to leave and Mara was waiting patiently for Paddy to finish saying his prayers and climb into bed when he suddenly stopped. Balancing precariously on one foot, he suddenly hopped around excitedly. "I remember now!" he cried as he raced to the door, his bare legs showing beneath the hem of his nightshirt.

"Paddy!" Mara called after him.

"Master Paddy," Jamie repeated in surprise as he bumped into her as she entered the room with a stack of freshly laundered linens piled high in her arms. "And just where d'ye think ye're off to, young man? 'Tis time ye was in bed and asleep, now come back here right now," she warned as he paused hesitantly in the opened doorway.

"But I'll forget in the morning, Jamie," he told her with a pleading look at Mara. "I'm just going down to get my missing soldier. I hid him, then forgot about him. I'll be just a minute," he added as he scampered out the door.

Paddy soundlessly made his way down the stairs, waiting at the foot. All that he heard were voices coming from behind the closed parlor doors. He quickly crossed the cold tiles of the floor and hurried to the closed door to the study. He entered the darkened room, not noticing the candles burning in a single candelabrum placed on the desk and sending a shadowy light throughout. Paddy walked without hesitation to the windowsill. With quick ease, he slid back the panel and removed the errant soldier from his hiding place. With a happy sigh he turned around and ran from the quiet room, closing the door behind him as he left.

The silence of the room continued for a minute after the door had been closed. Then one of the shadowy shapes near the wide expanse of bookcases moved, detaching itself from the wall as it steadily and purposefully made for the window, and the secret compartment that had just been so unbelievably revealed to the frustrated searcher.

A hand felt down into the black depths of the hollow paneling, jerking involuntarily when coming in contact with the bundle placed at the bottom. It withdrew, holding the bound documents and a leather diary. The figure moved surely across the room to the desk where the light from the candles flickered across a face tight with excitement, the nostrils flaring with heightened breathing while the hands, untying the ribbon, trembled slightly.

In mesmerized fascination the glowing eyes scanned the documents, one of which was a set of instructions for drawing up a new will naming Nicholas de Montaigne-Chantale heir. The other was the original will. The piece of paper naming Nicholas as the new heir was held with a steady hand until the edges began to curl and blacken as the flame from the candle touched it. It burned as it was dropped into a heavy ashtray. Deft hands quickly turned the pages of the diary, then systematically tore them from the binding and threw them on the small pyre burning brightly now in the ashtray. The document that had escaped the fire was carefully folded and placed inside a pocket, while the harmless diary was replaced within the secret panel, the incriminating remarks having been removed.

Moving stealthily, the figure blew out the candles and returned the study to darkness. Then, as a noise sounded in the hall beyond the study door, the figure slipped silently out the French windows to the safety of the darkness beyond, leaving the study looking undisturbed.

❧

"Au revoir, Mademoiselle O'Flynn," Celeste said as she was being assisted into her carriage. "Perhaps we will meet in New Orleans?" she said politely, knowing that would probably never happen. "I will be leaving for Charleston in April, right after Nicole's wedding. So if I do not have the pleasure of meeting you again, mademoiselle," Celeste said with a shrug of regret, "then I wish you good luck."

Mara smiled, knowing that she wouldn't see her again, for Mara O'Flynn had no intention of still being in Louisiana in the spring. "I wish you a pleasant journey," Mara told her. She stepped aside while Nicole was helped into the carriage, her face glowing.

"Au revoir, mademoiselle," she cried happily, her red velvet bonnet framing her dark curls and matching the new pelisse Mara suspected had come out of her trousseau. "I'm sorry you will not be coming to my wedding, for it will be the most beautiful ceremony ever," Nicole told her before settling back into the carriage with a dreamy expression.

"Good-bye, Damaris," Paddy called into the coach even though he couldn't see her. There was an awkward silence following his farewell as Paddy stared up hopefully, then glanced down at his boots as if finding them of sudden interest.

Suddenly an auburn head appeared at the carriage window and a pair of gray green eyes stared sadly at the group standing on the steps of Beaumarais. Her lips trembling, Damaris whispered, "Au revoir, Paddy."

Nicholas walked slowly down the steps and up to the window where Damaris sat watching him nervously. He reached inside the opened door of the carriage and swung her out of the coach, her squeal of fright startling the team of horses. As he whispered something in her ear, her next squeal was of joy. She wound her thin arms around his neck and kissed him warmly.

"You'll be good, little one, and mind what your mama says?" Nicholas ordered with a gentle smile as he returned her to the carriage.

"I will, Nicholas, I promise," Damaris cried, and was still waving from the carriage window as it turned off the oak-lined drive and onto the road heading to the river. They could now hear the whistle of the steamboat as it neared the Beaumarais levee.

"Now what on earth did you promise her to make such a change of spirit?" Mara asked as they walked back into the great house. A chill gust of wind whipped her skirts around her ankles and the first big drops of rain splattered against the ground.

"One of Sorcier's foals," Nicholas replied. With a devilish twinkle in his eye, he whispered, "but you seem surprised, my dear. I thought you, of all people, knew that I had a way with women, and do my very best to satisfy their most fervent desires."

Mara sent him a speaking glance, then couldn't resist taunting, "And have you satisfied the widow's?"

"Ah, it wouldn't be gentlemanly of me to say, now would it?" Nicholas responded. There was a gleam of satisfaction in his eyes as he caught the confused expression that crossed her face.

"And here I was thinkin' to meself that ye wasn't a gentleman. Now I'll have to be watchin' me manners for sure," Mara mocked.

"*C'est magnifique!*" Etienne laughingly complimented Mara from the doorway. "I've never heard a finer Irish accent."

"Why thank you, kind sir," Mara replied, "but 'tis me natural tongue."

"You should hear her French accent, Uncle," Nicholas commented lazily as he poured out two brandies, handing one to Etienne who had made himself comfortable on the sofa. "Mara's a good companion to have on a long journey, for one never knows who she will be next. Therefore, one can never become bored with her."

He raised his drink in a silent toast to her before taking a sip.

"Ah," Etienne sighed, "the quiet is so welcome. Please," he added apologetically, "don't misunderstand me, I quite adore the family. It is just that a baby's constant crying is nerve-racking, especially when not even your own grand-child. And Nicole, charming child that she is, is most tire-some at times," he explained with a smile that took the sting out of his words.

"Of course, I may just be getting old, and I suspect it is time I visited Paris again before it is too late. Well," Etienne said regretfully as he finished off his drink, "I must be off. Shall we dine at the same time, and maybe have a few hands of piquet, Mara? You did promise me you'd play."

"Of course, Etienne, I shall look forward to it," Mara

returned his smile as she watched him leave the room with an anticipatory gleam in his soft blue eyes.

"I'd be careful, my sweet, about what you wager," Nicholas advised, "for Etienne fancies himself quite a gambler."

Mara smiled mischievously, thinking the evening might not be so dull after all. "And I'm not Brendan O'Flynn's sister for nothing, mon cher."

Nicholas laughed, the rich sound startling Paddy who'd been sitting quiet as a mouse before the fire. He looked up nervously from his contemplation of the flames.

"No, I guess you're not, are you," he murmured curiously. "I shall have to remember that."

∾

Mara yawned, turning over as she stretched beneath the covers, then woke up as she felt the empty space beside her. Glancing around her in the darkness, she saw Nicholas's dim shape near the French windows.

"Nicholas?" she spoke into the cold air of the room.

"It's raining again."

Mara propped herself up on her elbows as she strained to see him in the dark. "And that worries you?"

Nicholas left the window and sat down on the edge of the bed. "Yes, very much, my dear."

"Why? Don't you have a lot of rain here? It's normal, isn't it?"

"Yes, it's expected, and that is why we, especially those of us living near the river, take certain precautions. It's the flooding I'm worried about, and with this continued rain it's going to come. The river's been rising steadily since dawn yesterday."

Mara frowned, beginning to feel some of the fear that was apparently worrying him. "Celeste mentioned that the first floor of Beaumarais had been flooded a couple of years ago. Could it happen again, do you think?" Mara asked as she sat up.

Nicholas shook his head. "I don't think it will get up that high again. But that doesn't matter, because it is the damage it did a couple of years ago that has me worried. The plantation's been allowed to rot. The levees are in a deplorable state and haven't been rebuilt up high enough to be effective should the waters rise much more. I don't know how extensive the damage was before. Beaumarais sits down too low, but in the past we've always had the levees to protect us, as well as a small army of field hands to keep it built up when the floods came. All I've got is a handful of house servants and some stableboys," Nicholas explained.

"But how could this have happened?" Mara demanded. "Wouldn't your father, or surely Alain, have seen to it?"

Nicholas rubbed his hand through his hair tiredly. "My father wasn't the same man he'd once been. I don't think he really cared. And Alain, well, he could only stand by and take orders. I know my father wanted to get the fields planted again, but by then Celeste would have none of it. All she could think about was selling out and moving back to Charleston. Alain couldn't do it by himself, and who could blame him for not really wanting to when he knew the place would be sold out from under him eventually?"

"What are you going to do if the river floods? Shouldn't we leave here?" Mara asked worriedly, thinking of Paddy and Jamie, neither of whom could swim.

"I don't think it will come to that. Alain says it won't, and he has lived here his whole life. He would know. But if I think there is a danger then I'll borrow some men from Amaryllis and get them to shore up the levee. I'm going to take the precaution of sending the livestock on over there tomorrow, and some things from the house. I'm relieved that Celeste took the girls and Jean-Louis away. I didn't want to frighten her unnecessarily, for I can imagine the hysterics it would have thrown her into, not to mention Nicole. I think she would have been more concerned about her wedding dress being ruined than her own life."

Mara sighed as she sank back against the pillows. "You're really concerned."

Nicholas rolled back onto the bed and took her in his arms. "Of course I am, I'd have to be a fool not to be. But I wouldn't put you or young Paddy in any. danger," he reassured her as he began to caress her face, smoothing away the lines of worry with his kisses.

"Now go to sleep, there's nothing we can do about it tonight," he murmured as he felt her relax against him trustingly.

Mara awoke to a ray of sunlight shining into her eyes through the window. She let consciousness seep slowly, knowing that as soon as it did she would feel the familiar nausea. Mara suddenly became aware of Nicholas's head, still beside her. Usually he had already risen by the time she awakened, and so had never witnessed her morning sickness. Mara willed herself to resist the queasiness she could already feel sneaking into her stomach, but when she felt the beads of cold perspiration breaking out on her forehead, she knew she hadn't succeeded. Carefully removing the covers, Mara slid from bed and quickly wrapped her robe around her shivering body. She raced against the nausea that was quickly overcoming her and, realizing she would not make it from the room in time, just barely managed to bend over the washbasin.

Mara took a deep breath and was pushing a tangled strand of hair from her face when a cool, wet handkerchief was pressed against her face and gently wiped across it.

Mara opened her eyes to see Nicholas leaning over her. He lifted her to her feet and, despite her feeble protest, carried her back to the bed. He tucked her beneath the covers.

"Are you all right?" he asked as he stared down at her with those penetrating eyes that wouldn't allow Mara to look away.

She managed a slight smile, "It must have been something I ate last night. Perhaps the fish?"

Nicholas continued to gaze down on her pale face. "I ate the fish as well, my sweet, and I'm not suffering any ill effects," he told her softly, a strange look entering his eyes. "Could it possibly be something else?"

Mara's eyes widened as she shook her head. "I really don't know what. This is the first time it's happened," she lied. "I think I was the only one to have the cream sauce. It must have been that. I'm feeling much better now, really I am," Mara reassured him as she smiled wider, her tone dismissing his worries.

Nicholas shrugged. "If you say so, ma petite. But why don't you have some breakfast sent up and stay in bed awhile longer? I shall be going out to check the levee with Alain shortly, so there is no reason for you to disturb yourself." Nicholas walked to the door, adding with a warning look, "But if you're not feeling better soon, I shall send for a doctor."

Mara stared gloomily at the closed door. "Damn," she whispered. That was all she needed, some doctor poking around. It wouldn't take him long to determine what was wrong with her.

Mara had dozed off when she was suddenly startled awake by the door opening. She breathed a sigh of relief when she saw Belle bustling in with a tray.

"Someone around here is sure asking a lot of personal questions," she told Mara as she placed the tray across Mara's lap.

"What do you mean?" Mara demanded as she took a sip of tea, relieved to find it going down without protest.

"May the good Lord forgive me for lying, but I've been punished for it by the fright it gave me to look into them green eyes of Master Nicholas's and say that I knew nothing," Belle said with a look of remembered fear. "Nearly shook my skirt off I was shaking so hard."

"You didn't say anything to him about my being sick?" Mara asked worriedly.

"Said nothing, like you asked, Miss Mara. Reckon this be women's business," she reassured her. "I didn't like doing it, but I did."

"Thank you, Belle," Mara told her simply, but she was deeply touched.

Belle opened the door and was about to step out when Paddy shot past her and into the room.

"Mara, Mara!" he greeted her excitedly. "Uncle Nicholas said I could ride with him up on Sorcier when he goes to look at the river. Is it all right? He said I had to tell you. Well," Paddy hesitated, looking shame-faced, "he did say *ask* if I could go."

Mara nodded her consent, knowing that this time he would

be safe. She was pleased that Paddy was back to calling him uncle, a sure sign that he was harboring no grudge.

Mara climbed out of bed after Paddy rushed out, and was on the gallery in time to see Nicholas, with Paddy perched in front of him, and Alain ride off down the drive. Mara shivered as the cold struck her and she quickly returned indoors, not envying them their ride in this weather.

"Warm enough?" Nicholas asked Paddy, whose small hand was clutching his coat sleeve.

Paddy glanced up at the hard face above him and smiled widely. "Sure, Uncle Nicholas, I'm having fun."

Nicholas smiled down at Paddy's dark head and then glanced over at Alain. "Did we used to get so much pleasure out of so small a treat?"

"Anytime I got the chance to get on the back of one of the master's fine riding horses I thought that was something special," Alain returned, then added seriously, "but do you think it wise to bring the little boy? This weather is not good for one who catches colds easily, as I am told he does."

Nicholas frowned. "I forgot about that. Maybe I should take him back."

"Oh, no, Uncle Nicholas!" Paddy cried. "You promised. I want to see the river. I'm all bundled up, Jamie made sure I had my scarf wrapped around my throat. Please," Paddy entreated, the big, hopeful eyes flashing the O'Flynn charm.

"I don't suppose it will hurt this once, eh, Alain?" Nicholas smiled.

Alain grinned good-naturedly. "Be a pity to disappoint him."

The horses' hooves pounded through the muddy road, sending thick clumps of mud flying in all directions. They splashed through puddles of water still filling the low places along the road and running rapidly through the ditches on each side.

As they neared the river, Nicholas sent Sorcier into a gallop, a frown crossing his face as he saw the trickling streams of water winding their way from the high bank and into the fields beyond. No additional water could be absorbed by the rain-soaked earth.

"Looks like the river's risen another foot since yesterday," Nicholas said grimly as he steered the big bay farther along the bank to where the land seemed firmer.

Alain urged his mount alongside the stallion, his eyes narrowed as he gazed at the river. "It'll go down soon," he predicted even as a loud clap of thunder sounded overhead.

"Eventually, yes." Nicholas brought Sorcier to a halt at the crest of the bank. As he surveyed the wide, swiftly moving river beyond, he asked, "But will the levee hold that long?"

Alain stared up and down the banks for a long moment, his eyes unfocused for a second as he searched his memory. "It'll hold, it always has," he said on a note of confidence.

Nicholas had been staring at him curiously, watching the play of emotion crossing his face. "This is where my father fell into the river, isn't it?"

Alain shook his dark head as he pointed upriver a short distance. "By the big oak with the drooping limbs that are almost under water."

He suddenly became aware of Nicholas's steady gaze and shifted uneasily in the saddle. "Is there something wrong?"

"How would you know exactly where he fell in?"

Alain smiled sadly. "You forget that I have lived here almost all my life, Nicholas. I know this river, my friend. I know the way it eddies and flows without reason, the sand bars it will leave where one does not expect them. Yes," Alain said with a loving look at the muddy expanse of water, "I would know where Monsieur Philippe fell into the river because of where they found his body."

"I see," Nicholas said, but Alain thought he did not quite understand.

"Also," Alain added modestly, "he told one of the stable-boys he was coming this way."

Nicholas's gaze sharpened with interest. "Did he say why?"

Alain shook his head regretfully. "I do not think so, but the slave who knew has been sold with so many others. When the stables were diminished, well, there was no need for so many stable hands."

Nicholas's lips tightened. "So many unanswered questions,"

he said to himself before turning his horse around and descending the bank. "We'd better head back. I think I'll go ahead and send the rest of the horses to Sandrose, as well as clear out some more valuables from the house." He took a last look at the river.

"Very well. But I think you're going to a lot of unnecessary trouble, Nicholas," Alain advised him.

"I'd rather go to the trouble now than see my father's portrait being washed downriver when the house is flooded," Nicholas said grimly.

"Will we get washed downriver too?" Paddy demanded, his eyes round with wonder. "Where's our boat? I didn't see one."

Nicholas sighed, chastising himself for having spoken unguardedly before the little boy. "You don't need to worry. We won't be taking any boat rides downriver for a while. And I don't want you saying anything about this to Mara, do you understand me, Paddy?" he warned.

It was a long day, busy with the activity of moving valuables from the house and loading them up in wagons to be taken to Sandrose. All the while it continued to thunder ominously in the distance. Jagged lightning struck through the black rain clouds time and time again until Mara expected to see the bottom ripped out of them and a deluge fall.

The following morning Nicholas awoke early, listening intently for the sound of rain. All that met his ears was silence. He reluctantly left the warmth of his bed and Mara's soft body and, walking to the window, stared out into the darkness that would lighten within the hour. He tapped his fingers against the pane thoughtfully, hardly daring to give rise to his hopes. They had gotten through the night, the levee holding firm. He glanced back at the dim outline of the canopied bed and felt a second's desire to climb back in and seek the inviting warmth of the woman who slept beside him each night.

He heard the stirrings of the house servants, however, and he shrugged into his robe. He'd have time for a quick breakfast before riding out to the levee. He wanted to be there with the first light of morning, to see how it had weathered the long night and swollen river.

When Mara awakened, the coldness of the room was being chased away by a bright fire crackling in the fireplace. Mara stretched luxuriantly, lazily snuggling beneath the satin quilt as she eyed Belle, who was just entering with a tray.

"That Miss Jamie, if she isn't the one," Belle exclaimed as she placed the tray on a small table drawn up close to the bed, then helped Mara into her bed jacket. "Did you know, Miss Mara, that she's got all her bags packed, as well as your clothes and the young master's?"

Mara stared up into Belle's indignant face. "She's packed everything?" she asked in confusion.

"Mumbling about the end coming," Belle told her as she placed the tray across Mara's lap, "and crossing herself. I swear I've never seen such a mournful face, even on an old hound dog."

Mara smiled. "Don't let her bother you. Jamie's always been one to see the darkest side of things. It's just her way," Mara explained, unconcerned.

"'Tis me way of staying alive, that it is," Jamie retorted sourly from the doorway. "Wouldn't be as old and wrinkled as I am today if I'd shrugged me shoulders at me feelings," she said as she pounded her thin chest with a tightly clenched fist.

Belle raised her eyes heavenward. She gave wide space to the little Irishwoman and left the room.

"You're going to have half the servants thinking you're a witch, Jamie," Mara commented as she sipped her tea and waited for the inevitable morning sickness.

"Can't help what folks are thinkin' about me," Jamie muttered irritably as she began to set out Mara's clothes. "I've got hot water comin' so ye'd best get yourself out of bed and into the tub, or ye'll be washin' yourself in river water instead of scented," she predicted with a black scowl.

Mara gave an exasperated sigh, but hurried to finish her breakfast, pleased that the nausea had not come. She laughed at some of Jamie's superstitious antics, but in the back of her mind was the thought that Jamie was often right.

❧

Nicholas sat astride Sorcier, looking down on the muddy Mississippi, cold dread spreading through him. The levee had held through the night, but it wouldn't through the day. Already huge chunks of earth were crumbling beneath the continual pressure of the tons of water surging against it.

Nicholas glanced around at Alain who was sitting barely an arm's reach away on his right side. Etienne sat silently on Nicholas's left, staring at the banks. Water was lapping gently over the tops.

"I wish now you had not persuaded me to accompany you, Nicholas, for this is a most distressing sight. Mon Dieu, but it is," Etienne said, shaking his white head in dismay.

Suddenly Sorcier jumped forward and came precariously close to the edge, his hooves slipping in the mud as his hind legs slid down into the muddy water. Nicholas fought mightily to pull the big bay's head up, his knees tightening against the heaving belly of the frightened horse. It dug its hooves into the slippery mud and tried to fight its way up the bank. A less powerful horse would never have managed to pull itself up, but Sorcier—and Nicholas was later to think he did it out of pure meanness—reached the top with a mighty leap, his coat muddied and dripping, while Nicholas's boots, thighs, and chest were soaked.

"My god, Nicholas," Etienne breathed, his face white. He stared in horror at his nephew. "You could have drowned."

"Are you all right?" Alain demanded as he moved between Nicholas and the dangerous edge of the riverbank. "That damned horse. I always thought he should be shot. He's a killer."

Nicholas was breathing heavily as he patted a soothing hand against Sorcier's wet neck. "He saved my life," Nicholas said in a cold voice. "Something startled him, and if he weren't such a big brute we would both have been swept downstream," he said as he glanced between the two men sitting on either side of him. He was about to say more when there was a sickening sound and all three men turned. Along the bank, only a few hundred yards away, the levee was giving way. A rush of water poured through it.

"It's gone!" Nicholas yelled above the roar of the water

coming through the break in the levee. "The whole damned bank will go within half an hour or less."

He turned his mount around and began to gallop back toward the trees that surrounded Beaumarais. He could see the line of oaks guarding the drive as he raced toward the great house, knowing that he didn't have much time to get everyone out safely. He glanced around to see Alain and Etienne not far behind him as their horses ate up the distance between the waters of the river and the house.

When Etienne and Alain caught up with him, Nicholas was issuing orders from Sorcier's back for the carriage and wagons to be hitched up.

Etienne stared across at Nicholas, dismay written across his aristocratic features. "What are you doing?" he demanded.

"I'm getting everyone out of here," Nicholas answered shortly.

"But why? The fields may be flooded, but we'll be safe enough in the top floor of the house."

Nicholas barely glanced at him as he swung down from Sorcier's back. "We've never had the levee go completely before, and I don't intend to be stranded here at Beaumarais until the waters go back down. I don't know how long that will be. Nor do I know how much higher the water will rise. I can't take the chance, Etienne," Nicholas told him. Pausing at the front door, he said, "You'd better get what things you'll be needing for a while because we're going to Sandrose. Just be thankful that you decided to remove some of your treasures yesterday while you had the chance. The carriage will be here at the front of the house.

Jamie was putting the finishing touches on Mara's hair when Nicholas burst into the room. Mara stared at him in incredulous silence for a second as her eyes went over his muddied boots and breeches.

"Get your cloak on, and anything else you need. We're leaving Beaumarais right now," he ordered abruptly as he walked on through to the gallery. "I'll get Paddy. A couple of stableboys will be up to get your trunks, but we haven't much time, the levee's gone."

"I warned ye," Jamie grumbled as she grabbed Mara's cape. "A foolish old woman am I? Why, ye'd be without a stitch to wear if I hadn't already packed up all your clothes."

Nicholas returned a minute later with Paddy holding his hand. "Ready?" he called into their room as he entered. Taking Mara by the elbow, he guided her out and down the stairs. They were near the foot of the staircase when Etienne entered the front of the house, a small leather bag gripped in one hand, a pile of books tucked beneath his arm. He glanced up as he heard them on the stairs and pointed to the study. "I just remembered some other books I want."

Nicholas watched impatiently as Etienne's dapper figure disappeared into the study. "Damn! We haven't time for searching through the library," Nicholas swore.

They waited for a minute, stepping aside as their trunks were carried down the stairs and to the waiting wagons. But when Etienne didn't reappear and they heard voices coming from the study, Nicholas followed, Mara and Paddy still with him.

"Etienne, hurry up, we haven't time for—" Nicholas began. He stopped as he saw Etienne standing rigid in the center of the room, two books held forgotten in his hand. The old man stared at the occupant of the big, leather chair beside the fire.

"Alain, what the devil?" Nicholas demanded. The fire had only recently been lit. Alain held a glass of brandy negligently in his hand. There was a gun placed within easy reach on the table beside his elbow.

"I'm not leaving Beaumarais," Alain spoke quietly, his hazel eyes staring boldly for once and without any show of deference.

"My God, Alain," Nicholas said incredulously, "the river's going to flood this floor under at least five feet of water."

A smile flickered briefly and humorlessly across Alain's handsome face before he took a sip of brandy. "How like the old man you look and sound," Alain spoke softly. "He was so damned arrogant. He feared nothing. Yet here you are, his son, fleeing Beaumarais with your tail between your legs. The great Nicholas de Montaigne-Chantale a coward. But then, only a coward would have shot his brother. Eh, Nicholas?"

"Alain, my son," Etienne began, "you don't know what you are saying."

Alain looked at Etienne contemptuously. "*Son?*" he asked.

Etienne blanched, the books he'd tucked beneath his arm falling to the floor with a thud. "W–what do you mean?"

"I think it's time for a revelation of truths, eh, Papa?" Alain spoke maliciously. "After all, shouldn't *mon frère*, Nicholas, know why he is going to lose Beaumarais?"

At Alain's words Nicholas's eyes widened in momentary surprise.

"Yes," Alain said with obvious enjoyment, "you are my brother—half-brother, actually. I am Alain de Montaigne-Chantale, not Ferrare, as they would have everyone believe. Ask him," Alain told Nicholas, nodding at Etienne, "if it is not the truth."

Nicholas shook his head as he looked at Alain. "You're crazed."

"Am I? Look at him!" Alain yelled, pointing a finger now at Etienne.

Nicholas slowly turned his head and stared at his uncle, seeing the truth in the painful sadness of Etienne Ferrare's eyes.

"Well?" Nicholas demanded.

Etienne nodded his head just barely. "He is Philippe's son."

"There! At last! After so many years of lies," Alain laughed triumphantly.

Nicholas continued to stare at Etienne for a moment before looking back at Alain, seeing for the first time certain similarities between Alain and himself. "So you are my half-brother? What does that prove?"

"So cool, so arrogantly spoken, mon frère, like the de Montaigne-Chantale that you are. Well I am not just a de Montaigne-Chantale. I am the eldest. *I* am heir to Beaumarais, not you, Nicholas. Never you," Alain spat.

He reached into his coat pocket and withdrew the document he had found in the secret windowsill. "A will, written by my father, Philippe, naming me heir to Beaumarais. I am master here," he stated, his eyes daring anyone to refute the claim.

Nicholas's narrowed gaze met Alain's. "Why now? Why not a year ago when my father died?" he demanded.

Alain's harsh laugh rang through the room. "Because that wily old fox hid it, that's why. I've been searching for this damned will since the day he died. How many sleepless nights did I spend searching this room for any sign of it. Never until now could I announce my rights to Beaumarais. And whom do I have to thank but a small boy who, while innocently playing, finds the secret panel that I'd searched for for so long," Alain said with mixed amusement and anger.

Nicholas and Mara both looked down at Paddy who was gaping at the overseer, his eyes round. "Me?"

"I was in here the other night when you came sneaking in to retrieve your toy soldier. You can imagine my surprise when you marched right over to the windowsill, slid back the panel, oh so casually, then left without even knowing I was here."

Nicholas moved slowly toward the windowsill. At Paddy's nod, he felt along the sill until, finding the latch, he slid it open to reveal the chamber inside. Reaching down he withdrew the diary and quickly thumbed through it as he moved back to stand in front of Alain. Nicholas's lips thinned grimly as he ran his thumb along the rough edges where pages had been torn from the diary.

"Oh, yes, he wrote it all down," Alain told Nicholas with a pitying smile, "and I enjoyed reading it before I burned it. You can prove nothing, Nicholas, nothing at all. As master of Beaumarais I shall be one of the most powerful men in Louisiana."

Mara was developing a sick feeling in the pit of her stomach as she stared at his glazed eyes and smiling lips.

"And what can't I prove against you, Alain? What have you to hide?" Nicholas asked softly.

"I have nothing to hide," Alain denied, his eyes sliding between the two men suspiciously. "I am master of Beaumarais and that is all that need concern you."

Etienne shook his head sadly. "Oh, Alain, you are master of nothing."

"If you and my father could have had your way, then I would have nothing," he charged. "My name and birthright were stolen from me by the two of you. I don't know why you agreed to pretend to be my father, but I do know that you aren't. All these years I've kept silent, just waiting, knowing that one day I would inherit Beaumarais. Who else could? I was his only son."

"But what of François and Nicholas?" Etienne asked quietly, a look of growing dread in his eyes. "They were his sons too."

"But François died, and Nicholas was dishonored," Alain said with a slight smile.

"And did you plan that, Alain?" Etienne suddenly demanded, his voice startling Nicholas. Never had he heard Etienne's voice raised in anger. If evil could come to life, then Alain was its personification as he sat staring at them, gloating. Mara stepped away from him, shivering with revulsion.

"All these years you have known the truth? You have waited patiently for the right time to make your identity known. When did you find out? How? Philippe and I never spoke of it."

"Once, you did," Alain told Etienne with a knowing look. "You and my father were discussing, no, arguing about my education, and whether or not I should stay in Paris any longer or return to New Orleans. Philippe wanted to make me manager of one of his other plantations, and eventually owner of it. Remember the argument, Papa?" Alain sneered. "Philippe said, 'After all, he is my son, a de Montaigne-Chantale. He should own land. It's in the blood, Etienne.' Mon Dieu, can you imagine how I felt? To know that I was *his* son, that I could have been master here except for François and Nicholas?"

"I remember that conversation very well," Etienne spoke, his voice thick with tears. He turned accusing eyes on Alain. "It was just a few days before Nicholas was accused of shooting François in the duel."

Nicholas took a step forward, stopping when he saw Alain's hand move to the butt of the gun. "You? You shot François, didn't you? My God, I never thought of you. Never."

"No, you wouldn't, for I was beneath the notice of the great de Montaigne-Chantales, wasn't I? Especially François.

He was the worst. Never a word to me, always riding with his nose in the air, his blond curls gleaming with the sunlight. But he was a fool, a hothead. Both of you played into my hands so easily, so gullibly that I still laugh to think of it. I saw you that day when you played your silly game. I stood behind the big oak and waited, and when you aimed your pistol, I aimed mine. When you pulled the trigger, so did I. Only I didn't aim to the side of François, I aimed for his heart."

Nicholas's lips thinned and whitened.

"I had everything then, for François was dead, you were ruined and sent away, and who was there but me for him to turn to? Everything went so well at first and we became very close…at least we were until that bitch gave birth to le petit Jean-Louis," Alain spat out the name on a wave of violent hate. "A son! A son after so many barren years. I could not believe it. I had dreaded the other two births, but they were girls. Then, suddenly, she gives him a son with the name de Montaigne-Chantale.

"He had made me his heir before that little bastard was born. I'd found it in his desk, my rights to Beaumarais." Alain spoke with the eagerness that he must have felt when he'd first found the will.

"But then he sent for his lawyer one day, and I knew he was going to change the will in favor of his new son. I confronted him with it. I told him that he couldn't write me out of it, that I was his son too. Hadn't I sweated over this land more than any of his other sons? He was shocked that I would demand my rights. I saw everything I had worked for slipping away. I think he suspected then that I had killed François, and he asked me so suddenly that I couldn't deny it. The look on his face…mon Dieu, but I shall never forget it. That look," Alain mumbled, his eyes glazing over in memory. "He struck me across the face, then ordered me from his presence. The next day, down at the levee, he told me to get off his land, that if I didn't he would shoot me down like the dog I was."

Nicholas and Etienne exchanged glances, neither having missed the pulse beating rapidly in Alain's throat, the cords standing out painfully as he struggled, against all the years of silence, to tell his story at last.

"I—I couldn't believe it! I hated him then, hated him for everything he'd stolen from me. I told him that I should be master of Beaumarais and that he couldn't drive me away like he did Nicholas. At the mention of your name he seemed to go crazy. He charged me, hitting me with his whip again and again, as if I were some field slave to grovel at his feet. He was so strong. I couldn't believe he would have such overwhelming strength, and so I hit him," Alain confessed, blinking. "I hit him hard across the face and he staggered backward, hitting his head on the oak tree. Then he rolled into the river. He floated for an instant, then he disappeared beneath the surface. That was the last I saw of him—until a few days later."

Nicholas's eyes never left Alain's face. He took a step forward.

"Don't!" Alain warned as he grabbed the pistol and aimed it at Nicholas's chest. "I don't want to shoot you, but I will. You can't prove anything against me, there is no proof, and I have the will. Everyone still believes you guilty of François's murder. You are the stranger here now, I'm not," he taunted him, an anticipatory gleam in his eye as Nicholas came closer. "Stop, Nicholas, I'm warning you, I don't want to have to kill you. I actually am grateful to you for returning in time to keep Celeste from selling Beaumarais to Amaryllis. I never thought I'd be glad to see you, but I was, especially when you turned out to be wealthy. I was worried at first that perhaps you knew something, but when you said nothing, and then started searching, well, I knew Philippe had told you nothing. I would prefer not having to put a bullet in you, mon frère," Alain repeated as Nicholas continued to tower over him.

"Damn you to hell," Nicholas whispered as he took another step, oblivious to the danger.

But Mara was aware of it. She pushed herself in front of him before he could take another step, and at the same instant, Alain pulled the trigger.

The loud report reverberated through the room and

mingled with Paddy's scream of terror as he saw the blood spurting from Mara's arm.

Nicholas felt Mara recoil against him and caught her in his arms. He glanced down at her face, his heart stopping. She managed a shaky smile, leaning against him.

"Mon Dieu, Alain," Etienne cried, his tears of shame and despair falling freely.

"The next bullet will go through you. I'm sorry, Mademoiselle O'Flynn, I didn't mean to shoot you. But I will shoot Nicholas," Alain promised.

"Master Nicholas! Master Nicholas!" the butler called frantically as he came rushing to the study door. "The river's comin', and comin' fast, sir!"

Nicholas glanced from the butler's black face, his fears clearly written across it, to Mara's pale one, then to the red of her blood dripping onto the rug.

Alain was watching, the gun still pointed directly at them.

"It's not over, Alain. And you're a fool if you think it is. Or that I'll let you live after what you've done," Nicholas promised.

He scooped Mara up into his arms, Looking at Etienne, he hesitated for one more moment. "Are you coming, Etienne?"

Nodding in confusion, Etienne turned around, stumbling slightly. With a nod from Nicholas the butler came forward, his eyes widening as they caught the flash of the gun. He gently took hold of Etienne's arm and guided him from the room.

Paddy clung to Nicholas's coattails as Nicholas walked from the room, leaving a triumphant Alain in sole possession of Beaumarais.

Nicholas lifted Mara into the coach, then Paddy. Looking around while Etienne was assisted inside, he assured himself that no one had been left behind, saw Sorcier tied to the back of the carriage, the wagons loaded with people and possessions. He signaled to the coachman and they pulled away from the house.

Nicholas sat down inside next to Mara, who was being fussed over by Jamie, and watched the little Irishwoman's professional administerings with a critical eye before asking, "How is she?"

"I'm fine, Nicholas, truly I am," Mara reassured him. She grimaced slightly under Jamie's probing fingers.

"'Tis just a scratch," Jamie diagnosed as she tied a clean, linen handkerchief around the fleshy part of Mara's upper arm. "But what I can't understand is why anyone would want to shoot Mara."

Nicholas looked at Mara for a long minute before saying quietly, "He was aiming at me until Mara stepped in front of me, shielding me with her body." Nicholas's palm gently cupped Mara's chin. "That was a damned foolish thing to do," he said.

"You're welcome," Mara replied softly as she stared out the window, avoiding Nicholas's gaze.

Etienne moved slightly in the corner of the coach where he had been huddled and looked around him despondently, as if becoming aware of his surroundings for the first time.

"Etienne," Nicholas spoke quietly, "can you tell me why all this happened? Why my father didn't claim Alain as his son?"

Etienne nodded, his eyes brimming. His lips trembled as he fought for control. "It was so long ago, and yet at times it seems as if it were only yesterday that Olivia was living here. How many years?" he mumbled, frowning. He was trying to recall events of well over a quarter century ago.

"Can it be *forty* years? So long ago it is hard to see it clearly anymore, except for the face of my Olivia," he said, the name a caress. "She was so beautiful, so exquisite, and so very much in love with Philippe. He saw her at one of the Quadroon Balls and set her up as his placée. They were happy for a while, but then he wed Danielle, my sister. She was also a great beauty, and the woman that Philippe genuinely loved. He was wild about her, the way he'd never been about another woman.

"But Danielle was delicate and very sensitive to her surroundings. She often brooded, and I think it was only Philippe's great love for her that kept her happy. She was very possessive of Philippe and it drove her mad to think of him with another woman. As every wife expected her husband to have a mistress in New Orleans, Danielle knew that Philippe would too. She begged him to give the woman up, and for Philippe, loving her as he did, that was easy.

"He set Olivia up in her own boardinghouse in the city where she would have a decent living, and he never saw her again after that—at least for some time. But I think sometimes that Danielle never believed he gave her up. It preyed upon her mind.

"For a while things were good between them. Then Danielle lost her first baby. She couldn't carry him the full time and she was very ill. After that she wanted a child so badly. I think she suspected she would lose Philippe if she didn't give him a son, and so she thought this was the only way of keeping him. Well, she tried," Etienne said sadly, "and lost yet another child, this time a son that she had prayed for. She was inconsolable, and thought she had been cursed by voodoo. She became a woman possessed, and for a couple of years she would not let anyone near her, especially Philippe. So, Philippe, he was no saint, he was a very virile man. And he was hurt. It was only natural that he would turn to someone who could give him the companionship he needed, and so he sought out Olivia again. For several years after that they were lovers, and Olivia gave Philippe a son. He was named Alain. Olivia satisfied Philippe's lusts, but it was still Danielle whom he loved so deeply, and gradually Danielle began to recover. Perhaps she sensed that if much more time passed she would lose Philippe forever. She became pregnant again, and because she had been so ill, she stayed in bed the whole time. Perhaps this is why she was able to give birth.

"That baby was Denise, your sister, and although it was not the son she wanted to give Philippe, it gave her hope that she could bear more children. She changed miraculously after that and was a completely different woman. Gone were the depressions that had seemed to drive her wild at times, and she and Philippe were very happy. But there were those who would tell her rumors of Olivia and Philippe, and he did not wish to have his happiness destroyed a second time—especially as Danielle was once again pregnant."

Etienne looked around at the silent occupants of the carriage. Then he took a deep breath and resumed.

"Philippe came to me for help. Please do not think that I am as self-sacrificing as this might lead you to believe. I took the responsibility of Olivia and Alain. It allayed Danielle's fears as nothing else would have, and it gave Alain a name. But you see, it was no great sacrifice for me, for I loved Olivia too, and I always had," Etienne admitted. "But Philippe had seen her first, and, well, next to his commanding and handsome figure I didn't seem like much. She had always had eyes only for Philippe."

"Françoise?" Nicholas spoke for the first time, his voice hoarse. "Is she my sister too?"

Etienne shook his head. "No, Françoise is my daughter. I think I made Olivia happy, and I think that she eventually came to be fond of me. But I know I never replaced Philippe in her heart. He was much as you, Nicholas, and I think once a woman has given her heart to you, it will never again be hers. It was that way with Olivia. But I was grateful for even a small piece of her heart, and she was faithful to me and kind."

"But Alain never knew that Philippe was his father?" Nicholas asked, touched by Etienne's confession.

"No, he was too young to remember Philippe. And after that I was always there. So I became his father," Etienne explained. "After Danielle died, there was no purpose in revealing it, for he had grown up knowing me. By then, you and François were Philippe's sons. Forgive me, Nicholas," Etienne said unhappily, "for believing you guilty of murdering François. Never did I imagine the truth." He put his face in his hands, rubbing his eyes clear of tears as he glanced up with a ravaged face. "Never did I believe it was Alain. Mon Dieu, but I never knew he had the slightest knowledge of his birth. Maybe if I'd given him more love…I don't know, but I suppose I always saw him as Philippe's son, and maybe I resented him. All those years he knew—and waited. How it must have panicked him when Celeste gave birth to a son and he saw all he had worked for slipping away from him. He must have been desperate. And so, one last time, he decided to do something about it."

"Does he really think he is master of Beaumarais?" Nicholas demanded.

Etienne shrugged, despair crossing his tired face. "He knows not what he is doing, Nicholas. This sickness has been eating away at him for all these years. To have lived with the thought that you killed your brother," Etienne said, then stopped abruptly with a look of contrition. "I'm sorry, Nicholas, for you would have lived with, that all these years.

"But Alain knew that he'd done it, and in cold blood. For many years he had the hope of becoming the heir, but then when Philippe found out the truth, he cut Alain out of his life as he would a gangrenous leg. It was too much for Alain, and I think he must have become insane. Certainly he must have after killing his father, for that is something a man cannot live with. And what was it all for? He could not find the will, and there was no way of proving his claim. He must have gone crazy with frustration as he waited for Celeste to sell Beaumarais. I see now why he was so pleased to see you and then for you to become owner of Beaumarais. It gave him more time to find the will, and with you here, time was no obstacle anymore. You realize," Etienne said in a shaky whisper, "that this morning near the levee he probably tried to kill you? What better way of disposing of you, Nicholas, than during the excitement of a flood, when so many tragic accidents happen. Poor Alain, I can pity him, yes," Etienne said with a note of firmness in his tremulous voice as he saw the hard look enter Nicholas's eyes. "I still have it in my heart to feel this, for he was my son in all but blood," Etienne spoke wearily.

"Don't ask me to, Etienne," Nicholas told him. "He destroyed my family. He destroyed Beaumarais and the life I knew. That I can never forgive," he said coldly. Mara knew with an instinctive fear that Nicholas would go back for Alain. One of them would not leave Beaumarais alive.

Mara gradually became aware of the carriage slowing down, moving with great reluctance along the road. Nicholas looked out at the deep mud that the carriage wheels were slicing through, noting the heavy coating of mud clinging to the rims. Suddenly the horses were halted and Nicholas opened the door and jumped out, his boots quickly disappearing beneath a foot of bright red mud.

"Are you all right, my dear?" Etienne inquired softly, a look of deep concern on his graven face.

Mara smiled slightly, her lips trembling with delayed reaction as she reached out and patted his blue-veined hand. "I'll be fine, but I'm worried about you, Etienne. You've suffered far more than I have. I'm so sorry," Mara told him simply.

"Look at all the water!" Paddy cried as he craned his neck out. A light drizzle was falling and drifted into the coach as a cold, wet breeze.

"Master Paddy," Jamie intoned with a disapproving look, "sit back down."

But Paddy continued to ignore her as he watched Nicholas returning through the muddy roadway. He scurried back into the coach as Nicholas's shoulders filled the opening.

"The river's flooded the low part of the road ahead. The horses won't go through it by themselves. The wagons will follow in our wake, and I'm going to take our team's head and guide them through. Some water will come into the coach but don't panic, just sit still and we'll be across in no time." Nicholas's green eyes met Mara's for an instant, his look reassuring her before he slammed the door and marched off through the mud.

Nicholas stared at the muddy torrent of water filling the hollow in the road, and with a sigh of regret that he didn't have the Swede's broad shoulder on the other side of the team, he plunged in, feeling the cold water swirling around his thighs as he fought against the swift current. Several times he nearly lost his footing on the slippery road bottom, his feet stepping blindly into deep holes.

He could feel the muscles in his arms and shoulders tightening, screaming out against the weight and strain of holding onto the harness. He continued until he began to feel the water receding around his thighs and the current lessening. He led the horses up the sloping road. The water was murky and slow near the high part of the road, and it was as he neared the crest that he felt the sudden sharp pain in his thigh, and then the stinging that penetrated even the numbing cold of his wet skin. He cursed as he caught a flash of something moving quickly beneath the surface. He moved up the last stretch of flooded road and led the carriage to safety.

Walking slowly, his legs feeling as if they were made of iron, he made his way back to the coach. He leaned against it, watching until the wagons cleared the stream and rolled up behind the coach. With a signal to the coachman to drive on, Nicholas climbed into the coach.

Mara started to say something to him as he stumbled onto the seat beside her, relief evident on her face, but his next actions froze her into silence. She watched him take a knife from his pocket and quickly and efficiently cut away the material of his breeches.

Etienne came out of his self-absorption, his eyes meeting Nicholas's over the flare of the match Nicholas was holding to the knife.

"Cottonmouth," Nicholas told him grimly as he stared down at the puffy, pinkish purple skin that surrounded two small punctures in his thigh, just above his knee. He glanced around the coach impatiently. "I need something to tie around my thigh."

Mara stared in horror at the ugly marks on his thigh. Then, with shaking fingers, she untied the thin ribbon around her ankle. Quickly slipping off her satin slipper, she pulled up her skirt and petticoat, all sense of propriety forgotten as she reached up beneath her drawers and rolled down her silk stocking, her slender white leg bare as she held out the needed tourniquet.

Nicholas smiled as he took the stocking and tied it around his upper thigh, above the wound. "I appreciate your sacrifice, ma petite," he murmured as he took the knife and pressed the red-hot blade against his flesh, making an X-shaped cut across each puncture.

Mara held her hand over her mouth, her teeth biting into

it as she watched him unflinchingly bend down and suck the wound clean of the poison, spitting out the venom after what must have been an excruciatingly painful procedure.

Nicholas fell back against the seat looking pale and weak as he tried to slow down his breathing. "Someone's got to tighten this tourniquet. I don't have the strength," he said quietly, his eyelids growing heavy over his darkening eyes.

"I might be small, but I'm strong as an ox," Jamie pronounced determinedly as she untied the stocking and pulled it tighter, the muscles in her wiry body straining with the effort.

The carriage bumped along, slowing down every so often when the road became almost impassable. The big wheels turned slower and slower under their buildup of thick mud. Mara was cradling Nicholas's head against her breast, oblivious to her own wound. She kept watching his pulse, which fluctuated rapidly in his neck.

Mara had never thought Sandrose could seem such a welcoming sight. They were a sorry-looking troupe of people who rolled up before the elegant doors, their carriage and wagons covered in red mud. The rain began to fall in earnest, blowing in cold sheets as the little party struggled from the carriage.

Amaryllis had been standing at the head of the steps staring down at the procession in silent amazement. As she saw Nicholas unconscious in Mara's blood-stained arms, she quickly issued orders. The servants who'd been standing curiously around the foot of the steps were sent in running groups to take charge of the wagons. Another group helped carry Nicholas to safety.

⁂

Nicholas was bedridden with fever for several days, while the storm continued its deluge. Even Sandrose felt its full fury as the water crept slowly and steadily higher, but the tall pilings kept Sandrose above its damaging effects. What had happened to Beaumarais and Alain no one knew, and only Etienne, perhaps, cared about the fate of his son.

Mara stared into the flames of a cheery fire burning in the parlor fireplace. The house was unusually quiet, for Sandrose was still full of guests, but it was too early in the morning for most of them to be stirring. She found the house silent and peaceful.

Mara walked over closer to the brightly burning logs and held out her hands, rubbing them together. The brown velvet of her jacket soaked up the heat as she stood before the crackling fire. The flames threw a flickering light across her pale features as she stared morosely into them and thought of Nicholas lying helplessly upstairs. She had been able to see him only once, and that was only because she'd gone in during the late-night hours when the house slept and Amaryllis's vigilance had been slack. For Amaryllis had left strict orders that Nicholas not be disturbed, and had allowed no one but herself access to his room.

Mara had selected her moment carefully and slipped inside the room silently, so as not to disturb the sleeping maid sitting in a chair near the bed. She had gazed down lovingly on his face, longing to reach out and touch the familiar features, but she had contented herself to stand beside his bed and watch over him for a few precious, stolen moments. Nicholas was going to be all right. He was a strong man and had fought off the deadly poison. Now he just needed to rest.

"Mademoiselle O'Flynn."

Mara turned abruptly. She waited expectantly, her hands clasped nervously together as she watched Amaryllis walk casually into the room.

"You are up early, mademoiselle," she said as she imperiously gestured for the maid who had followed her into the room to place the tea service near the sofa.

Amaryllis glanced up at Mara invitingly, a warm smile curving her mouth softly and making her look unbelievably beautiful. She was dressed in a morning gown of pale aqua with a wide, low neckline trimmed in elegant lace. The golden curls framing her face were held in place by two jeweled combs.

"Since you are English," Amaryllis began, and her tone sounded very condescending to Mara's sensitive ears, "I thought you might enjoy a cup of tea. That is one thing I admire about the English, that over a simple cup of tea they can sip away a rather uncomfortable situation. So civilized, wouldn't you say, mademoiselle?" Amaryllis inquired as she poured a steaming cup and handed it across to Mara.

Mara took a sip, her eyes glowing strangely as she replied politely, "A trifle weak I'm afraid, but quite palatable."

The half-smile curving her lips widened slightly at the look of discomfiture that momentarily crossed Amaryllis's perfect features. Brendan would have been proud, Mara thought with amusement. She took another sip and returned Amaryllis's look inquiringly.

Amaryllis's pale blue eyes narrowed with determination as her lips twisted into a tight smile. "I had hoped to save you any embarrassment, Mademoiselle O'Flynn," she began tentatively, as though extremely uncomfortable about what she must say, but Mara was not fooled. Amaryllis was not a very good actress. "But when a guest overstays his welcome, I'm afraid it is the hostess's unpleasant duty to have to ask them to leave."

Mara controlled her start of surprise well as she stared without blinking into Amaryllis's eyes. "I see. I do apologize for having not realized sooner that I was becoming an inconvenience to you. But I couldn't leave without knowing that Nicholas would recover."

"Quite," Amaryllis agreed, smiling with understanding, "and it is most admirable of you. But as you well know, Nicholas will recover fully. Of course, he will need rest, and what better place than at Sandrose where he will be given all the love and care he could wish for," Amaryllis told Mara, her meaning clear.

"I see," Mara said softly.

"I'm sure you do, Mademoiselle O'Flynn," Amaryllis replied eagerly. "You strike me as a very level-headed and understanding woman who knows something of the ways of the world. I will not pretend ignorance of the relationship that existed in the past between you and Nicholas, for I know that he is not a man to be denied, nor one to be turned down, whatever offer he makes. But you must have realized that it could only be a temporary arrangement, especially now that he has returned to Beaumarais, and to me. You can no longer have a place in his life."

"Nicholas and I have always known where we stand with each other," Mara said in such a cool voice and with such unconcern that Amaryllis was momentarily disconcerted, not realizing that it was taking every ounce of the young Irishwoman's acting ability not to give away her feelings. It was Mara's greatest performance, and would not be equaled ever again. "He need not have sent an emissary in his stead. It was quite unnecessary, for I had already made plans to leave Beaumarais as soon as possible. In fact, Nicholas and I had discussed the matter just a few days ago."

"My dear," Amaryllis reassured Mara with a patronizing look, "of course he didn't need to send me, but you see it was precisely because he was worried about you that he asked me to have a private word with you. He's been so ill that it hasn't been wise for him to see anyone. He will have to stay in bed for at least a week. So I'm afraid it has been impossible for him to speak with you personally. He wished to, my dear, but that is quite out of the question.

"He really hates to see you wasting your time around here when he knows how much you wish to return to New Orleans, and then from there to—where was it? Oh, yes, England? You will have noticed that the floodwaters are rapidly receding and already many of my guests are making plans to return to New Orleans. Edward, Mr. Ashford has already sent for the riverboat. In fact," Amaryllis paused meaningfully, "if you can manage to be ready it should be here tomorrow morning."

Mara eyed Amaryllis through lazily lowered lids. Had she not already made her decision to leave Nicholas, then nothing Amaryllis could have said or done would have driven her from his side. Amaryllis would have had to fight for Nicholas's affections, and Mara O'Flynn was an adversary the gentle-bred Amaryllis St. Laurens had not met the likes of before.

But this was the chance Mara had been waiting for. She would be able to leave Nicholas's life without his knowing of her love for him…or the child she carried. Yes, she would leave tomorrow. Mara wasn't surprised to hear that Edward Ashford would be leaving as well, for Amaryllis's treatment of him the past few days had been nothing short of rude, now that she had Nicholas within her reach.

As Amaryllis saw the half-smile on the Irishwoman's lips, she started to pat Mara's hand, then thought better of it as she caught the warning glint in her tawny eyes. "My dear, to be perfectly frank, I'd really prefer not to have one of Nicholas's ex-mistresses attending the wedding. We will be getting married as soon as possible. We are a bit provincial here in Louisiana, especially upriver here on our plantations. I'm sure it would offend most people to have you still here."

With admirable control Mara placed her teacup and saucer down on the table as she smiled across at her hostess. "I do understand completely, my dear. I'm sure you know as well as I do how fond memories of the past have a way of lingering on," Mara said with a commiserating look at Amaryllis. She stood up. "And I should really hate to be a constant reminder to Nicholas of," Mara paused delicately, her cheeks flushed slightly from the fire, "other times."

Amaryllis stared up at the beautiful Irishwoman in growing fury. "Will you need assistance in your packing, mademoiselle?" she inquired stiffly.

Mara shook her head. "I think not, thank you. I assume you have arranged for my travel accommodations?"

"You may rest assured that there will be space for you on the boat, Mademoiselle O'Flynn," Amaryllis promised her.

"Thank you," Mara murmured with a light smile, "you are too kind, madame."

Amaryllis stared in frustrated rage at the door that had closed behind the regal figure of that infuriating Irishwoman. She had the distinct impression that she had been bested during the exchange. Yet, Mara O'Flynn was leaving Sandrose—and Nicholas. That was the only important thing, Amaryllis reassured herself.

Escape me?
Never—
Beloved!
While I am I, and you are you.

—Browning

Chapter 15

"WELL, 'TISN'T THE ST. LOUIS HOTEL, FOR SURE," JAMIE SAID disagreeably as she looked around the dingy room. Its paint was peeling off in long strips across the walls. A chipped washbasin and matching pitcher sat squarely in the center of a scarred table. "I've seen better places along the docks in Dublin."

Mara sent Jamie an exasperated look but could really find nothing to say. The hotel room was deplorable, but what could she expect for next to nothing. And that was about what she had in her purse. Her last few dollars had gone for these cheap lodgings and food and would have to meet their demands for the next few days.

Mara sank down on the edge of the bed, her head in her hands. If she could barely afford to pay for this rat-infested hole, how could she hope to find enough money for their fares to England? Mara felt the bed sag beside her and glanced down fondly at Paddy's dark head.

"I don't like this place, Mara," he said unhappily. He looked up at her with big brown eyes full of puzzled reproach. "Why did we leave Uncle Nicholas? I didn't even get a chance to say good-bye. I would've too," he told her earnestly, his eyes full of bright tears. "I wasn't still mad at him, really I wasn't. Do you think he knows I still like him, Mara?" he begged.

Mara hugged him close. "Of course he does. He understands

that we had to leave, and since he was ill, he knew he wouldn't be able to see you to say good-bye."

Paddy hunched his shoulders dejectedly, his lower lip jutting out as he tried to control its trembling. "I don't see why we had to go. Didn't he want us?"

Mara ignored Jamie's snort and said simply, "We didn't belong there, Paddy, me love. But soon we'll be back in London, where we do belong. Then everything will be all right, you just wait and see," Mara promised.

She reluctantly got to her feet, her eyes straying to their trunks piled high in the corner of the small room. "It's too late today, but tomorrow I shall have to see about raising the money for our passage."

"And how d'ye reckon on doin' that, missie?" Jamie demanded gloomily.

Mara chewed her lip thoughtfully, then spoke confidently. "I'll sell what jewelry I have. It's good quality. It should bring something."

Jamie sniffed, leaving Mara in little doubt of her opinion on the success of that venture. With a determined stride, Jamie walked over to her small trunk and, quickly unlocking it, dug down deep inside. Mara watched in puzzlement. Holding herself proudly, she marched over to Mara. Taking her slender hand, she turned it over and placed a small bag in Mara's palm.

"Never had much need of spendin' me earnings all these years. And knowin' Master Brendan the way I did, well, I always thought I might have need of it someday to get him out of trouble. When he struck it rich in California, he was more than generous with me, to be sure. He was practically throwing it away, that he was! So I'm figurin' now's as good a time as any to be usin' it," Jamie said. Her tone of voice brooked no argument.

Mara stared down at the plump bag that contained the little woman's lifetime savings.

"Jamie," Mara whispered as she reached out and wrapped the startled woman in a warm embrace, the first such gesture Mara had made toward her since her mother had died in Paris. "Oh, Jamie, I can't accept such a sacrifice from you. It wouldn't be fair."

Jamie sniffed and drew herself up as much as she could, her thin chest puffed out with indignation. "I'll be the judge of what's fair or not, and I can be doin' whatever I please with me earnings. If ye won't be acceptin' them, well," she thought quickly, "then I'll be spendin' the money on a fur stole and muff, and maybe even a diamond tiara. Damned if I can't see it perched on me gray curls now!"

"Very well then, Mistress Jameson," Mara declared in mock severity, "since ye be part of the O'Flynn family, ye might as well have your say. Let's count this out and see how much we have."

"'Tisn't a fortune," Jamie cautioned her. She watched nervously as Mara opened the pouch. "But 'twill get us out of New Orleans."

Mara stared down at the jumble of money spread out in her lap, surprised at the amount. She hadn't really believed that Jamie could have this much. It was indeed no fortune, but it would pay for more than half the cost of their fares.

Mara looked up, a wide smile curving her lips, and at her expression Jamie sighed in satisfied relief. For the first time in her life, Jamie felt a real part of the O'Flynn family.

"Gee, Jamie's rich, Mara," Paddy exclaimed in awe as he fingered the pile of money.

"'Tis good money paid for honest work done," Jamie told him, secretly pleased to be the center of attention. "Ye be rememberin' that, Master Paddy."

"Someday I'm going to be rich too, only I'm going to have even more money than this," he proclaimed with an arrogant tilt of his chin, looking just like Brendan.

Mara pushed back his disorderly curls and silently promised herself and Paddy that he would be different from Brendan, that he would never have to resort to dishonest means, or even have to use his handsome face to achieve his goals. Paddy would have it differently. He must—as would her own child.

With the money from Jamie's savings and the small amount she'd received from the sale of her jewelry, Mara arranged passage on a ship bound for London, setting sail at the end of the week.

They managed quite well through the following days as they dined only once a day in a small restaurant near their hotel, and made do with fruits and bakery goods from the French Market for their other two meals.

Mara realized as she began to feel the tightness of her clothes that a few additions to her wardrobe would be necessary if she were to have anything to wear in the months to come. She found a dressmaker near the French Market who could make her several inexpensive gowns that would accommodate her thickening figure. But even at that low price she had been frightened by the cost. It was dark when Mara left the dressmaker's shop. It had been her last fitting, and a few minor adjustments had had to be made before she saw the gowns wrapped securely and exchanged for her money. With the package tucked beneath her arm, she made her way across the dark marketplace, now deserted.

The empty stalls gaped at her as she turned quickly up one of the narrow streets surrounding the square and hurried along the slippery banquette. A light drizzle began to fall and she heard laughing voices raised loudly behind her. She glanced over her shoulder to see a crowd of revelers, their faces concealed beneath strange masks, parading through the middle of the street. They stopped briefly beneath an iron-grilled balcony and called up to a young woman leaning over the railing, a lacy fan hiding the lower portion of her face as she flirted with them from the safety of her balcony high above the street.

Mara continued on, noticing more and more groups of noisy people crowding onto the narrow streets. Dressed in her dark, enveloping cape, she drew little attention from the garishly garbed masqueraders, some staggering already from the effects of their merrymaking, some still strong of voice as they serenaded their way through the old French Quarter. So this was what the season of Mardi Gras was all about. Mara remembered hearing about it from the guests at Sandrose, some of whom had seemed unable to talk of anything else.

As she crossed an intersection, her hurrying figure caught the attention of several masked men, their faces hidden behind grotesquely painted facades that leered nightmarishly in the light from the flaming torches carried by the carousers.

"Mademoiselle! Mademoiselle! *Où allez-vous? Attendez-moi!*" one of the costumed figures called out to her disappearing figure.

Mara left the revealing light and began to run along the narrow street near where she thought the hotel was. She was breathing heavily and felt a stitch in her side. She halted to catch her breath beneath the shadowy overhang of a balcony. Mara heard calling and looked nervously back down the street to see dark shapes moving along it. They were searching for her.

With a deep breath she pushed herself away from the cold stucco of the wall and disappeared into a narrow alley, leaving her seekers combing the street behind. She stumbled more than once in the darkness of the garbage-strewn alleyway but continued despite her tiredness. When she stepped out onto a street at the far end, she knew she was lost.

She glanced around frantically. It was so dark and the drizzle had now turned into a steady rain, the thunder that rumbled overhead promising more. Mara shivered with cold and fear as she saw the flickering torches dancing along the houses at the far corner of the street, and she turned in the opposite direction and headed into the darkness. Fifteen minutes later, or maybe a half an hour—Mara didn't know how long—but she stopped at a corner and looked around hopelessly. Where was she? She quickly stepped back into the shadows as a group of people paraded harmlessly past. It was then that she saw the street sign illuminated by their torches and remembered Françoise Ferrare. She lived along this street. Mara noticed the flower cart sitting on the opposite corner, torches lighting up the woman's display and guiding the merrymakers to her flowers. Mara laughed shakily as she realized she couldn't be far from Françoise's house. She trudged along the street, her package weighing heavily in her tired arms.

Suddenly Mara felt something grab her. She let out a scream as she stared up into a hideous face with bright red cheeks and bulging eyes, the nose sticking out half a foot. Sharp teeth glinted from a distorted, grinning mouth.

Mara couldn't even hear her own scream of terror as her heart pounded deafeningly in her chest. The monster's hands seemed to claw at her, swinging her around and around until she stared up dizzily into its demoniacal face. Mara glanced around wildly as she tried to fight free of the creature. She pushed and scratched at his scaly body, finally freeing herself as he fell back laughing. Without bothering to retrieve her fallen package, Mara ran as fast as she could up the street.

It was then that she saw the fence, and through the trees the pink shutters gleaming softly. With a deep sob she pushed against the gate, and it was then that she felt the first deep stab of pain inside her. Doubling over as it spread through her body, she staggered into the quiet darkness of the garden and then forced herself up the steps to the front door. She fell against it, sagging to her knees as if in prayer. "Oh, God, no. Please. I mustn't lose his baby, please, no," Mara clearly heard herself pleading before she gave in to the wave of blackness waiting to engulf her.

❧

Mara opened her eyes to see daylight streaming in through the windows. She wondered where she was, for the room was strange to her. It was a beautiful bedchamber decorated with gold-flocked wallpaper and blue-and-gold-striped, satin-upholstered chairs. Mara glanced up at the matching blue and gold canopy above her head and sighed. She breathed the light lavender scent of the lace-edged pillows, allowing her mind to drift aimlessly until she heard the door open. Looking up, she saw Françoise framed in the doorway. Suddenly the events of the night before came flooding back to her, and she gave a wounded cry as her hands reached down to where her baby should be.

"I've lost it, haven't I?" she cried out as Françoise hurried into the room, a look of concern crossing her beautiful face. "It's gone. I killed it, didn't I? I resented it at first, maybe even hated it. But I didn't really mean it. Oh, God, I've lost Nicholas's baby," Mara cried in anguish.

Françoise pulled up a chair, and grasping Mara's fluttering

hands, she held them between hers. "No!" she told her firmly, her eyes bright. "You have not lost *le petit bébé*. He is still with you, ma chérie." Taking Mara's hand, she placed it over her stomach. "See, it begins to show. It is no longer flat, and soon he will grow so big you will come to despair of it," Françoise laughed softly, her blue green eyes gentle.

Mara swallowed painfully on the tears that would not come. "I didn't lose it," she breathed.

"No, you didn't lose him," Françoise repeated firmly, relieved to see the despair leave Mara O'Flynn's eyes. "But you gave me such a scare. Mon Dieu," she said shaking her head, "but I thought you were dead. Never have I seen such a sight as you crumpled up on my front doorstep. I think I must have aged a lifetime when I heard you."

"I'm sorry, but I was lost, and those horrible people were out there in the most hideous masks. I was frightened," Mara admitted, slightly shamefaced. "I just don't know what came over me. And then when I thought I was losing the baby…" she trailed off, the pain of it still showing in her eyes.

"Oh, ma chérie," Françoise scolded her gently, "what on earth were you doing out so late? This is the worst time of the year to be on the streets at night."

"I had to pick up some gowns from the dressmaker. I didn't realize it would be like that out on the street. I know it is festival time, but still—they were so *wild*." Mara shuddered.

"It is this way every year around the Mardi Gras time. Some years are worse than others, for it is the season for festivals and balls, and a lot of carousing in the streets. No respectable person would be caught out on the streets at night during all of January, especially a woman. There are usually private balls and parties to attend, but for some it is just a chance to dress up in costumes so no one will recognize their foolish faces when they romp drunkenly through the streets making noise and trouble. It is bad sometimes and people usually end up fighting and getting hurt. This is just the beginning too, I'm afraid," Françoise said with a look of disgust. "It will continue for many days and nights."

Mara glanced down at her hands, twisting them

uncomfortably as she realized that Françoise might not know about Alain and all that had occurred at Beaumarais.

"You left Sandrose rather suddenly, causing quite a stir I believe," Françoise spoke suddenly.

Mara glanced up. "Then—"

Françoise nodded sadly. "Yes, I know of Alain."

For the first time Mara became aware of Françoise's appearance. She was dressed in black bombazine and crepe, the color of mourning.

Françoise seemed to become aware of Mara's curious look and explained softly, "Alain is dead."

"What?" Mara asked incredulously. "I don't understand. We left him at Beaumarais. What happened?" Mara asked with quickening heartbeats as she demanded, "Is Nicholas here?"

Françoise shook her head. "Non, Nicholas is not here," she answered, pausing strangely, "but my papa arrived yesterday and he told me all that had happened. I could scarcely believe what he was telling me, it is all so incredible, and tragic. Poor Papa," Françoise sighed, "he is so deeply grieved by what has happened, not only to Alain, but to everyone because of him."

Françoise rubbed her temple as she stared at Mara. "To think that Alain was capable of such acts, I am simply astounded. I always knew that he loved Beaumarais, but I never fully understood why he was so obsessive about it. To think that he was the son of Philippe de Montaigne-Chantale, and that he was the one who murdered François. So much sorrow.

"I find it hard to believe that he actually killed Philippe, his own father," Françoise whispered, dabbing at her eyes with a delicate handkerchief, "I suppose the manner in which he died was God's way of punishing him for his sins."

"What happened?"

"Papa says the river finally reclaimed the land where the great house had sat so royally for all those years, mocking the muddy waters below. Beaumarais is no more, it is gone," Françoise told her simply.

"Gone?" Mara repeated.

"The foundations of Beaumarais apparently could not resist the great weight of the waters flowing around it. In the past it must have eaten away underground where no one could see, and so she crumbled into the swamp she was built from. Alain was still in the house when it caved in. There are one or two columns still standing, but not much more. All is gone. Nicholas went back to Beaumarais to confront Alain, and it was he who found the house that way. The waters had risen above the middle of the stairs, which were still standing, only now they lead nowhere. It was beneath them that they found Alain's body," she ended, her voice thick. "Alain wanted Beaumarais so badly that he killed for it, only to have the house end up as his grave. Even though I know what I do about Alain, he was still the brother I grew up with, and I grieve deeply for his death. And I mourn because of the pain he caused for the people at Beaumarais, especially for Nicholas."

Beaumarais was destroyed. Nicholas had finally managed to return to his birthplace, only to have it stolen from him again. He had lost the house, but at least he had found the truth of the past. That would be some consolation to him, Mara thought sadly, wishing she were with him now to comfort him. But she wasn't, and never again would she be able to put her arms around him.

"How is Nicholas?" Mara asked hesitantly.

"Papa says that he is well recovered from the snakebite. Of course he is greatly upset by the loss of Beaumarais," Françoise told her, her blue green eyes narrowing thoughtfully as she gazed at the distracted woman.

"H-he is still at Sandrose?" Mara asked without meeting Françoise's eyes.

"Mais oui," Françoise laughed harshly, "you do not think that Amaryllis would let him out of her sight now that she has him there?"

At Mara's stricken look Françoise swore beneath her breath. "My cursed tongue. I am sorry, but since you are here in New Orleans and Nicholas still at Sandrose...well, I assumed you did not love him. Especially since you left so abruptly, and without saying good-bye to Papa, which upset him greatly, ma chérie. I am sure he will have something to say to you about that," Françoise warned Mara with a twinkle. "I am still confused, for now that I know you are to have Nicholas's child, ah," Françoise sighed, raising her eyes heavenward, "I have done it again, non? Nicholas does not know about the baby, eh? Or that you are so much in love with him? Mon Dieu, but it did not seem like Nicholas to turn you out knowing such a thing. What fools men can be at times. Bah, if he cannot see who is the better woman, then he deserves to be tied to that she-wolf."

Mara closed her eyes as she tried to block out the painful vision of Nicholas at Sandrose with Amaryllis. "It is difficult to explain, but although I love Nicholas with all of my heart, I know that he does not love me. Nor did I ever expect him to. I do not blame him, for he has reasons for the way he feels. But the one thing I will not have him feel for me is pity, and that is all that he would feel if he found out about the baby," Mara said. "I know now that I want his child more than anything else in the world. But Nicholas must never know about it."

Françoise stared at the proud Irishwoman helplessly, knowing there was nothing she could say. "I will bring you some hot tea and a little breakfast, non? And then you will feel better. I will have a bath prepared too, it will help relax you." Françoise told her as she stood up.

"Oh, my God!" Mara cried out suddenly. "Paddy and Jamie! They won't know where I've been. They'll be worried sick with fear. I must get back to them."

"Now, now," Françoise calmed her. "I will send one of my maids with the news that you are here. Where are you staying? The St. Louis?"

"No, at a place called Par Bonheur."

Françoise raised her elegant eyebrows incredulously. "Mon Dieu! C'est impossible that you could be staying in such a place. It should be called Par Malheur instead, for only by ill luck would someone step through its doors," Françoise spoke contemptuously, then with a look of utter contrition she clapped her hand across her mouth. "Mon Dieu, but I have done it again, non? I am so sorry, mademoiselle. Please forgive me, but I did not mean to insult you," she continued with increasing embarrassment.

"Please, you needn't apologize," Mara said with a forgiving smile, "for the place is deplorable. We are only staying there temporarily. In fact, we will be leaving New Orleans tomorrow for London."

Françoise stared at her in dismay. "You are leaving so soon? But Papa will be most disturbed. He was looking forward to visiting with you when he heard you were here. He will hardly have time to say hello."

"I would like to see him before I leave, but I can't delay our departure. I've already paid for our fares," Mara told her regretfully.

"Of course, I understand. I shall send someone immediately to inform these people of your whereabouts. Now, it will be best if you rest for a while. You will be quite safe here," she reassured Mara.

"Thank you. You've been very kind, Mademoiselle Ferrare."

"Françoise, please. Now lie back and think of pleasant thoughts, eh?" Françoise ordered with an appealing smile as she left the room.

Pleasant thoughts, Mara wondered. And then she smiled as she thought of her child. She knew now that she really did want him with every fiber of her being. This would be her part of Nicholas, something that no one could ever take away. She hoped desperately that it would be a boy and look just like Nicholas, with green eyes and black hair. Yes, Mara thought with a soft smile curving her lips, those were pleasant thoughts indeed.

❦

"If me hair wasn't already gray 'twould have turned that color, ye had me so scared," Jamie complained an hour later as she helped Mara dress, her eyes going over her critically as she hid her anxiety behind a scolding voice. "Goin' out by yourself in a town full of these hot-blooded French fools. 'Tis enough to have me wonderin' about your sanity."

She narrowed her gray eyes with concern when the expected retort didn't come. With a sniff she started brushing Mara's long hair and braiding it into a coronet. "Reckon 'tis a good thing we be leaving New Orleans after all," she mumbled as she noticed the sad droop to Mara's mouth. It seemed to Jamie as if the O'Flynn luck might have run out at last.

Etienne greeted Mara warmly when she entered the parlor a few minutes later, kissing her cheeks as he grasped her hands. "My dear Mara, it is so good to see you. But you gave us all such a fright! Why, my poor Françoise thought for sure you had committed the unpardonable and died on her front doorstep."

"Papa!" Françoise complained with a laugh.

"I may have a temper, and may not be entirely respectable, but I have never been accused of poor manners," Mara responded with some of the old spirit.

Etienne smiled at her as he settled her on the sofa. "Didn't I tell you, Françoise, that she was priceless? It is good to see you with a smile on your lips once again."

Mara reached out and took his hand. "Etienne, I am so sorry it had to end the way it did."

Etienne patted her hand reassuringly. "Thank you for that, my dear. But it was the only way, perhaps the easiest way for it to end. Alain is gone, and finally we must try and forget the past for it will do no good to remember it," he said. Then, with a sad smile, he added, "But perhaps sometimes I will remember him only as Olivia's little boy."

"Now we pretend none of it ever happened and we talk of other things," he declared adamantly and went on to do just that for the rest of the day and through dinner, which Françoise had insisted they stay and share. All too soon it came time for Mara to bid them farewell, sadly, not insulting them by promising to see them again in New Orleans. She knew she'd never return, and she suspected Etienne knew it too. But she did have his promise that he would see her the next time he was in London, and she believed he would keep that promise.

Once back at the cheap hotel everything seemed anti-climactic as they went about their preparations, packing for the long journey ahead.

The next morning seemed to dawn too soon as Mara dragged herself from the hard, cold bed she had shivered in most of the night. She had almost finished dressing when Jamie came bustling into the room. She had been down in the street overseeing the transfer of their luggage.

"Did ye already hire a carriage?" she demanded worriedly, her heavy cloak wrapped protectively around her thin figure and her bonnet tied securely over her gray curls.

Mara looked at Jamie's reflection in the mirror, a doubtful expression crossing her face. "No, I haven't had time to hire a wagon to take our trunks to the docks."

"I said, 'a carriage'—'cause that's what's sittin' outside right now, with a coachman sayin' he's waitin' for us," Jamie told her.

Mara picked up her cloak and folded it across her arm, then pulled on her kid gloves. She was wearing the same amber velvet she had worn on her arrival in New Orleans, the small velvet cap sitting well back on her head and trimmed with the same Brussels lace that edged her bodice jacket. "There must be some mistake," Mara said as she thought of the extra expense.

But there was no mistake, nor extra expense to be paid. Françoise Ferrare's coachman, sent especially to see them safely on board their ship, helped Mara into the carriage.

"Are we really leaving New Orleans, Mara?" Paddy asked dejectedly.

"Yes, Paddy, we're leaving New Orleans," Mara replied softly as she stared out at the iron-grilled balconies adorning pink and yellow stucco houses.

Once on board they were shown to their quarters, Paddy and Jamie sharing one while Mara was shown to a cabin of her own. She had made sure she had enough money to purchase one, for her condition would become more and more obvious as the voyage lengthened. It would save embarrassment all around if she could retreat to the privacy of her own cabin.

But when she had reserved the cabin, she'd had no idea it would be as nice as this one, with its mahogany-paneled walls and finely etched, crystal-shaded oil lamps. A fur rug, which looked as luxurious as sable, was folded across the foot of the berth. Mara pulled off her bonnet and gloves and threw them on top of the cloak she'd dropped across a chair. She walked over to the porthole and stared out, catching a glimpse of water beyond the bow of another ship docked alongside. She heard the activity on deck as the crew made preparations to set sail. Soon they would weigh anchor and sail out into the Mississippi River, which would carry them into the Gulf and far away from New Orleans.

A loud tapping on the cabin door drew Mara's attention from the limited view, and she turned as the door was swung open.

"We're going to be sailing in a few minutes, Mara!" Paddy exclaimed. "Do you want to go up on deck and watch?"

Mara shook her head. "I don't think so, Paddy."

Paddy looked disappointed. "Can I still go and watch? Jamie said she'd come with me," Paddy entreated.

"Yes, go on, but try to stay out of trouble," Mara told him as he rushed from the room with a hasty thank-you thrown over his shoulder. Mara sat in the silence of her cabin unaware of the time, or the damp chill creeping slowly in.

She leaned back against the side of the berth, her head bent as she stared blindly at her hands folded in her lap. She felt a strange tightness in her chest, as if something were welling up inside of her, something that she couldn't control any longer. She gradually became aware of the gentle rocking of the ship as it caught the current and drifted out into the Mississippi.

They were actually leaving New Orleans. Suddenly Mara realized the magnitude of it all. Never again would she see Nicholas Chantale, the Creole adventurer she had fallen so hopelessly in love with. It was all over, every dream was shattered.

Mara felt a sharp jab of pain behind her eyes as the pressure built, and suddenly her head ached unbearably. Mara frantically pulled at the hairpins holding her thick hair in place and, with a sigh, felt the heavy chignon fall into long strands around her shoulders. She ran her fingers through the thick tangle, but still her temples pounded with a merciless beat. Mara felt a constriction in her throat and swallowed painfully. Blinking her eyes rapidly, she felt a hot, burning sensation inside them, and suddenly she felt the unbelievable wetness on her cheeks and then a saltiness trickling into the corner of her mouth.

"Oh, God, it's been such a long time," she whispered as she began to weep, the deep sobs racking her slender body as she doubled over with all the pent-up pain and fury of her childhood, and of the last few years. She cried for Maud O'Flynn, her mother, and saw once again that room in Paris.

She cried for Brendan, for his dreams and failures, for his just wanting to *be* somebody in life, only to end up in a cold grave on a bleak hill far from home.

But most of all she cried for Nicholas, for the love she could never have and would never be able to give. Burying her head in the pillow on the berth, she cried for all of them, and for all the lost years. It felt as if her heart meant to explode.

Mara moaned as she continued to cry, terrified of the flood of emotion tearing her to pieces. She did not hear the cabin door, open, or the harsh words softly spoken. She did not feel the hard arms that closed around her shaking body and held her close to a warm chest, the heart beating strongly beneath her cheek.

Mara felt herself drifting to sleep. Then the enticing images of dreams began to flee as consciousness returned and she fought against opening her heavy eyes. She felt so warm, almost secure. She stretched, then suddenly stilled as she felt the hard muscle of an arm across her waist.

Mara's eyes flew open and met the green ones that had been intently watching her waken from exhausted slumber.

"Nicholas?" Her lips trembled as her golden eyes filled with fear. "Oh, God, don't be so cruel to torment me this way. It isn't real. He isn't here with me."

Nicholas's arms wrapped around her, holding her closer to his heart, the sable rug covering them warmly. "Feel me, hear my heart pounding with love for you, Mara," he said softly against her ear. "I'm very much alive, and here with you on this ship."

Mara looked up, her eyes clinging unblinkingly to his face as if afraid he would disappear. "Nicholas, oh, Nicholas... how can it be? I thought you were still at Sandrose. You are going to marry Amaryllis, and yet here you are with me. Why?" Mara cried, trying to pull free from his arms. But Nicholas continued to hold her close against him. "You hate me, you despise me. Have you forgotten who I am? I'm Mara O'Flynn, the Irish actress you once swore vengeance against."

"No," Nicholas corrected her gently as he touched his mouth softly to hers, "you are Mara O'Flynn, the woman I love."

Mara stared at him in confusion. "You can't love me."

Nicholas smiled. "I can see now that we shall always be arguing. So," he put the question to her, "why can't I be in love with you? You are with me."

Mara gazed at him in surprised silence.

Nicholas's smile widened. "I see I have finally found the way to render you speechless. I shall have to remember to keep telling you I love you, ma petite. But then, I don't think I shall ever forget to do that."

Mara felt a tear slide from the corner of her eye as she stretched out a tentative hand and touched Nicholas's hard cheek, her fingers caressing his lips. She whispered brokenly, "You love me? You aren't just saying that to be cruel, Nicholas?"

Nicholas's smile faded as he looked deeply into her eyes, willing her to open her mind and heart to him. He held Mara's face cupped within his hands as he said, very quietly, "Give me your love, Mara. Trust me with it, share it with me and don't keep it to yourself. I love you, Mara, and I need you more than anything else in this world. Will you believe in me and in my love?" Nicholas asked her, his green eyes never leaving her face as he searched for some sign of acceptance.

"I know you are wary, and still mistrustful," he began, a husky note in his voice, "and you have reason to be, for in the past there have been too many hurtful lies between us.

But I am opening my heart to you now, Mara, my love. When I heard that you had left Sandrose, I felt as if a part of me had died, and I was frightened for the first time in my life. I thought I had lost you, that I wouldn't be able to find you again."

"Why did you follow me?" Mara asked in bewilderment.

"Because I finally knew with no doubts to plague me that you loved me. Only a woman who loves a man deeply and with every breath in her body would have offered her life to protect his."

"I died a thousand times over when you threw yourself in front of me and Alain shot you," he said grimly, a brief flash of anguish showing in his eyes as he remembered.

"But what else could I have done?" Mara asked.

Nicholas dropped a light kiss on her forehead. "Exactly, my dear. *You* could have done nothing else but that act of foolhardy heroics, and it proved to me that you loved me—something your beautiful lips refused to admit."

Mara drew a deep breath. "I couldn't tell you how I felt when I thought you still hated me."

"That damned, lovable pride of yours—as well as my own pride—kept us apart. That, and a few other things of late," Nicholas said in a hard-edged voice, his green eyes narrowing. "I think you have something to tell me, don't you?"

"What do you mean?" Mara asked uncertainly, his tone of voice making her think of the old Nicholas, who had always been so disapproving.

"I mean, my sweet," Nicholas said unrelentingly despite the quivering of her lips, "that I wish to hear about my child. You neglected to tell me about him—or her."

"I couldn't," Mara admitted in a whisper. "You would have pitied me, Nicholas, and that I could not have lived with. You spoke with Françoise? That is how you found out?"

Nicholas shook his head. "No, that merely confirmed my suspicions. I'm no fool, my dear, and I believed you might be with child," Nicholas said, then laughed abruptly as he confessed. "Actually I think I was hoping you were, because then I'd have had even more of a hold over you. But you never said anything, except to keep pleading with me for your freedom. Now I know why," he said softly as he smoothed back a thick curl of her hair. "With that stiff-necked pride of yours you would have run off and had our child, never letting me know of its existence, raising him as your own. We have much to forgive each other for, I think," Nicholas said sadly.

"I love you, Nicholas," Mara spoke the precious words she had longed to have the right to say to him. Arching her neck backward, she raised her lips to his in a gentle kiss that sealed their love.

Relaxing in the warmth of his embrace, her arms holding him close to her, she asked shyly, "When did you come to love me?"

Nicholas rested his chin on top of her head and breathed in the sweet fragrance of her unbound hair. "It was a gradual process, although I suspect that part of me fell in love with your picture the first time I saw it."

"The locket," Mara murmured. "That's what started it all."

"Perhaps. Although I might have been attracted to your face, it was Mara O'Flynn, the woman, that I came to love. The allure of your beauty would have dimmed after a while. But the love I feel for who you are, Mara, will only grow brighter."

Mara felt the now-familiar wetness on her cheeks as she pressed her lips to his, her words of love becoming lost beneath the answering pressure of his mouth, their kiss taking on new sweetness and fire.

But there were still questions that needed to be answered, and so Mara asked the most painful one first. "What of Amaryllis?"

Nicholas smiled unpleasantly. "I left Amaryllis in little doubt of what I felt about her," he replied easily.

"She said you asked her to tell me to leave. She said that you and she would be marrying," Mara said huskily, the wound of that conversation still raw.

"She lied, my dear," Nicholas reassured her. "She was desperate. She knew I felt nothing for her, yet she couldn't admit defeat. I suppose she thought if she got rid of you, then I would turn to her. Her vanity allowed her to believe she could succeed. She hadn't counted on the fact that I was madly in love with you," Nicholas told Mara, feeling no pity for the old flame who, in selfish jealousy, might have destroyed his happiness. "She never told me you had left until just a few days ago. By then I'd found Alain, and I couldn't leave until I'd settled the affairs of the estate. I was like a man possessed until I managed to get away from Sandrose."

"But what of Beaumarais? Aren't you going to rebuild it, Nicholas?" Hugging him tightly, she said, "I'm so sorry about what happened to it. I know how much you loved that house. It was your home, and it's so unfair that you should lose it just as you returned to it."

Nicholas folded his arms behind his head and gazed up thoughtfully at the beams of the ceiling. "I came back to New Orleans thinking I wished only to discover the truth and reconcile with my father, but when I saw all the old, familiar places I began to relive the past, hoping to recapture it.

"Gradually I came to the realization that the past was dead and could not be reclaimed. I had changed too much in the years away from New Orleans, and my friends had not. They were the same stiff-necked Creoles they always had been, and I no longer belonged—nor did I wish to.

"I thought perhaps I was still in love with Amaryllis, and when I heard she was a widow, I thought maybe there might be another chance for happiness with her. But it didn't turn out that way. Every time I looked into Amaryllis's pale eyes, I saw a pair of golden ones baiting me, and when I kissed her lips, I remembered a half-smile and a taunting voice. You haunt me, my dear, and I know now that there is no escaping you. I don't want Beaumarais any longer. Let her go back to the swamp she was born from, for there are only ghosts left to inhabit her now."

Mara felt a relief and calm descend on her as she heard him. He was no longer held captive by the past, and they could start anew, in some other land. They would never have been able to begin again if they had stayed at Beaumarais. Mara laid her head on his chest and asked dreamily, "Where shall we be living in London?"

Deep laughter rumbled in his chest, and Mara propped herself up on her elbows as she stared into his face.

"London? Who said we were sailing to London, my love?" Nicholas declared with a grin that twitched the corners of his mouth. "We happen to be headed for California, and if we experience good weather the babe will be born there."

Mara opened her mouth, but it was a moment before any sound came out. "B-but I bought tickets on a ship sailing for London. I don't understand," she exclaimed weakly.

"You really should be more observant of your surroundings, ma petite," Nicholas scolded. "You see, under my orders you were brought to this ship, not to the one you had booked passage on. This is one of the faster clippers and should make the golden shores of California in three months or so."

Mara stared at Nicholas in mingled disbelief and suspicion. "You tricked me. But how?" she demanded. "Françoise and Etienne. Of course! I never even thought to ask how you knew where to find me. They were the only ones who knew."

"They send their love, my sweet," Nicholas told her, totally unrepentant. "I arrived at Françoise's late last night and discovered, to my great delight, that you had been there. I would have torn New Orleans apart trying to find you, my dear," Nicholas told her without exaggeration. "Luckily for me, this ship happens to belong to Armand de St. Jaubert. Remember? The father of little Gabriella? It was quite easy to make arrangements for our passage, even on such short notice. Etienne will handle all my affairs in New Orleans. He will have some of the heirlooms and keepsakes I had sent to Sandrose shipped out to us in California, and he will handle the sale of the land should I decide to sell. Although I think Amaryllis may not be quite so anxious to acquire it now that the house is gone. Nor may she have the funds now to do much speculating. I left her making plans to follow her ex-almost-fiancé to New Orleans. There was a desperate gleam in her eyes. She wishes to patch things up between them."

"So," Mara breathed, "we're going back to San Francisco."

Nicholas grasped her chin and turned her face to his. "You do want to return? There aren't too many bad memories there for you? And remember, my dear, should Brendan's wife still be there—which I doubt—you will be with me. She would not dare touch either you or Paddy," Nicholas promised her.

Mara smiled. "No, I don't fear her, or my memories of San Francisco. In fact, I think I'm rather pleased to be going back there," Mara added with an innocent look at him. "After all, I do have friends there."

"Ummm," Nicholas murmured. "I think by now the Swede will be safely wed to that redheaded landlady of yours, and I won't need to worry about him moping around with a long face. Of course, I shall be right by your side at all times, for by then you will be so big with our child that you will need a bit of assistance. And by the look in my eye no one will doubt who the father is, or whose woman you are," Nicholas added.

Mara's golden eyes darkened momentarily, and she said softly, "And what name shall the babe be born with?" For despite all his words of love and devotion, never once had Nicholas mentioned marriage.

Nicholas suddenly rolled over and Mara found herself staring up into his blazing eyes. "And what name did you think he would be born with, my dear?" he asked in a very quiet voice.

Mara swallowed. "Since I am not wed, the name O'Flynn is as good as any."

Nicholas narrowed his eyes until only a sliver of green shone from behind the thick fringe of black lashes covering them. "And I was thinking that this voyage would be an excellent opportunity for a honeymoon," Nicholas said casually, shrugging as if it were of little concern to him whether they were married or not.

"Did ye now?" Mara retorted, the sick feeling that had lurked in the pit of her stomach disappearing. Her lips curved in a smile of provocation. "And here I was thinkin' ye had to be married first. Well, that's what comes of bein' raised in the old country. Here am I, just a poor, Irish lass without the sense to be knowin' me own name anymore, or whether I'm to be your wife of not."

A smile curved Nicholas's mouth and a devilish light twinkled in his eyes. "Since you've assumed so many identities in your short but colorful life, Mara, *me love*, I think there might be room for one more. And the final one will be," he added in deadly seriousness, "Mara Chantale. It sounds right," he whispered as he enclosed her in his arms, holding her as if he would never free her, "as if it belongs to you, and only you."

Mara's arms encircled his strong neck and she gazed up at him with all her love revealed. Never had she looked more beautiful than she did at this moment, Nicholas thought humbly. He knew all too well the great effort it had taken for her to declare her love to him.

"'Tis a fine name. And to be sure, there's none other I'd care to be takin'," Mara answered as she reached up and met his seeking lips halfway.

The long voyage ahead of them was temporarily forgotten as they lost themselves in each other's love.

About the Author

Laurie McBain became a publishing phenomenon at age twenty-six with her first historical romance. She wrote seven romances, all of which were bestsellers, selling over eleven million copies. She is a winner of the Reviewer's Choice Award. Laurie lives in the San Francisco Bay Area, California.